COLLEEN McCULLOUGH

Antony and Cleopatra

HARPER

HarperCollins*Publishers*
77–85 Fulham Palace Road,
Hammersmith, London W6 8JB

www.harpercollins.co.uk

This paperback edition 2008
1

First published by HarperCollins*Publishers* 2007
1

A catalogue record for this book
is available from the British Library

ISBN-13: 978 0 00 722579 8

This novel is entirely a work of fiction.
The names, characters and incidents portrayed in it are
the work of the author's imagination, and, while
historical characters make appearances in the book,
this is a fictionalised account.

Set in Sabon by Palimpsest Book Production Limited,
Grangemouth, Stirlingshire

Mixed Sources
Product group from well-managed
forests and other controlled sources
www.fsc.org Cert no. SW-COC-1806
© 1996 Forest Stewardship Council
FSC

FSC is a non-profit international organisation established
to promote the responsible management of the world's forests.
Products carrying the FSC label are independently certified
to assure consumers that they come from forests that are managed
to meet the social, economic and ecological needs
of present and future generations.

Find out more about HarperCollins and the environment at
www.harpercollins.co.uk/green

For the unsinkable Anthony Cheetham
with love and enormous respect

CONTENTS

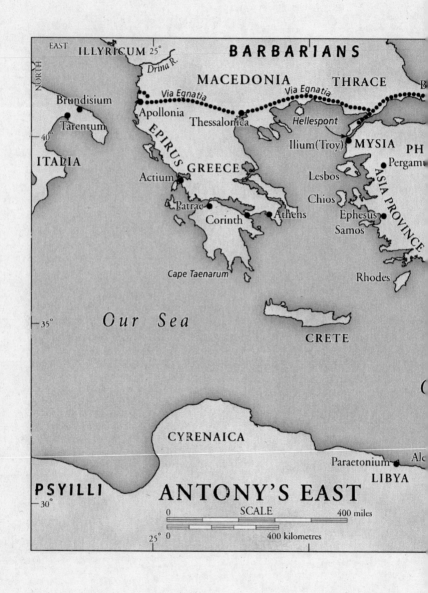

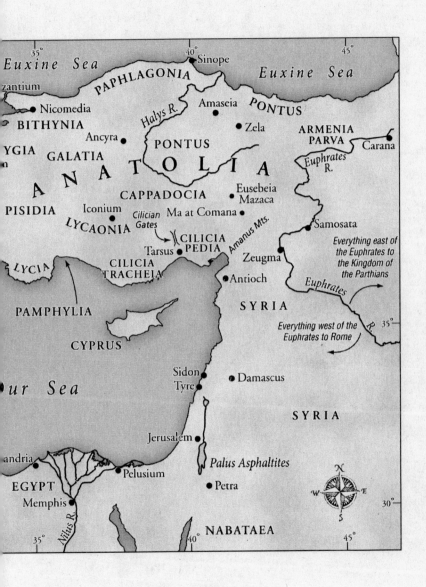

LONG-HAIRED GAUL

Oceanus
Atlanticus

WEST 0° EAST

NORTH

10°   5°   0°   5°

45°

Burdigala

AQUITANIA

Narbo

NEARER
SPAIN

Rhodanus

FURTHER
SPAIN

40°

Corduba

Gades

KINGDOM of
NUMIDIA

35°

KINGDOM of
MAURETANIA

10°   0°   5°

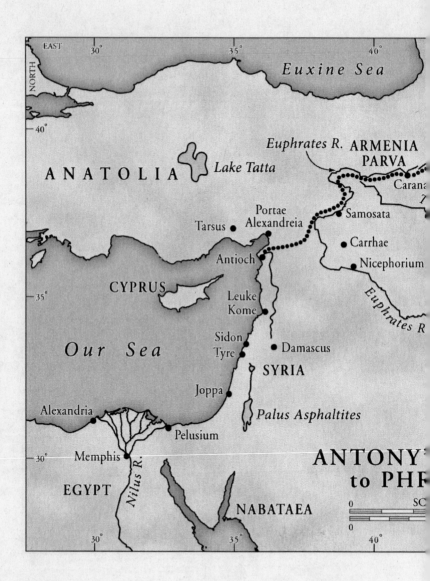

ARMENIA

Cyrus R.

Artaxata

ARMENIA

Araxes R.

Caspian
Sea

MEDIA
ATROPATENE

Lake
Thospitis

Lake Matiane

Tigris R.

PARTHIAN MEDIA

Phraaspa

Gyndes R.

Ecbatana

PARTHIAN

PARTHIAN PERSIS

Seleuceia-on-Tigris

Babylon

MESOPOTAMIA

Tigris R.

Susa

Euphrates R.

PARTHIAN
ELYMAIS

S MARCH
AASPA

Persepolis

Persian
Sea

ALE

400 miles

400 kilometres

THE HOME PROVINCES

EAST 8° 10° 12° 14° 16° 18°
NORTH

46°

ITALIAN GAUL

Aquileia

ILLYRICUM

Tergeste

ISTRIA

Mutina

Bononia

Genua

LIGURIA

Rubicon R.

Ariminum

Fanum Fortunae

LIBURNIA

DALMATIA

44°

Pisae

Arnus R.

Arretium

Ancona

Ilva I.

ITALIA

Asculum Picentum

Cosa

Reate

Adriatic Sea

Corsica

42°

Ostia

Rome

Fregellae

Beneventum

Circeii

Barium

Teanum Sidicinum

Neapolis

Tarentum

Brundisium

Cumae

Puteoli

Sardinia

Tuscan Sea

40°

Ionian Sea

38°

Messana

Rhegium

Lilybaeum

Mt Aetna

Tauromenium

Sicilia

Utica

Agrigentum

Syracuse

Carthage

AFRICA PROVINCE

36°

0 SCALE 200 miles

0 200 kilometres

8° 10° 12° 14° 16° 18°

PART I

Antony in the East

41–40 B.C.

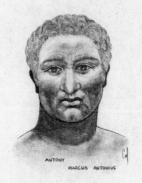

ANTONY

MARCUS ANTONIUS

ONE

Quintus Dellius was not a warlike man, nor a warrior when in battle. Whenever possible he concentrated upon what he did best, namely to advise his superiors so subtly that they came to believe the ideas were genuinely theirs.

So after Philippi, in which conflict he had neither distinguished himself nor displeased his commanders, Dellius decided to attach his meager person to Mark Antony and go east.

It was never possible, Dellius reflected, to choose Rome; it always boiled down to choosing sides in the massive, convulsive struggles between men determined to control – no, be honest, Quintus Dellius! – determined to *rule* Rome. With the murder of Caesar by Brutus, Cassius and the rest, everyone had assumed that Caesar's close cousin, Mark Antony, would inherit his name, his fortune, and his literally millions of clients. But what had Caesar done? Made a last will and testament that left everything to his eighteen-year-old great-nephew, Gaius Octavius! He hadn't even mentioned Antony in that document, a blow from which Antony had never really recovered, so sure had he been that he would step into Caesar's high red boots. And, typical Antony, he had made no plans to take second place. At first the youth everyone now called Octavian hadn't worried him; Antony was a man in his prime, a famous general of troops and owner of a large faction in the Senate, whereas Octavian was a sickly adolescent as easy to crush as the carapace of a beetle. Only it hadn't worked out that way, and Antony hadn't known how to deal with a crafty, sweet-faced boy with the intellect and wisdom of a seventy-year-old. Most of Rome had assumed that Antony, a notorious spendthrift in desperate need of Caesar's fortune to pay his debts, had been a part of the conspiracy to eliminate Caesar, and his conduct following the deed had only reinforced that. He made no attempt to punish the assassins; rather, he had virtually given them the full protection of the law. But Octavian, passionately attached to Caesar, had gradually eroded Antony's authority and forced him to outlaw them. How had he done that? By suborning a good percentage of Antony's legions to his own cause, winning over the People of Rome, and stealing the thirty thousand talents of Caesar's war chest so brilliantly that no one, even Antony, had managed to prove that Octavian was the thief. Once Octavian had soldiers and money, he gave Antony no choice but to admit him into power as a full equal. After that, Brutus and Cassius made their own bid for power; uneasy allies, Antony and Octavian had taken their legions to Macedonia and met the forces of Brutus and Cassius at Philippi. A great victory for Antony and Octavian that hadn't solved the vexed question of who would end in ruling as the First Man in Rome, an uncrowned king paying lip service to the hallowed illusion that Rome was a Republic, governed by an upper house, the Senate, and several Assemblies of the People. Together, the Senate and People of Rome: *Senatus Populusque Romanus*, SPQR.

Typically – Dellius's thoughts meandered on – victory at Philippi had found Mark Antony without a viable strategy to put Octavian out of the power equation, for Antony was a force of Nature, lusty, impulsive, hot-tempered and quite lacking foresight. His personal magnetism was great, of that kind which draws men by virtue of the most masculine qualities: courage, an Herculean physique, a well-deserved reputation as a lover of women, and enough brain to make him a formidable orator in the House. His weaknesses tended to be excused, for they were equally masculine: pleasures of the flesh, and heedless generosity.

His answer to the problem of Octavian was to divide the Roman world between them, with a sop thrown to Marcus Lepidus, high priest and owner of a large senatorial faction. Sixty years of on-again, off-again civil war had finally bankrupted Rome, whose people – and the people of Italia – groaned under poor incomes, shortages of wheat for bread, and a growing conviction that the betters who ruled them were as incompetent as they were venal. Unwilling to see his status as a popular hero undermined, Antony resolved that he would take the lion's share, leave the rotting carcass to that jackal Octavian.

So, after Philippi, the victors had carved up the provinces to suit Antony, not Octavian, who inherited the least enviable parts: Rome, Italia, and the big islands of Sicilia, Sardinia and Corsica, where the wheat was grown to feed the peoples of Italia, long since incapable of feeding themselves. It was a tactic in keeping with Antony's character, ensuring that the only face Rome and Italia saw would belong to Octavian, while his own glorious deeds elsewhere were assiduously circulated throughout Rome and Italia. Octavian to collect the odium, himself the stout-hearted winner of laurels far from the center of government. As for Lepidus, he had charge of the other wheat province, Africa, a genuine backwater.

Ah, but Marcus Antonius did indeed have the lion's share! Not only of the provinces, but of the legions. All he lacked was money, which he expected to squeeze out of that perennial golden fowl, the East. Of course he had taken all three of the Gauls for himself; though in the West, they were thoroughly pacified by Caesar, and rich enough to contribute funds for his coming campaigns. His trusted marshals commanded Gaul's legions, of which there were many; Gaul could live without his presence.

Caesar had been killed within three days of setting out for the East, where he had intended to conquer the fabulously rich and formidable Kingdom of the Parthians, using its plunder to set Rome on her feet again. He had planned to be away for five years, and had planned his campaign with all his legendary genius. So now, with Caesar dead, it would be Marcus Antonius – Mark Antony – who conquered the Parthians and set Rome upon her feet again. Antony had conned Caesar's plans and decided that they showed all the old boy's brilliance, but that he himself could improve on them. One of the reasons why he had come to this conclusion lay in the nature of the group of men who went East with him; every last one of them was a crawler, a sucker-up, and knew exactly how to play that biggest of fish, Mark Antony, so susceptible to praise, flattery and the fleshpots.

Unfortunately Quintus Dellius did not yet have Antony's ear, though his advice would have been equally flattering, balm to Antony's ego. So, riding down the Via Egnatia on a galled and grumpy pony, his balls bruised and his unsupported legs aching, Quintus Dellius waited his chance, which still hadn't come when Antony crossed into Asia and stopped in Nicomedia, the capital of his province of Bithynia.

Somehow, every potentate and client-king Rome owned in the East had sensed that the great Marcus Antonius would head for Nicomedia, and had scuttled there in their dozens, commandeering the best inns or setting up camp in style on the city's outskirts. A beautiful place on its dreamy, placid inlet, a place that most people had forgotten lay very close to dead Caesar's heart. But, because it had, Nicomedia still looked prosperous, for Caesar had exempted it from taxes, and Brutus and Cassius, hurrying west to Macedonia, had not ventured north enough to rape it the way they had raped a hundred cities from Judaea to Thrace. Thus the pink and purple marble palace in which Antony took up residence was able to offer legates like Dellius a tiny room in which to stow his luggage and the senior among his servants, his freedman Icarus. That done, Dellius sallied forth to see what was going on, and work out how he was going to snaffle a place on a couch close enough to Antony to participate in the Great Man's conversation during dinner.

Kings aplenty thronged the public halls, ashen-pale, hearts palpitating because they had backed Brutus and Cassius. Even old King Deiotarus of Galatia, senior in age and years of service, had made the effort to come, escorted by the two among his sons whom Dellius presumed were his favorites. Antony's bosom friend Poplicola had pointed out Deiotarus to him, but after that Poplicola admitted himself at a loss – too many faces, not enough service in the East to recognize them.

Smilingly demure, Dellius moved among the groups in their outlandish apparel, eyes glistening at the size of an emerald or the weight of gold upon a coiffed head. Of course he had good Greek, so Dellius was able to converse with these absolute rulers of places and peoples, his smile growing wider at the thought that, despite the emeralds and the gold, every last one of them was here to pay obsequious homage to Rome, their ultimate ruler. Rome, who had no king, whose senior magistrates wore a simple, purple-bordered white toga and prized the iron ring of some senators over a ton of gold rings; an iron ring meant that a Roman family had been in and out of office for five hundred years. A thought that made poor Dellius automatically hide his gold senatorial ring in a fold of toga; no Dellius had yet reached the consulship, no Dellius had been prominent a *hundred* years ago, let alone five. Caesar had worn an iron ring, but Antony did not; the Antonii were not quite antique enough. And Caesar's iron ring had gone to Octavian.

Oh, air, air! He needed fresh air!

The palace was built around a huge peristyle garden that had a fountain at its middle athwart a long, shallow pool. It was fashioned of pure white Parian marble on a fishy theme – mermen, tritons, dolphins – and it was rare in that it had never been painted to imitate real life's colors. Whoever had sculpted its glorious creatures had been a master. A connoisseur of fine art, Dellius gravitated to the fountain so quickly that he failed to notice that someone had beaten him to it, was sitting in a dejected huddle on its broad rim. As Dellius neared, the fellow lifted his head; no chance to avoid a meeting now.

He was a foreigner, and a noble one, for he wore an expensive robe of Tyrian purple brocade artfully interwoven with gold thread, and upon a head of snakelike, greasy black curls sat a skullcap made of cloth of gold. Dellius had seen enough Easterners to know that the curls were not *dirty* greasy; Easterners pomaded their locks with perfumed creams. Most of the royal supplicants inside were Greeks whose ancestors had dwelled in the East for centuries, but this man was a genuine Asian local of a kind Dellius recognized because there were many like him living in Rome. Oh, not clad in Tyrian purple and gold! Sober fellows who favored homespun fabrics in dark plain colors. Even so, the look was unmistakable; he who sat on the edge of the fountain was a Jew.

'May I join you?' Dellius asked in Greek, his smile charming.

An equally charming smile appeared on the stranger's jowly face; a perfectly manicured hand flashing with rings gestured. 'Please do. I am Herod of Judaea.'

'And I am Quintus Dellius, Roman legate.'

'I couldn't bear the crush inside,' said Herod, thick lips turning down. 'Faugh! Some of those ingrates haven't had a bath since their midwives wiped them down with a dirty rag.'

'You said Herod. No king or prince in front of it?'

'There should be! My father was Antipater, a prince of Idumaea who stood at the right hand of King Hyrcanus of the Jews. Then the minions of a rival for the throne murdered him. He was too well liked by the Romans, including Caesar. But I dealt with his killer,' Herod said, voice oozing satisfaction. 'I watched him die, wallowing in the stinking corpses of shellfish at Tyre.'

'No death for a Jew,' said Dellius, who knew that much. He inspected Herod more closely, fascinated by the man's ugliness. Though their ancestry was poles apart, Herod bore a peculiar likeness to Octavian's intimate Maecenas – they both resembled frogs. Herod's protruding eyes, however, were not Maecenas's blue; they were the stony glassy black of obsidian. 'As I remember,' Dellius continued, 'all of southern Syria declared for Cassius.'

'Including the Jews. And I personally am beholden to the man, for all that Antonius's Rome deems him a traitor. He gave me permission to put my father's murderer to death.'

'Cassius was a warrior,' Dellius said pensively. 'Had Brutus been one too, the result at Philippi might have been different.'

'The birds twitter that Antonius also was handicapped by an inept partner.'

'Odd how loudly birds can twitter,' Dellius answered with a grin. 'So what brings you to see Marcus Antonius, Herod?'

'Did you perhaps notice five dowdy sparrows among the flocks of gaudy pheasants inside?'

'No, I can't say that I did. Everyone looked like a gaudy pheasant to me.'

'Oh, they're there, my five Sanhedrin sparrows! Preserving their exclusivity by standing as far from the rest as they can.'

'That, in there, means they're in a corner behind a pillar.'

'True,' said Herod, 'but when Antonius appears, they'll push to the front, howling and beating their breasts.'

'You haven't told me yet why you're here.'

'Actually, it's more that the five sparrows are here. I'm watching them like a hawk. They intend to see the Triumvir Marcus Antonius and put their case to him.'

'What's their case?'

'That I am intriguing against the rightful succession, and that I, a gentile, have managed to draw close enough to King Hyrcanus and his family to be considered as a suitor for Queen Alexandra's daughter. An abbreviated version, but to hear the unexpurgated one would take years.'

Dellius stared, blinked his shrewd hazel eyes. 'A gentile? I thought you said you were a Jew.'

'Not under Mosaic law. My father married Princess Cypros of Nabataea. An Arab. And since Jews count descent in the mother's line, my father's children are gentiles.'

'Then – then what can you accomplish here, Herod?'

'Everything, if I am let do what must be done. The Jews need a heavy foot on their necks – ask any Roman governor of Syria since Pompeius Magnus made Syria a province. I intend to be King of the Jews, whether they like it or not. And I can do it. *If* I marry a Hasmonaean princess directly descended from Judas Maccabeus. Our children will be Jewish, and I intend to have many children.'

'So you're here to speak in your defence?' Dellius asked.

'I am. The deputation from the Sanhedrin will demand that I and all the members of my family be exiled on pain of death. They're not game to do that without Rome's permission.'

'Well, there's not much in it when it comes to backing Cassius the loser,' said Dellius cheerily. 'Antonius will have to choose between two factions that supported the wrong man.'

'But my father supported Julius Caesar,' Herod said. 'What I have to do is convince Marcus Antonius that if I am allowed to live in Judaea and advance my status, I will always stand for Rome. He was in Syria years ago when Gabinius was its governor, so he must be aware how obstreperous the Jews are. But will he remember that my father helped Caesar?'

'Hmm,' purred Dellius, squinting at the rainbow sparkles of the water jetting from a dolphin's mouth. 'Why should Marcus Antonius remember that, when more recently you were Cassius's man? As, I gather, was your father before he died.'

'I am no mean advocate, I can plead my case.'

'Provided you are permitted the chance.' Dellius got up and held out his hand, shook Herod's warmly. 'I wish you well, Herod of Judaea. If I can help you, I will.'

'You would find me very grateful.'

'Rubbish!' Dellius laughed as he walked away. 'All your money is on your back.'

Mark Antony had been remarkably sober since marching for the East, but the sixty men in his entourage had expected that Nicomedia would see Antony the Sybarite erupt. An opinion shared by a troupe of musicians and dancers who had hastened from Byzantium at the news of his advent in the neighborhood; from Spain to Babylonia, every member of the League of Dionysiac Entertainers knew the name Marcus Antonius. Then, to general amazement, Antony had dismissed the troupe with a bag of gold and stayed sober, albeit with a sad, wistful expression on his ugly-handsome face.

'Can't be done, Poplicola,' he said to his best friend with a sigh. 'Did you see how many potentates were lining the road as we came in? Cluttering up the halls the moment the steward opened the doors? All here to steal a march on Rome – and me. Well, I don't intend to let that happen. I didn't choose the East as my bailiwick to be diddled out of the goodies the East possesses in such abundance. So I'll sit dispensing justice in Rome's name with a clear head and a settled stomach.' He giggled. 'Oh, Lucius, do you remember how disgusted Cicero was when I spewed into your toga on the rostra?' Another giggle, a shrug. 'Business, Antonius, business!' he apostrophized himself. 'They're hailing me as the new Dionysus, but they're about to discover that for the time being I'm

9

dour old Saturn.' The red-brown eyes, too small and close together to please a portrait sculptor, twinkled. 'The new Dionysus! God of wine and pleasure – I must say I rather like the comparison. The best they did for Caesar was simply God.'

Having known Antony since they were boys, Poplicola didn't say that he thought God was superior to the God of This or That; his chief job was to keep Antony governing, so he greeted this speech with relief. That was the thing about Antony; he could suddenly cease his carousing – sometimes for months on end – especially when his sense of self-preservation surfaced. As clearly it had now. And he was right; the potentatic invasion meant trouble as well as hard work, therefore it behooved Antony to get to know them individually; learn which rulers should keep their thrones, which lose them to more capable men. In other words, which rulers were best for Rome.

All of which meant that Dellius held out scant hope that he would achieve his goal of moving closer to Antony in Nicomedia. Then Fortuna entered the picture, commencing with Antony's command that dinner would not be in the afternoon, but later. And as Antony's gaze roved across the sixty Romans strolling into the dining room, for some obscure reason it lit upon Quintus Dellius. There was something about him that the Great Man liked, though he wasn't sure what; perhaps a soothing quality that Dellius could smear over even the most unpalatable subjects like a balm.

'Ho, Dellius!' he roared. 'Join Poplicola and me!'

The brothers Decidius Saxa bristled, as did Barbatius and a few others, but no one said a word as the delighted Dellius shed his toga on the floor and sat on the back of the couch that formed the bottom of the U. While a servant gathered up the toga and folded it – a difficult task – another servant removed Dellius's shoes and washed his feet. He didn't make the mistake of usurping the *locus consularis*; Antony would occupy that, with Poplicola in the middle. His was the far end of the couch, socially the least desirable position, but for Dellius – what an elevation! He could feel the eyes boring into him, the minds behind them busy trying to work out what he had done to earn this promotion.

The meal was good, if not quite Roman enough – too much lamb, bland fish, peculiar seasonings, alien sauces. However, there was a pepper slave with his mortar and pestle, and if a Roman diner could snap his fingers for a pinch of freshly ground pepper, anything was edible, even German boiled beef. Samian wine flowed, though well watered; the moment he saw that Antony was drinking it watered, Dellius did the same.

At first he said nothing, but as the main courses were taken out and the sweeties brought in, Antony belched loudly, patted his flat belly and sighed contentedly.

'So, Dellius, what did you think of the vast array of kings and princes?' he asked affably.

'Very strange people, Marcus Antonius, particularly to one who has never been to the East.'

'Strange? Aye, they're that, all right! Cunning as sewer rats, more faces than Janus, and daggers so sharp you never feel them slide between your ribs. Odd, that they backed Brutus and Cassius against me.'

'Not really so odd,' said Poplicola, who had a sweet tooth and was slurping at a confection of sesame seeds bound with honey. 'They made the same mistake with Caesar – backed Pompeius Magnus. You campaigned in the West, just like Caesar. They didn't know your mettle. Brutus was a nonentity, but for them there was a certain magic about Gaius Cassius. He escaped annihilation with Crassus at Carrhae, then governed Syria extremely well at the ripe old age of thirty. Cassius was the stuff of legends.'

'I agree,' said Dellius. 'Their world is confined to the eastern end of Our Sea. What goes on in the Spains and the Gauls at the western end is an unknown.'

'True.' Antony grimaced at the syrupy dishes on the low table in front of the couch. 'Poplicola, wash your face! I don't know how you can stomach this honeyed mush.'

Poplicola wriggled to the back of the couch while Antony looked at Dellius with an expression that said he understood much that Dellius had hoped to hide: the penury, the New Man status, the vaunting ambition. 'Did any among the sewer rats take your fancy, Dellius?'

'One, Marcus Antonius. A Jew named Herod.'

'Ah! The rose among five weeds.'

'His metaphor was avian – the hawk among five sparrows.'

Antony laughed, a deep rich bellow. 'Well, with Deiotarus, Ariobarzanes and Pharnaces here, I'm not likely to have much time to devote to half a dozen quarrelsome Jews. No wonder the five weeds hate our rose Herod, though.'

'Why?' asked Dellius, assuming a look of awed interest.

'For a start, the regalia. Jews don't bedizen themselves in gold and Tyrian purple – it's against their laws. No kingly trappings,

11

no images, and their gold goes into their Great Temple in the name of all the people. Crassus robbed the Great Temple of two thousand gold talents before he set off to conquer the Kingdom of the Parthians. The Jews cursed him, and he died ignominiously. Then came Pompeius Magnus asking for gold, then Caesar, then Cassius. They *hope* I won't do the same, but they *know* I will. Like Caesar, I'll ask them for a sum equal to what Cassius asked for.'

Dellius wrinkled his brow. 'I don't – ah . . .'

'Caesar demanded a sum equal to what they gave Magnus.'

'Oh, I see! I beg pardon for my ignorance.'

'We're all here to learn, Quintus Dellius, and you strike me as quick to learn. So fill me in on these Jews. What do the weeds want, and what does Herod the rose want?'

'The weeds want Herod exiled under pain of death,' Dellius said, abandoning the avian metaphor. If Antony liked his own better, so would Dellius. 'Herod wants a Roman decree allowing him to live freely in Judaea.'

'And who will benefit Rome more?'

'Herod,' Dellius answered without hesitation. 'He may not be a Jew according to their lights, but he wants to rule them by marrying some princess with the proper blood. If he succeeds, I think Rome will have a faithful ally.'

'Dellius, Dellius! Surely you can't think *Herod* faithful?'

The rather faunlike face creased into a mischievous grin. 'Definitely, when it's in his best interests. And since he knows the people he wants to rule hate him enough to kill him if they get a tenth of a chance, Rome will always serve his interests better than they will. While Rome is his ally, he's safe from all but poison or ambush, and I can't see him eating or drinking anything that hasn't been thoroughly tasted, nor going abroad without a bodyguard of non-Jews he pays extremely well.'

'Thank you, Dellius!'

Poplicola intruded his person between them. 'Solved one problem, eh, Antonius?'

'With some help from Dellius, yes. Steward, clear the room!' Antony bellowed. 'Where's Lucilius? I need Lucilius!'

On the morrow, the five members of the Jewish Sanhedrin found themselves first on the list of supplicants Mark Antony's herald called. Antony was clad in his purple-bordered toga and carried the plain ivory wand of his high imperium: he made an imposing figure. Beside him was his beloved secretary, Lucilius, who had belonged to Brutus. Twelve lictors in crimson stood to either side of his ivory curule chair, the axed bundles of rods balanced between their feet. A dais raised them above the crowded floor.

The Sanhedrin leader began to orate in good Greek, but in a style so florid and convoluted that it took him a tediously long time to say who the five of them were, and why they had been deputed to come so far to see the Triumvir Marcus Antonius.

'Oh, shut up!' Antony barked without warning. 'Shut up and go home!' He snatched a scroll from Lucilius, unfurled it and brandished it fiercely. 'This document was found among Gaius Cassius's papers after Philippi. It states that only Antipater, chancellor to the so-called King Hyrcanus at that time, and his sons Phasael and Herod, managed to raise any gold for Cassius's cause. The Jews tendered nothing except a beaker of poison for Antipater. Leaving aside the fact that the gold was going to the *wrong* cause, it's clear to me that the Jews have far more love for gold than for Rome. When *I* reach Judaea, what will change from that? Why, nothing! In this man Herod I see someone willing to pay Rome her tributes and taxes – which go, I might remind you all, to preserve the peace and wellbeing of your realms! When you gave to Cassius, you simply funded his army and fleets! Cassius was a sacrilegious traitor who took what was rightfully Rome's! Ah, do you shiver in your shoes, Deiotarus? Well you should!'

I had forgotten, thought the listening Dellius, how pungently he can speak. He's using the Jews to inform all of them that he will not be merciful.

Antony returned to the subject. 'In the name of the Senate and People of Rome, I hereby command that Herod, his brother Phasael and all his family are free to dwell anywhere in any Roman land, including Judaea. I cannot prevent Hyrcanus from titling himself a king among his people, but in the eyes of Rome he is no more and no less than an ethnarch. Judaea is no longer a single land. It is five small regions dotted around southern Syria, and five small regions it will remain. Hyrcanus can have Jerusalem, Gazara and Jericho. Phasael the son of Antipater will be the tetrarch of Sepphora. Herod the son of Antipater will be the tetrarch of Amathus. And be warned! If there is any trouble in southern Syria, I will crush the Jews like so many eggshells!'

I did it, I did it! cried Dellius to himself, bursting with happiness. Antonius listened to *me*!

Herod was by the fountain, but not suffused with the joy that

Dellius expected to see. His face was pinched and white – what was the matter? What could be the matter? He had come a stateless pauper, he would leave a tetrarch.

'Aren't you pleased?' Dellius asked. 'You won without even needing to argue your case, Herod.'

'Why did Antonius have to elevate my brother too?' Herod demanded harshly, though he spoke to someone who wasn't there. 'He has put us on an equal footing! How can I wed Mariamne when Phasael is not only my equal in rank, but also my older brother? It's Phasael will wed her!'

'Come, come,' said Dellius gently. 'That's all in the future, Herod. For the moment, accept Antonius's judgement as more than you had hoped to gain. He's come down on your side – the five sparrows have just had their wings clipped.'

'Yes, yes, I see all that, Dellius, but this Marcus Antonius is clever! He wants what the far-sighted Romans all want – balance. And to put me alone on an equal footing with Hyrcanus is not a Roman enough answer. Phasael and I in one pan, Hyrcanus in the other. Oh, Marcus Antonius, you are clever! Caesar was a genius, but you are supposed to be a dolt. Now I find another Caesar.'

Dellius watched Herod plod off, his mind whirling. Between that brief conversation over dinner and this audience today, Mark Antony had done some research. *That* was why he'd hollered for Lucilius! And what frauds they were, he and Octavian! Burned all Brutus's and Cassius's papers, indeed! But like Herod, I deemed Antonius an educated dolt. He is not, he is not! thought Dellius, gasping. He's crafty *and* clever. He will put his hands on everything in the East, raising this man, lowering that man, until the client-kingdoms and satrapies are absolutely his. Not Rome's. *His*. He has sent Octavian back to Italia and a task so big it will break so weak and sickly a youth; but, just in case Octavian doesn't break, Antonius will be ready.

TWO

When Antony left the capital of Bithynia, all of the potentates save Herod and the five members of the Sanhedrin accompanied him, still declaring their loyalty to the new rulers of Rome, still maintaining that Brutus and Cassius had duped them, lied to them, coerced them – ai, ai, ai, *forced* them! Having scant patience for Eastern weeping and wailing, Antony didn't do what Pompey the Great, Caesar and the rest had done – invite the most important among them to join him for dinner, travel in his party. No, all the way from Nicomedia to Ancyra, the only town of any size in Galatia, Mark Antony pretended that his regal camp followers didn't exist.

Here, amid the rolling grassy expanses of the best grazing country east of Gaul, he had perforce to move into Deiotarus's palace and strive to be amiable. Four days of that were three too many, but during that time Antony informed Deiotarus that he was to keep his kingdom – for the moment. His second most favored son, Deiotarus Philadelphus, was gifted with the wild, mountainous fief of Paphlagonia (it was of no use to anybody), whereas his most favored son, Castor, got nothing, and what the old King should have made of *that* was now beyond his dwindling mental faculties. To all the Romans with Antony, it meant that eventually drastic changes would be made to Galatia, and not for the benefit of any Deiotarid. For information about Galatia, Antony talked to the old King's secretary, a noble Galatian named Amyntas who was young, well-educated, efficient and clear-sighted.

'At least,' said Antony jovially as the Roman column set off for Cappadocia, 'we've lost a decent percentage of our hangers-on! That gushing idiot Castor even brought the fellow who clips his toenails. Amazing, that a warrior like Deiotarus should produce such a perfect pansy.'

He was speaking to Dellius, who now rode an easy-gaited roan mare and had passed the grumpy pony to Icarus, previously doomed to walk. 'You've lost Pharnaces and his court too,' said Dellius.

'Pah! He ought never to have come.' Antony's lips curled in contempt. 'His father was a better man, and his grandfather much better still.'

'You mean the great Mithridates?'

'Is there any other? Now there was a man, Dellius, who almost beat Rome. Formidable.'

'Pompeius Magnus defeated him easily.'

'Rubbish! Lucullus defeated him. Pompeius Magnus just cashed in on the fruits of Lucullus's labors. He had a habit of doing that, did Magnus. But his vaingloriousness got him in the end. He began to believe his own publicity. Fancy anyone, Roman or otherwise, thinking he could beat Caesar!'

'You would have beaten Caesar with no trouble, Antonius,' said Dellius without a trace of sycophancy in his tone.

'*I*? Not if every god there is fought on my side! Caesar was in a class all his own, and there's no disgrace in saying that. Over fifty battles he generaled, and never lost a one. Oh, I'd beat Magnus if he still lived – or Lucullus, or even Gaius Marius. But Caesar? Alexander the Great would have gone down to him.'

The voice, a light tenor surprising in such a big man, held no resentment. Nor even, reflected Dellius, guilt. Antonius fully subscribes to the Roman way of looking at things: because he had lifted no finger against Caesar, he can sleep at night. To plot and scheme is no crime, even when a crime is committed thanks to the plotting and scheming.

Singing their marching songs lustily, the two legions and mass of cavalry Antony had with him entered the gorge country of the great red river, Halys, beautiful beyond Roman imagination, so rich and ruddy were the rocks, so tortured the planes of cliffs and shelves. There was ample flat ground on either bank of the broad stream, flowing sluggishly because the snows of the high peaks had not yet melted. Which was why Antony was marching over-land to Syria; winter seas were too dangerous for sailing, and Antony preferred to stay with his men until he could be sure they liked him better than they had Cassius, to whom they had belonged. The weather was chilly, but bitter only when the wind got up, and down in the bottom of the gorge country there was little wind. Despite its color, the water was potable for men as well as horses; central Anatolia was not a populous place.

The settlement of Eusebeia Mazaca sat at the foot of the vast volcano Argaeus, white with snow, for no one in history remembered its erupting. A blue city, small and impoverished; everyone had looted it time out of mind, for its kings were weak and too parsimonious to keep an army.

It was here that Antony began to realize how difficult it was going to be to squeeze yet more gold and treasure out of the East; Brutus and Cassius had plundered whatever King Mithridates the Great had overlooked. A realization that put him severely out of sorts and sent him with Poplicola, the brothers Decidius Saxa and Dellius to inspect the priest-kingdom of Ma at Comana, not far distant from Eusebeia Mazaca. Let the senile King of Cappadocia and his ludicrously incompetent son stew in their denuded palace! Perhaps at Comana he would find a hoard of gold beneath an innocent-looking flagstone − priests left kings for dead when it came to protecting their money.

Ma was an incarnation of Kubaba Cybele, the Great Earth Mother who had ruled all the gods, male and female, when humanity first learned to tell its history around the campfires. Over the aeons she had lost her power, save in places like the two Comanas, one here in Cappadocia, the other north in Pontus, and in Pessinus, not far from where Alexander the Great had cut the Gordian knot with his sword. Each of these three precincts was governed as an independent realm, its king also serving as high priest, and each lay within natural boundaries like Pontic cherries in a bowl.

Scorning an escort of troops, Antony, his four friends and plenty of servants rode into the beguiling little village of Cappadocian Comana, noting with approval its costly dwellings, the gardens promising a profusion of flowers in the coming spring, the imposing temple of Ma rising atop a slight hill surrounded by a grove of birches, with poplars down either side of a paved avenue that led straight to Ma's earthly house. Off to one side was the palace: like the temple, its Doric columns were blue with scarlet bases and capitals; the walls behind were a much darker blue, and the shingled roof edged in gilt.

A young man who looked in his late teens was waiting for them in front of the palace, clad in layers of green gauze, a round gold hat upon his head, which was shaven.

'Marcus Antonius,' said Antony, sliding from his dappled grey Public Horse and tossing its reins to one of the three servants he had brought with him.

'Welcome, Lord Antonius,' said the young man, bowing low.

'Just Antonius will do. We don't have any lords in Rome. What's your name, shaveling?'

'Archelaus Sisenes. I am Priest-king of Ma.'

'Bit young to be a king, aren't you?'

'Better to be too young than too old, Marcus Antonius. Come into my house.'

The visit started off with wary verbal fencing, at which King Archelaus Sisenes, even younger than Octavian, proved a match for Antony, whose good nature inclined him to admire a master of the art. As indeed he might have happily tolerated Octavian, had not Octavian been Caesar's heir.

But though the buildings were lovely and the landscaping good enough to please a Roman heart, an hour on the water clock was quite enough time to discover that whatever wealth Ma of Comana might once have possessed had vanished. With a ride of only fifty miles between them and the Cappadocian capital, Antony's friends were fully prepared to set out at dawn of the following day to rejoin the legions and continue the march.

'Will it offend you if my mother attends our dinner?' the Priest-king asked, tone deferential. 'And my young brothers?'

'The more the merrier,' said Antony, good manners to the fore. He had already found the answers to several vexed questions, but it would be prudent to see for himself what kind of family had produced this intelligent, precocious, fearless fellow.

Archelaus Sisenes and his brothers were a handsome trio, with quick wits, a thorough knowledge of Greek literature and philosophy, and even a smattering of mathematics.

None of which mattered the moment Glaphyra entered the room. Like all the Great Mother's female acolytes, she had gone into service for the Goddess at thirteen, but not, like the rest of that year's intake of pubescent virgins, to spread her mat inside the temple and offer her maidenhead to the first comer who fancied her. Glaphyra was royal, and chose her own mate where she wished. Her eye had lighted upon a visiting Roman senator, who sired Archelaus Sisenes without ever knowing that he had; she was all of fourteen when she bore the boy. The next son belonged to the King of Olba, descended from the archer Teucer, who fought with

18

his brother Ajax at Troy; and the father of the third was a handsome nobody guiding a team of oxen in a caravan from Media. After that, Glaphyra hung up her girdle and devoted her energies to bringing up her boys. At this moment she was thirty-four and looked twenty-four.

Though Poplicola wondered what drove her to appear for dinner when the guest of honor was a notorious philanderer, Glaphyra knew very well why. Lust did not enter the picture; she who belonged to the Great Mother had long ago abrogated lust as demeaning. No, she wanted more for her sons than a tiny priest-kingdom! She was after as much of Anatolia as she could get, and if Marcus Antonius was the kind of man gossip said he was, then he was her chance.

Antony sucked in his breath audibly – what a *beauty*! Tall and lissome, long legs and magnificent breasts, and a face to rival Helen's: lush red lips, skin as flawless as a rose petal, lustrous blue eyes between thick dark lashes, and absolutely straight flaxen hair that hung down her back like a sheet of hammered silver-gilt. Of jewels she wore none, probably because she had none to wear. Her blue, Greek-styled gown was plain wool.

Poplicola and Dellius were shoved off the couch so quickly that they were hard put to land on their feet; one huge hand was already patting the space where they had reclined.

'Here, with me, you gorgeous creature! What's your name?'

'Glaphyra,' she said, kicking off her felt slippers and waiting until a servant pulled warm socks over her feet. Then she swung her body onto the couch, but far enough away from Antony to prevent his hugging her, which he showed every sign of wanting to do. Gossip was certainly right in saying that he wasn't a subtle lover, if his greeting was anything to go by. Gorgeous creature, indeed! He thinks of women as conveniences; but I, resolved Glaphyra, must exert myself to become a more convenient convenience than his horse, his secretary or his chamber pot. And if he quickens me, I will offer to the Goddess for a girl. A girl of Antonius's could marry the King of the Parthians – what an alliance! As well that we are taught to suck with our vaginas better than a fellatrix can with her mouth! I will enslave him.

Thus it was that Antony lingered in Comana for the rest of winter, and when, early in March, he finally set out for Cilicia and Tarsus, he took Glaphyra with him. His ten thousand infantrymen hadn't minded this unexpected furlough; Cappadocia was a land of women whose men had been slaughtered on some battlefield or carted off to slavery. As these legionaries could farm as well as they soldiered, they enjoyed the break. Originally Caesar had recruited them across the Padus River in Italian Gaul, and, apart from the higher altitude, Cappadocia wasn't so very different to farm or graze. Behind them they left several thousand hybrid Romans in utero, properly prepared and planted land, and many thousands of grateful women.

They descended a good Roman road between two towering ranges, plunging into vast aromatic forests of pine, larch, spruce, fir, the sound of roaring water perpetually in their ears; until at the pass of the Cilician Gates the road was so steep it was stepped at five-pace intervals. Going down, a comb of Hymettan honey; had they been going up, the fragrant air would have been polluted by splendid Latin obscenities. With the snow melting fast now, the headwaters of the Cydnus River boiled and tumbled like a huge swirling cauldron, but once through the Cilician Gates the road became easier and the nights warmer. They were dropping rapidly toward the coast of Our Sea.

Tarsus, which lay on the Cydnus some twenty miles inland, came as a shock. Like Athens, Ephesus, Pergamum and Antioch, it was a city most Roman nobles knew, even if from a fleeting visit. A jewel of a place, hugely rich. But no more. Cassius had levied such a massive fine on Tarsus that, having melted down every gold or silver work of art, no matter how valuable, the Tarsians had been forced to sell the populace gradually into slavery, starting with the lowest born, and working their way inexorably upward. By the time that Cassius had grown tired of waiting and sailed off with the five hundred talents of gold that Tarsus had thus far managed to scrape together, only a few thousand free people were left out of what had been half a million. But not to enjoy their wealth; that had gone beyond recall.

'By all the gods I hate Cassius!' Antony cried, farther than ever from the riches he had expected. 'If he did this to Tarsus, what did he do in Syria?'

'Cheer up, Antonius,' Dellius said. 'All is not lost.' By now he had supplanted Poplicola as Antony's chief source of information, which was what he wanted. Let Poplicola have the joy of being Antony's intimate! He, Quintus Dellius, was well content to be the man whose advice Antony esteemed and, right at this dark moment, he had some useful advice. 'Tarsus is a big city, the center of all Cilician trade, but once Cassius hove in view, the whole of Cilicia Pedia stayed well away from Tarsus. Cilicia Pedia is rich and fertile, but no Roman governor has ever succeeded in taxing it. The region is run by brigands and renegade Arabs who get away with far more than Cassius ever did. Why not send your troops into Cilicia Pedia and see what's to be found? You can stay here – put Barbatius in command.'

Good counsel, and Antony knew it. Better by far to make the Cilicians bear the cost of victualling his troops than poor Tarsus, especially if there were bandit strongholds to be looted.

'Sensible advice that I intend to take,' Antony said, 'but it won't be anything like enough. Finally I understand why Caesar was determined to conquer the Parthians – there's no real wealth to be had this side of Mesopotamia. Oh, *curse* Octavianus! He pinched Caesar's war chest, the little worm! While I was in Bithynia, all the letters from Italia said he was dying in Brundisium, would never last ten miles on the Via Appia. And what do the stay-at-home letters have to say here in Tarsus? Why, that he coughed and spluttered all the way to Rome, where he's busy smarming up to the legion representatives. Commandeering the public land of every place that cheered for Brutus and Cassius when he isn't bending his arse over a barrel for apes like Agrippa to bugger!'

Get him off the subject of Octavian, thought Dellius, or he will forget sobriety and holler for unwatered wine. That snaky bitch Glaphyra doesn't help – too busy working for her sons. So he clicked his tongue, a sound of sympathy, and eased Antony back onto the subject of where to get money in the bankrupt East.

'There is an alternative to the Parthians, Antonius.'

'Antioch? Tyre, Sidon? Cassius got to them first.'

'Yes, but he didn't get as far as Egypt.' Dellius let the word 'Egypt' drop from his lips like syrup. 'Egypt can buy and sell Rome – everyone who ever heard Marcus Crassus talk knows *that*. Cassius was on his way to invade Egypt when Brutus summoned him to Sardis. He took Allienus's four Egyptian legions, yes, but, alas, in Syria. Queen Cleopatra cannot be impeached for that, but she didn't send any aid to you and Octavianus either. I think her in-action can be construed as worth a ten-thousand-talent fine.'

Antony grunted. 'Huh! Daydreams, Dellius.'

'No, definitely not! Egypt is *fabulously* rich.'

Half listening, Antony studied a letter from his warlike wife, Fulvia. In it she complained about Octavian's perfidies, and described the precariousness of Octavian's position in blunt, graphic terms. Now, she scrawled in her own hand, was the time to rouse Italia and Rome against him! And Lucius thought this too: Lucius was beginning to enlist legions. Rubbish, thought Antony, who knew his brother Lucius too well to deem him capable of deploying ten beads on an abacus. *Lucius* leading a revolution? No, he was just enlisting men for big brother Marcus. Admittedly Lucius was consul this year, but his colleague was Vatia, who would be running things. Oh, women! Why couldn't Fulvia devote herself to disciplining her children? The brood she had borne Clodius was grown and off her hands, but she still had her son by Curio and his own two sons.

Of course, by now Antony knew that he would have to postpone his expedition against the Parthians for at least another year. Not only did shortage of funds render it impossible; so did the need to watch Octavian closely. His most competent marshals, Pollio, Calenus and trusty old Ventidius, had to be stationed in the West with the bulk of his legions just to keep that eye on Octavian. Who had written him a letter begging that he use his influence to call off Sextus Pompeius, busy raiding the sea lanes to steal Rome's wheat like a common pirate. To tolerate Sextus Pompeius had not been a part of their agreement, Octavian whinged – did Marcus Antonius not remember how the two of them had sat down together after Philippi to divide up the duties of the three Triumvirs?

Indeed I remember, thought Antony grimly. It was after I won Philippi that I saw as through crystal that there was nowhere in the West to reap enough glory for me to eclipse Caesar. To surpass Caesar, I will have to crush the Parthians.

Fulvia's scroll fell to the desk top, curled itself up. 'Do you really believe that Egypt can produce that sort of money?' he asked, looking up at Dellius.

'Certainly!' said Dellius heartily. 'Think about it, Antonius! Gold from Nubia, ocean pearls from Taprobane, precious stones from the Sinus Arabicus, ivory from the Horn of Africa, spices from India and Aethiopia, the world's paper monopoly, and more wheat than there are people to eat it. The Egyptian public income is six thousand gold talents a year, and the sovereign's private income another six thousand!'

'You've been doing your homework,' said Antony with a grin.

'More willingly than ever I did when a schoolboy.'

Antony got up and walked to the window that looked out over the agora to where, between the trees, ships' masts speared the cloudless sky. Not that he saw any of it; his eyes were turned inward, remembering the scrawny little creature Caesar had installed in a marble villa on the wrong side of Father Tiber. How Cleopatra had railed at being excluded from the interior of Rome! Not in front of Caesar, who wouldn't put up with tantrums; but behind his back it had been a different story. All Caesar's friends had taken a turn trying to explain to her that she, an anointed queen, was religiously forbidden to enter Rome. Which hadn't stopped her complaining! Thin as a stick she had been, and no reason to suppose she'd plumped out since she returned home after Caesar died. Oh, how Cicero had rejoiced when word got around that her ship had gone to the bottom of Our Sea! And how downcast he had been when the rumor proved false. The least of Cicero's worries, as things turned out – he ought never to have thundered forth in the Senate against *me*! Tantamount to a death wish. After he was executed, Fulvia thrust a pen through his tongue before I exhibited his head on the rostra. Fulvia! Now there's a woman! I never cared for Cleopatra, never bothered to go to her soirées or her famous dinner parties – too highbrow, too many scholars, poets and historians. And all those beast-headed gods in the room where she prayed! I admit that I never understood Caesar, but his passion for Cleopatra was the biggest mystery of all.

'Very well, Quintus Dellius,' Antony said aloud. 'I will order the Queen of Egypt to appear before me in Tarsus to answer charges that she aided Cassius,' Antony said. 'You can carry the summons yourself.'

How wonderful! thought Dellius, setting off the next day on the road that led first to Antioch and then south along the coast to Pelusium. He had demanded to be outfitted in state, and Antony had obliged by giving him a small army of attendants and two squadrons of cavalry as a bodyguard. No traveling by litter, alas! Too slow to suit the impatient Antony, who had given him one month to reach Alexandria, a thousand miles from Tarsus. Which meant Dellius had to hurry. After all, he didn't know how long it was going to take to convince the Queen that she must obey Antony's summons, appear before his tribunal in Tarsus.

THREE

Chin on her hand, Cleopatra watched Caesarion as he bent over his wax tablets, Sosigenes at his right hand, supervising. Not that her son needed him; Caesarion was seldom wrong, and never mistaken. The leaden weight of grief shifted in her chest, made her swallow painfully. To look at Caesar's son was to look at Caesar, who at this age would have been Caesarion's image: tall, graceful, golden-haired, long bumpy nose, full humorous lips with delicate creases in their corners. Oh, Caesar, Caesar! How have I lived without you? And they *burned* you, those barbaric Romans! When my time is come, there will be no Caesar beside me in my tomb, to rise with me and walk the Realm of the Dead. They put your ashes in a jar and built a round marble monstrosity to accommodate the jar. Your friend Gaius Matius chose the epitaph: VENI · VIDI · VICI etched in gold on polished black stone. But I have never seen your tomb, nor want to. All I have is a huge lump of grief that never goes away. Even when I manage to sleep, it is there to haunt my dreams. Even when I look at our son, it is there to mock my aspirations. Why do I never think of the happy times? Is that the pattern of loss, to dwell upon the emptiness of today? Since those self-righteous Romans murdered you, my world is ashes doomed never to mingle with yours. Think on it, Cleopatra, and weep.

The sorrows were many. First and worst, River Nilus failed to inundate. For three years in a row, the life-giving water had not spread across the fields to wet them, soak in and soften the seeds. The people starved. Then came the plague, slowly creeping up the length of River Nilus from the cataracts to Memphis and the start of the Delta, then into the branches and canals of the Delta, and finally to Alexandria.

And always, she thought, I made the wrong decisions, Queen Midas on a throne of gold who didn't understand until it was too late that people cannot eat gold. Not for any amount of gold could I persuade the Syrians and the Arabs to venture down Nilus and collect the jars of grain waiting on every jetty. It sat there until it rotted, and then there were not enough people to irrigate by hand, and no crops germinated at all. I looked at the three million inhabitants of Alexandria and decided that only one million of them could eat, so I issued an edict that stripped the Jews and Metics of their citizenship. An edict that forbade them to buy wheat from the granaries, the right of citizens only. Oh, the riots! And it was all for nothing. The plague came to Alexandria and killed two million without regard for citizenship. Greeks and Macedonians died, people for whom I had abandoned the Jews and Metics. In the end, there was plenty of grain for those who did not die, Jews and Metics as well as Greeks and Macedonians. I gave them back the citizenship, but they hate me now. I made all the wrong decisions. Without Caesar to guide me, I proved myself a poor ruler.

In less than two months my son will be six years old, and I am childless, barren. No sister for him to marry, no brother to take his place should anything befall him. So many nights of love with Caesar in Rome, yet I did not quicken. Isis has cursed me.

Apollodorus hurried in, his golden chain of office clinking. 'My lady, an urgent letter from Pythodorus of Tralles.'

Down went the hand, up went the chin. Cleopatra frowned. 'Pythodorus? What does he want?'

'Not gold, at any rate,' said Caesarion, looking up from his tablets with a grin. 'He's the richest man in Asia Province.'

'Pay attention to your sums, boy!' said Sosigenes.

Cleopatra got up from her chair and walked across to an open section of wall where the light was good. A close examination of the green wax seal showed a small temple in its middle and the words PYTHO · TRALLES around its edge. Yes, it seemed authentic. She broke it and unfurled the scroll, written in a hand that said no scribe had been made privy to its contents. Too untidy.

Pharaoh and Queen, Daughter of Amun-Ra,
    I write as one who loved the God Julius Caesar for many years, and as one who respected his devotion to you. Though I am aware you have informants to keep you apprised of what is going on in Rome and the Roman world, I doubt

that any of them stands high in the confidence of Marcus Antonius. You will of course know that Antonius journeyed from Philippi to Nicomedia last November, and that many kings, princes and ethnarchs met him there. He did virtually nothing to alter the state of affairs in the East, but he did command that twenty thousand silver talents be paid to him immediately. The size of this tribute shocked all of us.

After visiting Galatia and Cappadocia, he arrived in Tarsus. I followed him with the two thousand silver talents that we ethnarchs of Asia Province had managed to scrape together. Where were the other eighteen thousand talents? he asked. I think I succeeded in convincing him that nothing like this sum is to be found, but his answer was one we have grown used to: pay him nine more years' tribute in advance, and we would be forgiven. As if we have salted away ten years' tribute against the day! They just do not listen, these Roman governors.

I crave your pardon, great Queen, for burdening you with our troubles, and our troubles are not why I am writing this in secret. This is to warn you that within a very few days you will receive a visit from one Quintus Dellius, a grasping, cunning little man who has wormed his way into Marcus Antonius's good opinion. His whisperings into Antonius's ear are aimed at filling Antonius's war chest, for Antonius hungers to do what Caesar did not live to do – conquer the Parthians. Cilicia Pedia is being scoured from end to end, the brigands chased from their strongholds and the Arab raiders back across the Amanus. A profitable exercise, but not profitable enough, so Dellius suggested that Antonius summon you to Tarsus and there fine you ten thousand *gold* talents for supporting Gaius Cassius.

There is nothing I can do to help you, dear good Queen, beyond warn you that Dellius is even now upon his way south. Perhaps with foreknowledge you will have the time to devise a scheme to thwart him and his master.

Cleopatra handed the scroll back to Apollodorus and stood chewing her lip, eyes closed. Quintus Dellius? Not a name she recognized, therefore no one with sufficient clout in Rome to have attended her receptions, even the largest; Cleopatra never forgot a name or the face attached to it. He would be a Vettius, some ignoble knight with smarm and charm, just the type to appeal to a boor like

Marcus Antonius. Him, she remembered! Big and burly, thews like Hercules, shoulders as wide as mountains, an ugly face whose nose strove to meet an upthrust chin across a small, thick-lipped mouth. Women swooned over him because he was supposed to have a gigantic penis – what a reason to swoon! Men liked him for his bluff, hearty manner, his confidence in himself. But Caesar, whose close cousin he was, had grown disenchanted with him – the main reason, she was sure, why Antonius's visits to her had been few. When left in charge of Italia he had slaughtered eight hundred citizens in the Forum Romanum, a crime Caesar could not forgive. Then he tried to woo Caesar's soldiers and ended in instigating a mutiny that had broken Caesar's heart.

Of course her agents had reported that many thought Antony was a part of the plot to assassinate Caesar, though she herself was not sure; the occasional letter Antony had written to her explained that he had had no choice other than to ignore the murder, forswear vengeance on the assassins, even condone their conduct. And in those letters Antony had assured her that, as soon as Rome settled down, he would recommend Caesarion to the Senate as one of Caesar's chief heirs. To a woman devastated by grief, his words had been balm. She *wanted* to believe them! Oh, no, he wasn't saying that Caesarion should be admitted into Roman law as Caesar's Roman heir! Only that Caesarion's right to the throne of Egypt should be sanctioned by the Senate. Were it not, her son would be faced by the same problems that had dogged her father, never certain of his tenure of the throne because Rome said Egypt really belonged to Rome. Anymore than she herself had been certain until Caesar entered her life. Now Caesar was gone, and his nephew Gaius Octavius had usurped more power than any lad of eighteen had ever done before. Calmly, cannily, quickly. At first she had thought of young Octavian as a possible father for more children, but he had rebuffed her in a brief letter she could still recite by heart.

Marcus Antonius, he of the reddish eyes and curly reddish hair, no more like Caesar than Hercules was like Apollo. Now he had turned his eyes toward Egypt – but not to woo Pharaoh. All he wanted was to fill his war chest with Egypt's wealth. Well, that would never happen – never!

'Caesarion, it's time you had some fresh air,' she said with brisk decision. 'Sosigenes, I need you. Apollodorus, find Cha'em and bring him back with you. It's council time.'

When Cleopatra spoke in that tone, no one argued, least of all her son, who took himself off at once, whistling for his puppy, a small ratter named Fido.

'Read this,' she said curtly when the council assembled, thrusting the scroll at Cha'em. 'All of you, read it.'

'If Antonius brings his legions, he can sack Alexandria and Memphis,' Sosigenes said, handing the scroll to Apollodorus. 'Since the plague, no one has had the spirit to resist. Nor do we have the numbers to resist. There are many gold statues to melt down.'

Cha'em was the high priest of Ptah, the creator god, and had been a beloved part of Cleopatra's life since her tenth year. His brown, firm body was wrapped from just below the nipples to mid-calf in a flaring white linen dress, and around his neck he wore the complex mixture of chains, crosses, roundels and breast-plate proclaiming his position. 'Antonius will melt nothing down,' he said firmly. 'You will go to Tarsus, Cleopatra, meet him there.'

'Like a *chattel*? Like a *mouse*? Like a whipped *cur*?'

'No, like a mighty sovereign. Like Pharaoh Hatshepsut, so great that her successor obliterated her cartouches. Armed with all the wiles and cunning of your ancestors. As Ptolemy Soter was the natural brother of Alexander the Great, you have the blood of many gods in your veins. Not only Isis, Hathor and Mut, but Amun-Ra on two sides – from the line of the pharaohs and from Alexander the Great, who was Amun-Ra's son and also a god.'

'I see where Cha'em is going,' said Sosigenes thoughtfully. 'This Marcus Antonius is no Caesar, therefore he can be duped. You must awe him into pardoning you. After all, you didn't aid Cassius, and he can't prove you did. When this Quintus Dellius arrives, he will try to cow you. But you are Pharaoh; no minion has the power to cow you.'

'A pity that the fleet you sent Antonius and Octavianus was obliged to turn back,' said Apollodorus.

'Oh, what's done is done!' Cleopatra said impatiently. She sat back in her chair, suddenly pensive. 'No one can cow Pharaoh, but . . . Cha'em, ask Tach'a to look at the lotus petals in her bowl. Antonius might have a use.'

Sosigenes looked startled. 'Majesty!'

'Oh, come, Sosigenes, Egypt matters more than any living being! I have been a poor ruler, deprived of Osiris time and time again! Do I care what kind of man this Marcus Antonius is? No, I do not! Antonius has Julian blood. If the bowl of Isis says there is enough Julian blood in him, then perhaps I can take more from him than he can from me.'

28

'I will do it,' said Cha'em, getting to his feet.

'Apollodorus, will Philopator's river barge sustain a sea voyage to Tarsus at this time of year?'

The Lord High Chamberlain frowned. 'I'm not sure, Majesty.'

'Then bring it out of its shed and send it to sea.'

'Daughter of Amun-Ra, you have many ships!'

'But Philopator built only two ships, and the ocean-going one rotted a hundred years ago. If I am to awe Antonius, I must arrive in Tarsus in a kind of state that no Roman has ever witnessed, not even Caesar.'

To Quintus Dellius, Alexandria was the most wondrous city in the world. The days when Caesar had almost destroyed it were seven years in the past, and Cleopatra had raised it in greater glory than ever. All the mansions down Royal Avenue had been restored, the Hill of Pan towered lushly green over the flat city, the hallowed precinct of Serapis had been rebuilt in the Corinthian mode, and where once siege towers had groaned and lumbered up and down Canopic Avenue, stunning temples and public institutions gave the lie to plague and famine. Indeed, thought Dellius, gazing at Alexandria from the top of Pan's hill, for once in his life great Caesar had exaggerated the degree of destruction he had wrought.

As yet he hadn't seen the Queen, who was, a lordly man named Apollodorus had informed him loftily, on a visit to the Delta to see her paper manufactories. So he had been shown his quarters – very sumptuous they were, too – and left largely to his own devices. To Dellius, that didn't mean simple sightseeing; with him he took a scribe, who jotted down notes using a broad stylus on wax tablets.

At the Sema, Dellius chuckled with glee. 'Write, Lasthenes! "The tomb of Alexander the Great, plus thirty-odd Ptolemies in a precinct dry-paved with collector's-quality marble in blue with dark green swirls ... Twenty-eight gold statues, man-sized ... An Apollo by Praxiteles, painted marble ... Four painted marble works by some unidentified master, man-sized ... A painting by Zeuxis of Alexander the Great at Issus ... A painting of Ptolemy Soter by Nicias ..." Cease writing. The rest are not so fine.'

At the Serapeum, Dellius whinnied with delight. 'Write, Lasthenes! "A statue of Serapis approximately thirty feet tall, by Bryaxis and painted by Nicias ... An ivory group of the nine Muses by Phidias ... Forty-two gold statues, man-sized ..."' He paused to scrape a gold Aphrodite, grimaced. '"Some, if not all, skinned rather than – ah – solid . . . A charioteer and horses in bronze by Myron . . ." Cease writing! No, simply add, "et cetera, et cetera . . ." There are too many more mediocre works to catalogue.'

In the agora, Dellius paused before an enormous sculpture of four rearing horses drawing a racing chariot whose driver was a woman – and what a woman! 'Write, Lasthenes! "*Quadriga* in bronze purported to be of a female charioteer named Bilistiche . . ." Cease! There's nothing else here but modern stuff, excellent of its kind but having no appeal for collectors. Oh, Lasthenes, on!'

And so it went as he cruised through the city, his scribe leaving rolls of wax behind like a moth its droppings. Splendid, splendid! Egypt is rich beyond telling, if what I see in Alexandria is anything to go by. But how do I persuade Marcus Antonius that we'll get more from selling them as works of art than from melting them down? Think of the tomb of Alexander the Great! he mused, a single block of rock crystal almost as clear as water; how fine it would look inside the Temple of Diana in Rome! What a funny little fellow Alexander was! Hands and feet no bigger than a child's, and what looked like yellow wool atop his head. A wax figure, surely, not the real thing – but you would think that, as he's a god, they would have made the effigy at least as big as Antonius! There must be enough paving in the Sema to cover the floor of a magnate's *domus* in Rome – a hundred talents' worth, maybe more. The ivory by Phidias – a thousand talents, easily.

The Royal Enclosure was such a maze of palaces that he gave up trying to distinguish one from another, and the gardens seemed to go on forever. Exquisite little coves pocked the shore beyond the harbor, and in the far distance the white marble causeway of the Heptastadion linked Pharos Isle to the mainland. And oh, the lighthouse! The tallest building in the world, taller by far than the Colossus at Rhodes had been. I thought Rome was lovely, burbled Dellius to himself; then I saw Pergamum and deemed it lovelier; but now that I have seen Alexandria, I am stunned, just stunned. Antonius was here about twenty years ago, but I've never heard him speak of the place. Too busy womanising to remember it, I suppose.

The summons to see Queen Cleopatra came the next day, which was just as well; he had concluded his assessment of the city's value, and Lasthenes had written it out on good paper, two copies.

The first thing he was conscious of was the perfumed air, thick with heady incenses of a kind he had never smelled before; then his visual apparatus took over from his olfactory, and he gaped at walls of gold, a floor of gold, statues of gold, chairs and tables of gold. A second glance informed him that the gold was a tissue-thin overlay, but the room blazed like the sun. Two walls were covered in paintings of peculiar two-dimensional people and plants, rich in colors of every description. Except Tyrian purple. Of that, not a trace.

'All hail the two Pharaohs, Lords of the Two Ladies Upper and Lower Egypt, Lords of the Sedge and Bee, Children of Amun-Ra, Isis and Ptah!' roared the lord high chamberlain, drumming his golden staff on the floor, a dull sound that had Dellius revising his opinion about thin tissue. The floor sounded *solid*.

They sat on two elaborate thrones, the woman on top of the golden dais and the boy one step beneath her. Each was clad in a strange raiment made of finely pleated white linen, and each wore a huge headdress of red enamel around a tubular cone of white enamel. About their necks were wide collars of magnificent jewels set in gold, on their arms bracelets, around their waists broad girdles of gems, on their feet golden sandals. Their faces were thick with paint, hers white, the boy's a rusty red, and their eyes were so hedged in by black lines and colored shapes that they slid, sinister as fanged fish, as no human eyes were surely intended to.

'Quintus Dellius,' said the Queen (Dellius had no idea what the epithet 'Pharaoh' meant), 'we bid you welcome to Egypt.'

'I come as Imperator Marcus Antonius's official ambassador,' said Dellius, getting into the swing of things, 'with greetings and salutations to the twin thrones of Egypt.'

'How impressive,' said the Queen, eyes sliding eerily.

'Is that all?' asked the boy, whose eyes sparkled more.

'Er – unfortunately not, Your Majesty. The Triumvir Marcus Antonius requires your presence in Tarsus to answer charges.'

'Charges?' asked the boy.

'It is alleged that Egypt aided Gaius Cassius, thereby breaking its status of Friend and Ally of the Roman People.'

'And that is a charge?' Cleopatra asked.

'A very serious one, Your Majesty.'

'Then we will go to Tarsus to answer it in person. You may leave our presence, Quintus Dellius. When we are ready to set out, you will be notified.'

And that was that! No dinner invitations, no reception to intro-duce him to the court – there must surely be a court! No Eastern monarch could function without several hundred sycophants to tell him (or her) how wonderful he (or she) was. But here was Apollodorus firmly ushering him from the room, apparently to be left to his own devices!

'Pharaoh will sail to Tarsus,' Apollodorus said, 'therefore you have two choices, Quintus Dellius. You may send your people home overland and travel with them, or you may send your people home overland and sail aboard one of the royal ships.'

Ah! thought Dellius. Someone warned them I was coming. There is a spy in Tarsus. This audience was a sham designed to put me – and Antonius – in our places.

'I will sail,' he said haughtily.

'A wise decision.' Apollodorus bowed and walked away, leaving Dellius to storm off at a hasty walk to cool his temper, sorely tried. How dared they? The audience had given him no opportunity to gauge the Queen's feminine charms or even discover for himself if the boy was really Caesar's son. They were a pair of painted dolls, stranger than the wooden thing his daughter dragged about the house as if it were human.

The sun was hot; perhaps, thought Dellius, it would do me good to paddle in the wavelets of that delicious cove outside my palace. Dellius couldn't swim – odd for a Roman – but an ankle-deep paddle was harmless. He descended a series of limestone steps, then perched on a boulder to unbuckle his maroon senatorial shoes.

'Fancy a swim? So do I,' said a cheerful voice – a child's, but deep. 'It's the funnest way to get rid of all this muck.'

Startled, Dellius turned to see the boy King, stripped down to a loincloth, his face still painted.

'You swim, I'll paddle,' said Dellius.

Caesarion waded in as far as his waist and then tipped himself forward to swim, moving fearlessly into deep water. He dived, came up with face a curious mixture of black and rusty red; then under again, up again.

'The paint's soluble in water, even salt,' the boy said, hip-deep now, scrubbing at his face with both hands.

And there stood Caesar. No one could dispute the identity of the father after seeing the child. Is *that* why Antonius wants to present him to the Senate and petition it to confirm him King of Egypt? Let anyone in Rome who knew Caesar see this boy, and he'll gather clients faster than a ship's hull does barnacles. Marcus Antonius wants to unsettle Octavian, who can only ape Caesar with thick-soled boots and practiced Caesarean gestures.

Caesarion is the real thing, Octavian a parody. Oh, clever Marcus Antonius! Bring Octavian down by showing Rome Caesar. The veteran soldiers will melt like ice in the sun, and they have so much power.

Cleopatra, cleansed of her regal make-up by the more orthodox method of a bowl of warm water, burst out laughing. 'Apollodorus, this is marvelous!' she cried, handing the papers she had read to Sosigenes. 'Where did you get these?' she asked while Sosigenes pored his way through them, chuckling.

'His scribe is fonder of money than statues, Daughter of Amun-Ra. The scribe made an extra copy and sold it to me.'

'Did Dellius act on instructions, I wonder? Or is this merely a way of demonstrating to his master that he's worth his salt?'

'The latter, Your Majesty,' said Sosigenes, wiping his eyes. 'It's so silly! The statue of Serapis, painted by *Nicias*? He was dead long before Bryaxis first poured bronze into a mold. And he missed the Praxiteles Apollo in the gymnasium – "a sculpture of no great artistic worth," he called it! Oh, Quintus Dellius, you are a fool!'

'Let us not underestimate the man just because he doesn't know a Phidias from a Neapolitan plaster copy,' Cleopatra said. 'What his list tells me is that Antonius is desperate for money. Money that I, for one, do not intend to give him.'

Cha'em pattered in, accompanied by his wife.

'Tach'a, at last! What does the bowl say about Antonius?'

The smoothly beautiful face remained impassive; Tach'a was a priestess of Ptah, trained almost from birth not to betray her emotions. 'The lotus petals formed a pattern I have never seen, Daughter of Ra. No matter how many times I cast them on the water, the pattern always stayed the same. Yes, Isis approves of Marcus Antonius as the sire of your children, but it will not be easy, and it will not happen in Tarsus. In Egypt, only in Egypt. His seed is spread too thinly, he must be fed on the juices and fruits that strengthen a man's seed.'

'If the pattern is so unique, Tach'a my mother, how can you be sure that is what the petals are saying?'

'Because I went to the holy archives, Pharaoh. My readings are only the last in three thousand years.'

'Ought I refuse to go to Tarsus?' Cleopatra asked Cha'em.

'No, Pharaoh. My own visions say that Tarsus is necessary. Antonius is not the God out of the West, but he has some of the same blood. Enough for our purposes, which are *not* to raise up a rival for Caesarion! What he needs are a sister to marry and some brothers who will be loyal subordinates.'

Caesarion walked in, trailing water. 'Mama, I've just talked to Quintus Dellius,' he said, flopping on a couch while a clucking Charmian hurried off to find towels.

'Did you, now? Where was that?' Cleopatra asked, smiling.

The wide eyes, greener than Caesar's and lacking that piercing quality, creased up in amusement. 'When I went for a swim. He was paddling. Can you imagine it? *Paddling*! He told me he couldn't swim, and that confession told me that he was never a *contubernalis* in any army that mattered. He's a couch soldier.'

'Did you have an interesting conversation, my son?'

'I led him astray, if that's what you mean. He suspected that someone warned us he was coming but, by the time I left him, he was sure we'd been taken by surprise. It was the news that we're sailing to Tarsus made him suspect. So I let it slip that late April is the time of year when we pull all the ships out of their sheds, go over them for leaks, and exercise them and their crews. What a fortunate chance! I said. Ready to go instead of struggling for ages to mend leaky ships.'

And he is not yet six years old, thought Sosigenes. This child has been blessed by all of Egypt's gods.

'I don't like that "we",' said the mother, frowning.

The bright, eager face fell. 'Mama! You can't mean it! I am to go with you – I *must* go with you!'

'Someone has to rule in my absence, Caesarion.'

'Not I! I am too young!'

'Old enough, and that's enough. No Tarsus for you.'

A verdict that ruptured the essential vulnerability of a five-year-old; an inconsolable sorrow welled up in Caesarion – that pain only a child can feel at being deprived of some new and passionately wanted experience. He burst into noisy tears, but when his mother went to comfort him, he shoved her away so fiercely that she staggered. He ran from the room.

'He'll get over it,' Cleopatra said comfortably. 'My, isn't he strong?'

Will he get over it? wondered Tach'a, who saw a different Caesarion – driven, split, achingly lonely. He's Caesar, not Cleopatra, and she doesn't understand him. It wasn't the chance to strut like a child king that made him hunger to go to Tarsus, it was the chance to see new places, ease his restlessness at this small world he inhabits.

* * *

Two days later the royal fleet was assembled in the Great Harbor, with Philopator's gigantic vessel tied up at the wharf in the little annex called the Royal Harbor.

'Ye gods!' said Dellius, gaping at it. 'Is everything in Egypt larger than in the rest of the world?'

'We like to think so,' said Caesarion who, for reasons known only to himself, had developed a habit of following Dellius around.

'It's a barge! It will wallow and sink!'

'It's a ship, not a barge,' said Caesarion. 'Ships have keels, barges do not,' he went on like a schoolmaster, 'and the keel of *Philopator* was carved from one enormous cedar hewn in the Libanus – we owned Syria then. *Philopator* was properly built, with a kelson, and bilges, and a flat-bottomed hull. It has loads of room below deck, and see? Both banks of oars are in outriggers. It's not topheavy, even from the weight of the outriggers. The mast is a hundred feet tall, and Captain Agathocles has decided to keep the lateen sail on board in case the wind's really good. See the figurehead? That's Philopator himself, going before us.'

'You know a lot,' said Dellius, who didn't understand much about ships, even after this lesson.

'Our fleets sail to India and Taprobane. Mama has promised me that, when I'm older, she'll take me to the Sinus Arabicus to see them set out. How I'd love to go with them!' Suddenly the boy stiffened and prepared for flight. 'There's my nursemaid! It's absolutely *disgusting* to have a nursemaid!' And off he ran, determined to elude the poor creature, no match for her charge.

Not long after, a servant came for Quintus Dellius; time to board his ship, which was not the *Philopator*. He didn't know whether to be glad or sorry; the Queen's vessel would undoubtedly lag far behind the rest, even if its accommodations were luxurious.

Though Dellius didn't know, Cleopatra's shipwrights had made changes to her vessel, which had survived its seagoing trials surprisingly well. It measured 350 feet from stem to stern, and 40 feet in the beam. Shifting both banks of rowers into outriggers had increased the space below deck, but Pharaoh couldn't be housed near laboring men, so below deck was given over to the hundred and fifty people who sailed in *Philopator*, most of them almost demented with terror at the very thought of riding on the sea.

The old stern reception room was turned into Pharaoh's domain, large enough for a spacious bedroom, another for Charmian and Iras, and a dining room that held twenty-one couches. The arcade of lotus-capital columns remained in place, ending forward of the mast in a raised dais, roofed with faïence tiles and supported by a new column at each corner. Forward of that was a reception room, now somewhat smaller than of yore in order that Sosigenes and Cha'em might have rooms of their own. And forward of that again, cunningly hidden in the bows, was an open cooking area. On river cruises most of the food preparation was done on shore; fire was always a risk on a wooden ship. But out to sea, no shore to cook on.

Cleopatra had brought along Charmian and Iras, two fair-haired women of impeccably Macedonian ancestry who had been her companions since babyhood. Theirs had been the job of selecting thirty young girls to travel with Pharaoh to Tarsus; they had to be beautiful in the face and voluptuous in the body, but none could be a whore. The pay was ten gold drachmae, a small fortune, but it wasn't the pay that reconciled them to the unknown, it was the clothes they were given to wear in Tarsus – flimsy gold and silver tissues, brocades glittering with metal threads, transparent linens in all the hues of the rainbow, wools so fine that they clung to the limbs as if wet. A dozen exquisitely lovely little boys had been purchased from the slave markets in Pelusium, and fifteen very tall barbarian men with fine physiques. Every male on show was outfitted in kilts embroidered to resemble peacock tails; the peacock, Cleopatra had decided, was to be the *Philopator* theme, and enough gold had been spent on buying peacock feathers to make an Antony weep.

On the first day of May the fleet sailed, and under sail, with *Philopator* scornfully showing the rest its stern cowl. The only wind that would have opposed their northerly heading, the Etesian, did not blow at this time of year. A brisk southeast breeze swelled the fleet's sails and made life much easier for the oarsmen. No tempest occurred to force them into harbor along the way, and the pilot, aboard *Philopator* in the lead, recognized every headland on the Syrian coast without hesitation. At Cape Heracleia, which faced the tip of Cyprus's tail, he came to see Cleopatra.

'Your Majesty, we have two choices,' he said, on his knees.

'They are, Palamedes?'

'To continue to hug the Syrian coast as far as the Rhosicum promontory, then cross the top of Sinus Issicus to the mouths of Cilicia Pedia's great rivers. That will mean sand bars and shoals – slow going.'

'And the alternative?'

36

'To strike into open water here and sail almost due northwest – possible with this wind – until we fetch up on the coast of Cilicia somewhere near the mouth of River Cydnus.'

'What is the difference in time at sea, Palamedes?'

'That is hard to say, Your Majesty, but perhaps as many as ten days. Cilicia Pedia's rivers will be flooding, an additional handicap if we hug the coast. But you must understand that the second choice is hazardous. A storm or a change in wind direction could send us anywhere from Libya to Greece.'

'We will take the risk and voyage upon the open sea.'

And the river gods of Egypt, perhaps not expected by Father Neptune to appear on the broad expanses of his kingdom, proved powerful enough to keep the fleet sailing unerringly for the mouth of the Cydnus River. Or perhaps Father Neptune, a properly Roman god, had concluded a contract with his Egyptian brethren. Whatever the reason, on the tenth day of May the fleet congregated seaward of the Cydnus bar. Not a good time to cross, with the swollen stream resisting entry; now the oarsmen would earn their wages! The passage was clearly marked with painted piles; between them barges worked indefatigably to dredge the sand and mud. No ship of the fleet was deep-drafted, especially tubby *Philopator*, built for river voyaging. Even so, Cleopatra ordered her fleet in ahead of her, wanting Dellius to have time to tell Antony she was here.

He found Antony bored and restless, but still sober.

'Well?' Antony demanded, glaring up at Dellius. One big hand gestured at the desk top, awash in scrolls and papers. 'Look at this! And all of it's either bills or bad news! Did you succeed? Is Cleopatra coming?'

'Cleopatra is here, Antonius. I traveled aboard her fleet, even now being assigned moorings downriver. Twenty triremes, all naval – no trade opportunities, I'm afraid.'

His chair scraped; Antony got up and went to the window, his movement making Dellius realize anew how graceful some big men could be. 'Where is she? I hope you told the city harbor master to assign her the choicest moorings.'

'Yes, but it's going to take some time. Her ship is as long as *three* Greek war galleys of olden times, so it can't exactly be slipped in between two merchantmen already tied up. The harbor master has to shift seven of them – he's not happy, but he'll do it. I spoke in your name.'

'A ship big enough to house a titan, eh? When am I going to see it?' Antony asked, scowling.

'Tomorrow morning, about an hour after dawn.' Dellius gave a contented sigh. 'She came without a murmur, and in huge state. I think she wishes to impress you.'

'Then I'll make sure she doesn't. Presumptuous sow!'

Which was why, as the sun nudged up over the trees east of Tarsus, Antony rode a drab horse to the far bank of Cydnus, a drab cloak wrapped about him, and no one in attendance. To see the enemy first is an advantage; soldiering with Caesar had taught him that. Oh, the air smells sweet! What am I doing in a sacked city when there are marches to be made, battles to be fought? he asked himself, knowing the answer. I am still here to see if the Queen of Egypt was going to answer my summons. And that other presumptuous sow, Glaphyra, is beginning to nag me in a way that Eastern women have perfected: sweetly, tearfully, larded with sighs and whimpers. Oh, for Fulvia! When *she* nags, a man knows he's being nagged – growl, snarl, roar! Nor does she mind a cuff over the ear – provided a man doesn't mind five nails raked down his chest in retaliation.

Ah, there was a good spot! He turned sideways and slid off the horse, making for a flat rock raised several feet above the bank. Sitting on it, he would have a perfect view of Cleopatra's ship sailing up the Cydnus to its moorings. He wasn't more than fifty paces from the river's channel; this was so near the edge that he could see a small bright bird nesting in the eaves of a warehouse alongside the quay.

Philopator came crawling up the river at the speed of a man walking at a fast clip, setting Antony agape long before it drew level with him. For what he could see was a figurehead amid a misty, golden halo; a brown-skinned man wearing a white kilt, a collar and belt of gold and gems, and a huge headdress of red and white. His bare feet skimmed the wavelets breaking on either side of the beak, and in his right hand he brandished a golden spear. Figureheads were known, but not so massive or so much a part of the prow. This man – some king of old? – *was* the ship, and he bore it behind him like a billowing cloak.

Everything seemed gold; the ship was gilded from the water line up to the very top of the mast, and what wasn't gold was painted in peacock blues and peacock greens, shimmering with a powdering of gold. The roofs of the buildings on deck were of faïence tiles in vivid blues and greens, and a whole arcade of lotus-headed columns marched down the deck. Even the oars were gold! And gems glittered everywhere! This ship alone was worth ten thousand gold talents!

Perfumes wafted, lyres and pipes sounded, a choir sang, all invisibly sourced; beautiful girls in gauzy gowns threw flowers from golden baskets; many beautiful little boys in peacock kilts hung laughing in the snow-white shrouds. The swelling sail, spread to help the oarsmen battle the current, was whiter than white, embroidered to display two entwined beast heads – a hooded serpent and a vulture – and a strange eye dripping a long black tear.

Peacock feathers had been clustered everywhere, but nowhere more lushly than about a tall gold dais in front of the mast. On a throne sat a woman clad in a dress of peacock feathers, her head burdened with the same red and white crown as the figurehead man wore. Her shoulders sparkled with the jewels in a wide gold collar, and a broad girdle of the same kind was cinched about her waist. Crossed on her breast she carried a shepherd's crook and a flail in gold worked with lapis blue. Her face was made up so heavily that it was quite impossible to see what she looked like; its expression was perfect impassivity.

The ship passed him by closely enough to see how wide it was, and how wonderfully made; the deck was paved in green and blue faïence tiles to match the roofs. A peacock ship, a peacock queen. Well, thought Antony, inexplicably angered, she will see who is cock of the walk in Tarsus!

He took the bridge to the city at a gallop, tumbled off the horse at the door to the governor's palace and strode in shouting for his servants.

'Toga and lictors, *now!*'

So when the Queen sent her chamberlain, the eunuch Philo, to inform Marcus Antonius that she had arrived, Philo was told that Marcus Antonius was in the agora hearing cases on behalf of the *fiscus*, and could not see Her Majesty until the morrow.

Such had actually been Antony's intention for days; it had been formally posted on the tribunal in the agora, so when he took his place on the tribunal he saw what he had expected – a hundred litigants, at least that many advocates, several hundred spectators and several dozen vendors of drinks, snacks, nibbles, parasols and fans. Even in May, Tarsus was hot. For that reason his court was shaded by a crimson awning that said SPQR on fringed flaps every few feet around its margins. Atop the stone tribunal sat Antony himself on his ivory curule chair, with twelve crimson-clad lictors to either side of him and Lucilius at a table stacked with scrolls. The most novel actor in this drama was a hoary centurion who stood in one corner of the tribunal; he wore a shirt of gold scales, golden greaves, a chest loaded with *phalerae*, *armillae* and torcs, and a gold helmet whose scarlet horsehair ruff spread sideways like a fan. But the chest loaded with decorations for valorous deeds wasn't what cowed this audience. It was the Gallic longsword the centurion held between his hands, its tip resting on the ground. It reminded the citizens of Tarsus that Marcus Antonius owned *imperium maius*, and could execute anyone for anything. If he took it into his head to issue an execution order, then this centurion would carry it out on the spot. Not that Antony had any intention of executing a fly or a spider; Easterners were used to being ruled by people who executed as capriciously as regularly, so why disillusion them?

Some of the cases were interesting, some entertaining as well. Antony waded through them with the efficiency and detachment that all Romans seemed to possess, be they members of the proletariat or the aristocracy. A people who understood law, method, routine, discipline, though Antony was less dowered with these essentially Roman qualities than most. Even so, he attacked his task with vigor, and sometimes venom. A sudden stir in the crowd threw a litigant off balance just as he reached the point whereat he would pass his case over to the highly paid advocate at his side; Mark Antony turned his head, frowning.

The crowd had parted, sighing in awe, to permit the passage of a small procession led by a nut-brown, shaven-headed man in a white dress, a fortune in gold chains around his neck. Behind him walked Philo the chamberlain in linen of blues and greens, face painted delicately, body glittering with jewels. But they were as nothing compared to the conveyance behind them: a spacious litter of gold, its roof of faïence tiles, nodding plumes of peacock feathers at its cornerposts. It was carried by eight huge men as black as grapes, with the same purple tint to their skins. They wore peacock kilts, collars and bracelets of gold, and flaring gold *nemes* headdresses.

Queen Cleopatra waited until the bearers gently set her litter down, then, without waiting for assistance in alighting, she slid lithely out of it and approached the steps of the Roman tribunal.

'Marcus Antonius, you summoned me to Tarsus. I am here,' she said in a clear, carrying voice.

'Your name is not on my roster of cases for today, madam! You will have to apply to my secretary, but I assure you that I will see that your name is first on my list in the morning,' said Antony with the courtesy due to a monarch, but no deference.

Inside, she was boiling. How dared this clodhopper of a Roman treat her like anyone else! She had come to the agora to show him up as the boor he was, display her immense clout and authority to the Tarsians, who would appreciate her position and not think too well of Antony for metaphorically spitting on her. He wasn't in the Roman forum now, these weren't Roman businessmen (all of them had quit the area as unprofitable). These were people akin to her Alexandrian people, sensitive to the prerogatives and rights of monarchs. *Mind* being pushed aside for the Queen of Egypt? No, they would preen at the distinction! They had all visited the wharf to marvel at *Philopator*, and had come to the agora fully expecting to find their cases postponed. No doubt Antony thought they would esteem his democratic principles in seeing them first, but that was not how an Eastern cerebral apparatus worked. They were shocked and disturbed, disapproving. What she was doing in standing so humbly at the foot of his tribunal was demonstrating to the Tarsians how arrogant the Romans were.

'Thank you, Marcus Antonius,' she said. 'If perhaps you have no plans for dinner, you might join me on my ship this evening? Shall we say, at twilight? It is more comfortable to dine after the heat has gone out of the air.'

He stared down at her, a spark of anger in his eyes; somehow she had put him in the wrong, he could see it in the faces of the crowd, fawning and bowing, keeping their distance from the royal personage. In Rome, she would have been mobbed, but here? Never, it seemed. Curse the woman!

'I have no plans for dinner,' he said curtly. 'You may expect to see me at twilight.'

'I will send my litter for you, Imperator Antonius. Please feel free to bring Quintus Dellius, Lucius Poplicola, the brothers Saxa, Marcus Barbatius and fifty-five more of your friends.'

Cleopatra hopped nimbly into her litter; the bearers picked up its poles and turned it around, for it was not a mere couch, it had a head and a foot to enable its occupant to be properly seen.

'Proceed, Melanthus,' said Antony to the litigant who the Queen's arrival had stopped in mid-sentence.

The rattled Melanthus turned helplessly to his highly paid

advocate, arms spread wide in bewilderment. Whereupon the man showed his competence by taking up the case as if no interruption had occurred.

It took his servants a while to find a tunic clean enough for Antony to wear to dinner on a ship; togas were too bulky to dine in, and had to be shed. Nor were boots (his preferred footwear) convenient; too much lacing and unlacing. Oh, for a crown of valor to wear upon his head! Caesar had worn his oak leaves for all public occasions, but only extreme valor in combat as a young man had earned him the privilege. Like Pompey the Great, Antony had never won a crown, brave though he had always been.

The litter was waiting. Pretending all this was great fun, Antony climbed in and ordered the bevy of friends, laughing and joking, to walk around the litter. The conveyance was admired, but not as much as the bearers, a fascinating rarity; even in the busiest, most varied slave markets, black men did not come up for sale. In Italia they were so rare that sculptors seized upon them, but those were women and children, and rarely pure-blooded like Cleopatra's bearers. The beauty of their skins, the handsomeness of their faces, the dignity of their carriage were marveled at. What a stir they would create in Rome! Though, thought Antony, no doubt she had them with her when she had lived in Rome. I just never saw them.

The gangplank, he noted, was gold save for its railings, of the rarest citrus wood, and the faïence deck was strewn with rose petals oozing a faint perfume when trodden upon. Every pedestal that held a golden vase of peacock feathers or a priceless work of art was chryselephantine – delicately carved ivory inlaid with gold. Beautiful girls whose supple limbs showed through tissue-fine robes ushered them down the deck between the columns to a pair of great gold doors wrought in bas relief by some master; inside was a huge room with shutters opened wide to let in every breeze, its walls of citrus wood and marquetry in gorgeous, complex designs, its floor a foot deep in rose petals.

She's taunting me! thought Antony. Taunting *me*!

Cleopatra was waiting, dressed now in filmy layers of gauze that shaded from dark amber underneath to palest straw on top. The style was neither Greek nor Roman nor Asian, but something of her own, waisted, flared in the skirts, the bodice fitting her closely to show small breasts beneath; her thin little arms were softened by billowing sleeves that ended at the elbows to allow room for bracelets up her forearms. Around her neck she wore a gold chain from which dangled, enclosed in a cage of finest golden wire, a single pearl the size and color of a strawberry. Antony's gaze was drawn to it immediately; he gasped, eyes going to her face in astonishment.

'I know that bauble,' he said.

'Yes, I suppose you do. Caesar gave it to Servilia many years ago to bribe her when he broke off Brutus's engagement to his daughter. But Julia died, and then Brutus died, and Servilia lost all her money in the civil war. Old Faberius Margarita valued it at six million sesterces, but when she came to sell it, she asked ten million. Silly woman! I would have paid twenty million to get it. But the ten million wasn't enough to get her out of debt, I heard. Brutus and Cassius lost the war, so that took care of one side of her fortune, and Vatia and Lepidus bled her dry, which took care of the other side.' Cleopatra spoke with amusement.

'It's true that she's Atticus's pensioner these days.'

'And Caesar's wife committed suicide, I hear.'

'Calpurnia? Well, her father, Piso, wanted to marry her to some mushroom willing to pay a fortune for the privilege of bedding Caesar's widow, but she wouldn't do it. Piso and his new wife made her life a misery, and she hated having to move out of the Domus Publica. She opened her veins.'

'Poor woman. I always liked her. I liked Servilia too, for that matter. The ones I loathed were the wives of the New Men.'

'Cicero's Terentia, Pedius's Valeria Messala, Hirtius's Fabia. I can understand that,' said Antony with a grin.

While they talked the girls were leading the fascinated group Antony had brought with him to their respective couches; when it was done, Cleopatra herself took his arm and led him to the couch at the bottom of the U, and placed him in the *locus consularis*. 'Do you mind if we have no third companion on our couch?' she asked.

'Not at all.'

No sooner was he settled than the first course came in: such an array of dainties that several noted gourmands among his party clapped their hands in delight. Tiny birds designed to be eaten bones and all, eggs stuffed with indescribable pastes, shrimps grilled, shrimps steamed, shrimps skewered and broiled with giant capers and mushrooms, oysters and scallops brought at the gallop from the coast; a hundred other equally delectable dishes meant to be eaten with the fingers. Then came the main course, whole lambs roasted on the spit, capons, pheasants, baby crocodile meat (it was superb, enthused the gourmands), stews and braises flavored in new ways, and whole roast peacocks arranged on golden dishes with all their feathers replaced in exact order and their tails fanned.

'Hortensius served the first roast peacock at a banquet in Rome,' Antony said, and laughed. 'Caesar said it tasted like an old army boot, except that the boot was tenderer.'

Cleopatra chuckled. 'He would! Give Caesar a mess of dried peas or chickpeas or lentils cooked with a knuckle of salted pork and he was happy. *Not* a food-fancier!'

'Once he dipped his bread in rancid oil and never noticed.'

'But you, Marcus Antonius, appreciate good food.'

'Yes, sometimes.'

'The wine is Chian. You shouldn't drink it watered.'

'I intend to stay sober, madam.'

'And why is that?'

'Because a man dealing with you needs his wits.'

'I take that as a compliment.'

'Age hasn't improved your looks,' he said as the sweetmeats came in, apparently indifferent to how any woman might take this news about her appearance.

'My charms were never in my looks,' she said, unruffled. 'To Caesar, what appealed were my voice, my intelligence and my royal status. Especially he liked the fact that I picked up languages as easily as he did. He taught me Latin, I taught him demotic and classical Egyptian.'

'Your Latin is impeccable.'

'So was Caesar's. That's why mine is.'

'You didn't bring his son.'

'Caesarion is Pharaoh. I left him behind to rule.'

'At *five*?'

'Nearly six, going on sixty. A wonderful boy. I trust that you intend to keep your promise and present him to the Senate as Caesar's heir in Egypt. He must have undisputed tenure of his throne, which means that Octavianus must be made to see that he is no threat to Rome. Just a good client-king of half-Roman blood that can be of no benefit to him in Rome. Caesarion's fate lies in Egypt, and Octavianus must be made to realize that.'

'I agree, but the time isn't ripe to bring Caesarion to Rome for ratification of our treaties with Egypt. There's trouble in Italia, and I can't interfere with whatever Octavianus does to solve those troubles. He inherited Italia as part of our agreement at Philippi – all I want from the place are troops.'

'As a Roman, don't you feel a certain responsibility for what is happening in Italia, Antonius?' she asked, brow pleated. 'Is it prudent and politic to leave Italia suffering so much from famine and economic differences between the businessmen, the landowners and the veteran soldiers? Ought not you, Octavianus *and* Lepidus have remained in Italia and solved its problems first? Octavianus is a mere boy, he can't possibly have the wisdom or the experience to succeed. Why not help him instead of hindering him?' She gave a gritty laugh and thumped her bolster. 'None of this is to my advantage, but I keep thinking of the mess Caesar left behind in Alexandria, and of how I had to get all its citizens cooperating instead of warring class against class. I failed because I didn't see that social wars are disastrous. Caesar left me the advice, but I wasn't clever enough to use it. But if it were to happen again, I would know how to deal with it. And what I see happening in Italia is a variation upon my own struggle. Forget your differences with Octavianus and Lepidus, work together!'

'I would rather,' Antony said between his teeth, 'be dead than give that posturing boy one iota of help!'

'The people are more important than one posturing boy.'

'No, they're not! I'm *hoping* Italia will starve, and I'll do whatever I can to speed the process up. That's why I tolerate Sextus Pompeius and his admirals. They make it impossible for Octavianus to feed Italia, and the less taxes the businessmen pay, the less money Octavianus has to buy land to settle the veterans. With the landowners stirring the pot, Octavianus will cook.'

'Rome has built an empire on the people of Italia from north of the Padus River all the way to the tip of Bruttium. Hasn't it occurred to you that in insisting that you be able to recruit troops in Italia, you're actually saying that no other place can produce such excellent soldiers? But if the country starves, they too will starve.'

'No, they won't,' Antony said instantly. 'The famine only drives them to re-enlist. It's a help.'

'Not to the women who bear the boys who will grow up into those excellent soldiers.'

'They get paid, they send money home. The ones who starve are useless – Greek freedmen and old women.'

Mentally exhausted, Cleopatra lay back and closed her eyes. Of the emotions that lead to murder she had intimate knowledge; her father had strangled his own daughter to shore up his throne, and would have killed her had not Cha'em and Tach'a hidden her in

Memphis as a growing child. But the very idea of deliberately drawing down famine and disease upon her people was utterly foreign to her. These feuding, passionate men possessed a ruthlessness that seemed to have no bounds – no wonder Caesar had died at their hands. Their own personal and familial prestige was more important than whole nations, and in that they were closer to Mithridates the Great than they would have cared to hear. If it meant that an enemy of the family would perish, they would walk over a sea of dead. They still practiced the politics of a tiny city-state, having no concept, it seemed to her, that the tiny city-state had turned into the most powerful military and commercial machine in history. Alexander the Great had conquered more, but on his death it vanished as smoke does into a wide sky; the Romans conquered a bit here and a bit there, but gave what they had conquered to an idea named Rome, for the greater glory of that idea. And yet they could not see that Italia mattered more than personal feuds. Caesar used to say it to her all the time: that Italia and Rome were the same entity. But Marcus Antonius would not have agreed.

However, she was a little closer to understanding what kind of man Marcus Antonius was. Ah, but too tired to prolong this evening! There would have to be more dinners, and if her cooks went insane dreaming up new dishes, then so be it.

'Pray excuse me, Antonius. I am for bed. Stay as long as you like. Philo will look after you.'

Next moment, she was gone. Frowning, Antony debated whether to go or stay, and decided to go. Tomorrow evening he would give a banquet for her. Odd little thing! Like one of those girls who starved themselves just at the age when they should be eating. Though they were anemic, weakly creatures, and Cleopatra was very tough. I wonder, he thought in sudden amusement, how Octavianus is coping with Fulvia's daughter by Clodius? Now there's a starved girl! No more meat on her than a gnat.

Cleopatra's invitation to a second dinner that evening came as Antony was setting out the following day for the courts, where he knew the Queen would not present herself again. His friends were so full of the wonders of that banquet that he cut his breakfast of bread and honey short, arrived at the agora before any of the litigants had expected him. Part of him was still fulminating at the direction in which she had led the more serious conversation, and they had not broached the subject of whether she had sided with

Cassius. That would keep a day or two, he supposed, but it did not augur well that clearly she was not intimidated.

When he returned to the governor's palace to bathe and shave in preparation for the evening's festivities aboard *Philopator*, he found Glaphyra lying in wait for him.

'Was I not asked last night?' she demanded in a thin voice.

'You were not asked.'

'And am I asked this evening?'

'No.'

'Ought I perhaps send the Queen a little note to inform her that I am of royal blood, and your guest here in Tarsus? If I did, she would surely extend her invitation to include me.'

'You could, Glaphyra,' said Antony, suddenly feeling jovial, 'but it wouldn't get you anywhere. Pack your things. I'm sending you back to Comana tomorrow at dawn.'

The tears cascaded like silent rain.

'Oh, cease the waterworks, woman!' Antony cried. 'You will get what you want, but not yet. Continue the waterworks, and you might get nothing.'

Only on the third evening at the third dinner aboard *Philopator* did Antony mention Cassius. How her cooks managed to keep on presenting novelties eluded him, but his friends were lost in an ecstasy of edibles that left them little time to watch what the couple on the *lectus medius* were doing. Certainly not making any amatory advances to each other and, with that speculation dead in the water, the sight of those gorgeous girls was far more thrilling – though some guests made a greater fuss of the little boys.

'You had better come to the governor's palace for dinner on the morrow,' said Antony, who had eaten well on each of the three occasions, but not made a glutton of himself. 'Give your cooks a well-deserved rest.'

'If you like,' she said indifferently; she picked at food, took a sparrow's portions.

'But before you honor my quarters with your royal presence, Your Majesty, I think we'd better clear up the matter of that aid you gave Gaius Cassius.'

'Aid? What aid?'

'Don't you call four good Roman legions aid?'

'My dear Marcus Antonius,' she drawled wearily, 'those four legions marched north in the charge of Aulus Allienus, who I was led to believe was a legate of Publius Dolabella's, the then legal governor of Syria. As Alexandria was threatened by plague as well as famine, I was glad to hand the four legions Caesar left there to Allienus. If he decided to change sides *after* he had crossed the border into Syria, that cannot be laid at my door. The fleet I sent you and Octavianus was wrecked in a storm, but you'll find no records of fleets donated to Gaius Cassius, anymore than he got money from me, or grain from me, or other troops from me. I do admit that my viceroy on Cyprus, Serapion, did send aid to Brutus and Cassius, but I am happy to see Serapion executed. He acted without orders from me, which makes him a traitor to Egypt. If you do not execute him, I certainly will on my way home.'

'Humph,' Antony grunted, scowling. He knew everything she said was true, but that was not his problem; his problem was how to twist what she said to make it look like lies. 'I can produce slaves willing to testify that Serapion acted under your orders.'

'Freely, or under torture?' she asked coolly.

'Freely.'

'For a minute fraction of the gold you hunger for more than Midas did. Come, Antonius, let us be frank! I am here because your fabulous East is bankrupt thanks to a Roman civil war, and suddenly Egypt looks like a huge goose capable of laying huge golden eggs. Well, disabuse yourself!' she snapped. 'Egypt's gold belongs to Egypt, which enjoys Friend and Ally of the Roman People status, and has never broken trust. If you want Egypt's gold, you'll have to wrest it from me by force, at the head of an army. And even then you'll be disappointed. Dellius's pathetic little list of treasures to be found in Alexandria is but one golden egg in a mighty pile of them. And that pile is so well concealed that you will never find it. Nor will you torture it out of me or my priests, who are the only ones who know whereabouts it is.'

Not the speech of someone who could be cowed!

Listening for the slightest tremor in Cleopatra's voice and watching for the slightest tension in her hands, her body, Antony could find none. Worse, he knew from several things Caesar had said that the Treasure of the Ptolemies was indeed secreted away so cunningly that no one could find it who didn't know how. No doubt the items on Dellius's list would fetch ten thousand talents, but he needed far more than that. And to march or sail his army to Alexandria would cost some thousands of talents of itself. Oh, curse the woman! I cannot bully or bludgeon her into yielding. Therefore I must find a different way. Cleopatra is no Glaphyra.

* * *

48

Accordingly a note was delivered to *Philopator* early the next morning to say that the banquet Antony was giving tonight would be a costume party.

'But I offer you a hint,' the note said. 'If you come as Aphrodite, I will greet you as the New Dionysus, your natural partner in the celebration of life.'

So Cleopatra draped herself in Greek guise, floating layers of pink and carmine. Her thin, mouse-brown hair was done in its habitual style, parted into many strips from brow to nape of neck, where a small knot of it was bunched. People joked that it resembled the rind of a canteloupe melon, not far from the truth. A woman like Glaphyra would have been able to tell him (had she ever seen Cleopatra in her pharaonic regalia) that this uninspiring style enabled her to wear Egypt's red and white double crown with ease. Tonight, however, she wore a spangled short veil of interwoven flowers, and had chosen to adorn her person with flowers at neck, at bodice, at waist. In one hand she carried a golden apple. The outfit was not particularly attractive, which didn't worry Mark Antony, not a connoisseur of women's wear. The whole object of the 'costume' dinner party was so that he could show *himself* to best advantage.

As the New Dionysus, he was bare from the waist up, and bare from mid-thigh down. His nether regions were draped in a flimsy piece of purple gauze, under which a carefully tailored loincloth revealed the mighty pouch that contained the fabled Antonian genitalia. At forty-three, he was still in his prime, that Herculean physique unmarred by more excesses than most men fitted into twice his tally of years. Calves and thighs were massive, but the ankles slender, and the pectorals of his chest bulged above a flat, muscled belly. Only his head looked odd, for his neck was as thick as a bull's, and dwarfed it. The tribe of girls the Queen had brought with her looked at him and gasped, near died inside for want of him.

'My, you don't have much in your wardrobe,' Cleopatra said, unimpressed.

'Dionysus didn't need much. Here, have a grape,' he said, extending the bunch he held in one hand.

'Here, have an apple,' she said, extending a hand.

'I'm Dionysus, not Paris. "Paris, you pretty boy, you woman-struck seducer,"' he quoted. 'See? I know my Homer.'

'I am consumed with admiration.' She arranged herself on the couch; he had given her the *locus consularis*, not a gesture the sticklers in his entourage appreciated. Women were women.

Antony tried, but the stripped-for-action look didn't affect Cleopatra at all. Whatever she lived for, it wasn't the physical side of love, so much was certain. In fact, she spent most of the evening playing with her golden apple, which she put into a glass goblet of pink wine and marveled at how the blue of the glass turned the gold a subtle shade of purple, especially when she stirred it with one manicured finger.

Finally, desperate, Antony gambled all on one roll of the dice: Venus, they must come up Venus! 'I'm falling in love with you,' he said, hand caressing her arm.

She moved it as if to brush off the attentions of an insect. '*Gerrae*,' she growled.

'It is not rubbish!' he said indignantly, sitting up straight. 'You've bewitched me, Cleopatra.'

'My wealth has bewitched you.'

'No, no! I wouldn't care if you were a beggar woman!'

'*Gerrae!* You'd step over me as if I didn't exist.'

'I'll prove that I love you! Set me a task!'

Her answer was immediate. 'My sister Arsinoë has taken refuge in the precinct of Artemis at Ephesus. She is under a sentence of death legally pronounced in Alexandria. Execute her, Antonius. Once she's dead, I'll rest easier, like you more.'

'I have a better way,' he said, sweat beading his forehead. 'Let me make love to you – here, now!'

Her head tilted, skewing the veil of blossoms. To Dellius, watching intently from his couch, she looked like a tipsy flower vendor determined on a sale. One yellow-gold eye closed, the other surveyed Antony speculatively. 'Not in Tarsus,' she said then, 'and not while my sister lives. Come to Egypt bearing me Arsinoë's head, and I'll think about it.'

'I can't!' he cried, gasping. 'I've too much work to do! Why do you think I'm sober? A war brewing in Italia, that accursed boy faring better than anyone could have expected – I can't! And how can you ask for the head of your own sister?'

'With *relish*. She's been after my head for years. If her plans succeed, she'll marry my son, then lop mine from my shoulders in the flicker of an eye. Her blood is pure Ptolemaic and she's young enough to have children when Caesarion is old enough. I am the granddaughter of Mithridates the Great – a hybrid. And my son, more hybrid yet. To many people in Alexandria, Arsinoë represents a return to the proper bloodlines. If I am to live, she must die.'

Cleopatra slid from the couch, discarding her veil, wrenching ropes of tuber roses and lilies from her neck and waist. 'Thank you for an excellent party, and thank you for an illuminating trip abroad. *Philopator* has not been so entertained these last hundred years. Tomorrow we sail home to Egypt. Come and see me there. And do look in on my sister at Ephesus. She's such an absolute chuckle. If you like harpies and gorgons, you'll just love her.'

'Maybe,' said Dellius, made privy to some of this the next morning as *Philopator* dipped golden oars in the water and started home, 'you frightened her, Antonius.'

'Frightened *her*? That cold blooded viper? Impossible!'

'She doesn't weigh much more than a talent, whereas you must weigh in the region of four talents. Perhaps she thinks you'd crush her to death.' He tittered. 'Or ram her to death! It's even possible that you would.'

'*Cacat!* I never thought of that!'

'Woo her with letters, Antonius, and get on with your duties as Triumvir east of Italia.'

'Are you trying to push me, Dellius?' Antony asked.

'No, no, of course not!' Dellius answered quickly. 'Just remind you that the Queen of Egypt is no longer on your horizon, whereas other people and events are.'

Antony swept the paperwork off his desk with a savage swipe that had Lucilius down on his hands and knees immediately, picking them up. 'I'm fed up with this life, Dellius! The East can rot – it's time for wine and women.'

Dellius looked down, Lucilius looked up, exchanged a speaking glance. 'I have a better idea, Antonius,' Dellius said. 'Why not get through a mountain of work this summer, then spend the winter in Alexandria at the court of Queen Cleopatra?'

FOUR

For the fourth year in a row, Nilus did not inundate. The only cheering news was that those along the river who had survived the plague seemed immune to it, as was equally true in the Delta and Alexandria. These folk were hardier, healthier.

Sosigenes had been visited by an idea, and issued an edict in Pharaoh's name; it ordered that the lowest sections of Nilus's banks be broken down a further five feet. If any water came over the tops of these prepared gaps, it would flow into huge ponds excavated in advance. All around the rims of the ponds stood treadmill water wheels ready to feed water into shallow channels snaking off across the parched fields. And when mid-July brought the inundation that was no inundation, the river rose just high enough to fill the ponds. This was a far easier way of irrigating by hand than the traditional shaduf, a single bucket that had to be dipped into the river itself.

And people were people, even in the midst of death; babies had been born, the population was increasing. But Egypt would eat.

The threat from Rome was in temporary abeyance; her agents told Cleopatra that from Tarsus Antony had gone to Antioch, paid calls on Tyre and Sidon, then taken ship for Ephesus. And there a screaming Arsinoë was dragged from sanctuary to be run through by a sword. The high priest of Artemis looked likely to follow her, but Antony, who disliked these Eastern bloodbath vengeances, intervened at the ethnarch's request and sent the man back to his precinct unharmed. The head would not be a part of Antony's baggage if and when he visited Egypt; Arsinoë had been burned whole. She had been the last true Ptolemy, and with her death that particular threat to Cleopatra vanished.

'Antonius will come in the winter,' said Tach'a, smiling.

'Antonius! Oh, my mother, he is no Caesar! How can I bear his hands upon me?'

'Caesar was unique. You cannot forget him, that I understand, but you must cease to mourn him and look to Egypt. What matter the feel of his hands when Antonius possesses the blood to give Caesarion a sister to marry? Monarchs do not mate for gratification of the self, they mate to benefit their realms and safeguard the dynasty. You will get used to Antonius.'

In fact, Cleopatra's greatest worry that summer and autumn was Caesarion, who hadn't forgiven her for leaving him behind in Alexandria. He was irreproachably polite, he worked hard over his books, he read voluntarily in his own time, he kept up his riding lessons, his military exercises and his athletic pursuits, though he would not box or wrestle.

'*Tata* told me that our thinking apparatus is located inside our heads and that we must never engage in sports that endanger it. So I will learn to use the *gladius* and the longsword, I will shoot arrows and throw rocks from slings, I will practice casting my *pilum* and my *hasta*, I will run, hurdle and swim. But I will not box or wrestle. *Tata* wouldn't approve, no matter what my instructors say. I told them to desist, not to come running to you – does my command count for less than yours?'

She was too busy marveling at how much he remembered about Caesar to hear the message implicit in his last words. His father died before the child turned four.

But it was not the argument over contact sport or other small dissatisfactions that gnawed at her; what hurt was his aloofness. She couldn't fault his attention when she spoke to him, especially to issue an order, but he had shut her out of his private world. Clearly he felt an ongoing resentment that she couldn't dismiss as petty.

Oh, she cried to herself, why do I always make the wrong decisions? Had I only known what effect excluding him from Tarsus would have, I would have taken him with me. But that would have been to risk the succession on a sea voyage – impossible!

Then her agents reported that the situation in Italia had deteriorated into open war. The instigators were Antony's termagant wife, Fulvia, and Antony's brother, the consul Lucius Antonius. Fulvia snared that famous fence-sitter and side-switcher Lucius Munatius Plancus and bewitched him into donating the veteran soldiers he was settling around Beneventum – two full legions – for her army; after which she persuaded that aristocratic dolt, Tiberius Claudius Nero, whom Caesar had so detested, to raise a slave revolt in Campania – not an appropriate task for one who had never in his life conversed with a slave. Not that Nero didn't try, just that he didn't even know how to start his commission.

Having no official position save his status as Triumvir, Octavian slid in careful Fabian circles on Lucius Antonius's perimeter as the two legions that Lucius himself had managed to recruit moved up the Italian peninsula toward Rome. The third Triumvir, Marcus Aemilius Lepidus, took two legions to Rome to keep Lucius out. Then the moment Lepidus saw the glitter of armor on the Via Latina, he abandoned Rome and his troops to a jubilant Fulvia (and Lucius, whom people tended to forget).

The outcome actually depended upon the ring of great armies fencing Italia in – armies commanded by Antony's best marshals, men who were his friends as well as his political adherents. Gnaeus Asinius Pollio held Italian Gaul with seven legions; in Further Gaul across the Alps sat Quintus Fufius Calenus with eleven legions; while Publius Ventidius and his seven legions sat in coastal Liguria.

By now it was autumn. Antony was in Athens, not far away, enjoying the entertainments this most sophisticated of cities had to offer. Pollio wrote to him, Ventidius wrote to him, Calenus wrote to him, Plancus wrote to him, Fulvia wrote to him, Lucius wrote to him, Sextus Pompey wrote to him, and Octavian was writing to him every single day. Antony never answered any of these letters – he had better things to do. Thus – as Octavian for one realized – Antony missed his great chance to crush Caesar's heir permanently. The veterans were mutinous, no one was paying taxes, and all Octavian could scrape up were eight legions. Every main road from Bononia in the north to Brundisium in the south reverberated to the rhythmic thud of hobnailed legionary *caligae*, most of them belonging to Octavian's avowed enemies. Sextus Pompey's fleets controlled both the Tuscan Sea to Italia's west and the Adriatic Sea to Italia's east, cutting off the grain supply from Sicilia and Africa. Had Antony hoisted his bulk off his plush Athenian couch and led all these elements in an outright war to squash Octavian, he would have won easily. But Antony chose not to answer his letters and not to move. Octavian breathed a sigh of relief, while Antony's own people assumed that Antony was too busy having a good time to bother with anything beyond pleasure.

But in Alexandria, reading her reports, Cleopatra fretted and fumed, considered writing to Antony to urge him into an Italian war. That would really remove the threat from Egypt! In the end she didn't write; had she, it would have been a wasted effort.

Lucius Antonius marched north on the Via Flaminia to Perusia, a magnificent town perched high on a flat-topped mountain in the middle of the Apennines. There he inserted himself and his six legions within Perusia's walls and waited to see not only what Octavian would do, but also what Pollio, Ventidius and Plancus would do. It never occurred to him that the latter three wouldn't march to his rescue – as Antony's men, they had to!

Octavian had put his spiritual brother Agrippa in command – a shrewd decision; when the two very young men concluded that neither Pollio and Ventidius nor Plancus were going to rescue Lucius, they erected massive siege fortifications in a ring all the way around Perusia's mountain. No food could reach the town and, with winter coming on, the water table was low, and lowering.

Fulvia sat in Plancus's camp and railed at the perfidy of Pollio and Ventidius, clustered miles away; she also railed in person at Plancus, who put up with it because he was in love with her. Her state of mind was alarmingly unstable: one moment frenzied tantrums, the next bursts of energy recruiting more men. But what ate at her most was a new hatred of Octavian. The super-cilious pup had sent his wife, Fulvia's daughter Clodia, back to her mother still virgo intacta. What was she going to do with a skinny girl who did nothing but weep and refuse to eat? *In a war camp?* Worst of all, Clodia insisted that she was madly in love with Octavian, and blamed Octavian's rejection on her mother.

By late October, Antony likened himself to Aetna just before an eruption. His colleagues felt the tremors and tried to avoid him, but that was not possible.

'Dellius, I'm going to winter in Alexandria,' he announced. 'Marcus Saxa and Caninius can stay with the troops at Ephesus. Lucius Saxa, you can come with me as far as Antioch – I'm making you governor of Syria. There are two legions of Cassius's troops in Antioch, they'll be enough for your needs. You can start by making the cities of Syria understand that I want tribute. Now, not later! Whatever a place paid Cassius, it will pay to me. For the moment I'm not changing my dispositions elsewhere – Asia Province is quiet, Censorinus is coping in Macedonia, and I can't see the need for a governor in Bithynia.' He stretched his arms above his head exultantly. 'A holiday! The New Dionysus is going to have a proper holiday! And what better place than at the court of Aphrodite in Egypt?'

He didn't write Cleopatra a letter either. She knew that he was coming only through her agents, who managed to give her two *nundinae* of notice. In those sixteen days she sent ships out in search of fare that Egypt did not stock, from the succulent hams of the Pyreneae to huge wheels of cheese. Though it wasn't usually on the menu, the palace kitchens could produce *garum* for flavoring sauces, and several breeders of suckling pigs for Roman residents of the city found their entire piggeries bought out. Chickens, geese, ducks, quails and pheasants were rounded up, though at this time of year there would be no lamb. More importantly, the wine had to be as good as plentiful; Cleopatra's court hardly touched it, and Cleopatra herself preferred Egyptian barley beer. But for the Romans it must be wine, wine, wine.

Rumors floated around Pelusium and the Delta that Syria was restless, although no one seemed to have concrete evidence as to the nature of the problem. Admittedly the Jews were in a ferment; when Herod had returned from Bithynia a tetrarch, there were howls from both sides of the Sanhedrin, Pharisee and Sadducee; that his brother Phasael was also a tetrarch didn't seem to matter as much. Herod was hated, Phasael tolerated. Some Jews were intriguing to spill Hyrcanus from the throne in favor of his nephew, a Hasmonaean prince named Antigonus; or, failing success, at least to strip Hyrcanus of the high priesthood and give *that* to Antigonus.

But with Mark Antony due to arrive any day, Syria didn't get the attention from Cleopatra that it deserved. It was a matter of some urgency only because Syria was right next door.

What preoccupied Cleopatra most was a crisis that hinged on her son. Cha'em and Tach'a had been instructed to take Caesarion to Memphis and keep him there until Antony left.

'I will not go,' Caesarion said very calmly, chin up.

They were far from alone, which annoyed her. So she answered curtly. 'Pharaoh orders it! Therefore you will go.'

'I too am Pharaoh. The greatest Roman left alive after my father was murdered is to visit us, and we will receive him in state. That means Pharaoh must be present in both incarnations, male and female.'

'Don't argue, Caesarion. If necessary, I'll have you taken to Memphis under guard.'

'That will look good to our subjects!'

'How dare you be insolent to me!'

'I am Pharaoh, anointed and crowned. I am son of Amun-Ra and son of Isis. I am Horus. I am the Lord of the Two Ladies and the Lord of the Sedge and Bee. My cartouche is above yours. Without going to war against me, you cannot deny me my right to sit on my throne. As I will when we receive Marcus Antonius.'

The sitting room was so silent that every word mother and son uttered rang around the gilded rafters. Servants stood on duty in every inconspicuous corner; Charmian and Iras were in attendance on the Queen, Apollodorus stood in his place, and Sosigenes sat at a table poring over menus. Only Cha'em and Tach'a were absent, happily planning the treats they were going to give their beloved Caesarion when he arrived at the precinct of Ptah.

The child's face was set mulishly, his blue-green eyes hard as polished stones. Never had his likeness to Caesar been so pronounced. Yet his pose was relaxed, no clenched fists or planted feet. He had said his piece; the next move was Cleopatra's.

Who sat in her easy chair with mind spinning. How to explain to this obstinate stranger that she acted for his own good? If he remained in the Royal Enclosure he was bound to be exposed to all manner of things beyond his ken – oaths and profanities, crudeness and coarseness, vomiting gluttons, people too hot with lust to care that they coupled on a couch or against a wall; goings-on that carried the seeds of corruption, vivid illustrations of a world she had resolved her son would never see until he was old enough to cope with it. Well she remembered her own years as a child in this selfsame palace, her dissolute father pawing his catamites, exposing his genitals to be kissed and sucked, dancing about drunkenly playing his silly pipes at the head of a procession of naked boys and girls. While she cowered out of sight and prayed he would not find her and have her raped for his pleasure. Killed, even, like Berenice. He had a new family by his young half-sister; a girl by his Mithridatid wife was expendable. So the years she had spent in Memphis with Cha'em and Tach'a lived in her memory as the most wonderful time of her whole life: safe, secure, *happy*.

The feasts in Tarsus had been a fairly good example of Mark Antony's way of life. Yes, he himself had remained continent, but only because he had to duel with a woman who was also a monarch. About the conduct of his friends he was indifferent, and some of them had disported themselves shamelessly.

But how to tell Caesarion that he wouldn't – *couldn't* – be here? Instinct said that Antony was going to forget continence, play the role of Neos Dionysus wholeheartedly. He was also her son's cousin. If Caesarion were in Alexandria, they couldn't be kept apart. And obviously Caesarion dreamed of meeting the great warrior, not understanding that the great warrior would present in the guise of the great reveler.

So the silence persisted until Sosigenes cleared his throat and pushed his chair back to stand.

'Your Majesties, may I speak?' he asked.

Caesarion answered. 'Speak,' he commanded.

'Young Pharaoh is now six, yet he is still under the care of a palace full of women. Only in the gymnasium and the hippodrome does he enter a world of men, and they are his subjects. Before they can talk to him, they must prostrate themselves. He sees nothing odd in this: he is Pharaoh. But with the visit of Marcus Antonius, young Pharaoh will have a chance to associate with men who are not his subjects, and who will not prostrate themselves. Who will ruffle his hair, cuff him gently, joke with him. Man to man. Pharaoh Cleopatra, I know why you wish to send young Pharaoh to Memphis, I understand—'

Cleopatra cut him short. 'Enough, Sosigenes! You forget yourself! We will finish this conversation after young Pharaoh has left the room – which he will do *now!*'

'I will not leave,' said Caesarion.

Sosigenes continued, visibly shaking in terror. His job – also his head – was in peril, but *someone* had to say it. 'Your Majesty, you cannot send young Pharaoh away, either now to finish this, or later to shield him from the Romans. Your son is crowned and anointed Pharaoh and King. In years he may be a child, but in what he is, he is a man. It is time that he associated freely with men who do not prostrate themselves. His father was a Roman. It is time he learned more of Rome and Romans than he could as a babe during the time when you lived in Rome.'

Cleopatra felt her face afire, wondered how much of what she experienced was written on it. Oh, bother the wretched boy, to take his stand so publicly! He knew how servants gossiped – it would be all over the palace in an hour, all over the city tomorrow.

And she had lost. Everybody present knew it.

'Thank you, Sosigenes,' she said after a very long pause, 'I appreciate your advice. It is the right advice. Young Pharaoh must stay in Alexandria to mingle with the Romans.'

The boy didn't whoop with glee or caper about. He nodded regally and said, gazing at his mother with expressionless eyes, 'Thank you, Mama, for deciding not to go to war.'

Apollodorus shooed everyone out of the room, including young Pharaoh; as soon as she was left alone with Charmian and Iras, Cleopatra burst into tears.

'It had to happen,' said Iras, the practical one.

'He was cruel,' said Charmian, the sentimental one.

'Yes,' said Cleopatra through her tears, 'he was cruel. All men are, it is their nature.' She mopped her face. 'I have lost a tiny fraction of my power – he has wrested it from me. By the time he is twenty, he will have all the power.'

'Let us hope,' said Iras, 'that Marcus Antonius is kind.'

'You saw him in Tarsus. Did you think him kind then?'

'Yes, when you let him. He was uncertain, so he blustered.'

'Isis must take him as her husband,' said Charmian, sighing, eyes misty. 'What man could be unkind to Isis?'

'To take him as husband is not to yield power. Isis will gather it,' said Cleopatra. 'But what will my son say when he realizes that his mother is giving him a stepfather?'

'He will take it in his stride,' said Iras.

Antony's flagship, an overlarge quinquereme high in the poop and bristling with catapults, was bidden tie up in the Royal Harbor. And there, waiting on the wharf under a golden canopy of state stood both incarnations of Pharaoh, though not clad in pharaonic regalia. Cleopatra wore a simple robe of pink wool and Caesarion a Greek tunic, oatmeal trimmed with purple. He had wanted to wear a toga, but Cleopatra had told him that no one in Alexandria could show the palace seamstresses how to make one. She thought that the best way to avoid giving Caesarion the news that he wasn't allowed to wear a toga because he wasn't a Roman citizen.

If it had been Caesarion's ambition to steal his mother's thunder, he succeeded; when Antony strode down the gangplank onto the wharf, his eyes were fixed on Caesarion.

'Ye gods!' he exclaimed as he reached them, 'Caesar all over again! Boy, you're his living image!'

Knowing himself tall for his age, Caesarion felt suddenly dwarfed; Antonius was *huge!* None of which mattered when Antony bent down and lifted him up effortlessly, settled him on a left arm bulging with muscles beneath many folds of toga. Behind him Dellius was beaming; it was left to him to greet Cleopatra, walk at her side up the path from the jetty, looking at the pair well in front, the boy's golden head thrown back as he laughed at some Antonian jest.

'They have taken to each other,' Dellius said.

'Yes, haven't they?' It was spoken tonelessly. Then she squared her shoulders. 'Marcus Antonius hasn't brought as many friends with him as I expected.'

'There were jobs to do, Your Majesty. I know Antonius hopes to meet some Alexandrians.'

'The Interpreter, the Recorder, the Chief Judge, the Accountant and the Night Commander are eager to attend on him.'

'The *Accountant?*'

'They are just names, Quintus Dellius. To be one of those five men is to be of pure Macedonian stock going back to the barons of Ptolemy Soter. They are the Alexandrian aristocrats,' Cleopatra said, sounding amused. What, after all, was Atticus if not an accountant, and would any Roman of patrician family scorn Atticus? 'We have not planned a reception for this evening,' Cleopatra went on. 'Just a quiet supper for Marcus Antonius alone.'

'I'm sure he'll like that,' said Dellius smoothly.

When Caesarion couldn't keep his eyes open, his mother firmly packed him off to bed, then dismissed the servants to leave her alone with Antony.

Alexandria didn't have a proper winter, just a slight chill in the air after sunset that meant the breeze walls were closed. After Athens, more extreme, Antony found it delightful; could feel himself relaxing as he hadn't in months. And the lady had been an interesting dinner companion – when she managed to get a word in edgeways; Caesarion had bombarded Antony with a staggering variety of questions. What was Gaul like? What was Philippi really like? How did it feel to command an army? And on, and on, and on.

'He wore you out,' she said now, smiling.

'More curiosity than a fortune-teller before she tells your fortune. But he's clever, Cleopatra.' A grimace of distaste twisted his face. 'As precocious as the other Caesar heir.'

'Whom you detest.'

'That's too mild a verb. Loathe, more like.'

'I hope you can find it in you to like my son.'

'Much better than I expected to.' His eyes traveled over the lamps set around the room, squinting. 'It's too bright,' he said.

In answer she slid from the couch, picked up a snuffer and quenched all save those flames that didn't shine in Antony's face. 'Have you a headache?' she asked, returning to the couch.

'Yes, as a matter of fact.'

'Would you like to retire?'

'Not if I can lie here quietly and talk to you.'

'Of course you can.'

'You didn't believe me when I said I was falling in love with you, but I spoke the truth.'

'I have silver mirrors, Antonius, and they tell me that I am not the kind of woman you fall in love with. Fulvia, for example.'

He grinned, his small white teeth flashing. 'And Glaphyra, though you never saw her. A delectable piece of work.'

'Whom clearly you did not love, to say that about her. But Fulvia you do love.'

'Used to, more like. At the moment she's a nuisance, with her war against Octavianus. A futile business, badly conducted.'

'A very beautiful woman.'

'Past her prime, at forty-three. We're much of an age.'

'She's given you sons.'

'Aye, but too young yet to know what they're made of. Her grandfather was Gaius Gracchus, a great man, so I hope for good boys. Antyllus is five, Iullus still a baby. A good mare, Fulvia. Four by Clodius – two girls, two boys – a boy by Curio, and mine.'

'The Ptolemies breed well too.'

'With only one chick in your nest, you can say that?'

'I am Pharaoh, Marcus Antonius, which means that I cannot mate with mortal men. Caesar was a god, therefore a fit mate for me. We had Caesarion quickly, but then –' she sighed – 'no more. Not for want of trying, I can assure you.'

Antony laughed. 'No, I can see why he wouldn't tell you.'

Stiffening, she lifted her head to look at him, her big, golden eyes reflecting the light of a lamp behind Antony's close-cropped curls. 'Tell me what?' she asked.

'That he'd sire no more children on you.'

'You lie!'

Surprised, he too lifted his head. 'Lie? Why should I?'

'How would I know your reasons? I simply know that you lie!'

'I speak the truth. Search your mind, Cleopatra, and you'll know that. Caesar, to sire a girl for his son to marry? He was a Roman through and through, and Romans do not approve of incest. Not even between nieces and uncles or nephews and aunts, let alone brothers and sisters. First cousins are considered a risk.'

The disillusionment crashed upon her like a massive wave: Caesar, of whose love she was so sure, had led her a dance of pure deception! All those months in Rome, hoping and praying for a pregnancy that never happened – and he knew, he knew! The God out of the West had deceived her, all for the sake of some stupid Roman shibboleth! She ground her teeth, growled in the back of her throat. 'He deceived me,' she said then, dully.

'Only because he didn't think you'd understand. I see that he was right,' said Antony.

'Were you Caesar, would you have done that to me?'

'Oh, well,' said Antony, rolling over to come a little closer to her, 'my feelings are not so fine.'

'I am destroyed! He cheated me, and I loved him so much!'

'Whatever happened is in the past. Caesar's dead.'

'And I have to have the same conversation with you that once I had with him,' Cleopatra said, furtively wiping her eyes.

'What conversation is that?' he asked, trailing a finger down her arm.

This time she didn't remove it. 'Nilus has not inundated in four years, Marcus Antonius, because Pharaoh is barren. To heal her people, Pharaoh must conceive a child with the blood of gods in its veins. Your blood is Caesar's blood – on your mother's side you are a Julian. I have prayed to Amun-Ra and Isis, and they have told me that a child of your loins would please them.'

Not exactly a declaration of love! How did a man answer such a dispassionate explanation? And did he, Marcus Antonius, want to commence an affair with such a cold-blooded little woman? A woman who genuinely believed what she said. Still, he thought, to sire gods on earth would be a new experience – one in the eye for old Caesar, the family martinet!

He took her hand, lifted it to his lips, and kissed it. 'I would be honored, my Queen. And while I can't speak for Caesar, I *do* love you.'

Liar, liar! she cried in her heart. You are a Roman, in love with nothing beyond Rome. But I will use you, as Caesar used me. 'Will you share my bed while you are in Alexandria?'

'Gladly,' he said, and kissed her.

It was pleasant, not the ordeal she had imagined; his lips were cool and smooth, and he didn't shove his tongue inside her mouth at this first, tentative exploration. Just lips against lips, gentle and sensuous.

'Come,' she said, picking up a lamp.

Her bedroom was not far away; these were Pharaoh's private quarters, on the small side. He pulled his tunic off – no loincloth underneath – and untied the bows that held her dress up at the shoulders. It fell in a puddle around her as she sat on the edge of the bed.

'Skin is good,' he murmured, stretching out beside her. 'I won't hurt you, my Queen. Antonius is a good lover; he knows what kind of love to give a frail little creature like you.'

As indeed he did. Their coupling was slow and amazingly pleasant, for he stroked her body with smooth hands and paid her breasts delightful attention. Despite his assurances that he would not, he would have hurt her had she not given birth to Caesarion, though he teased her into torment before he entered her, and knew how to use that enormous member in many ways. He let her come to climax before he did, and her climax astonished her. It seemed a betrayal of Caesar, yet Caesar had betrayed her, so what did it matter? And, greatest gift of all, he didn't remind her of Caesar in any respect. What she had with Antony belonged to Antony. Different, too, to find that within moments of each climax he was ready for her again, and almost embarrassing to count the number of her own climaxes. Was she so starved? The answer, obviously, was yes. Cleopatra the monarch was once again a woman.

Caesarion was thrilled that she had taken the great Marcus Antonius as her lover. In that respect he was not naive. 'Will you marry him?' he asked, dancing about in glee.

'In time, perhaps,' she said, profoundly relieved.

'Why not now? He is the mightiest man in the world.'

'Because it is too soon, my son. Let Antonius and I learn first if our love will bear the responsibilities of marriage.'

As for Antony, he was bursting with pride. Cleopatra was not the first sovereign he had bedded, but she was by far the most important. And, he had discovered, her sexual attentions lay halfway between those of a professional whore and a dutiful Roman wife. Which suited him. When a man embarked upon a relationship destined to last for more than a night, he needed neither one nor the other, so Cleopatra was perfect.

All of which may have accounted for his mood on the first evening when his mistress entertained him lavishly; the wine was superb and the water rather bitter, so why add water and spoil a great vintage? Antony let go of his good intentions without even realizing that he had, and got happily, hopelessly drunk.

The Alexandrian guests, all Macedonians of the highest stratum, looked on bewildered at first, then suddenly seemed to decide that there was much to be said for dissipation. The Recorder, an awesome man of huge conceit, whooped and giggled his way through the first flagon, then seized a passing female servant of beauty and began to make love to her. Within moments he was joined by the other Alexandrians, who proved that they were any Roman's equal when it came to participating in an orgy.

To Cleopatra, watching fascinated (and sober), it was a lesson of a kind she had never expected to need to learn. Luckily Antony didn't seem to notice that she didn't join in the hilarities; he was too busy drinking. Perhaps because he also ate hugely, the wine didn't reduce him to a helpless fool. In a discreet corner Sosigenes, somewhat more experienced in these matters than his queen, had placed chamber pots and bowls behind a screen where the guests could relieve themselves through any orifice, and also put out beakers of potions that rendered the next morning less painful.

'Oh, I enjoyed myself!' roared Antony the next morning, his rude health unimpaired. 'Let's do it again this afternoon!'

And so began for Cleopatra two months and more of constant, remorseless revels. And the wilder the goings-on became, the more Antony enjoyed them and the better he thrived. Sosigenes had inherited the task of dreaming up novelties to vary the tenor of these sybaritic festivities, with the result that the ships docking in Alexandria disgorged musicians, dancers, acrobats, mimes, dwarfs, freaks and magicians from all over the eastern end of Our Sea.

Antony adored practical jokes that sometimes verged on the cruel; he adored to fish; he adored to swim among naked girls; he adored to drive chariots, an activity forbidden to a nobleman in

Rome; he adored hunting crocodile and hippopotamus; he adored pranks; he adored rude poetry; he adored pageants. His appetites were so enormous that he would roar that he was hungry a dozen times each day; Sosigenes hit on the bright idea of always having a full dinner ready to be served, together with vast quantities of the best wines. It was an instant success, and Antony, kissing him soundly, apostrophized the little philosopher as a prince of good fellows.

There wasn't much Alexandria could do to protest against fifty-odd drunken people running up and down the streets in torchlit dances, banging loudly on doors and skipping away with bellows of delighted laughter; some of these annoying people were the chief officials of the city, whose wives sat at home weeping and wondering why the Queen permitted it.

The Queen permitted it because she had no choice, though her own participation in the capers was half-hearted. Once Antony dared her to drop Servilia's six-million-sesterces pearl into a goblet of vinegar and drink it; he was of that school that believed pearls dissolved in vinegar. Knowing better, Cleopatra did as dared, though drinking the vinegar was beyond her. The pearl, quite unharmed, was around her neck the next day. And the fish pranks never stopped. Having no luck as a fisherman, Antony paid divers to go down and attach live fish to his line; he would pull up these flapping creatures and boast of his fishing skills until one day Cleopatra, tired of his bombast, had a diver attach a putrid fish to his line. But he took the joke in good part, for that was his nature.

Caesarion watched the antics with amusement, though he never asked to go to the parties. When Antony was in the mood the pair of them would vanish on horseback to hunt crocodile or hippopotamus, leaving Cleopatra in anguish at the vision of her son mangled by massive trotters or long yellow teeth. But, give Antony his due, he protected the boy from danger, just gave him a wonderful time.

'You like Antonius,' she said to her son toward the end of January.

'Yes, Mama, very much. He calls himself Neos Dionysus, but he is really Herakles. He can balance me on one hand, can you imagine that? And throw the discus half a furlong!'

'I am not surprised,' she said dryly.

'Tomorrow we're going to the hippodrome. I'm going to ride with him in his chariot – four horses abreast, the hardest!'

'Chariot racing is not a seemly pastime.'

'I know, but it's such *fun*!'

And what did one say to that?

Her son had grown in leaps and bounds during the past two months; Sosigenes had been right. The company of men had freed him from that touch of preciousness she hadn't noticed until he lost it. Now he swaggered about the palace trying to roar like Antony, gave very funny imitations of the Accountant in his cups, and looked forward to every day with a sparkle and a zest he had never before displayed. And he was strong, lithe, naturally good at warlike sports – cast a spear with deadly accuracy, shot arrows straight into the center of the target, used his *gladius* with the verve of a veteran legionary. Like his father, he could ride a horse bareback at full gallop with his hands behind his back.

For herself, Cleopatra wondered how much longer she could tolerate Antony in revel mode; she was tired all the time, had bouts of nausea, and couldn't be far from a chamber pot. All signs of pregnancy, albeit too early to be wearisome or noticeable. If Antony didn't cease his gyrations soon, she would have to tell him that he must gyrate on his own. Strong she might be for a small woman, but pregnancy took a toll.

Her dilemma solved itself early in February when the King of the Parthians invaded Syria.

Orodes was an old man, long past war in person, and the intrigues natural to a succession of such magnitude taxed him. One of his ways of dealing with ambitious sons and factions was to find a war for the most aggressive among them, and what better war than against the Romans in Syria? The strongest of his sons was Pacorus, therefore to Pacorus must this war be given. And for once King Orodes had a loaded set of dice to throw; with Pacorus came Quintus Labienus who gave himself the nickname of Parthicus. He was the son of Caesar's greatest marshal, Titus Labienus, and had chosen to flee to the court of Orodes rather than yield to his father's conqueror. Internal strife at Seleuceia-on-Tigris had also brought forth a difference of opinion as to how the Romans could be defeated. In previous clashes, including the one that had resulted in the annihilation of Marcus Crassus's army at Carrhae, the Parthians had relied heavily upon the horse archer, an unarmored peasant trained to retreat at the gallop and let fly a murderous rain of arrows over his horse's rump as he twisted backward – the famous 'Parthian shot'. When Crassus fell at Carrhae, the General in command of the Parthian army had been an effeminate, painted prince named the Surenas, who devised a way to ensure that his horse archers did not run out of arrows: he loaded trains of camels with spare arrows and got them to his men. Unfortunately his success was so marked that King Orodes suspected the Surenas would aim next for the throne, and had him executed.

Since that day over ten years in the past, a controversy had raged as to whether it had been the horse archers who won Carrhae, or the cataphracts. Men clad in chain mail from head to foot, the cataphracts bestrode big horses also clad in chain mail. The source of the argument was social; horse archers were peasants, whereas cataphracts were noblemen.

So when Pacorus and Labienus led their army into Syria at the beginning of February in the year of the consulship of Gnaeus Domitius Calvinus and Gnaeus Asinius Pollio, its Parthian content consisted solely of cataphracts. The nobles had won the struggle.

Pacorus and Labienus crossed the Euphrates River at Zeugma and there separated. While Labienus and his mercenaries drove west across the Amanus into Cilicia Pedia, Pacorus and the cataphracts turned south for Syria. They swept all before them on both fronts, though Cleopatra's agents in the north of Syria concentrated on Pacorus, not Labienus. Word flew to Alexandria.

The moment Antony heard, he was gone. No fond farewells, no protestations of love.

'Does he know?' asked Tach'a of Cleopatra.

No need for clarification; Cleopatra knew what she meant. 'No. I didn't have a chance – all he did was bellow for his armor and apply the goad to men like Dellius.' She sighed. 'His ships are to sail to Berytus, but he wasn't sure enough of the winds to risk a sea voyage. He hopes to reach Antioch ahead of his fleet.'

'What doesn't Antonius know?' Caesarion demanded, most put out at the sudden departure of his hero.

'That in Sextilis you'll have a baby brother or sister.'

The child's face lit up, he leaped about joyfully. 'A brother or a sister! Mama, Mama, that's terrific!'

'Well, at least that's taken his mind off Antonius,' said Iras to Charmian.

'It won't take *her* mind off Antonius,' Charmian answered.

Antony rode for Antioch at a grueling pace, sending for this or that local potentate in southern Syria as he passed through, at times issuing his orders to them from horseback.

Alarming to find out from Herod that among the Jews opinion

was divided; a large group of Judaic dissenters actually seemed avid to be ruled by the Parthians. The leader of the pro-Parthian party was the Hasmonaean Prince Antigonus, Hyrcanus's nephew but no lover of Hyrcanus or the Romans. Herod neglected to inform Mark Antony that Antigonus was already dickering with Parthian envoys for the things he coveted – the Jewish throne and the high priest-hood. As Herod was not very interested in these furtive dealings or the Sanhedrin mood, Antony continued northward ignorant of how serious the Jewish situation was. For once Herod had been caught napping, too busy trying to cut his brother Phasael out for the hand of the Princess Mariamne to notice anything else.

Tyre was impossible to take except from within. Its stinking isthmus, fouled by hills of rotting shellfish carcasses, gave the center of the purple-dye industry the protection due an island, and no one would betray it from within; no Tyrian wanted to have to send purple dye to the King of the Parthians for a price fixed by the King of the Parthians.

In Antioch, Antony found Lucius Decidius Saxa striding up and down nervously, the watchtowers atop the massive city walls lined with men straining to see into the north; Pacorus would follow the Orontes River, and he wasn't far away. Saxa's brother had come from Ephesus to join him, and refugees were streaming in. Ejected from the Amanus, the brigand king Tarcondimotus told Antony that Labienus was doing brilliantly. By now he was supposed to have reached Tarsus and Cappadocia. Antiochus of Commagene, ruler of a client-kingdom that bordered the Amanus ranges on the north, was wavering in his Roman allegiance, said Tarcondimotus. Liking the man, Antony listened; a brigand, maybe, but clever and capable.

After inspecting Saxa's two legions, Antony relaxed a little. Once Gaius Cassius's men, these legionaries were fit and very experi-enced in combat.

More upsetting by far was the news from Italia. His brother Lucius was immured inside Perusia and under siege, while Pollio had *retreated* to the swamps at the mouth of the Padus River! It made no sense . . . Pollio and Ventidius vastly outnumbered Octavian! Why weren't they helping Lucius? Antony asked himself, entirely forget-ting that he hadn't answered their pleas for guidance – was Lucius's war a part of Antony's policy, or was it not?

Well, no matter how grave the situation in the East was, Italia was more important. Antony sailed for Ephesus, intending to go on to Athens as soon as possible. He had to find out more.

* * *

The monotony of the first stage of the voyage gave him time to think about Cleopatra and that fantastic winter in Egypt. Ye gods, how he had needed to break out! And how well the Queen had catered for his every whim. He truly did love her, as he loved all the women with whom he associated for longer than a day, and he would continue to love her until she did something to sour him. Though Fulvia had done more than merely sour, if the fragments of news he had from Italia were anything to go by. The only woman for whom his love had persisted in the teeth of a thousand thousand transgressions was his mother, surely the silliest woman in the history of the world.

As was true of most boys of noble family, Antony's father had not been in Rome overmuch, so Julia Antonia was – or was supposed to be – the one who held the family together. Three boys and two girls had not endowed her with a scrap of maturity; she was terrifyingly stupid. Money was something that fell off vines and servants people far cleverer than she. Nor was she lucky in love. Her first husband, father of her children, had committed suicide rather than return to Rome to face treason charges for his bungling conduct of a war against the Cretan pirates, and her second husband had been executed in the Forum Romanum for his part in the rebellion led by Catilina. All of which had happened by the time that Marcus, the eldest of the children, had turned twenty. The two girls were so physically huge and Antonian-ugly that they were married off to rich social climbers in order to bring some money into the family to fund the public careers of the boys, who had run wild. Then Marcus ran up massive debts and had to marry a rich provincial named Fadia, whose father paid a two-hundred-talent dowry. The goddess Fortuna seemed to smile on Antony; Fadia and the children she had borne him died in a summer pestilence, leaving him free to marry another heiress, his first cousin Antonia Hybrida. That union had produced one child, a girl who was neither bright nor pretty. When Curio was killed and Fulvia became available, Antony divorced his cousin to marry her. Yet another profitable alliance; Fulvia was the richest woman in Rome.

Not precisely an unhappy childhood and young manhood; more that Antony had never been disciplined. The only person who could control Julia Antonia and her boys had been Caesar; he wasn't the actual head of the Julian family, just its most forceful member. Over the years Caesar had made it plain that he was fond of them, but he was never an *easy* man, nor one whom the boys understood. That fatal lack of discipline combined with an outrageous love of debauchery had finally, in the grown man Mark Antony, turned Caesar away from him. Twice had Antony proven himself not to be trusted; to Caesar, one time too many. Caesar had cracked his whip – *hard*.

To this day, leaning on the rail watching the sunlight play on the wet oars as they came out of the sea, Antony wasn't sure whether he had *meant* to participate in the plot to murder Caesar. Looking back on it, he was inclined to think that he hadn't truly believed that the likes of Gaius Trebonius and Decimus Junius Brutus had the gumption or the degree of hatred necessary to go through with it. Marcus Brutus and Cassius hadn't mattered so much; they were the figureheads, not the perpetrators. Yes, the plot definitely belonged to Trebonius and Decimus Brutus. Both dead. Dolabella had tortured Trebonius to death, while a Gallic chieftain separated Decimus Brutus from his head for a bag of gold supplied by Antony himself. Surely, reflected Antony, that proved that he hadn't *really* plotted to kill Caesar! Mind you, he had long ago decided that a Rome without Caesar would be an easier one for him to live in. And the greatest tragedy was that it probably would have been, were it not for the emergence of Gaius Octavius, Caesar's heir. Who, aged eighteen, promptly set out to claim his inheritance, a precarious enterprise that saw him march twice upon Rome before his twentieth birthday. His second march had seen him elected Senior Consul, whereupon he had had the temerity to force his rivals, Antony and Lepidus, to meet in conference with him. What had resulted was the Second Triumvirate – Three Men to Reconstitute the Republic. Instead of one dictator, three dictators with (theoretically) equal power. Marooned on an island in a river in Italian Gaul, it was gradually borne upon Antony and Lepidus that this youth half their age could run rings around them for guile and ruthlessness.

What Antony couldn't bear to admit to himself, even in his gloomiest moments, was that thus far Octavian had demonstrated how uncanny Caesar's preference for him had been. Sickly, underage, too pretty, a real mama's boy, still Octavian had managed to keep his head above water that ought to have drowned him. Perhaps a part of it was having Caesar's name – he exploited it to the full – and another part of it was the blind loyalty of young men like Marcus Vipsanius Agrippa; but there could be no denying that most of Octavian's successful survival had to be laid at Octavian's door, and Octavian's door alone. Antony used to joke with his brothers that Caesar was an enigma, but compared to Octavian, Caesar was as transparent as the water in the Aqua Marcia.

FIVE

When Antony arrived in Athens in May, the governor Censorinus was very busy in the far north of Macedonia fighting barbarian incursions, therefore not present to greet his superior. Antony was not in a good mood; his friend Barbatius had turned out to be no friend. The moment Barbatius heard that Antony was having a wonderful time in Egypt, he quit his post with the legions in Ephesus and went to Italia. Where, as Antony now discovered, he had further muddied the waters that Antony had neglected to clear. What Barbatius said to Pollio and Ventidius had caused the one to retreat to the Padus marshes and the other to dither ineffectually just out of range of Octavian, Agrippa and Salvidienus.

The source of most of this extremely unpalatable news from Italia was Lucius Munatius Plancus, whom Antony found occupying the chief legate's apartment in the Athens residence.

'Lucius Antonius's whole enterprise was a disaster,' Plancus said, choosing his words. Somehow he had to deliver an accurate report without putting himself in a bad light, for at the moment he could see no opportunity to switch to Octavian's side, his only other option. 'On New Year's Eve the Perusians tried to break through Agrippa's siege walls – no luck. Neither Pollio nor Ventidius would move to engage Octavianus's armies, though Octavianus was badly outnumbered. Pollio kept insisting that – ah – he wasn't sure what you wanted him to do, and Ventidius would follow no one's lead except Pollio's. After Barbatius spun his tales of your – ah – debaucheries – his word, not mine!, Pollio was so disgusted that he refused to commit himself or his legions to getting your brother out of Perusia. The city fell not long into the new year.'

'And where were you and your legions, Plancus?' Antony asked, a dangerous spark in his eyes.

'Closer to Perusia than Pollio or Ventidius! I went to ground in Spoletium to form the southern jaw of a pincer strategy that never happened.' He sighed, shrugged. 'I also had Fulvia in my camp, and she was being very difficult.' He loved her, yes, but he loved his own skin more. Antonius wouldn't execute Fulvia for treason, after all. 'Agrippa had the gall to steal my best two legions, can you believe that? I had sent them to help Claudius Nero in Campania, then Agrippa appeared and offered the men better terms. Yes, Agrippa defeated Nero *with my two legions*! Nero had to flee to Sicilia and Sextus Pompeius. Apparently some elements in Rome were talking of killing wives and families, because Nero's wife, Livia Drusilla, took her small son and joined Nero.' At which point Plancus frowned, looked uncertain how to proceed.

'Out with it, Plancus, out with it!'

'Ah – your revered mother, Julia, fled with Livia Drusilla to Sextus Pompeius.'

'If I had stopped to think about her, which I didn't because I try not to, that is exactly the sort of thing she'd do. Oh, what a wonderful world we live in!' Antony clenched his fists. 'Wives and mothers living in army camps, behaving as if they knew which end of a sword was which – pah!' A visible effort, and he simmered down. 'My brother – I suppose he's dead, but you haven't yet managed to screw up the courage to tell me, Plancus?'

Finally he could convey a piece of good news! 'No, no, my dear Marcus! Far from it! When Perusia opened its gates, some local magnate got overenthusiastic about the size and splendor of his funeral pyre, and the whole city burned to the ground. A worse disaster than the siege. Octavianus executed twenty prominent citizens, but exacted no revenge on Lucius's troops. They were incorporated into Agrippa's legions. Lucius begged pardon, and was granted it freely. Octavianus gave him Further Spain to govern, and he left for it at once. He was, I think, a happy man.'

'And was this dictatorial appointment sanctioned by the Senate and People of Rome?' Antony asked, part relieved, part outraged. Curse Lucius! Always trying to outdo his big brother Marcus, never succeeding.

'It was,' said Plancus. 'Some objected to it—'

'Favored treatment for the bald-headed Forum demagogue?'

'Er – well, yes, the phrase was used. I can give you the names. However, Lucius *was* consul last year and your uncle Hybrida *is* censor, so most people felt that Lucius deserved his pardon and appointment. He should be able to have a nice little war with the Lusitani and triumph when he comes home.'

Antony grunted. 'Then he's wriggled out of things better than he deserves. Utter idiocy from start to finish! Though I'd be willing to bet that Lucius just followed orders. This was Fulvia's war. Where is she?'

Plancus opened his brown eyes wide. 'Here, in Athens. She and I fled together. At first we didn't think that Brundisium would let us – it's passionately for Octavianus, as always; but I gather Octavianus sent word that we were to be allowed to leave Italia, provided we took no troops with us.'

'So we have established that Fulvia is in Athens, but whereabouts in Athens?'

'Atticus gave her the use of his *domus* here.'

'Big of him! Always likes to have a foot in both camps, does our Atticus. But what makes him think I'm going to be glad to see Fulvia?'

Plancus sat mute, unsure what answer Antony wanted to hear.

'And what else has happened?'

'Don't you call that enough?'

'Not unless it's a full report.'

'Well, Octavianus got no money out of Perusia to fund his activities, though from somewhere he manages to pay his legions sufficient to keep their men on his side.'

'Caesar's war chest must be emptying fast.'

'Do you really think he took it?'

'Of course he took it! What's Sextus Pompeius doing?'

'Blocking the sea lanes and pirating all the grain from Africa. His admiral Menodorus invaded Sardinia and threw Lurius out, which means Octavianus has no source of grain left, save what he can buy from Sextus at grossly inflated rates – up to twenty-five or thirty sesterces the *modius*.' Plancus gave a small mew of envy. 'That's where all the money is – in Sextus Pompeius's coffers. What does he intend to do with it: take over Rome and Italia? Daydreams! The legions love big bonuses, but they'd not fight for the man who starves their grannies to death. Which is why, I daresay,' Plancus went on in a reflective voice, 'he has to enlist slaves and make freedmen admirals. Still, one day you're going to have to wrest the money off him, Antonius. If you don't, perhaps Octavianus will – and you need the money more.'

Antony sneered. 'Octavianus win a sea battle against a man as experienced as Sextus Pompeius? With Murcus and Ahenobarbus as allies? I'll deal with Sextus Pompeius when the time comes, but not yet. He spells failure for Octavianus.'

Knowing she looked her best, Fulvia waited eagerly for her husband. Though the few grey hairs didn't show in her mop of ice-brown hair, she had made her woman painstakingly pluck every one before dressing it in the latest fashion. Her dark red gown hugged the curves of her breasts before falling in a straight sheet that showed no hint of a protruding belly or thickened waist. Yes, thought Fulvia, preening, I carry my age very well. I am still one of Rome's most beautiful women.

Of course she knew about Antony's merry little winter in Alexandria; Barbatius had tattled far and wide. But that was a man's thing, and none of her business. Did he philander with a Roman woman of high estate, it would be different. Her claws would be out in a moment. But when a man was away for months, sometimes years on end, no sensible wife stuck in Rome would think the worse of him for getting rid of his dirty water. And darling Antonius had a penchant for queens, princesses, women of the high foreign nobility. To bed one of them made him feel as much like a king as any republican Roman could tolerate. Having met Cleopatra when she stayed in Rome before Caesar's assassination, Fulvia understood that it was her title and her power that had attracted Antony. Physically she was far from the lusty, strapping women he preferred. Also, she was enormously wealthy, and Fulvia knew her husband; he would have been after her money.

So when Atticus's steward appeared to tell her that Marcus Antonius was in the atrium, Fulvia gave a shudder to settle her draperies and flew down the long, austere corridor from her rooms to where Antony was waiting.

'Antonius! Oh, *meum mel*, how wonderful to see you!' she cried from the doorway.

He had been studying a magnificent painting of Achilles sulking by his ships, and turned at the sound of her voice.

After that, Fulvia didn't know what exactly happened, his movements were so fast. What she felt was a crashing slap to the side of her face that knocked her sprawling. Then he was looming over her, his fingers locked in her hair, and dragging her to her feet. The open-handed blows rained on her face, no less huge and hurtful than another man's fist; teeth loosened, her nose broke.

'You stupid *cunnus*!' he roared, still striking her. 'You stupid, stupid *cunnus*! Who do you think you are, Gaius Caesar?'

74

Blood was gushing from her mouth and nose, and she, who had met every challenge of an eventful life with fierce fire, was helpless, shattered. Someone was screaming, and it must have been her, for servants came running from all directions, took one look, and fled.

'Idiot! Strumpet! What do you mean, going to war against Octavianus *in my name*? Frittering away what money I had left in Rome, Bononia, Mutina? Buying legions for the likes of Plancus to lose? Living in a war camp? Who do you think you are, to assume that men like Pollio would take orders from you? *A woman*? Bullying and bluffing my brother *in my name*? He's a moron! He always was a moron! If I needed any further proof of that, his throwing in with a woman is it! You're beneath contempt!'

Spitting with rage, he pushed her roughly to the floor; still screaming, she scrambled away like a crippled beast, tears flowing now faster than the blood.

'Antonius, Antonius! I thought to please you! Manius said it would please you!' she cried thickly. 'I was continuing your fight in Italia while you were busy with the East! Manius said!'

It came out in mumbled snatches; hearing 'Manius', suddenly his temper died. Her Greek freedman, a serpent. In truth, he hadn't known until he saw her how angry he was, how the fury had festered in him throughout his voyage from Ephesus. Perhaps had he done as he had originally planned and sailed straight from Antioch to Athens, he might not have been so enraged.

More men than Barbatius were talking in Ephesus, and not all about his winter with Cleopatra. Some joked that, in his family, he wore the dresses while Fulvia wore the armor. Others sniggered that at least *one* Antonian had waged a war, even if a female. He had had to pretend he didn't overhear any of these remarks, but his temper built. Learning the full story from Plancus had not helped, nor the grief that had consumed him until he found out that Lucius was safe and well. Their brother, Gaius, had been murdered in Macedonia, and only the execution of his killer had assuaged the pain. He, their big brother, *loved* them.

Love for Fulvia, he thought, looking down at her scornfully, was gone forever. Stupid, stupid *cunnus*! Wearing the armor and publicly emasculating him.

'I want you gone from this house by tomorrow,' he said, her right wrist in his hold, dragging her into a sitting position under Achilles. 'Let Atticus keep his charity for the deserving. I'll be writing to him today to tell him that, and he can't afford to offend me, no matter how much money he has. You're a disgrace as a wife and a woman, Fulvia! I want nothing more to do with you. I will send you notice of divorce immediately.'

'But,' she said, sobbing, 'I fled without money or property, Marcus! I need money to live!'

'Apply to your bankers. You're a rich woman and *sui iuris*.' He began yelling for the servants. 'Clean her up and then kick her out!' he said to the steward, who was almost fainting in fear. He turned on his heel and was gone.

Fulvia sat against the wall for a long time, hardly conscious of the terrified girls who bathed her face, tried to staunch the bleeding and the tears. Once she had laughed at hearing of this or that woman and her broken heart, believing that no heart could break. Now she knew differently. Marcus Antonius had broken her heart beyond mending.

Word flew around Athens of how Antony had treated his wife, but few who heard had much sympathy for Fulvia, who had done the unforgivable: usurped men's prerogatives. The tales of her exploits in the Forum when married to Publius Clodius came out for an airing, together with the scenes she created outside the Senate House doors, and her possible collaboration with Clodius when he had profaned the rites of the Bona Dea.

Not that Antony cared what Athens said. He, a Roman man, knew that the city's Roman men would think no worse of him.

Besides, he was busy writing letters, an arduous task. His first was curt and short, to Titus Pomponius Atticus, informing him that Imperator Marcus Antonius, Triumvir, would thank him if he kept his nose out of Marcus Antonius's affairs, and have nothing to do with Fulvia. His second was to Fulvia, informing her that she was hereby divorced for unwomanly conduct, and that she was forbidden to see her two sons by him. His third was to Gnaeus Asinius Pollio, asking him what on earth was going on in Italia, and would he kindly keep his legions ready to march south in case he, Marcus Antonius, was denied entry to the country by the Octavianus-loving populace of Brundisium? His fourth was to the ethnarch of Athens, thanking that worthy for his city's kindness and loyalty to (implied) the right Romans; therefore it pleased Imperator Marcus Antonius, Triumvir, to gift Athens with the island of Aegina and some other minor isles associated with it. That ought to make the Athenians happy, he thought.

He might have written more letters, were it not for the arrival of Tiberius Claudius Nero, who paid him a formal call the moment he had installed his wife and toddling son in good lodgings nearby.

'Faugh!' Nero exclaimed, nostrils flaring. 'Sextus Pompeius is a barbarian! Though what else could one expect from a member of an upstart clan from Picenum? You can have no idea what kind of headquarters he keeps – rats, mice, rotting garbage. I didn't dare expose my family to the filth and disease, though they weren't the worst Pompeius had to offer. We hadn't unpacked our belongings before some of his dandified "admiral" freedmen were sniffing around my wife – I had to chop a slice out of some low fellow's arm! And would you believe it, Pompeius actually *sided* with the cur? I told him what I thought, then I put Livia Drusilla and my son on the next ship for Athens.'

Antony listened to this with dreamy memories in his head of how Caesar felt about Nero – '*inepte*' was the kindest word Caesar could find to describe him. Gaining more from what Nero didn't say, Antony decided that Nero had arrived at Sextus Pompeius's lair, strutted around it like a cockerel, carped and criticized, and finally made himself so intolerable that Sextus had thrown him out. A more insufferable snob than Nero would be hard to find, and the Pompeii were very sensitive about their Picentine origins.

'So what do you intend to do now, Nero?' he asked.

'Live within my means, which are not limitless,' Nero said stiffly, his dark, saturnine countenance growing even prouder.

'And your wife?' Antony asked slyly.

'Livia Drusilla is a good wife. She does as she's told, which is more than you can say about your wife!'

A typical Neronian statement; he seemed to have no inbuilt monitor to warn him that some things were best left unsaid. I ought, thought Antony savagely, to seduce her! What a life she must lead, married to this *inepte*!

'Bring her to dinner this afternoon, Nero,' he said jovially. 'Think of it as money saved – no need to send your cook to the market until tomorrow.'

'I thank you,' Nero said, unwinding to his full, spindling height. Left arm cuddling folds of toga, he stalked out, leaving Antony chuckling softly.

Plancus came in, horror written large upon his face. 'Oh, *Edepol*, Antonius! What's Nero doing here?'

'Apart from insulting everyone he meets? I suspect that he made himself so unwelcome in Sextus Pompeius's headquarters that he was told to leave. You can come to dinner this afternoon and share the joys of his company. He's bringing his wife, who must be a terrible bore to put up with him. Just who is she?'

'His cousin – fairly close, actually. Her father was a Claudius Nero adopted by the famous tribune of the plebs, Livius Drusus, hence her name, Livia Drusilla. Nero is the son of Drusus's blood brother, Tiberius Nero. Of course she's an heiress – a lot of money in the Livius Drusus family. Once, Cicero hoped Nero would marry his Tullia, but she preferred Dolabella. A worse husband in most ways, but at least he was a merry fellow. Didn't you move in those circles when Clodius was alive, Antonius?'

'I did. And you're right, Dolabella was good company. But it's not Nero gives your face that look, Plancus. What's up?'

'A packet from Ephesus. I had one too, but yours is from your cousin Caninius, so it ought to say more.' Plancus sat in the client's chair facing Antony across the desk, eyes bright.

Antony broke the seal, unrolled his cousin's epistle and mumbled his way through it, a long business accompanied by frowns and curses. 'I wish,' he complained, 'that more men had taken Caesar's hint and put a dot over the beginning of a new word. I do it now, so do Pollio, Ventidius and – though I hate to say it – Octavianus. Turns a continuous scrawl into something a man can read almost at a glance.' He went back to his mumbling, finally sighed and put the scroll down.

'How can I be in two places at once?' he asked Plancus. 'By rights I should be in Asia Province shoring it up against attack from Labienus, instead I'm forced to sit closer to Italia and keep my legions within call. Pacorus has overrun Syria and all the petty princelings have thrown in their lot with the Parthians, even Amblichus. Caninius says that Saxa's legions defected to Pacorus – Saxa was forced to flee to Apamaea, then took ship for Cilicia. No one has heard from him since, but rumor has it that his brother was killed in Syria. Labienus is busy overrunning Cilicia Pedia and eastern Cappadocia.'

'And of course there are no legions east of Ephesus.'

'Nor will there be in Ephesus, I'm afraid. Asia Province will have to fend for itself until I can sort out the mess in Italia. I've already sent to Caninius to bring the legions to Macedonia,' said Antony, sounding grim.

'Is that your *only* course?' Plancus asked, paling.

'Definitely. I've given myself the rest of this year to deal with Rome, Italia and Octavianus, so for the rest of this year the legions will be camped around Apollonia. If they're known to be on the

Adriatic, that will tell Octavianus that I mean to squash him like a bug.'

'Marcus,' Plancus wailed, 'everyone is fed up with civil war, and what you're talking is civil war! The legions won't fight!'

'My legions will fight for *me*,' said Antony.

Livia Drusilla entered the governor's residence with all her usual composure, creamy lids lowered over her eyes, which she knew were her best feature. Hide them! As always, she walked a little behind Nero because a good wife did, and Livia Drusilla had vowed to be a good wife. Never, she had sworn, hearing what Antony had done to Fulvia, would she put herself in that position! To don armor and wave a sword about, one would have to be a Hortensia, who had only done it to demonstrate to the leaders of the Roman state that the women of Rome from highest to lowest would never consent to being taxed when they didn't have the right to vote. Hortensia won the encounter, a bloodless victory, at considerable embarrassment to the Triumvirs Antony, Octavian and Lepidus.

Not that Livia Drusilla intended to be a mouse; she simply masqueraded as someone small and meek and a trifle timid. Huge ambition burned in her, inchoate because she had no idea how she was going to seize that ambition, turn it into a productive thing. Certainly it was shaped in an absolutely Roman mold, which meant no unfeminine behavior, no putting herself forward, no unsubtle manipulating. Not that she wanted to be another Cornelia the Mother of the Gracchi, worshipped by some women as a truly Roman goddess because she had suffered, borne children, seen them die, never complained of her lot. No, Livia Drusilla sensed that there had to be another way to reach the heights.

The trouble was that three years of marriage had shown her beyond all doubt that the way was not through Tiberius Claudius Nero. Like most girls of her exalted station, she hadn't known Nero very well before they married, for all that he was her close cousin. Nothing in him, on the few occasions when they had met, had inspired anything in her save contempt for his stupidity and an instinctive detestation of his person. Dark herself, she admired men with golden hair and light eyes. Intelligent herself, she admired men with great intelligence. On neither count could Nero qualify. She had been fifteen when her father Drusus had married her to his first cousin Nero, and in the house where she grew up there had been no priapic wall paintings or phallic lamps whereby a girl might learn something about physical love. So union with Nero had revolted her. He too preferred golden-haired, light-eyed lovers; what pleased him in his wife were her noble ancestry and her fortune.

Only how to be shriven of Tiberius Claudius Nero when she was determined to be a good wife? It didn't seem possible unless someone offered him a better marriage, and that was highly unlikely. Her cleverness had shown her very early in their marriage that people disliked Nero, tolerated him only because of his patrician status and his consequent right to occupy all the offices that Rome offered her nobility. And oh, he *bored* her! Many were the tales she had heard about Cato Uticensis, Caesar's greatest enemy, and his tactless, prating personality, but to Livia Drusilla he seemed an ecstatic god compared to Nero. Nor could she like the son she had borne Nero ten months after their wedding; little Tiberius was dark, skinny, tall, solemn and a trifle sanctimonious, even at two years of age. He had fallen into the habit of criticizing his mother because he heard his father do so and, unlike most small children, he had spent his life thus far in his father's company. Livia Drusilla suspected that Nero preferred to keep her and little Tiberius close in case some pretty fellow with Caesarean charm tampered with his wife's virtue. What an irritation that was! Didn't the fool know that she would never demean herself in that way?

The housebound existence she had led until Nero embarked upon his disastrous Campanian venture in Lucius Antonius's cause had not allowed her as much as a glimpse of any of the famous men all Rome talked about; she hadn't laid eyes on Marcus Antonius, Lepidus, Servilius Vatia, Gnaeus Domitius Calvinus, Octavianus, or even Caesar, dead in her fifteenth year. Therefore today was exciting, though nothing in her demeanor showed that: she was going to dine with Marcus Antonius, the most powerful man in the world!

A pleasure that almost didn't happen when Nero discovered that Antony was one of those disgracefully fast fellows who let women recline on the men's couches.

'Unless my wife has a chair, I am leaving!' Nero said with his customary tact.

Had Antony not already found the little oval face of Nero's wife bewitching, the upshot of that remark would have been a roar and expulsion; as it was, Antony grinned and commanded that a chair be brought for Livia Drusilla. When the chair came he had it placed opposite his own position on the couch, but as there were only the three male diners, Nero couldn't very well object to that. It wasn't as if she was around a corner from him, though Nero did think it more evidence of Antony's uncouth nature that he had relegated him to the end of the couch and put a puffed-up nobody like Plancus in the middle.

Removal of her wrap revealed that Livia Drusilla wore a fawn dress with long sleeves and a high neck, but nothing could disguise the charms of her figure or her flawless ivory skin. As thick and black as night, with the same indigo tinge to its lustre, her hair was done plainly, drawn back to cover her ears and knotted on the nape of her neck. And her face was exquisite! A small, lush red mouth, enormous eyes fringed with long black lashes like fans, pink cheeks, a small but aquiline nose, all combined to form perfection. Just when Antony became annoyed at not being able to decide what color her eyes were, she moved her chair and a thin ray of sun lit them. Oh, amazing! They were a very dark blue, but striated in a magical way with strands of whitish fawn. Like no eyes he had ever seen before, and – eerie. Livia Drusilla, I could eat you up! he said to himself, and set out to make her fall in love with him.

But it wasn't possible. She was not shy, answered all of his questions frankly yet demurely, wasn't afraid to add a tiny comment when it was called for. However, she would introduce no topic of conversation of her own volition, and said or did nothing that Nero, watching suspiciously, could fault. None of that would have mattered to Antony had a single spark of interest flared in her eyes, but it didn't. If he had been a more perceptive man, he would have known that the faint *moue* crossing her face from time to time spoke of distaste.

Yes, he would beat a wife who grossly erred, she decided, but not as Nero would, coldly, with total calculation. Antonius would do it in a terrible temper, though afterward, cooled down, he wouldn't rue the deed, for her crime would be unpardonable. Most men would like him, be drawn to him, and most women desire him. Life during those few days in Sextus Pompeius's lair at Agrigentum had exposed Livia Drusilla to low women, and she had learned a lot about love, and men, and the sexual act. It seemed that women preferred men with large penises because a large penis made it easier for them to achieve climax, whatever that was (she had not found out, afraid to ask for fear of being laughed at). But she did find out that Marcus Antonius was famous for the immensity of his procreative equipment. Well, that was as maybe, when now she could discover nothing in Antonius to like or admire.

81

Especially after she realized that he was trying his hardest to elicit a response from her. It gave her tremendous satisfaction to deny him that response, which taught her a little about how a woman might acquire power. Only not intriguing with an Antonius, whose lusts were transient, unimportant even.

'What did you think of the Great Man?' Nero asked as they walked home in the brief, fiery twilight.

Livia Drusilla blinked; her husband didn't usually ask her what she thought about anyone or anything. 'High in birth, low in character,' she said. 'A vulgar boor.'

'Emphatic,' he said, sounding pleased.

For the first time in their relationship, she dared to ask him a political question. 'Husband, why do you cleave to a vulgar boor like Marcus Antonius? Why not to Caesar Octavianus, who by all descriptions is not a boor, nor vulgar either?'

For a moment he stopped absolutely still, then turned to look at her, more in surprise than irritation. 'Birth outweighs both. Antonius is better born. Rome belongs to men with the proper ancestry. They and only they should be permitted to hold high offices, govern provinces, conduct wars.'

'But Octavianus is Caesar's nephew! Wasn't Caesar's birth unimpeachable?'

'Oh, Caesar had it all – birth, brilliance, beauty. The most august of the august patricians. Even his plebeian blood was the best – mother Aurelian, grandmother Marcian, great-grandmother Popillian. Octavianus is an imposter! A tinge of Julian blood, the rest trash. Who are the Octavii of Velitrae? Utter nobodies! Some Octavii are fairly respectable, but not those from Velitrae. One of Octavianus's great-grandfathers was a rope maker, another a baker. His grandfather was a banker. Low, low! His father made a lucky second marriage to Caesar's niece. Though *she* was tainted – her father was a rich nobody who bought Caesar's sister. In those days the Julii had no money, they had to sell daughters.'

'Is a nephew not a quarter Julian?' she ventured boldly.

'*Great*-nephew, the little poseur! One-eighth Julian. The rest is abominable!' barked Nero, getting worked up. 'Whatever possessed the great Caesar to choose a low-born boy as his heir escapes me, but of one thing you may be sure, Livia Drusilla – I will never tie myself to the likes of Octavianus!'

Well, well, thought Livia Drusilla, saying no more. That is why so many of Rome's aristocrats abhor Octavianus! As a person of the finest blood, I should abhor him too, but he intrigues me. He's risen so far! I admire that in him because I understand it. Perhaps every so often Rome must create new aristocrats; it might even be that the great Caesar realized that when he made his will.

Livia Drusilla's interpretation of Nero's reasons for hewing to Mark Antony was a gross oversimplification – but then, so was Nero's reasoning. His narrow intellect was undeveloped; no number of additional years could make him anymore than he had been when a young man serving under Caesar. Indeed, he was so dense that he had no idea Caesar had disliked him. Water off a duck's back, as the Gauls said. When your blood is the very best, what possible fault could a fellow nobleman find in you?

To Mark Antony, it seemed as if his first month in Athens was littered with women, none of whom was worth his valuable time. Though was his time truly valuable, when nothing he did bore fruit? The only good news came from Apollonia with Quintus Dellius, who informed him that his legions had arrived on the west coast of Macedonia, and were happy to bivouac in a kinder climate.

Hard on Dellius's heels came Lucius Scribonius Libo, escorting the woman surest to blight Antony's mood: his mother.

She rushed into his study strewing hairpins, stray seed for the bird her servant girl carried in a cage, and strands from a long fringe some insane seamstress had attached to the edges of her stole. Her hair was coming adrift in wisps more grey than gold these days, but her eyes were exactly as her son remembered them: eternally cascading tears.

'Marcus, Marcus!' she cried, throwing herself at his chest. 'Oh, my dearest boy, I thought I'd never see you again! Such a dreadful time of it I've had! A paltry little room in a villa that rang night and day with the sounds of unmentionable acts, streets slimed with spittle and the contents of chamber pots, a bed crawling with bugs, nowhere to have a proper bath—'

With many shushes and other soothing noises, Antony finally managed to put her in a chair and settle her down as much as anyone could ever settle Julia Antonia down. Only when the tears had diminished to something like their usual rate did he have the opportunity to see who had entered behind Julia Antonia. Ah! The sycophant to end all sycophants, Lucius Scribonius Libo. Not glued to Sextus Pompey – grafted to him to make a sour rootstock produce sweet grapes.

Short in height and meager in build, Libo had a face that reinforced the inadequacies of his size and betrayed the nature of the beast within: grasping, timid, ambitious, uncertain, selfish. His moment had come when Pompey the Great's elder son had fallen in love with his daughter, divorced a Claudia Pulchra to marry her, and obliged Pompey the Great to elevate him as befitted his son's father-in-law. Then when Gnaeus Pompey followed his father into death, Sextus, the younger son, had married his widow. With the result that Libo had commanded naval fleets and now acted as an unofficial ambassador for his master, Sextus. The Scribonian women had done well by their family; Libo's sister had married two rich, influential men, one a patrician Cornelius, by whom she had borne a daughter. Though Scribonia the sister was now in her early thirties and deemed ill-omened – twice widowed was once too often – Libo did not despair of finding her a third husband. Comely to look at, proven fertile, a two-hundred-talent dowry – yes, Scribonia the sister would marry again.

However, Antony wasn't interested in Libo's women; it was his own bothering him. 'Why on earth bring her to me?' he asked.

Libo opened his fawn-colored eyes wide, spread his hands. 'My dear Antonius, where else could I bring her?'

'You could have sent her to her own *domus* in Rome.'

'She refused with such hysteria that I was forced to push Sextus Pompeius out of the room – otherwise he would have killed her. Believe me, she wouldn't go to Rome, kept screeching that Octavianus would execute her for treason.'

'Execute Caesar's cousin?' Antony asked incredulously.

'Why not?' Libo asked, all innocence. 'He proscribed Caesar's cousin Lucius, your mother's brother.'

'Octavianus and I *both* proscribed Lucius!' Antony snapped, goaded. 'However, we did not execute him! We needed his money, that simple. My mother is penniless, she stands in no danger.'

'Then you tell her that!' said Libo with a snarl; it was he, after all, who had had to suffer Julia Antonia on a fairly long sea voyage.

Had either man thought to look her way – he did not – he might have seen that the drowned blue eyes held a certain cunning and that the profusely ornamented ears were picking up every word uttered. Monumentally silly Julia Antonia might be, but she had a healthy regard for her own wellbeing and was convinced that she would be much better off with her senior son than stranded in Rome without an income.

By this time the steward and several female servants had arrived, their faces displaying some trepidation. Unmoved by this evidence of servile fear that they were about to be burdened with a problem, Antony thankfully passed his mother over to them, all the while assuring her that he wasn't going to send her to Rome. Finally the deed was done and peace descended on the study; Antony sat back in his chair with a sigh of relief.

'Wine! I need wine!' he cried, suddenly erupting out of the chair. 'Red or white, Libo?'

'A good strong red, I thank you. No water. I've seen enough water in the last three *nundinae* to last me half a lifetime.'

Antony grinned. 'I fully understand. Chaperoning my mama is no picnic.' He poured a large goblet almost to its brim. 'Here, this should numb the pain – Chian, ten years old.'

Silence reigned for some time as the two bibbers buried their snouts in their goblets with appropriate sounds of content.

'So what brings you to Athens, Libo?' Antony asked, breaking the silence. 'And don't say my mother.'

'You're right. Your mother was convenient.'

'Not for me,' Antony growled.

'I'd love to know how you can do that,' Libo said brightly. 'Your speaking voice is light and high, but in a trice you can turn it into a deep-throated growl or roar.'

'Or bellow. You forgot the bellow. And don't ask me how. I don't know. It just happens. If you want to hear me bellow, keep on evading the subject, by all means.'

'Er – no, that won't be necessary. Though if I may continue about your mother for a moment longer, I suggest that you give her plenty of money and the run of the best shops in Athens. Do that, and you'll never see or hear her.' Libo smiled down at the bubbles beading the rim of his wine. 'Once she learned that your brother Lucius was pardoned and sent to Further Spain with a proconsular imperium, she was easier to deal with.'

'Why are you here?' Antony said again.

'Sextus Pompeius thought it a good idea for me to see you.'

'Really? With a view to what end?'

'Forming an alliance against Octavianus. The two of you united would crush Octavianus to pulp.'

The small full mouth pursed; Antony looked sideways. 'An alliance against Octavianus . . . Pray tell me, Libo, why I, one of the three men appointed by the Senate and People of Rome to reconstitute the Republic, should form an alliance with a man who is no better than a pirate?'

Libo winced. 'Sextus Pompeius is the governor of Sicilia in full accordance with the *mos maiorum*! He does not regard the Triumvirate as legal or proper, and he deplores the proscription edict that falsely outlawed him, not to mention stripped him of his property and inheritance! His activities on the high seas are purely to convince the Senate and People of Rome that he has been unjustly condemned. Lift the sentence of *hostis*, lift all the bans, embargoes and interdictions, and Sextus Pompeius will cease to be – er – a pirate.'

'And he thinks I'll move in the House that his status as a public enemy and all the bans, embargoes and interdictions be lifted if he aids me in ridding Rome of Octavianus?'

'Quite so, yes.'

'I take it he's proposing outright war, tomorrow if possible?'

'Come, come, Marcus Antonius, all the world can see that you and Octavianus must eventually come to blows! Since between you – I discount Lepidus – you have *imperium maius* over nine-tenths of the Roman world and you control its legions as well as its incomes, what else can happen when you collide than full-scale war? For over fifty years the history of the Roman Republic has been one civil war after another – do you honestly believe that Philippi was the end of the final civil war?' Libo kept his tone gentle, his face serene. 'Sextus Pompeius is tired of outlawry. He wants what is due to him – restoration of his citizenship, permission to inherit his father Magnus's property, the restitution of said property, the consulship, and a proconsular imperium in Sicilia in perpetuity.' Libo shrugged. 'There is more, but that will do to go on with, I think.'

'And in return for all this?'

'He will control and sweep the seas as your ally. Include a pardon for Murcus and you will have his fleets too. Ahenobarbus says he's independent, though as big a . . . pirate. Sextus Pompeius will also guarantee you free grain for your legions.'

'He's holding me to ransom.'

'Is that a yea or a nay?'

'I will not treat with pirates,' Antony said in his usual light voice. 'However, you can tell your master that if he and I should meet upon the water, I expect him to let me go wherever it is I'm going. If he does that, we shall see.'

'More yea than nay.'

'More nothing than anything – for the time being. I do not *need* Sextus Pompeius to squash Octavianus, Libo. If Sextus thinks I do, he's mistaken.'

'If you should decide to ship your troops across the Adriatic from Macedonia to Italia, Antonius, you won't welcome fleets in the plural preventing you.'

'The Adriatic is Ahenobarbus's patch, and he'll not hamper me. I am unimpressed.'

'So Sextus Pompeius cannot call himself your ally? You will not undertake to speak for him in the House?'

'Absolutely not, Libo. The most I'll agree to do is not to hunt him down. If I did hunt him down, he'd be the one crushed to pulp. Tell him he can keep his free grain, but that I expect him to sell me grain for my legions at the usual wholesale price of five sesterces the *modius*, not a bronze farthing more.'

'You drive a hard bargain.'

'I'm in a position to do so. Sextus Pompeius is not.'

And how much of this obduracy, wondered Libo, is because he now has his mother around his neck? I *told* Sextus it was not a good idea, but he wouldn't listen.

Quintus Dellius entered the room, arm in arm with yet another sycophant, Sentius Saturninus.

'Look who's just arrived from Agrigentum with Libo!' Dellius cried delightedly. 'Antonius, have you any of that Chian red?'

'Pah!' spat Antony. 'Where's Plancus?'

'Here, Antonius!' said Plancus, going to embrace Libo and Sentius Saturninus. 'Isn't this nice?'

Very nice, thought Antony sourly. Four servings of syrup.

Moving his army to the Adriatic coast of Macedonia hadn't begun as anything more than an exercise designed to frighten Octavian; having abandoned all thought of contending with the Parthians until his income improved, Antony had at first wanted to leave his legions in Ephesus, but his visit to Ephesus had changed his mind. Caninius was too weak to control so many senior legates unless cousin Antony was nearby. Besides, the idea of frightening Octavian was too delicious to resist. But somehow everyone assumed that the war they expected to erupt between the two Triumvirs was finally going to push ahead, and Antony found himself in a dilemma. *Ought* he crush Octavian now? As campaigns went, it would be a cheap one, and he had plenty of transports to ferry his legions across a little sea to home territory, where he could pick up Octavian's legions to supplement his own, and free up Pollio and Ventidius – fourteen extra legions from them alone! Ten more once Octavian was defeated. And whatever was in the Treasury to put in his war chest.

Still, he wasn't sure . . . When Libo's advice about Julia Antonia proved correct and he never saw her, Antony relaxed a little. His Athenian couch was comfortable and the army content in Apollonia – time would tell him what to do. It didn't occur to him that in postponing this decision, he was telling his world that he lacked resolution about his future course of action.

PART II

Octavian in the West

41–39 B.C.

CAIUS JULIUS CAESAR OCTAVIANUS

SIX

She looked so old and tired, his beloved Lady Roma. From where he stood at the top of the Velia, Octavian could see down into the Forum Romanum and beyond it to the Capitoline Mount; if he turned to face the other way, he could look across the swamps of the Palus Ceroliae all the way along the Sacra Via to the Servian Walls.

Octavian loved Rome with a fierce passion alien to his nature, which tended to be cool and detached. But Goddess Roma, he believed, had no rival on the face of the globe. How he hated to hear this one say that Athens outshone her as the sun does the moon, hear that one say that Pergamum on its heights was far lovelier, hear another say that Alexandria made her look like a Gallic *oppidum*! Was it her fault that her temples were decayed, her public buildings grimy, her squares and gardens neglected? No, the fault lay with the men who governed in her name, for they cared more about their reputations than they did about hers, who made them. She deserved better, and if he had anything to do with it, she would receive better. Of course there were exceptions: Caesar's glorious Basilica Julia, the masterpiece that was his Forum, the Basilica Aemilia, Sulla's Tabularium. But, even on the Capitol, temples as grand as Juno Moneta were in sad need of fresh paint. From the eggs and dolphins of the Circus Maximus to the shrines and fountains of the crossroads, poor Goddess Roma was shabby, a gentlewoman in decline.

If we only had one-tenth of the money Romans have squandered on warring against each other, Roma would be unparalleled for beauty, Octavian thought. Where does it go, all that money? A question that had occurred to him often, and to which he had only an approximate answer, an educated guess: into the purses

91

of the soldiers to be spent on useless things or hoarded according to their natures; into the purses of manufacturers and merchants who took their profits from warmongering; into the purses of foreigners; and into the purses of the very men who waged the wars. But if that last is true, he wondered, why did I not make any profit?

Look at Marcus Antonius, his thoughts went on. He has stolen hundreds of millions, more of them to keep up his hedonistic lifestyle than to pay his legions. And how many millions has he given away to his so-called friends in order to look like a big man? Oh, I have stolen too – I got away with Caesar's war chest. If I had not, I would be dead today. But, unlike Antonius, I never give a brass farthing away. What I disburse from my hidden treasure-trove I expect to see put to good use, as in paying my army of agents. I cannot survive without my agents. The tragedy is that none of it dare I spend on Roma herself. Most of it goes to pay the legions' massive bonuses. A bottomless pit that perhaps has only one real asset: it distributes personal wealth more equally than in the old days when the plutocrats could be numbered on the fingers of both hands, and the soldiers didn't have enough income to belong even to the Fifth Class. That's not true anymore.

The vista of the Forum blurred as his eyes filled with tears. Caesar, oh, Caesar! What might I have learned if you had lived? It was Antonius enabled them to kill you – he was a part of the plot, I know it in my bones. Believing that he was Caesar's heir and urgently needing Caesar's vast fortune, he succumbed to the blandishments of Trebonius and Decimus Brutus. The other Brutus and Cassius were nothings, mere figureheads. Like many before him, Antonius hungers to be the First Man in Rome. Were I not here, he would be. But I am here, and he's afraid that I will usurp that title as well as Caesar's name, Caesar's money. He's right to be afraid. Caesar the God – Divus Julius – is on my side. If Rome is to prosper, I *must* win this struggle! Yet I have vowed never to go to war against Antonius, and I will keep that vow.

The zephyr breeze of early summer stirred his mass of bright gold hair; people noticed it first, then noticed the identity of its owner. They stared, usually with a scowl. As the Triumvir present in Rome, it was he who got most of the blame for the hard times – expensive bread, monotonous supplementary foods, high rents, empty purses. But to every scowl he returned Caesar's smile, a thing so powerful that the scowls became answering smiles.

Though even in Rome Antonius liked to strut around in armor, Octavian always wore his purple-bordered toga; in it he looked small, slight, graceful. The days when he had worn boots with platform soles were gone. Rome now knew him as Caesar's heir beyond doubt, and many called him what he called himself – Divi Filius, the son of a god. It remained his greatest advantage, even in the face of his unpopularity. Men might scowl and mutter, but mamas and grannies cooed and gushed; Octavian was too clever a politician to discount the impact of mamas and grannies.

From the Velia he walked through the lichen-whiskered ancient pillars of the Porta Mugonia and ascended the Palatine Mount at its less fashionable end. His house had once belonged to the famous advocate Quintus Hortensius Hortalus, Cicero's rival in the courts. Antonius had blamed the son for the death of his brother Gaius, and had him proscribed. Which didn't worry young Hortensius, dead in Macedonia, his corpse thrown on Gaius Antonius's monument. Like most of Rome, Octavian was well aware that Gaius Antonius had been so incompetent that his demise had been a positive blessing.

The *domus Hortensia* was a very big and luxurious house, though not the size of Pompey the Great's palace on the Carinae. That, Antonius had snaffled; when Caesar learned of it, he made his cousin pay for it. Upon Caesar's death, the payments stopped. But Octavian hadn't wanted a house ostentatious enough to be called a palace, just wanted something large enough to function as offices as well as residence. The *domus Hortensia* had been knocked down to him at the proscription auctions for two million sesterces, a fraction of its real value. That kind of thing happened often at the proscription auctions, when so much first-class property was sold at one and the same moment.

At the fashionable end of the Palatine, all the crowded houses vied for views of the Forum Romanum, but Hortensius hadn't cared about outlook. He cared about space. A noted fish fancier, he had huge ponds devoted to gold and silver carp, and grounds and gardens more usual in villas outside the Servian Walls, like the palace Caesar had built for Cleopatra under the Janiculan Hill. Its grounds and gardens were legendary.

The *domus Hortensia* stood atop a fifty-foot cliff overlooking the Circus Maximus, where on days of parades or chariot races over a hundred and fifty thousand Roman citizens jammed its bleachers to marvel and cheer. Sparing the circus no glance, Octavian entered his house through the garden and ponds behind it, proceeding into a vast reception room that Hortensius had never used, so infirm was he when he added it on.

Octavian liked the house's design, for the kitchens and the servants' quarters were off to one side in a separate structure that contained latrines and baths for servile use. The baths and latrines for the owner, his family and guests were inside the main pile and made of priceless marbles. Like most such on the Palatine, they were situated above an underground stream that fed into the immense sewers of the Cloaca Maxima. To Octavian, they were a main reason for his purchasing this *domus*; he was the most private of persons, especially when it came to voiding his bowels and bladder. No one must see, no one must hear! As was true when he bathed, at least once each day. Thus military campaigns were a torment only made bearable by Agrippa, who contrived to give him privacy whenever possible. Quite why he felt so strongly about this, Octavian didn't know, as he was well made; save that, without properly arranged clothes, men were vulnerable.

His valet met him, signalling anxiety; Octavian hated the slightest mark on tunic or toga, which made life hard for the man, perpetually busy with chalk and clear vinegar.

'Yes, you can have the toga,' he said absently, shed it, and walked out into an internal peristyle garden that had the finest fountain in Rome, of rearing horses with fish's tails, Amphitryon riding a shell chariot. The painting was exquisite, so lifelike that the water god's weedy hair glimmered and glowered greenish, his skin a network of tiny, silvery scales. The sculpture sat in the middle of a round pool whose pale green marble had cost Hortensius ten talents to buy from the new quarries at Carrara.

Through a pair of bronze doors bearing scenes of Lapiths and centaurs in bas relief, Octavian entered a hall that had his study to one side and the dining room to the other. Thence he passed into a huge atrium whose *impluvium* pool beneath the *compluvium* in the roof shimmered mirrorlike from an overhead sun. And finally through another pair of bronze doors he came onto the loggia, a vast open-air balcony. Hortensius had liked the idea of an arbor as shelter from strong sun, and erected a series of struts over part of the area, then planted grapevines to train over them. With the years they had festooned the frame into a dappled haven, pendant at this season with dangling bunches of pale green beads.

Four men sat in big chairs around a low table, with a fifth chair vacant to complete the circle. Two jugs and a number of beakers sat on the table, of plain Arvernian pottery – no golden goblets or Alexandrian glass flagons for Octavian! The water jug was bigger than the wine one, which held a very light, sparkling white vintage from Alba Fucentia. No connoisseur of oenological bent would have sniffed contemptuously at this wine, for Octavian liked to serve the best of everything. What he disliked were extravagance and imported anythings. The produce of Italia, he was fond of telling those prepared to listen, was superlative, so why play the snob by flaunting wines from Chios, rugs from Miletus, wools dyed in Hierapolis, tapestries from Corduba?

Cat-footed, Octavian gave no warning of his advent, and stood in the doorway for a moment to observe them; his 'council of elders', as Maecenas called them, punning on the fact that Quintus Salvidienus, at thirty-one, was the oldest of the group. To these four men – and to them alone – did Octavian voice his thoughts; though not all his thoughts. That privilege was reserved for Agrippa, his coeval and spiritual brother.

Marcus Vipsanius Agrippa, aged twenty-two, was everything a Roman nobleman ought to be in looks. He was as tall as Caesar had been, heavily muscled in a lean way, and possessed of an unusual yet handsome face whose brows beetled below a shelf of forehead and whose strong chin was tucked firmly beneath a stern mouth. Discovering that his deep-set eyes were hazel was difficult thanks to the bristling brows obscuring them. Yet Agrippa's birth was so low that a Tiberius Claudius Nero sneered – who had ever heard of a family named *Vipsanius?* Samnite, if not Apulian or Calabrian. Italian scum at any rate. Only Octavian fully appreciated the depth and breadth of his intellect, which ran to the generaling of armies, the building of bridges and aqueducts, the invention of gadgets and tools to make labor easier. This year he was Rome's urban praetor, responsible for all civil law suits and the apportioning of criminal cases to the various courts. A heavy job, but not heavy enough to satisfy Agrippa, who had also taken on some of the duties of the aediles. These worthies were supposed to care for Rome's buildings and services; apostrophizing them as a scabby lot of idlers, he had assumed authority over the water supply and sewerage, much to the dismay of the companies that the city contracted to run them. He talked seriously of doing things to prevent the sewers backing up whenever the Tiber flooded, but feared it would not happen this year, as it necessitated a thorough mapping of many miles of sewers and drains. However, he had managed to get some action on the Aqua Marcia, the best of

Rome's existing aqueducts, and was constructing a new one, the Aqua Julia. Rome's water supply was the best in the world, but the city's population was increasing and time was running out.

He was Octavian's man to the death, not blindly loyal but insightfully so; he knew Octavian's weaknesses as well as his strengths, and suffered for him as Octavian never suffered for himself. There could be no question of ambition. Unlike almost all New Men, Agrippa truly understood to the core of his being that it was Octavian, with the birth, who must retain ascendancy. His was the role of *fides Achates*, and he would always be there for Octavian . . . who would elevate him far beyond his true social status: what better fate than to be the Second Man in Rome? For Agrippa, that was more than any New Man deserved.

Gaius Cilnius Maecenas, aged thirty, was an Etruscan of the oldest blood; his family were the lords of Arretium, a busy river port on the bend of the Arnus where the Annian, Cassian and Clodian roads met as they traveled from Rome to Italian Gaul. For reasons best known to himself, he had dropped his family name, Cilnius, and called himself plain Gaius Maecenas. His love of the finer things in life showed in his softly plump physique, though he could, when push came to shove, undertake grueling journeys on Octavian's behalf. The face was a trifle froglike, for his pale blue eyes had a tendency to pop out – exophthalmia, the Greeks called it.

A famous wit and raconteur, he had a mind as broad and deep as Agrippa's, but in a different way; Maecenas loved literature, art, philosophy, rhetoric, and collected not antique pots but new poets. As Agrippa jokingly observed, he couldn't general a bun fight in a brothel, but he did know how to stop one. A smoother, more persuasive talker than Maecenas no one had yet found, nor a man more suited for scheming and plotting in the shadows behind the curule chair. Like Agrippa, he had reconciled himself to Octavian's ascendancy, though his motives were not as pure as Agrippa's. Maecenas was a grey eminence, a diplomat, a dealer in men's fates. He could spot a useful flaw in a trice and insert his sweet words painlessly into the weakness to produce a wound worse than any dagger could make. Dangerous, was Maecenas.

Quintus Salvidienus was a man from Picenum, that nest of demagogues and political nuisances that had bred such luminaries as Pompey the Great and Titus Labienus. But he hadn't won his laurels in the Forum Romanum; his were earned on the battlefield, where he excelled. Fine-looking in the face and body, he had a thatch of bright red hair that had given him his cognomen, Rufus, and shrewd, far-sighted blue eyes. Inside himself he cherished high ambitions, and had tied his career to the tail of Octavian's comet as the quickest way to the top. From time to time the Picentine vice stirred in him, which was to contemplate changing sides if it seemed prudent to do so. Salvidienus had no intention of ending on a losing side, and wondered sometimes if Octavian really had what it took to win the coming struggle. Of gratitude he had little, of loyalty none, but he had hidden these so successfully that Octavian, for one, did not dream that they existed in him. His guard was good, but there were occasions when he wondered if Agrippa suspected, so, whenever Agrippa was present, he watched what he said and did closely. As for Maecenas – who knew what that oily aristocrat sensed?

Titus Statilius Taurus, aged twenty-seven, was the least man among them, and therefore knew the least about Octavian's ideas and plans. Another military man, he looked what he was, being tall, solidly built and rather beaten around the face – a swollen left ear, scarred left brow and cheek, broken nose. Yet he was, withal, a handsome man with wheat-colored hair, grey eyes, and an easy smile that belied his reputation as a martinet when he commanded legions. He had a horror of homosexuality and would not have anyone so inclined under his authority, no matter how well born. As a soldier he was inferior to Agrippa and Salvidienus, but not by much; what he lacked was their genius for improvisation. Of his loyalty there was no doubt, chiefly because Octavian dazzled him; the undeniable talents and brilliance of Agrippa, Salvidienus and Maecenas were as nothing compared to the extraordinary mind of Caesar's heir.

'Greetings,' said Octavian, going to the vacant chair.

Agrippa smiled. 'Where have you been? Making eyes at Lady Roma? Forum or Mons Aventinus?'

'Forum.' Octavian poured water and drank it thirstily, then sighed. 'I was planning what to do when I have the money to set Lady Roma to rights.'

'Planning is all it can be,' said Maecenas wryly.

'True. Still, Gaius, nothing is wasted. What plans I make now don't have to be made later. Have we heard what our consul Pollio is up to? Ventidius?'

'Skulking in eastern Italian Gaul,' Maecenas said. 'Rumor has it that shortly they'll be marching down the Adriatic coast to help

Antonius land his legions, which are clustered around Apollonia. Between Pollio's seven, Ventidius's seven and the ten Antonius has with him, we're in for a terrible drubbing.'

'I will *not* go to war against Antonius!' Octavian cried.

'You won't need to,' said Agrippa with a grin. 'Their men won't fight ours, on that I'd stake my life.'

'I agree,' said Salvidienus. 'The men have had a gut-full of wars they don't understand. What's the difference to them between Caesar's nephew and Caesar's cousin? Once they belonged to Caesar himself, that's all they remember. Thanks to Caesar's habit of shifting his soldiers around to plump out this legion or thin down that legion, they identify with Caesar, not a unit.'

'They mutinied,' Maecenas said, voice hard.

'Only the Ninth can be said to have mutinied directly against Caesar, thanks to a dozen corrupt centurions in the pay of Pompeius Magnus's cronies. For the rest, blame Antonius. *He* put them up to it, no one else! He kept their centurions drunk and bought their spokesmen. He *worked* on them!' Agrippa said contemptuously. 'Antonius is a mischief maker, not a political genius. He lacks any subtlety. Why else is he even *thinking* of landing his men in Italia? It makes no sense! Have you declared war on him? Has Lepidus? He's doing it because he's afraid of you.'

'Antonius is no bigger a mischief maker than Sextus Pompeius Magnus Pius, to give him his full name,' said Maecenas, and laughed. 'I hear that Sextus sent *tata*-in-law Libo to Athens to ask Antonius to join him in crushing you.'

'How do you know that?' Octavian demanded, sitting upright.

'Like Ulysses, I have spies everywhere.'

'So do I, but it's news to me. What did Antonius answer?'

'A sort of a no. No official alliance, but he won't impede Sextus's activities, provided they're directed at you.'

'How considerate of him.' The extraordinarily beautiful face puckered, the eyes looked strained. 'As well, then, that I took it upon myself to give Lepidus six legions and send him off to govern Africa. Has Antonius heard of that yet? My agents say no.'

'So do mine,' Maecenas said. 'Antonius won't be pleased, Caesar, so much is sure. Once Fango was killed, Antonius thought he had Africa in the sinus of his toga. I mean, who counts Lepidus? But now that the new governor is dead too, Lepidus will walk in. With Africa's four legions and the six he took there with him, Lepidus has become a strong player in the game.'

'I am aware of that!' Octavian snapped, nettled. 'However,

Lepidus loathes Antonius far more than he loathes me. He'll send Italia grain this autumn.'

'With Sardinia gone, we're going to need it,' said Taurus.

Octavian looked at Agrippa. 'Since we have no ships, we have to start building some. Agrippa, I want you to doff your insignia of office and go on a journey all the way around the peninsula from Tergeste to Liguria. You'll be commissioning good stout war galleys. To beat Sextus, we need fleets.'

'How do we pay for them, Caesar?' Agrippa asked.

'With the last of the planks.'

A cryptic reply that meant nothing to the other three, but was crystal clear to Agrippa, who nodded. 'Planks' was the codeword Octavian and Agrippa employed when they spoke of Caesar's war chest.

'Libo returned to Sextus empty-handed, and Sextus took—er—umbrage. Not sufficient umbrage to plague Antonius, but umbrage nonetheless,' Maecenas said. 'Libo didn't like Antonius any better in Athens than he had in other places, therefore Libo is now an enemy dropping poison about Antonius in Sextus's ear.'

'What particularly piqued Libo?' Octavian asked curiously.

'With Fulvia gone, I think he had rather hoped to secure a third husband for his sister. What cleverer way to cement an alliance than a marriage? Poor Libo! My spies say he baited his hook with great variety. But the subject never came up, and Libo sailed back to Agrigentum a disappointed man.'

'Hmmm.' The golden brows knotted, the thick fair lashes came down over Octavian's remarkable eyes. Suddenly he slapped both hands upon his knees and looked determined. 'Maecenas, pack your things! You're off to Agrigentum to see Sextus and Libo.'

'With what purpose?' Maecenas asked, misliking the mission.

'Your purpose is to make a truce with Sextus that enables Italia to have grain this autumn, and for a reasonable price. You will do whatever is necessary to achieve that end, is that understood?'

'Even if there's a marriage involved?'

'Even if.'

'She's in her thirties, Caesar. There's a daughter, Cornelia, almost old enough for marriage.'

'I don't care how old Libo's sister is! All women are the same from the waist down, so what does age matter? At least she won't have the taint of a strumpet like Fulvia on her.'

No one commented upon the fact that, after two years, Fulvia's daughter had been sent back to her virgo intacta. Octavian had married the girl to appease Antony, but had never slept with her. However, that couldn't happen with Libo's sister. Octavian would have to sleep with *her*, preferably fruitfully. In all things of the flesh he was as big a prude as Cato the Censor, so pray that Scribonia was neither ugly nor licentious. Everyone looked at the floor of tessellated tiles and pretended to be deaf, dumb, blind.

'What if Antonius attempts to land in Brundisium?' Salvidienus asked, to change the subject a little.

'Brundisium is fortified within an inch of its life; he won't get a single troop transport past the harbor chain,' Agrippa said. 'I supervised the fortification of Brundisium myself, you know that, Salvidienus.'

'There are other places he can land.'

'And undoubtedly will, but with all those troops?' Octavian looked tranquil. 'However, Maecenas, I want you back from Agrigentum in a tearing hurry.'

'The winds are against,' Maecenas said, sounding desolate. Who needed to spend any part of summer in a cesspit like Sextus Pompey's Sicilian township of Agrigentum?

'All the better to bring you home quickly. As for getting there – *row*! Take a gig to Puteoli and hire the fastest ship and the best oarsmen you can find. Pay them double their going rate. Now, Maecenas, now!'

And so the group broke up; only Agrippa stayed.

'What's your latest count on the number of legions we have to oppose Antonius?'

'Ten, Caesar. Though it wouldn't matter if all we had were three or four. Neither side will fight. I keep saying it, but every ear is deaf except yours and Salvidienus's.'

'I heard you because in that fact lies our salvation. I refuse to believe I'm beaten,' Octavian said. He sighed, smiled ruefully. 'Oh, Agrippa, I hope this woman of Libo's is bearable! I haven't had much luck with wives.'

'They've been someone else's choice, no more than political expedients. One day, Caesar, you'll choose a woman for yourself, and she won't be a Servilia Vatia or a Clodia. Or, I suspect, a Scribonia Libone, if the deal with Sextus comes off.' Agrippa cleared his throat, looked uneasy. 'Maecenas knew, but has left me to tell you the news from Athens.'

'News? What news?'

'Fulvia opened her veins.'

For a long moment Octavian said nothing, just stared at the

Circus Maximus so fixedly that Agrippa fancied he had gone away to some place beyond this world. A mass of contradictions, was Caesar. Even in his mind, Agrippa never thought of him as Octavianus; he had been the first person to call Octavian by his adopted name, though now all his adherents did. No one could be colder, or harder, or more ruthless; yet, it was plain to see, looking at him now, that he was grieving for Fulvia, a woman he had loathed.

'She was a part of Rome's history,' Octavian finally said, 'and she deserved a better end. Have her ashes come home? Does she have a tomb?'

'To my knowledge, no on both counts.'

Octavian got up. 'I shall speak to Atticus. Between us, we will give her a proper burial, as befits her station. Aren't her children by Antonius quite young?'

'Antyllus is five, Iullus is two.'

'Then I'll ask my sister to keep an eye on them. Three of her own aren't enough for Octavia, she's always got someone else's children in her care.'

Including, thought Agrippa grimly, your half-sister, Marcia. I will never forget that day on the heights of Petra when we were on our way to meet Brutus and Cassius – Gaius sitting with the tears streaming down his face, mourning the death of his mother. But she isn't dead! She's the wife of his stepbrother, Lucius Marcius Philippus. Another one of his contradictions, that he can grieve for Fulvia, while pretending that his mother doesn't exist. Oh, I know why. She had only donned her widow's weeds for a month when she began an affair with her stepson. That might have been hushed up, had she not become pregnant. He'd had a letter from his sister that day in Petra, begging him to understand their mother's plight. But he wouldn't. To him, Atia was a whore, an immoral woman not worthy to be the mother of a god's son. So he forced Atia and Philippus to retire to Philippus's villa at Misenum, and forbade them to enter Rome. An edict he has never lifted, though Atia is ill and her baby girl a permanent member of Octavia's nursery. One day it will all come back to haunt him, though he cannot see that, anymore than he has ever laid eyes on his half-sister. A beautiful child, fair as any Julian, for all that her father is so dark.

Then came a letter from Further Gaul that put all thought of Antony or his dead wife out of Octavian's mind, and postponed the date of a marriage Maecenas was busy arranging for him in Agrigentum.

'Esteemed Caesar,' it said, 'I write to inform you that my beloved father, Quintus Fufius Calenus, has died in Narbo. He was fifty-nine years old, I know, but his health was good. Then he fell down dead. It was over in a moment. As his chief legate, I now have charge of the eleven legions stationed throughout Further Gaul: four in Agedincum, four in Narbo, and three in Glanum. At this time the Gauls are quiet, my father having put down a revolt among the Aquitani last year, but I quail to think what might yet happen if the Gauls get wind of my command and inexperience. I felt it right to inform you rather than Marcus Antonius, though the Gauls belong to him. He is so far away. Please send me a new governor, one with the necessary military skills to keep the peace here. Preferably quickly, as I would like to bring my father's ashes back to Rome in person.'

Octavian read and reread the rather bald communication, his heart fluttering in his chest. For once, happy flutterings. At last a twist of fate that favored him! Who could ever have believed that Calenus would die?

He sent for Agrippa, busy winding up his tenure of the urban praetorship so that he could travel for long periods; the urban praetor could not be absent from Rome for more than ten days.

'Forget the odds and ends!' Octavian cried, handing him the letter. 'Read this and rejoice!'

'Eleven veteran legions!' Agrippa breathed, understanding the import immediately. 'You have to reach Narbo before Pollio and Ventidius beat you to it. They have fewer miles to cover, so pray the news doesn't find them quickly. Young Calenus isn't his father's bootlace, if this is anything to go by.' Agrippa waved the sheet of paper. 'Imagine it, Caesar! Further Gaul is about to drop into your lap without a *pilum* raised in anger.'

'We take Salvidienus with us,' Octavian said.

'Is that wise?'

The grey eyes looked startled. 'What makes you question my wisdom in this?'

'Nothing I can put a finger on, except that governing Further Gaul is a great command. Salvidienus might let it go to his head. At least I presume that you mean to give him the command?'

'Would you rather have it? It's yours if you want it.'

'No, Caesar, I don't want it. Too far from Italia and you.' He sighed, shrugged in a defeated way. 'I can't think of anyone else.

102

Taurus is too young, the rest you can't trust to deal smartly with the Bellovaci or the Suebi.'

'Salvidienus will be fine,' Octavian said confidently, and patted his dearest friend on the arm. 'We'll start for Further Gaul at dawn tomorrow, and we'll travel the way my father the god did – four-mule gigs at the gallop. That means the Via Aemilia and the Via Domitia. To make sure we have no trouble commandeering fresh mules often enough, we'll take a squadron of German cavalry.'

'You ought to have a full-time bodyguard, Caesar.'

'Not now, I'm too busy. Besides, I don't have the money.'

Agrippa gone, Octavian walked across the Palatine to the Clivus Victoriae and the *domus* of Gaius Claudius Marcellus Minor, who was his brother-in-law. An inadequate and indecisive consul in the year that Caesar had crossed the Rubicon, Marcellus was the brother and first cousin of two men whose hatred of Caesar had been beyond reason. He had skulked in Italy while Caesar fought the war against Pompey the Great, and had been rewarded after Caesar won with the hand of Octavia. For Marcellus the union was a mixture of love and expedience; a marriage tie to Caesar's family meant protection for himself and the massive Claudius Marcellus fortune, now all his. And he truly did love his bride, a priceless jewel. Octavia had borne him a girl, Marcella Major, a boy whom everyone called Marcellus, and a second girl, Marcella Minor, who was known as Cellina.

The house was preternaturally quiet. Marcellus was very ill, ill enough that his ordinarily gentle wife had issued iron instructions about servant chatter and clatter.

'How is he?' Octavian asked his sister, kissing her cheek.

'It's only a matter of days, the physicians say. The growth is extremely malignant, it's eating up his insides voraciously.'

The large aquamarine eyes brimmed with tears that only fell to soak her pillow after she retired. She genuinely loved this man whom her stepfather had chosen for her with her brother's full approval; the Claudii Marcelli were not patricians, but of very old and noble plebeian stock, which had made Marcellus Minor a suitable husband for a Julian woman. It had been Caesar who hadn't liked him, Caesar who at first had disapproved of the match.

Her beauty grew ever greater, her brother thought, wishing he could share her sorrow. For though he had consented to the marriage, he had never really taken to the man who possessed his beloved Octavia. Besides, he had plans, and the death of Marcellus Minor was likely to further them. Octavia would get over her loss. Four years older than he, she had the Julian look: golden hair, eyes with blue in them, high cheekbones, a lovely mouth, and an expression of radiant calmness that drew people to her. More importantly, she had a full measure of the famous gift meted out to most Julian women: she made her men happy.

Cellina was newborn and Octavia was nursing the babe herself, a joy she wouldn't relinquish to a wet nurse. But it meant that she hardly ever went out, and often had to absent herself from the presence of visitors. Like her brother, Octavia was modest to the point of prudishness, would not bare her breast to give her child milk in front of any man except her husband. Yet one more reason why Octavian loved her. To him, she was Goddess Roma personified and, when he was undisputed master of Rome, he intended to erect statues of her in public places, an honor not accorded to women.

'May I see Marcellus?' Octavian asked.

'He says no visitors, even you.' Her face twisted. 'It's pride, Caesar, the pride of a scrupulous man. His room smells, no matter how hard the servants scrub, or how many sticks of incense I burn. The physicians call it the smell of death and say it's ineradicable.'

He took her into his arms, kissed her hair. 'Dearest sister, is there anything I can do?'

'Nothing, Caesar. You comfort me, but nothing comforts him.'

No use for it; he would have to be brutal. 'I must go far away for at least a month,' he said.

She gasped. 'Oh! Must you? He can't last half a month!'

'Yes, I must.'

'Who will arrange the funeral? Find an undertaker? Find the right man to give the eulogy? Our family has become so *small*! Wars, murders . . . Maecenas, perhaps?'

'He's in Agrigentum.'

'Then who is there? Domitius Calvinus? Servilius Vatia?'

He lifted her chin to look directly into her eyes, his mouth stern, his expression one of subtle pain. 'I think that it must be Lucius Marcius Philippus,' he said deliberately. 'Not my choice, but socially the only one who won't make Rome talk. Since no one believes that our mother is dead, what can it matter? I'll write to him and tell him he may return to Rome, take up residence in his father's house.'

'He'll be tempted to throw the edict in your teeth.'

'Huh! Not that one! He'll knuckle under. He seduced the mother of the Triumvir Caesar, Divi Filius! It's only she has saved his skin. Oh, I'd dearly love to cook up a treason charge and serve *that* as a treat for his Epicurean palate! Even my patience has its limits, as he well knows. He'll knuckle under,' Octavian said again.

'Would you like to see little Marcia?' Octavia asked in a trembling voice. 'She's so sweet, Caesar, honestly!'

'No, I wouldn't!' Octavian snapped.

'But she's our sister! The blood is linked, Caesar, even on the Marcian side. Divus Julius's grandmother was a Marcia.'

'I don't care if she was Juno!' Octavian said savagely, and stalked out.

Oh dear, oh dear! Gone before she could tell him that, for the time being at any rate, Fulvia's two boys by Antonius had been added to her nursery. When she went to see them she had been shocked to find the two little fellows without any kind of supervision, and ten-year-old Curio gone feral. Well, she didn't have the authority to take Curio under her wing and tame him, but she could take Antyllus and Iullus as a simple act of kindness. Poor, poor Fulvia! The spirit of a Forum demagogue cooped up inside a female shell. Octavia's friend Pilia insisted that Antonius had beaten Fulvia in Athens, even *kicked* her, but that Octavia just couldn't credit. After all, she knew Antonius well, and liked him very much. Some of her liking stemmed out of the fact that he was so different from the other men in her life; it could be wearing to associate with none but brilliant, subtle, devious men. Living with Antonius must have been an adventure, but beat his wife? No, he'd never do that! Never.

She went back to the nursery, there to weep quietly, taking care that Marcella, Marcellus and Antyllus, old enough to notice, didn't see her tears. Still, she thought, cheering up, it would be wonderful to have Mama back in her life! Mama suffered so from some disease of the bones that she had been forced to send little Marcia to Rome and Octavia; but in the future she would be just around the corner, able to see her daughters. Only when would brother Caesar understand? Would he ever? Somehow Octavia didn't think so. To him, Mama had done the unforgivable.

Then her mind returned to Marcellus; she went to his room immediately. Aged forty-five the year he had married Octavia, he had been a man in his prime, slender, well kept, erudite in education, good-looking in a Caesarish way. The ruthless attitude of Julian men was entirely missing in him, though he had a certain cunning, a deviousness that had enabled him to elude capture when

Italia went mad for Caesar Divus Julius, had enabled him to make a splendid marriage that brought him into Caesar's camp unplucked. For which he had Antony to thank, and had never forgotten it. Hence Octavia's knowledge of Antony, a frequent caller.

Now the beautiful, twenty-seven-year-old wife beheld a stick man, eaten away to desiccation by the thing that gnawed and chewed at his vitals. His favorite slave, Admetus, sat by his bed, one hand enfolding Marcellus's claw, but when Octavia entered Admetus rose quickly and gave her the chair.

'How is he?' she whispered.

'Asleep on syrup of poppies, *domina*. Nothing else helps the pain, which is a pity. It clouds his mind dreadfully.'

'I know,' said Octavia, settling herself. 'Eat and sleep, do. It will be your shift again before you know it. I wish he'd let someone else take a turn, but he won't.'

'If I were dying so slowly and in so much pain, *domina*, I would want the right face above me when I opened my eyes.'

'Exactly so, Admetus. Now go, please. Eat and sleep. And he has manumitted you in his will, he told me so. You will be Gaius Claudius Admetus, but I hope you stay on with me.'

Too moved to speak, the young Greek kissed Octavia's hand.

Hours went by, their silence broken only when a nursemaid brought Cellina to be fed. Luckily she was a good baby; didn't cry loudly even when hungry. Marcellus slept on, oblivious.

Then he stirred, opened dazed dark eyes that cleared when they saw her.

'Octavia, my love!' he croaked.

'Marcellus, my love,' she said with a radiant smile, rising to fetch a beaker of sweet watered wine. He sucked at it through a hollowed reed, not very much. Then she brought a basin of water and a cloth. She peeled back the linen cover from his skin and bones, removed his soiled diaper, and began to wash him with a featherlight hand, talking to him gently. No matter where she was in the room, his eyes followed her, bright with love.

'Old men shouldn't marry young girls,' he said.

'I disagree. If young girls marry young men, they never grow or learn except tritely, for both are equally green.' She took the basin away. 'There! Does that feel better?'

'Yes,' he lied, then suddenly spasmed from head to toes, a rictus of agony tugging at his teeth. 'Oh, Jupiter, Jupiter! The pain, the pain! My syrup, where's my syrup?'

106

So she gave him syrup of poppies and sat down again to watch him sleep until Admetus arrived to relieve her.

Maecenas found his task made easier because Sextus Pompey had taken offense at Mark Antony's reaction to his proposal. 'Pirate' indeed! Willing to agree to a fly-by-night conspiracy to badger Octavian, but not willing to declare a public alliance. 'Pirate' was not how Sextus Pompey saw himself – ever had, ever would. Having discovered that he loved being at sea and commanding three or four hundred war ships, he saw himself as a maritime Caesar, incapable of losing a battle. Yes, unbeatable on the waves and a big contender for the title of First Man in Rome. In that respect he feared both Antony and Octavian, even bigger contenders. What he needed was an alliance with one of them against the other, to reduce the number of contenders. Three down to two. In actual fact he had never met Antonius, hadn't even managed to be in the crowds outside the Senate doors when Antony had thundered against the Republicans as Caesar's tame tribune of the plebs. A sixteen-year-old had better things to do, and Sextus was not politically inclined, then or now. Whereas he had once met Octavian, in a little port on the Italian instep, and found a formidable foe in the guise of a sweet-faced boy, twenty to his own twenty-five. The first thing that had struck him about Octavian was that he beheld a natural outlaw who would never put himself in a position where he might be outlawed. They had done some dealing, then Octavian had resumed his march to Brundisium and Sextus had sailed away. Since then, allegiances had changed; Brutus and Cassius were defeated and dead; the world belonged to the Triumvirs.

He hadn't been able to credit Antony's short-sightedness in choosing to center himself in the East. Anyone with a modicum of intelligence could see that the East was a trap, gold the bait on its terrible barbed hook. Dominion over the world would go to the man who controlled Italia and the West, and that was Octavian. Of course it was the hardest job, the least popular, which was why Lepidus, given Lucius Antonius's six legions, had scuttled off to Africa, there to play a waiting game and accumulate more troops. Another fool. Yes, Octavian was to be feared the most because he hadn't balked at taking on the hardest task.

If he had consented to a formal alliance, Antony would have made Sextus's grab for First Man in Rome status easier. But no, he refused to associate with a pirate!

'So it goes on as it is,' Sextus said to Libo, his dark blue eyes stony. 'It will just take longer to wear Octavianus down.'

'My dear Sextus, you will never wear Octavianus down,' said Maecenas, turning up in Agrigentum a few days later. 'He has no weaknesses for you to work on.'

'*Gerrae!*' Sextus snapped. 'To start with, he has no ships and no admirals worthy of the name. Fancy sending an effete Greek freedman like Helenus to wrest Sardinia off me! I have the fellow here, by the way. He's safe and unharmed. Ships and admirals – two weaknesses. He has no money, a third. Enemies in every walk of life – four. Shall I go on?'

'They're not weaknesses, they're deficiencies,' said Maecenas, savoring a mouthful of tiny shrimps. 'Oh, these are delicious! Why are they so much tastier than the ones I eat in Rome?'

'Muddier waters, better feeding grounds.'

'You do know a lot about the sea.'

'Enough to know that Octavianus can't beat me on it, even if he did find some ships. Organizing a sea battle is an art all its own, and I happen to be the best at it in Rome's entire span of history. My brother, Gnaeus, was superb, but not in my class.' Sextus sat back and looked complacent.

What is it about this generation of young men? wondered the fascinated Maecenas. At school we learned that there would never be another Scipio Africanus, another Scipio Aemilianus, but each of them was a generation apart, unique in his time. Not so today. I suppose the young men have been given a chance to show what they can do because so many men in their forties and fifties have died or gone into permanent exile. This specimen isn't thirty yet.

Sextus came out of his self-congratulatory reverie. 'I must say, Maecenas, that I'm disappointed that your master didn't come to see me in person. Too important, is he?'

'No, I assure you,' said Maecenas, at his oiliest. 'He sends his profuse apologies, but something has come up in Further Gaul that made his presence there mandatory.'

'Yes, I heard, probably before he did. Further Gaul! What a cornucopia of riches will become his! The best of the veteran legions, grain, hams and salt pork, sugar beets . . . Not to mention the land route to the Spains, though he doesn't have Italian Gaul yet. No doubt he will when Pollio decides to don his consular regalia, though rumor has it that won't be for some time. Rumor has it that Pollio is marching his seven legions down the Adriatic coast to assist Antonius when he lands at Brundisium.'

Maecenas looked surprised. 'Why should Antonius need military help to land in Italia? As the senior of the Triumvirs, he's free to come and go as he pleases.'

'Not if Brundisium has anything to do with it. Why do the Brundisians hate Antonius so? They'd spit on his ashes.'

'He was very hard on them when Divus Julius left him behind there to get the rest of the legions across the Adriatic the year before Pharsalus,' said Maecenas, ignoring the darkening of Sextus's face at mention of the battle that had seen his father crushed, the world changed. 'Antonius can be unreasonable, never more so than at that time, with Divus Julius breathing down his neck. Besides, his military discipline was slack. He let the legionaries run wild – raping, looting. Then, when Divus Julius made him Master of the Horse, he took out a lot of his spleen at Brundisium on Brundisium.'

'That would do it,' said Sextus, grinning. 'However, it does look a bit like an invasion when a Triumvir brings his entire army with him.'

'A show of strength, a signal to Imperator Caesar—'

'*Who?*'

'Imperator Caesar. We don't call him Octavianus. Nor does Rome.' Maecenas looked demure. 'Perhaps that's why Pollio hasn't come to Rome, even as her elected junior consul.'

'Here's some less palatable news for Imperator Caesar than Further Gaul,' Sextus said waspishly. 'Pollio has won Ahenobarbus over to Antonius's side. Won't Imperator Caesar love *that*!'

'Oh, side, side,' Maecenas exclaimed, but without passion. 'The only side is Rome's. Ahenobarbus is a hothead, Sextus, as you well know. He "belongs" to nobody save Ahenobarbus, and he revels in roaring up and down his little patch of sea playing at being Father Neptune. No doubt this means you'll be having more to do with Ahenobarbus yourself in future?'

'I don't know,' said Sextus, looking inscrutable.

'More to the point, that busy bird rumor says that you're not getting on well with Lucius Staius Murcus these days.'

'Murcus wants the co-command,' Sextus said before he could put a brake on his tongue. That was the trouble with Maecenas, he lulled his listeners into a cosy rapport that somehow turned him from Octavian's creature into a trusted friend. Annoyed at his indiscretion, Sextus tried to pass it off with a shrug. 'Of course he can't have the co-command, I don't believe in them. I succeed

109

because I make all the decisions myself. Murcus is an Apulian goatherder who thinks he's a Roman nobleman.'

Look at who's talking, thought Maecenas. So it's goodbye to Murcus, eh? By this time next year he'll be dead, accused of some transgression or other. This haughty young reprobate brooks no equals, hence his predilection for freedmen admirals. His romance with Ahenobarbus won't last any longer than it takes Ahenobarbus to call him a Picentine upstart.

All useful information, but not why he was here. Abandoning the shrimps and the fishing for news, Maecenas got down to his real business, which was to make it clear to Sextus Pompey that he had to give Octavian and Italia a chance to survive. For Italia, that meant full bellies; for Octavian, that meant hanging on to what he had.

'Sextus Pompeius,' Maecenas said very earnestly two days later, 'it is not my place to sit in judgement upon you, or upon anyone else. But you cannot deny that the rats of Sicilia eat better than the people of Italia, your own country from Picenum, Umbria and Etruria to Bruttium and Calabria. Home of your city, which your father adorned for such a long time. In the six years since Munda you've made thousands of millions of sesterces reselling wheat, so it isn't money you're after. But if, as you insist, it is to force the Senate and People of Rome to restore your citizenship and all its attendant rights, then surely you must see that you will require powerful allies inside Rome. In fact, there are only two who wield the power necessary to help you – Marcus Antonius and Imperator Caesar. Why are you so determined that it be Antonius, a less rational and, if I dare say it, a less reliable man than Imperator Caesar? Antonius called you a pirate, wouldn't listen to Lucius Libo when *you* made the overtures. Whereas now it is Imperator Caesar making the overtures. Doesn't that *shout* his sincerity, his regard for you, his wish to help you? You'll hear no aspersions about pirates from Caesar Imperator's lips! Cast your vote for him! Antonius is not interested, and that's unarguable. If there are sides to choose, then choose the right one.'

'All right,' Sextus said, sounding angry. 'I'll cast my vote for Octavianus. But I require concrete guarantees that he'll work for me in the Senate and Assemblies.'

'Imperator Caesar will do that. What evidence of his good faith will satisfy you?'

'How would he feel about marrying into my family?'

'Overjoyed.'

'He has no wife, I understand?'

'None. Neither of his marriages was consummated. He felt that the daughters of strumpets might become strumpets themselves.'

'I hope he can get it up for this one. My father-in-law, Lucius Libo, has a sister, a widow of the utmost respectability. You can take her on approval.'

The pop-eyes widened even more, as if the news of this lady came as a thrilling surprise. 'Sextus Pompeius, Imperator Caesar will be honored! I know something of her . . . *eminently* suitable.'

'If the marriage goes through, I'll let the African grain fleets go through. And I'll sell all comers from Octavianus to the smallest dealer *my* wheat at thirteen sesterces the *modius*.'

'An unlucky number.'

Sextus grinned. 'For Octavianus, maybe, but not for me.'

'You never can tell,' said Maecenas softly.

When Octavian set eyes on Scribonia he was secretly pleased, though the few people present at their wedding would never have guessed it from his unsmiling demeanor and the careful eyes that never gave away his feelings. Yes, he *was* pleased. Scribonia didn't look thirty-three, she looked his own age, twenty-three next birthday. Her hair and eyes were dark brown, her smooth skin clear and milky, her face pretty, her figure excellent. She had not worn the flame and saffron of a virgin bride, but chosen pink in gauzy layers over a cerise petticoat. The scant words they exchanged at the ceremony revealed that she wasn't shy, but was not a chatterbox either, and further conversation afterward told him that she was literate, well read, and spoke much better Greek than he did. Perhaps the only quality that gave him qualms was her sense of the ridiculous. Not owning a well-developed sense of humor himself, Octavian feared those who did, especially if they were women – how could he be sure they weren't laughing at him? Still, Scribonia was hardly likely to find a husband so far above her station as the son of a god humorously *or* peculiarly funny.

'I'm sorry to part you from your father,' he said.

Her eyes danced. 'I'm not, Caesar. He's an old nuisance.'

'Really?' he asked, startled. 'I've always believed that parting from her father is a blow for a female.'

'That particular blow has fallen twice before you, Caesar, and each time it falls, it hurts less. At this stage, it's more a pat than a slap. Besides, I never imagined that my third husband would be

111

a beautiful young man like you.' She giggled. 'The best I was hoping for was a spry eighty-year-old.'

'Oh!' was all he could manage, floundering.

'I heard that your brother-in-law Gaius Marcellus Minor has died,' she said, taking pity on his confusion. 'When should I go to pay my condolences to your sister?'

'Yes, Octavia was sorry not to be able to come to my wedding, but she's overcome with grief, quite why I don't know. I think emotional excesses are a trifle unseemly.'

'Oh, not *unseemly*,' she said gently, discovering more about him by the moment, and a part of her dismayed at what she learned. Somehow she had envisioned Caesar as in the mold of a Sextus Pompeius – brash, conceited, callow, very male, somewhat smelly. Instead she had found the composure of a venerable consular laid atop a beauty that she suspected would come to haunt her. His luminous, silvery eyes honed his looks to spectacular, but they hadn't gazed on her with any desire. This was his third marriage too, and if his behavior in sending his two previous wives back to their mothers untouched was anything to go by, these political brides were accepted from necessity, then placed in storage to be returned in the same condition as they came in. Her father had told her that he and Sextus Pompey had a bet going: Sextus had laid long odds that Octavian wouldn't go through with it, whereas Libo believed that Octavian would go through with it for the sake of the people of Italia. So if the marriage was consummated and issue resulted to prove that, Libo stood to win a huge sum. News of the bet had made her rock with laughter, but she knew enough of Octavian already to know that she didn't dare tell him about it. Odd, that. His uncle Divus Julius would have shared her mirth, from what she knew about him. Yet in the nephew, not a spark.

'You may see Octavia at any time,' he was saying to her, 'but be prepared for tears and children.'

That was all the conversation they managed to hold together before her new serving maids put her into his bed.

The house was very large and made of gloriously colored marbles, but its new owner hadn't bothered furnishing it properly or hanging any paintings on the walls in places clearly designed for that purpose. The bed was very small for such a huge sleeping room. She had no idea that Hortensius had abhorred the tiny cubicles Romans slept in, so caused his own sleeping room to be the size of another man's study.

'Tomorrow your servants will install you in your own suite of rooms,' he said, getting into the bed in pitch darkness; he had snuffed out the candle in the doorway.

That became the first evidence of his innate modesty, which she would find difficult to overcome. Having shared the marriage bed with two other men, she expected urgent fumbling, pokes and pinches, an assault that she assumed was structured to arouse her to the same degree of want, though it never had.

But that was not Caesar's way (she must, *must*, *must* remember to call him Caesar!). The bed was too narrow not to feel his naked length alongside hers, yet he made no attempt to touch her otherwise. Suddenly he climbed on top of her, used his knees to push her legs apart, and inserted his penis into a sadly juiceless receptacle, so unprepared was she. However, it didn't seem to put him off; he worked diligently to a silent climax, removed himself from her and the bed with a muttered word that he must wash, and left the room. When he didn't come back she lay there bewildered, then called for a servant and a light.

He was in his study, seated behind a battered old desk loaded with scrolls, loose sheets of paper under his right hand, which held a simple, unadorned reed pen. Her father Libo's pen was sheathed in gold, had a pearl on top. But Octavian – Caesar – clearly cared nothing for those kinds of appearances.

'Husband, are you well?' she asked.

He had looked up at the advent of another light; now he gave her the loveliest smile she had ever seen. 'Yes,' he said.

'Did I displease you?' she asked.

'Not at all. You were very nice.'

'Do you do this often?'

'Do what?'

'Um – ah – work rather than sleep?'

'All the time. I like the peace and quiet.'

'And I've disturbed you. I'm sorry. I won't again.'

He put his head down absently. 'Goodnight, Scribonia.'

Only hours later did he lift his head again, remember that little encounter. And thought with a sense of enormous relief that he liked his new wife. She understood the boundaries and, if he could quicken her, the pact with Sextus Pompey would hold.

Octavia was not at all what she had expected, Scribonia discovered when she went to pay that condolence call. To her surprise, she found her new sister-in-law tearless and cheerful. It must have shown in her eyes, for Octavia laughed, pressed her into a comfortable chair.

'Little Gaius told you I was prostrate with grief.'

'Little Gaius?'

'Caesar. I can't get out of the habit of calling him Little Gaius because that's how I see him – as a dear little boy toddling around behind me making a thorough nuisance of himself.'

'You love him very much.'

'To distraction. But these days he's so grand and terribly important that big sisters and their "Little Gaiuses" do not sit well. However, you appear to be a woman of good sense, so I trust you not to tell him what I say about him.'

'Dumb and blind. Also deaf.'

'The pity of it is that he never had a proper childhood. The asthma plagued him so dreadfully that he couldn't mix with other boys or do his military exercises on the Campus Martius.'

Scribonia looked blank. 'Asthma? What is that?'

'He wheezes until he goes black in the face. Sometimes he nearly dies of it. Oh, it's awful to watch!' Octavia's eyes looked at an old, familiar horror. 'It's worst when there's dust in the air, or around horses from the chaff. That's why Marcus Antonius was able to say that Little Gaius hid in the marshes at Philippi and contributed nothing to the victory. The truth is that there was a shocking drought. The battlefield was a thick fog of dust and dead grass – certain death. The only place where Little Gaius could find relief was in the marshland between the plain and the sea. It is a worse grief to him that he appeared to be avoiding combat than the loss of Marcellus is to me. I do not say that lightly, believe me.'

'But people would understand if only they knew!' Scribonia cried. 'I too heard that canard, and I simply assumed it was true. Couldn't Caesar have published a pamphlet or something?'

'His pride wouldn't let him. Nor would it have been prudent. People don't want senior magistrates who are likely to die early. Besides, Antonius got in first.' Octavia looked miserable. 'He isn't a bad man, but he's so healthy himself that he has no patience with those who are sickly or delicate. To Antonius, the asthma is an act, a pretext to excuse cowardice. We're all cousins, but we're all very different, and Little Gaius is the most different. He's desperately driven. The asthma is a symptom of it, so the Egyptian physician who ministered to Divus Julius said.'

Scribonia shivered. 'What do I do if he can't breathe?'

'You'll probably never see it,' said Octavia, having no trouble seeing that her new sister-in-law was falling in love with Little Gaius. Not a thing she could avert, but understandably a thing that was bound to lead to bitter sorrow. Scribonia was a lovely woman, but not capable of fascinating either Little Gaius or Imperator Caesar. 'In Rome his breathing is usually normal unless there's drought. This year has been halcyon. I don't worry about him while he's here, nor should you. He knows what to do if he has an attack, and there's always Agrippa.'

'The stern young man who stood with him at our wedding.'

'Yes. They're not like twins,' Octavia said with the air of one who has puzzled a conundrum through to its solution. 'No rivalry exists between them. It's more as if Agrippa fits into the voids in Little Gaius. Sometimes when the children are being particularly naughty, I wish I could split myself into two of me. Well, Little Gaius has succeeded in doing that. He has Marcus Agrippa, his other half.'

By the time that Scribonia left Octavia's house, she had met the children, a tribe whom Octavia treated as if all of them were born of her own womb, and learned that next time she came, Atia would be there. Atia, her mother-in-law. She also dug deeper into the secrets of this extraordinary family. How *could* Caesar pretend that his mother was dead? How great were his pride and hauteur, that he couldn't excuse the understandable lapse of an otherwise unimpeachable woman? According to Octavia, the mother of Imperator Caesar Divi Filius could have absolutely no failings. His attitude spoke volumes about what he expected from a wife. Poor Servilia Vatia and Clodia, virgins both, but hampered by having morally unsatisfactory mothers. As he did himself, and better Atia was dead than living proof of it.

Yet, walking home between two gigantic and fierce German guards, his face filled her thoughts. Could she make him love her? Oh, pray she could make him love her! Tomorrow, she resolved, I will offer to Juno Sospita for a pregnancy, and to Venus Erucina that I please him in bed, and to the Bona Dea for uterine harmony, and to Vediovis just in case disappointment is lurking. And to Spes, who is Hope.

SEVEN

Octavian was in Rome when the news came from Brundisium that Marcus Antonius, accompanied by two legions, had attempted to enter its harbor, but been rebuffed. The chain had been cranked up, the bastions manned. Brundisium didn't care what status the monster Antonius enjoyed, the letter said, nor did it care if the Senate ordered it to admit him. Let him enter Italia anywhere he liked: just not through Brundisium. Since the only other port within the area able to land two legions was Tarentum, on the far side of the heel, a foiled and furious Antonius had had to land his men in much smaller ports around Brundisium, thus scattering them.

'He should have gone to Ancona,' Octavian said to Agrippa. 'He'd have been able to link up with Pollio and Ventidius there, and by now would be marching on Rome.'

'Were he sure of Pollio, he would have,' Agrippa replied, 'but he isn't sure of him.'

'Then you believe Plancus's letter tattling of doubts and discontent?' Octavian waved a single sheet of paper.

'Yes, I do.'

'So do I,' Octavian said, grinning. 'Plancus is in a cleft stick – he'd prefer Antonius, but he wants to keep an avenue open to me in case the time comes to hop the fence to our side of it.'

'You have too many legions around Brundisium for Antonius to band his men together again until Pollio arrives, which my scouts say won't happen for at least a *nundinum*.'

'Time enough for us to reach Brundisium, Agrippa. Are our legions placed across the Via Minucia?'

'Perfectly placed. If Pollio wants to avoid a fight, he'll have to march to Beneventum and the Via Appia.'

Octavian put his pen in its holder and gathered his papers together in neat piles that comprised correspondence with bodies and persons, drafts of laws, and detailed maps of Italia. He rose. 'Then it's off to Brundisium,' he said. 'I hope Maecenas and *my* Nerva are ready? What about the neutral one?'

'If you didn't bury yourself under a landslide of papers, Caesar, you'd know,' Agrippa said in a tone only he dared use to Octavian. 'They've been ready for days. And Maecenas has sweet-talked the neutral Nerva into coming along.'

'Excellent!'

'Why is he so important, Caesar?'

'Well, when one brother elected Antonius and the other me, his neutrality was the only way the Cocceius Nerva faction could continue to exist should Antonius and I come to blows. Antonius's Nerva died in Syria, which left a vacancy on his side. A vacancy that saw Lucius Nerva in a lather of sweat – did he dare choose to fill it? In the end, he said no, though he would not choose me either.' Octavian smirked. 'With his wife wielding the lash, he's tied to Rome, therefore – neutrality.'

'I know all that, but it begs the question.'

'You'll have an answer if my scheme succeeds.'

What had jerked Mark Antony off his comfortable Athenian couch was a letter from Octavian.

'My very dear Antonius,' it said, 'it grieves me sorely to have to pass on the news I have just received from Further Spain. Your brother Lucius died in Corduba not very long into his tenure as governor. From all the many reports I have read of the matter, he simply dropped dead. No lingering, no pain. The physicians say it was a catastrophe originating in the brain, which autopsy revealed was full of blood around its stem. He was cremated in Corduba, and the ashes were sent to me along with documentation sufficient to satisfy me on all counts. I hold his ashes and the reports against your coming. Please accept my sincere condolences.' It was sealed with Divus Julius's sphinx ring.

Of course Antony didn't believe a word of it beyond the fact that Lucius was dead; within a day he was hurrying to Patrae and orders had gone to western Macedonia to embark two legions from Apollonia immediately. The other eight were put on stand-by for shipment to Brundisium as soon as he summoned them.

Intolerable that Octavian should have the news first! And why had no word come to him ahead of that letter? Antony read the missive as a challenge thrown down: your brother's ashes are in

Rome – come and get them if you dare! Did he dare? By Jupiter Optimus Maximus and all the gods, he dared!

An informative letter from Plancus to Octavian sped off from Patrae, where the enraged Antony was obliged to wait until his two legions were confirmed as sailed. It went (had Antony only known of its contents, it would not have) together with Antony's curt order to Pollio to get his legions moving down the Via Adriatica; at the moment they were in Fanum Fortunae, where Pollio could move on Rome along the Via Flaminia, or hug the Adriatic coast to Brundisium. A quailing Plancus begged a place on Antony's ship, judging his chances of slipping through the lines to Octavian easier on Italian soil. By now he was desperately wishing that he hadn't sent that letter – could he be sure Octavian wouldn't leak its contents back to Antony?

His guilt made Plancus an edgy, anxious companion on the voyage, so when, in mid-Adriatic, the fleet of Gnaeus Domitius Ahenobarbus hove in sight, Plancus soiled his loincloth and almost fainted.

'Oh, Antonius, we're dead men!' he wailed.

'At the hands of Ahenobarbus? Never!' said Antony, nostrils flaring. 'Plancus, I do believe you shit yourself!'

Plancus fled, leaving Antony to wait for the arrival of a rowboat heading for his ship. His own standard still fluttered from the mast, but Ahenobarbus had lowered his.

Squat, dark and bald, Ahenobarbus clambered neatly up a rope ladder and advanced on Antony, grinning from ear to ear. 'At last!' the irascible one cried, hugging Antony. 'You're moving on that odious little insect, Octavianus, aren't you? Please say you are!'

'I am' was Antony's answer. 'May he choke on his own shit! Plancus just shit himself at sight of you, and I would have put his courage higher than Octavianus's. Do you know what Octavianus did, Ahenobarbus? He murdered Lucius in Further Spain, then had the gall to write and inform me that he's the proud owner of Lucius's ashes! He dares me to collect them! Is he mad?'

'I'm your man through thick and thin,' Ahenobarbus said huskily. 'My fleet is yours.'

'Good,' said Antony, extricating himself from a very strong embrace. 'I may need a big warship with a solid bronze beak to break Brundisium's harbor chain.'

But not a sixteener with a twenty-talent bronze beak could have broken the chain strung across the harbor mouth; anyway, Ahenobarbus didn't have a ship half as large as a sixteener. The chain was anchored between two concrete piers reinforced with iron pieces, and each of its bronze links was fashioned from metal six inches thick. Neither Antony nor Ahenobarbus had ever seen a more monstrous barrier, nor a population so jubilant at the sight of their frustrated attempts to snap that barrier. While the women and children cheered and jeered, the men of Brundisium subjected Ahenobarbus's battle quinquereme to a murderous hail of spears and arrows that finally drove it offshore.

'I can't do it!' Ahenobarbus yelled, weeping in rage. 'Oh, but when I do, they're going to suffer! And where did it come from? The old chain was a tenth this one's size!'

'That Apulian peasant Agrippa installed this one,' Plancus was able to say, sure he no longer smelled of shit. 'When I left to seek refuge with you, Antonius, the Brundisians were quick to explain its genesis. Agrippa has fortified this place better than Ilium was, including on its land sides.'

'They won't die quickly,' Antony snarled. 'I'll impale the town magistrates on stakes up their arses and drive them in at the rate of an inch a day.'

'Ow, ow!' said Plancus, flinching at the thought. 'What are we going to do?'

'Wait for my troops and land them wherever we can to north and south,' said Antony. 'Once Pollio arrives – he's taking his sweet time! – we'll squash this benighted place from its land side, Agrippa's fortifications or no. After a siege, I suppose. They know I won't be kind to them – they'll resist to the end.'

So Antony withdrew to the island off Brundisium's harbor mouth, there to wait for Pollio and try to discover what had become of Ventidius, curiously silent.

Sextilis had ended and the Nones of September were gone, though the weather was still hot enough to make island living an ordeal. Antony paced; Plancus watched him pace. Antony growled; Plancus pondered. Antony's thoughts never left the subject of Lucius Antonius; Plancus's ranged far and wide on one subject too, but a more fascinating one – Marcus Antonius. For Plancus was seeing new facets in Antony, and didn't like what he saw. Wonderful, glorious Fulvia wove in and out of his mind – so brave and fierce, so . . . so *interesting*. How could Antony have beaten a woman, let alone his wife? The granddaughter of *Gaius Gracchus*!

He's like a small child with its mother, Plancus thought, brushing at tears. He should be in the East fighting the Parthians – that's his duty. Instead, he's here on Italian soil, as if he hasn't the courage to abandon it. Is it Octavianus who eats at him, or is it insecurity? At his core, does Antonius believe he can win future laurels? Oh, he's brave, but generaling armies doesn't demand bravery. It's more an intellectual exercise, an art, a talent. Divus Julius was a genius at it, Antonius is Divus Julius's cousin. But, to Antonius, I suspect that fact is more a burden than a delight. He's so terrified of failing that, like Pompeius Magnus, he won't move unless he has superior numbers. Which he has here in Italia, between Pollio, Ventidius and his own legions just across a small sea. Sufficient to crush Octavianus, even now Octavianus has Calenus's eleven from Further Gaul. I gather that they're still in Further Gaul under the command of Salvidienus, writing to Antonius regularly in an attempt to switch sides. One little item I didn't tell Octavianus.

What Antonius fears in Octavianus is that genius Divus Julius had in such abundance. Oh, not as a general of armies! As a man of infinite courage, the kind of courage Antonius is beginning to lose. Yes, his fear of failure grows, whereas Octavianus starts to dare all, to gamble on unpredictable outcomes. Antonius is at a disadvantage when dealing with Octavianus, but even more so when dealing with foes as foreign as the Parthians. Will he ever wage that particular war? He rants about lack of money, but is that lack really the sum total of his reluctance to fight the war he should be fighting? If he doesn't fight it, he'll lose the confidence of Rome and Romans; he knows that too. So Octavianus is his excuse for lingering in the West. If he drives Octavianus out of the arena, he'll have so many legions that he could defeat a quarter of a million men. Yet, with sixty thousand men, Divus Julius defeated over three hundred thousand. Because he went about it with genius. Antonius wants to be master of the world and the First Man in Rome, but can't work out how to go about it.

Pace, pace, pace, up and down, up and down. He's insecure. Decisions loom, and he's insecure. Nor can he embark upon one of his famous fits of 'inimitable living' – what a joke, to call his cronies in Alexandria the 'Society of Inimitable Livers'! Now here he is, in a situation where he can't binge his way to forgetfulness. Haven't his colleagues realized, as I have, that Antonius debauched is simply demonstrating his innate weakness?

Yes, concluded Plancus, it is time to change sides. But can I do that at the moment? I doubt it, in the same way as I doubt Antonius. Like him, I'm short on steel.

* * *

Octavian knew all this with more conviction than Plancus, yet he couldn't be sure which way the dice would fall now Antony had arrived outside Brundisium; he had staked everything on the legionaries. Then their representatives came to tell him they would not fight Antony's troops, be they his own, or Pollio's, or Ventidius's. An announcement that saw Octavian limp with relief. It only remained to see if Antony's troops would fight for him.

Two *nundinae* later, he had his answer. The soldiers under the command of Pollio and Ventidius had refused to fight their brothers at arms.

He sat down to write Antony a letter.

My dear Antonius, we are at an impasse. My legionaries refuse to fight yours, and yours refuse to fight mine. They belong to Rome, they say, not to any one man, even a Triumvir. The days of massive bonuses, they say, are past. I agree with them. Since Philippi I have known that we can no longer sort out our differences by going to war against each other. *Imperium maius* we may have but, in order to enforce that, we must have command of willing soldiers. We do not.

I therefore propose, Marcus Antonius, that each of us chooses a single man as his representative to try to find a solution to this impasse. As a neutral participant whom both of us deem fair and impartial, may I nominate Lucius Cocceius Nerva? You are at liberty to dispute my choice and nominate a different man. My delegate will be Gaius Maecenas. Neither you nor I should be present at this meeting. To attend it would mean ruffled tempers.

'The cunning rat!' cried Antony, screwing up the letter.

Plancus picked it up, smoothed it out and read it. 'Marcus, it's the logical solution to your predicament,' he faltered. 'Consider for a moment, please, where you are and what you face. What Octavianus suggests may prove a salve to heal injured feelings on both sides. Truly, it is your best alternative.'

A verdict echoed by Gnaeus Asinius Pollio several hours later when he arrived by pinnace from Barium.

'My men won't fight, nor will yours,' he said flatly. 'I for one can't change their minds, nor will yours change theirs; and from all reports Octavianus is in like straits. The legions have decided for us, so it's up to us to find an honorable way out. I have told my men that I will arrange a truce. Ventidius has done the same. Give in, Marcus, give in! It's not a defeat.'

'Anything that enables Octavianus to wriggle out of the jaws of death is a defeat,' Antony said stubbornly.

'Nonsense! His troops are as disaffected as ours.'

'He's not even game to confront me! It's all to be done by agents like Maecenas – ruffled tempers? I'll give him ruffled tempers! And I don't care what he says, I'm going to his little meeting to represent myself!'

'He won't be present, Antonius,' Pollio said, eyes fixed on Plancus, rolling his eyes skyward. 'I have a far better scheme. Agree to it, and I'll go as your representative.'

'You?' Antony asked incredulously. '*You?*'

'Yes, I! Antonius, I've been consul for eight-and-a-half months, yet I haven't been able to go to Rome to don my consular regalia,' Pollio said, exasperated. 'As consul, I outrank Gaius Maecenas and a paltry Nerva combined! Do you really think I'd let a weasel like Maecenas dupe me? Do you?'

'I suppose not,' Antony said, beginning to yield. 'All right, I'll agree to it. With some conditions.'

'Name them.'

'That I am free to enter Italia *through Brundisium*, and that you be permitted to go to Rome to assume your consulship without any impediments put in your way. That I retain my right to recruit troops in Italia. And that the exiles be allowed to go home immediately.'

'I don't think any of those conditions will be a problem,' said Pollio. 'Sit down and write, Antonius.'

Odd, thought Pollio as he rode down the Via Minucia toward Brundisium, that I always manage to be where the great decisions are made. I was with Caesar – Divus Julius, indeed! – when he crossed the Rubicon, and on that river isle in Italian Gaul when Antonius, Octavianus and Lepidus agreed to divide up the world. Now I'll be presiding over the next momentous occasion – Maecenas is not a fool, he won't object to my assuming the chair. What extraordinary luck for a writer of modern history!

Though his family had not been prominent until his advent, Pollio owned an intellect formidable enough to have made him one of Caesar's favorites. A good soldier and a better commander, he had advanced with Caesar after Caesar became Dictator, and never had had any doubt where his loyalties lay until after Caesar was murdered. Too pragmatic and unromantic to side with Caesar's heir, he had only one man left to whom to hew – Marcus Antonius. Like many of his peers, he found the eighteen-year-old Gaius Octavius farcical, couldn't begin to fathom what a peerless man like Caesar could see in such a pretty boy. He believed too that Caesar hadn't expected to die so soon – he was as tough as an old army boot – and that Octavius had been a temporary heir, just a ploy to exclude Antony until he could judge whether Antony would settle down. Also to see what time would make of the mama's boy who now denied his mama's existence. Then Fate and Fortuna had exacted the ultimate penalty from Caesar, allowed a group of embittered, jealous, short-sighted men to murder him. How Pollio rued that, despite his ability to chronicle contemporary events with detachment and impartiality. The trouble was that at the time Pollio had no idea what Caesar Octavianus would make of his unexpected rise to prominence. How could any man foresee the steel and gall inside an inexperienced youth? Caesar, he had long realized, was the only one who had seen what Gaius Octavius was made of. But, even when Pollio had come to understand what lay within Octavian, it was already too late for a man of honor to follow him. Antonius was not the better man, he was simply the alternative pride permitted. Despite his failings – and they were many – at least Antony was a *man*.

As little as he knew Octavian did Pollio know his principal ambassador, Gaius Maecenas. In all physical respects Pollio was a medium man: height, size, coloring, facial appeal. Like most such, particularly when high intelligence was a part of the package, he mistrusted those who were definitely not medium men in any respect. Had Octavianus not been so vain (boots with three-inch soles, for pity's sake!) and pretty, he would have fared better in Pollio's estimation right after Caesar's assassination. And so it was with Maecenas, plump and plain of face, pop-eyed, rich and spoiled. Maecenas simpered, steepled his fingers, pursed up his lips, looked amused when there was nothing to be amused about. A poseur. Detestable or annoying characteristics. Yet he had volunteered to treat with this poseur because he knew that once Antony simmered down, he would choose Quintus Dellius as his delegate. That could not be allowed to happen; Dellius was too venal and hungry for such delicate negotiations. It was possible that Maecenas was equally venal and hungry but, as far as Pollio could see, Octavianus hadn't made many mistakes when he selected his inner circle. Salvidienus was a mistake, but his days were numbered. Greed always antagonized Antony, who would feel no compunction at striking him down as soon as his usefulness was at an end. But Maecenas had made no overtures, and he did own one quality Pollio admired: he loved literature and was the enthusiastic patron of several promising poets, including Horace and Virgil, the best versifiers since Catullus. Only that inspired any hope in Pollio that a conclusion satisfying both parties could be reached. But how was he, a plain soldier, going to survive the kind of food and drink a connoisseur like Maecenas was bound to provide?

'I hope you don't mind ordinary food and well-watered wine?' Maecenas asked Pollio the moment he arrived at the surprisingly modest house on Brundisium's outskirts.

'Thank you, I prefer it,' Pollio said.

'No, thank *you*, Pollio. May I say before we get down to our real business that I enjoy your prose? I don't tell you that in a spirit of sycophancy, because I doubt you're susceptible to the fine art of sucking up; I tell you because it's the truth.'

Embarrassed, Pollio passed the compliment off tactfully but lightly by turning to greet the third member of the team, Lucius Cocceius Nerva. Neutral? How could such a neutral man be anything else? No wonder his wife ruled him.

Over a dinner of eggs, salads, chicken and crunchy fresh bread, Pollio found himself liking Maecenas, who seemed to have read everybody from Homer to Latin luminaries like Caesar and Fabius Pictor. If there was one thing lacking in any army camp, he reflected, it was an in-depth conversation about literature.

'Of course Virgil is Hellenistic in style, but then, so was Catullus – oh, what a poet!' said Maecenas with a sigh. 'I have a theory, you know.'

'What?'

'That the most lyrical exponents of poetry or prose all have some Gallic blood. Either they come from Italian Gaul or their ancestors did. The Celtae are a lyrical people. Musical too.'

'I agree,' said Pollio, relieved to find no sweeties on the menu. 'Leaving aside *"Iter"* – a remarkable poem! – Caesar is typically unpoetical. Exquisite Latin, yet bald and spare. Aulus Hirtius had been with him long enough to do a fair imitation of his style in the commentaries Caesar didn't live to write, but they lack the master's deftness. However, Hirtius does give some things away that Caesar never would have. Like what drove Titus Labienus to defect to Pompeius Magnus after the Rubicon.'

'Never a boring writer, though.' Maecenas giggled. 'Ye gods, what a bore Cato the Censor is! Like being forced to listen to the maiden speech of a political hopeful mounting the rostra.'

They laughed together, at ease with each other, while Nerva the Neuter, as Maecenas had named him, dozed gently.

On the morrow they got down to business, in a rather bleak room furnished with a large table, two wooden chairs with backs but no arms, and an ivory curule chair. Seeing it, Pollio blinked.

'It's yours,' said Maecenas, taking a wooden chair and directing Nerva to the other, which faced it. 'I know you haven't assumed it yet, but your rank as junior consul of the year demands that you chair our meetings, and you should sit on ivory.'

A nice and very diplomatic touch, thought Pollio, seating himself at the head of the table.

'If you want a secretary present to take the minutes, I have a man,' Maecenas went on.

'No, no, we'll do this alone,' Pollio said. 'Nerva will act as secretary and take the minutes. Can you do shorthand, Nerva?'

'Thanks to Cicero, yes.' Looking pleased at having something to do, Nerva put a stack of blank Fannian paper under his right hand, chose a pen from among a dozen, and discovered that someone had thoughtfully dissolved a cake of ink.

'I'll start by summarizing the situation,' Pollio said crisply. 'Number one, Marcus Antonius is not satisfied that Caesar Octavianus is fulfilling his duties as a Triumvir. A, he has not ensured that the people of Italia are well-fed. B, he has not suppressed the piratical activities of Sextus Pompeius. C, he has not settled enough retired veterans on their portions of land. D, Italia's merchants are suffering through hard times for business. E, Italian landowners are angry at the draconian measures he has adopted to separate them from their land in order to settle the veterans. F, more than a dozen towns throughout Italia have been illegally stripped of their public lands, again in order to settle veterans. G, he has raised taxes to an intolerable height. And H, he is filling the Senate with his own minions.

'Number two, Marcus Antonius is not satisfied at the way Caesar Octavianus has usurped the governance and legions of one of his provinces, Further Gaul. Both governance and legions are at the command of Marcus Antonius, who should have been notified of the death of Quintus Fufius Calenus and allowed to appoint the new governor, as well as dispose of Calenus's eleven legions as he sees fit.

'Number three, Marcus Antonius is not satisfied at the waging of a civil war inside Italia. Why, he asks, did not Caesar Octavianus solve his difference of opinion with the late Lucius Antonius in a peaceful way?

'Number four, Marcus Antonius is not satisfied at being refused entry to Italia through Brundisium, its major Adriatic port, and doubts that Brundisium defied Italia's resident Triumvir, Caesar Octavianus. Marcus Antonius believes that Caesar Octavianus issued orders to Brundisium to exclude his colleague, who is not only entitled to enter Italia, but also entitled to bring legions with him. How does Caesar Octavianus know that these legions have been imported for the purposes of war? They might as easily be going to retirement.

'Number five, Marcus Antonius is not satisfied that Caesar Octavianus is willing to allow him to recruit new troops inside Italia and Italian Gaul, as he is lawfully entitled to do.

'That is all,' Pollio concluded, having said every word of that without reference to notes.

Maecenas had listened impassively while Nerva scribbled away – to some effect, apparently, since Nerva didn't ask Pollio to repeat any of what he had said.

'Caesar Octavianus has faced untold difficulties in Italia,' Maecenas said in a quiet, pleasant voice. 'You will forgive me if I do not tabulate and enumerate in your own succinct style, Gnaeus Pollio. I am not governed by such merciless logic – my style inclines toward storytelling.

'When Caesar Octavianus became the Triumvir of Italia, the Islands and the Spains, he found the Treasury empty. He had to confiscate or buy sufficient land upon which to settle over one hundred thousand retired veteran soldiers. *Two million iugera!* So he confiscated the public lands of the eighteen *municipia* that had supported Divus Julius's killers – a fair and just decision. And whenever he acquired any money, he bought land from the proprietors of *latifundia*, on the premise that these individuals were behaving exploitatively by grazing vast areas once under the plough for wheat. No grower of grain was approached, for Caesar Octavianus planned to see a great increase in locally grown grain once these *latifundia* were split up as allotments for veterans.

'The relentless depradations of Sextus Pompeius had deprived Italia of wheat grown in Africa, Sicilia and Sardinia. The Senate and People of Rome had grown lazy about the grain supply, assuming that Italia could always be fed on grain grown overseas.

Whereas Sextus Pompeius has proved that a country relying on the importation of wheat is vulnerable, can be held to ransom. Caesar Octavianus doesn't have the money or the ships to drive Sextus Pompeius off the high seas, nor to invade Sicilia, his base. For that reason he concluded a pact with Sextus Pompeius, even going as far as marrying Libo's sister. If he has taxed, it is because he has no alternative. This year's wheat is costing thirty sesterces the *modius* from Sextus Pompeius – wheat already bought and paid for by Rome! From somewhere, Caesar Octavianus has to find forty million sesterces every month – imagine it! Nearly five hundred million sesterces a year! Paid to Sextus Pompeius, a common pirate!' cried Maecenas so earnestly that his face reflected a rare passion.

'Over eighteen thousand talents,' said Pollio thoughtfully. 'And of course the next thing you're going to say is that the silver mines of the Spains were just beginning to produce when King Bocchus invaded, so now they're closed again and the Treasury beggared.'

'Precisely,' said Maecenas.

'Taking that as read, what happens next in your story?'

'Rome has been dividing up land on which to settle first the poor and then the veterans since the time of Tiberius Gracchus—'

'I've always thought,' Pollio interrupted, 'that the worst sin of omission the Senate and People committed was to refuse to give Rome's retiring veterans a pension over and above what's banked for them out of their pay. When consulars like Catulus and Scaurus denied Gaius Marius's propertyless Head Count soldiers a pension, Marius rewarded them with land in *his* name. That was sixty years ago, and ever since the veterans have looked to their commanders for reward, not to Rome herself. A terrible mistake. It gave the generals power they should never have been allowed to have.'

Maecenas smiled. 'You're telling my story for me, Pollio.'

'I beg your pardon, Maecenas. Continue, please.'

'Caesar Octavianus *cannot* free Italia from Sextus without help. He has begged that help from Marcus Antonius many times, but Marcus Antonius is either deaf or illiterate, for he doesn't answer those letters. Then came internal war, a war that was *not* provoked in any way by Caesar Octavianus! He believes that the true instigator of Lucius Antonius's rebellion – for so it seemed to those of us in Rome – was a freedman named Manius, in the clientele of Fulvia. Manius convinced Fulvia that Caesar Octavianus was – er – *stealing* Marcus Antonius's birthright. A very strange accusation that she believed. In turn, she persuaded Lucius Antonius to use the legions he was recruiting on Marcus Antonius's behalf and march on Rome. I don't think it's necessary to say anymore on the subject, save to assure Marcus Antonius that his brother was not prosecuted, but allowed to assume his proconsular imperium and go to govern Further Spain.'

Fishing through a number of scrolls near him, Maecenas found one, and flourished it. 'I have here the letter that Quintus Fufius Calenus's son wrote, not to Marcus Antonius, as he should have, but to Caesar Octavianus.' He handed it to Pollio, who read it with the ease of a highly literate man. 'What Caesar Octavianus saw in it was alarming, for it betrayed Calenus Junior's weakness and lack of decision. As a veteran of Further Gaul, Pollio, I'm sure I do not have to tell you how volatile the long-haired Gauls are, and how quick they are to scent an uncertain governor. For this reason and this reason alone, Caesar Octavianus acted swiftly. He had to act swiftly. Knowing that Marcus Antonius was a thousand miles farther away, he took it upon himself to travel immediately to Narbo, there to install a *temporary* governor, Quintus Salvidienus. Calenus's eleven legions are exactly where they were – four in Narbo, four in Agedincum, and three in Glanum. What did Caesar Octavianus do wrong in acting thus? He acted as a friend, a fellow Triumvir, the man on the spot.'

Maecenas sighed, looked rueful. 'I daresay that the most truthful charge that can be laid against Caesar Octavianus is that he found himself unable to control Brundisium, which was ordered to allow Marcus Antonius to come ashore together with as many legions as he cared to bring to their homeland, be it for a nice vacation or retirement. Brundisium defied the Senate and People of Rome, it is as simple as that. What Caesar Octavianus hopes is that he will be able to persuade Brundisium to cease its defiance. And that is all,' Maecenas concluded, smiling sweetly.

At which point the arguments began, but not with passion or rancor. Both men knew the truth of every matter raised, but both men also knew that they had to be loyal to their masters, and had decided the best way to do the latter was to argue convincingly. Octavian for one would read Nerva's minutes closely, and if Mark Antony did not, he would at least pump Nerva about the meeting.

Finally, just before the Nones of October, Pollio decided he had had enough.

'Look,' he said, 'it's clear to me that the way things were arranged after Philippi was slipshod and ineffective. Marcus Antonius was full of his own importance, and despised Octavianus for his conduct at Philippi.' He rounded on Nerva, beginning to scribble. 'Nerva, don't you dare write down a word of this! It's time to be frank, and as great men don't like frankness, it's best we don't tell them. That means you can't let Antonius bully you, hear me? Spill the beans about this, and you're a dead man – I will kill you myself, understand?'

'Yes!' squeaked Nerva, dropping his pen in a hurry.

'I adore it!' said Maecenas, grinning. 'Proceed, Pollio.'

'The Triumvirate is ridiculous as it stands at the moment. How did Antonius ever think he could be in several places at once? For that's what happened after Philippi. He wanted the lion's share of everything, from provinces to legions. So what emerged? Octavianus inherits the grain supply and Sextus Pompeius, but no fleets to put Sextus down, let alone transport an army capable of taking Sicilia. If Octavianus was a military man, which he is not, nor ever claimed to be, he would have known that his freedman Helenus – obviously a persuasive fellow – couldn't take Sardinia. Mostly because Octavianus doesn't have enough troop transports. He's shipless. The provinces were allocated in the most muddle-headed way imaginable. Octavianus gets Italia, Sicilia, Sardinia, Corsica, Further and Nearer Spain. Antonius gets the entire East, but that isn't enough for him. So he takes all the Gauls as well as Illyricum. Why? Because the Gauls contain so many legions still under the Eagles and not wishful of retiring. I know Marcus Antonius very well, and he's a good fellow, brave and generous. When he's at the top of his form, no one is more capable or clever. But he's also a glutton who can't curb his appetite, no matter what it is he fancies devouring. The Parthians and Quintus Labienus are running amok all over Asia and a good part of Anatolia. But here we sit, outside Brundisium.'

Pollio stretched, then hunched his shoulders. 'It's our duty, Maecenas, to even things up and out. How do we do that? By drawing a line between West and East, and putting Octavianus on one side of it, and Antonius on the other. Lepidus can have Africa, that goes without saying. He's got ten legions there, he's safe and secure. You'll get no arguments from me that Octavianus has by far the harder task because he has Italia: impoverished, worn out and hungry. Neither of our masters has any money. Rome is close to bankruptcy, and the East so exhausted it can't pay any significant tributes. However, Antonius can't have things all his way, and he has to be made to see that. I propose that Octavianus be given a better income by governing all the West – Further Spain, Nearer Spain, Further Gaul in all its parts, Italian Gaul, and Illyricum. The Drina River is a natural frontier between Macedonia and Illyricum, so it will become the border between West and East. It goes without saying that Antonius will be as free to recruit troops in Italia and Italian Gaul as Octavianus. Italian Gaul, incidentally, should become a part of Italia in all respects.'

'Good man, Pollio!' Maecenas exclaimed, smiling broadly. 'I couldn't begin to say it as well as you just have.' He gave a mock shiver. 'For one thing, I wouldn't have dared be so hard on Antonius. Yes, my friend, very well said indeed! Now all we have to do is persuade Antonius to agree. I don't foresee any arguments from Caesar Octavianus. He's had a terrible time of it, and of course the journey from Rome brought on his asthma.'

Pollio looked amazed. '*Asthma?*'

'Yes. He almost dies of it. That's why he hid in the marshes at Philippi. So much dust and chaff in the air!'

'I see,' Pollio said slowly. 'I see.'

'It's his secret, Pollio.'

'Does Antonius know?'

'Of course. They're cousins, he's always known.'

'How does Octavianus feel about letting the exiles come home?'

'He won't object.' Maecenas seemed to consider something, then spoke. 'You ought to know that Octavianus will never go to war against Antonius, though I don't know whether you can convince Antonius of that. No more civil wars. He'll hew to it, Pollio. That's really why we're here. No matter what the provocation, he won't go to war against a fellow Roman. His way is diplomacy, the conference table, negotiations.'

'I didn't realize he felt so strongly about it.'

'He does, Pollio, he does.'

Persuading Antony to accept the terms Pollio had outlined to Maecenas took a full *nundinum* of ranting, punching holes in walls, tears and yells. Then he began to calm down; his rages were so devastating that even a man as strong as Antony couldn't sustain that level of energy for more than a *nundinum*. From rage he plummeted to depression and finally to despair. The moment he landed at the bottom of his pit, Pollio struck; it was now or never. A Maecenas couldn't have dealt with Antony, but a soldier like Pollio, a man Antony respected and loved, knew exactly what to do. He had, besides, the confidence of some stalwarts back in Rome who would, if necessary, reinforce his strictures.

'All right, all right!' Antony cried wretchedly, hands in his hair. 'I'll do it! You're sure about the exiles?'

'Absolutely.'

'I insist on some items you haven't mentioned.'

'Mention them now.'

'I want five of Calenus's eleven legions shipped to me.'

'I don't think that will be a problem.'

'And I won't agree to combining my forces with Octavianus's to sweep Sextus Pompeius from the seas.'

'That's not wise, Antonius.'

'Ask me do I care? I don't care!' Antony said savagely. 'I had to appoint Ahenobarbus governor of Bithynia, he was so furious at the terms you've drawn up, and that means I don't have enough fleets to fall back on without Sextus's. He stays in case I need him, that has to be made clear.'

'Octavianus will agree, but he won't be happy.'

'Anything that makes Octavianus unhappy makes me happy!'

'Why did you conceal Octavianus's asthma?'

'Pah!' spat Antony. 'He's a *girl*! Only girls get sick, no matter what the sickness. His asthma is an excuse.'

'Not conceding Sextus Pompeius may cost you.'

'Cost me what?'

'I don't quite know,' Pollio said, frowning. 'It just will.'

Octavian's response to the terms Maecenas brought him was very different. Interesting, thought Maecenas, how much his face has changed over this last twelve-month. He's grown out of his prettiness, though he'll never not be beautiful. The mass of hair is shorter, he doesn't care about his prominent ears anymore. But the major change is in his eyes, quite the most wonderful I have ever seen, so large, luminous and silvery-grey. They have always been opaque, he has never betrayed what he's thinking or feeling with them, but now there's a certain stony hardness behind their brilliance. And the mouth I've longed to kiss, knowing I will never be permitted to kiss it, has firmed, straightened. I suppose that means he's grown up. Grown up? He was never a boy! Nine days before the Kalends of October, he turned a whole twenty-three. While Marcus Antonius is now forty-four. Truly a marvel.

'If Antonius refuses to aid me in my battle against Sextus Pompeius,' said Octavian, 'he must pay a price.'

'But what? You don't have the leverage to exact one.'

'Yes, I do, and Sextus Pompeius gave me my lever.'

'And that is?'

'A marriage,' Octavian said, face tranquil.

'Octavia!' Maecenas breathed. 'Octavia . . .'

'Yes, my sister. She's a widow, there's no impediment.'

'Her ten months of mourning aren't over.'

'Six of them are, and all of Rome knows she can't be pregnant: Marcellus suffered a long, agonizing death. It won't be hard to get a dispensation from the pontifical colleges and the seventeen tribes the lots throw up to vote in the religious *comitium*.' Octavian smiled complacently. 'They'll be falling all over each other to do anything that might avert a war between Antonius and me. In fact, I predict that no marriage in the annals of Rome will prove so popular.'

'He won't agree.'

'*Antonius?* He'd copulate with a cow.'

'Can't you hear what you're saying, Caesar? I know how much you love your sister, yet you'd inflict Antonius upon her? He's a drunkard and a wife beater! I beg you, think again! Octavia is the loveliest, sweetest, nicest woman in Rome. Even the Head Count adore her, just as they did Divus Julius's daughter.'

'It sounds as if you want to marry her yourself, Maecenas,' Octavian said slyly.

Maecenas bridled. 'How can you joke about something as – as *serious* as this? I like women, but I also pity them. They lead such uneventful lives, their only political importance lies in marriage – about the most you can say for Roman justice is that the majority of them control their own money. Relegation to the periphery of public affairs may irk the Hortensias and the Fulvias, but it doesn't irk Octavia. If it did, you wouldn't be sitting here so smug and certain of her obedience. Isn't it time she was let wed a man she truly wants to wed?'

'I won't force her to it, if that's what you're getting at,' said Octavian, unmoved. 'I'm not a fool, you know, and I've attended enough family dinners since Pharsalus to have realized that Octavia is more than half in love with Antonius. She'll go to her fate willingly – gladly, even.'

'I don't believe it!'

'It's the truth. Far be it from me to understand what women see in men but, take my word for it, Octavia is keen on Antonius. That fact and my own union with Scribonia gave me the idea. Nor do I doubt Antonius when it comes to wine and wife beating. He may have attacked Fulvia, but the provocation must have been severe. Under all that bombast he's sentimental about women. Octavia will suit him. Like the Head Count, he'll adore her.'

'There's the Egyptian queen – he won't be faithful.'

'What man on duty abroad is? Octavia won't hold infidelity against him: she's too well brought up.'

Throwing his hands in the air, Maecenas departed to stew over the unenviable lot of a diplomat. Did Octavian really expect that he, Maecenas, would conduct these negotiations? Well, he would not! Cast a pearl like Octavia in front of a swine like Antonius? Never! Never, never, never!

Octavian had no intention of depriving himself of these particular negotiations; he was going to enjoy them. By now Antony would have forgotten things like that scene in his tent after Philippi, when Octavian had demanded Brutus's head – and got it. Antony's hatred had grown so great it obscured all individual events; it was enough in and of itself. Nor did Octavian expect that a marriage to Octavia would change that hatred. Maybe a poetical kind of fellow like Maecenas would assume such to be Octavian's motive, but Octavian's own mind was too sensible to hope for miracles. Once Octavia became Antony's wife, she would do exactly as Antony wanted; the last thing she would do was to attempt to influence how Antony felt about her brother. No, what he hoped for in achieving this union was to strengthen the hopes of ordinary Romans – and the legionaries' – that the threat of war had vanished. So when the day came that Antony, in the throes of some new passion for a new woman, rejected his wife, he would go down in the estimation of millions of Roman citizens everywhere. Since Octavian had vowed that he would never engage in civil war, he had to destroy not only Antony's *auctoritas* – his official public standing – but also his *dignitas*, the public standing he possessed due to his personal actions and achievements. When Caesar the God crossed the Rubicon into civil war, he had done it to protect his *dignitas*, which he had held dearer than his life. To have his deeds stripped from the official histories and records of the Republic and be sent into permanent exile was worse than civil war. Well, Octavian wasn't made of such stuff; to him, civil war was worse than disgrace and exile. Also, of course, he wasn't a military genius sure to win. Octavian's way was to corrode Mark Antony's *dignitas* until it reached a nadir wherein he was no threat. From that point on, Octavian's star would continue to rise until he, not Antony, was the First Man in Rome. It wouldn't happen overnight; it would take many years. But they were years Octavian could afford to concede; he was twenty-one years younger than Antony. Oh, the prospect of years and years of struggling to feed Italia, find land for the never-ending flood of veterans!

He had Antony's measure. Caesar the God would have been knocking on King Orodes's palace door in Seleuceia-on-Tigris by now, but where was Antony? Laying siege to Brundisium, still in his own country. Prate though he might about being there to defend his entitlements as a Triumvir, he was actually there so he couldn't be in Syria fighting the Parthians. Prate though he might about single-handedly winning Philippi, Antony knew he couldn't have won without Octavian's legions, composed of men whose loyalty he couldn't command, for it belonged to Octavian.

I would give almost anything, Octavian thought after he had written his note to Antony and sent it off by a freedman courier, I would give almost anything to have Fortuna drop something in my lap that would send Antonius crashing down for good. Octavia isn't it, nor probably would his rejection of her be it, did he decide to reject her once he tired of her goodness. I am aware that Fortuna smiles upon me – I have had so many close shaves that I am always beardless. And every time, it has been luck that yanked me back from the abyss. Like Libo's hunger to find an illustrious husband for his sister. Like Calenus's death in Narbo and his idiot son's petitioning me instead of Antonius. Like the death of Marcellus. Like having Agrippa to general armies for me. Like my escapes from death each time the asthma has squeezed all the breath out of me. Like having my father Divus Julius's war chest to keep me from bankruptcy. Like Brundisium's refusing Antonius entry, may Liber Pater, Sol Indiges and Tellus grant Brundisium future peace and great prosperity. I didn't issue any orders to the city to do what it has, anymore than I provoked the futility of Fulvia's war against me. Poor Fulvia!

Every day I offer to a dozen gods, Fortuna at their head, to give me the weapon I need to bring Antonius down faster than age will inevitably do it. The weapon exists, I know that as surely as I know I have been chosen to set Rome on her feet permanently, to achieve lasting peace on the frontiers of her empire. I am the Chosen One whom Maecenas's poet Virgil writes about and all Rome's prognosticators insist will herald in a golden age. Divus Julius made me his son, and I will not fail his trust in me to finish what he started. Oh, it will not be the same world as Divus Julius would have made, but it will satisfy and please him. Fortuna, bring me more of Caesar's fabled luck! Bring me the weapon, and open my eyes to recognize it when it comes!

Antony's reply came by the same courier. Yes, he would see Caesar Octavianus under a flag of truce. But we are not at war! Octavian thought, breath taken away by something other than asthma. How does his mind work, to think that we are?

Next day Octavian set out on the Julian Public Horse – it was a small one, but very handsome with its creamy coat and darker mane and tail. To ride meant he couldn't wear a toga, but as he didn't want to appear warlike, he wore a white tunic with the broad purple stripe of a senator down its right shoulder.

Naturally Antony was in full armor, silver-plated, and with Hercules slaying the Nemean lion worked on its contoured cuirass. His tunic was purple, so was the *paludamentum* flowing from his shoulders, though by rights it should have been scarlet. As ever, he looked fit and well.

'No built-up boots, Octavianus?' he asked, grinning.

Though Antony had not, Octavian held out his right hand so obviously that Antony was obliged to take it, wring it so hard he crunched fragile bones. Face expressionless, Octavian endured it.

'Come inside,' Antony invited, holding the flap of his tent aside. That he chose to inhabit a tent rather than commandeer a private home was evidence of his confidence that the siege of Brundisium would not be a long business.

The tent's public room was generous but, with the flap down, very dark. To Octavian, an indication of Antony's wariness. He didn't trust his face not to betray his emotions. Which didn't worry Octavian. Not faces but thought patterns concerned him, for they were what he had to work on.

'I'm so pleased,' he said, swallowed by a chair much too big for his slight frame, 'that we have reached the stage of drafting out an agreement. I felt it best that you and I in person should thrash out those matters on which we haven't quite reached accord.'

'Delicately put,' said Antony, drinking deeply from a goblet of wine he had ostentatiously watered.

'A beautiful thing,' Octavian remarked, turning his own vessel in his hands. 'Where was it made? Not Puteoli, I'd wager.'

'In some Alexandrian glassworks. I like drinking from glass, it doesn't absorb the flavor of earlier wines the way even the best ceramic does.' He grimaced. 'And metal tastes . . . metallic.'

Octavian blinked. '*Edepol*! I didn't realize you're such a connoisseur of something that merely *holds* wine.'

'Sarcasm will get you nowhere,' Antony said, unoffended. 'I was told all that by Queen Cleopatra.'

'Oh, yes, that makes sense. An Alexandrian patriot.'

Antony's face lit up. 'And rightly so! Alexandria is the most beautiful city in the world; leaves Pergamum and even Athens shivering in the shade.'

Having sipped, Octavian put his chalice down as if it burned. Here was another fool! Why rave about a city's beauty when his own city faded to nothing from lack of care? 'You may have as many of Calenus's legions as you wish, that goes without saying,' he lied. 'In fact, nothing about your conditions fazes me save only your refusal to help me rid the seas of Sextus Pompeius.'

Frowning, Antony got to his feet and pulled the tent flap wide open, apparently deciding it was necessary to see Octavian's face properly after all. 'Italia is your province, Octavianus. Have I asked for *your* help in governing mine?'

'No, you haven't, but nor have you sent Rome's share of the Eastern tributes to the Treasury. I'm sure I don't have to tell you that, even as Triumvir, the Treasury is supposed to gather in the tributes and pay Rome's provincial governors a stipend, out of which they fund their legions and pay for public works in their provinces,' Octavian said blandly. 'Of course I understand that no governor, least of all a Triumvir, simply collects what the Treasury demands – he always asks for more, keeps the surplus for himself. A time-honored tradition I have no quarrel with. I too am a Triumvir. However, you've sent *nothing* to Rome in the two years of your governorship. Had you, I would be able to buy the ships I need to deal with Sextus. It may suit you to use pirate ships as your fleets, since all the admirals who sided with Brutus and Cassius decided to become pirates after Philippi. I'm not above using them myself, were it not that they grow fat picking at *my* carcass! What they're busy doing is proving to Rome and all Italia – the source of our best soldiers – that a million soldiers can't help two shipless Triumvirs. You *should* have grain from the Eastern provinces to feed your legions right fatly! It's not my fault that you've let the Parthians overrun everywhere except Bithynia and Asia Province! What's saved your bacon is Sextus Pompeius – as long as it suits you to stay sweet with him, he sells you Italia's grain at a modest price – grain, may I remind you, bought and paid for by Rome's Treasury! Yes, Italia is my province, but my only sources of money are the taxes I must squeeze from all Roman citizens living in Italia. They are not enough to pay for ships as well as buy stolen wheat from Sextus Pompeius for thirty sesterces the *modius!* So I ask again, where are the Eastern tributes?'

Antony listened in growing ire. 'The East is bankrupt!' he shouted. 'There isn't any tribute to send!'

'That's not true, and even the least Roman from end to end of Italia knows that,' Octavian countered. 'Pythodorus of Tralles brought you two thousand silver talents to Tarsus, for instance. Tyre and Sidon paid you a thousand more. And raping Cilicia Pedia yielded you four thousand. A total of one hundred and seventy-five million sesterces! Facts, Antonius! *Well-known facts!*'

Why had he ever consented to see this despicable little gnat? Antony asked himself, squirming. All he had to do to gain the ascendancy was remind me that whatever I do in the East somehow leaks back to every last Roman citizen in Italia. Without saying it, he's telling me that my reputation is suffering. That I'm not yet above criticism, that the Senate and People of Rome can strip me of my offices. And yes, I can march on Rome, execute Octavianus and appoint myself Dictator. *But I was the one who made a huge fuss out of abolishing the dictatorship!* Brundisium has proved that my legionaries won't fight Octavianus's. That fact alone is why the little *verpa* can sit here and defy me; be open about his antagonism.

'So I'm none too popular in Rome,' he said sullenly.

'Candidly, Antonius, you're not at all popular, especially after laying siege to Brundisium. You've felt at liberty to accuse me of putting Brundisium up to refusing you entry, but you're well aware I didn't. Why should I? It profits me nothing! All you've actually done is throw Rome into a frenzy of fear, expecting you to march on her. Which you cannot do! Your legions won't let you. If you genuinely want to retrieve your reputation, you have to prove that to Rome, not to me.'

'I won't join you against Sextus Pompeius, if that's what you're angling for. All I have are a hundred warships in Athens,' Antony lied. 'Not enough to do the job, since you have none. As matters stand, Sextus Pompeius prefers me to you, and I'll not do anything to provoke him. At the moment, he leaves me alone.'

'I didn't think you would help me,' Octavian said calmly. 'No, I was thinking more of something visible to *all* Romans from the top of the heap to the very bottom.'

'What?'

'Marriage to my sister, Octavia.'

Jaw dropped, Antony stared at his tormentor. 'Ye gods!'

'What's so unusual about it?' Octavian asked softly, smiling. 'I've just concluded a similar kind of marital alliance myself, as I'm sure you know. Scribonia is very pleasant – a good woman, pretty, fertile . . . I hope tying myself to her keeps Sextus at bay, for a while at any rate. But she can't begin to compare with Octavia, can she? I am offering you Divus Julius's great-niece – known and loved by every stratum in Rome as Julia was, beautiful to look at, enormously kind and thoughtful, an obedient wife, and the mother of three children, including a boy. As Divus Julius expected of *his* wife, she's above suspicion. Marry her, and Rome will assume that you mean Rome no harm.'

'Why should it do that?'

'Because to be cruel to such a public paragon as Octavia would brand you a monster in every Roman's eyes. Not the most stupid among them would condone ill-treatment of Octavia.'

'I see. Yes, I see,' said Antony slowly.

'Then we have a deal?'

'We have a deal.'

This time Antony shook Octavian's hand gently.

The Pact of Brundisium was sealed on the twelfth day of October, in Brundisium's town square, and in the presence of a horde of cheering, beaming people who threw flowers at Octavian's feet and controlled their behavior sufficiently not to spit at Antony's feet. His perfidies were neither forgotten nor forgiven, but this day signified a victory for Octavian and Rome. There wasn't going to be another civil war. Which pleased the legions strung around the city even more than it pleased Brundisium.

'So what do you think about this?' Pollio asked Maecenas as they traveled up the Via Appia in a four-mule gig.

'That Caesar Octavianus is a master of intrigue and a far better negotiator than I.'

'Did you think of offering Antonius the dearly beloved sister?'

'No, no! It was his idea. I suppose I thought the chances of his agreeing to it so remote that it never even popped into my mind. Then when he told me the day before he went to see Antonius, I assumed he'd be sending me to do the offering – brr! I quailed in my shoes! But no. Off he went himself, unescorted.'

'He couldn't send you because he needed it man to man. What

he said, only he could say. I gather he pointed out to Antonius that he'd lost the love and respect of most Romans. In such a way that Antonius believed him. The crafty little *mentula* – I beg your pardon! – crafty little – um – ferret then presented Antonius with the chance to mend his reputation by marrying Octavia. Brilliant!'

'I concur,' said Maecenas, envisioning Octavian as a *mentula* or a ferret, and smiling.

'I shared a gig with Octavianus once,' Pollio said, tone of voice musing. 'From Italian Gaul to Rome after the formation of the Triumvirate. He was twenty years old, but he spoke like a venerable consular. About the grain supply, and how the Apennines made it easier for Rome to get her grain from Africa and Sicilia than from Italian Gaul. Trotted out numbers and statistics like the most idle senior civil servant you ever heard. Only he wasn't trying to get out of work, he was tabling the work he considered must be done. Yes, a memorable journey. When Caesar made him his heir, I thought he'd be dead within months. That journey taught me that I'd been mistaken. No one will kill him.'

Atia brought the news of her fate to Octavia, and in tears. 'My darling girl!' she cried, falling on Octavia's neck. 'My ingrate of a son has betrayed you! *You!* The one person in the world I thought safe from his machinations, his coldness!'

'Mama, be explicit, please!' said Octavia, helping Atia sit down. 'What has Little Gaius done to me?'

'Betrothed you to Marcus Antonius! A brute who kicked his wife! A monster!'

Stunned, Octavia slumped into a chair and stared at her mother. *Antonius?* She was to marry Marcus Antonius? Shock was followed by a slowly seeping warmth that suffused her whole body. In a trice her lids went down to veil her eyes from Atia, done with weeping, beginning to fulminate.

'Antonius!' shrieked Atia loudly enough to bring servants running, only to be waved out impatiently. 'Antonius! A boor, a scavenger, a . . . a . . . oh, there aren't words to describe him!'

While Octavia thought, am I to be lucky at last, have a man I want as my husband? Thank you, thank you, Little Gaius!

'Antonius!' roared Atia, flecks of foam at the corners of her mouth. 'Dearest girl, you must screw up the courage to say no! No to him, and no to my wretched son!'

While Octavia thought, I have dreamed of him for so long,

hopelessly, sadly. In the old days, when he was in Italia and came to call on Marcellus, I used to find excuses to be present.

'Antonius!' howled Atia, pounding her fists on the chair arms, thump, thump, thump. 'He's sired more bastards than any other man in the history of Rome! Not a faithful bone in him!'

While Octavia thought, I used to sit and feast my eyes on him, offer to Spes that he'd visit again soon. Yet careful that I never gave myself away. Now this?

'Antonius!' whimpered Atia, the tears gathering again as her impotence gained the upper hand. 'I could plead until next summer, and my traitor of a son wouldn't listen!'

While Octavia thought, I will make him a good wife, I will be whatever he wants me to be, I won't complain about mistresses or beg to accompany him when he returns to the East. So many women, all more experienced than I am! He will grow tired of me, I know it in my bones. But nothing can ever take away the memories of my time with him after it is over. Love understands, and love forgives. I was a good wife to Marcellus, and I have mourned him as a good wife does. But I pray to all Rome's goddesses of women that I have long enough with Marcus Antonius to last for the rest of my life. For he is my true love. After him, there can be no one. No one . . .

'Hush, Mama,' she said aloud, eyes open and shining. 'I will do as my brother says and marry Marcus Antonius.'

'But you're not in Gaius's hand, you're *sui iuris*!' Then Atia recognized the look in those splendid aquamarine eyes, and gaped. '*Ecastor*!' she exclaimed feebly. 'You're in love with him!'

'If love is to long for his touch and his good esteem, then I must be,' said Octavia. 'Do you know when it is to happen?'

'According to Philippus, Antonius and your callous brother have made a pact at Brundisium that there will be no civil war. The whole country is wild with joy, so the pair of them elected to make a regular spectacle out of their journey to Rome. Up the Via Appia to Teanum, then up the Via Latina. Apparently they won't arrive here until the end of October. The marriage is to take place very shortly after that.' The mother's face twisted. 'Oh, please, dearest daughter, refuse it! You're *sui iuris*, your fate is in your own hands!'

'I shall accept gladly, Mama, whatever you say or however much you beseech me. I know what Antonius is like, and that makes not a scrap of difference. There will always be mistresses, but he has never had a satisfactory wife. Look at them,' Octavia went on, warming to her theme. 'First Fadia, the illiterate daughter of a dealer in everything from slaves to grain. I never saw her, of course, but apparently she was as unattractive as she was dull. But Antonius didn't divorce her, he just didn't come home much. She bore him a son and a daughter, bright little things by all accounts. That Fadia and her children died of the summer paralysis cannot be blamed on Antonius. Then came Antonia Hybrida, daughter of a man who tortured his slaves. They say Antonia Hybrida tortured her slaves too, but that Antonius "beat it out of her" – can you condemn Antonius for curing his wife of such a horrible habit? I do remember her vaguely, also the child. The poor little girl was so fat and plain – but, far worse, slightly simple.'

'That's what comes of marrying close relatives,' said Atia grimly. 'Antonia Tertia is sixteen now, but she'll never find a husband, even one of low birth.' Atia sniffed. 'Women are fools! Antonia Hybrida fell into a depression after Antonius divorced her, which he did with cruel words. Yet she loved him. Is that the fate you want? Is it?'

'Whether Antonia Hybrida loved Antonius or not, Mama, the fact remains that she was not an interesting wife. Whereas for all her faults, Fulvia was. Her troubles I lay at the door of far too much money, that *sui iuris* status you keep throwing at me – and her first husband, Publius Clodius. He encouraged her to run wild in the Forum, engage in behavior that isn't condoned in high-born women. But she wasn't too bad until after Philippi, when she found out that Antonius would be permanently in the East for years, and wasn't planning any trips to Rome. Her freedman Manius got at her, worked on her. And on Lucius Antonius. But she paid the price, not Lucius.'

'You're determined to find excuses,' said Atia, sighing.

'Not excuses, Mama. My point is that none of Antonius's wives was a good wife. I intend to be a perfect wife, the kind Cato the Censor would have approved of, the awful old bigot. Men have whores and mistresses for bodily gratification, the sort of relief they cannot obtain from their wives because wives are not supposed to know how to please a man bodily. Wives who know too much about gratifying a man are suspect. As a virtuous wife, I will fare no differently or better than any other virtuous wife. But I will make sure that, whenever I see Antonius, I am an educated, interesting confidant as well as a pleasure to spend time with. After all, I grew up in a political household, listened to men like Divus Julius and Cicero, and I am exceptionally well schooled. I will also be a wonderful mother for his children.'

'You're already a wonderful mother for his children!' Atia snapped tartly, having listened to this tall order with despair. 'I suppose the moment you're married you'll demand to take charge of that dreadful boy, Gaius Curio? What a dance he'll lead you!'

'There's not a child born I can't tame,' said Octavia.

Atia rose, wringing her knotted, crippled hands. 'I will say this for you, Octavia, you're not as sheltered as I thought. Perhaps there's more Fulvia in you than you realize.'

'No, I'm quite different,' Octavia said, smiling, 'though I do know what you're trying to say. What you forget, Mama, is that I am the full sister of Little Gaius, which means I am one of the cleverest women Rome has produced. The quality of my mind has given me a self-confidence my life thus far hasn't put on display to anyone from Marcellus to you. But Little Gaius is well aware what lies inside me. Do you think he doesn't know how I feel about Marcus Antonius? There's nothing Little Gaius misses! And nothing he can't use to further his own career. He loves me, Mama. That should have told you everything. Little Gaius, force me into a marriage I wouldn't welcome? No, Mama, no.'

Atia sighed. 'Well, since I'm here, I'd like to see the contents of your nursery before it grows even larger. How is little Marcia?'

'Beginning to show her true colors. *Very* self-willed. She won't be forced into an unwelcome marriage!'

'I heard a whisper that Scribonia is pregnant.'

'So did I. How lovely! Her Cornelia is a nice girl, so I imagine this child will have a good disposition too.'

'Well, it's too early for her to know whether she's carrying a boy or a girl,' Atia said briskly as they walked toward the sound of baby wails, toddler giggles and small child arguments. 'Though I hope it will be a girl for Little Gaius's sake. He has such a high opinion of himself that he won't welcome a son and heir from such a mother. As soon as he can, he'll divorce her.'

Thank the gods for the proximity of the nursery! We are too close to dangerous ground, thought Octavia. Poor Mama, always on the periphery of Little Gaius's life, unseen, unmentioned.

EIGHT

By the time the cavalcade got to Rome, Mark Antony was in a very good mood. His reception by the crowds which lined the roads every inch of the way had been ecstatic: so ecstatic, in fact, that he was beginning to wonder if Octavian had exaggerated his unpopularity. A suspicion accentuated when every senator inside Rome at this moment came thronging out in full regalia to greet not Octavian, but him. The trouble was that he couldn't be sure; there was too much evidence of Italia's and Rome's relief at the ebbing of civil war. Perhaps it was the Pact of Brundisium that brought all his old adherents back wholeheartedly to his side. If he had been able to sneak around Italia and Rome in disguise a month ago, he might have heard disillusioned words and abuse of himself. As it was, he hovered between doubt and elation, neatly balanced, cursing Octavian only under his breath and out of habit.

The prospect of marriage to Octavian's sister didn't worry him; rather, it contributed to his good mood. Though his eye would never of its own volition have alighted on her as a wife, he had always liked her, found her physically attractive, and had even envied his friend Marcellus's luck in espousing her. From Octavian he had learned that she had taken in Antyllus and Iullus after Fulvia died, which reinforced his impression that she was as good a person as her brother was bad. That often happened in families – look at himself versus Gaius and Lucius. They all got the Antonian physique, but marred in Gaius's case by a shambling gait and in Lucius's by a bald head; only he had inherited the Julian cleverness. Careless strewer of his seed though he was, Antony liked those of his children whom he knew, and had just had a brilliant idea about his daughter by Antonia Hybrida, whom he pitied in an offhand way. In fact, his children occupied more of his mind as he reached Rome than they usually did, for he found a letter from Cleopatra waiting there.

My dearest Antonius, I write this on the Ides of Sextilis, in the midst of such halcyon weather that I wish you could be here to enjoy it with me – and with Caesarion, who sends his love and good wishes. He is growing apace, and his exposure to Roman men (especially you) has been of great benefit to him. He is currently reading Polybius, having cast aside the letters of Cornelia the Mother of the Gracchi – no wars, no exciting events. Of course he knows his father's books off by heart.

I do not know whereabouts in the world this may catch up with you, but sooner or later it will. One hears that you are in Athens, a moment later that you are in Ephesus, even that you are in Rome. No matter. This is to thank you for giving Caesarion a brother *and* a sister. Yes, I have given birth to twins! Do they run in your family? They do not run in mine. I am delighted, of course. In one blow you have secured the succession and provided Caesarion with a wife. Little wonder that Nilus rose high into the Cubits of Plenty!

How well she knows me, he thought to himself. Realizes that I don't read long letters, so keeps hers short. Well, well! I did my duty splendidly. Two of them, no less, a pigeon pair. But to her, they're simply adjuncts to enhance Caesarion. Her passion for Caesar's son knows no bounds.

He dashed off a letter to her.

Dear Cleopatra, what terrific news! Not one, but two little Antonians to follow big brother Caesarion around, the way my brothers followed me. I'm marrying Octavianus's sister, Octavia, very shortly. Nice woman, very beautiful too. Did you ever meet her in Rome? It solved my difficulties with Octavianus for the moment and pacified the country, which won't countenance a civil war. Nor, from what Maecenas said, will Octavianus. That ought to mean that I can march in and stamp on Octavianus, except that the soldiers are a part of the national conspiracy to outlaw civil war. Mine won't fight his; his won't fight mine. Without willing troops, a general is as impotent as a eunuch in a harem. Speaking of potency, we must have another roll in the papyrus sometime. If I get bored, watch out for my arrival in Alexandria to do a bit of inimitable living.

There. That would do. Antony poured a small puddle of melted red wax on the bottom of the single sheet of Fannian paper, and pushed his signet ring into it: Hercules Invictus in the middle, IMP· M· ANT· TRI· around its edge. He'd had it made after that conference on the river island in Italian Gaul. What he yearned for was the chance to make M· ANT· a DIV· ANT· for Divus Antonius, but that wasn't likely as long as Octavian existed.

Of course he had to go around to the *domus Hortensia* for his men's party before the wedding, and found Octavian's complacency so irritating that he couldn't help himself, had to lash out with invigorating venom.

'What's your opinion of Salvidienus?' he asked his host.

Octavian looked besotted at mention of the name. I really do believe that he's a secret turd pusher, thought Antony.

'The very best of good fellows!' Octavian exclaimed. 'He's doing extremely well in Further Gaul. As soon as he can free them up, you'll have your five legions. The Bellovaci are giving a lot of trouble.'

'Oh, I know all about *that*. What a fool you are, Octavianus!' Antony said contemptuously. 'The very best of good fellows is negotiating with me to change sides in our non-war – has been almost since he arrived in Further Gaul.'

Octavian's face gave nothing away, neither astonishment nor horror; even when it had shone with affection for Salvidienus, its eyes had not genuinely participated. Did they ever? Antony wondered, unable to remember one time in his experience that they had. The eyes never told you what he really thought about anything. They just . . . watched. Watched the behavior of everyone, including himself, as if they and the mind behind them stood twenty paces away from his body. How could two orbs so luminous be so opaque?

Octavian spoke, easily, diffidently even. 'Do you consider, Antonius, that his conduct is treasonous?'

'Depends how you look at it. To switch allegiance from one Roman of good standing to another of equal standing may be . . . ah . . . treacherous, but it's not treasonous. However, if said conduct is aimed at inciting civil war between those two equals, then it's definitely treasonous,' Antony said, enjoying himself.

'Have you any tangible evidence to suggest that Salvidienus should be put on trial for *maiestas?*'

'Talents of tangibility.'

'Would you, if I asked it, tender your evidence at trial?'

'Of course,' said Antony in mock surprise. 'It's my duty to a fellow triumvir. If he's convicted, you're short one very good general of troops – fortunate for me, eh? *If* there were a civil war, I mean, naturally. Because I wouldn't enlist him in my ranks, Octavianus, let alone have him as my legate. Was it you who said that traitors might be made use of, but never liked or trusted, or was it your divine daddy?'

'Who said it doesn't matter. Salvidienus must go.'

'Across the Styx, or into permanent exile?'

'Across the Styx. After trial in the Senate, I think. Not in *comitia* – too public. In the Senate, behind closed doors.'

'Good thinking! Difficult for you, however. You'll have to send Agrippa to Further Gaul now it's an official part of your Triumvirate. If it were mine, I could send any one of several – Pollio, for instance. Now I'll be able to send Pollio to relieve Censorinus in Macedonia, and send Ventidius to hold Labienus and Pacorus at bay until I can deal with the Parthians in person,' said Antony, twisting the knife.

'There is absolutely nothing to stop your dealing with them in person at once!' Octavian said caustically. 'What, *afraid* to go too far from me, Italia and Sextus Pompeius, in that order?'

'I have good reason to stay near all three of you!'

'You have no reason whatsoever!' Octavian snapped. 'I will not war against you under any circumstances, though I will war against Sextus Pompeius the moment I'm able.'

'Our pact forbids that.'

'In a pig's eye it does! Sextus Pompeius was declared a public enemy, written on the tablets as *hostis*, a law you were party to, remember? He's not the governor of Sicilia or anywhere else, he's a pirate. As Rome's *curator annonae*, it is my duty to hunt him down. He impedes the free flow of grain.'

Taken aback at Octavian's fearlessness, Antony decided to terminate their conversation, if so it could be called. 'Good luck,' he said ironically, and strolled away in the direction of Paullus Lepidus to verify the rumor that Lepidus the Triumvir's brother was about to marry Scribonia's Cornelian daughter. If it is true, he thinks he's a canny fellow, thought Antony, but it won't advance him a notch higher, apart from her huge dowry. Octavianus will divorce

Scribonia as soon as he's defeated Sextus, which means I'll have to ensure that day never comes. Give Octavianus a big victory, and all Italia will worship him. Is the little worm aware that one reason I stay so close to Italia is to keep the name Marcus Antonius alive in Italian eyes? Of course he is.

Octavian gravitated to Agrippa's side. 'We're in trouble again,' he said ruefully. 'Antonius has just told me that our dear Salvidienus has been in contact with him for months with a view to changing his allegiance.' The eyes looked dark grey. 'I confess it came as a blow. I didn't think Salvidienus such a fool.'

'It's a logical move for him, Caesar. He's a red-haired man from Picenum – when have such ever been trustworthy? He's dying to be a bigger fish in a bigger sea.'

'It means I'll have to send you to govern Further Gaul.'

Agrippa looked shocked. 'Caesar, no!'

'Who else is there? It also means I can't move against Sextus Pompeius anytime soon. Luck is with Antonius, she always is.'

'I can do the shipyards between Cosa and Genua as I travel, but from Genua I'll be on the Via Aemilia Scaura to Placentia – not enough time to hug the coast all the way. Caesar, Caesar, it will be two years before I can come home if I do the job properly!'

'You must do it properly. I want no more of these uprisings among the Long-hairs, and I think Divus Julius was wrong to let the Druids go about their business. It seems mostly to consist of stirring up discontent.'

'I agree.' Agrippa's face brightened. 'I do have an idea how to keep the Belgae in order.'

'What?' Octavian asked, curious.

'Settle hordes of Ubii Germans on the Gallic bank of the Rhenus. Every tribe from the Nervii to the Treveri will be so busy trying to push the Germans back to their own bank of the river that they won't have the leisure to rebel.' He looked wistful. 'I'd love to imitate Divus Julius and cross into Germania!'

Octavian broke into laughter. 'Agrippa, if you want to teach the Suebi Germans a lesson, I'm sure you will. On the other hand, we need the Ubii, so why not gift them with better land? They're the best cavalry Rome has ever fielded. All I can say, my dearest friend, is that I'm very glad you chose me. I can bear the loss of hundreds of Salvidienuses, but I could never bear the loss of my one and only Marcus Agrippa.'

Agrippa glowed, reached out an impulsive hand to clasp it

around Octavian's forearm. *He* knew that he was Caesar's man to the death, but he loved to see Caesar acknowledge that fact by word or deed. 'More importantly, whom will you use while I'm on service in Further Gaul?'

'Statilius Taurus, of course. Sabinus, I suppose. Calvinus goes without saying. Cornelius Gallus is clever and reliable, as long as he's not wrestling with a poem. Carrinas in Spain.'

'Lean heaviest on Calvinus' was Agrippa's reply.

Like Scribonia, Octavia didn't think it right to wear flame and saffron to her wedding. Having good taste, she chose a color she knew became her, pale turquoise, and with the gracefully draped dress she wore a magnificent necklace and earrings that Antony had given her when he had walked around to the late Marcellus Minor's house to see her the day before the ceremony.

'Oh, Antonius, how beautiful!' she breathed, studying the set in wonder. Made of massive gold, the necklace sat flat like a narrow collar, and was rich with flawless turquoise cabochons. 'The stones have no dark patches to spoil their blueness.'

'I thought of them when I remembered the color of your eyes,' Antony said, pleased at her patent delight. 'Cleopatra gave them to me for Fulvia.'

She didn't look away, nor let a fraction of the light die out of those much-admired eyes. 'Truly, they are beautiful,' she said, up on her toes to kiss his cheek. 'I'll wear them tomorrow.'

'I suspect,' Antony went on heedlessly, 'that they weren't up to Cleopatra's standards when it comes to jewels – she gets a lot of gifts. So you might say she gave me her castoffs. I got none of her money,' he ended bitterly. 'She's a . . . oops, sorry.'

Octavia smiled the way she did at little Marcellus when he was naughty. 'You may be as profane as you like, Antonius. I am not a sheltered young maiden.'

'You don't mind marrying me?' he asked, thinking he ought.

'I have loved you with all my heart for many years,' she said, making no attempt to hide her emotions. Some instinct told her that he liked being loved, that it predisposed him to love in return, and she wanted that desperately.

'I would never have guessed!' he said, amazed.

'Of course not. I was Marcellus's wife, and loyal to my vows. Loving you was something for myself, quite separate and private.'

He could feel the familiar slide in his belly, the visceral reaction that warned him he was falling in love. And Fortuna was on his side, even in this. Tomorrow Octavia would belong to him. No need to worry that she might look at another man when she hadn't looked at him through the seven years she belonged to Marcellus Minor. Not that he had ever worried about any of his wives; all three had been faithful to him. But this fourth was the pick of the bunch. Cool, sleek and elegant, of Julian blood, a Republican princess. A man would have to be dead not to be moved by her.

He bent his head and kissed her on the mouth, suddenly very hungry for her. The kiss was returned with lightheaded feeling but, before it could burn her, she broke it and moved away.

'Tomorrow,' she said. 'Now come and see your sons.'

The nursery was not a very big room, and seemed at first glance to be overcrowded by small children. His quick soldier's eye made the count six ambulant, and one jigging in a cot. An adorable, fair little girl of about two planted a vicious kick on the shin of a dark, handsome little boy about five. He promptly gave her a push-slap with the palm of his hand that sat her down on her bottom with a thump just audible before the howls started.

'Mama, Mama!'

'If you dole out pain, Marcia, you have to expect to get it back,' Octavia said without a scrap of sympathy. 'Now stop your racket, or I'll slap you for starting something you can't finish.'

The other four, three around the little boy's age, and one a trifle younger than the blond termagant, had spied Antony and stood with their mouths open, as did Marcia the kicker and her victim, whom Octavia introduced as Marcellus. At five, Antyllus had vague memories of his father, but wasn't quite sure that this giant was really his father until Octavia assured him of the fact. Then he simply stared, too afraid to hold out his arms for a hug. At not quite two, Iullus burst into noisy tears when the giant advanced on him. Laughing, Octavia picked him up and gave him to Antony, who soon had him smiling. The moment he did, Antyllus held out his arms for that hug, and was picked up too.

'Handsome little chaps, aren't they?' she asked. 'They'll be as big as you when they grow up. Half of me can't wait to see how they look in cuirass and *pteryges*, and half of me dreads it, for then they'll have passed out of my keeping.'

Antony answered something, his mind elsewhere; it was Marcia who gnawed at him. Marcia? *Marcia?* Whose was she, and why did she call Octavia Mama? Though, he noted, Antyllus and Iullus also called her Mama. The one in the cot, fair as Marcia, was her own youngest, Cellina, he was told. But whose was Marcia? She had a Julian look, otherwise he would have deemed her a Philippan cousin rescued from some dire fate by this child-obsessed woman. For obsessed she clearly was.

'Please, Antonius, may I have Curio?' Octavia asked, her eyes begging. 'I didn't feel I could take him without your permission, but he badly needs stability and supervision. He's nearly eleven, and dreadfully wild.'

Antony blinked. 'You're welcome to the brat, Octavia, but why would you want to saddle yourself with yet another child?'

'Because he's unhappy, and no boy of his age should be. He misses his mama, ignores his pedagogue – a very silly, inadequate man – and is mostly to be found in the Forum making a nuisance of himself. Another year or two, and he'll be stealing purses.'

Antony grinned. 'Well, his father my friend did enough of that in his day! Curio the Censor, *his* father, was a tightfisted, narrow-minded autocrat who used to lock Curio up. I'd break him out, and we'd create chaos. Maybe you're what this Curio needs.'

'Oh, thank you!' Octavia closed the nursery door on a chorus of protests; apparently she usually spent a longer time with them when she came, and they blamed the giant, even Antyllus and Iullus.

'Who exactly is Marcia?' he asked.

'My half-sister. Mama bore me, her first, at eighteen, and Marcia at forty-four.'

'You mean she's Atia's by Philippus Junior?'

'Yes, of course. She came to me when Mama couldn't look after her properly. Mama's joints are swollen and terribly painful.'

'But Octavianus has never mentioned her existence! I know he pretends that his mother is dead, but a half-sister . . . ! Ye gods, it's ludicrous!'

'Two half-sisters, actually. Don't forget that our father had a girl by his first wife. She's in her forties now.'

'Yes, but . . . !' Antony kept shaking his head like a boxer on the receiving end of too many punches.

'Oh, come, Antonius, you know my brother! Though I love him dearly, I *can* see his faults. He's too conscious of his status to want a half-sister twenty years his junior – so undignified! Also, he feels Rome won't take him seriously if his youth is reinforced by a baby sister who is public knowledge. It didn't help that Marcia was conceived so soon after our poor stepfather's death. Rome has long forgiven Mama her slip, but Caesar never will. Besides, Marcia came to me before she could walk, and people lose count.' She chuckled. 'Those who meet the members of my nursery assume she's mine because she looks like me.'

'Do you love children *so* much?'

'Love is too small a word, too abused and misused. I would give my life for a child, literally.'

'Without caring whose the child is.'

'Exactly. I have always believed that children are people's chance to do something heroic with their lives – try to see that all their own mistakes are rectified rather than repeated.'

Next morning the late Marcellus Minor's servants took the children to Pompey the Great's marble palace on the Carinae, those doomed to stay and mind Marcellus Minor's house weeping because they were losing the lady Octavia. The house they now had to care for belonged to little Marcellus, but he would not be able to live in it for years to come. Antony, who was executor of the will, had decided not to rent it out in the meantime, but his secretary, Lucilius, was a strict supervisor and caretaker. No chance to idle and let the place decay.

At twilight Antony carried his new bride over the threshold of Pompey's palace, a house that had seen Pompey carry Julia over the same threshhold into six years of bliss that had ended with her death in childbirth. Let that not be my fate, Octavia thought, a little breathless at the ease with which her husband scooped her up, then set her down to receive the fire and the water, pass her hands through them and thereby assume her station as mistress of the household. What seemed like a hundred servants watched, sighing and cooing, breaking into soft applause. The lady Octavia's reputation as the kindest and most understanding of women had gone before her. The older among them, especially the steward Egon, dreamed that the place would bloom as it had under Julia; to them, Fulvia had been demanding, yet uninterested in domestic matters.

It hadn't escaped Octavia's attention that her brother looked as pleased as complacent, though precisely why was beyond her. Yes, he hoped to heal the breach by masterminding this marriage, but what could he possibly gain from it if it foundered, as all who attended the ceremony privately judged it would? Yet more frightening was Octavia's presentiment that Caesar was *counting* on its collapse. Well, she vowed, it won't fail because of me!

Her first night with Antony was sheer pleasure, a far greater pleasure than all her nights with Marcellus Minor combined. That her new husband liked women was evident in the way he touched her, rumbled his own delight in being close to her. Somehow he stripped her of a lifetime's inhibitions, welcomed her caresses and small purrs of astonished joy, let her explore him as if he had never been explored before. For Octavia he was a perfect lover, sensuous as well as sensual, and not, as she had expected, concerned only with his own desires. Words of love and acts of love fused into a fiery continuum of bliss so wonderful she wept. By the time she fell into a dazed and ecstatic sleep, she would have died for him as cheerfully as she would have for a child.

And in the morning she learned that Antony too was affected in equal measure; when she tried to leave the bed to see to her duties, it all began again, more beautifully because of the slight sense of familiarity, and more satisfying because of her increased awareness of what she needed and he was so happy to provide.

Oh, excellent! thought Octavian when he saw the couple two days later at a dinner given by Gnaeus Domitius Calvinus. I was right: they are so opposite that they have enchanted each other. Now I just have to wait for him to grow tired of her. He will. He will! I must offer to Quirinus that he leaves her for an alien love, not a Roman one, and to Jupiter Best and Greatest that Rome will profit from his inevitable disenchantment with my sister. *Look* at him, oozing love, sloppy with it! As full of sentimentality as a fifteen-year-old girl. How I despise people who succumb to such a trivial, unappealing disease! It will never happen to me, so much I know. My mind rules my emotions, I am not vulnerable to this saccharine business. How can Octavia fall for his act? She'll hold him in thrall for at least two years, but longer than that – hardly likely. Her goodness and sweetness of nature are a novelty to him, but as he's neither good nor sweet natured, his fascination with virtue will pall, then pass in a typically Antonian tempest of revulsion.

I will work indefatigably to spread word of this marriage far and wide, set my agents to talking of it incessantly in every city, town and *municipium* in Italia and Italian Gaul. Until now I have kept them pleading my own case, enumerating the perfidies of Sextus Pompeius, describing the indifference of Marcus Antonius to his homeland's plight. But, during this coming winter, they will cease most of that in favor of singing the praises not of this union per se, but of the lady Octavia, sister of Caesar and the personification of everything a Roman matron should be. I will erect those statues of her, as many as I can afford, and keep adding to them until the peninsula groans under their weight. Ah, I can see it now! Octavia, chaste and virtuous as Lucretia the dishonored; Octavia, more worthy of respect than a Vestal Virgin; Octavia, tamer of the irresponsible lout Marcus Antonius; Octavia, the person who single-handedly saved her country from the evils of civil war. Yes, Octavia Pudica must have *all* the credit! By the time my agents get through with the business, Octavia Pudica will be as close to a goddess as Cornelia the Mother of the Gracchi! So that when Antonius abandons her, every Roman and Italian will condemn him as a brute, a heartless monster ruled by lust.

Oh, if only I could see into the future! If only I knew the identity of the woman for whom Antonius will desert Octavia Pudica! I will offer to every Roman god that she be someone every Roman and Italian can hate, hate, hate. If possible, shift the blame of Antonius's conduct to her influence over him. I will paint her as wicked as Circe, as vain as Helen of Troy, as malignant as Medea, as cruel as Clytemnestra, as lethal as Medusa. And if she is none of those, I will make her seem all of those. Set my agents to a new whispering campaign, create a demon out of this unknown woman in the same way as I am about to create a goddess out of my sister.

There are more ways to bring a man down than to go to war against him – how wasteful that is in lives and prosperity! How much money it costs! Money that should be going to the greater glory of Rome.

Watch out for me, Antonius! But you won't, because you think me as ineffectual as effeminate. I am not Divus Julius, no, but I *am* a worthy heir to his name. Veil your eyes, Antonius, be blind. I'll get you, even at the cost of my beloved sister's happiness. If Cornelia the Mother of the Gracchi had not had a life pervaded by pain and disappointment, Roman women would not lay flowers on her tomb. So will it be for Octavia Pudica.

NINE

Dazzled by the vision of the Triumvir Antony and the Triumvir Octavian walking around together like old and dear friends, Rome rejoiced that winter, hailing it as the beginning of the Golden Age that the prognosticators kept insisting was knocking on humanity's door. Helped by the fact that both the Triumvir Antony's wife and the Triumvir Octavian's wife were pregnant. Having ascended so high into the aether of creative transfiguration that he didn't know how to get down again, Virgil wrote his fourth *Eclogue* and predicted the birth of the child who would save the world. The more cynical were laying bets on whether the Triumv ir Antony's son or the Triumvir Octavian's son was the Chosen Child, and nobody stopped to think of daughters. The Tenth Era would not be ushered in by a girl, so much was sure.

Not that all was really well. The secret trial of Quintus Salvidienus Rufus was talked about, even if no one but the members of the Senate knew what evidence was presented and what Salvidienus said as he and his advocates conducted his defence. The verdict shocked; it was a relatively long time since a Roman had been put to death for treason. Exiles aplenty, yes; proscription lists aplenty, yes; but not a formal trial in the Senate that exacted the death penalty, which could not be levied upon a Roman citizen, hence the fiasco of first removing citizenship before a head could be removed. There had been a treason court and, though it had not functioned in some years, it was still on the tablets. So why secrecy, and why the Senate?

No sooner had the Senate disposed of Salvidienus than Herod was seen flaunting his Tyrian purple and gold outfit on the streets of Rome. He put up at the inn on the corner of the Clivus Orbius, quite the most expensive hostelry in town, where from its best suite of rooms he began to distribute largesse to certain needy senators. His petition to the Senate to appoint him King of the Jews was properly presented in the Senaculum before a senatorial gathering that numbered slightly over a quorum only because of his liberal largesse and the presence of Mark Antony at his side. The whole business was hypothetical anyway, since Antigonus was King of the Jews with the sanction of the Parthians and unlikely to be dethroned at any time in the foreseeable future; Parthians or no, the vast majority of the Jews wanted Antigonus.

'Where did you get all this money?' Antony asked as they went into the Senaculum, a tiny building adjacent to the Temple of Concord at the foot of the Capitoline Mount. Here the Senate saw foreigners, who were not permitted into the House.

'From Cleopatra,' said Herod.

The massive hands clenched. '*Cleopatra?*'

'Yes, and what's so amazing about that?'

'She's too stingy to give money to anyone.'

'But her son isn't, and he rules her. Besides, I had to agree to pay her the revenues from Jericho balsam when I'm king.'

'Ah!'

Herod got his *senatus consultum*, which officially confirmed him as King of the Jews.

'Now all you have to do is win your kingdom,' said Quintus Dellius over a delicious dinner; the inn's cooks were famous.

'I know, I know!' Herod snapped.

'It wasn't I who pinched Judaea,' Dellius said reproachfully, 'so why take it out on me?'

'Because you're here under my nose shoveling sow's udder into your maw at the rate of one drop of Jericho balsam per bite! Do you think Antonius will ever get off his arse to fight Pacorus? He hasn't even mentioned a Parthian campaign.'

'He can't. He needs to be within watching distance of that sweet boy, Octavianus.'

'Oh, the whole world knows that!' Herod said impatiently.

'Speaking of sweet things, Herod, what's happened to your hopes of Mariamne? Won't Antigonus have her married already?'

'He can't marry her himself, he's her uncle, and he's too afraid of his relatives to give her to one of them.' Herod grinned and flopped over on his back, flapping pudgy hands. 'Besides, he doesn't have her. I do.'

'*You* do?'

'Yes, I took her away and hid her just before Jerusalem fell.'

'Aren't you the clever one?' Dellius spotted a new delicacy. 'How many drops of Jericho balsam are there in these stuffed wrens?'

These and various other incidents paled before the true, on-going problem Rome had faced ever since the death of Caesar: the grain supply. Having promised faithfully to be good, Sextus Pompey was back raiding the sea lanes and making off with shipments of wheat before the wax on the Pact of Brundisium was fully cured. He grew bolder, actually sending detachments of men ashore on to Italian soil wherever there was a concentration of granaries, and stole wheat no one had dreamed vulnerable. When the price of public grain soared up to forty sesterces for a six-day ration, rioting broke out in Rome and every Italian city of any size. There was a free grain dole available to the poorest citizens, but Divus Julius had halved it to one hundred and fifty thousand recipients by introducing a means test. But that, screamed the furious crowds, was when wheat fetched ten sesterces the *modius*, not forty! The free grain dole list should be expanded to include people who couldn't afford to pay quadruple the old price. When the Senate refused this demand, the rioting grew more serious than at any time since the days of Saturninus.

An awkward situation for Antony, obliged to witness at first hand how critical an issue the grain supply had become, and aware that he, and no one else, had enabled Sextus Pompey to continue operating.

Stifling a sigh, Antony abandoned all thought of using two hundred talents he had put aside for his pleasures on those same pleasures; instead, he used it to buy sufficient grain to feed an extra hundred and fifty thousand citizens, thereby earning an unmerited adulation from the Head Count. Where had this wind-fall come from? No less than Pythodorus of Tralles. He had offered this plutocrat his daughter Antonia – homely, obese and mentally dull – in return for two hundred talents of hard cash. Pythodorus, still in his prime, had jumped at the offer; bawling like a mother-less calf, Antonia was already on her way to Tralles and something called a husband. Bawling like a calfless cow, Antonia Hybrida proceeded to let all of Rome know what had happened to her daughter.

'What a despicable thing to do!' Octavian cried, seeking his *inimicus* Antony out.

'Despicable? *Despicable?* First of all, she's my daughter and I can marry her to whomsoever I please!' roared Antony, taken aback at this new manifestation of Octavian's temerity. 'Secondly, the price I got for her has fed twice as many citizens for a month and a half! Talk about ingratitude! You can criticize, Octavianus, when you produce a daughter capable of doing a tenth as much for the Head Count paupers as mine has!'

'*Gerrae*,' said Octavian scornfully. 'Until you got to Rome and saw for yourself what was going on, you had every intention of keeping the money to pay your ever-mounting bills! The poor girl hasn't a particle of sense to help her understand her fate – you might at least have sent her mother with her instead of leaving the woman in Rome to mourn her loss into any ear willing to listen!'

'Since when have you grown feelings? *Mentulam caco!*'

While Octavian retched with disgust at this obscenity, Antony stormed off in a rage that even Octavia found it difficult to mollify.

At which point Gnaeus Asinius Pollio, a fully fledged consul at last by virtue of his having assumed his regalia, made his offering and taken his oath of office, stepped into the picture. He had wondered what he might do to ennoble two months' worth of office, and now he had the answer: bring Sextus Pompey to his senses. A certain fairness of mind told him that this lesser son of a greater man had a modicum of right on his side; seventeen when his father was murdered in Egypt, not yet twenty when his older brother died after Munda, he had had to stand by impotent while a vindictive Senate and People forced him into a life of outlawry by refusing to allow him an opportunity to repair the fortunes of his family. All it would have taken to avoid this present ghastly situation was a senatorial decree allowing him to come home and inherit his father's position and wealth. But the former was deliberately tarnished to enhance the reputation of his enemies, and the latter had long-since disappeared into the bottomless pit of funding civil war.

Still, thought Pollio, summoning Antony, Octavian and Maecenas to a meeting at his house, I can attempt to make our Triumvirs see that something positive has to be done.

'If it isn't,' he said over watered wine in his study, 'it will not be very long before everyone present in this room will be dead at the hands of the mob. Since the mob has no idea how to rule, a new set of masters of Rome will come into being – men whose names I cannot even guess, they will rise so high from such depths. Now, this is not what I want as an end to my life. What I want is to retire, my brow wreathed in laurels, to write a history of our turbulent times.'

'Such a beautiful turn of phrase,' Maecenas murmured when his two superiors said nothing at all.

'What are you saying exactly, Pollio?' Octavian asked after a long pause. 'That we who have suffered this irresponsible thief for years, seen the Treasury's coffers depleted because of his activities, should now turn around and *laud* him? Tell him that all is forgiven and he can come home? Pah!'

'Here, now,' said Antony, looking statesmanlike, 'that's a little harsh, isn't it? Pollio's contention that Sextus isn't all bad has some justice. Personally, I've always felt Sextus was hard done by, hence my reluctance, Octavianus, to stamp on the boy – young man, I mean.'

'You hypocrite!' Octavian cried, angrier than anyone there had ever seen him. 'Easy for you to be kind and understanding, you lump of inertia, idling away your winters in debauchery while I struggle to feed four million people! And where is the money I need to do that? Why, in that pathetic, dispossessed, incredibly wronged boy's vaults! For vaults he must have, he's squeezed me out of so much! And when he squeezes me, Antonius, he squeezes Rome and Italia!'

Maecenas reached out and laid his hand on Octavian's shoulder; it looked gentle, but the fingers bit in so hard that Octavian winced, shrugged it off.

'I didn't ask you to come here today to listen to what are essentially personal differences,' Pollio said strongly. 'I've asked you in order to see if between us we can work out a way to deal with Sextus Pompeius that will be considerably cheaper than a war on the sea. The answer is negotiation, not conflict! And I expected you for one to see that, Octavianus.'

'I'd sooner make a pact with Pacorus that gave him all the East,' said Octavian.

'You're beginning to sound as if you don't want a solution,' Antony said.

'I do want a solution! The *only* one! Namely, to burn every last one of his ships, execute his admirals, sell his crews and soldiers into slavery, and leave him free to emigrate to Scythia! For until we admit that is what we have to do, Sextus Pompeius will continue to starve Rome and Italia at his whim! The wretch has neither substance nor honor!'

'I propose, Pollio, that we send an embassage to Sextus and ask him to meet us in conference at – Puteoli? Yes, Puteoli sounds good,' said Antony, radiating goodwill.

'I agree,' said Octavian promptly, which startled the others, even Maecenas. Had his outburst been calculating, then, rather than spontaneous? What was he up to?

Some time later Pollio changed the subject, Octavian having acquiesced to a conference at Puteoli without argument.

'It's going to be up to you, Maecenas,' Pollio said. 'I intend to leave at once for my proconsulship in Macedonia. The Senate can have suffect consuls elected for the rump of the year. One *nundinum* in Rome is enough for me.'

'How many legions do you want?' Antony asked, relieved to discuss something inarguably in his purlieu.

'Six should do it.'

'Good! That means I can give Ventidius eleven to take to the East. He'll have to hold Pacorus and Labienus where they are for the moment.' Antony smiled. 'A good old muleteer, Ventidius.'

'Maybe better than you think,' Pollio said dryly.

'Huh! I'll believe that when I see it. He didn't exactly shine while my brother was penned up inside Perusia.'

'Nor did I, Antonius!' Pollio snapped. 'Perhaps our inactivity was due to a certain Triumvir's not answering his letters.'

Octavian rose. 'I'll go, if you don't mind. The mere mention of letters is enough to remind me that I have a hundred of them to write. It's times like that when I wish I had Divus Julius's ability to keep four secretaries busy at once.'

Octavian and Maecenas gone, Pollio glared at Antony.

'Your trouble, Marcus, is that you're lazy and slipshod,' he said bitingly. 'If you don't get off your *podex* soon and do something, you might find that you've left it too late to do anything.'

'Your trouble, Pollio, is that you're a meticulous fusspot.'

'Plancus is grumbling, and he heads a faction.'

'Then let him grumble in Ephesus. He can go to govern Asia Province, the sooner the better.'

'And Ahenobarbus?'

'Can continue to govern Bithynia.'

'And what about the client-kingdoms? Deiotarus is dead and Galatia gone to rack and ruin.'

'Oh, don't worry, I have some ideas,' Antony said comfortably. He yawned. 'Ye gods, how I loathe Rome in winter!'

TEN

The Pact of Puteoli was concluded with Sextus Pompey late in the summer. What Antony thought, he didn't divulge, but Octavian knew that Sextus wouldn't behave like an honorable man; at heart he was a Picentine warlord degenerated into a pirate, and incapable of keeping his word. In return for agreeing to allow the free passage of grain to Italia, Sextus received official acknowledgement of his governorships of Sicilia, Sardinia and Corsica; he also received the Greek Peloponnese, a thousand silver talents, and the right to be elected consul in four years' time, with Libo to follow him as consul the following year. A farce, as everybody understood who had a brain larger than a pea. How you must be laughing, Sextus Pompeius, thought Octavian, fresh from the fray.

In May, Octavian's wife Scribonia gave birth to a girl, whom Octavian named Julia. Far too late for Virgil to rectify that embarrassing eclogue. Shivering in fear, the esteemed poet prayed that Antony would not have a son and put all his eggs into an Antonian basket. Late in June, Octavia gave birth to . . . a daughter, Antonia. Virgil could breathe again, and say that this longed-for Chosen Child was still to come.

One of the clauses of the contract with Sextus Pompey said that whatever exiles remained could come home. That included the exclusive Tiberius Claudius Nero, who hadn't felt that the Pact of Brundisium offered him sufficient protection. So he had stayed on in Athens until now, when he decided he could go back to Rome with relative impunity. It was difficult, as Nero's fortune had dwindled to an alarming low. Part of that was his own fault, as he had invested unwisely in the *publicani* companies who farmed the revenues of Asia Province and found themselves ejected after Quintus Labienus and his Parthian mercenaries invaded Caria,

Pisidia, Lycia – their richest pickings. But part of it too was through no fault of his own, save that a cleverer man would have remained in Italy to foster his wealth rather than fled to leave it at the disposal of unscrupulous Greek freedmen and inert bankers.

Thus the Tiberius Claudius Nero who returned home in the early autumn was so financially chastened that he proved poor company for his wife. His pecuniary resources just stretched to the hire of one litter and an open cart for his baggage. Though he had given Livia Drusilla permission to share this conveyance, she declined without offering either of her reasons: one, that the bearers were a thin, sorry lot, just able to lift the litter with Nero and his son aboard; and two, that she loathed being close to her husband and son. As the party traveled at walking pace, Livia Drusilla walked. The weather was idyllic – a warm sun, a cool breeze, plenty of shade, a haunting perfume of browned grass and the aromatic herbs farmers grew to discourage pests through winter. Nero preferred to go on the road, Livia Drusilla to use its verge, where daisies made a white carpet for her feet, and early apples and late pears could be plucked from wind-sown orchard escapees. As long as she didn't stray out of sight of Nero in the litter, the world was her own.

At Teanum Sidicinum they left the Via Appia in favor of the inland Via Latina; those who continued to Rome on the Via Appia through the Pomptine Marshes risked their lives, for the region was riddled with the ague.

Just outside Fregellae they put up in a modest hostelry that could offer a proper bath, something Nero ordered avidly.

'Don't empty the water after my son and I have finished,' he commanded. 'My wife can use it.'

In their room he gazed at her with a frown; heart beating faster, she wondered what her face had betrayed, but stood, demure and complaisant, to receive what she knew from long experience was going to be a homily.

'We draw near to Rome, Livia Drusilla, and I shall require that you exert every possible effort not to overspend,' he instructed her. 'Little Tiberius will need a pedagogue next year – an unwelcome expense – but it is up to you to economize sufficiently in the meantime to make that less of a burden. No new dresses, no jewelry, and definitely no special servants like hairdressers or cosmeticians. Is that quite clear?'

'Yes, husband,' Livia Drusilla answered dutifully, and with an internal sigh. Not because she yearned for hairdressers or their

161

like, but because she hungered so desperately for peace, for a secure, uncritical life. She wanted a haven wherein she could read whatever she wanted, or choose a menu irrespective of cost, or not be held responsible for servile embezzlements. She wanted to be adored, to see ordinary faces light up at the mention of her name. Like Octavia, the exalted wife of Marcus Antonius, whose statues stood in the marketplaces of Beneventum, Capua, Teanum Sidicinum. What had *she* done, after all, except marry a Triumvir? Yet people hymned her as if she were a goddess, prayed that one day they would see her journey between Rome and Brundisium. People kept raving about her, attributing the peace to her. Oh, would that she was an Octavia! But who cared about the wife of a patrician nobleman if his name was Tiberius Claudius Nero?

He was staring at her, puzzled; Livia Drusilla came out of her reverie with a jolt, licked her lips.

'You have something you wish to say?' he asked coldly.

'Yes, husband.'

'Then speak, woman!'

'I am expecting another baby. Another son, I think. My symptoms are identical to those I had with Tiberius.'

First came shock, then, crowding on its heels, displeasure. His mouth turned down, he ground his teeth. 'Oh, Livia Drusilla! Couldn't you have managed things better? I can't afford a second baby, especially another son! You'd better go to the Bona Dea and ask for the medicine as soon as we're in Rome.'

'I fear it may be a little late for that, *domine*.'

'*Cacat*!' he said savagely. 'How long?'

'Almost two months, I think. The medicine should be taken within six *nundinae*, I am already seven.'

'Even so, you will take it.'

'Certainly.'

'Of all the nuisances!' he cried, throwing his clenched fists in the air. 'Go away, woman! Go away and let me bathe in peace!'

'Do you still want Tiberius to join you?'

'Tiberius is my joy and consolation, of course I do!'

'Then may I go for a walk to see the old town?'

'As far as I'm concerned, wife, you can walk over a cliff!'

Fregellae had been a ghost town for eighty-five years, sacked by Lucius Opimius for rebelling against Rome in the days when the peninsula had been tessellated with Italian states interspersed with Roman 'colonies' of citizens. The injustice of this cavalier treatment had finally led the Italian states to unite and attempt to throw off the Roman yoke. The bitter war that ensued had many causes, but it commenced with the assassination of Livia Drusilla's adoptive grandfather, the tribune of the plebs, Marcus Livius Drusus.

Perhaps because she knew all that, sore of heart and fighting tears, his granddaughter drifted among crumbled walls and old buildings still standing. Oh, how *dared* Nero treat her so! How could he blame her pregnancy on her, who, if given the opportunity, would never enter his bed? Detestation, she was discovering, had grown amain since Athens; the dutiful wife was no less dutiful, but she abominated every moment of that duty.

Of her grandfather she knew, but what she didn't know was that fifty years earlier Lucius Cornelius Sulla had taken this same walk, pondering what the slaughter had been for, looking at the crimson poppies fertilized by Italian and Roman blood, the sleek domes of skulls with yellow daisies fluttering in their orbits like coquettish eyes, and asked himself the question no man has ever been able to answer – why do we go to war on our brothers? And, like him, as she walked, Livia Drusilla saw a Roman advancing on her through the shimmer of tears, and wondered if he were real or surreal. At first she looked about furtively for a place to hide, but as he drew closer she subsided on to the selfsame column drum Gaius Marius had used as a seat, and waited for the man to reach her.

He was wearing a purple-bordered toga, and was crowned with a cap of luxuriant gold hair; his gait was graceful and assured, the body under its capacious wrapping slender, young. Then, when he was within scant paces of her, his face swam into focus. Very smooth, beautiful, stern yet gentle, with silver eyes fringed in gold. Livia Drusilla gaped, mouth falling open.

Octavian too had needed to escape; sometimes people wearied him, no matter how well meant their attentions or how indisputable their loyalty. And old Fregellae lay close by Fabrateria Nova, the town built to replace it. Soaking up the sun, he lifted his face to the cloudless sky and let his mind wander without direction, something he didn't do very often. This ruined place held an odd seduction, perhaps because of its quietness; the hum of bees instead of human marketplace chatter, the faint song of some lyrical bird rather than a marketplace busker. Peace! How beautiful, how needed!

It may have been because he allowed his mind this grace of liberty that a loneliness invaded him; for once in his busy life he became conscious that no one in it was there just for *him*—oh, yes, Agrippa, yet that wasn't what he meant. Someone just for *him* in the way a mother or a wife should be, that delicious compound of femininity and selfless devotion Octavia gave to Antonius or—curse her!—Mama had given to Philippus Junior. But no, he wouldn't think of Atia and her unchastity! Better to think of his sister, the sweetest Roman woman who ever lived. Why should so much contentment be given to a boor like Antonius? Why didn't he have his own Octavia, different though she would be from his sister?

He became aware that someone was walking the desolate stone stumps of Fregellae, a woman who, upon sight of him, looked ready to flee; then she sank onto a column drum and sat, the tears on her cheeks glinting in the strong light. At first he thought her a visitation, then, pausing, acknowledged that she was real. The most bewitching little face turned first to him, then stared at the ground. A pair of beautiful hands fluttered, were folded on her lap; no jewels adorned them, but nothing else about her spoke of humble origins. This was a great lady, he knew it in his bones. Some instinct within him leaped free of its cage and shrieked so ecstatically that suddenly he understood its godly message: she had been sent to him, a divine gift he couldn't—wouldn't!—spurn. Almost he cried aloud to his divine father, then shook his head. Speak to *her*, break the spell!

'Do I disturb you?' he asked, smiling a wonderful smile.

'No, no!' she gasped, wiping the last of the tears from her face. 'No!'

He sat down at her feet, gazing up at her with a quizzical expression, and those amazing eyes suddenly tender. 'For a moment I thought you were the goddess of the marketplace,' he said, 'in mourning for the fate of Fregellae. But you aren't a goddess – yet. One day I'll turn you into one.'

Heady stuff! She didn't understand, deemed him slightly mad. Yet in an instant, in less time than it takes lightning to strike, she fell totally in love. 'I had a little leisure,' she said, throat tight, 'and I wanted to see the ruins. They're so peaceful – how I long for peace!' The last was said with passion.

'Oh, yes, once men are finished with a place, it's shorn of all its terrors. It emanates the peace of death, but you're too young to be preparing for death. My great-great uncle, Gaius Marius, once met another of my great-great uncles, Lucius Sulla, here amid the desolation. A kind of respite. Both of them were busy making other towns as dead as Fregellae, you see.'

'And have you done that too?' she asked.

'Not deliberately. I'd rather build than destroy. Though I will never rebuild Fregellae. It's my monument to you.'

More madness! 'You joke, and I am an undeserving object.'

'How could I joke, when I've seen your tears? Why weep?'

'Self-pity,' she said honestly.

'The answer of a good wife. You are a good wife, aren't you?'

She looked at her plain gold wedding ring. 'I try to be, but sometimes it's hard.'

'It wouldn't be were I your husband. Who is he?'

'Tiberius Claudius Nero.'

His breath hissed. 'Ah! That one. And you are?'

'Livia Drusilla.'

'Of a fine old family. An heiress too.'

'Not anymore. My dowry is gone.'

'Nero spent it, you imply.'

'After we fled, yes. I'm really a Claudian of the Nerones.'

'So your husband is your first cousin. Have you children?'

'One, a boy aged four.' Her black lashes dropped. 'And one in my womb. I am to take the medicine,' she said – *Ecastor*, what made her tell a complete stranger that?

'Do you want to take the medicine?'

'Yes, and no.'

'Why yes?'

'I don't like my husband or my firstborn.'

'And why no?'

'Because I have a feeling there will be no more children from my womb. Bona Dea spoke to me when I offered to her in Capua.'

'I've just come from Capua, but I didn't see you there.'

'Nor I, you.'

A silence fell, honeyed and serene, its periphery of birds singing and small insects chirruping in the grass an intrinsic part of it, as if even silence was layered.

I am in the grasp of an enchantment, Livia Drusilla thought. 'I could sit here forever,' she said huskily.

'And I, but only if you were with me.'

Fearing that he would move to touch her and she would not have the strength to push him away, she broke the mood in a brisk

165

voice. 'You wear the *toga praetexta*, but you're too young. Does that mean you're one of Octavianus's minions?'

'I am no minion. I am Caesar.'

She jumped to her feet. 'Octavianus? You are Octavianus?'

'I decline to answer to that name,' he said, but not angrily. 'I am Caesar, Divi Filius. One day I will be Caesar Romulus by a decree of the Senate ratified by the People. When I've conquered my enemies and have no peer.'

'My husband is your avowed enemy.'

'Nero?' He laughed, genuinely amused. 'Nero is a nothing.'

'He is my husband and the arbiter of my fate.'

'You are his property, more like. I know him. Too many men lump their wives in with their beasts and their slaves. A great pity, Livia Drusilla. A wife should be a man's most precious colleague, not a chattel.'

'Is that how you regard your wife?' she asked as he scrambled up. 'As your colleague?'

'Not this present wife, no. She doesn't have the intelligence, poor woman.' His toga was a little awry; he twitched it into the proper folds. 'I must go, Livia Drusilla.'

'And I, Caesar.'

They turned to walk together in the direction of the inn.

'I'm on my way to Further Gaul,' he said at the fork in the track. 'It was going to be a prolonged stay, but now I've met you, it can't be. I'll return before winter is old.' His white teeth were striking against his brown skin as he smiled. 'And when I return, Livia Drusilla, I will marry you.'

'I am married, and true to my vows.' She drew herself up, her dignity touching. 'I am no Servilia, Caesar. I will not break my vows even with you.'

'That's why I'll marry you!'

And off he went down the left-hand path without looking back, though his voice was clearly audible. 'Yes, and Nero would never divorce you for the likes of me to marry, would he? What a terrible situation! How can it ever be resolved?'

Livia Drusilla stared after him until he vanished. Only then did she recollect the function of feet and commence to walk. Caesar Octavianus! Of course it was a farrago of nonsense; for all she knew, he said similar things to every pretty young female he met. Power gave men inflated ideas of their desirability – look at how Marcus Antonius had set out to charm her. The only problem with this line of reasoning was that she had been revolted by Antonius, but fallen in love with Caesar. One look, and she was lost.

When she had offered eggs and milk to the sacred snake who dwelled in Bona Dea's shrine at Capua, he had appeared from out of his slit in a glide of glittering scales the sun had turned bright gold, nosed at the milk, swallowed both eggs, then lifted his wedge of a head to gaze at her with still, cold eyes. And she had gazed back fearlessly, hearing him speak an alien language inside her, and reached out her hand to stroke him. He had put his chin upon her fingers and flickered his tongue, in and out, in and out, and told her – what *had* he told her? As if through dense grey fog she fought to remember, and fancied that it had been a message for her from the Bona Dea: that if she was fully prepared to make the sacrifice, the Bona Dea would gift her with the world. It had been the day upon which she was sure of this second pregnancy. No one ever saw the sacred snake. He waited until the night before he came out to drink his milk and eat his eggs. But he had manifested himself to her in brilliant sun, a long golden serpent as thick as her arm. Bona Dea, Bona Dea, gift me with the world and I will restore your worship to what it was before men intruded!

Nero was reading a sheaf of scrolls. When she entered he looked up, frowning direfully.

'An overlong walk, Livia Drusilla, for one who tramps the road all day?'

'I had conversation with a man in the ruins of Fregellae.'

Nero stiffened. 'Wives do not converse with strange men!'

'He wasn't a strange man. He was Caesar Divi Filius.'

That provoked a diatribe that Livia Drusilla had heard many times before, so she felt at liberty to leave her husband with a light word about using the bath water before it grew absolutely cold. Which she did, though it took courage after she had absorbed the sight of the scum of dead skin and body oils floating on the surface, smelled the stench of sweat. Knowing Nero, he had probably urinated in it; certainly little Tiberius would have. Using a rag, she skimmed as much of the detritus off as she could before sinking into the barely tepid water. Thinking to herself that she would gladly abandon wifely virtue for any man who offered her a fresh, hot, sweetly perfumed bath in a lovely marble tub only she ever used. And after she managed to banish things like urine and scum from her mind, she dreamed that this man was Caesar Octavianus; that he had meant what he said.

* * *

He had meant what he said, though he spent the walk back to the *duumvir*'s house in Fabrateria castigating himself for the clumsiest overtures of love ever made. See what happens when you tempt the gods? he asked, smiling wryly. I despised mawkish sentimentality, deemed men weak who protested that one look had transfixed them with Cupid's dart. Yet here I am with an arrow protruding from my chest, oceans deep in love with a girl I do not even know. How can that be? How can I, so rational and detached, have succumbed to an emotion that wars with everything I believe in? It was a visitation from some god, it has to have been! Otherwise it makes no sense! I *am* rational and detached! Therefore, why do I feel this incredible rush of—of—love? Oh, she moved me unbearably! I wanted to take all her troubles on my own shoulders, I wanted to smother her in kisses, I wanted to be with her for the rest of my life! Livia Drusilla. The wife of a pretentious snob like Tiberius Claudius Nero. Out of the same litter basket, another Claudian. The branch of the Claudii cognominated Pulcher produces quirky, independent, unorthodox consuls and censors, whereas the branch cognominated Nero is famous for producing nonentities. And Nero is a nonentity—a proud, stubborn, petty man who will never agree to divorce his wife at the behest of Caesar Octavianus.

Her face danced before his eyes, maddened him. Stripey eyes, black hair, skin like creamy milk, lush red lips. Could this be a simple sexual drive, then? Could he be suffering from the same ailment that perpetually got Marcus Antonius into hot water? No, that he wouldn't believe! Whatever this alien emotion was, there had to be a better reason for it than mere penile itch. Perhaps, Octavian wondered as a gig took him back to Rome, each of us has a natural mate, and I have found mine. Like turtle doves. The wife of another man, and pregnant with his child. Which makes no difference. She belongs to me—*to me*!

Hugging his secret, he soon found that there was no one to whom he could confide it, even had he wanted to. With the grain fleets docking safely in Puteoli and Ostia and the price of wheat down where it should be for this year at least, Antony had decided to remove himself back to Athens, and was taking Octavia and her brood with him. Octavia might have been the only person he could trust with this awful emotional dilemma, but she was transparently happy with Antony, and immersed in travel preparations. Both put her at risk of letting a confidence slip to her husband, who would crow and tease insufferably. Ha ha ha, Octavianus, you too can be ruled by your prick! Octavian could hear it now. So he waved the Antonian ménage off with his secret undivulged, and turned to wondering if Agrippa might prove to have words of wisdom about it when he reached Narbo, near the Spanish border and a month's journey from Rome.

His state of mind tormented him, for passion sat awkwardly upon one whose cerebral habits were coolly logical and emotions resolutely suppressed. Confused, fretting, yearning, Octavian lost his appetite for food and came near to losing his reason. The weight fell off him visibly, as if some furnace of hot air evaporated it, and he couldn't even begin to think in Greek. To think in Greek was a crotchet, something he did with iron determination because it was so hard. Yet here he was, with half a hundred communications to dictate in Greek, obliged to dictate in Latin with curt instructions to his secretaries to make their own translations.

Maecenas wasn't in Rome, perhaps just as well; which meant that it was Scribonia who, on the very eve of Octavian's departure for Further Gaul, nerved herself to say something.

She had been very happy throughout a tranquil pregnancy, and bore baby Julia quickly, easily. The little mite was undeniably beautiful, from her flaxen wisps of hair to her big blue eyes, too light ever to go brown as the months went by. Never remembering Cornelia as a joy, Scribonia settled to mothering her babe, more in love with her aloof, meticulous husband than ever. That he didn't love her was not a huge sorrow, for he treated her kindly, with unfailing courtesy and respect, and promised that, as soon as she had fully recovered from her parturition, he would visit her bed again. Next time let it be a son! she prayed, offering to Juno Sospita, Magna Mater and Spes.

But something had happened to Octavian on his way back to Rome from a visit to the legion training camps dotted around the old army city of Capua. Scribonia had her own eyes and ears to tell her this, but she also had several servants, including Gaius Julius Burgundinus, who was Octavian's steward and a grandson of Divus Julius's beloved German freedman, Burgundus. Though he always stayed in Rome as steward of the *domus Hortensia*, there were so many of his brothers, sisters, cousins, aunts and uncles in Octavian's clientele that some were always in attendance on their patron whenever he traveled. And, said Burgundinus, big with news, Octavian had gone for a walk in Fregellae and returned in a mood no one had ever seen before. A visitation from a god, was Burgundinus's own theory, but it was simply one of many.

169

Scribonia feared a mental malady, for the calm and collected Octavian was touchy, short-tempered and critical of things he usually ignored. Had she known him as well as Agrippa did, she would have seen all of it as evidence of self-detestation, and been right. As it was, she attempted to remind him that he needed his strength, therefore had to eat.

'You need your strength, my dear, so you have to eat,' she said at the specially delicious dinner she had chosen. 'You're off to Narbo tomorrow, and you won't be served any of your favorite dishes. Please, Caesar, eat!'

'*Tace*!' he snapped, and slid off the couch. 'Mend your ways, Scribonia! You're turning into a shrew.' He stopped, one foot off the ground as a servant struggled to buckle his shoe. 'Hmm! A good word, that! A true shrew, a *grue*-some shrew, a new shrew!'

From that moment until she heard the sounds of his departure the next morning, she didn't set eyes on him. Running, the tears streaming down her face, she was just in time to catch sight of his golden head as it disappeared into the gig, hood up against the rain, pouring down. Caesar was leaving Rome, and Rome wept.

'He went without saying goodbye to me!' she cried to Burgundinus, at her elbow, his face downcast.

He held out a scroll, looking anywhere but at her. '*Domina*, Caesar commanded that I give you this.'

I hereby divorce you.

My grounds are these: shrewishness, old age, bad manners, incompatibility and extravagance.

I have instructed my steward to move you and our child to my old *domus* at the Ox Heads near the Curiae Veteres, where you will reside and bring up my daughter as befits her exalted station. She is to be highly educated, not set to spin and weave. My bankers will pay you an adequate allowance, and you are to have the full use of your dowry. Bear in mind that I can put a stop to this generous settlement at any time, and will do so if I hear any rumors that your behavior is immoral. In that event, I will return you to your father and take custody of Julia myself, nor will you be let see her.

It was sealed with the sphinx. Scribonia dropped it from fingers grown suddenly numb, and sank onto a marble bench to sit with her head between her knees, fighting faintness.

'It is all over,' she said to Burgundinus, standing near.

'Yes, *domina*,' he said gently; he had liked her.

'But I did nothing! I am not a shrew! I am not any of those awful things he lists! *Old age*! I am not yet thirty-five!'

'Caesar's orders are that you be moved today, *domina*.'

'But I did nothing! I do not deserve this!'

Poor lady, you irritated him, thought Burgundinus, bound to dumbness by cliental ties. He will tell the whole world that you are a shrew so that he can save his own face. Poor lady! And poor little baby Julia.

Marcus Vipsanius Agrippa was in Narbo because the Aquitani had been giving trouble, obliging him to teach them that Rome still produced superlative troops and highly competent generals.

'I sacked Burdigala, but I didn't burn it,' he said to Octavian when that worthy arrived after a grueling journey that had seen him succumb to the asthma for the first time in two years. 'No gold or silver, but a mountain of good strong iron-tyred wagon wheels, four thousand excellently cooped barrels, and fifteen thousand able-bodied men to sell as slaves in Massilia. The vendors are rubbing their hands together in glee – it's been some time since the markets have had such first-class merchandise. I didn't think it politic to enslave any women or children, but I always can if you wish it.'

'No, if *you* wish it. Profits from slaves are yours, Agrippa.'

'Not during this campaign, Caesar. The males will fetch two thousand talents, and I have a better use for those than to put them in my purse. My needs are simple, and you will always look after me.'

Octavian sat up straighter, his eyes gleaming. 'A scheme! You have a scheme! Enlighten me!'

In answer, Agrippa rose to fetch a map and spread it out on his homely desk. Leaning over it, Octavian saw that it depicted in considerable detail the area around Puteoli, a hundred miles south-west of Rome, and Campania's chief port.

'The day will come when you have sufficient warships to put down Sextus Pompeius,' Agrippa said, keeping his voice carefully neutral. 'Four hundred ships, I estimate. But where is there a harbor big enough to shelter half that many? Brundisium. Tarentum. However, both those ports are separated from the Tuscan coast by the Straits of Messana, where Sextus lies in perpetual wait. So we cannot anchor our fleets in either Brundisium or Tarentum. Take the Tuscan Sea harbors: Puteoli is too congested by commercial shipping, Ostia is beset by mud flats, Surrentum is overcrowded by fishing boats, and Cosa has to be kept for steeling the iron sows from Ilva. Added to which, they are vulnerable to attack from Sextus, even if they could accommodate four hundred big ships.'

'I am aware of all this,' Octavian said tiredly; the asthma had sapped him. His fist came down on the map. 'Useless, useless!'

'There is an alternative, Caesar. I have been thinking about it ever since I started visiting shipyards.' Agrippa's big, well-shaped hand hovered over the map, its index finger on two little lakes near Puteoli. 'Here is our answer, Caesar. The Lucrine Lake and the Avernian Lake. The first is very shallow and its water is warmed by the Fields of Fire. The second is bottomless, with water so cold it must lead straight to the Underworld.'

'Well, it's very dark and gloomy, at any rate,' said Octavian, something of a religious skeptic. 'No farmer will fell the forest around it for fear of angering the *lemures*.'

'The forest must go,' Agrippa said briskly. 'I intend to join the Lucrine Lake to the Avernian by digging several big canals. Then I'll break down the dyke that keeps the sea from overflowing into the Lucrine Lake and flood it. The sea water will pass down the canals and gradually turn Lake Avernus salty.'

Octavian's face was a study in awe and disbelief. 'But . . . but the dyke was built atop the spit that separates Lake Lucrinus from the sea to make sure that the lake waters are exactly the right temperature and salinity to grow oysters,' he said, his mind fixed on the *fiscus*. 'To let in the sea would utterly destroy the oyster beds – Agrippa, you'd have hundreds of oyster farmers howling for your citizenship, your blood and your head!'

'They can have their oysters back after we beat Sextus once and for all,' said Agrippa curtly, not a scrap concerned about ruining an industry that had been in existence for generations. 'What I pull down they can put up again later. If this is done as I envision it, Caesar, we'll have a huge expanse of calm, sheltered water in which to anchor all our fleets. Not only that, we'll be able to train their crews and marines in the art of sea battles without ever needing to worry about Sextus on a raid. The entry will be too narrow to get his ships in more than two at a time. And to make sure he can't lurk offshore waiting for us to come out two at a time, I'm going to build two big tunnels between Avernus and the beach at Cumae. Our ships can row through those tunnels with impunity and emerge to take Sextus on the flank.'

The realization broke on Octavian with the shock of immersion in icy water. 'You are Caesar's equal,' he said slowly, so dazed that he forgot to call his adoptive father Divus Julius. 'That is a Caesarean plan, a masterpiece of engineering.'

'I, Divus Julius's equal?' Agrippa looked astonished. 'No, Caesar, the idea is common sense and the execution a matter of hard work, not engineering genius. Going from one shipyard to the next, I've had a lot of time to think. And one thing I overlooked is the fact that ships can't propel themselves. Certainly we'll have some established, fully crewed fleets, but perhaps two-thirds will be new vessels without crews. Most of the galleys I've commissioned are fives, though I've taken threes from yards not equipped to build something close to two hundred feet long and twenty-five feet in the beam.'

'Quinqueremes are very clumsy,' Octavian said, revealing that he was not a complete ignoramus when it came to war galleys.

'Yes, but fives have a size advantage and can carry *two* nasty beaks of solid bronze. I've gone for the modified five – no more than two men to an oar in three banks – two, two, and one. Ample deck space for a hundred marines as well as catapults and ballistas. At an average of thirty banks to a side, that's three hundred oarsmen per vessel. Plus thirty sailors.'

'I begin to see your problem. But of course you have solved it. Three hundred times three hundred oarsmen – a total of ninety thousand. Also forty-five thousand marines and twenty thousand sailors.' Octavian stretched like a contented cat. 'I am no general of troops or admiral of fleets, but I am a master of the fine Roman science of logistics.'

'So you'd rather have a hundred and fifty marines per ship than a hundred?'

'Oh, I think so. Swarm over the enemy like ants.'

'Twenty thousand men will do me to start,' said Agrippa. 'I mean to start by building the harbor, and for that, someone can press ex-slaves wandering around Italia in search of *latifundia* that your land commissioners have not broken up for veterans. I'll pay them out of my slave sale profits, feed and house them too. If they're any good, they can train as oarsmen later on.'

'Incentive employment,' Octavian said with a smile. 'That's clever. The poor wretches haven't the wherewithal to go home, so why not offer them shelter and full bellies? Sooner or later they drift to Lucania and become bandits. This way is better.' He clicked his tongue. 'It's going to be slow; much slower than I had hoped. How long, Agrippa?'

'Four years, Caesar, including the one coming but not the one just going.'

'Sextus will never adhere to the pact for a third of that.' The thick gold lashes fell, hiding the eyes. 'Especially now I've divorced Scribonia.'

'*Cacat!* Why?'

'She's such a shrew I can't bear living with her. Whatever I want, she doesn't. So she nags. Nag, nag, nag.'

Agrippa's shrewd gaze never swerved from Octavian's face. So the wind's changed direction, has it? Blowing now from a quarter I can't recognize. Caesar's plotting, the signs are unmistakable. Only what's he plotting that requires the divorce of Scribonia? Shrewish? A nagger? Not in a fit, Caesar. You can't fool me.

'I'll need several men to supervise work on the lakes,' he said. 'Do you mind if I choose them? Probably army engineers from my own legions. But they'll need protecting by someone with clout. A propraetor, if you have one spare.'

'No, I have a proconsul spare.'

'A proconsul? Not Calvinus, alas. A pity you sent him to Spain. He'd be ideal.'

'He's needed in Spain. Mutinous troops.'

'I know. The trouble there started with Sertorius.'

'Sertorius was over thirty years ago! How is he to blame?'

'He enlisted the local peoples and taught them to fight like Romans. So now the Spanish legions are mostly that – Spanish. A fierce lot, but they don't drink in Roman discipline with their mother's milk. One reason I'll not try the same experiment in the Gauls, Caesar. But getting back to the subject, who?'

'Sabinus. Even if there was a province begging for a new governor – which there isn't – Sabinus doesn't want it. He wants to stay in Italia and participate in fleet manoeuvres when they happen.' He grinned briefly. 'It won't be uplifting listening to him when he discovers that's four years off. I wouldn't trust him with legions, but I think he'll make an excellent supervisor of engineers for Portus Julius. That's what we'll call your harbor.'

Agrippa laughed. 'Poor Sabinus! He'll never live it down, that one bungled battle while Caesar was conquering Further Gaul.'

'He was self-important then, and he's self-important now. I'll send him to you for a thorough grounding in what has to be done. Will you be here in Narbo?'

'Not unless he's quick, Caesar. I'm going to Germania.'

'Agrippa! Seriously?'

'Very. The Suebi are boiling and they've grown used to the sight of what's left of Caesar's bridge across the Rhenus. Not that I'm going to use it. I'm going to build my own bridge, and farther upstream. The Ubii are eating out of my hand, so I don't want them or the Cherusci to take alarm. Therefore I'll dive into pure Suebi country.'

'And into the forest?'

'No. I could, but the troops are afraid of the Bacenis – too dark and gloomy. They think there's a German behind every tree, not to mention bears, wolves and aurochs.'

'And is there? Are there?'

'Behind some, at any rate. Fear not, Caesar, I'll be careful.'

Since it was politic that Caesar's heir show himself to the Gallic legions, Octavian stayed long enough to visit every one of the six legions camped around Narbo, walking among the soldiers and giving them Caesar's old smile; many of them were veterans of the Gallic wars, enlisted yet again from sheer boredom at civilian life.

That has to stop, Octavian thought as he made his rounds, his right hand feeling like pulp from so many hearty handshakes. Some of these men have become considerable landowners from a dozen enlistments; they are discharged, they collect their ten *iugera* each, and a year later they're back for another campaign. In, out, in, out, each time accumulating more land. Rome has to have a standing army, its men enlisted to serve for twenty years without discharge. Then, at the end, they will receive a monetary pension rather than land. Italia is only so big, and settling them in the Gauls or Spains or Bithynia or wherever doesn't please them; they are Romans, and long for an old age at home. My divine father settled the Tenth around Narbo because they mutinied, but where are those men now? Why, in Agrippa's legions.

An army should be where the dangers are, ready to fight in a *nundinum*. No more of this sending praetors to recruit, equipping and training troops in a tremendous hurry around Capua, then sending them on a thousand-mile march to face the enemy at once. Capua will continue to be the training ground, yes, but the moment a soldier is satisfactory, he ought to go immediately to some frontier to join a legion already there. Gaius Marius threw the legions open to enlistment of pauper Head Count – oh, how the *boni* hated him for that! To the *boni* – the good men – Head Count paupers had nothing to defend: not land nor property. But Head Count soldiers turned out to be even braver than the old propertied men, and now Rome's legions are exclusively composed of the Head Count. Once the *proletarii* had had nothing to give Rome save children; now they gave Rome their valor and their lives. A brilliant move, Gaius Marius!

Divus Julius was an odd one. His legionaries worshipped him long before he was deified, but he never bothered to initiate the changes the army was crying for. He didn't even think of it as an army, he thought of it as legions. And he was a constitutional man, one who disliked changing the constitution, the *mos maiorum*, for all that the *boni* said to the contrary. But Divus Julius had been wrong about the *mos maiorum*.

A new *mos maiorum* is long overdue. The phrase may mean the way things have always been done, but people's memories are short, and a new *mos maiorum* will soon turn into a hallowed relic. It's time for a different political structure, one more suited to rule a far-flung empire. Can I, Caesar Divi Filius, let myself be held to ransom by a handful of men determined to strip me of my political power? Divus Julius let that happen to him, had to cross the Rubicon into rebellion to save himself. But a good *mos maiorum* would never have let Cato Uticensis, the Marcelli and Pompeius Magnus push my divine father into outlawry. A good *mos maiorum* would have protected him, for he did nothing that that puffed-up toad Pompeius Magnus hadn't done a dozen times. It was a classic case of one law for this man, Magnus, but another law for that man, Caesar. Caesar's heart had broken at the stain on his honor, just as it broke when the Ninth and Tenth mutinied. Neither would have happened if he had kept a closer eye on and more control of everything from his insane political opponents to his shiftless relatives. Well, that is not going to happen to me! I am going to change the *mos maiorum* and the way Rome is governed to suit me and my needs. I will not be outlawed. I will not wage civil war. What I have to do will be done legally.

He spoke of all that to Agrippa over dinner on his last day in Narbo, but he didn't discuss his divorce, or Livia Drusilla, or the dilemma of choice facing him. For he could see as in the full flush of a summer sun that Agrippa must be kept apart from his emotional tribulations. They were a burden unsuited to Agrippa, who was not his twin or his divine father, but the military and civil executive of his own creating. His invincible right arm.

So he kissed Agrippa on both cheeks and climbed into his gig for the long journey home, made even longer by his resolution to visit every other legion in Further Gaul. They must all see and meet Caesar's heir, they must all be bound to him personally. For who knew where or when he would need their allegiance?

Even with that punishing schedule, he was home again well before the end of the year, his priorities mentally assembled in definite order, some of them extremely urgent. But first on his list was Livia Drusilla. Only with that matter settled would he be able to bend his mind to more important things. For in and of itself it was not an important thing; it owed its power only to a weakness in him, a deficiency he couldn't fathom, and had given up trying to. Therefore, get it over and done with.

Maecenas was back in Rome, happily married to his Terentia, whose great-aunt, the formidably ugly widow of the august Cicero, thoroughly approved of such a charming man from such a good family. Having been some years older than Cicero, she was past seventy now, but still controlled her enormous fortune with an iron hand and an encyclopedic knowledge of religious laws permitting her to wriggle out of paying taxes. Caesar's civil war against Pompey the Great had seen her family scattered and ruined; the only one left alive was her son, an irascible drunkard whom she despised. So there was room for a man in her tough old bosom, and Maecenas fitted himself there very comfortably indeed. Who knew? Perhaps one day he'd fall heir to her money. Though privately he informed Octavian that he was convinced she'd outlive all of them, and find a way to take her money with her when she finally went.

So Maecenas was available to do the negotiating with Nero; the only problem with that lay in the fact that Octavian still had not breathed a word of his passion for Livia Drusilla to a single soul, even Maecenas. Who would listen gravely, then proceed to try to talk him out of this bizarre union. Nor, given Nero's stupidity and intractability, would Maecenas enjoy his usual advantages. In his mind Octavian had equated his non-affair with the privacy of bodily functions; no one must see or hear. Gods did not excrete, and he was the son of a god who one day would be a god himself. There was much about the State religion that he dismissed as sheer claptrap, but his skepticism did not extend to Divus Julius or his own status, which he didn't think of in the Greek fashion. There was no Divus Julius sitting atop a mountain or dwelling in the temple Octavian was building for Divus Julius in the Forum; no, Divus Julius was a disembodied force whose addition to the pantheon of forces had augmented Roman power, Roman might,

Roman military excellence. Some of it pervaded Agrippa, he was sure of it. And much of it pervaded him; he could feel it surging through his veins, and had learned the trick of steepling his fingers to build the force ever higher.

Did such a man confess his weaknesses to another man? No, he did not. He might confess his frustrations, his trials, his bouts of practical depression. But never the weaknesses or flaws in his character. Therefore to use Maecenas was out of the question. He would have to conduct these negotiations himself.

On the twenty-third day of September each year he had his birth anniversary, and now had celebrated twenty-four of them. A fog had descended over the years just after his divine father's assassination; he didn't remember quite how he had marshaled the strength to embark upon his career, aware that some of his deeds were due to the folly of youth. But they had turned out well, and that was what he recollected. Philippi formed a watershed, for after it he remembered everything with crystal clarity. He knew why. In the aftermath of Philippi he had faced down Antony and won. A simple demand: the head of Brutus. That was when his future had unfolded before his mental gaze, and he had seen his way. Antony had given in after a performance that went from terrifying rage to bathetic tears. Yes, he had given in.

His encounters with Antony hadn't been numerous since, but at each of them he had found himself stronger, until, at the last such, he had spoken his mind without even the faintest falter in his breathing. He wasn't Antony's equal anymore; he was Antony's superior. Perhaps because Divus Julius had never managed to break him, Cato Uticensis came into his mind, and he knew at last what Divus Julius had always known: that no one can break a man who has no idea he owns an imperfection. Take Cato Uticensis out of the equation, and you had . . . Tiberius Claudius Nero. Another Cato, but a Cato without an intellect.

Octavian went to call on Nero at an hour of the short morning that would see him arrive after the last of Nero's clients had gone, but before Nero himself could sally forth to sniff the damp winter air and see what was going on in the Forum. Had Nero been a lawyer of repute, he might have been defending some noble villain against accusations of peculation or fraud, but his advocacy was not prized; he would act for his friends in the fourth or fifth position if they asked, but none had recently. His circle was small, comprised of ineffectual aristocrats like himself, and most of it had followed Antony to Athens, preferring that to living in Octavian's Rome of taxes and riots.

It would have given Nero untold satisfaction to have declined to see this unwelcome caller, but civility said that he ought, and punctiliousness said that he must.

'Caesar Octavianus,' he said stiffly, rising to his feet, but not moving from behind his desk, or extending a hand. 'Pray be seated.' He did not offer wine or water, simply sank back into his chair and gazed at that detested face, so smooth, appallingly young. It reminded him that he was now in his mid-forties and had not yet been consul; he had been praetor the year of Philippi, no help to anyone's career, least of all his. If he couldn't mend his fortunes, he would never be consul, for to get himself elected would take massive bribes. Nearly a hundred men were standing for the praetorship next year and the Senate was talking of letting sixty or more actually hold office; that would release a flood of ex-praetors to contest every consulship for the next generation.

'What do you want, Octavianus?' he asked.

Out with it: best so. 'I want your wife.'

An answer that left Nero bereft of words; dark eyes wide, he gaped and gobbled, choked, had to get clumsily to his feet and run for the water jug. 'You jest,' he said then, chest heaving.

'Absolutely not.'

'But . . . but that's ridiculous!' Then the implications of the request began to sink in. Mouth tight, he returned to his desk to sit down again, hands clenched around the homely contours of a cheap pottery beaker; his set of gilt goblets and flagons had vanished. 'You want my wife?'

'Yes.'

'That she's unfaithful is bad enough, but with *you* . . . !'

'She hasn't been unfaithful. I've only met her once, in the ruins of Fregellae.'

Deciding that Octavian's request wasn't carnal, but rather a mystery, Nero asked, 'What do you want her for?'

'Marriage.'

'She *has* been unfaithful! The child is yours! I curse her, I curse her, the *cunnus*! Well, you'll not get her the easy way, you filthy prick! Out my door she goes, her disgrace spread far and wide!' The beaker spilled, the hands that held it shaking.

'She is innocent of any transgression, Nero. As I've said, I met her only the once, and from start to finish of that encounter she behaved with complete decorum – such exquisite manners! You chose well in your wife. Which is why I want her as my wife.'

Something in the usually opaque eyes said that Octavian spoke the truth; his cerebral apparatus already taxed to its limits, Nero resorted to logic. 'But people don't just go around asking men for their wives! It's ludicrous! What do you expect me to say? I don't *know* what to say! You can't be serious! This sort of thing just isn't *done!* You do have a trace of noble blood, Octavianus, you ought to know it isn't done!'

Octavian smiled. 'As I understand it,' he said in ordinary tones, 'a senescent Quintus Hortensius once went around to Cato Uticensis and asked if he could marry Cato's daughter, a child at the time. Cato said no, so he asked for one of Cato's nieces. Cato said no, so he asked for Cato's wife. And Cato said yes. Wives, you see, are not of the same blood, though I admit yours is. That wife was Marcia, who was my stepsister. Hortensius paid through the nose for her, but Cato wouldn't take a bronze farthing. The money went entirely to my stepfather, Philippus, chronically short of cash. An Epicure of the most expensive kind. Perhaps if you viewed my request in the same light as Cato did Hortensius's, it would make it more credible. If you prefer, believe that, like Hortensius, I was visited by a dream Jupiter who said I must marry your wife. Cato found that a reasonable reason. Why shouldn't you?'

A new thought had dawned on Nero as he listened to this: he was playing host to a madman! Quiet enough at the moment, but who knew when he might erupt into utter mania? 'I'm going to call my servants and have you thrown out,' he said, thinking that, phrased thus, it didn't sound too incendiary, wouldn't provoke violence.

But before he could open his mouth to bellow for help, his visitor leaned across the desk and clasped his arm. Nero went as still as a mouse transfixed by the stare of the basilisk.

'Don't do that, Nero. Or at least, let me finish first. I am not mad, I pledge my word on that. Do I behave like a madman? I simply want to marry your wife, which necessitates that you divorce her. But not in disgrace. Cite religious reasons, everyone accepts those, and honor is preserved on both sides. In return for your yielding me this pearl beyond price, I will undertake to lighten your present financial difficulties. In fact, I'll conjure them out of existence better than a Samian magician. Come now, Nero, wouldn't you like that?'

The eyes looked suddenly away, focusing beyond Octavian's

right shoulder, and the thin, saturnine face took on an expression of cunning. 'How do you know I'm financially embarrassed?'

'All Rome knows,' Octavian said coolly. 'You should have banked with Oppius or the Balbi, you really should. The heirs of Flavus Hemicillus are a shifty lot, anyone save a fool could see that. Unfortunately you happen to be a fool, Nero. I heard my divine father say so on several occasions.'

'What is going *on*?' Nero cried, mopping up the spilled water with a napkin, as if in this trifling task he might banish the confusions of the last quarter-hour. 'Are you making fun of me? Are you?'

'Anything but, I do assure you. All I ask is that you divorce your wife immediately upon religious grounds.' He reached into the sinus of his toga and pulled out a piece of folded paper. 'They are detailed in this, to save your getting a headache thinking of some. In the meantime, I'll make my own arrangements with the College of Pontifices and the Quindecimviri regarding my marriage, which I intend to celebrate as quickly as I can.' He rose. 'Of course it goes without saying that you will have full custody of both your children. When the second one is born, I'll send it to you at once. A pity they won't know their mother, but far be it from me to block a man's right to his children.'

'Ah . . . um . . . ah,' said Nero, unable to assimilate the deftness with which he had been manoeuvred into all this.

'I imagine her dowry is gone beyond recall,' said Octavian, a trace of contempt in his voice. 'I'll pay your outstanding debts – anonymously – give you an income of a hundred talents a year, and help you bribe if you seek the consulship. Though I'm not in a position to guarantee you'll be elected. Even the sons of gods cannot dam the spate of public opinion effectively.' He walked to the door, turned to look back. 'You will send Livia Drusilla to the House of the Vestals as soon as you divorce her. The moment you've done that, our business is concluded. Your first hundred talents are already lodged with the Brothers Balbi. A good firm.'

And out he went, shutting the door quietly behind him.

Much of what had transpired was fading fast, but Nero sat and tried to make sense of what he could, which was chiefly to do with the alleviation of his money worries. Though Octavian hadn't said it, a healthy streak of self-preservation told Nero that he had two alternatives: tell the whole world, or be silent forever. If he talked, the debts would remain unpaid and the promised income would be withdrawn. If he kept his mouth shut, he would be able to take up his rightful position in Rome's highest stratum, something he prized more than any wife. Therefore he would be silent.

He opened the piece of paper Octavian had given him and conned the few lines of its single column with painful slowness. Yes, yes, this would salve his pride! Religiously impeccable. For it was dawning upon him that if Livia Drusilla were damned as an unfaithful wife, he would wear the horns of a cuckold and be laughed at. Old man with luscious young wife, along comes young man, and . . . Oh, that would *never* do! Let the world make what it would of this fiasco; he for one was going to behave as if nothing more salacious than a religious impediment had occurred. He drew a piece of paper forward and began to write out the bill of divorcement, then, the deed done, he summoned Livia Drusilla.

No one had thought to tell her that Octavian had visited, so she appeared looking exactly as she always did – submissive and demure, the quintessential goodwife. Beautiful, he decided as he studied her. Yes, she *was* beautiful. But why had Octavian's fancy alighted upon her? Upstart though he was, he could have his pick. Power drew women like moths to a flame, and Octavian had power. What on earth did she have that he had detected in one meeting, yet six years of marriage hadn't revealed to a husband? Was he, Nero, blind, or was Octavian deluded? The latter, it had to be the latter.

'Yes, *domine*?'

He handed her the bill of divorcement. 'I am divorcing you immediately, Livia Drusilla, on religious grounds. Apparently a verse in the new addition to the Sibylline Books has been interpreted by the Quindecimviri as pertaining to our marriage, which must be dissolved. You are to pack your belongings and go to the House of the Vestals at once. Naturally I will have sole custody of our son. When you've given birth to the one in your womb, it must be sent to me. That will acknowledge its paternity.'

Shock struck her mute, numbed her feelings, dazed her mind. But she stood her ground without swaying; the only outward sign of the blow was a suddenly pallid face.

'May I see the children?' she asked when she could.

'No. That would render you *nefas*.'

'So I must give up the one still in my womb?'

'Yes, the moment it is born.'

'What is to happen to me? Will you refund my dowry?'

'No, I will not refund your dowry or any part of it.'

'Then how am I to live?'

'How you manage to live is no longer my concern. I've been instructed to send you to the House of the Vestals, that is all.'

She turned on her heel and went back to her tiny domain, so cluttered with things she detested, from her distaff to her loom, used to spin thread to weave fabric no one ever wore, for she was not an adept at either craft and had no wish to be one. The place was smelly at this time of year; she was expected to bind bunches of dried fleabane to keep pests at bay, and she was *nundinae* behind because she hated the job. Oh, for the days when Nero had given her a few sesterces to hire books from Atticus's lending library! Now it had come down to spin, weave and bind.

The baby began to kick at her cruelly – his brother all over again. It might be an hour before he ceased his pummelling, getting his exercise at her expense. Soon her bowel would rebel, she would have to run for the latrine and pray no one was there to hear her. The servants considered her beneath their notice, smart enough to know that Nero considered her beneath his notice. Thoughts whirling, she sat on her weaving stool and looked through her window at the colonnade and the dilapidated peristyle garden beyond it.

'Keep still, you – you *thing*!' she cried to the baby.

As if by magic, the pounding ceased – why hadn't she thought of doing that before? Now she could start to think.

Freedom, and from a quarter no one could have dreamed of, least of all her. A verse in the latest Sibylline Book! She knew that fifty years ago Lucius Cornelius Sulla had commissioned the Quindecimviri to search the world for fragments of the partially burned Sibylline Books – what were fragments doing outside Rome? But she had always thought of this collection of abstruse couplets and quatrains as completely aethereal, having no relation to ordinary people or ordinary events. Earthquakes, wars, invasions, fires, the death of mighty men, the birth of children destined to save the world: that was what the prophetic books were all about.

Though she had asked Nero what she would live on, Livia Drusilla wasn't worried about that inside herself. If the gods had deigned to notice her – as clearly they had – and relieve her of this ghastly marriage, then they would not let her descend to soliciting men outside Venus Erucina's, or starve. The exile in the House of the Vestals must be a temporary thing; a Vestal was adlected at six or seven years of age, and had to maintain her virginity for the thirty years of her service, for her virginity represented Rome's luck. Nor did the Vestals take women in – she must be special indeed! What lay in the future she couldn't begin to guess, nor did she try to guess. It was enough that she was free, that her life was going somewhere at last.

She had a small trunk in which she packed her few clothes whenever she traveled; by the time that the steward came a short hour later to enquire if she was ready to make the walk from the Germalus of the Palatine down into the Forum Romanum, it was packed and roped, and she was wrapped in a warm mantle against the cold, the threatening snow. Shoes with high cork soles upon her feet to keep them out of occasional muck, she hurried as fast as the shoes let her in the wake of the servant hefting her trunk and complaining loudly of his woes to all and sundry. Getting down the Vestal Steps took some time, but after that it was a short, level walk past the little round Aedes Vestae to the side entrance of the Vestals' half of the Domus Publica. There a servant woman handed her trunk to a brawny Gallic woman, and led her to a room that held a bed, a table and a chair.

'The latrines and baths are down that corridor,' said the housekeeper, for such she was. 'You are not to dine with the holy ladies, but food and drink will be brought to you here. The Chief Vestal says that you may exercise in their garden, but not at an hour when they use it themselves. I am instructed to ask you if you like to read?'

'Yes, I love to read.'

'What books would you like?'

'Anything in Latin or Greek that the holy ladies deem suitable,' said Livia Drusilla, well trained.

'Have you any questions, *domina?*'

'Just one. Do I have to share the bath water?'

Three *nundinae* went by in a dreamy peace feathered by flakes of snow; understanding that her gravid presence must be against all Vestal precepts, Livia Drusilla made no attempt to see her hostesses, nor did any, even the Chief Vestal, come to visit her. She passed the time in reading, tramping up and down the garden and bathing ecstatically in clean, hot water. The Vestals enjoyed better facilities than Nero's *domus* had offered; the seats in their latrines were of marble, their baths were made of Egyptian granite, and their food was delicious. Wine, she discovered, was a part of the menu.

'It was Ahenobarbus Pontifex Maximus who refurbished the Atrium Vestae sixty years ago,' the housekeeper explained, 'and then Caesar Pontifex Maximus installed hypocaust heating in all the living areas as well as the record rooms.' She clicked her tongue. 'Our basement was given over to the storage of wills, but Caesar Pontifex Maximus worked out how to take enough of it to make the best hypocaust in Rome. Oh, how we miss him!'

A *nundinum* after the New Year, the housekeeper brought her a letter. Unfurling it and spreading it between two porphyry weights, Livia Drusilla settled to read, easy because of the dot above each new word. Why didn't Atticus's copyists do that?

To Livia Drusilla, love of my life, greetings. As this tells you, I, Caesar Divi Filius, did not forget you after we met at Fregellae. It took some time to work out a way to get you free of Tiberius Claudius Nero without scandal or odium. I instructed my freedman, Helenus, to search the new Sibylline Book until he found a verse that could be held as pertaining to you and Nero. Of itself, this was insufficient. He also had to find a verse pertaining to you and me, more difficult. The excellent fellow – I was so pleased to have him back in my fold after a year's imprisonment with Sextus Pompeius – is really a far better scholar than he is an admiral or a general. I am so happy to be able to write this that I feel like Icarus soaring up into the aether. Please, my Livia Drusilla, do not cast me down! The disappointment would kill me, if the fall didn't. Here is your and Nero's verse:

> Husband and wife, black as night
> Joined together are Rome's blight
> Sundered they must be, and swift
> Or Rome's forever set adrift

Yours and mine is roses in Campania by comparison:

> The son of a god, fair and gold of hair
> Must take as bride the mother of two
> Black as night, of a foundered pair
> Together they will build Rome anew

Do you like that? I did, when I read it. Helenus is a very clever fellow, an expert with manuscripts. I have raised him to the status of chief secretary.

On the seventeenth day of this month, January, you and I

are to be joined in wedlock. When I took the two verses to the Quindecimviri – I am one of the Fifteen Men – they agreed that my interpretation was the true one. All impediments and obstacles were swept aside and a *lex curiata* has been passed sanctioning your divorce from Nero and our union.

The Chief Vestal, Appuleia, is my cousin, and agreed to shelter you until we could marry. I have agreed that, as soon as Rome is on her feet, I will separate the Vestals from the Pontifex Maximus in their own house. I love you.

She removed the paperweights and let the scroll curl up, then got to her feet and slipped through her door. The stone stair to the basement wasn't far away; she scurried along the corridor to it and was down it before anyone saw her. In the Atrium Vestae all the servants were female and free women, including those who chopped the wood and fed it to the furnaces that turned it into charcoal. Yes, she was lucky! The stoking had been done, but it was not yet time to rake the glowing coals into the hypocaust, there to heat the higher floors. Like a shadow she approached the nearest furnace and thrust the scroll into its flames.

Now why did I do that? she asked herself when she was safe in her room, breathing hard from the effort. Oh, come, Livia Drusilla, you know why! Because he has chosen you, and no one must ever suspect that he has taken you into his confidence so early. This is a house of women, and everything is everyone's business. They would not have dared to break his seal, but the moment my back was turned, they would be there reading my letter.

Power! He will give me power! He wants me, he needs me, he will marry me! Together we will build Rome anew. The Sibylline Book speaks the truth, no matter whose pen wrote the verse. If my two verses are anything to go by, all the thousands of verses must be very silly. But no one has ever asked that an ecstatic prophet should be a Catullus or a Sappho. A well-trained mind can coin rubbish like that in a trice.

Today are the Nones. In twelve days I will be the bride of Caesar Divi Filius; I can rise no higher. Therefore it behooves me to work for him with might and main, for if he falls, I fall.

On the day of her wedding, Livia Drusilla finally saw the Chief Vestal, Appuleia. This awe-inspiring lady was not yet twenty-five years old, but that was how it sometimes went in the College of Vestals; several of the women reached the retiring age of thirty-five at much the same moment, leaving younger women as their successors. Appuleia could look forward to at least ten years as Chief Vestal, and was carefully molding herself into a gentle tyrant. No lovely young Vestal was going to be accused of unchasteness under *her* reign! The punishment if found guilty was to be buried alive with a jug of water and a loaf of bread, but it was a very long time since that had happened, for the Vestals prized their status and regarded men as more alien than a striped African horse.

Livia Drusilla looked up; Appuleia was very tall.

'I hope you realize,' said the Chief Vestal, looking grim, 'that we six Vestals have put Rome at peril by taking a pregnant woman into our house.'

'I do realize it, and I thank you.'

'Thanks are irrelevant. We have made the offerings and all is well, but for no one except the son of Divus Julius would we have agreed to shelter you. It is a mark of your extreme virtue that no harm has come to us or to Rome, but I will rest easier when you are wed and out of here. Had Lepidus Pontifex Maximus been in residence, he might have refused you succor at our hands, but Vesta of the Hearth says you are necessary to Rome. Our own books say that too.' She produced an evil-smelling, straight robe of a depressing pale brown. 'Dress now. The little Vestals have woven you this shift from wool that has never been fulled or dyed.'

'Where am I going?'

'Not far. Just to the temple in the Domus Publica that we share with the Pontifex Maximus. It hasn't been used for any public ceremony since Caesar Pontifex Maximus lay in state after his cruel death. Marcus Valerius Messala Corvinus, the senior priest in Rome at the moment, will preside, but the Flamens will be there, as will the Rex Sacrorum.'

Skin prickling uncomfortably from the dismal hairshirt, Livia Drusilla followed the white-clad form of Appuleia through the huge rooms where the Vestals toiled at their testamentary duties, for they had custody of several million wills belonging to Roman citizens all over the world, and could put their hands on a specific one within an hour.

A giggling Vestal about ten years old had done Livia Drusilla's hair in the six locks and placed a crown of seven coils of wool upon her brow. Over that went a veil that rendered her nine parts blind, so thick and coarse was it. No flame and saffron cloth fine enough to draw through the eye of a darning needle for this bride! She was dressed to marry Romulus, not Caesar Divi Filius.

Owning no windows, the temple was a tangle of blackness and pools of yellow light, terrifyingly holy and, so Livia Drusilla fancied, haunted by the shades of every man who had molded Rome's religion for a thousand years, right back to Aeneas. Numa Pompilius and Tarquinius Priscus lurked there arm in arm with Ahenobarbus Pontifex Maximus and Caesar Pontifex Maximus, watching silent as the tomb from the impenetrable darkness of every cranny.

He was waiting, and had no friends to attend him. She recognized him only from the glitter of his hair, a flickering focal point under a huge gold chandelier that must have held a hundred wicks. Various men in particolored togas stood far back, some clad in *laena* and *apex*, shoes without laces or buckles. Her breath caught as she finally understood; this was to be a marriage in the oldest form, *confarreatio*. He was marrying her for life; their union could never be dissolved, unlike an ordinary union. Appuleia's hands pressed her down upon a conjoined seat draped with a sheepskin while the Rex Sacrorum did the same to Octavian. Other people stood in the shadows, but who they were she couldn't see. Then Appuleia, acting as *pronuba*, flung a huge veil over both of them. Clad in the glory of a toga striped in purple and crimson, Messala Corvinus bound their hands together and said a few words in an archaic language Livia Drusilla had never heard before. Then Appuleia broke a cake of *mola salsa* in half and gave it to them to eat – a cloying unpleasantness of salt and dry spelt flour.

The worst part was the sacrifice that followed, a messy struggle between Messala Corvinus and a squealing, screaming pig that had not been properly drugged – whose fault was that, who didn't want this marriage? It would have escaped had it not been for the groom, who leaped from under the veil and grabbed the pig by one hind trotter, quietly laughing to himself. He was jubilant.

Somehow it was done. Those witnessing and verifying the act of *confarreatio* – five members of the Livii and five members of the Octavii – melted away when it was over. A faint cry of '*Feliciter*!' came on the heavy air, rank with blood.

A litter was waiting outside on the Sacra Via; she was put into it by men holding torches, for the ceremony had dragged on into the night. Livia Drusilla put her head on a soft pillow and let her eyelids fall. Such a long day for one entering her eighth month! Had any other woman ever been subjected to this? Surely it was unique in the annals of Rome.

So she dozed as the litter heaved and creaked its hilly way up onto the Palatine, and was deeply asleep when the curtains parted to admit the glare of torches.

'What? Where?' she asked, confused, as hands helped her out.

'You are home, *domina*,' said a female voice. 'Come, walk with me. A bath is ready. Caesar will join you afterward. I am the chief among your servants, and my name is Sophonisba.'

'I am so hungry!'

'There will be food, *domina*. But first, a bath,' Sophonisba said, easing her out of the smelly bridal regalia.

It is a dream, she thought, conducted to a huge room that contained a table, two chairs, and, pushed into the corners, three tattered, lumpy couches. Octavian came in as she sat on one of the chairs; he was followed by several servants bearing dishes and plates, napkins, finger bowls, spoons.

'I thought we'd eat country style, sitting at a table,' he said, occupying the other chair. 'If we use a couch, I can't look into your eyes.' His own eyes, gone gold in the lamplight, shone eerily. 'Dark blue, with little fawnish stripes. How amazing!' He reached out to take her hand, kissed it. 'You must be starving, so tuck in,' he said. 'Oh, this is one of the greatest days of my life! I have married you, Livia Drusilla, *confarreatio*. There is no escape from me, none.'

'I don't want to escape,' she said, biting into a boiled egg and following that up with a wedge of crisp white bread dipped in oil. 'Oh, I am starving!'

'Have a baby chicken. The cook basted it in honey and water.'

Silence fell while she ate and he made an attempt to, busy watching her and noting that she was a dainty eater with exquisite manners. And, unlike his ugly members, her hands were perfectly formed, fingers tapering to manicured oval nails; they floated when they moved. Lovely, lovely hands! Rings, she must wear superb rings.

'A strange wedding night,' she said when she couldn't fit in another morsel. 'Do you intend to bed me, Caesar?'

He looked horrified. 'No, of course not! I can't think of anything more repellent, for me as well as for you. There's time enough, little one. Years and years. First you must have Nero's child, and recover from that. How old are you? How old were you when you married Nero?'

'I am twenty-one, Caesar. I married Nero when I was fifteen.'

'That's disgusting! No girl should be married at fifteen – it isn't

Roman. Eighteen is the proper age. No wonder you were so unhappy. I swear that you won't be unhappy with me. You'll have leisure and love.'

Her face changed, became frustrated. 'I have had too much leisure, Caesar, that has been my greatest trouble. Reading and writing letters, spinning, weaving – nothing that *mattered*! I want a job of some kind, proper work! Nero kept few women servants, but the Atrium Vestae swarmed with women carpenters, plasterers, tilers, bricklayers, physicians, dentists – there was even a veterinarian who came to minister to Appuleia's lapdog. I envied them!'

'I hope the lapdog was a bitch,' he said, smiling.

'Definitely. Lady cats and lady dogs. Theirs is a lovely life in the Atrium Vestae, I think. Peaceful. But the Vestals have work to do, and, from what the housekeeper said, it obsesses them. Everyone of value must have work and, because I have none, I have no value. I love you, Caesar, but what am I to do when you aren't here?'

'You won't be idle, so much I promise you. Why do you think I married you, of all women? Because I looked into your eyes and saw the spirit of a true workmate there. I need a true helper by my side, someone I can trust, literally with my life. There are so many things I don't have time for, things better suited to a woman, and when we are lying together in our bed, I am going to ask for counsel from a woman – you. Women see things differently, and that is important. You are educated and highly intelligent, Livia Drusilla. Take my word for it, I intend to work you.'

Now it was her turn to smile. 'How do you know I have all those qualities? A look into my eyes that didn't see their stripes hints at baseless assumptions.'

'I was too busy with your spirit to see physical things.'

'Yes, I understand that.'

Octavian got up hastily, then sat down again. 'I was going to lead you to lie on that couch – you must be exhausted,' he said. 'But it wouldn't rest your bones, it would punish them. So that's your first job, Livia Drusilla. Furnish this basilica of a place as befits the First Man in Rome.'

'But it isn't women's work to buy furniture! That is the man's privilege.'

'I don't care whose privilege it is, I don't have the time.'

Visions of color schemes and styles were crowding into her head; she beamed. 'How much money may I spend?'

'As much as it needs. Rome is poor and I've spent much of my inheritance alleviating her woes, but I'm not a pauper yet. Citrus wood, chryselephantine, ebony, enamels, Carrara marble . . . whatever you like.' Suddenly he seemed to remember something, and did get to his feet. 'I'll be back in a moment,' he said.

When he returned he was carrying something wrapped in a red cloth, put it on the table. 'Open it, my beloved wife. It's your wedding gift.'

A necklace and earrings lay within the cloth, of pearls the color of moonlight, seven strings connected to a pair of gold plates that rested on the back of the neck and hooked together. The earrings each had seven pearl tassels linked to a gold plate that rested on the ear lobe, a hook welded to its back.

'Oh, Caesar!' she breathed, entranced. 'They're *beautiful*!'

He grinned, delighted at her delight. 'As I'm rather noted for my parsimony, I won't tell you how much they cost, but I was lucky. Faberius Margarita had just got them in. The pearls are so perfectly matched that he thinks it was made for a queen – Egypt or Nabataea, probably, since they bring the pearls from Taprobane. But this never adorned a royal neck or royal ears, because it was stolen. Probably quite a long time ago. Faberius found it in Cyprus and bought it for – well, not quite as much as I paid for it, but not cheaply, at any rate. I give it to you because old Faberius and I both believe no one has ever worn it, or prized it. Therefore it is yours to wear as its first owner, *meum mel*.'

She let him link the pearls around her neck, slip the hooks through the holes in her ears, then stood and let him admire her, so filled with joy that she couldn't speak. Servilia's strawberry pearl paled into insignificance when compared to this – seven whole strands! Old Clodia had a necklace with two strands, but not even Sempronia Atratina could boast more than three.

'Bedtime,' he said then, briskly, and took her elbow. 'You have your own suite of rooms, but if you prefer a different one – I don't know what kind of view you like – just tell Burgundinus, our steward. Do you like Sophonisba? Will she do?'

'I'm straying in the Elysian Fields,' she said, allowing him to guide her. 'So much trouble and expense on my behalf! Caesar, I looked at you and loved you, but now I know that every day that I am with you will see me love you more.'

PART III

Victories and Defeats

39–37 B.C.

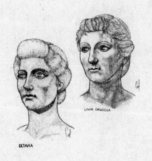

OCTAVIA   LIVIA DRUSILLA

ELEVEN

Publius Ventidius was a Picentine from Asculum Picentum, a big walled city on the Via Salaria, the old salt road that connected Firmum Picenum with Rome. Six hundred years ago the peoples of the Latin plain had learned to mine salt from the flats of Ostia; salt was a scarce and highly marketable commodity. Very soon the trade passed into the hands of merchants living in Rome, a tiny city on the Tiber River fifteen miles upstream from Ostia. Historians like Fabius Pictor stated categorically that it was salt that made Rome the biggest city in Italia, and its people the most powerful.

Be that as it may, when Ventidius was born into a wealthy and aristocratic Asculan family the year before Marcus Livius Drusus was assassinated, Asculum Picentum had become the hub of southern Picenum. Set in a valley between the foothills and the high peaks of the Apennines, well protected by its towering walls from raids by the Marrucini and the Paeligni, the neighboring Italian tribes, Asculum was the center of a prosperous area of apple, pear and almond orchards, which meant it also sold excellent honey, as well as jam made from what fruit was not suitable to be sent fresh to the Forum Holitorium in Rome. Its women ran a cottage industry producing fine fabrics in a particularly fetching shade of blue obtained from a flower peculiar to the region.

But Asculum became notorious for quite a different reason: it was here that the first atrocity of the Italian War was committed when the inhabitants, fed up with being discriminated against by a small number of resident Roman citizens, slaughtered two hundred resident Romans and a visiting Roman praetor at a performance of a Plautus play. When two legions under Divus Julius's uncle, Sextus Caesar, arrived to exact punishment, it shut its gates and underwent a two-year siege. Sextus Caesar died of a lung complaint during a very cold winter, and was succeeded by Gnaeus Pompeius Strabo Carnifex. This cross-eyed Picentine warlord was proud of the achievements that had earned him the nickname of the Butcher, but was to be eclipsed by his son, Pompey the Great. Accompanied by his seventeen-year-old son and his son's friend Marcus Tullius Cicero, Pompey Strabo proceeded to demonstrate that he utterly lacked mercy. He devised a way to divert the city's water supply, which was obtained from an aquifer layer beneath the bed of the Truentius River. But submission wasn't nearly enough for Pompey Strabo, bent on teaching the Asculans that they couldn't murder a Roman praetor by tearing him literally into small pieces. He flogged and beheaded every male Asculan between the ages of fifteen and seventy, an exercise in logistics that was hard to solve. Having left five thousand headless bodies to rot in the marketplace, Pompey Strabo then drove thirteen thousand women, children and old men out of the city and into the teeth of a bitter winter without food or warm clothing. It was after this orgy of butchery that Cicero, sickened beyond measure, transferred to the service of Sulla in the southern theater of the war.

Little Ventidius was four years old, and was spared the fate of his mother, grandmother, aunts and sisters, all of whom perished in the Apennine snows. For he was one of a number of very young boys whom Pompey Strabo saved to walk in his triumph – a triumph that scandalized men of decency in Rome. Triumphs were supposed to be held for victories over foreign foes, not Italians. Thin, hungry, covered in sores, little Ventidius was pushed and prodded along that two-mile march from the Campus Martius to the Forum Romanum, then expelled from Rome to fend for himself. He was now five years of age.

But the Italians, be they Picentines or Marsi, Marrucini or Frentani, Samnites or Lucani, were of the same race as the Romans, and just as hard to kill. Stealing food when he couldn't beg it, Ventidius got as far as Reate, which was Sabine country. There a mule farmer named Considius gave him employment mucking out the stables of his brood mares. These sturdy horses of special blood-lines were mated with stud donkeys to produce superb mules that went for high prices to the Roman legions, which couldn't exist without top-quality mules at the rate of six hundred to the legion. That Reate was the center of this industry lay in its situation on the Rosea Rura, a bowl of perfect grazing grass; be it actual fact or mere superstition, everyone believed that mules raised on the Rosea Rura were better than any others.

He was a good little boy, wiry and strong, and worked himself to a standstill. With his mop of fair curls and a pair of bright blue eyes, Ventidius soon discovered that if he looked at the women of the establishment with a mixture of longing and admiration, he would get extra rations and blankets to cover himself when he slept in a nest of aromatic straw.

At twenty he was a big young man, heavily muscled due to hard labor, and remarkably knowledgeable about breeding mules. Cursed with a ne'er-do-well son, Considius promoted Ventidius to manage his estate while the son went off to Rome, there to drink, dice and whore himself to death. That left Considius with one child, a daughter, who had long fancied Publius Ventidius, and now was emboldened to ask her father if she could marry him. Considius said yes; when he died, he willed his five hundred *iugera* of the Rosea Rura to Ventidius.

Because Ventidius was as intelligent as he was hard working, he made a greater success of his muleteering than some Sabines who had been engaged in the industry for centuries; he even managed to survive those ten hideous years when the lake that fed Rosea Rura grass was drained to provide an irrigation canal for the strawberry farmers of Amiternum. Luckily the Senate and People of Rome regarded mules as more important than strawberries, so the canal was filled in and the Rosea Rura regained its fertility.

But he didn't really want to spend his life as a muleteer. When the Gadetanian banker Lucius Cornelius Balbus became Caesar's *praefectus fabrum*, responsible for supplying his legions, Ventidius cultivated Balbus and secured an audience with Caesar. To whom he confided his secret ambition: Ventidius wanted to enter Roman politics, reach the praetorship, and general armies.

'I'll be a mediocre politician,' he said to Caesar, 'but I know I can general the legions.'

Caesar believed him. Leaving his mule ranch to the care of his eldest son and Considia, he became one of Caesar's legates, and upon Caesar's death transferred his allegiance to Mark Antony. Now here it was at last, the great command he had dreamed of.

'Pollio has got eleven legions together, and doesn't need more than seven,' Antony said to him before he left Rome. 'I can give you eleven, and Pollio will donate you four of his. Fifteen legions and whatever cavalry you can rake up in Galatia should see you able to hold your own against Labienus and Pacorus. Choose your own legates, Ventidius, and remember your limitations. You are to conduct a containing action against the Parthians until I can finally get into the field myself. Leave the beating to me.'

'Then, Antonius, with your permission I'll take Quintus Poppaedius Silo with me as my chief legate.' Ventidius grinned, trying to conceal his elation. 'He's a good man, inherited his father's military skill.'

'Splendid. Sail from Brundisium as soon as the equinoctial gales have blown themselves out – you can't march the Via Egnatia, it's too slow. Sail to Ephesus and start your campaign by driving Quintus Labienus out of Anatolia. If you get to Ephesus by May, you'll have plenty of time.'

Brundisium had no objection to lowering its mighty harbor chain and allowing Ventidius and Silo to load their 66,000 men, 6,000 mules, 600 wagons and 600 field pieces aboard 500 hundred troop transports that had magically appeared at the harbor entrance from some undisclosed source. A part of Antony's hoard, probably.

'The men will be crammed in like sardines in a jar, but they won't have much opportunity to grumble about sailing all the way,' said Silo to Ventidius. 'They can do the rowing. We should fit everything in, even the artillery.'

'Good. Once we round Cape Taenarum the worst will be over.'

Silo looked anxious. 'What about Sextus Pompeius, who now owns the Peloponnese and Cape Taenarum?'

'Antonius assured me that he won't attempt to stop us.'

'I hear he's very busy in the Tuscan Sea again.'

'I don't care what he does in the Tuscan Sea, as long as he leaves the Ionian Sea alone.'

'Where did Antonius get so many transports? There are more here than Pompeius Magnus or Caesar managed to gather.'

'He collected them after Philippi and hung onto them, hauled them out of the water along the Adriatic shore of Macedonia and Epirus. A good many of them were beached around the Bay of Ambracia, where he's also got a hundred warships. In fact, Antonius has more warships than Sextus. Unfortunately they're coming to the end of their seagoing lives, shipsheds notwithstanding. He has a huge fleet at Thasos, and another in Athens. He pretends the Athenian one is the only one, but now you know that isn't true. I'm trusting you, Silo. Don't disappoint me.'

'My mouth is sewn shut, you have my oath on it. But why is Antonius hanging onto them, and why the secrecy?'

Ventidius looked surprised. 'Against the day when he goes to war with Octavianus.'

'I pray that day never comes,' said Silo, shivering. 'The secrecy means he has no intention of defeating Sextus.' He seemed puzzled, angry. 'When my father led the Marsi and then all the Italian peoples against Rome, transports and war fleets belonged to the State, not to individual commanders. Now that Italia and Rome are on an equal footing as far as entitlements go, the State is sitting on the back benches while its commanders occupy the front benches. There's something wrong when men like Antonius regard the property of the State as their private property. I'm loyal to Antonius and will remain loyal, but I cannot approve of the way things are.'

'Nor can I,' Ventidius said gruffly.

'It's the innocents will suffer if it comes to civil war.'

Ventidius thought about his childhood and grimaced. 'I suppose the gods are more prone to protect those rich enough to offer them the best sacrifices. What's a dove or a chicken compared to a pure white bull? Besides, it's better to be a genuine Roman, Silo, we both know that.'

A handsome man, with his father's unsettling yellow-green eyes, Silo nodded. 'Well, with Marsi in your legions, Ventidius, we'll win in the East. A holding action? Is that what *you* want?'

'No.' Ventidius looked scornful. 'This is my best chance at a decent campaign, so I intend to go as far as I can as fast as I can. If Antonius wants the glory, he should be here in my place, not keeping one eye on Octavianus and the other on Sextus. Does he think all of us, from Pollio to me, don't know?'

'Do you really think we can beat the Parthians?'

'We can have a good try, Silo. I've seen Antonius general, and he's no better than I am, if as good. Certainly he's no Caesar!' His ship slid over the submerged harbor chain and heeled into a northwest wind. 'Ah, I like the sea! Goodbye, Brundisium, goodbye Italia!' cried Ventidius.

In Ephesus the fifteen legions sat down in several immense camps around that port city, one of the most beautiful in the world. Its houses had marble façades, it boasted a huge theater, had dozens of magnificent temples, and the precinct of Artemis in her guise as fertility goddess, for which reason her statues showed her girdled from shoulders to waist with bulls' testicles.

While Silo went the rounds of the fifteen legions and kept a stern eye on training and drills, Ventidius found a rock with a natural seat in it and sat down to think in peace and quiet. He had noticed a detachment of five hundred slingers sent by Polemon, the son of Zeno, who was attempting to rule Pontus without official sanction from Antony.

After he paused to watch them practice, the slingers had fascinated Ventidius. Astonishing, how far a man with a very shallow leather pouch on a supple leather thong could throw a stone missile! More than that, the missile flew through the air at an amazing velocity. Hard enough to drive a Parthian horse archer from the battlefield? Now *that* was a question!

From the first day of planning this campaign, Ventidius had intended to be content with nothing less than a triumph. So he had fretted about the legendary Parthian horse archer, who pretended to flee the field and fired his arrows backward over his horse's haunches. With perfect logic, Ventidius had assumed that the bulk of the Parthian troops would be horse archers, who never ventured close enough to the infantry to be cut down. But perhaps these slingers . . .

No one had told him that Pacorus had pinned his success upon cataphracts: warriors in chain mail from head to foot mounted on big horses in chain mail from head to knees. Pacorus had no horse archers at all. The reason for this shocking lack of information about the enemy was thanks to Mark Antony, who hadn't asked for a report on the Parthian forces. Nor had any other Roman. Like Ventidius, everyone at Antony's side had simply assumed that the Parthian army was more horse archer than cataphract. Such had a Parthian army always been: why should this one be different?

Thus Ventidius sat and thought about slingers as he planned a campaign directed mainly at horse archers, who didn't run out of arrows anymore, even through the longest battle.

What if, wondered Ventidius, he was to rake up every slinger the East had, and train them to lob their missiles at the horse archers? No use turning a legionary into a slinger; he would elect flogging and beheading rather than doff his shirt of mail and pick up a sling instead of a *gladius*.

However, a stone wasn't a satisfactory missile. For one thing, slingers couldn't throw any old rock; they spent a great deal of precious time searching river beds for the right stones – smooth, rounded, about a pound in weight. And unless the stone hit a fragile part of the body, particularly the skull, it caused atrocious bruising but no lasting harm. An enemy fighter would be out of the battle, but healed enough to join battle several days later. That was the trouble with stones and arrows; they were clean weapons, and clean weapons rarely killed. The sword was a dirty weapon, caked with the blood of every body it had encountered, and veteran legionaries wiped their blades but never washed them. Its edges were kept sharp enough to split a hair; when it slid into flesh it carried poisons with it that would cause the wound to fester, perhaps kill.

Well, he couldn't make a festering sling missile, thought Publius Ventidius, but he could make a more lethal one. From his experience with field artillery, he knew that the biggest boulders did the most damage, not so much from their own massiveness but from their ability to shatter whatever they hit and send pieces of it flying. If the catapult or ballista was really efficient, it sent missiles at higher speed than an instrument whose rope spring was damp or hadn't been wound as tightly as possible. Lead. A pound of lead occupied a much smaller volume than a pound-weight stone of the hardest rock. Therefore it would gather momentum inside the sling pouch, which could be swung faster, and fly farther than a stone due to its velocity. And when it hit, it would change its shape, flatten or even develop a spine. Lead missiles were not unknown, but they were designed to be flung from small field artillery over the top of city walls, as at Perusia, and that was a blind exercise of debatable effectiveness. A lead ball thrown by an expert slinger at a specific target from, say, two hundred feet, might turn out to be extremely useful.

He had the legion artificers make a small number of pound-weight lead balls, warning them that, if his idea bore fruit, they would have to make thousands upon thousands of pound-weight lead balls; the chief artificer cunningly countered by suggesting that thousands upon thousands of pound-weight lead balls would be better contracted out to a private supplier.

'A private supplier will fleece us,' said Ventidius, manfully keeping a straight face.

'Not if I detail half a dozen legionary journeymen to weigh each ball and check it for humps, lumps and bumps, General.'

Having agreed to this arrangement, provided the chief artificer also supplied the lead and made sure it wasn't adulterated by the addition of a cheaper metal like iron, Ventidius carried a bag of lead balls to the slinger practice range, laughing to himself. You never could get the better of a resourceful, clever legionary, no matter how hard you tried or how senior your rank. They grew up much as he had done, hand-to-mouth, and they weren't even afraid of three-headed dogs.

Xenon, the chief of the slingers, was at his station.

'Try one of these,' said Ventidius, handing the balls over.

Xenon balanced the small object in the declivity of his sling and swung the weapon until it whistled. An expert flick, and the lead ball screamed through the air to land on the midriff of a bolster. Together they walked to inspect the damage; Xenon gave a squeak, too amazed to yell.

'General, look!' he said when he was able.

'I'm already looking.'

The missile hadn't punched a hole in the soft leather, it had torn an irregular, gaping aperture, and rested at the bottom of a moil of earth and gravel.

'The trouble with your bolsters,' said Ventidius, 'is that they contain no true skeleton. I suspect that these lead balls will behave differently when they hit something with a skeleton. Therefore we'll try the missile on a condemned mule.'

By the time the mule had been found, five hundred slingers were gathered as closely as possible around the test site; word had spread that the Roman commander had invented a new projectile.

'Rump facing the path of the ball,' Ventidius ordered. 'It will be used on fleeing horses about the mule's size. A horse down is an archer down. The Parthians may keep up the supply of arrows, but horses? I doubt there'll be many spare ones.'

The mule was so maimed that it had to be put out of its misery at once, its hide torn open, its nether innards mangled. When dug from the carcass, the missile was no longer a ball; it resembled a flattish dish with a ragged perimeter: the result, it appeared, of hitting solid bone on its way in.

'Slingers!' Ventidius hollered, 'you have a new weapon!'

Cheers went up from every side.

To Xenon he said, 'Send word to Polemon that I need fifteen hundred more slingers and a thousand talents of lead left over from his silver mines. Pontus has just become a very important ally.'

Of course it wasn't as simple as that. Some of the slingers found the smaller missile harder to throw, and some, hidebound, refused to see its excellence. But gradually even the most obdurate slingers grew expert in throwing lead, and swore by their new kind of weapon. Modifications to the sling pouch also helped, as use proved that a lead ball wore the flimsier slings out faster than a stone did.

At about the moment when content among the slingers was widespread, fifteen hundred extra slingers arrived from Amaseia and Sinope, with more expected from Amisus, farther away. No fool, Polemon counted on his generosity and speed paying big dividends later on.

Ventidius wasn't idle while sling training went on, nor was he entirely pleased. The new governor of Asia Province, Lucius Munatius Plancus, had installed himself at Pergamum, well to the north of Labienus's incursions, situated in Lycia and Caria. But a Pergamite in Labienus's pay sought Plancus out and convinced him that Ephesus had fallen and Pergamum was the next Parthian target. Flustered, not very brave, and prone to listen to false counsel, Plancus had packed up in a panic and fled to the island of Chios, sending word to Antony, still in Rome, that nothing could stop Labienus.

'And all this,' said Ventidius in a letter to Antony, 'while I was busy landing fifteen legions in Ephesus! The man is a dupe and a coward, and must *not* be dowered with troops. I have not bothered to contact him, deeming it a waste of time.'

'Well done, Ventidius,' said Antony's letter, arriving just as Ventidius and his army were about to march. 'I admit that I gave him the governorship to get him out from under my feet – a little like Ahenobarbus in Bithynia, except that Ahenobarbus is no coward. Let Plancus stay on Chios, the wine is superlative.'

When shown this reply, Silo chuckled. 'Excellent, Ventidius, except that we'll be leaving Asia Province without a governor.'

'I've thought of that,' Ventidius said complacently. 'Since Pythodorus of Tralles is now Antonius's son-in-law, I've summoned him to Ephesus. He can collect the tributes and taxes in *tata*-in-law Antonius's name, and send them to the Treasury in Rome.'

'Oooh!' said Silo, strange eyes wide. 'I doubt that will please Antonius! His orders are, directly to him.'

'No order that's been given to me, Silo. I am loyal to Marcus Antonius, but more loyal to Rome. Tributes and taxes exacted in her name must go to the Treasury. Similarly with any spoils we might collect. If Antonius wants to complain, he can do so – but only after we've beaten the Parthians.'

He was feeling his oats, Ventidius, for the leaderless thanes of Galatia had massed every horse trooper they could find and come to Ephesus eager to show this unknown Roman general what good horse troopers could do. Ten thousand of them, all too young to have perished at Philippi, and anxious to preserve their grassy plains from the depredations of Quintus Labienus, too close for comfort.

'I'm riding with them, but not headlong,' Ventidius said to Silo. 'It's your job to get the infantry on the road, quick-smart. I want no fewer than thirty miles a day from my legions, and I want them on the most direct route to the Cilician Gates. That is, up the Maeander and across northern Pisidia to Iconium. Take the caravan road from there to southern Cappadocia, where you'll pick up the Roman road that leads to the Cilician Gates. It's a five-hundred-mile march, and you have twenty days. Understood?'

'Completely, Publius Ventidius,' said Silo.

It was not the habit of a Roman commander to ride: most much preferred to walk, for a number of reasons. For one, comfort; a man on horseback had no relief for the weight of his legs, which hung down limply. For another, infantry liked their commanders to walk; it put them on the same level, literally as well as metaphorically. For a third, it kept the cavalry in their place; Roman armies were largely composed of infantry, more valued than horsed troops, which over the centuries had become non-Roman, an auxiliary force of Gauls, Germans, Galatians.

However, Ventidius was more used to riding than most, due to his career breeding mules. It tickled him to remind his loftier colleagues that the great Sulla had always ridden a mule, and that Sulla had made Caesar the God ride a mule when a young man. What he wanted was to keep a stern eye on his cavalry, led by a Galatian named Amyntas, who had been secretary to old King Deiotarus. If Ventidius was right, Labienus would retreat before such a large cavalry force until he found a place where his ten thousand Roman-trained infantry could beat ten thousand horse. Nowhere in Caria, or in central Anatolia; he could do it in Lycia and southern Pisidia, but to retreat in that direction would render his communications with the Parthian army tenuous. His instincts, and they were right, would lead him across the same ground Ventidius had outlined to Silo as the legions' route, but days ahead of the legions. Ten thousand horse on his heels would force him to flee too fast to keep his baggage train, loaded down with loot only ox wagons could carry. It would fall to Silo; Ventidius's job was to keep Labienus hurrying back toward Cilicia Pedia and a Parthian army just on the far side of the Amanus range, the geographical barrier between Cilicia Pedia and northern Syria.

There was only one way Labienus could pass from Cappadocia into Cilicia, for the immensely tall and rugged Taurus Mountains cut central Anatolia off from anywhere east of it; the snows of the Taurus never melted, and what passes there were lay at ten and eleven thousand feet, especially in the Anti-Taurus segment. Except for the Cilician Gates. It was at the Cilician Gates that Ventidius expected to catch up with Quintus Labienus.

The young Galatian troopers were at that exact age that produces the finest, bravest warriors: not old enough to have wives and families, not old enough to think of joining battle with the enemy as anything to be afraid of. Only Rome had managed to turn men older than twenty into superlative soldiers, and that was a mark of Rome's superiority. Discipline, training, professionalism, a secure, ineradicable knowledge that each man was a part of a vast, unbeatable machine. Without his legions, Ventidius knew he could not defeat Labienus; what he had to do was pin the renegade to one spot, make it impossible for him to negotiate the Cilician Gates, and wait for his legions to arrive. In trusting Silo, he was handing the coming battle over to Silo.

Labienus did the expected. His intelligence network had told him of the enormous force sitting in Ephesus, and when he heard the name of its commander, he knew he had to retreat from western Anatolia in a hurry. His booty was considerable, for he had touched places that Brutus and Cassius had not. Pisidia was full of shrines to Kubaba Cybele and her consort, Attis; Lycaonia full of temple precincts to deities forgotten to the rest of the world since Agamemnon had ruled Greece; and Iconium a town where Median and Armenian gods had temples. So he tried desperately to haul his baggage train along with him – an exercise in futility. He abandoned it fifty miles west of Iconium, its wagoneers too terrified of the pursuing Roman horde to think of stealing its contents. They fled, leaving the two-mile-long train of bellowing, thirsty oxen deserted. Ventidius paused only to free the beasts so they could find water, and trotted on. When, in the fullness of time, the loot made its way to the Treasury, it amounted to five thousand silver talents. No priceless works of art, but a great deal of gold, silver and gems. It would, he thought as his rump lifted and fell to the gait of his mule, be a fitting adornment at his triumph.

The country around the Cilician Gates was not good horse country; its forests of various kinds of pine grew too closely to permit of grass, and no horse would eat such redolent foliage. Each trooper carried as much fodder with him as he could, one reason why Ventidius hadn't hurried. But the troopers were crafty, gathered every tender fern shoot they could find; to Ventidius they looked like the *lituus* of an augur, finished on top with a curlicue. Between the fodder his army still had and the fern shoots, he estimated they could survive for ten days. Enough, if Silo was sufficiently tough to push his legions on at thirty miles a day. Caesar could always get more miles than that out of legionaries, but Caesar was unique. Oh, that march from Placentia to relieve Trebonius and the rest at Agedincum! And what gratitude, to kill the man who rescued you. Ventidius hawked, spat at an imaginary Gaius Trebonius.

Labienus had arrived at the top of the pass two days before and managed to fell sufficient trees to make a camp in proper Roman style, using the logs to make high walls, digging ditches around the periphery, and erecting towers at intervals atop the walls. However, his troops were Roman-trained, not Roman, which meant that there were faults in the camp design – cutting corners, Ventidius called it. When he arrived, Labienus made no attempt to come out from behind his fortifications and give battle, but Ventidius had not expected him to. He was waiting for Pacorus and his Parthians to come from Syria; that was the prudent thing to do. It was also a risky waiting game. His scouts would have found Silo and the legions, just as Ventidius's scouts by now had ascertained that there were no Parthians within several days' ride of the Cilician Gates. Farther east than that Ventidius did not dare send scouts. The most cheering fact was that Silo couldn't be too far away, judging from the speed at which Labienus constructed his camp.

Three days later, Silo and the fifteen legions came down the flanks of the Taurus; they had beaten the Parthian relief, still some distance away and obliged to climb from the coast at Tarsus, exhausting work for horses as well as men.

'There,' said Ventidius to Silo, pointing as they met; he had no time to waste. 'We build our camp above Labienus, and on rising ground.' He chewed his lip, came to a decision. 'Send young Appius Pulcher and five of the legions north to Eusebeia Mazaca – ten will be enough to fight in this country, it's too rugged for mass deployments of that size, and I don't have the room to make a camp square miles in area. Tell Pulcher to occupy the town and be prepared to march at a moment's notice. He can also report on the state of affairs in Cappadocia – Antonius is anxious to know whether there's an Ariarthrid capable of ruling.'

One didn't use horse troopers to build a camp; they weren't

Roman and they had no idea how to go about manual labor. Now Silo had come up he could go about erecting something that would give his soldiers shelter but not inform them that this was going to be a long stay. Labienus was worried enough to huddle within his walls and look up the scarred slope to where Ventidius's camp was growing rapidly; his only consolation was that, in taking the high ground, Ventidius had left him an escape route down into Cilicia at Tarsus. A fact of which Ventidius was equally aware, though not concerned. He preferred to chase Labienus out of Anatolia at this time; such a steep, stump-riddled site was no place for a decisive battle. Just a *good* battle.

Four days after Silo had arrived, a scout came to tell the Roman commanders that the Parthians had skirted around Tarsus and taken the road up to the Cilician Gates.

'How many of them?' Ventidius asked.

'Five thousand or thereabouts, general.'

'All archers?'

The man looked blank. 'No archers. They're cataphracts to the last man, general. Didn't you know?'

Ventidius's blue eyes met Silo's green, both pairs startled. 'What a cock-up!' Ventidius cried when the scout had gone. 'No, we didn't know! All that work with the slingers, and for nothing!' He braced himself, managed to look determined. 'Well, it will have to hinge on the terrain. I'm sure Labienus thinks we're fools to have offered him a chance at flight, but I'm now more committed to chopping up cataphracts than I am to his mercenaries. Call a meeting of the centurions for tomorrow at dawn, Silo.'

The plan was careful and meticulously worked out.

'I haven't been able to ascertain whether Pacorus is leading his army in person,' Ventidius said to his six hundred centurions at the meeting, 'but what we have to do, boys, is tempt the Parthians into charging us uphill without infantry support from Labienus. That means we line our walls and shout awful insults at the Parthians – in Parthian. I have a fellow who has written down a few words and phrases that five thousand men have to learn off by heart. Pigs, idiots, sons of whores, savages, dogs, turd eaters, peasants. Fifty centurions with the loudest voices will have to learn how to say "Your father is a pimp!" and "Your mother sucks cock!" and "Pacorus is a pig keeper!" – Parthians don't eat pork and regard pigs as unclean. The whole idea is to work them into such a rage that they forget tactics and *charge*. In the meantime

Quintus Silo will have opened the camp gates and broken down the side walls to let nine legions out in a hurry. It's your other job, boys, to tell your men not to be afraid of these big *mentulae* on their big horses. They come in like Ubii foot warriors, under and around the horses, and chop at horse legs. Once a horse is down, swing the sword at its rider's face or anywhere else not protected by chain mail. I'm still going to use my slingers, though I can't be sure they'll be of any help. And that's it, boys. The Parthians will be here tomorrow fairly early, so today has to be spent learning Parthian insults and talking, talking, talking. Dismissed, and may Mars and Hercules Invictus be with us.'

It was more than a good battle; it was a sweet one, an ideal blooding for legionaries who had never set eyes on a cataphract before. The mailed horsemen looked more fearsome than experience showed they actually were, and responded to the barrage of insults with a rage that overcame all common sense. Up the stump-spidered hill they came, shaking the ground, screaming their war cries, some of the horses falling needlessly as their riders crashed into stumps or tried to hurdle them. Their mail-clad opponents, tiny by comparison, issued out of the forest to either side of the camp and danced nimbly into a forest of equine legs, hacking, chopping, turning the Parthian charge into a frenzy of squealing horses and floundering riders, helpless against the blows that rained on faces and stabbed at underarms. A good thrust with a *gladius* penetrated belly mail, though it wasn't very good for the blade.

And, much to his delight, Ventidius discovered that the lead missiles flung by his slingers punched rents in the Parthian mail and went on to kill.

Sacrificing a thousand of his infantry to fight a rearguard action, Labienus fled down the Roman road into Cilicia, thankful to be alive. Which was more than could be said for the Parthians, cut to pieces. Perhaps a thousand of them followed Labienus, the rest dead or dying on the field of the Cilician Gates.

'What a bloodbath,' said an exultant Silo to Ventidius when, six hours after it began, the battle was over.

'How have we fared, Silo?'

'Oh, excellently. A few cracked heads that got in the way of hooves, several crushed under fallen horses; but, all up, I'd say about two hundred casualties. And fancy those lead bullets! Even chain mail can't stop them.'

Frowning, Ventidius walked the field, unmoved by the suffering all around him; they had dared the might of Rome, and found that a fatal thing to do. A number of legionaries were passing through the heaps of dead and dying, killing horses and men who would not survive. Few who stayed were lightly injured, but those who were would be gathered together and kept for ransom, for the cataphract warrior was a nobleman whose family could afford to ransom him. If no ransom came, a man would be sold into slavery.

'What do we do about the mountains of dead?' Silo asked, and sighed. 'This isn't country with topsoil beyond a foot or two, so it's going to be hard to dig pits to bury them, and the wood's too green to burn as pyres.'

'We drag them into Labienus's camp and leave them there to rot,' said Ventidius. 'By the time we come back this way, if come back we do, they'll be bleached bones. There's no habitation for many miles, and Labienus's sanitary arrangements are good enough to ensure that the Cydnus won't be polluted.' He huffed. 'But first, we search for booty. I want my triumphal parade to be a good one – no Macedonian imitation triumph for Publius Ventidius!'

And that remark, thought Silo with a secret grin, is a slap at Pollio, waging the same old war in Macedonia.

In Tarsus, Ventidius discovered that Pacorus had not been present at the battle, perhaps one reason why it had been so easy to work the Parthians into a furore. Labienus was still fleeing east across Cilicia Pedia, his column in wild disarray between the leaderless cataphracts and a few mercenary grumblers with the influence to stir up trouble among more placid infantrymen.

'We have to keep on his tail,' said Ventidius, 'but this time it's you can ride with the cavalry, Silo. I'll bring the legions on myself.'

'Was I too slow getting to the Cilician Gates?'

'*Edepol*, no! Confidentially, Silo, I'm getting too old for long rides. My balls are sore and I have a fistula. You'll fare better, you're much younger. A man nearly fifty-five is doomed to use his feet.'

A servant appeared in the doorway. '*Domine*, Quintus Dellius is here to see you, and asking to be accommodated.'

Blue eyes met green in another of those glances only close friendship and similar tastes permit; it spoke volumes, though not a word was said.

'Send him in, but don't worry about the accommodation.'

'My very dear Publius Ventidius! And Quintus Silo too! How nice to see you.' Dellius settled himself in a chair before he was offered one, and looked significantly at the wine flagon. 'A drop of something light, white and bright would be good.'

Silo poured, handed the goblet over as he spoke to Ventidius. 'If there's nothing else, I'll be about my business.'

'Tomorrow at dawn for both of us.'

'My, my, so much earnestness!' said Dellius, sipping, then pulling a face. 'Ugh! What is this piss, third pressing?'

'I wouldn't know because I haven't tried it,' Ventidius said curtly. 'What do you want, Dellius? And you'll have to put up at an inn tonight, because the palace is full. You can move in tomorrow and have the place all to yourself. We're off.'

Bridling indignantly, Dellius sat up straight and glared. Since that memorable dinner when he had shared Antony's couch two years ago, he had become so used to deference that he expected it even from crusty Military Men like Publius Ventidius. Now, to find it missing . . . His fawnish eyes encountered Ventidius's, and he went red; they glared contempt. 'Well, really!' he cried. 'That is the outside of enough! I have a propraetorian imperium and I *insist* that I be accommodated immediately! Throw Silo out if you've no one else to throw.'

'I'd not throw the meanest *contubernalis* out for a crawler like you, Dellius. My imperium is proconsular. What do you want?'

'I bear a message from the Triumvir Marcus Antonius,' Dellius said coldly, 'and I expected to deliver it in Ephesus, not in a rat's nest like Tarsus.'

'Then you should have moved faster,' Ventidius said without sympathy. 'While you've been bobbing around in a boat, I've been doing battle with the Parthians. You may carry a message from me to Antonius – tell him that we beat an army of Parthian cataphracts at the Cilician Gates, and have Labienus on the run. What's your message? Anything that exciting?'

'It isn't wise to antagonize me,' said Dellius in a whisper.

'Ask me do I care? Your message? I have work to do.'

'I am instructed to remind you that Marcus Antonius is most anxious to see King Herod of the Jews placed upon his throne as soon as possible.'

Incredulity was written large on Ventidius's face. 'You mean Antonius sent you all this way just to tell me *that*? Tell him I will be glad to put Herod's fat arse on a throne, but first I have to eject Pacorus and his army from Syria, which may take some time. However, assure the Triumvir Marcus Antonius that I will bear his instruction in mind. Is that all?'

Puffed up like an adder, Dellius lifted his lip in a snarl. 'You will rue this conduct, Ventidius!' he hissed.

'I rue a Rome that encourages suckers-up like you, Dellius. See yourself out.'

Ventidius departed, leaving Dellius to simmer. How dared the old muleteer treat *him* like that! For the time being, however, he decided, abandoning the wine and getting to his feet, the old nuisance would have to be suffered. He'd beaten a Parthian army and chased Labienus out of Anatolia – news Antony would love as much as he loved Ventidius. Whose comeuppance can wait, Dellius thought to himself; when I see my opportunity, I'll strike. But not yet. No, not yet.

Commanding his Galatian troopers with valor and shrewdness, Quintus Poppaedius Silo penned Labienus in halfway through the pass across Mount Amanus called the Syrian Gates, and waited for Ventidius to bring up the legions. It was November, but not very cold; the autumn rains hadn't come, which meant the ground was battle hard, battle worthy. Some Parthian commander had brought two thousand cataphracts up from Syria to aid Labienus, but to no avail. For a second time the mailed horse warriors were cut to pieces, but this time Labienus's infantry perished as well.

Pausing only to write a jubilant letter to Antony, Ventidius went on into Syria to find the Parthians absent. Pacorus had not been at the battle of Amanus either; rumor had it that he had gone home to Seleuceia-on-Tigris months ago, taking Hyrcanus of the Jews with him. Labienus had escaped, taken ship for Cyprus at Apameia.

'That will profit him nothing,' said Ventidius to Silo. 'I believe Antonius put one of Caesar's freedmen in Cyprus to govern on his behalf – Gaius Julius – um – Demetrius, that's it.' He reached for paper. 'Get this off to him at once, Silo. If he's the man I think he is – my memory grows muddled about anyone's Greek freedmen – he'll search the island from Paphos to Salamis very efficiently. Diligently, in fact.'

That done, Ventidius scattered his legions in several winter camps, and settled to wait for whatever the following year would bring. Comfortably ensconced in Antioch and with Silo in Damascus, he spent his leisure dreaming of his triumph, the prospect of which became ever more alluring. The battle at Mount Amanus had yielded two thousand silver talents and some nice works of art to decorate the floats in his parade. Eat your own arse, Pollio! My triumph will eclipse yours by miles.

The winter furlough didn't last as long as Ventidius expected; Pacorus returned from Mesopotamia with every cataphract he could find – but no horse archers. Herod turned up in Antioch with the news, apparently obtained from one of Antigonus's minions who had soured about the prospect of perpetual Parthian rule.

'I've established an excellent rapport with the fellow – a Zadokite named Ananeel who yearns to be High Priest. As I don't intend to be High Priest myself, he'll do as well as any other, so I promised it to him in return for accurate information about the Parthians. I had him whisper to his Parthian contacts that, having occupied northern Syria, you intend to lay a trap for Pacorus at Nicephorium on the river Euphrates because you expect him to cross it at Zeugma. Pacorus now believes this, and will ignore Zeugma, travel on the east bank all the way north to Samosata. I imagine he'll take Crassus's short cut up the Bilechas, isn't that ironic?'

Though he couldn't warm to Herod, Ventidius was fully shrewd enough to realize that this greedy toad of a man had nothing to gain by lying; whatever information Herod disgorged would be the truth. 'I thank you, King Herod,' he said, feeling none of the revulsion Dellius inspired. Herod wasn't a sycophant, for all of his obliging guise; he was simply determined to eject Antigonus the usurper and king it over the Jews. 'Rest assured that the moment the Parthian threat is no more, I'll help you get rid of Antigonus.'

'I hope the wait isn't too long,' said Herod, sighing. 'My women-folk and my betrothed are marooned atop the most hideous crag of rock in the world. I've had word from my brother Joseph that they're very low on food. I fear I can't assist them.'

'Would some money help? I can give you enough to travel to Egypt and buy supplies and transport there. Can you get it to this hideous crag without being detected leaving Egypt?'

Herod sat up eagerly. 'I can escape detection easily, Publius Ventidius. The crag has a name – Masada – and it's a long way down the Palus Asphaltites. A camel train going overland from Pelusium would avoid Jews, Idumaeans, Nabataeans and Parthians.'

'A fearsome list,' said Ventidius with a grin. 'Then, while I deal with Pacorus, I suggest you do that. Cheer up, Herod! This time next year will see you in Jerusalem.'

Herod managed to look humble and diffident, no mean feat. 'I . . . er . . . how do I . . . ah . . . apply for this grant of money?'

'Just see my quaestor, King Herod. I'll tell him to give you whatever you ask for – within reason, that is.' The bright blue eyes twinkled. 'Camels are expensive, I know, but I'm a muleteer by trade. I have a fair idea what anything with four feet costs. Just deal honestly with me, and keep the information coming.'

Eight thousand cataphracts emerged out of the northeast at Samosata, and there crossed the Euphrates while it was at its winter ebb. Leading in person this time, Pacorus struck west for Chalcis along the road that led to Antioch, through verdant country that offered him no challenge, country he knew well from his previous incursions. It had water and grass aplenty and, apart from a low mountain named Gindarus, the terrain was easy, relatively flat. Comfortable because he knew that every minor prince in the area was on his side, he approached the flank of Gindarus with his horsemen stretched out for miles behind him, grazing their way toward Antioch, which they didn't know was now in Roman hands again. Herod's agents had done their work well, and Antigonus of the Jews, who might have been expected to keep his channels to Pacorus open, was too absorbed in subjugating those Jews who still felt rule under the Romans was less alien.

A scout came galloping to inform him that a Roman army sat upon Gindarus, well dug in. A relief to Pacorus, summoning his cataphracts into battle order; he hadn't liked not knowing where the new Roman army was.

He repeated all the mistakes his subordinates had at the Cilician Gates and Mount Amanus, still imbued with contempt for foot soldiers faced with mailed giants on mailed horses. The mass of cataphracts charged uphill and into a rain of lead missiles that pierced their mail at a range beyond arrows; thrown into disorder, horses screaming from balls that crashed between their eyes, the Parthian vanguard foundered. At which moment the legionaries waded fearlessly into the fray, dodging among the milling horses to hack at their knees, drag the riders down to die with sword thrusts through their faces. Their long spears were useless in such a melee, their sabres still mostly sheathed. With no hope of getting his rearguard through the confusion in front of them, and no way to find the Roman flank, Pacorus watched in horror as the legionaries drew ever closer to his own position atop a small mound. But he fought, as did the men around him, defending his person to the last. When Pacorus fell, those of them who could rallied around his body on foot and tried to contend with genuine foot soldiers. By nightfall most of the eight thousand were dead, the few survivors riding hard for the Euphrates and home, leading Pacorus's horse as proof that he was dead.

In actual fact he wasn't when the battle ended, though he bore a fatal wound in his belly. A legionary finished him off, stripped him of his armor and took it to Ventidius.

'The ground was ideal,' Ventidius wrote to Antony, in Athens with his wife and her brood of children. 'I will have Pacorus's golden armor to display at my triumph; my men have hailed me imperator on the field three times, as I can testify should you require it. There was no point in fighting a holding action at any stage in this campaign, which progressed naturally into the series of three battles. Of course I understand that the conclusiveness of my campaign is no cause for complaint from you. Simply, it has given you a Syria safe and sound wherein to marshal your armies – including mine, which I will put into winter camp around Antioch, Damascus and Chalcis – for your great campaign against Mesopotamia.

'However, it has come to my ears that Antiochus of Commagene concluded a treaty with Pacorus that yielded Commagene to Parthian overrule. He also gifted Pacorus with food and provender, a fact that enabled Pacorus to drive into Syria unaffected by the usual problems besetting a large force of cavalry. Therefore in March I intend to lead seven legions north to Samosata and see what King Antiochus has to say about his treachery. Silo and two legions will proceed to Jerusalem to put King Herod on his throne.

'King Herod has been a great help to me. His agents spread misleading information among the Parthian spies, which enabled me to find myself that ideal ground while the Parthians were in full ignorance of my whereabouts. In him, I believe Rome has an ally worth his salt. I gave him a hundred talents to go to Egypt and buy provisions for his family and the family of King Hyrcanus, which he installed in some mountain retreat incapable of being taken. However, my campaign has yielded ten thousand silver talents in spoils, which are on their way to the Treasury in Rome even as I write. Once I have held my triumph and the spoils have been released, you will profit considerably. My own share, from the sale of slaves, will not be great, as the Parthians fought to the bitter end. I did collect about a thousand men from the army of Labienus, and have sold them.

'As regards Quintus Labienus, I have just had a letter from Gaius Julius Demetrius in Cyprus, who informs me that he captured

214

Labienus and put him to death. I deplore this last fact, as I do not think a mere Greek freedman, even one of the late Caesar's, has sufficient authority to execute. But I leave the final judgement in that to you, as I must.

'Rest assured that when I reach Samosata I will deal hard by Antiochus, who has forfeited Commagene's status as Friend and Ally. I trust this finds you and yours well.'

TWELVE

Life in Athens was pleasant, especially since Mark Antony had patched up his differences with Titus Pomponius Atticus, the most treasured Roman in Athens, witness his *cognomen* of Atticus, which meant Athenian at heart. Lover of Athenian boys would have been more to the point, but that was discreetly ignored by every Roman, even one as homophobic as Antony. In much earlier days Atticus had developed the discipline never to indulge his taste for boys anywhere save in homophilic Athens, where he had built a mansion and been very good to the city over the years. A man of great culture and a noted literatus, Atticus had a hobby that eventually earned him a lot of money: he published the works of famous Roman authors from Catullus to Cicero and Caesar. Each new opus was copied in editions that varied from several dozens to several thousands. A hundred scribes chosen for accuracy and legibility were comfortably housed in a building on the Argiletum near the Senate, busy these days on the poetry of Virgil and Horace. Tacked onto this scriptorium were premises that functioned as a lending library, a concept that had actually been invented by the Brothers Sosius, his rival publishers next door. Their career in publishing predated that of Atticus's, but they lacked his immense wealth and had to hasten more slowly; recently the late Brothers Sosius had produced political hopefuls, one of whom was attached to Antony as a senior legate.

In middle age Atticus had married a cousin, Caecilia Pilia, who bore him a girl, Caecilia Attica, his only child and heir to his fortune. A bout with the summer paralysis had left Pilia an invalid; she died shortly after the battle of Philippi, leaving Atticus to rear Attica on his own. Born two years before Caesar crossed the Rubicon, she was now thirteen years old, tenderly fathered by a sophisticate who never concealed any of his activities from her, believing that ignorance would only render her vulnerable to mischief-making gossip. Notwithstanding this, Atticus worried about his one chick now that she was attaining maturity – whom could he choose as her husband in five years' time?

Remarkable shrewdness and an uncanny knack of maintaining good relations with every faction in Rome's upper class had thus far ensured Atticus's survival, but upon the death of Caesar the world changed so radically that he feared for both his own survival and the welfare of his daughter. His one weakness had been sympathy for the more shady among Rome's matrons; it had led him to succor Servilia, the mother of Brutus and mistress of Caesar, Clodia, the sister of Publius Clodius and a notorious man-eater, and Fulvia, who had been the wife of no less than three demagogues in Clodius, Curio and Antony.

Sheltering Fulvia had almost caused his ruin, despite his power in the knight-run world of Rome's commerce; for a terrible moment it had looked as if everything from his grain importations to his vast *latifundia* in Epirus would go on the auction block to benefit Antony, but upon receipt of Antony's curt letter ordering him to abandon Fulvia, he did just that. Though in private he wept bitterly when she opened her veins, the fate of Attica and his fortune mattered more.

So when Antony arrived in Athens with Octavia and her nursery full of children, Atticus set out to ingratiate himself with both husband and wife. He found the Triumvir much calmed and soothed, and correctly laid the credit for that at Octavia's door. They were patently happy together, but not in the manner of younger newlyweds, who never wanted any company save their own. Antony and Octavia were eager for company, attended every lecture, symposium and function the Capital of Culture could offer, and entertained at home frequently. Yes, a year of marriage had improved Antony, in the same way that famous boor, Pompey the Great, had improved after he married Caesar's enchanting daughter, Julia.

Of course the old Antony still inhabited that Herculean shell – brash, hot-tempered, aggressive, hedonistic and *lazy*.

It was the last, Antony's laziness, that occupied most of Atticus's thoughts as he strolled down a narrow Athenian alley on his way to dinner with Antony in the governor's residence; it was April of the year in which Appius Claudius Pulcher and

Gaius Norbanus Flaccus were consuls, and (along with the rest of Athens) Atticus knew that the Parthians had been driven back to their own lands. Not by Antony, but by Publius Ventidius. In Rome people were saying that the Parthian incursions had simply fallen apart, crumbled so suddenly that Antony hadn't had time to join Ventidius in Cilicia or Syria. But Atticus knew better; nothing had prevented Antony from being where the military action was. Nothing, that is, except Antony's most fatal weakness: a laziness that led to perpetual procrastination. He seemed blind to the pace of events, comfortably telling himself that all would happen when *he* wanted it to. As long as Julius Caesar had been alive to push him, the weakness had not seemed so fatal and, after Caesar's murder, Octavian had pushed. But Philippi had been such a great victory for Antony that the weakness had suddenly mushroomed. Just as it had when Julius Caesar had left him in charge of all Italia while he went to Greece to fight Pompey the Great. And what had Antony done with this immense responsibility? Harnessed four lions to a chariot, assembled an entourage of magicians, dancing girls and clowns, and roistered heedlessly. *Work?* What was that? Rome ran herself; as the man in charge, he could do precisely what he wanted, which was to roister. Though it had no basis in reality, he seemed to believe that, since he was Marcus Antonius, everything would turn out the way he thought it should. And when everything didn't, Antony blamed everyone but himself.

Underneath Octavia's calming influence, he had not really changed. Pleasure ahead of work, always. Pollio and Maecenas had rearranged triumviral boundaries more sensibly, an act which should have completely freed Antony to lead his armies. But apparently he wasn't yet ready to do that, and his excuses were hollow. Octavian represented no genuine threat and, despite his protestations, he had enough money to go to war. His legions already existed, were properly equipped, and supplied with cheap grain by Sextus Pompey. So what had stopped him?

By the time he arrived at the governor's residence, Atticus had worked himself into the sour rage old men feel, and found to his dismay that he and Antony would be dining alone; pleading some illness in the nursery, Octavia had begged off. That meant she couldn't coax or cajole Antony into a good mood. Heart sinking, Atticus realized that it was going to be an uncomfortable meal.

'If Ventidius were here, I'd try him for treason!' was Antony's opening statement.

Atticus laughed. 'Rubbish!' he said.

Antony looked startled, then rueful. 'Yes, yes, I see why you say it's rubbish, but the war against the Parthians was *mine*! Ventidius exceeded his orders.'

'You should have been in the command tent yourself, my dear Antonius!' Atticus said with a snap. 'Since you weren't, what do you have to complain about when your deputy succeeded so well that he didn't even have many casualties? You ought to be offering to Mars Invictus.'

'He was supposed to wait for me,' Antony said stubbornly.

'Nonsense! Your problem is that you want two ways of life at one and the same moment.'

The fleshy face betrayed Antony's irritation at such blunt words, but the eyes lacked the red spark that blazed a warning of impending doom. 'Two ways of life?' he asked.

'Yes. The most famous man of our day strutting across the Athenian stage to a loud chorus of admiration – that's one. The most famous man of our day leading his legions to victory – that's the other.'

'There's lots to do in Athens!' Antony said indignantly. 'It's not I who is out of step, Atticus, it's Ventidius. He's like a boulder running downhill! Even now he's not content to rest on his laurels. Instead, he's taken himself and seven legions up the Euphrates to kick King Antiochus on the shins!'

'I know. You showed me his letter, remember? What Ventidius is or is not doing isn't the point. The point is that you're in Athens, not in Syria. Why don't you admit it, Antonius? You're a procrastinator.'

In answer, Antony bellowed with laughter. 'Oh, Atticus!' he gasped when he was able. 'You're impossible!' Suddenly he sobered, scowled. 'In the Senate I'd have to put up with couch generals criticizing me, but this isn't the Senate, and you're courting my displeasure.'

'I am not a member of the Senate,' Atticus said, incensed enough to have lost his fear of this dangerous man. 'A public career is open to criticism from all walks, including mere businessmen like me. I say again, Marcus Antonius, you are a procrastinator.'

'Well, perhaps I am, but I do have an agenda. How can I go any farther east than Athens when Octavianus and Sextus Pompeius are still up to their tricks?'

'You could squash both those young men, and you know it. In fact, you ought to have squashed Sextus years ago, and left Octavianus to his own devices in Italia. Octavianus is no real threat to you, Antonius, but Sextus is a boil that needs lancing.'

'Sextus keeps Octavianus busy.'

His temper snapped. Atticus leaped off the couch and came around to confront his host across the low, narrow table loaded with food, his normally amiable face twisted into fury. 'I am fed up with hearing you say that! Grow up, Antonius! You can't be the virtually absolute ruler of half the world and think like a schoolboy!' He clenched his fists and shook them. 'I've wasted a great deal of my precious time in trying to work out what's the matter with you, why you can't act like a statesman. Now I know. You're pig-headed, idle, and not nearly as intelligent as you believe you are! A better organized world would never have made you its master!'

Jaw dropped, too stunned to speak, Antony watched him gather up his shoes and toga and stalk toward the door. Then he too leaped off the couch, reached Atticus in time to halt his progress.

'Titus Atticus, please! Lie down again, please!' The rictus of a smile peeled his lips back from his teeth, but he managed to keep his grip of Atticus's arm gentle.

The rage died; Atticus seemed to shrink, then let himself be drawn back to the couch and once more ensconced in the *locus consularis*. 'I'm sorry,' he muttered.

'No, no, you're entitled to your opinions,' Antony said quite jovially. 'At least I know what you think of me.'

'You asked for it, you know. Whenever you start to use Octavianus as an excuse for lingering west of where you ought to be, I am sorely tried,' said Atticus, breaking bread.

'But Atticus, the boy's a complete idiot! I *worry* about Italia, I really do.'

'Then help Octavianus instead of hindering him.'

'Not in a thousand years!'

'He's in dire straits, Antonius. The grain from this coming harvest looks never to arrive, thanks to Sextus Pompeius.'

'Then Octavianus ought to stay in Rome paddling his fingers up Livia Drusilla's skirts instead of mounting invasions of Sicilia with sixty ships. *Sixty ships*! No wonder he was trounced.' One huge but shapely hand reached for a tiny chicken. The food seemed to soothe him; he looked sideways at Atticus with a grin. 'Just grant me a successful campaign against the Parthians next year and I'll give Octavianus all the help he needs when I'm done.' He looked suspicious. 'Surely you don't *like* Octavianus?'

'I am indifferent,' said Atticus, sounding detached. 'He has odd ideas about how Rome should function – ideas that won't benefit me or any other plutocrat. Like Divus Julius, I think he intends to weaken the First Class and the upper end of the Second Class to strengthen the lower classes. Oh, not the Head Count, I give him that. He's no demagogue. Were he simply a cynical exploiter of popular gullibility, I wouldn't be concerned. But I think he firmly believes that Caesar is a god, and he the son of a god.'

'His pushing for the deification of Caesar is a mark of insanity,' said Antony, feeling better.

'No, Octavianus isn't insane. In fact, I don't think I've ever seen a saner man than he.'

'I may be a procrastinator, but he has delusions of grandeur.'

'Perhaps so, but I hope you've retained sufficient impartiality to see that Octavianus is something new to Rome. I have reason to believe that he employs a small army of agents throughout Italia working strenuously to perpetuate the fiction that he is as like Caesar as two peas in a pod. Like Caesar, he's a brilliant orator with huge crowd appeal. His ambition knows no bounds, which is why, in a few years' time, he's going to face a very serious situation,' Atticus said soberly.

'What can you mean?' Antony asked, at a loss.

'When Caesar's Egyptian son is older, he's bound to visit Rome. My Egyptian connections tell me that the boy is Caesar's image, and in more than mere looks. He's a prodigy. His mama maintains that all she wants for Caesarion is a secure throne and the status of Friend and Ally of the Roman People, and that may be so. But if he's Caesar's image and Rome sets eyes on him, he might very well filch Rome, Italia *and* the legions off Octavianus. Who at best is an imitation Caesar. You won't be affected because you will have gone into an enforced retirement by then – Caesarion is hardly nine years old. But in thirteen or fourteen years he'll be a man grown. Octavianus's struggles with you and Sextus Pompeius will pale to insignificance compared to Caesarion.'

'Hmmm,' said Antony, and changed the subject.

An unsettling dinner, for all that Antony's digestion stayed its usual hearty self. Some reflection enabled him to shrug off Atticus's criticisms of his own conduct – how could he know what problems

Antony faced anent Octavian? After all, he was seventy-four years old; despite his trim, agile figure and his business acumen, senility must be setting in.

It was Atticus's comments about Caesarion that stayed with him. Frowning, he cast his mind back to that three-month sojourn in Alexandria, now over two years in the past. Was Caesarion truly almost nine? What he remembered was a gallant little boy, game for every exploit from hunting hippopotamus to hunting crocodile. Fearless. Well, so had Caesar been. Cleopatra tended to lean on him despite his age, though that hadn't surprised Antony. She was emotional and not always wise, whereas her son was ... was *what*? Tougher, certainly. But what else? He didn't know.

Oh, why didn't he have more patience with the fine art of correspondence? Cleopatra did write to him from time to time, and it hadn't escaped Antony that her letters were mostly about Caesarion, his cleverness and natural authority. But he hadn't really taken much notice, deeming her remarks the waffles of a besotted mother. Married to Octavia, he knew all about besotted mothers. A vague itch stirred in him to visit Alexandria and see for himself what Caesarion was becoming, but at the moment it was impossible. Though, he thought, it would afford him terrific pleasure to discover that Octavian had a rival cousin more to be feared than Marcus Antonius.

He sat down to write to Cleopatra.

My dearest girl, I have been thinking about you as I sit here in Athens metaphorically impotent. The literal state has not yet been visited upon me, I hasten to add, and I feel the best friend welded to my groin begin to stir at the memory of you, your kisses. Athens, you perceive, has improved my literary style – there's little else to do here than read, patronize the Academy and other philosophical haunts, and talk to men like Titus Pomponius Atticus, who comes to dinner.

Can Caesarion really be nearing his ninth birthday? I suppose he must, but it sorrows me to think that I've missed two precious years of his childhood. Believe that as soon as I can, I'll come to you. My own twins must be close to two – where does the time go? I have never seen them at all. I know you called my boy Ptolemy and my girl Cleopatra, but I think of them as the Sun and the Moon, so maybe when you have Cha'em in residence, you could officially call my boy Ptolemy Alexander Helios, and my girl Cleopatra Selene? He's the sixteenth Ptolemy and she's the eighth Cleopatra, so it would be good if they had their private names, wouldn't it?

Next year I will definitely be in Antioch, though I may not have time to visit Alexandria. No doubt you've heard that Publius Ventidius exceeded his mandate from me by going to war and throwing the Parthians out of Syria? It did not please me, since it smacks of hubris. Instead of putting Herod on his throne, he went off to Samosata, which, I am just informed, has shut its gates to withstand siege. Still, it must be the size of a village, so it shouldn't take more than a *nundinum* to reduce.

Octavia is delightful, though sometimes I find myself wishing she had more of her brother's obnoxiousness. There's something intimidating about a woman who has no faults, and she has no faults, take my word for that. If she complained occasionally, I'd think better of her, since I know she thinks I don't spend enough time with the children, only three of whom are mine. In which case, why not spit it out? But does she? Not Octavia! She just looks sorrowful. Still, I must count myself lucky. There's no woman in all of Rome more desirable; I am deeply envied, even by my enemies.

Write and tell me sometime how you are, and how Caesarion is. Atticus made some penetrating remarks about him and his relationship to Octavianus. Hinted there might be future danger in it for him. Whatever you do, don't send him to Rome until I can accompany him. That's an order, and don't be a Ventidius. Your boy is too like Caesar to be welcomed kindly by Octavianus. He'll need allies in Rome, strong support.

In late May Antony received a letter from Octavian on the usual subject – his difficulties with Sextus Pompey and the grain supply – but this one implored Antony to meet him in Brundisium immediately. Accompanied only by a squadron of German horse guards, a grumbling Antony left Athens for Corinth to catch the ferry to Patrae. But before departing he testily repeated his grievances to Dellius, starting with his resentment of Ventidius.

'He's still sitting in front of Samosata conducting that ridiculous snail's-pace siege! I mean, it puts him in Cicero's league! The whole of Rome knew that Cicero couldn't general a fox in a henhouse, even with Pomptinus doing the actual fighting.'

'Cicero?' Dellius asked incredulously, sidetracked; he was too young to remember much about Cicero's earlier exploits. 'When on earth did the Great Advocate conduct a siege? This is the first I've heard about any military exploits.'

'He went out to govern Cicilia ten years after he was consul and got mired down in a siege in eastern Cappadocia – a literal village named Pindenissus. It took him and Pomptinus ages to reduce it.'

'I see,' said Dellius, who was indeed seeing, but not sieges conducted by the most unwarlike consul Rome had ever produced. 'I was under the impression that Cicero was a good governor.'

'Oh, he was – if you approve of the kind of man who makes it impossible for Roman businessmen to make provincial profits. But Cicero isn't the point, Dellius. Ventidius is. I hope that by the time I return from seeing Octavianus he's got the gates of Samosata reduced to pieces and is busy counting the booty.'

Antony wasn't away nearly as long as Dellius expected, but he had his tale ready when the Triumvir of the East stormed into his Athens residence fuming about Octavian, who hadn't turned up, nor sent word as to why. To add insult to injury, once again Brundisium refused to lower its harbor chain and admit the visitor. Instead of going to another port to land, Antony turned around and came back to Athens in high dudgeon.

Dellius half listened to the diatribe, too used to Antony's hatred for Octavian to take much notice. This was an ordinary temper tantrum, not one of those *nundinum*-long affairs that would terrify a Hector, so Dellius waited for the period of calm that followed the ranting and raving. Once it ensued, Antony buckled down to work again as if he found the outburst beneficial.

Most of his work at this time concerned the vital decisions he had to make about which man would rule each of the many kingdoms and principalities dotted around the East – places Rome did not administer in person as provinces. Antony in particular was firmly convinced that client-kings were the correct solution, not extra provinces. It was shrewd policy that saw the local rulers inherit the odium of tax and tribute collection.

His desk was piled high with reports about every candidate for each job. Each man had a dossier that would be gone into thoroughly; Antony often asked for additional information, and sometimes commanded that this or that candidate appear in Athens.

However, it wasn't long before he returned to the subject of Samosata and the siege, his displeasure undiminished.

'It's the end of June and still no word,' Antony said with a scowl. 'There sit Ventidius and seven legions before a town the size of Aricia or Tibur! It's scandalous!'

Now was his chance to pay Ventidius back for that humiliating interview in Tarsus! Dellius struck. 'You're right, Antonius, it's scandalous. From what *I* hear, anyway.'

Arrested, Antony focused his gaze on Dellius's sorrowful face, irritation dying before curiosity. 'What do you mean, Dellius?'

'That Ventidius's investment of Samosata is a scandal. Or so, at least, a correspondent of mine in the Sixth Legion said in his last letter to me. It arrived yesterday, surprisingly fast.'

'And the name of this legate?'

'I'm sorry, Antonius, I can't tell you that. I gave my word that I wouldn't divulge my source of information.' Dellius spoke softly, eyelids lowered. 'I was told in strictest confidence.'

'Are you at liberty to tell me the nature of the scandal?'

'Certainly. That the siege of Samosata goes nowhere because Ventidius accepted a thousand-talent bribe from Antiochus of Commagene. If the siege drags on long enough, Antiochus hopes that you'll order Ventidius and his legions to pack up and leave.'

Stunned, Antony said nothing for a long moment. Then his breath hissed between his teeth, his fists clenched. 'Ventidius accept a bribe? *Ventidius*? No! Your informant is mistaken.'

The small head snaked from side to side to intimate a sad skepticism. 'I understand your reluctance to believe ill of such an old comrade in arms, Antonius, but tell me this – why should my friend in the Sixth lie? What profits it him? More than that, it appears the bribe is common knowledge among the legates of all seven legions. Ventidius has made no secret of it. He's fed up with the East and yearns to go home to celebrate his triumph. There is also a rumor that he doctored the account books he's sent to the *aerarium* along with the spoils of his entire campaign. That, in fact, he's skimmed another thousand talents off the booty. Samosata is such a mean place that he knows he won't get much out of it, so why try to take it at all?'

Antony leaped to his feet, roaring for his steward.

'Antonius! What do you mean to do?' Dellius asked, paling.

'What any commander-in-chief does when his second-in-command betrays his trust!' said Antony curtly.

The steward edged in apprehensively. 'Yes, *domine*?'

'Pack my chest, including armor and weapons. And whereabouts is Lucilius? I need him.'

Off went the steward in a hurry; Antony began to pace.

'What are you going to do?' Dellius repeated, sweating now.

'Go to Samosata, of course. You can come with me, Dellius. Rest assured, I'll get to the bottom of this.'

His whole life flashed before Dellius's eyes; he swayed, gurgled, fell to the floor and went into convulsions. The next thing Antony was on his knees beside him, shouting for a physician. Who took an hour to arrive, during which time Dellius was put to bed, apparently *in extremis*.

Not that Antony had remained with him; as soon as Dellius was carried away, he was rapping orders to Lucilius and making sure the servants knew how to pack for a campaign – a fool decision, not to have his batman or his quaestor with him!

Octavia walked in with the physician, her face alarmed. 'My dear Antonius, what is the matter?' she asked.

'I'm off to Samosata in less than an hour. Lucilius found a ship I can hire to take me to Portae Alexandreia. That's on the Sinus Issicus, the closest I can get.' He grimaced, remembered to kiss her hand. 'From there I have a three-hundred-mile ride, *meum mel*. If Auster blows, the voyage will take almost a month, but if he doesn't, more like two months. Add the ride, and you have two to three months just getting there. Oh, *curse* Ventidius! He's betrayed me.'

'I refuse to believe that,' she said, standing on tiptoe to kiss his cheek. 'Ventidius is an honorable man.'

Antony's eyes went over her head to the physician, bowing low and trembling at the knees. 'Who are you?' he demanded.

'Oh, this is Themistophanes,' said Octavia. 'He's the doctor who has just seen Quintus Dellius.'

Having forgotten all about Dellius, Antony blinked. 'Oh! Oh, yes. How is he? Still alive?'

'Yes, lord Antonius, he lives. A crisis of the liver, I think. He managed to tell me that he is to go to Syria with you today, but he cannot – I am firm about that. He needs poultices of charcoal, verdigris, bitumen and oil applied to his chest several times a day, as well as regular purgations and phlebotomy,' the physician said, looking terrified. 'An expensive treatment.'

'Oh, well, he'd better stay here,' said Antony, annoyed that he wouldn't have Dellius to point out the tattling legate. 'Apply to my secretary, Lucilius, for your fees.'

Another hug and kiss for Octavia, and Antony was gone. She stood, bemused, then lifted her shoulders in a shrug and smiled. 'Well, that's the last I'll see of him until winter,' she said. 'I must break the news to the children.'

Upstairs, safely tucked in his bed, Dellius thanked all the gods for giving him the presence of mind to collapse. From what Themistophanes said, he was in for considerable discomfort, if not outright pain – a small price to pay for salvation. That Antony would set out for Samosata was the one thing he hadn't bargained for; why would he, when he hadn't moved a muscle to eject the Parthians? Perhaps, Dellius decided, it would be a good idea to make a miraculous recovery and spend some months in Rome being nice to Octavian.

Auster did blow, and the ship, carrying no cargo save Antony and his gear, could afford to have two shifts of oarsmen aboard. But a south wind wasn't ideal and the ship's captain disliked the open sea, so hugged the coastline all the way from making landfall in Lycia to Portae Alexandreia. Just as well, thought the restless Antony, that Pompey the Great had scoured all the pirates out of those convenient coves and strongholds along Pamphylia and Cilicia Tracheia. Otherwise he would have been captured and held to ransom like many Romans, including Divus Julius.

Even reading was difficult, as the ship had a tendency to bob up and down; though Our Sea had no ocean swell, it was choppy and could be dangerous in a storm. Those at least he was spared at this summer season, the best time of year to sail. About the only way he could assuage his impatience was to play dice with the crew for mere sesterces and, even then, he was careful to lose. He also walked the deck around and around, kept his muscles in condition by lifting water barrels and other feats of strength beyond the crew. Hardly a night went by that the captain didn't insist on putting into port or anchoring off some deserted beach. A seven-hundred-mile voyage at the rate of thirty miles a day on a good day. At times Antony felt as if he'd never get there.

When all else failed, he leaned on the ship's rail and stared into the water, hoping to spot some gigantic sea monster, but the closest he came to that were the big dolphins that leaped and frolicked around the hull, playing games amid the two rudder oars and flying past like marine hares. Then he discovered that gazing so for too long provoked a wave of loneliness in him, a sense of abandonment, of weariness and disenchantment, and wondered what was happening to him.

In the end he concluded that the defection of Ventidius had destroyed some part of his core, imbued him not with his customary rage, which was a kind of fighting spirit, but with black despair. Yes, he thought, I dread the meeting with him. I dread to find the proof of his perfidy right there under my nose. What can I do? Fire him, of course. Banish him to Rome and that wretched triumph he's so set upon. But with whom do I replace him? Some whining cur like Sosius? Who else is there, than Sosius? Canidius is a good man. And my cousin Caninius. Yet – if Ventidius could accept a bribe, why not any of them, not attached to me by years in Further Gaul and Caesar's civil war campaigns? I am forty-five, but the rest are ten and fifteen years younger. Calvinus and Vatia are for Octavianus, and so too, I am told, Appius Claudius Pulcher, the most important consul since Calvinus. Maybe that's the nucleus of it? Infidelity. Disloyalty.

In exactly a month, his ship docked at Portae Alexandreia, and he had to set about finding mounts for his servants. He had brought Clemency with him, his dappled grey Public Horse, which was tall and strong enough to bear him. Still in that null, grey mood, he rode for Samosata.

Which, as he came up the Euphrates, loomed like a black brick. Shocked, Antony discovered that Samosata was a big city with the same kind of walls as Amida, for it had belonged to the Assyrians when they ruled all this part of the world. Black basalt of the kind the Greeks called Cyclopean – smooth, immensely high, and impervious to rams or siege towers. From that moment on he knew that Dellius had misled him; what he didn't know was whether Dellius had done so deliberately, or simply been duped by his Sixth Legion correspondent. This was no Cappadocian village in a tufa cliff; this was a daunting task even for a Caesar, whose siege experience had been very different. Nothing Ventidius had seen in any of Caesar's wars could have prepared him for this.

Still, there was always the possibility that Ventidius had taken a bribe anyway . . . Stiff and sore, Antony slid off Clemency in the camp assembly area, right alongside the general's quarters.

Ventidius came out to see what all the fuss was about, a solid man who looked his age, tight grey curls turning his pate into something that resembled astrakhan. His face lit up.

'Antonius!' he cried, coming to embrace Antony. 'What in Jupiter's name brings you to Samosata?'

'I wanted to see how the siege is going.'

'Oh, that!' Ventidius laughed jubilantly. 'Samosata asked for terms two days ago. The gates are open and Antiochus is gone, the crafty *irrumator*.'

'On the giving end, is he?'

'Well, in that respect. In every other, he takes.'

Ventidius gave Antony a field chair and went to the flagons. 'Horrible red, worse white, or nice Euphrates water?'

'Red, half and half with Euphrates water. Good, is it?'

'Tasty for water. The city has neither an aqueduct nor any sewers. They dig wells rather than take their drinking water from the river, then dig their cesspits right alongside their wells.' He pulled a face. 'The fools! Enteric fevers are rife in summer *and* winter. I've built an aqueduct for my men and forbidden them to come in contact with the Samosatans. The river is so deep and wide that I've just pushed the camp sewers back into it. Our swimming holes are upstream, though the current's dangerous.' The hospitality taken care of, Ventidius sank into his curule chair and stared at Antony shrewdly. 'There's more to it than curiosity about my siege, Antonius. What's wrong?'

'Someone in Athens told me that you'd taken a thousand-talent bribe from Antiochus to keep the siege going.'

'*Cacat!*' Ventidius sat up straight, the pleasure fading from his eyes. He grunted. 'Well, your arrival says you believed the worm – who is he? I think I'm entitled to know.'

'First, a question. Are you having trouble with the command chain in the Sixth?'

Ventidius's eyes widened. '*The Sixth?*'

'Yes, the Sixth.'

'Antonius, I haven't had the Sixth here since April. Silo is having trouble putting Herod on his throne, and asked for another legion. I sent him the Sixth.'

Feeling suddenly sick, Antony got to his feet and walked across to a window in the mud-brick wall. That answered everything except why Dellius had made his story up. How had Ventidius offended him?

'My informant was Quintus Dellius, who said he corresponded with a legate in the Sixth. This legate told him about the bribe, and insisted the whole army knew.'

Ventidius's color had paled. 'Oh, Antonius, that hurts! I'm cut to the quick! How could you take the word of a miserable little pander like Dellius without even writing to me to ask what's going on? Instead, here you are in person! That says you believed him implicitly. *Against me!* What kind of proof did he offer?'

Antony forced himself to turn from the window. 'He didn't. Said his informant wanted to be anonymous. But it went farther than that – the bribe, I mean. You were also accused of doctoring the account books for the Treasury.'

Tears coursing down his seamed face, Ventidius turned one shoulder on Antony. 'Quintus Dellius! A sycophant, a sucker-up, a contemptible crawler! And on his word alone, you've made this journey? I could spit on you! I should spit on you!'

'I have no excuse,' said Antony miserably, wishing there was somewhere he could go – anywhere but here, anywhere! 'It's life in Athens, I suppose. So far from the action, wading through endless mountains of paper, out of it completely – Ventidius, I cry pardon from the bottom of my heart.'

'You can cry pardon from here to your pyre and back, Antonius. It will make no difference.' He wiped the tears away with the back of one hand. 'We're finished, you and I. Finished. I've taken Samosata and I throw my account books open to whomsoever you choose as an auditor. You'll find no discrepancies, not even a bronze farthing. I ask leave of you, my commander, to let me return to Rome. I insist on my triumph, but I've fought my last campaign for Rome. Once I've laid my laurels at the feet of Jupiter Optimus Maximus, I'm going home to Reate to breed mules. I've nearly broken my back fighting your wars for you, and the only thanks you give me is an accusation from the likes of Dellius.' He got up and went to a door. 'Through there are my own quarters, but by tonight I'll be out of them. You can move in and make what dispositions you want. You *trusted* me! And now, this.'

'Publius, please! *Please!* We can't part enemies!'

'You're not my enemy, Antonius. Your worst enemy is yourself, not a Picentine muleteer who walked in Strabo's triumph fifty years ago. You're why we Italians still have the short end of the stick – Dellius is a Roman, after all. That makes his word better than mine, that makes him better than me. I'm sick of Rome, I'm sick of war, field camps, the company of none but men. And don't rely on Silo – he's another Italian, he might take a bribe. He'll be going home with me.' Ventidius sucked in a breath. 'Good luck in the East, Antonius. It suits you, it really does. Corrupted arse lickers, cock twiddlers, greasy oriental potentates who lie even to themselves . . .' His face twisted in pain. 'That reminds me: Herod is

230

here. So is Polemon of Pontus, and Amyntas of Galatia. You won't lack company, even if Dellius was too craven to come.'

After Ventidius shut the door behind him, Antony threw his watered beverage through the window and poured the beaker full of the strong, slightly toxic wine.

It couldn't have been worse, nor could he have conducted an interview more ineptly. Ventidius is right, Antony thought as he gulped the liquid until it was gone. When he got up to refill his cheap pottery vessel, he brought the flagon back with him. Yes, Ventidius is right. Somewhere along the way I've lost myself, my direction, my self-esteem. I couldn't even flog myself into a rage! What he said was true. Why did I believe Dellius? It all seems so long ago, that day in Athens when Dellius poured his poison into my eager ear. Who is Dellius? How could I possibly have taken credence in a tale that had no evidence to back it up, let alone proof? I *wanted* to believe it, that's all I can think. I wanted to see my old friend disgraced, I hungered for it. And why? Because he fought a war that belonged to me, a war I couldn't be bothered fighting myself. That might have meant hard work. It's become Roman tradition for the commander-in-chief to take all the credit. Gaius Marius started it when he took the credit for the capture of Jugurtha. He should not have. Sulla did the deed, expertly, brilliantly. But Marius just couldn't bear to share the laurels, so he never even mentioned it in dispatches. If Sulla hadn't published his memoirs, no one would ever have known the truth.

I wanted to pack the campaign against the Parthians in snow, preserve the final confrontation for myself after a better man softened them up. Then Ventidius stole my thunder. A titan bold enough to see how to do it – crack, boom! Away went my thunder. How angry I was, how frustrated! I underestimated him and Silo – it never even occurred to me how good they were. And that is why I believed Dellius. There can be no other reason. I wanted to destroy Ventidius's achievements, I wanted to see him disgraced, maybe even put to the sword like Salvidienus. That was my doing too, though Salvidienus was less of a man, less of a commander. I was so absorbed in Octavianus that I let the East slip from my hands, gave the reins to Ventidius, my trusty muleteer.

He began to weep, rocking back and forth on the flimsy cross-legged stool with its leather seat, watching the teardrops fall into the wine, drinking his own grief as a black dog drinks blood. Oh, the sorrow, the regret! No one would ever look at him in the same way again. His honor was stained beyond removal.

When Herod rushed through the door an hour later, he found Antony so drunk that he wasn't recognized or acknowledged.

Ventidius came in, saw Antony, and spat on the floor.

'Find his servants and tell them to put him to bed,' Ventidius said curtly. 'Through there, in my quarters. By the time he's conscious again, I'll be halfway to Syria.'

And more than that Herod could not find out.

Antony told Herod two days later, sober but unusually affected by the wine.

'I believed Dellius,' he said miserably.

'Yes, that was unwise, Antonius.' Herod tried to look chirpy. 'Still, it's over and done with. Samosata is taken, Antiochus has fled to Perse, and the booty surpasses all expectations. A good conclusion to the war.'

'How did Ventidius take the place?'

'He's an inventor, so he saw what he had to do. He built a gigantic ball from pieces of solid iron, attached it to a chain, and suspended the chain from a tower. Then he harnessed up fifty oxen and pulled the ball far back behind the tower. When its chain was stretched straight, he severed the connection between the ball and the beasts. It swung like a monstrous fist and struck the walls with a hideous noise – I covered my ears. And the walls just . . . fell down! Within a day he'd demolished enough to get his soldiers inside in thousands. It turned out that the Samosatans didn't have any other defense than their fortifications. No troops good or bad – nothing!'

'I heard he invented a lead sling missile too.'

'A terrifying weapon!' Herod exclaimed. He put a hand on Antony's arm. 'Come, Antonius, you're in command now that Ventidius has gone. You should at least inspect the place and see what the iron ball did. Those walls had stood for five hundred years, but nothing stands before a Roman army. You don't look as if you're very hungry, but your legates are . . . er . . . milling around helplessly, unsure what to do next. So I've arranged a dinner in my house. Do come! It will make everybody feel better, including you.'

'My head aches.'

'No surprise, considering the piss you drank. I've also got in some bearable wine, if that's what you want.'

Antony sighed, extended his hands and stared at them. 'They look as if they can take hold of anything, don't they?' he asked, shivering. 'But they lost control.'

'Nonsense! A good meal of fresh bread and lean meat will put all to right.'

'What's happening in Judaea?'

'Very little. Silo is an excellent man, but two legions were not enough, and by the time a third one arrived, Antigonus had gone to earth in Jerusalem. It's a hard city to take, harder than this Assyrian outpost. Ventidius was very good to me, by the way.'

Antony winced. 'Don't rub it in! How?'

'He gave me enough money to go to Egypt and restock Masada, where my family and Hyrcanus's family are. But I'm not getting any younger, Antonius, and the Jews need . . . well, a tyrant. They're arming and drilling.'

Since no legate was imprudent enough to mention Ventidius, by the end of his first *nundinum* at Samosata, Antony was able to feel genuinely in command. But guilt over Ventidius meant that the city suffered atrociously at Antony's hands. The entire population was sold into slavery at Nicephorium, where a representative of the new King of the Parthians, Phraates, bought them as a job lot. He was short of labor, having executed a significant proportion of his people from lowest to highest. His own sons were the first to die, but he missed a nephew, one Monaeses, who fled to Syria and disappeared. Very vexing for Phraates, who loved being king.

Samosata's walls were torn down. Antony wanted to use them to bridge the Euphrates, but discovered that the river was so deep and strong that it swept the stones away like snippets of chaff. Finally he scattered the stones far and wide.

By the time all was done, a chill had crept into the night air. Antony had deposed Antiochus, fined him heavily, and put his brother Mithradates on the throne. Publius Canidius was placed in charge of the legions, which went into camp near Antioch and Damascus; he was to prepare for a campaign into Armenia and Media the following year – under Antony's *personal* command. Gaius Sosius was created the governor of Syria, and instructed to put Herod on his throne as soon as the winter furlough was over.

In Portae Alexandreia Antony boarded a ship whose captain was willing to brave open waters. The wound was slowly healing; he could look his fellow Romans in the eye again without wondering what they were thinking. But oh, he needed a sweet feminine breast to bury his head in! The only trouble was that the sweet feminine breast he yearned for belonged to Cleopatra.

THIRTEEN

When Agrippa returned from two years in Further Gaul, covered in glory, he and the two legions he had brought with him camped on the Campus Martius outside the *pomerium*; the Senate had voted him a triumph, which meant he was religiously forbidden to enter Rome herself. It went without saying that he expected Caesar to be waiting for him in the flap of the splendid red tent erected to house the general in his temporary exile, but – no Caesar. No senators either. Well, perhaps he was early, Agrippa thought as he directed his batman to take his things inside; he was too eager to see Caesar in the distance to seek shelter himself. His eyes were capable of seeing the flash of metal two miles away, or a nigh-invisible scratch on something held in his hand, so he drew a sigh of relief when he spotted a large armed guard of Germans emerge from the Fontinalis Gate, coming down the hill toward the Via Recta. Then he frowned; in their midst was a litter. Caesar, in a litter? Was he ill?

Anxious and impatient, he disciplined himself to wait where he was, not run toward the awkward conveyance, which eventually drew up amid a hail of jubilant congratulations from the Germans.

When Maecenas flopped out of it, Agrippa gasped.

'Inside,' said the Arch Manipulator, making for the tent.

'What is it? What's the matter? Is Caesar ill?'

'No, not ill, just in a fine old stew,' Maecenas said, looking strained. 'His house is fenced around with guards, and he dare not move outside it. He's had to fortify it, can you believe that? A wall and a ditch on the Palatine!'

'Why?' Agrippa asked, bewildered.

'Don't you know? Can't you guess? When is it ever anything except the grain supply? Taxes? High prices?'

234

Mouth set, Agrippa stared at the Eagle standards planted in the ground outside his tent, each wreathed in the laurels of victory. 'You're right, I should have known. What's the latest chapter in this eternal epic? Ye gods, it begins to be as painful as suffering through Thucydides!'

'That conniving slug Lepidus – *sixteen legions* under his command! – let Sextus Pompeius make off with the entire African grain shipment. Then that treacherous cur Menodorus had a row with Sabinus – didn't like being under his authority – and deserted back to Sextus. He didn't take more than six warships with him, but he did tell Sextus the route of the Sardinian harvest, so that went too. The Senate has no choice, it must buy grain from Sextus, who is charging forty sesterces the *modius*. That means State wheat will cost fifty sesterces the *modius*, while the private vendors are talking of charging sixty. If the State is to be able to buy sufficient for the free grain dole, it has to charge fifty from those who must pay. When the Roman People heard, they went wild. Riots, gang warfare – Caesar had to import a legion from Capua to guard the State granaries, so the Vicus Portae Trigeminae is awash with soldiers and the Port of Rome deserted.' Maecenas drew a breath and held out shaking hands. 'It is a crisis, a real crisis.'

'What about Ventidius's spoils from his triumph?' Agrippa asked. 'Can't they balance the books and keep the price at forty to the People?'

'They might have, except that Antonius insisted he be given half as Triumvir and commander-in-chief in the East. Since the Senate is still full of his creatures, it voted that he should have five thousand talents,' Maecenas said gloomily, passion worn out. 'Add the legions' share, and all that's left are two thousand. A mere fifty million sesterces, against a grain bill from Sextus of nearly five hundred million sesterces. Caesar asked if he could pay the bill in increments, but Sextus said no. Up front, or no grain at all. One more month will see the granaries empty.'

'And no money to defray the costs of an all-out war against the *mentula*!' said Agrippa savagely. 'Well, I'm bringing another two thousand in spoils – that's a hundred million of the grain bill when they're added to what's left of Ventidius's. What we ought to do is put the Senate in the middle of the Forum and let the mobs stone every last member to death! But of course they've all fled Rome, haven't they?'

'Oh, yes. Huddling in their villas. It's not only Rome in a ferment, the whole of Italia is rioting. Not their fault, they say, blaming everything on Caesar's bad government. I curse them!'

Agrippa moved to the tent flap. 'It has to stop, Maecenas. Come, let's go to Caesar.'

Maecenas stared aghast. 'Agrippa! You can't! Cross the *pomerium* into Rome, and you lose your triumph!'

'Oh, what's a triumph when Caesar needs me? I'll triumph for some other war.' And off strode Agrippa, unaccompanied, still in his dress armor, his long legs swallowing the distance. His mind was running in circles, for it knew there was no answer, while his spirit insisted there had to be an answer. Caesar, Caesar, you can't let a common pirate hold you and the Roman People to ransom! I curse you, Sextus Pompeius, but I curse Antonius more.

All Maecenas could do was to crawl into his litter and hope to be at the *domus Livia Drusilla* an hour later, escorted by his armed guard. Agrippa, alone! The mob would tear him to pieces.

The city was in turmoil, every shutter of every shop pulled down and locked; the walls were thick with graffiti, some protesting the grain prices, but most vilifying Caesar, Agrippa was quick to note as he marched down the Hill of the Bankers. Gangs roamed armed with rocks, cudgels, an occasional sword, but no one challenged him – this was a warrior, the most aggressive among them could see that at a glance. The detritus from rotten eggs and vegetables dripped down venerable bank fronts and porticoes, the stink of sewage hung on the air from chamber pots no one was courageous enough to carry to the nearest public latrine to empty; never in his most morbid dreams had Agrippa thought to see Rome so degraded, so soiled, so marred. The only thing missing was the reek of smoke; insanity hadn't quite taken over, then. Careless of his safety, Agrippa shouldered his way through the howling crowds in the Forum, where statues had been torn down and the rich colors of the temples almost obliterated by graffiti and filth. When he reached the Ringmaker's Steps he took them four at a time, shoving aside anyone in his path. Across the Palatine, and there in front of him stood a high, hastily assembled wall, on top of which stood a line of German guards.

'Marcus Agrippa!' one cried as he flung out an arm; the drawbridge across a wide ditch fell, the portcullis behind it was raised. By this time a loud chorus of 'Marcus Agrippa!' was joined by cheers. He walked in to be surrounded by whooping Ubii.

'Keep watch, boys!' he shouted over his shoulder, flashing them a grin, and walked on into a desolation of slimy fish ponds, weeds, an abandoned garden transformed into a camp for Germans, who were not fussy.

Inside the *domus Livia Drusilla* he saw at once that the new wife had made her mark already. The place had changed beyond recognition. He strode into an exquisitely furnished room, its walls glowing with frescoes, its plinths and herms of beautiful marbles. Burgundinus appeared wrathfully, face wreathed in smiles as soon as he discovered who was gouging the priceless floor with hobnailed boots.

'Where is he, Burgundinus?'

'In his study. Oh, Marcus Agrippa, it's so good to see you!'

Yes, he was in his study, but not at a battered desk hemmed in by book buckets and stands of overflowing pigeonholes. This desk was huge and made of ribboned green malachite; the archival disorder was reduced to the same neatness as Caesar's desk had always displayed, and two scribes sat at less ornate but highly presentable desks while a clerk ambled around filing scrolls.

The face that lifted in irritation to see who disturbed him had aged, looked in its late thirties – not from lines or wrinkles, but thanks to black stains around washed-out eyes, furrows in the broad brow, an almost lipless mouth.

'Caesar!'

The malachite inkwell went flying; Octavian leaped up amid fluttering papers and bounded across the room to clutch at Agrippa in an ecstatic embrace. Then realization dawned. He stepped back, horrified. 'Oh, no! Your triumph!'

Agrippa hugged him, kissed his cheeks. 'There will be other triumphs, Caesar. Did you really think I'd stay outside when Rome is in so much tumult you can't venture out? If a civilian sees my face, he doesn't recognize it, so I came to you.'

'Where's Maecenas?'

'Littering back,' said Agrippa, grinning.

'You mean you came without an escort?'

'No mob can face down a fully armed centurion, and that's who they thought I was. Maecenas needed the guard more than I did.'

Octavian dashed away his tears, closed his eyes. 'Agrippa, my own Agrippa! Oh, this is the turning point, I know it!'

'Caesar?' asked a new voice, low and slightly husky.

Octavian turned in Agrippa's arms, but didn't move from them. 'Livia Drusilla, my life is complete again! Marcus has come home.'

Agrippa beheld a small oval face, its skin a flawless ivory, its mouth lushly full, its great dark eyes shining. If she found the situation strange, nothing of that showed, even in the depths of those very expressive eyes. Her face broke into smiles of genuine delight, and she put her hand lightly on Agrippa's arm, stroking it as tenderly as a lover.

'Marcus Agrippa, how wonderful,' she said, then frowned. 'But your triumph . . . !'

'He's given it up to see me,' Octavian said, taking his wife by one hand and putting his other arm around Agrippa's shoulders. 'Come, let's sit somewhere more private and comfortable. Livia Drusilla has provided me with a most efficient workforce, but I have lost my isolation.'

'Is the new look of Caesar's house your work, lady?' Agrippa asked, sinking into a gilded chair upholstered in soft purple brocade and accepting a crystal goblet of unwatered wine. He sipped, laughed. 'A much better vintage than you used to serve, Caesar! I take it no water means this is a celebration?'

'None more important than your return. She's a marvel, my Livia Drusilla.'

To Agrippa's surprise, Livia Drusilla didn't absent herself, though a wife should. She chose a large purple chair and sat in it with her feet tucked under her, taking a goblet from Octavian with a nod of thanks. Oho! The lady was privy to councils!

'Somehow I have to survive yet another year of this,' Octavian said, putting down his wine after that toast. 'Unless you think we can move this coming year?'

'No, Caesar, we can't. Portus Julius won't be ready until the summer, so Sabinus said in his last letter to me, which gives me eight months to arm and train. Sextus Pompeius's defeat has to be complete, too complete ever to see him rise again. Though from somewhere we have to find at least a hundred and fifty warships. The dockyards of Italia can't provide enough.'

'There's only one source able to provide them, and that is our so-dear Antonius,' Octavian said bitterly. 'He and he alone is the cause of all this! He has the Senate eating out of his hand, no god can tell me why! You'd think the fools would know better, living in the midst of so much agony, but no! Loyalty to Marcus Antonius counts for more than starving bellies!'

'That hasn't changed since the days of Catulus and Scaurus,' Agrippa said. 'Are you writing to him?'

'I was, when you appeared at the door. Wasting sheet after sheet of good-grade paper trying to find the right words.'

'How long is it since you've seen him?'

'Over a year ago, when he took Octavia and the children to Athens. I wrote last spring asking him to meet me at Brundisium, but he tricked me by coming minus his legions and so quickly on the heels of my summons that I was still in Rome waiting for his answer. So he went back to Athens and sent me a nasty letter, threatening to put my neck under his sword if I failed to turn up at our next meeting. Then he went off to Samosata, so . . . no meeting. I'm not even sure he's returned to Athens.'

'Leaving that aside, Caesar, what can we do about the grain supply? Somehow we have to feed Italia, and more cheaply than Maecenas says we can.'

'Livia Drusilla says I have to borrow whatever's necessary from the plutocrats, but I shrink from that.'

Well, well, *good* counsel from the little blackbird! 'She's right, Caesar. Borrow rather than tax.'

Her eyes flew to Agrippa's face, astonished; today had been a meeting she dreaded, convinced that Caesar's most beloved friend would be her enemy – why should he not? Men didn't welcome women in council, and while she knew that her ideas were the right ones, men like Statilius Taurus, Calvisius Sabinus, Appius Claudius and Cornelius Gallus hated to see her star rising. To find that Agrippa was on her side was a greater gift than the child that had so far failed to come.

'They'll soak me.'

'Better than a first-quality sponge,' Agrippa said, smiling. 'However, the money is there, and until Antonius gets off his arse to regulate the East, they're not making any profits in the East, their greatest source of revenue.'

'Yes, I see that,' Octavian said a little stiffly, not sure he wanted to be overwhelmed by sound advice about things he had worked out for himself. 'What I dislike is paying back interest they'll levy at twenty per cent compound.'

Time to retreat: Agrippa looked confused. 'Compound?'

'Yes, interest on the interest. That will make them Rome's creditors for the next thirty or forty years,' said Octavian.

'You doubt yourself, dearest Caesar, and you shouldn't,' said Livia Drusilla. 'Come, think! You know the answer.'

The old smile dawned; he chuckled. 'Sextus Pompeius's vaults of ill-gotten gains, you mean.'

'She means,' said Agrippa, sending her a look of gratitude.

'That has occurred to me, but what I dislike even more than

borrowing from the plutocrats is paying the contents of Sextus's vaults over to the plutocrats when it's all over.' Suddenly he looked sly. 'I shall offer them twenty per cent compound, and toss my net wide enough to catch a few of Antonius's senators in it. I doubt anyone will turn me down at those terms, do you? I may even have to pay over a year's worth of Sextus's ill-gotten gains, but once I get rid of Antonius and make the Senate mine, I can do what I want. Reduce the interest rate by enacting laws – the only ones who will object to that are the biggest fish in our money sea!'

'He has not been idle in other respects,' said Livia Drusilla.

Octavian looked blank for a moment, then laughed. 'Oh, the "Grow More Wheat in Italia!" campaign! Yes, I've gone into yet more debt on behalf of Rome. My figures revealed that a farmer with a large family needs two hundred *modii* of wheat a year to feed everyone. But one *iugerum* yields far more than that, and of course the farmer sells his surplus unless the creatures of the field and whatever other omens he believes tell him that a drought or a flood is coming. In which case, he ensiles more grain. However, the signs say that we're not due for drought or flood next year. So I'm offering to pay wheat farmers thirty sesterces the *modius* for their surplus. A sum that the private vendors to whom they usually sell will not be prepared to match. What I'm hoping is to see some of our veterans actually *grow* something on their allotments. Most of them rent their land to vignerons because they like to drink wine – that's how the mind of a retired soldier works, it seems to me.'

'Anything that means having to buy less grain from Sextus next harvest is good, Caesar,' Agrippa said, 'but will it answer? How much do you think to buy?'

'Half of our needs,' Octavian said calmly.

'It will cost, but not what Sextus will ask for. Maecenas said Lepidus hadn't acted to preserve the African supply – what's going on there?' Agrippa asked.

'He's getting too big for his boots,' said Livia Drusilla, casting that stone to see if Agrippa looked to her husband for confirmation. But he didn't, simply accepted the statement – and her – as equal to Octavian's. Oh, Agrippa, I love you too!

Agrippa's armor creaked as he tried to get more comfortable – too many backless field chairs.

'He doesn't know, Caesar,' she said, eyes glowing. 'Tell him, then let the poor man divest himself of that awful cuirass.'

'*Edepol!* I forgot!' Octavian exclaimed, and jigged in delight.

'In less than a month, Marcus, you will be senior consul of Rome.'

'Caesar!' Agrippa breathed, stunned. A wave of joy spread through him, transfigured his stern face. 'Caesar, I am not – I am not worthy!'

'No one in the world is worthier, Marcus. All I've done is handed you a bruised and bleeding Rome, hungry and all but beaten. I had to concede the junior consulship to Caninius for no better reason than that he's Antonius's cousin, but on terms – he'll be succeeded by Statilius Taurus as suffect in Julius. The Senate is shivering, for you showed enough of your steel when you were *praetor urbanus* to make them understand you won't be merciful.'

'What you haven't said, Caesar, is how much this appointment must be resented by the men with the blood. Mine is base.'

'Appointment?' Octavian asked, grey eyes widening. 'My dear Agrippa, you were elected *in absentia*, a boon they wouldn't grant to Divus Julius. And your blood isn't base, it's good, legitimate Roman blood. I know whose sword I'd rather have at my side, and it doesn't belong to a Fabius or a Valerius. *Or* a Julius.'

'Oh, this is terrific! It means I can get to work on Portus Julius with consular authority! Only you or Antonius could impede me, and you won't, and he can't. Thank you, Caesar, thank you!'

'Would that all my decisions were greeted with such pleasure,' Octavian said wryly, eyes meeting his wife's. 'Livia Drusilla is right, you must get into more comfortable clothes. For myself, I have to go back to writing that letter to Antonius.'

'No, don't,' Agrippa said, half out of his chair.

'Don't?'

'Don't.' Agrippa managed to extricate himself. 'It's gone beyond letters. Send Maecenas.'

'The wheel in a rut,' said Livia Drusilla, coming to press her cheek against Agrippa's. 'We have become the wheel in a rut, Caesar. Agrippa is right. Send Maecenas.'

She slipped away then to her own suite of rooms, which held a large sitting room furnished in the most luxurious way, but no other ostentation, even in her sleeping cubicle. There was a big closet, for Livia Drusilla loved clothes, but by far the roomiest area was her private *tablinum*, her study that didn't ape that of a man – it was that of a man. Since she had come to Caesar without a dowry or a servant, the freedmen who acted as her secretaries belonged to him, and she had had the clever idea of rotating them between his study and hers so that everyone clerical knew what was going on and could pinch-hit in a crisis.

She went straight to her prayer cubicle, another one of her ideas, where altars were set up to Vesta, Juno Lucina, Opsiconsiva and the Bona Dea. If her theology was a little muddled, that was because she hadn't been as educated in the State religion as a male child; simply, she held those four godly forces the ones she must pray to. Vesta, for giving her a proper home; Juno Lucina, for a child; Opsiconsiva, to increase Rome's wealth and power; and the Bona Dea because she knew the Bona Dea had brought her to Caesar's side to be his helpmate as well as his wife.

A golden cage of white doves hung from a stand; making kissing sounds, she took one to each altar, there to offer it. But not to kill; the moment each bird had rested on the altar, she carried it to the window and threw it into the air, watching it fly away with hands crossed on her bosom, face uplifted raptly.

For months she had listened to her husband rave about his beloved Marcus Agrippa – listened not in skepticism, but in despair. How could she possibly compete with this paragon? Who had cradled Caesar's head in his lap on that terrible voyage from Apollonia to Barium after Divus Julius had been assassinated; who brought him around whenever his asthma threatened to kill him; who had always been there until the defection of Salvidienus had exiled him to Further Gaul. Marcus Agrippa, the coeval. The same birthday, though not in the same month. Agrippa was born on the twenty-third day of Julius, Octavian on the twenty-third day of September, both in the same year. They were now twenty-five, and had been together for nine years.

Any other woman might have plotted to drive a wedge between them, but Livia Drusilla was not so stupid or so credulous. They shared a bond she knew instinctively no one could break, so why waste her essence trying? No, what she had to do was ingratiate herself with Marcus Agrippa, get him on her side – or, at least, bring him to see that her side was Caesar's side. In her mind she had envisioned a titanic struggle; naturally he would view her with jealousy and distrust. Not for one moment did she believe what rumor said: that they were lovers in every way. Perhaps the seeds of that lay in Caesar, but had been resolutely put away for all time, he had told her. Not admitting they existed, but giving her the gist of a conversation he had had with Divus Julius in a gig galloping through Further Spain. Seventeen. He had been an inexperienced and sickly *contubernalis*, privileged to serve with the greatest Roman who ever lived. And Divus Julius had warned him that his beauty allied to his delicate look would lead to allegations that he serviced men – in homophobic Rome, a hideous handicap for a public career. No, he and Agrippa were not lovers. What they had was a deeper tie than the flesh, a unique fusion of their spirits. And, understanding that, she had been terrified of Marcus Agrippa, the one she wouldn't succeed in winning as her ally. That his blood was beneath the contempt of a Claudius Nero had ceased to matter; if Agrippa was an intrinsic part of Caesar's miraculous survival, then his blood to the new Livia Drusilla was as good as her own. Better, even.

Today the meeting had come and gone, leaving her as light-hearted as the vision of a butterfly on the wind. For she had learned that Marcus Agrippa truly did love as few were able or willing to love – without self, without conditions, without fear of rivals, without craving favors or distinction.

There are three of us now, she thought, watching Opsiconsiva's dove soar above the pines so high that its wingtips gleamed gold from the sinking sun. There are three of us to nurture Rome, and three is a lucky number.

The last dove belonged to the Bona Dea, her private offering that concerned herself only. But as it flew upward, an eagle dropped out of the sky to grab it, carry it away. An eagle . . . Bona Dea. What can that mean? Do not ask, Livia Drusilla! No, do not ask.

Maecenas never minded being sent to negotiate in places like Athens, where he kept a small residence he had no intention of ever sharing with his wife, a typical Terentia Varrone – haughty, proud, extremely conscious of her status. Here, like Atticus, he could indulge his homosexual side discreetly and delightfully. But that must wait; first, he had to see Marcus Antonius, who was said to be in Athens, though Athens hadn't set eyes on him. Apparently he was not in a mood for philosophy or lectures.

And, indeed, when Maecenas sallied forth to pay his respects to the Great Man, he found him absent; it was Octavia who welcomed him, sat him in an Attic chair he couldn't find beautiful.

'Why is it,' he said to Octavia, accepting wine, 'that the Greeks, so brilliant at everything, have never truly appreciated the curve? If there's anything I dislike about Athens, it's the mathematical rigidity of its right angles.'

'Oh, they have some affection for the curve, Maecenas. There is no column capital half as lovely as the Ionic to me. Like an unfurled scroll, each end curling up. I know Corinthian acanthus leaves have become more popular on capitals, but they are *too* much. To me, they reflect a certain decadence,' said Octavia, smiling.

She looked, thought Maecenas, a little careworn, though she couldn't yet be thirty. Like her brother, she had developed dark stains around those luminous aquamarine eyes, and her mouth had a sadder curve. Speaking of curves. Was the marriage in trouble? Surely not! Even a lusty, rip-roaring type like Marcus Antonius couldn't fault Octavia, as wife or woman.

'Where is he?'

Her eyes clouded, she shrugged. 'I have no idea. He's been back a *nundinum*, but I've hardly seen him. Glaphyra has come to town, escorted by her two younger sons.'

'No, Octavia, he wouldn't philander under your nose!'

'I have told myself that, and I *think* I believe myself.'

The Arch Manipulator leaned forward in that angular chair. 'Come, my dear, it isn't Glaphyra eating at you. You have too much good sense for that. What is really the matter?'

Her eyes looked blind, her hands moved helplessly. 'I am at a loss, Maecenas. All I can tell you is that Antonius has changed in some way I can't put my finger on. I expected him to return full of good health and hollering for diversion – he always loves to visit a theater of war, it rejuvenates him. But he came back – oh, I don't know, *blighted*. Is that the right word? As if his trip had drained him of something he desperately needs to keep up his good opinion of himself. There have been other changes – he has fallen out with Quintus Dellius, whom he sent packing. And he won't see Plancus, here on a visit from Asia Province. Just took the tribute Plancus brought and ordered him back to Ephesus. Plancus is beside himself, but the most I can get out of Antonius is that he can't trust any of his friends. That all they do is lie to him. Pollio wanted to confer with him here about Caesar's difficulties in Italia – he's having trouble keeping Antonius's senatorial faction up to the mark, whatever that means. But he wasn't allowed to come!'

'I heard that his most serious falling out was with Publius Ventidius,' Maecenas said.

'Well, all Rome must know about that,' she said wryly. 'He made a terrible mistake in thinking that Ventidius took a bribe.'

'Perhaps that's what's the matter.'

'Perhaps,' she said, then turned her head. 'Ah! Antonius!'

He entered with that lightness of foot and grace that always amazed Maecenas; big, muscle-bound men were supposed to lumber. The smooth-skinned face was lowering, but not because of some transient mood, Maecenas fancied; this was its usual expression these days, he divined. When Antony saw Maecenas he propped, scowled.

'Oh, you!' he said, flinging himself into a chair but not reaching for the wine. 'I suppose your arrival was inevitable, though I rather thought your slimy master would continue to write me begging letters.'

'No, he felt it was time for a begging Maecenas.'

Octavia rose. 'I'll leave you in private,' she said, ruffling the auburn curls as she passed Antony's chair. 'Behave yourselves.'

Maecenas laughed, Antony did not.

'What does Octavianus want?'

'What he always wants, Antonius. Warships.'

'I don't have any.'

'*Gerrae!* The Piraeus is stuffed with them.' Maecenas set his wine to one side and steepled his fingers. 'Antonius, you cannot go on avoiding a meeting with Caesar Octavianus.'

'Hah! It wasn't I who failed to show up at Brundisium.'

'You sent no word of your coming, and you moved so swiftly that you caught Caesar Octavianus on the wrong foot, still in Rome. Then you didn't wait until he could make the journey.'

'He had no intention of making the journey. He just wanted to see me hop at his command.'

'No, he wouldn't do that.'

The argument went around and around for several hours, during which they ate a meal – in no mood to relish the dainties Octavia's cooks had put together – and during which Maecenas watched his quarry like a cat a mouse, still yet quivering with anticipation. Octavia, you are closer to the mark than you realize, he thought; blighted is exactly the right word to describe this new Antonius.

Finally he slapped his hands on his thighs and produced a noise of exasperation, the first sign he had made of impatience. 'Antonius, admit that, without your help, Caesar Octavianus cannot defeat Sextus Pompeius!' he said.

Antony lifted his lip. 'I admit that freely.'

'Then hasn't it occurred to you that all the money you need to regulate the East and invade the Kingdom of the Parthians is sitting in Sextus's vaults?'

'Well, yes . . . That has occurred to me.'

'Then if it has, why don't you start redistributing wealth in the proper way, the Roman way? Does it really matter that Caesar Octavianus will see his troubles dissolve if Sextus is defeated? Your troubles are what concern you, Antonius, and, like Caesar Octavianus's, they will melt into nothing once Sextus's vaults are thrown open. Isn't that more important to you than the fate of Caesar Octavianus? If you come back from the East with a brilliant campaign under your belt, who can rival you?'

'I don't trust your master, Maecenas. He'll think of a way to keep the contents of Sextus's vaults for himself.'

'That might be true if Sextus had less in them. I think you will admit that Caesar Octavianus has a head for figures, for the minutiae of accounting?'

Antony couldn't help laughing. 'At heart, he's another Atticus!'

'Then think about this. Whether it's grown in Sicilia on his land, or pilfered from the grain fleets of Africa and Sardinia, Sextus doesn't pay for the wheat he sells Rome – and you. This has been an ongoing fact since well before Philippi. Conservatively, the amount of grain he's stolen over the past six years comes to – in roundish figures – at least eighty million *modii*. Granting him a few greedy admirals and overheads – but not nearly as many overheads as Rome and you bear – Caesar Octavianus and his abacus have arrived at an average of twenty sesterces the *modius* in clear profit. Not fanciful! His price to Rome this year was forty, and it has never been less than twenty-five. Well, that means Sextus's vaults must contain in the neighborhood of one thousand eight hundred million sesterces. Divide by twenty-five thousand, and that's a staggering *seventy-two thousand talents*! Why, with half that, Caesar Octavianus can feed Italia, buy land to settle veterans *and* reduce taxes! While your half will let your legionaries wear silver mail shirts and put ostrich feather plumes in their helmets! The Treasury of Rome has never been as rich as Sextus Pompeius is right now, even after his father doubled its contents.'

Antony listened in rapt fascination, his spirits soaring. A dunce at arithmetic he might have been as a schoolboy (he and his brothers had played truant most of the time), but he had no trouble following Maecenas's lesson, and he knew that this had to be an accurate estimation of Sextus's present wealth. Jupiter, what a *cunnus*! Why hadn't he sat down with his abacus and come up with it? Octavian was right, Sextus Pompeius had bled Rome of all her wealth. Money didn't just disappear! Sextus had it!

'I see your point,' he said curtly.

'Then will you come in person to see Caesar Octavianus in the spring?'

'As long as the place isn't Brundisium.'

'Ah – how about Tarentum? A longer voyage, but not as arduous as Puteoli or Ostia. And it's on the Via Appia, very convenient for a visit to Rome afterward.'

That didn't suit Antony. 'No, the meeting has to be early in the spring, and brief. No squabbling or dickering. I have to be in Syria by summer to commence my invasion.'

That isn't going to happen, Antonius, Maecenas thought to himself. I've whetted your appetite by producing sums that a glutton like you can't resist. By the time you come to Tarentum, you will have realized how enormous the carcass is, and you'll want the lion's share. Born in the month of Sextilis, the Lion. Whereas Caesar is a cusp child, half the cool, meticulous Virgin, half the balance of the Scales. Your Mars is in the Lion too, but Caesar's Mars is in a far stronger constellation, the Scorpion. And his Jupiter is in the Sea Goat, together with his ascendant. Riches and success. Yes, I chose the right master. But then, I have the Scorpion's shrewdness and the ambivalence of the Fishes.

'Is that agreeable?' Antony rapped, apparently a repetition.

Jerked out of his astrological analysis, Maecenas started, then nodded. 'Yes. Tarentum on the Nones of April.'

'He took the bait,' Maecenas informed Octavian, Livia Drusilla and Agrippa when he arrived back in Rome just in time for the New Year and Agrippa's inauguration as senior consul.

'I knew he would,' Octavian said smugly.

'How long have you had that bait tucked in the sinus of your toga, Caesar?' Agrippa asked.

'From the very beginning, before I was Triumvir. It is just a matter of adding each year to the earlier ones.'

'Atticus, Oppius and the Balbi have indicated that they'll be willing to lend again to buy the next harvest,' Livia Drusilla said, smiling rather venomously. 'While you were away, Maecenas, Agrippa took them to see Portus Julius. They are beginning at last to believe that we will defeat Sextus.'

'Well, they can tot up figures better than Caesar,' Maecenas said. 'They know now their money is safe.'

Agrippa's inauguration went smoothly. Octavian watched the night skies with him during his vigil, and his perfect white bull accepted the hammer and the knife of *popa* and *cultarius* so calmly that the watching senators suppressed twinges of apprehension – a year of Marcus Vipsanius Agrippa was a year too many. Since Gaius

Caninius Gallus's white bull eluded the hammer and almost bolted before the stunning blow was finally administered, it didn't seem likely that Caninius would have the mettle to deal with this low-born, vulgar fellow.

Rome still rioted, but it was a hard winter; the Tiber froze, snow fell and didn't melt, a perishing north wind blew incessantly. None of which encouraged huge crowds in the Forum and squares, all of which permitted Octavian to venture from behind his walls, though Agrippa forbade him to tear them down. In the end, State grain sold for forty sesterces the *modius* – thanks to the plutocrat loans and a shocking interest bill – and Agrippa's increased activity on Portus Julius meant work was available for any man willing to quit Rome for Campania. The crisis wasn't over, but it had lessened.

Octavian's agents began to talk about the conference to be held at Tarentum on the Nones of April, predict that Sextus's days were numbered. The good times would return, they hymned.

This time Octavian wouldn't be late; he and his wife arrived in Tarentum well before the Nones, together with Maecenas and his brother-in-law, Murena. Wanting the conference to have the air of a fête, Octavian decorated the port city with wreaths and garlands, hired every mummer, magician, acrobat, musician, freak and specialty act Italy could produce, and erected a wooden theater for the staging of mimes and farces, the favorite fare of ordinary people. The great Marcus Antonius was coming to revel with Caesar Divi Filius! Even had Tarentum suffered at Antony's hands in the past – it had not – all resentments would have been forgotten. A festival of spring and prosperity, that was how the people saw it.

When Antony sailed in the day before the Nones, all Tarentum was lined up along the waterfront, cheering wildly, especially when the people realized that he had brought the hundred and twenty warships of his Athenian fleet with him.

'Wonderful, aren't they?' Octavian asked Agrippa as they stood at the harbor mouth looking for the flagship, which hadn't come in first. 'I count four admirals so far, but no Antonius. He must be wagging his tail in the rear. That's Ahenobarbus's standard – a black boar.'

'Apt,' said Agrippa, more interested in the ships. 'Every one of them is a decked five, Caesar. Bronze beaks, many double, plenty of room for artillery and marines. Oh, what I wouldn't give for a fleet like this!'

'My agents assure me he has more at Thasos, Samothrace and

Lesbos. Still in good condition, but in five years they won't be. Ah, here comes Antonius!'

Octavian pointed at a magnificent galley with a high poop to allow a roomy cabin beneath it, its deck bristling with catapults. His standard was a gold lion on a scarlet background, mouth open in a roar, black mane, a black-tipped tail. 'Apt,' Octavian said.

They began to walk back in the direction of the jetty chosen to receive the flagship, which the pilot was directing in a rowboat. No hurry; they would beat it easily.

'You must have your own standard, Agrippa,' Octavian said as he inspected the town spread around the shores, its houses white, its public buildings painted in bright colors, the umbrella pines and poplars in its squares strung with lanterns and bunting.

'I suppose I should,' Agrippa said, taken aback. 'What do you recommend, Caesar?'

'A pale blue background with the word FIDES written large in crimson,' Octavian said immediately.

'And your naval standard, Caesar?'

'I won't have one. I'll fly SPQR in a laurel wreath.'

'What about admirals like Taurus and Cornificius?'

'They'll fly Rome's SPQR, like me. Yours will be the only personal standard, Agrippa. A mark of distinction. It's you will win for us against Sextus, I know it in my bones.'

'At least his ships can't be mistaken, flying crossed bones.'

'Distinctive' was Octavian's reply. 'Oh, what wretch did that? Shameful!'

He referred to the red carpet that some official belonging to the *duumviri* had laid down the full length of the jetty, a sign of kingliness that horrified Octavian. But no one else seemed perturbed; it was the scarlet of a general, not the purple of a king. And there he was, jumping from the ship to the red matting, looking as fit and healthy as ever. Octavian and Agrippa waited together under the awning at the base of the jetty, with Caninius, the junior consul, one pace behind, and behind him seven hundred senators, all Mark Antony's men. The *duumviri* and other officials of the city had to be content with a position farther back still.

Of course Antony wore his gold dress armor; a toga didn't sit well on his bulk, made him look overweight. An equally muscular man, though more slender, Agrippa didn't care how he looked, so wore his purple-bordered toga. He and Octavian came forward to greet Antony, Octavian seeming a frail and delicate child between those two splendid warriors. Yet it was Octavian who dominated, perhaps because of that, perhaps because of his beauty, his thick thatch of bright golden hair. In this southern Italian town where Greeks had settled centuries before the first Romans penetrated the peninsula, bright gold hair was a rarity, and much admired.

It is done! Octavian thought. I've managed to get Antonius onto Italian soil, and he's not leaving it until he gives me what I want, what Rome must have.

Amid showers of spring petals thrown by little girls, they paraded to the complex of buildings set aside for them, smiling and waving at the ecstatic crowds.

'An afternoon and night to settle in,' said Octavian at the door of Antony's residence. 'Shall we get straight down to our business – I understand you're in a hurry – or shall we gratify the people of Tarentum by going to the theater tomorrow? They're playing an Atellan mime.'

'Not Sophocles, but more to everybody's taste,' Antony said, looking relaxed. 'Yes, why not? I've brought Octavia and the children with me – she was desperate to see her *little* brother.'

'No more desperate than I to see her. She hasn't met my wife – yes, I brought mine too,' said Octavian. 'Then shall we say the theater tomorrow morning, and a banquet tomorrow afternoon? After that – definitely down to business.'

When he walked into his own residence, Octavian found Maecenas in fits of laughter.

'You'll never guess!' Maecenas managed to gasp, wiping his eyes, then broke into a fresh paroxysm. 'Oh, it's funny!'

'What?' Octavian asked, allowing a servant to divest him of the toga. 'And where are the poets?'

'That's just it, Caesar! The poets!' Maecenas managed to command himself, occasionally swallowing, eyes still streaming. 'Horatius, Virgilius, Virgilius's shield companion Plotius Tucca, Varius Rufus and a few more minor luminaries set off from Rome a *nundinum* ago to elevate the intellectual tone of this Tarentum festivity, but . . .' he choked, giggled, composed himself . . . 'they went to Brundisium instead! And Brundisium won't let them go, determined to have its own festival!' He howled with laughter.

Octavian managed a smile, Agrippa rumbled a chuckle, but neither of them could appreciate the situation as Maecenas did, lacking his knowledge of the woolly-mindedness of poets.

When he found out, Antony roared quite as loudly as Maecenas, then sent a courier to Brundisium with a bag of gold for them.

* * *

Not expecting Octavia and the children, Octavian hadn't put Antony in a house big enough to accommodate everyone without the noise of the nursery disturbing him, but Livia Drusilla came up with a novel solution.

'I have heard of a house nearby whose owner is willing to donate it for the duration of the conference,' she said. 'Why don't I move into it together with Octavia and the children? If I am there as well, then Antonius can't complain of second-class treatment for *his* wife.'

Octavian kissed her hand, smiled into those wonderful stripey eyes. 'Brilliant, my love! Do so, immediately.'

'And, if you don't mind, we won't attend the play tomorrow. Not even Triumvirs can have their wives sit with them. I can never hear from the women's rows at the back and, besides, I don't think Octavia is anymore enamored of farces than I am.'

'Ask Burgundinus for a purse, and shop your way around the town. I know you have a weakness for pretty clothes, and you may find something you like. As I remember, Octavia likes to shop.'

'Don't worry about us,' said Livia Drusilla, very pleased. 'We may not find anything to wear, but it will be a chance to get to know each other.'

Octavia was curious about Livia Drusilla; like all of Rome's upper stratum, she had heard the story of her brother's peculiar passion for another man's wife, pregnant with his second child, that divorce on religious grounds, the sheer mystery surrounding him, her, the passion. Was it mutual? Did it exist at all?

The Livia Drusilla whom Octavia met was very different from the girl she had still been when she married Octavian. No demure, mouselike wife, this! thought Octavia, remembering the reports of Livia Drusilla. She beheld an elegantly dressed young matron whose hair was piled up in the latest fashion and who wore the correct amount of plain (but solid) gold jewellery. Compared to her, Octavia felt a nicely dressed frump – not surprising after a relatively long time in Athens, where women didn't mix in general society. Of course Roman wives insisted upon attending dinners given by Roman men, but those given by Greek men were closed to them; husbands only. So the center of feminine fashion was Rome, and never had Octavia realized that more than she did now, looking at her new sister-in-law.

'A very clever idea to put us both in the same house,' said Octavia when they were settled over sweet watered wine and honey-cakes still warm from the clay oven, a delicacy of the region.

'Well, it gives our husbands latitude,' said Livia Drusilla, smiling. 'I imagine Antonius would rather have come without you.'

'Your imagination is absolutely right,' Octavia said wryly. She leaned forward impulsively. 'But I don't matter! Tell me all about you and . . .' It was on the tip of her tongue to say 'Little Gaius', but something stopped her, warned her that that would be a mistake. Whatever she was, Livia Drusilla was neither sentimental nor feminine, so much was plain. 'You and Gaius,' she amended. 'One hears such idiotic tales, and I would like to know the truth.'

'We met in the ruins of Fregellae, and fell in love,' said Livia Drusilla in ordinary tones. 'That was our only meeting until we married *confarreatio*. I was seven months gone by then with my second son, Tiberius Claudius Nero Drusus, whom Caesar sent to his father to be reared.'

'Oh, you poor thing!' Octavia cried. 'It must have broken your heart.'

'Not at all.' Octavian's wife nibbled at a cake daintily. 'I dislike my children because I dislike their father.'

'You dislike a *child*?'

'Why not? They grow into the selfsame adults we dislike.'

'Have you seen them? Especially your second one – what do you call him for short?'

'His father chose Drusus. And no, I haven't seen him. He's thirteen months old now.'

'Surely you miss him!'

'Only when I got the milk sickness.'

'I . . . I . . .' Octavia floundered, and stammered into silence. She knew what people said of Little Gaius – that he was a cold fish. Well, he had married another cold fish. Yet both of them burned, just not for the things she, Octavia, held important. 'Are you happy?' she asked, trying to find some common ground.

'Yes, very. My life is so interesting these days. Caesar is a genius, the quality of his mind fascinates me. Such a privilege, to be his wife! And his helpmate. He listens to my advice.'

'Does he really?'

'All the time. We look forward to our night talks.'

'Night talks?'

'Yes, when we go to bed. He saves all the day's headaches to discuss with me in privacy.'

Pictures of this bizarre union danced before Octavia's eyes: two young and extremely attractive people cuddled together in their bed *talking*. Did they . . . did they . . . ? Perhaps after their conversation was finished, she concluded, then came out of her reverie with a start when Livia Drusilla laughed, bells tinkling.

'The moment he's thrashed his problems out, he falls asleep,' she said tenderly. 'He says he's never slept so well in all his life. Isn't that splendid?'

Oh, you're still a child! thought Octavia, understanding. A fishlet caught in my brother's net. He's molding you into what he needs, and conjugality isn't one of his needs. Has he even consummated your *confarreatio* marriage? You're so proud of that, when the truth is it binds you to him irrefutably. If it has been consummated, that's not what you yearn for either, you poor little fishlet. How perceptive he must be, to have met you once and seen what I see now – a hunger for power equal only to his own. Livia Drusilla, Livia Drusilla! You will lose your childishness, but never know the true happiness of a woman as I have known it, know it now . . . Rome's first couple, presenting an iron face to the world, fighting side by side to control every person and every situation you meet. Of course you've gulled Agrippa. He's as smitten with you as my brother is, I imagine.

'What of Scribonia?' she asked, changing the subject.

'She's well, though not happy,' said Livia Drusilla, sighing. 'I visit her once a week now that the city has settled down a bit – it's difficult to get out when the street gangs are rioting. Caesar put guards at her house too.'

'And Julia?'

For a moment Livia Drusilla looked blank, then her face cleared. 'Oh, *that* Julia! Funny, I always think of Divus Julius's daughter whenever I hear that name. She's very pretty.'

'She's two, so she must be walking and talking. Is she bright?'

'I really wouldn't know. Scribonia dotes on her.'

Suddenly Octavia felt tears close at hand, and rose. 'I am so tired, my dear. Do you mind if I have a nap? There's plenty of time to see the children – we'll be here for days.'

'*Nundinae*, more like,' said Livia Drusilla, obviously not enthralled at the prospect of meeting a tribe of small children.

Maecenas's private prediction was right; having spent the winter in Athens assimilating the size of the sum in Sextus Pompey's vaults, Antony wanted the lion's share.

'Eighty per cent of it to me,' he announced.

'In return for what?' Octavian asked, face impassive.

'The fleet I've brought to Tarentum and the services of three experienced admirals – Bibulus, Oppius Capito and Atratinus. Sixty of the ships are commanded by Oppius, the other sixty by Atratinus, while Bibulus acts as overall admiral.'

'And for twenty per cent, I am to provide another three hundred ships at least, plus a land army for the invasion of Sicilia.'

'Correct,' said Antony, looking at his nails.

'You don't feel that's a rather disproportionate split?'

Grinning, Antony leaned forward with an air of subtle menace. 'Put it this way, Octavianus – without me, you can't beat Sextus. Therefore I'm the one who dictates the terms.'

'Negotiating from a position of power. Yes, I understand that. But I don't agree, on two grounds. The first, that we will act in concert to eliminate a burr under *Rome's* saddle, not yours or mine. The second, that I need more than twenty per cent to repair Sextus's ravages and pay off Rome's debts.'

'I don't give a turd in a cesspit what you want or need! If I am to participate, I get eighty per cent.'

'Does that mean you'll be present in Agrigentum when we open Sextus's vaults?' asked Lepidus.

His arrival had come as a shock to Antony and Octavian, secure in the knowledge that the third Triumvir and his sixteen legions were safely tucked out of the way in Africa. How he had heard of the conference soon enough to make himself a part of it, Antony did not know, whereas Octavian suspected Lepidus's eldest son, Marcus, who was in Rome to marry Octavian's untouched first bride, Servilia Vatia. Someone had tattled, and Marcus had contacted Lepidus at once. If great spoils were in the offing, the Aemilii Lepidi must have their fair share.

'No, I won't be in Agrigentum!' Antony snapped. 'I'll be well on the way to reducing the Parthians.'

'Then how do you expect the division of what's in Sextus's vaults to follow your dictate?' Lepidus asked.

'Because if it doesn't, Pontifex Maximus, you'll be out of your priestly job and everything else! Do I care about your legions? No, I do not! The only legions worth their salt belong to me, and I won't be in the East forever. Eighty per cent.'

'Fifty per cent,' said Octavian, face still expressionless. He looked at Lepidus. 'And for you, Pontifex Maximus, nothing. Your services won't be required.'

'Nonsense, of course they will,' said Lepidus complacently. 'However, I'm not greedy. Ten per cent will do me nicely. You, Antonius, are not doing enough to warrant forty per cent, but I'll agree to that, as you're such a glutton. Octavianus has the most debts due to Sextus's activities, so he should get fifty per cent.'

'Eighty, or I take my fleet back to Athens.'

'Do so, and you get nothing,' said Octavian, leaning forward in subtle menace, an act he did better than Antony did. 'Do not mistake me, Antonius! Sextus Pompeius is going to go down next year, whether you donate a fleet or not. As a loyal and dutiful Triumvir, I am offering you a chance to share in the spoils of his defeat. *Offering*. Your war in the East, *if* successful, will benefit Rome and the Treasury, therefore a share will help fund that war. For no other reason do I offer. But Lepidus has a point. If I use his legions as well as Agrippa's to invade a very large and mountainous island once Sextus's fleets are no more, Sicilia will fall more quickly, and with less loss of life. So I am willing to concede our Pontifex Maximus ten per cent of the spoils. I need fifty per cent. That leaves you with forty. Forty per cent of seventy-two thousand is twenty-nine. That's about what Caesar had in his war chest for his campaign against the Parthians.'

Antony listened in obviously growing ire, but said nothing.

Octavian swept on. 'However, by the time we mount this all-out war against Sextus, he will have added twenty thousand talents to his hoard – the price of this year's harvest. That means he'll be sitting on about ninety-two thousand talents. Ten per cent of that is over nine thousand talents. Your forty, Antonius, goes up to about thirty-seven thousand. Think on that, do! A huge return for a minor investment – one fleet only, no matter how good.'

'Eighty,' Antony repeated, but wavering.

How much, Maecenas wondered, has he come prepared to take? Not eighty per cent – he must know he'd never get away with that. But clearly he's forgotten the addition of another harvest to the spoils. It depends on how much he's spent in his mind. On the old figures, thirty-six thousand. Accepting ten per cent less on the new figures, he comes out slightly ahead of that, if what he had counted on getting was fifty per cent.

'Remember,' said Octavian, 'whatever goes to you, Antonius, and to you, Lepidus, is paid in Rome's name. Neither of you will spend your share on Rome herself. Whereas my entire fifty per cent will go straight into the Treasury. I know the general is entitled to ten per cent, but I will take nothing. What would I use it for, if I did? My divine father left me more than enough in property for my needs, and I have bought the only Roman *domus* I'll ever require. It's already furnished. So my personal wants are quite nonexistent. My share goes wholly to Rome.'

'Seventy per cent,' said Antony. 'I'm the senior partner.'

'In what? Certainly not the war against Sextus Pompeius,' said Octavian. 'Forty per cent, Antonius. Take it or leave it.'

The wrangling went on for a month, at the end of which Antony should have been well on his way to Syria. That he remained where he was could be laid entirely at the door of Sextus's hoard, for he was determined to come out of the negotiations with enough to equip twenty legions superbly, and twenty thousand cavalry. Many hundreds of pieces of artillery. An enormous baggage train capable of carrying all the food and fodder his massive army would eat. Trust Octavian to imply that he would keep his percentage for himself! He would not, which Octavian well knew. It meant the finest army Rome had ever fielded. Oh, and the plunder at the end of his campaign! It would make Sextus Pompey's hoard look miserable.

Finally the percentages were agreed: fifty for Octavian and Rome, forty for Antony and the East, and ten for Lepidus in Africa.

'There are other things,' said Octavian. 'Things that have to be thrashed out now, not later.'

'Oh, Jupiter!' growled Antony. 'What?'

'The Pact of Puteoli, or Misenum, or whatever you want to call it, gave Sextus proconsular imperium over the Islands as well as the Peloponnese. And he is to be consul the year after next. Those are all things that must be stopped immediately. The Senate must re-enact its decree of *hostis*, forbid Sextus fire and water within a thousand miles of Rome, strip him of his so-called provinces and remove his name from the *fasti* – he cannot be consul, ever.'

'How can any of that be done immediately? The Senate meets in Rome,' Antony objected.

'Why, when the subject is war? When it discusses war, the Senate must meet outside the *pomerium*. And Tarentum is definitely outside the *pomerium*. There are over seven hundred of your tame senators here, Antonius, busy smarming up to you so assiduously that their noses have turned quite brown,' Octavian said acidly. 'We also have the Pontifex Maximus here, and you are an augur, and I am priest and augur. There is no impediment, Antonius, none at all.'

'The Senate must convene in an inaugurated building.'

'Of which, no doubt, Tarentum has its share.'

'You've forgotten one thing, Octavianus,' said Lepidus.

'Pray enlighten me.'

'The name Sextus Pompeius is on the *fasti* already – that's what happens when we choose the consuls years in advance and then simply pretend to have them elected. To strike it off would be *nefas*.'

Octavian giggled. 'Why strike it off, Lepidus? I don't see the need. Have you forgotten there's another Sextus Pompeius of the same family strutting around Rome? There's no reason he can't be consul the year after next – he was one of the sixty praetors who served last year.'

Every face broke into a broad grin.

'Brilliant, Octavianus!' Lepidus cried. 'I know the fellow – Pompeius Strabo's brother's grandson. He'll be flattered to death.'

'Just flattered to near death will do, Lepidus.' Octavian stretched, yawned, managed to look like a contented cat. 'Do you suppose this means we can conclude a Pact of Tarentum and repair to Rome to spread the joyous news that the Triumvirate has been renewed for a further five years, and the days of Sextus Pompeius the pirate are numbered? You must come, Antonius, it's already too late for a campaign this year.'

'Oh, Antonius, how delightful!' Octavia cried when he told her. 'I can see Mama, and visit little Julia for myself – Livia Drusilla is indifferent to her plight, won't exert herself to persuade little . . . Caesar Octavianus, I mean . . . to keep in touch with his daughter. I fear for the mite.'

'You're pregnant again,' said Antony, light dawning.

'You guessed! How amazing! It's barely a fact yet, and I was waiting until I was sure before I told you. I hope it's a son.'

'Son, daughter, what does it matter? I have plenty of both.'

'Indeed you do,' said Octavia. 'More than any other man of distinction, especially if you include Cleopatra's twins.'

A smile flashed. 'Irked, my dear?'

'*Ecastor*, no! Just rather proud of your virility, I think,' she said with an answering smile. 'I confess that sometimes I find myself wondering about her – Cleopatra. Is she well? Is life pleasant for her? She's faded out of consciousness to most of Rome, including my brother. A pity in a way, since she has a son by Divus Julius as well as your twins. Perhaps one day she will return to Rome. I would like to see her again.'

He reached for her hand, kissed it. 'One thing I'll say for you, Octavia – you don't have a jealous bone in your body.'

In Rome, Antony found two letters waiting for him: one from Herod and one from Cleopatra. Considering Cleopatra's of less moment, he snapped the wax seal on Herod's letter first.

My dear Antonius, I am King of the Jews at last! It wasn't easy, given the military ineptitude of Gaius Sosius – no Silo, he! A good peacetime governor, but not up to the task of disciplining the Jews. However, he paid me a signal honor by giving me two very good legions of Roman troops and letting *me* lead them south to Judaea. Antigonus came out of Jerusalem to meet me at Jericho, and I utterly routed him.

He then fled to Jerusalem, which underwent siege. It fell when Sosius sent me two more good legions. He came with them himself. When the city fell he wanted to sack it, but I talked him out of it. What I wanted and Rome needed, I said to him, was a prosperous Judaea, not a pillaged desert. Eventually, he agreed. We have put Antigonus in chains and sent him to Antioch. Once you are in Antioch, you can decide what to do with him, but I strongly urge execution.

I have freed my family and the family of Hyrcanus from Masada, and married Mariamne. She is pregnant with our first child. Since I am not a Jew, I did not appoint myself High Priest. That honor went to a Zadokite, Ananeel, who will do exactly as I tell him. Of course I have opposition, and there are some who conspire to take up arms against me, but nothing will come of it. My foot is now firmly on the Jewish neck, and will never be lifted while there is life in my body.

Please, I beg you, Marcus Antonius, give me back a whole and contiguous Judaea instead of these five separate places! I need a seaport, and would be happy with Joppa. Gaza is a little too far south. The best news is that I have wrested the bitumen fisheries off Malchus of Nabataea, who sided with the Parthians and refused me, his own nephew, succor.

I close thanking you most profusely for your support. Rest assured that Rome will never regret making me King of the Jews.

Antony let the scroll curl up and sat for a moment with his hands behind his head, smiling at his thoughts of the semitic toad.

Maecenas in eastern guise, but owning a ruthlessness and savagery that Maecenas completely lacked. The thing was, what would benefit Rome's interests in southern Syria most? A reunited Judaic kingdom, or a fragmented one? Without expanding his geographical borders by one mile, Herod had enriched himself mightily by acquiring the balsam gardens of Jericho and the bitumen fisheries of the Palus Asphaltites. The Jews were warlike and made excellent soldiers – did Rome need a wealthy Judaea ruled by a highly intelligent man? What would happen if Judaea engulfed all of Syria south of the Orontes River? Where would its king look next? To Nabataea, which would give him one of the two great fleets engaged in trade with India and Taprobane. More wealth. After that, he'd look to Egypt, less of a hazard than any attempted expansion north into Rome's provinces. Hmmm . . .

He picked up Cleopatra's letter, broke the seal, and read it more quickly by far than he had Herod's. Not that they were so very different, Herod and Cleopatra: not an ounce of sentimentality in either of them. As always, she had written a litany of praise for Caesarion, but that wasn't sentimentality, that was the lioness and her cub. Caesarion apart, it was the letter of a sovereign rather than an ex-mistress. Glaphyra would do well to emulate her Egyptian counterpart.

Cleopatra's beaky little face swam before his inner gaze, the golden eyes shining as they did when she was happy – was she happy? Such a businesslike letter, softened only by love for her older son. Well, she was a ruler first, a woman second. But at least she had more to talk about than Octavia, immersed in her pregnancy and loving being in Rome again. Though she didn't see a great deal of Livia Drusilla, whom she considered cold and calculating. Not that she'd said so – when did his present wife ever commit a social solecism, even in private to her husband? But Antony knew because he shared Octavia's dislike; the girl was so absolutely Octavian's creature. What did Octavian have, that he could grab and hold certain chosen people with talons of steel? Agrippa. Maecenas. And now Livia Drusilla.

Suddenly he was filled with loathing of Rome, of Rome's tight little ruling class, Rome's greed, Rome's inexorable goals, Rome's divine right to rule the world. Even the Sullas and the Caesars abnegated their own desires before Rome, offered everything they did on Rome's altars, fed Rome with their strength, their deeds, the *animus* that drove them. Was that what was wrong with him? Was he incapable of that kind of dedication to an abstraction, an idea? Alexander the Great didn't think of Macedon the way Caesar had Rome; he thought of himself first, he dreamed of his own godhead, not his country's might. Of course, that was why his empire fell apart as soon as he died. Rome's empire would never fall apart because of one man's death, or even the deaths of many men. A Roman man had his place in a temporary sun, he never thought of himself as *the* sun. Alexander the Great had. And perhaps Marcus Antonius did too. Yes, Marcus Antonius wanted a sun of his own, and his sun was not Rome's. No, it was *not* Rome's!

Why had he let that lot in Tarentum whittle his percentage down? All he had to do was sail away with his fleet, but he hadn't. Thinking he was staying in order to ensure the safety and welfare of his troops when he invaded the Kingdom of the Parthians. Being fobbed off with mere promises! Yes, I promise that I'll give you twenty thousand well-trained legionaries, said Octavianus, lying through his teeth. I promise I'll send your forty per cent the moment we open Sextus's vault door. I promise you'll be consul. I promise you'll be the senior Triumvir. I promise to care for your interests in the West. I promise this, I promise that. Lies, lies, all lies!

Consider, Antonius. *Think!* You have over seven hundred out of the thousand senators. You can rally voters in the upper classes and control laws, elections. But somehow you can never get to him, Caesar Octavianus. That's because he's here in Rome, and you're not. Even this interminable summer, while you are physically here, you can't marshal your forces to destroy him. The senators are waiting to see how much they'll get out of Sextus Pompeius's coffers – those among them, that is, who haven't disappeared to their seaside villas for a summer out of stinking, sweltering Rome. And the People are losing sight of you. Now you're back, a lot of them don't recognize you at a glance anymore, though it's only two years since you were last here. They may hate Octavianus, but he's a familiar and much-loved hate – the kind of man whom every man thinks he has to love to hate. Whereas I am not even seen as Rome's savior these days. They have waited too long for me to assert myself. Five years since Philippi, and I haven't managed to do what I said I'd do in the East. The knights loathe me more than they do Octavianus – he owes them millions upon millions, which makes him theirs. I don't owe them anything, but I haven't succeeded in making the East a safe place to conduct business, and that they can't forgive.

The month of Julius has come and gone, Sextilis is fast disappearing into that maw I don't understand. Why does time fly so quickly? Next year – it *must* be next year! If it isn't, I will be a has-been, an also-ran. While that little turd wins.

Octavia came into the room, hesitated with a tentative smile, then continued when he beckoned her.

'Don't look afraid,' he said, voice deep. 'I won't eat you.'

'I didn't think you would, my dear. I just wondered when we were leaving for Athens.'

'On the Kalends of September.' He cleared his throat. 'I'll be taking you, but not the children. By the end of the year I'll be in Antioch, which means an exile for you in Athens. The children would be better off in Rome, under your brother's protection.'

Her face fell, her eyes filled with unshed tears. 'Oh, that will be hard!' she said, voice breaking. 'They need me.'

'You can stay here if you want,' he said curtly.

'No, Antonius, I can't. My place is with you, even if you are not in Athens very often.'

'Whatever you like.'

FOURTEEN

There was a new Quintus Dellius in Antony's life, a tall and extremely elegant senator of a fairly old family that had, for instance, produced a Vestal Virgin close to a hundred years ago, and disclaimed any blood relationship to Sulla's beloved centurion who saved a legion from the German Cimbri and won a Grass Crown. No, the Fonteii Capitones were genuine Roman plebeian aristocrats. His name was Gaius Fonteius Capito, and he was as handsome as any Memmius, as well educated as any Mucius Scaevola. Nor was Fonteius a sycophant; he enjoyed Antony's company, brought out the best in Antony, and, as a loyal client, was pleased to do Antony a service, but he owned himself.

When Antony quit Rome and Italia at the beginning of September, embarking himself and Octavia on his flagship at Tarentum, he took Fonteius with him. The hundred and twenty ships of his fleet had been joined by twenty more quinqueremes that Octavia had donated to her brother out of her private fortune; all one hundred and forty were still at anchor in Tarentum, busy building ship-sheds so the vessels could be drawn up out of the water before winter.

It was still a little early for equinoctial gales, thus Antony was anxious to be gone, hoping to sail before a following wind and a following sea all the way around Cape Taenarum at the foot of the Peloponnese, and thus up to Athens to anchor in the Piraeus.

But, three days out, they encountered a terrible storm that forced them to seek shelter on Corcyra, a beautiful isle off the Greek Peloponnese. The tossing sea hadn't been kind to Octavia, nearing the end of her seventh month, so she greeted *terra firma* with gratitude.

'I hate to see you delayed,' she said to Antony, 'but I confess I hope we have several days here. My baby must be a soldier, not a sailor.'

He didn't smile at her little joke, too impatient to be on his way to be moved by his wife's suffering, or her gallant attempts not to be a nuisance. 'As soon as the captain says we can put out, we sail again,' he said brusquely.

'Of course. I'll be ready.'

That evening she didn't appear for supper, pleading a stomach still churning from its maritime ordeal, and Antony was tired of the usual group who surrounded him, jockeying for his attention, forcing him to assume a bonhomie he didn't feel. In fact, the only one he was drawn to was Fonteius, whom he bade join him for supper, just the two of them.

Shrewd in the manner of a natural diplomat, and fonder of Antony than he was of himself, Fonteius accepted gracefully. He had long divined that Antony wasn't happy, and maybe tonight was his chance to probe Antony's wound, see if he could find the poisoned dart.

It was an ideal evening for intimate talk; the lamp flames flickered crazily in tendrils of the wind roaring outside, rain hissed against the shutters, a small torrent gurgled as it rushed down the hill. Coals glowed red in several braziers to take the chill out of the room, and the servants moved like *lemures* in and out of the shadows.

Perhaps because of the atmosphere, or perhaps because Fonteius knew exactly how to trigger the right responses, Antony found himself pouring out his fears, dilemmas and anxieties with little logic or order.

'Where is my place?' he asked Fonteius. 'What do I want? Am I a true Roman, or has something happened to make me less a Roman than I used to be? Everything at my fingertips, great power – and yet – and yet . . . I seem to have no place to call my own. Or is place the wrong word? I don't *know*!'

'It might be that you have become too isolated,' said Fonteius, picking his way delicately. 'You love to revel, to be with the men you deem your friends and the women you desire. The face you show to the world is bold, brazen, uncomplicated. But I see many complications beneath that exterior. One of them led you to a peripheral participation in the murder of Caesar – no, don't deny it! I do not blame you, I blame Caesar. He killed you too, by making Octavianus his heir. I can only imagine how deeply that cut you! You had spent your life to that time in Caesar's service, and a man of your temperament couldn't see why Caesar condemned some of your actions. Then he left a will that didn't even mention you. A cruel blow that utterly destroyed your *dignitas*. For men wondered why Caesar left his name, his legions, his money and his power to a pretty-boy youth rather than to you, his cousin and a man in his prime. They interpreted Caesar's will as a sign of his colossal displeasure at your conduct. That wouldn't have mattered were it not that he was Caesar, the idol of the people – they have made him a god, and gods do not make wrong decisions. Therefore – you were not worthy to be Caesar's heir. You could never become another Caesar. *Caesar* made that impossible, not Octavianus. He stripped you of your *dignitas*.'

'Yes, I see,' said Antony slowly, hands clenching. 'The old boy spat on me.'

'You are not naturally insightful, Antonius. You like to deal with concrete facts, and you have Alexander the Great's propensity to use a sword on knotty problems. You don't have Octavianus's ability to burrow beneath society's skin, to whisper defamations as truths in a way people come to believe. The source of your troubled thoughts is the stain upon your reputation that Caesar put there. Why, for instance, did you choose the East as your Triumvirate? You probably think you did because of the riches and the wars you could fight there. But I don't think that's why at all. I think it was an honorable way to get out of being in Rome and Italia, where you would have had to display yourself before people who know Caesar despised you. Dig down inside yourself, Antonius! Find your injury, identify it for what it is!'

'Luck!' said Antony, shocking Fonteius. Then, louder, '*Luck*! Caesar's luck was proverbial, it was a part of his legend. But, when he cut me out of his will, he passed his luck to Octavianus. How else has the little worm survived? He has Caesar's luck, that's how! While I lost mine. Lost it! And that's the crux of it, Fonteius. Whatever I do is unlucky – how does anyone deal with that? I know I can't.'

'But you can, Antonius!' Fonteius cried, recovering from this extraordinary development. 'If you choose to regard your present melancholy as loss of luck, then make your own luck in the East! It's not a task beyond you. Retrieve your reputation with the knights by creating an East perfect for business opportunities! And take yourself an Eastern adviser, someone of the East and for the East.' He paused, thinking of Pythodorus of Tralles, bound to Antony by marital ties. 'An adviser with power, influence, wealth. You have five more years as Triumvir thanks to the Pact of Tarentum – use them! Create a bottomless well of luck!'

Prickles of exhilaration sparkled through Antony, banishing his gloominess. Suddenly he saw his way clear, how to regain his luck.

'Would you undertake a long voyage for me on winter seas?' he asked Fonteius.

'Anything, Antonius. I'm genuinely concerned for your future, which isn't in harmony with Octavianus's Rome. That's another factor causing melancholy – that the Rome Octavianus is intent upon making is alien to the Roman men who prize Rome as she used to be. Caesar started tampering with the rights and prerogatives of the First Class, and Octavianus is determined to continue that work. I think that, when you find your luck, you should aim at bringing Rome back to what she used to be.' Fonteius lifted his head, listened to the sounds of wind and rain, smiled. 'The gale is blowing itself out. Where do you want me to go?' It was a rhetorical question: Tralles and Pythodorus, he knew.

'To Egypt. I want you to see Cleopatra and persuade her to join me in Antioch before winter is over. Will you do that?'

'It is my pleasure, Antonius,' Fonteius said, concealing his dismayed disappointment. 'If there's a ship in harbor here in Corcyra seaworthy enough to sail the Libyan Ocean, I'll go at once.' A rueful look appeared. 'However, my purse isn't deep. I'll need money.'

'Money you shall have, Fonteius!' Antony huffed, his face transfigured with happiness. 'Oh, Fonteius, thank you for showing me what to do! I must use the East to force Rome to reject the machinations of Caesar and Caesar's heir!'

When Antony passed by the door of Octavia's room on his way to his own, he was still fizzing with excitement, and full of a new urgency to reach Antioch. No, he wouldn't stop in Athens! He would sail directly to Antioch. The decision made, he opened Octavia's door and entered to find her snuggled up in bed. He sat on the edge of it and pushed a wisp of hair off her brow, smiling.

'My poor girl!' he said tenderly. 'I should have left you in Rome, not subjected you to the Ionian Sea near the equinox.'

'I'll be better in the morning, Antonius.'

'And so you may be, but here you stay until you can obtain passage to Italia,' he said. 'No, don't protest! I'll have no arguments, Octavia. Go back to Rome and have our baby there. You miss the children, who are in Rome. I'm not going to Athens, I'm going straight to Antioch, no place for you.'

Sadness washed over her; she gazed into those reddish eyes with pain in her own. How she knew it, she had no idea, but this was going to be the last time she ever saw Marcus Antonius, her beloved husband. Goodbye on the island of Corcyra – who could ever have predicted that?

'I will do whatever you think best,' she said, swallowing.

'Good!' He got up, leaned to kiss her.

'But I will see you in the morning, won't I?'

'You will, definitely you will.'

When he was gone she rolled over, pushed her face into the pillow. Not to weep; the agony was too great for tears. What she looked at was the loneliness.

Fonteius got away first. A Syrian merchantman had also put in to wait out the tempest, and since its captain had to brave the Libyan Sea anyway, he said, he wasn't averse to an extra stop in Alexandria for a nice fat fee. His holds were loaded with Gallic iron-tyred wagon wheels, copper pots from Nearer Spain, some firkins of *garum* flavoring, and, to fill up the spaces, linen canvas from the lands of the Petrocorii. This meant his vessel sat low but well in the water, and he was willing to give up his cabin under the poop for this foppish senator with his seven servants.

Fonteius waved Antony goodbye, still stunned. How horribly it had all gone wrong! And how presumptuous he had been, to think that he could read the mind of Antonius, let alone manipulate it! Why had the man fixed on luck, of all things? A phantasm, a figment of the imagination. Fonteius didn't believe luck existed as an entity of itself, no matter what people said about Caesar's luck. Yet Antony had soared over the top of the truth he ought to have seen, to fix on luck. *Luck!* As for Cleopatra . . . ! Ye gods, what was he thinking about, to choose her as his Eastern adviser? She'd tweak and twist, compounding his confusion. The blood of King Mithridates the Great flowed in her veins, along with a bevy of murdering, amoral Ptolemies, and a few Parthians to boot. To Fonteius, she was a distillation of all that was worst about the East.

Fonteius wanted civil war, if civil war was what it took to get rid of Octavian. And the only man who could successfully beat Octavian was Mark Antony. Not the Antony whom Fonteius had seen emerging over the past years; it needed the Antony of Philippi. Cleopatra? Oh, Antonius, a bad choice! He had been friendly with Caesar's widow, Calpurnia, before she took her life, and Calpurnia had given him a fairly comprehensive sketch of the Cleopatra she and other women had known in Rome. A sketch that didn't inspire hope in Antony's ambassador.

Who arrived in Alexandria after a month's passage due to a storm that forced them to spend six days in Paraetonium – what a place! But the captain had found *laserpicium* there, and tossed enough canvas overboard to make room for twenty amphorae of it.

'My fortune is made!' he told Fonteius jubilantly. 'With Marcus Antonius coming to live in Antioch, there will be so much overindulgence in food that I'll be able to ask a fortune for one dose! At several thousand spoonfuls per amphora – ah, bliss!'

Though he hadn't been to Alexandria before, Fonteius wasn't very impressed by the city's undeniable beauty, its layout of wide streets. Maecenas, he reflected, would have called it a desert of right angles. However, thanks to each succeeding Ptolemy's passion for erecting a new palace, the Royal Enclosure had charm. Two dozen palaces at least, plus an audience chamber.

There, amid a blaze of gold that had awed every Roman who had seen it, he met two marionettes. That was the only word he could attribute to them, they were so stiff, wooden, and painted. A pair of dolls made in Saturnia or Florentia, their strings manipulated by an invisible master. The audience was brief; he was not asked to state his business, simply to convey greetings from the Triumvir Marcus Antonius.

'You may go, Gaius Fonteius Capito,' said the white-faced doll on the higher throne.

'We thank you for coming,' said the red-faced doll on the lower throne.

'A servant will conduct you to dinner with us this afternoon.'

Removal of the maquillage and paraphernalia revealed two small people, though the boy wasn't going to be a small man. Fonteius knew his age – ten – and thought he looked more like thirteen or fourteen, save that puberty had not yet started. Caesar's image! Another player on the stage of the future, and an unexpected but immensely urgent reason why Antony should not be associating with this woman. Caesarion was the sole object of her affections, it shone out of her magnificent golden eyes every time they rested on him. For the rest, she was skinny, tiny, almost ugly. The eyes and a beautiful skin saved her; she also had a low, melodious and cleverly used voice. Both of them spoke to him in Latin he could not fault.

'Did Marcus Antonius send you to warn us he is coming here?' the boy asked eagerly. 'Oh, I have missed him!'

'No, Your Majesty, he isn't coming here.'

The bright face fell, its vivid blue eyes looked away. 'Oh.'

'A disappointment,' the mother observed. 'Why are you here, then?'

'By this time Marcus Antonius should have taken up residence in Antioch,' said Fonteius, thinking that the freshwater shrimp he was eating lacked flavor. With Our Sea at the foot of her palace steps, why didn't she direct her fishing fleets to catch saltwater ones? While his mind dealt with this conundrum, his lips continued to speak. 'He plans to make his stay there a permanent one, for two reasons.'

'One of which,' said the boy, 'is its proximity to the lands of the Parthians. He'll jump off from Antioch.'

The rude little monster! thought Fonteius. Butting in to an adult conversation! What's more, his mother thinks that's normal as well as wonderful. All right, little monster, let's see how smart you really are! 'And the second reason?' Fonteius asked.

'It's truly East, which can't be said of Asia Province, and certainly not of Greece or Macedonia. If Antonius is to regulate the East, he should be situated somewhere truly East, and Antioch or Damascus is ideal,' said Caesarion, unabashed.

'Then why not Damascus?'

'A better climate, but too far from the sea.'

'Just what Antonius himself said,' Fonteius answered, too much the diplomat to let his displeasure show.

'So why are you here, Gaius Fonteius?' the Queen asked.

'To invite you, Your Majesty, to Antioch. Marcus Antonius is very anxious to see you, but more than that. He is in need of advice from someone who is Eastern by birth and culture, and thinks you are by far the best candidate.'

'He considered other people?' she asked sharply, frowning.

'No, I did,' said Fonteius quietly. 'I brought forward names, but Antonius spoke only the one – yours.'

'Ah!' She lay back on her couch and smiled like the tawny cat which lay at her elbow. One thin hand went out to stroke the creature's back, and it turned its smile on her.

'You like cats,' he said.

'Cats are sacred, Gaius Fonteius. Once upon a time, perhaps

twenty-five years ago, a Roman businessman in Alexandria killed a cat. The people tore him into little pieces.'

'Brr!' he said with a shiver. 'I am used to grey cats with stripes or spots, but I have never seen one this color.'

'She is Egyptian. I call her Bastella – to call her Bast would be sacrilegious, but I got good omens for the Latin diminutive.' Cleopatra turned from the cat, reached to eat a date. 'So Marcus Antonius commands me to come to Antioch?'

'Not commands, Your Majesty. Requests.'

'In a pig's eye!' said Caesarion, chuckling. 'He commands.'

'You may tell him I will come.'

'And I!' said the boy quickly.

A curious little dumb show followed between mother and son; no word was said, though she yearned to speak. A tussle of wills. That the boy won it was no surprise to Fonteius: Cleopatra had not been born an autocrat; circumstances had made her one. Whereas Caesarion was an autocrat formed in the womb. Just like his *tata*. Fonteius experienced a frisson of fear that streaked down his backbone and stood his hair on end. Imagine what Caesarion would be like when fully grown! The blood of Gaius Julius Caesar and the blood of Eastern tyrants. He would be unstoppable. And it is because Cleopatra knows it that she will pimp and pander for poor Antonius. Caring nothing for Antonius or his fate. Wanting her son by Caesar to rule the world.

Fonteius was advised to set off overland, accompanied by an Egyptian guard Cleopatra said was necessary: Syria was full of brigands since the various principates had foundered during the Parthian occupation.

'I will follow you as soon as I can,' she told Fonteius, 'but I do not think it will be before the new year. If Caesarion insists upon coming, I'll have to arrange for a regent and a council, though Caesarion won't be staying in Antioch more than a few days.'

'Does he know that?' Fonteius asked slyly.

'Certainly,' Cleopatra said stiffly.

'What about Antonius's children?'

'To see them, Antonius must come to Alexandria.'

A month later Fonteius found Antony in residence in Antioch, and working hard. Lucilius ran to obey one order after another, while Antony sat at his desk and reviewed stacks of papers, a very few scrolls. His only recreation was parading his troops, back in winter camp after a brisk campaign into Armenia that Publius Canidius had conducted as efficiently as Ventidius had the previous campaigns; Canidius himself had stayed in the north with ten of the legions, waiting for the spring, the rest of the legions, the cavalry, and Marcus Antonius. The only thing Canidius did wrong in Antony's eyes was to warn him in every letter that King Artavasdes of Armenia was not to be trusted, for all his protestations of loyalty to Rome and of enmity for the Parthians. A prophecy Antony chose to ignore, more wary of the other Artavasdes, King of Media. He too was making overtures of friendship.

'I see the city is filling up with potentates and would-be potentates,' Fonteius said as he sank into a chair.

'Yes, I've finally got all of them sorted out, so I summoned them to hear their fates,' Antony said with a grin. 'Is she . . . is she coming?' he added, the amusement fading before anxiety.

'As soon as she can. That impudent brat Caesarion has insisted on coming with her, so she has to find a regent.'

'Impudent brat?' Antony asked, frowning.

'So *I* consider him. Insufferable, actually.'

'Oh, well, he participates in the monarchy as his mother's equal – both of them are Pharaoh.'

'Pharaoh?' Fonteius asked.

'Aye, supreme ruler of river Nilus, the true kingdom of Egypt. Alexandria is considered non-Egyptian.'

'I agree with that, at any rate. Very Greek indeed.'

'Oh, not inside the Royal Enclosure.' Antony tried to look disinterested. 'When exactly is she coming?'

'Early in the new year.'

Crestfallen, Antony waved a vague hand of dismissal. 'Tomorrow I'm going to hand out Rome's largesse to all the potentates and would-be potentates,' he said. 'In the agora. Custom and tradition say I should wear a toga, but I hate the things. I'm wearing gold armor. Have you got a dress set with you?'

Fonteius blinked. 'No, Antonius, not even a workaday set.'

'Then Sosius can lend you some.'

'Is armor . . . er . . . legal?'

'Outside Italia, anything the Triumvir decides is legal. I thought you knew that, Fonteius.'

'I confess I didn't.'

Antony had set up a tall tribunal in the agora, the biggest open space in Antioch, and there he seated himself in military splendor, with Sosius the governor and his legates seated atop the tribunal in less prominent positions, and poor Fonteius, uncomfortable enough because of the borrowed armor, all on his own. When exactly, he wondered, did Antony start using twenty-four lictors? The only magistrate entitled to so many was the Dictator, and Antony himself had abolished the dictatorship. Yet here he sat, with a dictatorial number of lictors! Something that Octavian in Rome did not dare to do, Divi Filius notwithstanding.

It was a closed meeting; those present had formal invitations. Guards blocked the many entrances, much to the ire of Antiochites not used to being excluded from their own public spaces.

No prayers were said or auguries taken, an interesting and odd omission. Antony simply launched into speech, using his high voice, which carried farther.

'After many moons of deep thought, careful consideration, many interviews and inspections of documents, I, Imperator and Triumvir Marcus Antonius, have come to a decision about the East.

'First, what is the East? I do not include Macedonia and its prefectures that cover Greece proper, the Peloponnese, Cyrenaica and Crete, to be a part of the East. Though my Triumvirate includes them, they belong geographically and physically to the world of Our Sea. The East is Asia – that is, all land east of the Hellespont, the Propontis, and the Thracian Bosporus.'

Hmmm, thought Fonteius, this is going to be interesting! I begin to see why he chose to display Rome's armed might rather than her civilian government.

'There will be three Roman provinces in the East, each under the direct control of Rome through a governor! First, the province of Bithynia, which will include the Troad and Mysia, and have its eastern boundary at the Sangarius River. Second, the province of Asia, incorporating Lydia, Caria and Lycia! And third, the province of Syria, bordered by the Amanus ranges, the western bank of the Euphrates River, and the deserts of Idumaea and Arabia Petraea. However, southern Syria will also incorporate kingdoms, satrapies and principalities, as will the western bank of the Euphrates!'

The small crowd stirred, some faces eager, some downcast. To one side and under heavy guard stood several Eastern-looking men chained together. Who are they? Fonteius asked himself. Never mind, I'm bound to find out.

'Amyntas, come forward!' Antony shouted.

A young man in Greek garb stepped out of the crowd.

'Amyntas, son of Demetrius of Ancyra, in Rome's name I appoint you King of Galatia! Your realm includes all four Galatian tet-

271

rarchies, Pisidia, Lycaonia, and all regions from the south bank of the Halys River to the coast of Pamphylia!'

A huge gasp went up; Antony had just given Amyntas a bigger kingdom than ambitious old Deiotarus had ever ruled.

'Polemon, son of Zeno of Laodiceia, in Rome's name I appoint you King of Pontus and Armenia Parva, including all lands on the north bank of the Halys River!'

Polemon's was a familiar face; he had done a lot of dancing to Antony's tune in Athens. Now he had his reward, a big one.

'Archelaus Sisenes, son of Glaphyra, Priest-king of Ma, in Rome's name I appoint you King of Cappadocia, commencing east of the great bend in the river Halys and incorporating all lands on its south bank from that point to the Tarsian coast and the coast of Cilicia Pedia. Your eastern boundary is the Euphrates River above Samosata. I may designate small areas within your realm as better ruled by another, but in effect such is yours.'

Another very pleased young man, thought Fonteius, and look at his mother! Rumor says she sucked it out of Antonius with her vagina. Clever to choose young men. Clients for decades.

More minor now, the appointments continued; Tarcondimotus, others. But then came the executions, something Fonteius had not counted on. Lysanias of Chalcis, Antigonus of the Jews, Ariarathes of Cappadocia. Oh, I am not a warrior! cried Fonteius to himself, hanging onto his gorge as the reek of blood stole upward in the hot sun and the sticky flies came in syrupy swarms. Antony viewed the carnage indifferently; Sosius fainted. That I refuse to do, said Fonteius silently, thanking every god there was when finally he could depart for the governor's palace. Of course Antony stayed behind; he was giving a feast for the new rulers and their hordes of followers right there in the agora, as the palace was not endowed with big rooms or spacious courtyards. If Fonteius hadn't known better, he would have said that the governor's palace in Antioch had once been a particularly vile caravanserai, not the home of kings like Antiochus and Tigranes.

On the morrow he met his first genuine Parthian, a refugee named Monaeses from the court of the new king, Phraates. Tricked out in ringleted curls, an artificial wig-beard held on by gold wires looped behind each ear, a frilly skirt, fringed jacket, and huge amounts of gold.

'I'm thinking of making him King of the Skenite Arabs,' said Antony, pleased with his dispositions. Seeing the look on Fonteius's face, he seemed surprised. 'Now why the disapproval? Because he's a Parthian? I *like* him! Phraates murdered the whole family except for Monaeses, who was clever enough to escape.'

'Or was his escape assisted?' Fonteius asked.

'Why on earth should it have been?' Antony demanded.

'Because the whole world knows you're planning to invade the Kingdom of the Parthians, that's why! No matter how obsessed a king may be at being deposed by his own flesh and blood, he'd be stupid not to save *one* heir! I think Monaeses is here as a Parthian spy. Besides, he's very proud and haughty. I can't think he'd be thrilled at the thought of kinging it over a bunch of desert Arabs.'

'*Gerrae!*' Antony exclaimed, unimpressed by any of this. 'I think Monaeses is a good man, and I'll take a bet that I'm right. A thousand denarii?'

'Done!' said Fonteius.

The chief reason Cleopatra took her time about traveling to Antioch had nothing to do with finding a regent or a council; that alternative was always set up ready to go. She wanted time to think and time to arrive at the proper moment. Not too fast, not too slow. And what was she going to ask for when she reached Antioch? This summons had come by a very different man than Quintus Dellius; Fonteius was an aristocrat and devoted to Antony; he wasn't in it for the money. Too sophisticated to be caught out, nonetheless he gave out an aura of apprehension – no, *worry*. That was it, worry! Though life for the past four years had been uneventful, senior Pharaoh hadn't relaxed her vigilance one iota. Her agents in the East and the West reported regularly; there was little she did not know, including who expected to get what from Antony when he got around to making his dispositions. The moment Fonteius said that Antony was already in Antioch, she knew why he had wanted her there in a hurry: he intended to have the Queen of Egypt stand below his dais with a lot of dirty peasants and receive . . . *nothing*. Just stand there as a statement that Egypt too was under the Roman parasol. In the shade.

Fury engulfed her. She shook with it, hardly able to catch her breath. So he wants me there to witness his lordly acts, does he? Well, by Serapis, I'll not do it! Let him put me to death, but I'll not do it! Watch him appoint this peasant king and that peasant prince? Never! Never, never, never! And when I do come to Antioch, Marcus Antonius, I will be asking for more than you

273

have the power to give me. But you will give it to me, power or not! Fonteius is worried about you, therefore you've developed a weak spot dangerous enough for Fonteius to think it imperils you.

As November started its downhill slide, the Queen knew all of Antony's dispositions in Antioch. They seemed logical, sensible, even far-sighted. Except, that is, for his last decision: to make Monaeses the Parthian the new King of the Skenite Arabs. Antonius, Antonius, you fool! *You idiot!* No matter if the man is a genuine refugee from his uncle's beheading axe, you don't make an Aryan Arsacid king of any kind of Arab! It is beneath him. It is an insult. A mortal insult. And if he is an agent for Uncle Phraates, it will steel him in his enmity. You may rule the East, but you are of the West. You don't begin to understand Eastern peoples, how they feel, how they think.

War with the Parthians could not be allowed to happen, she resolved. Only how could she persuade Antony of that? For no other reason was she going to Antioch. Rome was a menace to her throne but, if the Parthians conquered, she would lose it, and Caesarion would meet the same fate as all promising young men: execution. Antony was stirring up an ant's nest.

At this time of year she would have to journey overland, a complicated progress because Egypt had to stun the people of every land she and Caesarion traveled through. Lumbering wagons of supplies and royal paraphernalia, a thousand-strong segment of the Royal Guard, mule carts, prancing horses and, for the Queen, her litter with its black bearers. A month on the road; she would set out on the Nones of December, not a day before.

And in all of this, Mark Antony the man, the lover, never rose to the surface of Cleopatra's mind, too busy plotting and scheming about what she wanted and how she was going to get it. Somewhere deep down she had vague recollections that he had been a pleasant diversion, but wearying in the end; she had never grown close to loving him. She dismissed him as a means; she had quickened, Nilus had inundated, Caesarion had a sister to marry and a brother to support him. At this stage, all Antony could give her was power – which necessitated that she strip him of some of his. A tall order, Cleopatra.

PART IV

The Queen of Beasts

36–33 B.C.

CLEOPATRA

FIFTEEN

On the Nones of January and in the teeth of an unusually bitter wind, Cleopatra and Caesarion entered Antioch. Wearing the Double Crown and riding in her litter, the Queen sat like Fonteius's doll, face painted, body clad in finely pleated white linen, neck, arms, shoulders, waist and feet blazing with gold and jewels. Wearing the military version of the Double Crown, Caesarion rode a mettlesome red horse, red being the color of Montu, God of War, his face painted red, his body clad in Egyptian pharaonic armor of linen and golden scales. Between the purple tunics and silver armor of the thousand Royal Guards, the glitter of trapped horses carrying officers and bureaucrats, and the royal litter with Caesarion riding alongside it, Antioch hadn't seen a parade like this since the last Seleucus had been King of Syria.

Antony had been busy to some purpose. Acknowledging the truth of Fonteius's contention that the governor's palace was a cara-vanserai, he had razed several blocks of adjacent dwellings to the ground and built an annex he thought fit to house Egypt's Queen.

'It isn't an Alexandrian palace,' he said, escorting Cleopatra and her son around it, 'but it's a great deal more comfortable than the old residence.'

Caesarion was alight with joy, grieving only that he had grown far too much to ride Antony's hip anymore. Disciplining himself not to skip, he walked solemnly and tried to look regal. Not diffi-cult, in all that loathed paint. 'I hope there's a bath,' he said.

'Ready and waiting, young Caesar,' Antony said with a grin.

The three didn't meet again until mid-afternoon, when Antony served dinner in a *triclinium* so new that it still smelled of plaster and the various pigments used to enhance its bleak walls with frescoes of Alexander the Great and his closest marshals, all mounted on high-stepping horses. Since it was too cold to open the shutters, incense burned to cut the reek. Cleopatra was too polite and aloof to comment, but Caesarion felt no such compunction.

'The place stinks,' he said, clambering onto a couch.

'If it's unbearable, we can repair to the old palace.'

'No, I'll stop noticing it in a few moments, and the fumes have lost their power to poison.' Caesarion chuckled. 'Catulus Caesar committed suicide by shutting himself in a freshly plastered room with a dozen braziers and all the apertures stuffed to prevent the entrance of outside air. He was my grandfather's first cousin.'

'You've been studying your Roman history.'

'Of course.'

'What about Egyptian history?'

'Right back to verbal records, before the hieroglyphs.'

'Cha'em tutors him,' Cleopatra said, speaking for the first time. 'Caesarion will be the best-educated king ever.'

This exchange set the tenor for the dinner: Caesarion talked incessantly, his mother interpolated an occasional remark to verify one of his statements, and Antony lay on a couch pretending to listen when he wasn't answering one of Caesarion's questions.

Though he was fond of the boy, he saw the truth of Fonteius's observation; Cleopatra had given Caesarion no real sense of his limitations, and he felt confident enough to participate as an adult in all conversation. That might have been permissible, did he not have the habit of butting in. His father would have put a stop to such conduct – well did Antony remember him when Antony had been Caesarion's age! Whereas Cleopatra was a doting mother saddled with an imperious, extremely strong-willed son. No good.

Finally, the sweeties having come and gone, Antony acted. 'Off you go, young Caesarion,' he said curtly. 'I want to talk to your mother in private.'

The boy bridled, mouth open to protest; then he caught the red spark in Antony's eyes. His resistance collapsed like a pricked bladder. A shrug of resignation, and he was gone.

'How did you do that?' she asked, relieved.

'Spoke and looked like a father. You give the boy too much latitude, Cleopatra, and he won't thank you for it later.'

She didn't answer, too busy trying to plumb this particular Mark Antony. He never seemed to age as other men did, nor show any outward signs of dissipation. His belly was flat, the muscles of his arms above the elbows betrayed no hint of the flaccid sag of middle age, and his hair was as auburn as ever, free of grey.

What changes there were lay in his eyes – the eyes of a man who was troubled. But why was he troubled? It was going to take time to find out.

Is it Octavianus responsible? Ever since Philippi he's had to contend with Octavianus in a war that isn't a war. A duel of wits and will, fought without one sword drawn or one blow landed. He could see that Sextus Pompey was his best weapon, but when the perfect opportunity arrived to unite with Sextus and bring in his own marshals Pollio and Ventidius, he didn't take it. At that moment he could have crushed Octavianus. Now he never will, and he's beginning to understand that. While ever he thought there was a chance to crush Octavianus, he lingered in the West. That he is here in Antioch says he has given up the struggle. Fonteius saw it in him, but how? Did Antonius confide in him?

'I've missed you,' he said abruptly.

'Have you?' she asked casually, as if not very interested.

'Yes, more and more. Funny, that. I always thought missing a person wore off as time went on, but my longing for you grows worse. I couldn't have waited much longer to see you.'

A feminine tactic: 'How is your wife?'

'Octavia? Sweet as ever. The loveliest person.'

'You shouldn't say that of one woman to another woman.'

'Why not? Since when has Marcus Antonius been in love with virtue, or goodness or kindness in a woman? I . . . pity her.'

'That means you think she loves you.'

'I have no doubt of it. Not a day goes by that she doesn't tell me she loves me, in a letter if we're not together. I have a pigeon-hole full of them already, here in Antioch.' He pulled a grotesque face. 'She tells me how the children are, what brother Octavianus is up to – at least as she knows it – and whatever else she thinks I might find amusing. Though she never mentions Livia Drusilla. She doesn't approve of Octavianus's wife's attitude to his daughter by Scribonia.'

'Has she borne a child herself? I've not heard of it.'

'No. Barren as the Libyan desert.'

'Then perhaps it is Octavianus's fault.'

'I don't care whose fault it is!' he snapped.

'You should, Antonius.'

In answer, he moved to her couch, drew her close. 'I want to make love to you.'

Ah, she had forgotten his smell, how it stirred her! Clean, sun-kissed, devoid of the faintest Eastern tinge. Well, he ate the foods of his own people; he hadn't succumbed to the cardamoms and cinnamons so beloved of Easterners. Therefore his skin didn't give off their residual oils.

A glance around told her that the servants had gone, and that no one, even Caesarion, would be permitted through the doors. Her hand covered the back of his, she moved it to one breast, fuller since the birth of the twins. 'I've missed you too,' she lied, feeling the stir bloom and spread through her. Yes, he had pleased her as a lover, and Caesarion would benefit from a second brother. Amun-Ra, Isis, Hathor, give me a son! I am but thirty-three, not old enough to make childbirth a hazard for a Ptolemy.

'I've missed you too,' she whispered. 'Oh, this is *lovely!*'

Vulnerable, consumed with doubts, unsure what his future held in Rome, Antony was ripe for Cleopatra's picking, and fell of his own accord into the palm of her hand. He had come to an age that saw him in desperate need of more than mere sex from a woman; he yearned for a true partner, and none could he find among his female friends, or his mistresses, or, most of all, his Roman wife. This queen among women—indeed, this king among men—was his equal in every way: power, strength, ambition permeated her to the marrow. Being with her was like fitting himself against crests and hollows that mated his mind and core to hers. When he spoke, she seemed to have read his thoughts; when he moved, she seemed able to anticipate that movement; when he came to a decision about the merest trifle or the greatest riddle, she reached the same decision even before him. Something about her screamed of magic, of an eerie enchantment, but he sensed – nay, was convinced! – that she was with him, for him, his equal in everything. And always on *his* side. Concerned with nothing except him. Oh, Caesarion, yes, but that was natural, and he couldn't grudge her that devotion. The boy was, after all, his own cousin, and only ten years old.

So Antony fell in love with Cleopatra as he had never loved any woman, neither wife nor mistress. He hung upon her every word, eager for a glance of approval, a touch, the slightest hint of love returned.

And she, aware of all this, took her time about exacting her wants, which were not of the flesh or of the spirit. Gaius Fonteius, Poplicola, Sosius, Titius and young Marcus Aemilius Scaurus were all in Antioch, but this new Mark Antony hardly noticed them anymore. Gnaeus Domitius Ahenobarbus turned up, his governorship of Bithynia just too out of things for such a busybody of a man. He had always disliked Cleopatra, and what he saw in Antioch only reinforced that dislike. Antony was her slave.

'Not like a son with his mother,' Ahenobarbus said to Fonteius, in whom he sensed an ally, 'but a dog with its master.'

'He'll get over it,' Fonteius said, sure Antony would. 'He's closer to fifty now than forty, he's been consul, imperator, triumvir – everything except the undisputed First Man in Rome. And since his ill-spent youth with Curio and Clodius, he's been a famous womanizer without ever yielding his essence to a woman. That's now overdue, hence Cleopatra. Face it, Ahenobarbus! She is the most powerful *woman* in the world, and fabulously rich. He has to have her, and he has to keep her against all comers.'

'*Cacat!*' snapped Ahenobarbus. 'It's she leading him, not he, her! He's turned as soft as a mushy pudding!'

'Once he's away from Antioch and in the field, the old Marcus Antonius will return,' Fonteius comforted, positive he was right.

Much to Cleopatra's surprise, when Antony told Caesarion it was time to go to Alexandria, there to rule as King and Pharaoh, the boy went without a murmur of protest. He hadn't spent as much time with Antony as he had hoped, but they had managed to ride out of Antioch several times and spend a day hunting wolves and lions, which wintered in Syria before returning to the Scythian steppes. Nor was he to be fooled.

'I'm not an idiot, you know,' he said to Antony after their first kill, a male lion.

'What do you mean?' Antony asked, startled.

'This is settled country, too populous for lions. You brought him in from the wilderness so we'd have some sport.'

'You're a monster, Caesarion.'

'Gorgon, or Cyclops?'

'A new breed entirely.'

Antony's last words to him as he set out for Egypt were more serious. 'When your mother returns,' he said, 'make sure that you mind her better. At the moment you ride roughshod over her opinions and her wishes. That's your father in you. But what you lack is his perception of reality, which he understood was something quite outside his own self. Cultivate that quality, young Caesar, and when you grow up, nothing will stop you.'

And I, thought Antony, will be too old to care what you make of your life. Though I think I've been more of a father to you than

I have to my own sons. But then, your mother matters terribly to me, and you are the center of her world.

She waited five *nundinae* to strike. By then almost all the newly appointed kings and potentates had visited Antioch to pay their respects to Antony. Not to her. Who was she, except another client monarch? Amyntas, Polemon, Pythodorus, Tarcondimotus, Archelaus Sisenes, and, of course, Herod. Very full of himself!

She started with Herod. 'He hasn't repaid the money he owes me, nor my share of the balsam revenues,' she said to Antony.

'I wasn't aware he owed you money or balsam revenues.'

'Indeed he does! I lent him a hundred talents to take his case to Rome. The balsam was part of the repayment.'

'I'll remind him by couriered letter tomorrow.'

'Remind, nothing! He hasn't forgotten, he just doesn't intend to honor his debts. Though there is a way to enforce payment.'

'Really? What?' asked Antony warily.

'Cede me the balsam gardens of Jericho and the bitumen fisheries of the Palus Asphaltites. Free and clear, all mine.'

'Jupiter! That's tantamount to half the revenues of Herod's entire kingdom! Leave him and his balsam alone, my love.'

'No, I will not! I don't need the money and he does, that's true, but he doesn't deserve to be left alone. He's a fat slug!'

A moment's thought provoked amusement; Antony's eyes began to twinkle. 'Is there anything else you demand, my sparrow?'

'Full sovereignty over Cyprus, which had always belonged to Egypt until Cato Uticensis annexed it to Rome. Cyrenaica, another Egyptian possession pilfered by Rome. Cilicia Tracheia. The Syrian coast as far as the River Eleutherus – it has been Egyptian more often than not. Chalcis. In fact, an entirely Egyptian southern Syria would suit me beautifully, so you'd better cede me all of Judaea. Crete would be good. Rhodes too.'

He sat with jaw dropped and little eyes wide, hardly knowing whether to roar with laughter or outrage. Finally, 'You joke.'

'Joke? *Joke*? Just who are your new allies, Antonius? *Your* allies, not Rome's! You've given away most of Anatolia and a good part of Syria to a parcel of ruffians, traitors and brigands! In fact, Tarcondimotus *is* a brigand! To whom you've handed the Syrian Gates and the entire Amanus! You dowered the son of your mistress with Cappadocia, and gave Galatia to a common clerk! You married your daughter with a double dose of Julian blood to a grubby Asian Greek usurer! You set a *freedman* to rule Cyprus! Oh, what glory you've spread far and wide to such a wonderful bunch of allies!' She was working up her temper with masterly precision, eyes gone to the feral glow of a cat, lips peeled back, face a mask of pure venom. 'And where is Egypt in all these brilliant dispositions?' she hissed. 'Passed over! Not even mentioned! How Tarcondimotus for one must be laughing! As for Herod – that slimy toad, that rapacious spawn of a pair of grasping nonentities!'

Where was his rage? Where was his trustiest tool, the hammer he had used to crush the pretensions of mightier opponents than Cleopatra? Not a flash of the old familiar fire warmed his veins, chilled to ice under her Medusan glare. Amazement overwhelmed him, a bewilderment so great he couldn't think straight, had to resort to political actor's tricks.

'You cut me to the quick!' he gasped, hands clawing at the unforgiving air. 'I meant no insult!'

Her seeming rage was permitted to die, but not mercifully. 'Oh, I know what I have to do to get the territories I ask for,' she said conversationally. 'Your bum-boys got their lands gratis, but Egypt has to pay. How many gold talents is Cilicia Tracheia worth? The balsam and the bitumen are debts, I refuse to pay for them. But Chalcis? Phoenicia? Philistia? Cyprus? Cyrenaica? Crete? Rhodes? Judaea? My treasure vaults are overflowing, dear Antonius, as well you know. That was your intention all along, was it not? Make Egypt pay thousands upon thousands of gold talents for every *plethron* of land! What other, less deserving minions get for nothing, Egypt will have to buy! You hypocrite! You mean, miserable twister!'

Tears could be a man's weapon too; he broke down and wept, apparently devastated that this woman whom he loved so much could round on him as if she hated him.

'Oh, stop crying!' she snapped, tossing him a napkin as a plutocrat might toss a bronze farthing to someone who has just done him a huge service. 'Wipe your eyes! It's time to get down to bargaining.'

'I didn't think of Egypt as wanting more territory,' he said, not knowing what else to say.

'Oh, really? And what led you to make that assumption?'

'Egypt is so self-contained.' Eyes still swimming, he stared at her. Think, Antonius, *think*! 'What would you do with Cilicia Tracheia? Crete? Rhodes? Cyrenaica, even? You rule a land that has great difficulty in maintaining an army to defend its own borders.' To talk collected his wits, helped him find arguments that held water in the face of these incredible demands.

'I would add those lands to the kingdom my son will inherit; I would use them as his training ground. Egypt's laws are set in stone, but other places are crying out for a wise ruler's hands, and Caesarion will be the wisest of the wise,' she said.

How to answer that? 'Cyprus I can see, Cleopatra. You're absolutely right, it has always belonged to Egypt. Caesar gave it back to you, but when he died, it reverted to Rome. I'd be happy to cede you Cyprus. In fact, I had every intention of doing so – didn't you notice I withheld it from all my grants?'

'Big of you,' she said caustically. 'And Cyrenaica?'

'Cyrenaica is a part of Rome's wheat supply. Not a chance.'

'I refuse to go home with less than your pimps and toadies!'

'They're not pimps and toadies, they're decent men.'

'What will you take for Phoenicia and Philistia?'

So be it, the greedy *meretrix*! Once he had realized that his forty thousand silver talents from Sextus Pompey's hoard might be years in the coming, he had fretted. Whereas here sat the Queen of Egypt, ready and able to pay. She didn't love him a bit – the disillusion! But she could give him that splendid army, right now. Good, he felt more lucid. 'Let's talk down payments. You'll want complete sovereignty and all profits. Over time, a hundred thousand gold talents each. But I'll take one per cent down payment. A thousand gold talents for Phoenicia, Philistia, Cilicia Pedia, Chalcis, Emesa, the Eleutherus River and Cyprus. No Crete, Cyrenaica or Judaea. Balsam and bitumen, free.'

'A total of seven thousand gold talents.' She stretched and made a small, purring sound. 'It's a deal, Antonius.'

'I want the seven thousand *now*, Cleopatra.'

'In return for official deeds, signed and sealed by you in your function as Triumvir in charge of the East.'

'When I have the gold – and count it – you'll have your papers. The seal of Rome affixed, plus my own triumviral seal. I'll even throw in my personal seal.'

'That's satisfactory. I'll start a fast courier for Memphis in the morning.'

'Memphis?'

'It's quicker, take my word for that.'

Which left them without any idea of where to go next. She had come to get what she could, and got more than she had hoped for; he had needed her strength and guidance desperately, and got nothing. The physical bond was frail, the mental nonexistent. A very long moment went by as they stared at each other without anything further to say. Then Antony sighed.

'You don't love me at all,' he said, committing his disenchantment to sounds that reverberated around him like goat bells – hollow, clashing. 'You came to Antioch like any other woman – to shop.'

'It's true that I came to get Caesarion's share of the booty,' she answered, her eyes human enough now to look a little sad. 'I do love you, however. If I did not, I would have gone about my task in a different way. You don't see it, but I spared you.'

'The gods preserve me from a Cleopatra who didn't spare me!'

'Oh, you wept, which to you means I unmanned you. But no one can unman you, Antonius, except yourself. Until Caesarion is grown – ten more years at least – Egypt needs a consort, and I have only one name in mind. Marcus Antonius. You're not a weakling, but you lack purpose. I see it as clearly as Fonteius must have seen it.'

His brow knitted. 'Fonteius? Have you been comparing notes?'

'Not at all. Simply, I sensed that he was worried about you. Now I see why. You don't love Rome as Caesar did, and your rival in Rome is over twenty years your junior. Short of his death, he must outlast you, and I can't see Octavianus dying young, despite his asthma. Murder? An ideal answer – if it could be done. But it can't be. Between Agrippa and the German guards, he's invulnerable. Octavianus dismiss his lictors the way Caesar did? Not if he were offered Sextus Pompeius on a golden platter! If you were older, it would be easier on you, but twenty years are not enough, though too many. Octavianus must be twenty-six this year. My agents say he's more manly now the blush of youth has gone. You're forty-six, and I have turned thirty-two. You and I are more ideally matched for age, and I would have Egypt regain its old power. Unlike the Kingdom of the Parthians, Egypt belongs on Your Sea. With you as my consort, Antonius, think what we might do in the next ten years!'

Was what she proposed feasible? It wasn't Roman, but Rome was eluding his grasp, tendrils of smoke in perfumed Eastern air. Yes, he was thrown off balance, but not so much that he didn't understand what she was proposing, and what the issues were. His hold over his adherents in Rome was slipping; Pollio had gone, and Ventidius, Sallust, all the great marshals except Ahenobarbus. How much longer could he hang onto his seven hundred senatorial clients, unless he paid long visits to Rome at fairly frequent intervals? Was it worth the effort? Could he take more effort on board, when Cleopatra did not love him? Not always a rational man, he couldn't work out what she had done to him; only that he loved her. From the day she arrived in Antioch, he was defeated, and that was a mystery beyond his capacity to solve.

She was speaking again. 'With Sextus Pompeius to defeat, it will be some years before Octavianus and Rome are in any condition to look at what's happening in the East. The Senate is a body of clucking old hens, impotent to wrest government from Octavianus – or you. Lepidus, I discount.'

She slid off her couch and came to lie beside him, her cheek on one sinewy forearm. 'I'm not advocating sedition, Antonius,' she said in soft, honeyed tones. 'Far from it. All I am saying is that, in concert with me, you can make the East a better and a stronger place. How can that be injurious to Rome? How can that diminish Rome? On the contrary. For instance, it prevents the rise of another Mithridates or Tigranes.'

'I'd become your consort in the blink of an eye, Cleopatra, if I could honestly believe that some of it was for me, because of me. Must every atom of it be Caesarion's?' he asked, lips brushing her shoulder. 'Lately I've come to understand that, before I die, I want to stand alone and colossal in the full blaze of the sun – no shade of any kind! Not Rome's shade, not Caesarion's shade. I want to end my life as Marcus Antonius, neither Roman nor Egyptian. I want to be a true singularity. I want to be Antonius the Great. And you don't offer me that.'

'But I do offer you greatness! You cannot be Egyptian, that is foregone. If you're Roman, only you can cast that off. It's just a skin, no harder to shed than a snake, his.' Her mouth nuzzled the side of his face. 'Antonius, I *do* understand! You yearn to be greater than Julius Caesar, which means conquering new worlds. But in the Parthians, you're looking at the wrong world. Turn your head West, not farther East! Caesar never really conquered Rome – he succumbed to Rome. Antonius can only earn the cognomen Great by conquering Rome.'

That was only the opening round of an ongoing battle that lasted until March, the Antiochean spring. A titanic struggle fought in the darkness of their tangled emotions, in the silence of their unspoken doubts and mistrusts. The secrecy was urgent and complete; if Ahenobarbus, Poplicola, Fonteius, Furnius, Sosius or any other Roman in Antioch guessed that Antony was selling in perpetuity and without tribute what belonged to Rome in perpetuity and was merely leased to client-kings in return for tribute, then there would be a convulsion so great that Antony might find himself in chains and shipped back to Rome. Cleopatra's deeded territories had to seem innocently deeded until Antony's power base was much stronger. So what was public knowledge in one way was known only to Antony and Cleopatra in another way. To his fellow Romans, they had to appear ordinary cessions to get the gold to fund the army. Once he was unconquerable in the East, it no longer mattered what was known. She had tried to persuade Caesar to make himself King of Rome, and failed. Antony was more malleable material, especially in his present state of mind. And the East hungered for a strong king. Who better than a Roman, trained in law and government, not given to caprices or killing sprees? Antonius the Great would weld the East into an entity formidable enough to contend with Rome for world supremacy. Thus did Cleopatra dream, knowing full well that she had a long way to go, and farther still before she could crush Antonius the Great in favor of Caesarion, King of Kings.

Antony succeeded in duping his colleagues. Ahenobarbus and Poplicola witnessed Cleopatra's documents without reading what they contained, and sniggered at her gullibility. So much gold!

But Antony's worst conflict he could confide in no one. The Queen was adamantly against his Parthian campaign, and grudged her gold to funding it. She dreaded to see the army horribly reduced by Parthian attacks, dreaded to see the army too thinned out to do what she intended it would do: go to war against Rome and Octavian. Plans she had revealed to Antony in part only, but there in her mind constantly. Caesarion must rule Caesar's world as well as Egypt and the East, and nothing, including Mark Antony, was going to stop that.

To Antony's horror, he learned that Cleopatra intended to march with him on campaign, and expected to have the major say in the war councils. Canidius was waiting in Carana after a successful strike north into the Caucasus, and she was so looking forward to meeting him, she kept saying. Try though he did, Antony couldn't convince her that she was unwelcome, that his legates wouldn't tolerate her.

So in the space of one *nundinum* he got rid of the men most likely to rebel against her presence. He sent Poplicola to Rome to cheer up his seven hundred senators, and Furnius to govern Asia Province. Ahenobarbus went back to governing Bithynia, and Sosius was to continue in Syria.

Then the most natural and inevitable of events saved him: a pregnancy. Limp with relief, he was able to tell his legates that the Queen was traveling with the legions only as far as Zeugma on the Euphrates, then going home to Egypt. Amused and admiring, his legates assumed that the Queen's love for Antony was so great that she could hardly bear to be parted from him.

Thus it was a very contented Cleopatra who kissed Mark Antony goodbye at Zeugma, and commenced the long land trek back to Egypt; though she might have sailed, she had good reason not to. A reason named Herod, King of the Jews. When he learned of the loss of his balsam and bitumen, he had come at the gallop from Jerusalem to Antioch. But when he saw Cleopatra sitting beside Antony in the audience chamber, he turned around and rode home again. An action that told Cleopatra that Herod preferred to wait until he could see Antony alone. It also meant that Herod saw what the Roman men had not: that she dominated the Triumvir in charge of the East, clay in her busy, interfering hands.

No matter what his private feelings, however, Herod had no choice other than to welcome the Queen of Egypt to his capital and house her royally in his new palace, a sumptuous building.

'In fact, I see new buildings going up everywhere,' Cleopatra said to her host over dinner, thinking to herself that the food was awful and Queen Mariamne an ugly bore. Fecund, however; two sons already. 'One looks suspiciously like a fortress.'

'Oh, it is a fortress,' said Herod, unruffled. 'I shall call it the Antonia, after our Triumvir. I'm also building a new temple.'

'And some new structures at Masada, I hear.'

'It was a cruel exile for my family, but a handy place. I'm giving it better housing, more granaries, food rooms and water cisterns.'

'A pity I won't see it. The coast road is more comfortable.'

'Especially for a lady with child.' He waved a dismissing hand at Mariamne, who rose and departed immediately.

'You have sharp eyes, Herod.'

'And you an insatiable appetite for territory, according to my reports from Antioch. Cilicia Tracheia! What do you want that rocky stretch of coast for?'

'Among other things, to restore Olbia to Queen Aba and the line of the Teucrids. I didn't get the only city, however.'

'Cilician Seleuceia is too strategically important to the Romans, my dear ambitious Queen. Incidentally, you can't have my income from the balsam and the bitumen. I need it too badly.'

'I already have both the balsam and the bitumen, Herod, and here,' she said, fishing a paper out of a jeweled bag of gold net, 'are instructions from Marcus Antonius directing you to collect the revenues on my behalf.'

'Antonius wouldn't do this to me!' cried Herod, reading.

'Antonius would, and has. Though it was my idea to make you do the collecting. You should have paid your debts, Herod.'

'I will outlast you, Cleopatra!'

'Nonsense. You're too greedy and too fat. Fat men die early.'

'While skinny women live forever, you imply. Not in your case, Queen. My greed is as nothing compared to yours. You won't be content with less than the entire world. But Antonius isn't the man to get it for you. He's losing his grip on what part of the world he already has, haven't you noticed?'

'Pah!' she spat. 'If you mean his campaign against the King of the Parthians, that is simply something he has to get out of his mind before he turns his energies to more feasible objectives.'

'Objectives *you* invent for him!'

'Rubbish! He's quite capable of seeing them for himself.'

Herod flung himself back on his couch and clasped his podgy, beringed fingers on his belly. 'How long have you been plotting what I think you're plotting?'

The golden eyes went wide, gazed at him ingenuously. 'Herod! I, plotting? Your imagination grows fevered. The next thing you'll be babbling in delirium. What could I plot?'

'With Antonius wearing a ring through his nose and trailing vast numbers of legions behind him, my dear Cleopatra, my guess is that you're out to overturn Rome in favor of Egypt. What better time to strike than while Octavianus is weak and the western provinces in need of his best men? There's no limit to your ambitions, your lusts. What surprises me is that no one appears to have woken up to your designs save me. Poor Antonius, when he does!'

'If you're wise, Herod, you'll keep your speculations inside your head, not drip them off the end of your tongue. They're insane, baseless.'

'Give me the balsam and the bitumen, and I'm silent.'

She slid off the couch and into her backless slippers. 'I wouldn't give you the smell of a sweaty rag, you abomination!' And out she went, her trailing draperies making sibilant sounds as of soft, fell voices whispering spells.

SIXTEEN

The day after Cleopatra left Zeugma for Egypt, Ahenobarbus turned up, breezy and unapologetic.

'You're supposed to be on your way to Bithynia,' Antony said, looking displeased, feeling overjoyed.

'That was your scheme to get rid of me while ever you thought the Egyptian harpy was going to campaign with you. No Roman man could stomach that, Antonius, and I'm surprised you thought you could – unless you've given up being a Roman man.'

'No, I haven't!' Antony said irritably. 'Ahenobarbus, you have to understand that Cleopatra's willingness to lend me huge amounts of gold is all that got this expedition going! She seemed to think that the loan entitled her to participate in the endeavor but, by the time we got this far, she was happy to go home.'

'And I was happy to abandon my journey to Nicomedia. So, my friend, enlighten me as to recent events.'

Antonius looks very well, Ahenobarbus thought, better than I have seen him look since Philippi. He has something to do worthy of his steel, and it's the fulfilment of a dream besides. Much and all as I loathe the Egyptian harpy, I'm grateful to her for the loan of her gold. He'll pay it back out of one short campaign segment.

'I've obtained a source of information about the Parthians,' Antony said. 'A nephew of the new Parthian king, name of Monaeses. When Phraates slaughtered his entire family, Monaeses managed to flee to Syria because he wasn't at the court at the time. He was in Nicephorium, sorting out a trade dispute with the Skenites. Of course he daren't go home – there's a price on his head. It seems King Phraates has married the nubile daughter of some minor Arsacid house and intends to breed a new lot of heirs. The bride's family all went to the sword, or the axe, or whatever it is the Parthians use. This new litter of sons will be years growing up, therefore years off being a danger to Phraates. Whereas Monaeses is a grown man and has a following. Ruthless, these Eastern monarchs.'

'I hope you remember that when you're dealing with Cleopatra,' Ahenobarbus said dryly.

'Cleopatra,' said Antony a trifle haughtily, 'is different.'

'And you, Antonius, are love-struck,' said the uncompromising one bluntly. 'I hope your judgement of this Monaeses is sounder.'

'Sound as a Bryaxis bronze.'

But when Ahenobarbus met Prince Monaeses, his belly caved in hollowly. Trust this man? Never! He couldn't look you in the eye, for all his fine Greek and aping of Greek manners.

'Don't give him the tip of your little finger!' Ahenobarbus cried. 'Do, and he'll take your arm off at the shoulder! Can't you see that he's the one King Phraates kept in reserve, trained in western ways, in case it became necessary to put a spy in our midst? Monaeses didn't escape slaughter, he was spared to do his Parthian duty – lure us to ruin and defeat!'

Antony's reply was a laugh; nothing Ahenobarbus or any of the other doubters could say would swerve him from his opinion that Monaeses was as solid as Cleopatra's gold.

Most of the army was waiting in Carana with Publius Canidius, but Antony brought six more legions with him as well as ten thousand Gallic horse troopers and a total of thirty thousand foreign levies made up of Jews, Syrians, Cilicians and Asian Greeks. He had left one legion at Jerusalem to ensure Herod's continued tenure of the throne – Antony was a loyal friend, if sometimes a gullible one – and seven legions to garrison Macedonia, always restless.

The Euphrates had cut a wide valley between Zeugma and its upper reaches at Carana; there was plenty of grazing for horses, mules and oxen. Samosata came and went, the valley began to close in a little, and the road became rougher as the vast force pressed on into Melitene. Not far north of Samosata the army passed the baggage train, a disappointment, as Antony had started it twenty days earlier from Zeugma than the army, and had thought this would see both units reach Carana at the same moment. But he had confidently expected the oxen to walk fifteen and more miles a day, whereas not all the whips and curses in the world could get more than ten from them, as he now discovered.

The baggage train was Antony's pride and joy, the biggest any

Roman army had ever assembled. Literally hundreds of catapults, ballistas, onagers and smaller artillery trundled along behind the required number of oxen each piece needed, plus several battering rams capable of breaking down ordinary town gates, and one eighty-foot-long monster capable of breaking down, as Antony jokingly put it to Monaeses, 'even the gates of Ilium of old!' That was just the war machinery. In wagon after wagon came the supplies – wheat, barrels of salt pork, sides of heavily smoked bacon, oil, lentils, chickpeas, salt, spare parts, tools and equipment for the legion artificers, charcoal, sows of smelted iron for steeling, huge beams and planks, saws for cutting trees or soft rock like tufa, ropes and hawsers, canvas, extra tents, poles, harness: everything an efficient *praefectus fabrum* could think an army the size of this one might need to replenish what it carried with it as well as undertake a siege. In single file the train measured fifteen miles long, but it traveled on a broad front three miles thick; two under-strength legions of four thousand men each were permanently seconded to guarding such an immense and precious adjunct of war; Oppius Statianus was in command, and grumbling about it to anyone who would listen.

They included Antony when the army passed by.

'All very well while we can march like this,' Statianus said tactlessly, 'but those mountains up ahead spell narrow valleys to me, and if we have to string the wagons out, both our communications and our defences won't last.'

Not an opinion Antony wanted to hear, or was prepared to listen to. 'You're an old woman, Statianus,' he said, kicking his horse onward. 'Just get more miles a day out of them!'

The mobile forces reached Carana fifteen days after leaving Zeugma, a distance of three hundred and fifty miles, but the baggage train didn't arrive for twelve more days, despite its head start. Which meant that Antony was in a foul mood; when he was, he would listen to no one, from friends like Ahenobarbus to marshals like Canidius, fresh from an expedition to the Caucasus and extremely well informed about mountains.

'Italia is ringed around by the Alpes,' Canidius said, 'but they're like a child's toy bricks compared to these peaks. Look all around the bowl Carana sits in, and you're looking at hundreds of mountains around fifteen thousand feet high. Go north or east, and they just get taller, more precipitous. The valleys are notches scarcely wider than the boiling streams that fill them. It is the middle of April already, which means you have until October to do your campaigning. Six months, and winter will be here. Carana is the biggest saucer of relatively level land between here and the great flats where the Araxes flows into the Caspian Sea. All I had were ten legions and two thousand cavalry, but I found even a force of that size unwieldy in this country. Still, I daresay you know what you're doing, so I don't intend to argue.'

Like Ventidius, Canidius was a Military Man of ignoble origins; only his great skill as a general of troops had enabled him to rise. He had attached himself to Mark Antony after Caesar's death, and was fonder of Antony than of Antony's martial capabilities. However, after Ventidius's triumph in Syria, Canidius knew that he wouldn't be put in command of an enterprise like the one Antony now proposed to lead into the Kingdom of the Parthians by, so to speak, the back door. A tortuous undertaking that would require the genius of a Caesar, and Antony was no Caesar. For one thing, he liked sheer size, whereas Caesar had detested big armies. To him, ten legions and two thousand cavalry were as many men as any commander could deploy with success; larger than that, and orders became scrambled, lines of communication imperiled by distance and time. Canidius agreed with Caesar.

'Has King Artavasdes come?' Antony asked.

'Which one?'

Antony blinked. 'I meant Armenia.'

'Aye, he's here, waiting with tiara in hand for an audience. But so is Artavasdes of Media.'

'*Media?*'

'That's right. Both of them got the wind up after my jaunt to the Caucasus, and both have decided that Rome is going to win this encounter with the Parthians. Artavasdes of Armenia wants his seventy valleys in Media Atropatene returned to him, and Artavasdes of Media wants to rule the Kingdom of the Parthians.'

Antony roared with laughter. 'Canidius, Canidius, what luck! Only how can we tell them apart by their names?'

'I call Armenia, Armenia, and Media, Media.'

'Don't they have some physical attributes I can use?'

'Not this pair! They're as like as twins – all that intermarriage, I suppose. Frilly skirts and jackets, wig beards, lots of curls, hooked noses, black eyes and black hair.'

'They sound Parthian.'

'All the same stock, I imagine. Are you ready to see them?'

'Does either speak Greek?'

'No, nor Aramaic. They speak their own languages, and Parthian.'

'Just as well, then, that I have Monaeses.'

However, Antony didn't have Monaeses for long. Having acted as interpreter at several rather strange audiences between people who had no idea how their opposites thought, Monaeses elected to return to Nicephorium – he was, as he reminded Antony, King of the Skenite Arabs, and ought to put his new kingdom on a war footing. With profuse thanks and assurances that the three men he had found to act as interpreters would do better at it than he, Monaeses left for the south.

'I wish I could trust him,' Canidius said to Ahenobarbus.

'I wish *I* could trust him, but I don't. Since events are in motion and can't be stopped now, all either of us can do, Canidius, is to offer to the gods that we're wrong.'

'Or, if right, that there's nothing Monaeses can do to upset Antonius's plans.'

'I'd be happier if our army was a great deal smaller. He's like a child over his Armenian cataphracts! But as a veteran of Armenian and Parthian cataphracts, I can tell you that the Armenian sort aren't to be compared with the Parthian,' said Canidius with a sigh. 'Their armor is thinner and weaker, their horses not much bigger than ours at home – I'd sooner call them lancers in mail than proper cataphracts. But Antonius is ecstatic at being gifted with sixteen thousand of them.'

'Sixteen thousand more horses to feed,' said Ahenobarbus.

'And can we trust Armenia or Media anymore confidently than we can trust Monaeses?' Canidius asked.

'Armenia, perhaps. Media, not at all. How far is it from here to Artaxata?' Ahenobarbus asked.

'Two hundred miles, maybe slightly fewer.'

'Do we have to go there?'

'Into the belly of the Armenians, you mean. Unfortunately, yes. I've never been enthusiastic about this back-door approach, though it would have merit were the terrain less ghastly. We hit Phraaspa, then Ecbatana, then Susa, then into Mesopotamia. And does he think that the baggage train will keep up? Surely not!'

'Oh, he's Marcus Antonius,' said Ahenobarbus. 'He belongs to the school of general who believes that if he wants something enough, it will happen. And he can be very good in a campaign of the Philippi kind. But how will he cope with the unknown?'

'It all boils down to two things, Ahenobarbus. The first: is Monaeses a traitor? The second: can we trust Armenia? If the answer to the first is a negative and the answer to the second an affirmative, Antonius will succeed. Not otherwise.'

This time the baggage train had set off for Artaxata, the capital of Armenia, almost the moment it had arrived in Carana, much to the wrath of Oppius Statianus, deprived of a rest, a bath, a woman and a chance to talk to Antony. He had intended to give Antony a list of things he thought could well remain in Carana, thus cutting down the size of the train and perhaps speeding up its pace a little. But no, the orders came to keep on going, and take *everything*. The moment Oppius Statianus reached Artaxata, he was to start the journey to Phraaspa. Again no rest, no bath, no woman and no chance to talk to Antony.

Antony was edgy and anxious to start his campaign, convinced that he was stealing a march on the Parthians with his back-door approach. Oh, no doubt someone had warned them that Phraaspa would be the first Parthian city to come under assault – there were too many Easterners and foreigners of all descriptions to keep a secret as big as this one – but Antony was relying upon his pace, which he intended be as headlong as any march Caesar ever commanded. A Roman army would be at Phraaspa months before it was expected.

So he didn't linger in Artaxata, he marched as soon as possible in the straightest line he could. It was five hundred miles from Artaxata to Phraaspa, and in some ways the terrain was neither as rugged nor as high as the country they had traversed from Carana to Artaxata. But, Antony's Median and Armenian guides told him, he was marching in the wrong direction for ease of passage. Every range, every fold, every furrow, ran east to west and, while it would have been much easier to march east of Lake Matiane – a huge body of water – the only pass through the mountains meant marching down its west side, a matter of crossing many ranges up and down, up and down. At the south end of the lake the army had to strike east before turning to come down upon Phraaspa; a new range of peaks fifteen thousand and more feet high lay to the west.

Sixteen legions, ten thousand Gallic cavalry, fifty thousand foreign troops both horsed and on foot, and sixteen thousand Armenian cataphracts – one hundred and forty thousand men – began the march. More than fifty thousand of them were mounted.

Not even Alexander the Great had commanded such a multitude, thought Antony exultantly, absolutely sure that no force on earth could beat him. What an adventure, what a colossal undertaking! He'd eclipse Caesar at last.

They encountered the baggage train disappointingly soon; it had not yet crossed the mountain pass to come down to Lake Matiane, so it had nearly four hundred miles to go. Though Canidius urged Antony to lessen his pace and stay within fairly easy distance of the baggage train, Antony refused. With some justice; if he kept his pace down to that of the baggage train, he would be too late at Phraaspa to take it before winter, even if it put up no serious resistance. Besides, they were romping along, despite the constant up and down of the mountains. Antony contented himself with a message to Statianus that he should separate some elements of the train from others, and try to speed things up by lightening the weight of the wagons best suited to forging ahead.

The message never reached Statianus. Unbeknownst to scouts or foraging parties, Artavasdes of Media had joined forces with Monaeses; forty thousand cataphracts and horse archers dogged the Roman route just too far away for their dust to be noticed. When the baggage train crossed the pass coming down to Lake Matiane, its wagons were in single file, thanks to the narrowness of the very poor road, and Statianus decided to keep them in single file until the terrain flattened a little. Ten thousand Median cataphracts attacked every part of the train simultaneously. His communications shattered, Statianus didn't know what was happening where or when, couldn't send his two legions in any direction with certainty. As he dithered, his men were slaughtered; those who survived the attack were killed afterward to make sure Antony had no idea what had happened to his supplies. And what a prize! Within a day every last wagon was rumbling north and east to Media proper, well out of Antony's way. His force now had only the month's provisions it carried with it, and no artillery or siege equipment.

That accomplished, Monaeses took the Parthian segment, thirty thousand strong, in Antony's wake, but without attacking. He now had the two silver Eagles of Statianus's legions to add to the nine in Ecbatana: seven from Crassus, and now four from Antony.

The oblivious Antony reached Phraaspa intact, to find that it was far from the rude, mud-brick place of his imagination; it was a city the size of Attaleia or Tralles, immured behind huge bastions of stone and equipped with several mighty gates. One look told

Antony that he would have to besiege it. So he sat down with his army to pen the inhabitants inside, very relieved that the country around Phraaspa was heavy with wheat in ripe ear that no Parthian had thought to burn, as well as thousands of plump sheep. They'd eat.

Day succeeded day without any sign of the baggage train.

'Plague take Statianus, where is he?' Antony demanded, aware that one in every two of his foraging parties wasn't returning.

'I'll try to locate him,' said Polemon, who had decided to accompany his slingers. He rode off with a thousand of his light cavalry, waving cheekily at the Parthians atop Phraaspa's walls, absolutely confident in Antony and his magnificent army.

Day succeeded day, but Polemon didn't return.

With no timber to fell, only Roman numbers kept the Phraaspans within their fortifications; it was clear that the city was well provisioned and had water sources. A long siege, a slow siege. The month of Julius had come and gone, Sextilis began to follow it, and still no sign of the baggage. Oh, for that eighty-foot ram! It would have made splinters out of the Phraaspan gates.

'Face it, Antonius,' said Publius Canidius after the army had been camped outside Phraaspa for seventy days, 'the baggage train isn't coming because it no longer exists. We have no wood to build siege towers, no catapults, no ballistas, no anything. Thus far we have lost twenty-five thousand foreign levies sent out to forage, and today I had a flat refusal to budge from the Cilicians, Jews, Syrians and Cappadocians. Admittedly that's twenty-five thousand fewer mouths to feed, but we're not bringing in enough from the fields to keep up bodies and morale much longer. Somewhere out beyond our scouts – those who manage to come back, anyway – is a Parthian army doing what Fabius Maximus did to Hannibal.'

His belly seemed permanently filled with lead these days, a sign that Antony could no longer ignore for what it was: the knowledge of defeat. Phraaspa's dark walls mocked, and he was as lost, as impotent in fact as he had felt in premonition for many, many months. Years, even. All leading up to this . . . *failure*. Was this why he had become no trouble? Because he had lost his luck? And where was the enemy? Why didn't the Parthians attack, if they had spirited away his supplies? An even worse, more awful dread invaded him: he was not even going to be offered the chance of battle, of dying gloriously on a field as Crassus had, redeeming in his last hours all the hideous mistakes of a bungled campaign. For that reason alone, Crassus's name was spoken with respect, with sorrow for his sightless head fixed to Artaxata's walls. But Antony's name? Who would remember it, if there wasn't going to be a battle?

'They don't intend to attack us while we sit here, do they?' he asked Canidius.

'That's how I read them, Marcus,' Canidius said, keeping the compassion out of his voice; he knew what Antony was thinking.

'And I read them that way too,' said Ahenobarbus, scowling. 'We're not going to be offered battle; they want us to die slowly, and of things more mundane than sword cuts. We've also had a traitor in our midst to tell them everything – Monaeses.'

'Oh, I don't want it to end this way!' Antony cried, ignoring the reference to Monaeses. 'I need more time! Phraaspa can't be living on full rations – no city has that much within its walls, even Ilium! If we persist a while longer, I say Phraaspa will surrender.'

'We could storm it,' said Marcus Titius.

No one bothered to answer; Titius was a quaestor, young and foolish, game for anything.

Antony sat in his ivory curule chair and stared into the distance, his face almost rapt. Finally he came out of his reverie to look at Canidius. 'How much longer can we last here, Publius?'

'It's the beginning of September. Another month at most, and that's too long. If we don't get inside Phraaspa's walls before winter, then we must retreat to Artaxata by the same route we came. Five hundred miles. The legionaries will do it in thirty days if they're pushed, but most of the auxiliaries we have left are foot, and they can't begin to match that pace. It means splitting the army to preserve the legions. The Gallic troopers who have lived through foraging will be all right – there should still be grass. Unless thousands of cataphracts have cut it into mud and sod. As you well know, Antonius, without scouts we're groping like blind men in the middle of a basilica.'

'That we are.' Antony gave a wry grin. 'They say Pompeius Magnus turned back three days short of the Caspian Sea because he couldn't stand the spiders, but I'd cheerfully take a million of the biggest, hairiest spiders imaginable just to have a reliable report of what's waiting out there if we do decide to retreat.'

'I'll go,' said Titius eagerly.

The rest stared at him.

'If Armenian scouts haven't come back, Titius, why do you think you will?' Antony asked; he was fond of Titius, and tried to let him down gently. 'No, I thank you for the offer, but we have to go on sending out Armenians. No one else could survive.'

'But that's just it!' Titius said earnestly. 'They're enemy, Marcus Antonius, no matter what else they purport to be. We all know the Armenians are as treacherous as the Medians. Let me go! I promise I'll take care of myself.'

'How many men do you want to take?'

'None, Publius Canidius. Just me on a local pony. One the color of the fields. I'll wear goatskin trousers and coat, blend in too. And maybe I'll take a dozen local ponies with me so I look like a horse breeder or a horse shepherd or something.'

Antony laughed and clapped Titius on the back. 'Why not? Yes, Titius, you go! Just . . . come back.' He managed a wide grin. 'You *have* to come back! The only quaestor I've ever known worse than you at totting up figures was Marcus Antonius, but he served a more demanding master – Caesar.'

No one from the command tent was there to see Marcus Titius begin his mission because no one wanted to carry the memory of his perky, freckled face into the future as more than that wretched nuisance of a quaestor, Titius, in charge of the army's finances and utterly incapable of managing his own.

He had been gone a *nundinum* when the wind changed direction and began to blow out of the north. With it came rain and sleet. And on that day some Phraaspans atop their walls roasted sheep, the smell of it floating through the vast encampment on the plain; a way of telling the besiegers that Phraaspa had plenty of food for the winter, that it would not surrender.

Antony called a war council – not a meeting of his intimates, but a gathering that included all his legates and tribunes, plus the *primipilus* and *pilus prior* centurions: sixty men altogether. An ideal size for personal communication; he could be heard by everyone without the nuisance of having heralds follow his words and transmit what he said onward, outward. Those commanded to be there exchanged significant looks: no foreigners were present. A meeting for the legions rather than the army.

'Without siege equipment we cannot take Phraaspa,' Antony began, 'and today's little exhibition says the Phraaspans are still eating well. We've been sitting here for a hundred days and have denuded the surrounding countryside, but at a price – the loss of two-thirds of our mounted auxiliaries.' He drew a breath and tried to appear sternly resolute, the general in total command of himself as well as the situation. 'It's time to go, boys,' he said. 'We know from today's weather that it swings from summer straight to real winter, and on the last day of September. Tomorrow, the Kalends of October, we march for Artaxata. One thing the Phraaspans won't be prepared for is the speed of legions on the move. By the time they get up tomorrow morning, all that will be left of us are campfires. Order the men to carry a month's supply of grain – century mules are to be used for food and kindling, and the mules drawing wagons will be turned into pack animals – what we can't carry on our backs and mules will have to be left behind. Food and burnables.'

Most had been expecting this announcement, but no one liked hearing it. However, of one thing Antony could be sure – these men were Roman, and would not mourn the fate of the auxiliaries, tolerated but never esteemed.

'Centurions, between now and the first sign of dawn, every legionary has to know the situation and understand what he must do to survive the march. I have no idea what lies out there just waiting for us to retreat, but Roman legions don't give in, nor will they on this coming march. The terrain means it will take us about a month to reach Artaxata, especially if the rain and sleet continue. They mean muddy ground and freezing conditions. Every man is to dig his socks out of his pack – if he has rabbit- or ferret-skin ones, all the better. Keeping dry is going to be a lot of the battle, for it's the only kind we're going to get, boys. The Parthians are out there using Fabian tactics – they'll pick off the stragglers but they won't engage us in mass. Worst is the fact that there's not even enough wood for kindling between here and Artaxata, so no fires for warmth. Any man who burns his picket stake, section of breastworks or *pilum* shaft will be flogged and beheaded – we may need them to fight Parthian raids off. Nor can we trust any foreign levies, including the Armenians. The only troops Rome expects us to preserve are her legions.'

A small silence fell, broken by Canidius.

'March formation, Antonius?' he asked.

'*Agmen quadratum* where the ground is flat enough, Canidius, and where it isn't, in square anyway. I don't care how narrow a track may be, we never march in rank and file, is that understood?'

Murmurs from all sides.

Ahenobarbus's mouth was open to ask another question when a stir started on the perimeter of the group; some men moved aside to permit Marcus Titius a passage to Antony's spot, faces wreathed in broad smiles, some slapping the young quaestor on the back.

'Titius, you dog!' cried Antony in delight. 'Did you find the Parthians? What's the true situation?'

'Yes, Marcus Antonius, I found them,' said Titius, face grim. 'Forty thousand of them, commanded by our friend Monaeses – I saw him clearly on several occasions, and he was riding around in gold chain mail and had a coronet on his helmet. A Parthian prince at least as important as Pacorus was, by Ventidius's description.'

The news about Monaeses came as no surprise by now, even to Antony, his staunchest supporter. King Phraates had tricked them, put a traitor in their midst.

'How far away are they?' Fonteius asked.

'About thirty miles, and right between us and Artaxata.'

'Cataphracts? Horse archers?' Canidius asked.

'Both, but more horse archers.' Titius grinned briefly. 'I suppose they're short of cataphracts after Ventidius's campaign – about five thousand, no more. But hordes of archers. An entirely horsed army, and they've done a fine job of cutting up the ground – with this rain, our soldiers are going to be floundering through mud.' He stopped, looked a question at Antony. 'At least, I presume we're planning to retreat?'

'That we are. You came back in the nick of time, Titius. A day later, and you'd have found us gone.'

'Anything else to report?' Canidius asked.

'Only that they don't act like warriors sniffing battle. More like a force determined to stay on the defensive. Oh, they'll raid us, but unless Monaeses is a better general than I think he is after watching him prance around looking important, we should be able to hold off whatever he throws at us if we have enough warning.'

'Warning we won't need, Titius,' Ahenobarbus said. 'We march *agmen quadratum*, and when we can't do that, we march in square.'

The meeting calmed into a discussion on logistics – which of the fourteen legions should go first, which last, how frequently the men on the outside of each square should be rested by being pulled in and replaced, how big the squares should be, how many pack mules could be contained within each square at its smallest size – a thousand and one decisions that had to be made before the first foot in its socked *caliga* started the march.

Finally Fonteius asked what no one else would. 'Antonius, the auxiliaries. Thirty thousand infantrymen. What happens to them?'

'If they can keep up, they can form our rearguard – in square.

But they won't keep up, Fonteius, we all know that.' Antony's eyes grew moist. 'I am very sorry for it, and as Triumvir of the East I am responsible for them, but the legions must be preserved at all costs. Funny, I keep thinking we have sixteen, but we don't, of course. Statianus's two are long gone.'

'Including noncombatants, eighty-four thousand men. Enough to make a formidable front while ever they can march *agmen*. We have four thousand Gallic troopers and four thousand more Galatians to protect our flanks, but if there's not much grass, they'll be in trouble before we've gone half the distance,' said Canidius.

'Send them ahead, Antonius,' said Fonteius.

'And cut up the ground even more? No, they travel with us and on our flanks. If they can't deal with the number of archers and cataphracts Monaeses throws at them, they can at least come inside the squares. My Gallic horse especially are precious to me, Fonteius. They volunteered for this campaign, and it's half a world away from home,' Antony said, and lifted his hands. 'All right, dismissed. We march at first light, and I want everyone moving by sunrise.'

'The men aren't going to like retreating,' Titius said.

'I am well aware of that!' Antony said sharply. 'For which reason, I intend to do a Caesar. I'm going to be in every column talking to the men in person, even if it takes me a *nundinum*.'

Agmen quadratum was a formation that saw an army of sufficient strength spread in column across a wide front, ready in an instant to wheel and take up battle stations. It also permitted the formation of squares very quickly. Now was the time when the densest soldier understood the days, months, even years of remorseless drilling; his maneuvers had to be automatic responses, no thought involved.

With the auxiliary infantry tacked on behind this mile-wide front of legionaries, the retreat began in good order, though into the teeth of a biting north wind that froze the mud and turned it into a jagged field of knifelike edges – slippery, punishing, lacerating.

The best the legions could do was twenty miles a day, but even that was too fast for the auxiliaries. On the third day, with Antony still visiting his soldiers full of jokes and predictions of victory next year now that they knew what they were up against, Monaeses and the Parthians attacked the rear, the archers picking off dozens of men in one sortie. Few died, but those too wounded to keep up had to be left behind; as the enormous expanse of Lake Matiane loomed like a sea, all but a handful of the auxiliaries had vanished, whether to execution at Parthian hands or to a life of slavery, no one knew.

Morale was surprisingly high until the country became so steep that the columns had to be abandoned in favor of squares. While ever he could, Antony kept his squares a cohort in size, which meant six centuries of men marching four-deep around the four sides of a square, the shields of the outermost file slung protectively, as when forming a tortoise. Inside the hollow middle were the noncombatants, the mules, and what tiny part of the artillery had always traveled with the centuries – scorpions firing wooden darts and very small catapults. If attacked, a square turned with all four sides out to fight, the rear rank of soldiers holding long siege spears to go for the bellies of horses persuaded to jump inside – not something Monaeses was prepared to do, it seemed. If cataphracts were becoming scarce in Parthian lands thanks to old Ventidius, big horses took even longer to breed.

The days went on at a dismal pace of between seventeen and nineteen miles up and down, up and down, everyone now aware of the Parthians shadowing them. Skirmishes developed between Galatian and Gallic cavalry and the cataphracts, but the army pushed on in good order and reasonable spirits.

Until, climbing into ever higher peaks to hazard the eleven-thousand-foot pass, they encountered a blizzard the like of which Italia never saw. Blinding snow like a featureless white wall, howling gales, the kind of surface that dropped away underfoot leaving men stranded thigh-deep in powdery crystals.

The worse conditions became, the more cheerful Antony and his legates became, rationing out sections of the army between them, jollying the men, telling them how brave they were, how hardy and uncomplaining. Squares were down now to maniples, and only three men deep. Over the pass, it would have to be century squares, but neither Antony nor anyone else thought the pass a likely site for attack – no room.

The worst of it was that, though each legionary's pack held warm breeches, socks, the wonderful waterproof circular *sagum*, and neck scarves, still he froze, unable to warm himself by a fire. With two-thirds of the march completed, the army had finally run out of its most precious commodity – charcoal. No one could bake bread, cook pease pottage; the men trudged now chewing raw grains of wheat, their only sustenance. Hunger, frostbite and sickness began to be so severe that even Antony couldn't cheer the most sanguine among his soldiers, who muttered about dying in the snow, of never seeing civilization again.

'Just let us get over the pass!' Antony cried to his Armenian guide, Cyrus. 'You've led us true for two *nundinae* – don't let me down, Cyrus, I beg you!'

'I won't, Marcus Antonius,' the man said in atrocious Greek. 'Tomorrow will see the front squares start to cross, and after that I know where we can get charcoal.' His dark face grew darker. 'Though I should warn you, Marcus Antonius, not to trust the King of Armenia. He has always been in contact with his brother of Media, and both of them are the creatures of King Phraates. Your baggage train was too tempting, I am afraid.'

This time Antony listened; but there were still a hundred miles to go to Artaxata, and the mood of the legions was growing steadily bleaker, creeping toward insurrection.

'Mutiny, even,' Antony said to Fonteius with half his troops on one side of the ranges and the other half still crossing or waiting to cross. 'I daren't let my face be seen.'

'That's true for all of us,' Fonteius answered cheerlessly. 'They've been on raw wheat for seven days, their toes are black and dropping off, their noses too. Terrible! And they're blaming you, Marcus – you, and only you. The malcontents are saying that you should never have let the baggage train out of your sight.'

'It isn't really me,' Antony said drearily, 'it's the nightmare of a fruitless campaign that didn't give them a chance to show their stuff in battle. As they see it, all they did was sit in a camp for a hundred days looking at a city giving them the *medicus* – up your arse, Romans! Think you're great? Well, you're not. I understand . . .' He broke off when Titius hurried up, looking afraid.

'Marcus Antonius, there's mutiny in the air!'

'Tell me something I don't know, Titius.'

'No, but this is *serious*! Tonight or tomorrow or both. At least six legions are involved.'

'Thank you, Titius. Now go and balance the books, or count up how much the soldiers are owed, or something – anything!'

Off went Titius, for once unable to come up with a solution.

'It will be tonight,' Antony said.

'Yes, I agree,' said Fonteius.

'Will you help me fall on my sword, Gaius? One of the most vexing things about such heavy chest and arm muscles is that they curtail my reach. I can't get a decent hold on my sword hilt to make the thrust deep and sure.'

Fonteius didn't argue. 'Yes,' he said.

The pair huddled inside a small leather tent all that night, waiting for the mutiny to begin. To Antony, already devastated, this was a fitting end to the worst campaign a Roman general had waged since Carbo was chopped to pieces by the German Cimbri, or Caepio's army died at Arausio, or – most horrible of all – Paullus and Varro were annihilated by Hannibal at Cannae. Not a single shining fact to illuminate the abyss of total defeat! At least the armies of Carbo, Caepio, Paullus and Varro had perished fighting! Whereas his grand army was never offered one tiny opportunity to show its mettle – no battles, just impotence.

I cannot blame my soldiers for mutinying, Antony thought as he sat with his unsheathed sword in his lap, ready. Impotence. That's what they feel, just as badly as I do. How can they tell their grandsons about Marcus Antonius's expedition into Median Parthia without spitting at the memory? It's shabby, decomposed, utterly beggared of pride or distinction. *Miles gloriosus*, that's Antonius. The vainglorious soldier. Perfect material for a farce. Strutting, posturing, full of himself and his own importance. But his success is as hollow as he is. A caricature as a man, a joke as a soldier, a failure as a general. Antonius the Great. Hah.

And then the mutiny vanished into the thin air of that high pass as if no legionaries had ever talked of it. Morning saw the men keep on crossing, and by mid-afternoon the pass was way behind. From somewhere Antony found the strength to go among the men, pretending that he for one had never even heard a whisper of mutiny.

Twenty-seven days after breaking camp before Phraaspa, the fourteen legions and handful of cavalry reached Artaxata, their bellies filled by a little bread and as much horsemeat as they could force down. Cyrus the guide had told Antony where to plunder enough charcoal for cooking.

The first thing Antony did in Artaxata was to give Cyrus the guide a bag of coins and two good horses, and push him off at the gallop by the quickest route south. Cyrus's mission was urgent – and secret, especially from Artavasdes. His destination was Egypt, where he was to seek an audience with Queen Cleopatra; the coins Antony had given him, struck in Antioch the previous winter, were his passport to the Queen. He was instructed to beg her to come to Leuke Kome bearing aid for Antony's troops. Leuke Kome was a small port near Berytus in Syria, a less public place by far than ports like Berytus, Sidon, Joppa. Cyrus went with gratitude and speed; to have stayed in Armenia once the Romans departed would have been a death sentence, for he had led the Romans well, and that was not what Armenian Artavasdes had wanted. The Romans were supposed to wander, lost, without food or fuel, until every last one of them was dead.

But, with fourteen understrength legions warmly camped on the outskirts of Artaxata, King Artavasdes had no choice other than to fawn and beseech Antony to winter there. Not trusting a word that Artavasdes said, Antony refused to linger. He forced the King to open his granaries; then, adequately provisioned, he marched on for Carana in the face of storms and snow. The legionaries, it seemed inured now, trudged over those last two hundred miles immensely cheered because they had fires at night. Wood was scarce in Armenia too, but the Armenians of Artaxata hadn't dared to argue when Roman soldiers descended on their woodpiles and confiscated them. The thought of Armenians perishing from the cold did not move the Romans in the slightest. *They* hadn't marched chewing raw wheat thanks to Eastern treachery!

Antony reached Carana, from whence the expedition had set out the previous Kalends of May, halfway through November. All of his legates had seen the melancholy, the confusion, but only Fonteius knew how close Antony had come to suicide. Knowing this, but very reluctant to confide it to Canidius, Fonteius took it upon himself to persuade Antony to continue south to Leuke Kome. Once there, he could, if necessary, send another message to Cleopatra.

But first, Antony was made to know the worst by an inflexible Canidius. Theirs had not been an always amicable relationship, for Canidius had seen the shape of the future early in the campaign, and been all for retreat immediately. Nor had he approved of the way the baggage train had been assembled and conducted. However, all of that was in the past, and he had come to terms with himself, his own ambitions. His future lay with Mark Antony, no matter what.

'The census is in and complete, Antonius,' he said dourly. 'Of the auxiliary foot, some thirty thousand, none has survived. Of the Gallic cavalry, six out of ten thousand, but their horses are gone. Of the Galatian cavalry, four out of ten thousand, but their horses are gone. All slaughtered for food over the last hundred miles. Out of sixteen legions, two – Statianus's – have vanished, their fate unknown. The other fourteen have sustained heavy but not mortal casualties, mostly frostbite. Men missing toes will have to be retired and sent home by wagon. They can't march without toes. Each legion save for Statianus's two was up to strength – nearly five thousand soldiers, over a thousand noncombatants. Now, each legion is down to fewer than four thousand, and perhaps five hundred noncombatants.' Canidius drew a breath and looked anywhere but at Antony's face. 'Here are the figures. Auxiliary foot, thirty thousand. Auxiliary cavalry, ten thousand, but twenty thousand horses. Legionaries, fourteen thousand will never fight again, plus another eight thousand from Statianus. And noncombatants, nine thousand. A total of seventy thousand men, twenty thousand horses. Twenty-two thousand of them are legionaries. Half the army, though not the best half. By no means all dead, yet they may as well be.'

'It will look better,' said Antony, mouth quivering, 'if we say a third dead, a fifth incapacitated. Oh, Canidius, to lose so many without fighting a battle! I can't even claim a Cannae.'

'At least no one passed beneath the yoke, Antonius. It isn't a disgrace; it's simply a disaster due to weather.'

'Fonteius says I should continue to Leuke Kome to wait for the Queen, send her another message if necessary.'

'Good thinking. Go, Antonius.'

'Bring the army on as best you can, Canidius. Fur or leather socks for everyone, and when you encounter a snowstorm, wait it out in a good camp. Hugging the Euphrates will be a little warmer, I imagine. Just keep them moving, and promise them a wander in the Elysian Fields when they reach Leuke Kome – warm sun, lots to eat, and every whore I can round up in Syria.'

Clemency had gone the way of all the horses once charcoal had appeared between the mountain pass and Artaxata. Legs dangling nearly to the ground, Antony set off from Carana on a local pony, accompanied by Fonteius and Marcus Titius.

He reached Leuke Kome a month later, to find the little port bewildered at his advent; Cleopatra had not come, nor was there any word from Egypt. Antony sent Titius off to Alexandria, but with little hope; she hadn't wanted him to undertake this campaign, and she was not a forgiving woman. There would be no aid, no money to patch up what remained of his legions, and while to him it was at least something of an achievement to have got the legions out decimated but not annihilated, she was more likely to mourn for the lost auxiliary levies.

Depression clamped down and became a despair so dark that

Antony took to the wine flagon, unable to face the thoughts of icy cold, of rotting toes, of mutiny on one terrible night, of rank after rank of hating faces, of troopers loathing him for the loss of their beloved horses, of his own pathetic decisions, always wrong and always disastrous. He, and no one else, bore the blame for so many deaths, so much human misery. Oh, unbearable! So he drank himself into oblivion, and kept on drinking.

Twenty and thirty times a day he would reel out of his tent, a brimming beaker in one hand, stagger the short distance to the shore, and look toward the shipless, sailless harbor mouth.

'Is she coming?' he would ask anyone near. 'Is she coming? Is she coming?' They thought him mad, and ran away the moment they saw him emerge from his tent. Is who coming?

Back inside he would bolt to drink some more, then outside: 'Is she coming? Is she coming?'

January became February, then the end of February, and she never came, nor sent a message. Nothing from Cyrus or Titius.

Finally Antony's legs wouldn't bear him anymore; he lolled over the wine flagon in his tent and tried to say 'Is she coming?' to anyone who entered.

'Is she coming?' he asked the movement of the tent flap at the beginning of March, a meaningless gabble to those who didn't know from long experience what he was trying to say.

'She is here,' said a soft voice. 'She is here, Antonius.'

Soiled, stinking, Antony somehow managed to get to his feet; he fell on his knees and she sank down beside him, cradling his head against her breast as he wept and wept.

She was horrified, though that was just a word; it didn't even begin to describe the emotions that roiled in Cleopatra's mind and devastated her body during the days that followed as she talked to Fonteius and Ahenobarbus. Once Antony had wept himself to sleep and could be bathed, put into a more comfortable bed than his military camp stretcher, the painful process of sobering up and doing without the wine taxed Cleopatra's ingenuity to its limits. He was not a good patient – he refused to talk, grew angry when denied wine, and seemed to regret ever having wanted Cleopatra there.

Thus it had to be Fonteius and Ahenobarbus who talked to her, the former very willing to help in any way he could, the latter making no attempt to disguise his dislike and contempt for her.

So she tried to divide the horrors she was told into categories, in the hope that, by approaching things logically, sequentially, she might see more clearly how to go about the healing of Mark Antony. If he was to survive, he *must* be healed!

From Fonteius she got the full story of that doomed campaign, including the night when suicide had seemed the only alternative. Of the blizzards, ice and thigh-deep snow she had no comprehension, having seen snow only during her two winters in Róme, and they were not hard, she had been assured at the time; the Tiber hadn't frozen over, and the sparse snowfalls had been an enchantment, an utterly silent world coated in white. Not, she divined, remotely comparable to the retreat from Phraaspa.

Ahenobarbus concentrated more on painting graphic pictures for her, of feet rotting from frostbite, of men chewing raw wheat, of Antony driven mad by the treachery of everyone from his allies to his guides.

'You paid for this debacle,' he said, 'without ever stopping to think of equipment that wasn't included and should have been, like warmer clothing for the legionaries.'

What could she answer? That such were not her concerns, but lay within the province of Antony and his *praefectus fabrum*? If she did, Ahenobarbus would attribute her answer to self-preservation at Antony's expense; clearly Ahenobarbus would hear no criticism of Antony; preferring to lay the blame at her door just because her money had funded the expedition.

So she said, 'Everything was already in place when my money became available. How was Antonius going to conduct his campaign if my money hadn't turned up?'

'There would have been no campaign, Queen! Antonius would have continued to sit in Syria, in colossal debt to the purveyors of everything from mail shirts to artillery.'

'And you would rather he went on that way than have the money to pay and be able to conduct his campaign?'

'Yes!' snapped Ahenobarbus.

'That implies that you don't consider him a capable general.'

'Infer what you like, Queen. I say no more.' And Ahenobarbus stormed off, radiating hatred.

'Is he right, Fonteius?' she asked her sympathetic informant. 'Is Marcus Antonius incapable of commanding a great enterprise?'

Surprised and flustered, Fonteius privately cursed Ahenobarbus's irascible tongue. 'No, Your Majesty, he's not right, but nor was he saying quite what you thought. If you hadn't accompanied the army to Zeugma with the intention of going farther, and spoken your mind at councils, men like Ahenobarbus would have had no criticism to make. What he was saying was that *you* bungled the venture by insisting that it be conducted in a certain way; that, without you, Antonius would have been a different man, and not gone down to defeat without a battle.'

'Oh, that isn't fair!' she said, gasping. 'I laid no kind of command on Antonius! None!'

'I believe you, lady. But Ahenobarbus never will.'

When the army began to limp into Leuke Kome three *nundinae* after the Queen of Egypt had arrived there, it found the little harbor choked with ships and a number of camps spread around the town's outskirts. Cleopatra had brought physicians, medicines, what seemed like a legion of bakers and cooks to feed the soldiers better fare than their noncombatant servants gave them, comfortable beds, clean soft clothing; she had even gone to the trouble of having her slaves pluck all the sea urchins from the shallows of a large beach so everyone could bathe free of the worst scourge that beaches at this end of Our Sea produced. If Leuke Kome wasn't exactly the Elysian Fields, to the average legionary it seemed akin to them. Spirits soared, especially among the men whose toes hadn't perished.

'I'm very grateful,' Publius Canidius said to her. 'My boys need a real holiday, and you've enabled them to have it. Once they've mended, they'll forget the worst of their ordeals.'

'Except for rotten toes and noses,' Cleopatra said bitterly.

SEVENTEEN

Portus Julius was finished in time for Agrippa to train his oarsmen and marines all through the mild winter that saw Lucius Gellius Poplicola and Marcus Cocceius Nerva assume the consulship on New Year's Day. As usual, partisan won out over neutral; the impartial third at negotiations to frame the Pact of Brundisium, Lucius Nerva, lost to the brother who was Octavian's adherent. There in Rome to hold a watching action for Antony, Poplicola was given the job of governing Rome; Octavian didn't want him trying to claim any victories over Sextus Pompey for Antony's faction, still large and very vocal.

Sabinus had been an adequate superviser of the construction of Portus Julius and wanted the high command, but his tendency to be hard to get on with rendered him unsuitable in Octavian's eyes; while Agrippa was busy at Portus Julius, Octavian went to the Senate with his proposals.

'Having been consul, you rank with Sabinus,' he said to Agrippa when that worthy came to Rome to report, 'so the Senate and People have decreed that you, not Sabinus, will be commander-in-chief on the land, and admiral-in-chief on the water. Under me, of course.'

Two years governing Further Gaul, a consulship and Octavian's trust in his initiative had worked upon Agrippa powerfully. Where once he would have blushed and disclaimed, now he simply swelled a little and looked pleased. His degree of self-importance – none – had not altered, but his confidence in himself had mushroomed without manifesting Antony's fatal flaws; no laziness, erratic attention to detail or reluctance to deal with correspondence from Marcus Agrippa! When Agrippa received a letter, it was answered immediately, and so succinctly that its recipient experienced no doubt whatsoever about the nature of its contents.

311

All Agrippa said in response to the news of his huge job was 'As you wish, Caesar.'

'However,' Octavian went on, 'I would humbly ask that you find me a tiny fleet or a couple of legions to command. I want to serve in this war personally. Since I married Livia Drusilla I seem to have lost the asthma entirely, even around horses, so I ought to be able to survive without incurring a new lot of canards about my cowardice.' It was said matter-of-factly, but a glassy look in his eyes betrayed his determination to scotch the slur of Philippi for good.

'I had planned to do so anyway, Caesar,' Agrippa said, smiling. 'If you have the time, I'd like to discuss war plans.'

'Livia Drusilla should be here.'

'I agree. Is she in, or out buying clothes?'

Octavian's wife had few faults, but clothing was certainly one such. She loved to dress well, had perfect taste, and her jewelry, augmented by her husband regularly, was the envy of every woman in Rome. That the habitually parsimonious Octavian didn't object to her extravagance lay in the fact that he wanted his wife to be above all others in every way; she must look and conduct herself like an uncrowned queen, thus establishing her ascendancy over other women. One day that would be very important.

'In, I think.' Octavian clapped his hands and told the man who answered to fetch the lady Livia Drusilla.

In she came a moment later, clad in floating draperies of a very dark blue, sewn with an occasional sapphire that flashed when light caught it. Her necklace, earrings and bracelets were of sapphires and pearls, and the buttons that pinched her sleeves together at intervals were also of sapphires and pearls.

Agrippa blinked, dazzled.

'Delicious, my dear,' said Octavian, sounding seventy years old; she had that effect on him.

'Yes, I can't understand why sapphires are so unpopular,' she said, settling herself in a chair. 'I find their darkness subtle.'

Octavian nodded to the scribes and clerks, lingering with ears flapping. 'Go and have lunch, or count the fish in the one pond the Germans haven't plundered,' he said to them. And to Agrippa, 'Oh, not to live behind fortified walls! Tell me that this year I will be able to pull them down, Agrippa!'

'This year, definitely, Caesar.'

'Speak, Agrippa.'

But first Agrippa spread out a big map on the large table that served as a culling area for the myriad papers a busy Triumvir collected in the course of his duties: Italia from Adriatic to Tuscan Sea, Sicilia, and Africa Province.

'I've just taken a count, and can tell you that we'll have four hundred and eleven ships,' Agrippa said. 'All but a hundred and forty of them are in Portus Julius, ready and waiting.'

'Antonius's hundred and twenty plus Octavia's twenty, in Tarentum,' Octavian said.

'Exactly. If they were intended to sail through the Straits of Messana, they would be vulnerable, but they won't go near the Straits. They will take a southward curve and make Sicilian land-fall at Pachymus Cape, then creep northward up the coast to attack Syracuse. This fleet goes to Taurus, who will also have four legions of land troops. After he takes Syracuse he's to set off across the slopes of Aetna, reducing the countryside as he goes, and bring his legions to Messana, where the strongest resistance is bound to be concentrated. But Taurus will need help, both in taking Syracuse and on his land march afterward.' The hazel eyes buried under Agrippa's jutting forehead gleamed suddenly green. 'The most dangerous task of all is a bait consisting of sixty big fives specially chosen to withstand a heavy sea battle – I'd prefer not to lose them, if possible, even though they are a bait. This fleet will sail from Portus Julius through the Straits to reinforce Taurus. Sextus Pompeius will do what he always does – lurk in the Straits. And he'll pounce on our bait fleet like a lion on a deer. The aim is to keep Sextus's attention riveted on the Straits and, by inference, Syracuse – why else would a fleet of stout fives be sailing south than to attack Syracuse? With any luck, my own fleet, following behind the bait fleet, will steal a march on Sextus and succeed in landing legions at Mylae.'

'I'll command the bait fleet,' Octavian said eagerly. 'Give me that task, Agrippa, please! I'll take Sabinus with me so he won't feel passed over for an important job.'

'If you want the bait fleet, Caesar, it's yours.'

'Thus far, a two-pronged attack directed at the eastern end of the island,' said Livia Drusilla. 'You'll move from the west toward Messana, Agrippa, while Taurus approaches Messana from the south. But what about the western end of Sicilia?'

Agrippa's face took on an unhappy expression. 'For that, lady, I am afraid we have to use Marcus Lepidus and some of the too many legions he has accumulated in Africa Province. It's a short sail from Africa to Lilybaeum and Agrigentum, one better undertaken by

Lepidus. Sextus may have his headquarters in Agrigentum, but he won't linger in that neighborhood with so much going on around Syracuse and Messana.'

'I never thought he would linger there, but his money vaults will,' Livia Drusilla said, and looked steely. 'Whatever we do, we can't let Lepidus make off with Sextus Pompeius's hoard. Which he will try to do.'

'Absolutely,' Octavian said. 'Unfortunately he was privy to our dickerings with Antonius, so he knows full well that Agrigentum is vital. And that militarily it's not a first target. We'll have to beat Sextus around Messana, separated from Agrigentum by half the island and several mountain ranges. But I see Agrigentum as another bait. Lepidus can't afford to confine his activities to the western end if he's to preserve his status as Triumvir and a major contributor to victory. So what he'll do is garrison Agrigentum with several legions until he can return to empty the vaults. Therefore we don't let him return.'

'How do you plan to do that, Caesar?' Agrippa asked.

'I'm not sure yet. Just take my word for it, that's what will happen to Lepidus.'

'I believe you,' said Livia Drusilla, looking smug.

'And I,' said Agrippa, looking loyal and devoted.

Unwilling to run the risk of equinoctial gales, Agrippa didn't mount his attack until early summer, after word had come from Africa and Lepidus that he was ready and would sail on the Ides of Julius. Statilius Taurus, who had by far the longest voyage to make, was to sail from Tarentum thirteen days earlier, on the Kalends, while Octavian, Octavian's friend Messala Corvinus and Sabinus set off from Portus Julius the day before the Ides, and Agrippa on the day after the Ides.

It had been agreed that Octavian would land just south of the toe of the Italian boot, at Tauromenium, and have the bulk of the legions in his charge; Taurus was to join up with him there after crossing Mount Aetna. Messala Corvinus was to march the legions through Lucania to Vibo, from which port they would cross to Tauromenium.

All of which would have been fine, had it not been for an unseasonal storm that did more damage to Octavian's bait fleet than Sextus Pompeius did in pouncing. Octavian himself was stranded on the Italian side of the Straits together with half his legions; the other half, having landed at Tauromenium, waited for Taurus to come up and Octavian to come over. A long wait. Even after the storm blew itself out two *nundinae* later, Octavian and Messala Corvinus were frustrated by the damage done to their troop transports. By the time they were repaired, it was well into Sextilis, and the whole island was involved in land fighting.

Lepidus had no troubles at all. He landed in Lilybaeum and Agrigentum on time, disembarked twelve legions, and struck both north and east across the mountains, aiming for Messana. Just as Octavian had predicted, he garrisoned Agrigentum with four more legions, sure that it would be he and no one else who returned to pick over the contents of Sextus Pompey's vaults.

But it was Agrippa who won the campaign. Knowing the size of Taurus's Tarentum fleet and overestimating the size of Octavian's bait fleet, Sextus Pompey pulled in every ship he owned and concentrated them in the Straits, determined to hold Messana and therefore the eastern end of the island. With the result that Agrippa's two hundred and eleven quinqueremes and triremes sent a small Pompeian fleet to the bottom off Mylae, and landed the four legions in his wake there, safe and sound. Agrippa then raided far along the north coast in a westerly direction before rallying his warships and lurking offshore at Naulochus.

It seemed not to have entered Sextus Pompey's mind that the despised Octavian would – or could – gather so many ships and troops against him. Bad news followed bad news: Lepidus was reducing the western end of Sicilia, Agrippa was reducing the north coast, and Octavian himself had finally made it across the Straits. Sicilia swarmed with soldiers, but few of them belonged to Sextus Pompey. Filled with dread and despair, Pompey the Great's younger son decided to stake everything on a huge naval engagement, and sailed to meet Agrippa.

The two fleets met at Naulochus, Sextus convinced that, as well as having the numbers, he also had the skill. Over three hundred galleys admiraled and crewed superbly, with himself in overall command – what did an Apulian lout like Marcus Agrippa think he was doing, to take on Sextus Pompeius, unbeaten at sea for ten long years? But Agrippa's ships were more aggressive, and armed with a typically Agrippan secret weapon – the *harpax*. He had taken an ordinary tossing grapnel and turned it into something that could be fired from a scorpion at a much longer distance than an arm's throw. The enemy vessel was then winched in, all the while bombarded with scorpion darts, boulders and flaming bundles of hay. As this was going on, the Agrippan ship turned bow on and ran down the enemy vessel's side to shear off its oars. That done, the marines boarded across *corvus* gangplanks and finished the process by killing everyone who hadn't leaped into the water, there to drown or be fished out as a prisoner of war. According to Agrippa's way of thinking, beaks for ramming were all very well, but they rarely sank a ship and mostly allowed it to get away. The *harpax*, sheared oars and marines to follow invariably meant a doomed quarry.

Tears streaming down his face, Sextus Pompey watched his combined fleets destroyed. At the very last moment, he turned his flagship into the south and ran, determined that he wouldn't be led in chains through the Forum Romanum to be tried for treason in secret in the Senate, like Salvidienus. For he knew well that his status would protect him from the usual fate of one declared *hostis*: to be killed by the first man who saw him. That, he could have borne.

He hid in a cove and negotiated the Straits during darkness, then set his course eastward to round the Peloponnnese and seek shelter with Antony, who he knew was absent on his campaign; he would go to earth somewhere sympathetic until Antony returned. Mitylene on the island of Lesbos had let his father have asylum; it would do the same for the son, Sextus was sure.

Land resistance was negligible, especially after the third day of September, the day on which Agrippa won at Naulochus. Sextus's 'legions' were made up of brigands, slaves and freedmen, poorly trained and not valorous. All Sextus had used them for was to terrorize the local populace; against true Roman legions they stood no hope of winning. Most surrendered, crying for mercy.

Lepidus reveled in his superiority, and took his time crossing the island. Even so, he arrived before Messana ahead of Octavian, encountering the most determined resistance on the straight coast north of Tauromenium. When Lepidus reached Messana, he found its Pompeian governor, Plinius Rufus, offering to surrender to Agrippa. An insult Lepidus would not brook. He sent to Plinius Rufus at once, demanding that the surrender be to him, not to Agrippa the low-bred nobody. That might have passed muster, save that he accepted the submission in his own name, not Octavian's.

When Octavian arrived in Agrippa's camp, he found Agrippa seething: a new experience! In all their years together, he never remembered Agrippa in a towering rage.

'Do you know what that *cunnus* did?' Agrippa roared, lashing a metaphorical tail. 'Said he was the victor over Sicilia, not you, the Triumvir of Rome, Italia and the Islands! Said . . . said . . . oh, I can't think for the life of me, I am so furious!'

'Let's go and see him,' Octavian soothed, 'sort our differences out and get an apology. How's that?'

'Nothing short of his head will satisfy me,' Agrippa muttered.

Lepidus, however, was not in a conciliatory mood. He received Octavian and Agrippa wearing his scarlet *paludamentum* and a pretty set of gold armor, its cuirass tooled to show Aemilius Paullus on the battlefield at Pydna, a famous victory. At fifty-five, Lepidus wasn't young, and felt his eclipse by mere youths acutely. It was now or never, as far as he was concerned; time to make that bid for power, which always seemed to elude him. His rank was equal to Antony's and Octavian's, yet no one took him seriously, and that had to change. Every 'legion' of Sextus's troops he found was incorporated into his own army, with the result that Messana saw his tally stand at twenty-two legions – and that didn't even include the four guarding Agrigentum and the ones he had left to police Africa Province. Yes, time to act!

'What do you want, Octavianus?' he asked haughtily.

'My due,' Octavian said quietly.

'You're due nothing. I beat Sextus Pompeius, not you or your low-bred minions.'

'How odd, Lepidus. Why did I think it was Marcus Agrippa who beat Sextus Pompeius? He staked his all on a sea battle at which you were not present.'

'You can have the seas, Octavianus, but you can't have this island,' said Lepidus, drawing himself up. 'As Triumvir with equal powers to yours, I declare that henceforth Sicilia is a part of Africa, and will be ruled from Africa by me. Africa is mine, apportioned out to me at the Pact of Tarentum for another five years. Except,' Lepidus went on with a smirk, 'that five years are not sufficient. I'm taking Africa, including Sicilia, in perpetuity.'

'The Senate and People will deprive you of both if you're not careful, Lepidus.'

'Then let the Senate and People go to war against me! I have thirty legions under my command. I order you to take yourself and your minions to Italia, Octavianus! Leave my province now!'

'Is that your final word?' Octavian asked, his hand clenched on Agrippa's forearm to make sure he didn't draw his sword.

'It is.'

'Are you truly prepared for another civil war?'

'I am.'

'Thinking that Marcus Antonius will back you when he returns from the Kingdom of the Parthians. But he won't, Lepidus. Believe me, he won't.'

'I don't care whether he does or not. Now leave while you still have life in your body, Octavianus.'

'I have been Caesar for some years now, but you're still just . . . Lepidus the ignominious.'

Octavian turned and walked out of Messana's best mansion, his hand still keeping Agrippa's from his sword.

'Caesar, how dare he! Don't tell me we have to fight him!' Agrippa cried, prising Octavian's fingers from his arm at last.

His most beautiful smile curved Octavian's lips; the eyes he directed at Agrippa looked luminous, innocent, endearingly young. 'Dear Agrippa! No, we won't have to fight, I promise.'

More than that, Agrippa couldn't learn. Octavian simply said there would be no civil war, not even a tiny warlet, a skirmish, a duel, a drill.

Next morning at dawn Octavian disappeared; by the time a frantic Agrippa found him, it was all over. Alone and togate, he had entered Lepidus's enormous encampment and gone among the many thousands of soldiers, smiling at them, congratulating them, and making them his own. They swore mighty oaths to Tellus, Sol Indiges and Liber Pater that Caesar was their only commander, that Caesar was their darling, their gold-haired mascot, *divi filius*.

Sextus Pompey's eight legions of motley recruits were disbanded that same day, and milled around under heavy guard speculating about their fate in a fairly complacent mood; from Lepidus they had been promised freedom, and as they knew little of Octavian, they fully expected the same kind of treatment.

'Your race is run, Lepidus,' Octavian said when the astounded Lepidus stormed into his tent. 'Because you are related by blood to my divine father, I will spare your life and not subject you to a treason trial in the Senate. But I will have that selfsame body strip you of your Triumvirate and all your provinces. You will retire to private life and never again leave it, even to seek the censorship. However, you may retain your status as Pontifex Maximus. It is given for life, and it will remain yours while you live. I require you to sail aboard my ship with me, but you will be put off at Circeii, where you have a villa. You will not enter Rome for any reason, nor will you be allowed to tenant the Domus Publica.'

Face drawn, Lepidus listened, his throat working convulsively. When he could find nothing to say in reply, he sagged onto a chair and covered his face with a fold of toga.

Octavian was as good as his word. Full of Antony's cliental adherents it might be, but the Senate enacted the decrees about Lepidus asked of it without a murmur. Lepidus was forbidden to enter Rome, and stripped of all his public duties, honors, provinces.

The harvest that year sold for ten sesterces the *modius*, and Italia rejoiced. When the vaults in Agrigentum were breached by Octavian and Agrippa, they yielded the staggering sum of a hundred and ten thousand talents. Antony's forty per cent, forty-four thousand talents, were divided off and sent to him at Antioch the moment his Athenian fleet was free to sail. To prevent theft, it was locked in metal-banded oak chests, each nailed shut and sealed with a dollop of lead that bore a replica of Octavian's sphinx signet, IMP.CAES.DIV.FIL.TRI. Each ship carried six hundred and sixty-six chests, one fifty-six-pound talent to a chest.

'That ought to please him,' Agrippa said, 'though he won't like your keeping Octavia's twenty galleys.'

'Oh, they'll go to Athens next year, with two thousand picked troops aboard, and Octavia as an extra present. She misses him.'

But Rome's share, sixty per cent now that Lepidus was out of the equation, didn't reach Rome intact after all. The sixty-six thousand chests were loaded aboard the troop transports that first had to call into Portus Julius and there disgorge the twenty legions that Octavian was bringing home – some for retirement, most to stay under the Eagles for reasons that none save Octavian knew.

Word of the enormous treasure had spread. The legion representatives at the end of the Sicilian campaign were not an admirable lot, nor imbued with patriotism. When Octavian and Agrippa had marched them to Capua and inserted them into a camp on its outskirts, twenty legion representatives came as a delegation to Octavian, talking mutiny unless he paid every man a hefty bonus.

They meant it, so much Octavian could see. He listened to their spokesman expressionlessly, then asked, 'How much?'

'A thousand denarii – four thousand sesterces – each,' said Lucius Decidius. 'Otherwise all twenty legions will run amok.'

'Does that include the noncombatants?'

Obviously not; the faces looked bewildered. Decidius was a quick thinker, however. 'For them, a hundred denarii each.'

'Pray pardon me while I sit down with my abacus and work out how much that amounts to,' Octavian said, apparently unruffled.

He proceeded to do just that, the ivory beads whizzing back and forth across their thin rods faster than any untutored legion representative could credit. Oh, he was a treat, was young Caesar!

'That is fifteen thousand, seven hundred and forty-four silver talents,' he said a few moments later. 'In other words, the usual contents of Rome's Treasury, whole and entire.'

'*Gerrae*, it ain't!' said Decidius, who could read and write, but was hopeless at sums. 'You're a swindler and a liar!'

'I assure you, Decidius, that I am neither. I simply speak the truth. To prove this, when I pay you – yes, I will pay you! – I'll put the money in one hundred thousand bags of a thousand for the men, and twenty thousand bags of a hundred for the noncombatants. Denarii, not sesterces. I'll pile these bags on the assembly ground, and I suggest that you find enough legionaries who can count to verify that each bag does indeed hold the requisite amount of money. Though I advise you to weigh them – it's quicker!

'Oh, I forgot to say that it's four thousand denarii each for the centurions,' said Decidius quickly.

'Too late, Decidius! Centurions get the same as rankers. I agreed to your original request, and I refuse to alter it after the fact, is that clear? I am going somewhat farther – after the fact, because I am a Triumvir and allowed that privilege – by telling you that you can't have this bonus and expect land. This is your retirement payout, and it finishes us free and clear. If you get land, it will be at my pleasure. Fritter away what should be in the Treasury with my best wishes, but do not ask for more, now or in the future. Because Rome will pay no more big bonuses. In future, Rome's legions will be fighting for Rome, not for a general nor in a civil war. And in future, Rome's legions will get their pay, their savings and a small bonus when they retire. No more land, no more anything the Senate and People don't sanction. I am instituting a standing army of twenty-five legions, all of whose men will serve for twenty years without discharge. A career, not a job. A torch carried for Rome, not a candle for a general. Do I make myself understood? It's over, Decidius, on this day.'

The twenty representatives listened in growing horror, for there was something of Caesar about that beautiful young face, now it was neither as beautiful nor as young as it used to be. They knew he meant what he said. As representatives, they were the most militant and the most venal of their kind, but even the most militant

320

and venal of men can hear the closing of a door, and one closed on that day. Perhaps the future would hold mutinies too, but Caesar was saying that it would carry the death penalty for all involved.

'You can't execute a hundred thousand of us,' Decidius said.

'Oh, can't I?' Octavian's eyes grew wider, more luminous. 'How long would you last if I were to tell the three *million* people of Italia that you are holding them to ransom, taking money out of their purses? Because you wear a mail shirt and a sword? It's not a good enough reason, Decidius. If the people of Italia knew, they'd tear a hundred thousand of you into little pieces.' He waved a contemptuous hand. 'Be off, all of you! And look at the size of your bonuses when I pile my bags up on the assembly ground. Then you'll know how much you asked for.'

They filed out looking sheepish but determined.

'Have you their names, Agrippa?'

'Yes, every last one. And a few more besides.'

'Break them up and mix them up. I think it's better that each meets an accident, don't you?'

'Fortuna is capricious, Caesar, but death in battle is easier to arrange. A pity the campaigns are over.'

'Not at all!' said Octavian in the most cordial of voices. 'Next year we are going to Illyricum. If we don't, Agrippa, the tribes will unite with the Bessi and the Dardani and pour over the Carnic Alps into Italian Gaul. That's the lowest and easiest way into Italia, and the only reason it hasn't been used to invade is lack of unity among the tribes. Who are becoming Romanized – in the wrong way. Legion representatives are going to be heroic, and a lot will die in the process of winning a crown for valor. By the way, I'm going to award you a Naval Crown.' He giggled. 'It will suit you, Agrippa – all that gold.'

'Thank you, Caesar, that's very nice of you. But Illyricum?'

'No, mutiny. It's going to go out of fashion, or my name is not Caesar and I am not the son of a god. Pah! I've just lost near sixteen thousand talents for a paltry campaign that saw more men drown than perish at the end of a sword. If for no other reason than exorbitant bonuses, there can be no more civil wars. The legions are going to fight in Illyricum for Rome, and only Rome. It will be a proper campaign, with no element of commander worship or dependence on him to grant bonuses. Though I'm going along to fight too, it's your campaign, Agrippa. You, I trust.'

'You're amazing, Caesar.'

Octavian looked genuinely surprised. 'Why?' he asked.

'You faced them down, that scabby lot of utter villains. They came here this morning to intimidate you, and you turned the table, intimidating them. They left very frightened men.'

Came the smile that (or so Livia Drusilla thought) could melt a bronze statue. 'Oh, Agrippa, they may be utter villains, but they're such *children*! I know that at least one in every eight legionaries must be able to read and write, but in future, when they belong to a standing army, they're all going to have to be literate – *and* numerate. Winter camp is going to be stuffed with teachers. If they had any real idea of how much their greed has just cost Rome, they'd think again. That's why the lessons begin now, with those bags.' He sighed, looked rueful. 'I must send for a full cohort of Treasury clerks. Here I sit until it's done, Agrippa, right under my own eyes. No peculation, embezzlement or fraud on the farthest horizon.'

'Will you palm them off with cistophori? There were a lot of them in Sextus's hoard, and I remember the story about the great Cicero's brother being paid in cistophori.'

'The cistophori will be melted down and minted as sesterces and denarii. My utter villains and the men they represent will be paid in denarii, as they demanded.' A dreamy look suffused his eyes. 'I'm trying to visualize how high the piles of bags will be, but even my imagination boggles.'

It was January before Octavian could return to Rome, his task concluded. He turned the event itself into something of a circus, compelling every one of a hundred and twenty thousand men to file past the assembly ground and look at the small mountains of bags, then made a speech that was more in dead Caesar's mode than in his own. His method of disseminating what he said was novel; he himself stood atop a high tribunal and addressed those centurions his agents informed him were the really influential men, while each of his agents gave the same speech to one century of troops, not read from a paper, but declaimed from memory. It astonished Agrippa, who knew all about Octavian's agents, but had never realized how many of them there were. A century consisted of eighty soldiers and twenty noncombatant servants; there were sixty centuries to the legion, and twenty legions assembled to see the bags, hear the speech. *Twelve hundred agents!* No wonder he knew everything there was to know. Son of Caesar he might pretend to be, but the truth was that Octavian resembled no one, even his divine father. He was something absolutely new, as perceptive men like the late Aulus Hirtius had understood very early in his career.

As for his agents, they were men who were virtually unemployable in any other capacity – the kind of gossipy, idle fellows who loved being paid a small wage just to loiter around a marketplace and talk, talk, talk. When one reported a valuable item of information back to his superior in a long, carefully structured chain, he would receive a few denarii as a reward, but only if the information proved accurate. Octavian had agents in the legions as well, but they were only paid for information; Rome paid their wages.

By the time the meeting was dismissed, the legions knew that only the veterans of Mutina and Philippi would be retiring; that next year the bulk of them would be fighting in Illyricum – and that mutiny would not be tolerated for any reason, least of all bonuses. The slightest hint of it, and backs would be bared for the lash, then heads would roll.

Agrippa triumphed at last for his victories in Further Gaul; Calvinus, loaded with Spanish plunder and a fearsome reputation for treating mutinous soldiers cruelly, sheathed the scarred little Regia, Rome's oldest temple, in costly marbles and adorned its exterior with statues; Statilius Taurus was given the job of governing Africa and reducing its legions to two; the grain was flowing as the grain should, and at the old price; and a very happy Octavian ordered the fortifications around the *domus Livia Drusilla* pulled down. He built a comfortable barracks for the Germans at the end of the Palatine, on the corner where the Via Triumphalis met the Circus Maximus, and appointed them as a special bodyguard. Though he walked behind twelve lictors, as was the custom, he and his lictors walked surrounded by Germans in armor. A new phenomenon for Rome, unused to seeing armed troops inside the sacred boundary of the city save in times of emergency.

Though the legions belonged to Rome, the Germans belonged to Octavian and Octavian alone. There were six hundred of them, the *cohors praetorii*, officially designated protectors of magistrates, senators and triumvirs, but no magistrate or senator was under any illusions; when needed, they would answer only to Octavian, who suddenly became special in a way even Caesar had not. Rich and powerful senators and knights had always hired bodyguards, but they were motley lots of ex-gladiators who had never looked truly military. Octavian outfitted his Germans in spectacular gear, and kept them fresh and the Head Count entertained by having them perform their drills inside the Circus Maximus every day.

No one booed or hissed or spat at him anymore when Octavian walked the city streets or appeared in the Forum Romanum; he had saved Rome and Italia from starvation without assistance from Marcus Antonius, whose loaned fleet somehow never got a mention. The job of organizing Italia was given to Sabinus, who found he relished the work, consisting as it did of confirming deeds to land, assessing the public lands of the various towns and *municipia*, taking censuses of veterans, wheat farmers, anyone Octavian considered valuable or noteworthy, and repairing roads, bridges, public buildings, harbors, temples and granaries. Sabinus also was dowered with a team of praetors to hear grievance lawsuits, of which there were many; Romans of all Classes were litigious.

Twenty days after the battle of Naulochus, Octavian had turned twenty-seven; he had been at the heart of Roman politics and war for nine whole years. Longer at a stretch than even Caesar or Sulla, who had been absent from Rome for years at a time. Octavian was a Roman fixture. This showed in many ways, but particularly in his bearing. Slight, not tall, his togate form moved with grace, dignity and a strange aura of power – the power of one who had survived against all the odds, and emerged triumphant. The people of Rome, from highest to lowest, had grown used to seeing him, and, like Julius Caesar, he was not too grand to talk to anyone. This, despite the German bodyguard, who knew better than to intervene when he pushed through their ranks to chat to a citizen. If their swords were loose in their scabbards, they had learned to conceal their anxiety, exchanging remarks in broken Latin with those in the crowd not trying to get to Caesar. Looking gorgeous.

By the New Year, when that serendipitous Pompeian with the same name, Sextus Pompeius, had assumed the consulship together with Lucius Cornificius, news of great victories in the East began to arrive in Rome, spread by Antony's agents at the instigation of Poplicola. Antony had conquered the Parthians, won vast tracts for Rome, accumulated untold treasure. His partisans were overjoyed, his enemies confounded. Octavian, the most important unbeliever, sent special agents to the East to find out whether these rumors were true.

On the Kalends of March he convened the Senate, something he didn't ordinarily do. Whenever he did, the senators turned up to the last man, out of curiosity and a growing respect. He wasn't there yet; there were still senators who called him Octavianus, refused to give him the title of Caesar, but their number was diminishing. And his survival for nine perilous years had added an element of fear. If his power grew greater still and Mark Antony didn't come home soon, nothing would stop him from becoming whatever he wanted to be. That was where the fear came in.

As Triumvir in charge of Rome and Italia, he occupied an ivory curule chair on the magistrates' dais at the end of the new Curia his divine father had built, such a long process that it was not finished until the year of Sextus Pompey's defeat. As his imperium was *maius*, he outranked the consuls, whose ivory curule chairs were to either side of his, and farther back.

He rose to speak, holding no notes, spine straight, hair a golden nimbus in a building whose sheer size made it rather dim. Light poured in through clerestory windows high above, and was swallowed by the gloom of an interior big enough to hold a thousand men in two banks of three tiers, one to either side of the dais. They sat on small stools – those who had been senior magistrates on the bottom tier, more junior magistrates on the middle tier, and the *pedarii*, forbidden to speak, on the top tier. As there was no party system, whether a man chose to sit to right or to left of the dais was not significant, though those belonging to a faction tended to cluster together. Some took verbatim notes in shorthand for their own archives, but six clerks took verbatim records for the Senate as a body, copied out afterward, impressed with the seals of the consuls, and inserted into the archives held next door in the Senate offices.

'Honored consuls, consulars, praetors, ex-praetors, aediles, ex-aediles, tribunes of the plebs, ex-tribunes of the plebs, and conscript fathers, I am here to report on what has been done. I regret that I could not make this report any earlier, but it was necessary that I travel to Africa Province to install Titus Statilius Taurus as its governor and see for myself what kind of mess the ex-Triumvir Lepidus had created. A considerable mess, consisting chiefly in the accumulation of a staggering number of legions which he later used in an attempt to take over government. A situation I dealt with, as you know. But never again will any promagistrate of any rank or imperium be permitted to recruit, arm and train legions in his province, or import legions to his province without the express consent of the Senate and People of Rome.

'Very well, onward. My oldest legions, veterans of Mutina and Philippi, will be discharged and given land in Africa and in Sicilia, the latter a bigger mess than Africa, in crying need of good governance, proper farming and a prosperous populace. These veterans will be settled on one to two hundred *iugera* of land that must grow wheat alternating with legumes every fourth year. The old *latifundia* of Sicilia will be subdivided, save for one given to Imperator Marcus Agrippa. He will act as overall supervisor of veteran growers, thus relieving them of the burden of selling their crop, which he will do in their names and pay them fairly. The legion representatives of these troops are happy with my arrangements, and anxious to be retired.

'Their going will leave Rome with twenty-five good legions, sufficient men to cope with whatever wars Rome is compelled to wage. Very shortly they will be serving in Illyricum, which I intend to subdue during this year, next year, and perhaps the year after. It is high time that the people of eastern Italian Gaul were protected against raids by the Iapudes, Delmatae and other Illyrian tribes. If my divine father had lived, this would have been done. So now it falls to me, and I will do it in conjunction with Marcus Agrippa. For I myself cannot and will not leave Rome for more than a matter of months. Good governance happens at first hand, and mine is the hand the Senate and People of Rome have honored with the task of establishing good governance.'

Octavian stepped down from the curule dais, steered a course around the long wooden bench below it that accommodated the ten tribunes of the plebs, and walked to the centre of the tessellated floor. There he spoke, turning in very slow circles so that every senator had a good view of him and saw his face as much as the back of his head. The nimbus of gold light followed, imbued his slight figure with an aura of unworldliness.

'We have had riots and unrest ever since Sextus Pompeius began to interfere with the grain supply,' he went on, level-voiced, calm. 'The Treasury was empty, people starved, the price of goods soared to a height which meant that none without means could live as all Romans should live – with dignity and a modicum of comfort. Those who could not afford one slave multiplied. The *capite censi* who did not have a soldier's wage coming in were in such dire straits that there were times when no shop in Rome dared open. Not their fault, conscript fathers! Our fault, for not dealing with Sextus Pompeius. We had neither the fleets nor the money to deal with him, as all of you well know. It took four years of scrimping and saving to assemble the ships we needed, but last year it was done, and Marcus Agrippa swept Sextus Pompeius from the seas forever.'

His voice changed, took on a steely edge. 'I have dealt with Sextus Pompeius's land troops as harshly as I have with his sailors and oarsmen. Those of slave status have been returned to their masters with a request that they never be freed. If their former masters could not be found because Sextus Pompeius had killed them, these slaves have been impaled. Yes, true impalement! A stake driven up through the rectum into the vital organs. Freedmen and foreigners have been flogged and branded on the forehead. Admirals have been executed. The ex-Triumvir Marcus Lepidus wanted to draw them into his legions, but Rome neither needs nor should tolerate such scum. They have died or face a life of slavery, as is right and proper.

'Rome's consuls, praetors, aediles, quaestors and tribunes of the soldiers have certain duties which they will acquit with zeal and efficiency. The consuls frame laws and authorize enterprises. The praetors hear lawsuits, civil and criminal. The quaestors take care of Rome's moneys, be they attached to the Treasury or to some governor, port, or other. The aediles attend to Rome herself by seeing that the water supply, sewerage, markets, buildings and temples are cared for. As Triumvir in charge of Rome and Italia, I will be watching these magistrates closely, and expect them to be good magistrates.'

He smiled, teeth flashing white, and looked a little impish. 'I appreciate the gilded statue of me placed in the Forum that says I have restored order on land and sea, but I appreciate good governance more. Nor is Rome yet so rich that she can afford to dedicate statues out of her revenues. Spend wisely, conscript fathers!'

He went for a stroll down the floor, then returned to the dais and stood to make what everyone expected to be his peroration, very relieved that it was a short – if rather terrifying – speech.

'Last, but by no means least, conscript fathers, it has come to my attention that Imperator Marcus Antonius has won great victories in the East, that his brow is wreathed in laurels and his plunder massive. He penetrated the lands of the Parthian king as far as Phraaspa, a mere two hundred miles from Ecbatana, and everywhere was triumphant. Armenia and Media lie under his foot, their kings his vassals. Therefore let us vote him a thanksgiving of twenty days for his valorous deeds! All who agree, say aye!'

The roar of 'Aye!' was drowned by cheers and drumming feet; Octavian's eyes roamed the tiers, counting. Yes, still about seven hundred adherents.

* * *

'I got in first,' he said complacently to Livia Drusilla when he returned home, 'and left his creatures no opportunity to shout the news of Antonius's deeds from the benches.'

'Does no one know yet of Antonius's failure?' she asked.

'It seems not. By moving that he be given a thanksgiving, I made it impossible for anybody to argue.'

'And averted any motions to vote him victory games or things that would become public knowledge right down to the Head Count,' she said, satisfied. 'Excellent, my love, excellent!'

He pulled her against his side on the couch and kissed her eyelids, her cheeks, her delicious mouth. 'I feel like making love,' he murmured into her ear.

'Then let us,' she whispered, taking his hand.

Entwined, they left Livia Drusilla's sitting room to enter her sleeping cubicle. Now, while he was alight with pleasure! Now, now! she thought, pulling off their clothes and stretching out on the bed voluptuously. Kiss my breasts, kiss my belly, kiss what lies beneath, cover me in kisses, fill me with your seed!

Six *nundinae* later, Octavian convened the Senate again, armed with a mountain of evidence he knew he wouldn't need, but must have on hand just in case. This time he commenced by announcing that there was sufficient in the Treasury to remit some taxes and reduce others, and followed that up by declaring that proper Republican government would return as soon as the campaign in Illyricum was concluded. Triumvirs would not be necessary, consular candidates could put up their names without triumviral approval, the Senate would reign supreme, the Assemblies meet regularly. All of this was greeted with cheers and loud applause.

'However,' he said to the House in ringing tones, 'before I conclude I must discuss affairs in the East. That is, the affairs of Imperator Marcus Antonius. First of all, Rome has received very little in tribute from Marcus Antonius's provinces since he assumed his Triumvirate in the East shortly after Philippi, some six and a half years ago. That I, Triumvir in Rome, Italia and the Islands, have just been able to reduce some taxes and remit others, is by my own endeavor, with no contribution or help from Marcus Antonius. And before someone on the front or middle benches leaps up to tell me that Marcus Antonius donated a hundred and twenty ships to me for the campaign against Sextus Pompeius, I must tell all of you that he charged Rome for the use of those ships. *Yes, he charged Rome!* Do I hear you ask, "How much?"

Forty-four thousand talents, conscript fathers! A sum that represents forty per cent of the hoard in Sextus Pompeius's vaults! The other sixty-six thousand talents went to Rome, not to me. I repeat, *not to me*! They went to pay massive public debts and regulate the grain supply. I am Rome's servant and have no wish to be Rome's master! I profit from her only if that profit be a time-honored custom. Those hundred and twenty ships cost three hundred and sixty-six talents apiece, and were loaned by Antonius, not given. A new quinquereme costs a hundred talents, but we had to hire Marcus Antonius's fleet. There was no money in the Treasury, and we couldn't afford to postpone our campaign against Sextus Pompeius for yet another year. So, in Rome's name, I agreed to this extortion – for extortion it is!'

By this time the benches were in turmoil, their occupants yelling insults or praise, Antony's seven hundred tame senators aware that they were on the defensive, and doubly vocal because of it. Face composed, Octavian waited the furore out.

'Ah, but did the Treasury get those sixty-six thousand silver talents?' Poplicola asked. 'No! Only fifty thousand talents were deposited! What happened to the other sixteen thousand? Didn't they wind up in your vaults, Octavianus?'

'They did not,' said Octavian, voice gentle. 'They were paid to Rome's legions to avert a very serious mutiny. A subject that I intend to discuss with the members of this House on another occasion, for it must stop. Today the House is discussing Marcus Antonius's administration of the East. It is a sham, conscript fathers! A sham! Rome's magistrates from me on down get no news of Antonius's activities in the East, anymore than Rome's Treasury gets tribute from the East!'

He paused to survey the benches, first to the right, then to the left, eyes resting longest on the Antonians, who were starting to shrink. Yes, he thought, they know. Did they think I wouldn't find out? Did they think me sincere when I had them vote Antonius a thanksgiving?

'Everything in the East is a sham,' he said loudly, 'up to and including Marcus Antonius's reported victories against the Parthians. There have been no victories, conscript fathers. None at all. Instead, Antonius has gone down in defeat. Before he took up his Triumvirate, the summer palace of the King of the Parthians at Ecbatana held seven Roman Eagles, lost when Marcus Crassus and seven legions were exterminated at Carrhae. A shame that all true Romans deplore! The loss of an Eagle means the loss of a legion in circumstances where the enemy holds and controls the field after the battle is over. These seven Eagles stand for Rome's shame, for they were the only ones an enemy holds. Yes, I use the past tense! On purpose! For in the six and a half years during which Marcus Antonius has governed the East, four more of our Eagles have gone to the summer palace in Ecbatana! Lost by Marcus Antonius! The first two belonged to the two legions Gaius Cassius left in Syria, to whom Antonius entrusted Syria's defence when he roistered his way to Athens after the Parthians invaded. But what was his duty? Why, to remain in Syria and drive the enemy out! He did not. He fled to Athens to continue his dissolute style of life. His governor, Saxa, was killed. So was Saxa's brother. Did Antonius return to avenge them? No, he did not! He governed what he had left of the East from Athens, and when the Parthians were driven out, their conqueror was Publius Ventidius, a common muleteer! A good man, a superb general, a man of whom Rome can be proud, proud, *proud*! While his chief roistered in Athens and made little trips across the Adriatic to torment me, a colleague, for not achieving my objectives as stated in our agreement. But I have achieved my objectives, and when the time came I was there in person. That I entrusted command in my campaign to Marcus Agrippa was pure common sense. He's a far better general than I am – or, I suspect, than Marcus Antonius is! For I gave Marcus Agrippa a free hand, while Antonius strapped Ventidius hand and foot. He was to hold the Parthians in readiness for his chief when his chief felt like getting off his over-muscled arse, be that five months or five years! Luckily for Rome, Ventidius ignored his orders and threw the Parthians out. For I cannot help but think, conscript fathers, that if Ventidius had obeyed his orders, Antonius would have led the legions to defeat! Just as now!'

He stopped speaking, for no other reason than to wallow in the profound silence of eight hundred men, most of them Antonians, stricken, wondering how much Octavian knew, dreading the coming denouement. No bellows of protest, not one!

'Last May,' Octavian said in ordinary tones, 'Antonius led a mighty force from Carana in Little Armenia eastward on a long march. Sixteen Roman legions – ninety-six thousand men – and an auxiliary force of cavalry and infantry from his provinces, another fifty thousand strong – paused in Artaxata, the capital of Armenia, before embarking on a journey into unknown country guided by some Armenians whom Antonius trusted. One of the tragedies of my story, conscript fathers, is that Marcus Antonius demonstrated an uncanny ability to trust the wrong men. His advisers could protest until the skies fell, but Antonius would not listen to sage counsel. He trusted where he ought not to have trusted, commencing with the King of Armenia, and then the King of Media. The two Artavasdes first pulled the wool over his eyes, then fleeced him. Our poor sheep Antonius lost his baggage train, the largest ever assembled by a Roman commander, and in the process lost two stout legions led by Gaius Oppius Statianus of the eminent banking family. Two more silver Eagles went to Ecbatana, making four lost by Antonius for a total of eleven adorning King Phraates's summer palace! A tragedy? Yes, of course. But more than that, conscript fathers – *a calamity*! What foreign foe is going to fear the might of Rome when Roman troops lose their Eagles?'

This time the silence was broken by soft sobs; by no means all of the senators had heard the story, and even most of those who had had not heard the details.

Octavian resumed. 'Without his siege equipment, spirited away by King Artavasdes of Media along with the rest of the baggage, Marcus Antonius sat futilely before the city of Phraaspa for over a hundred days, unable to take it. His foraging parties were at the mercy of the lurking Parthians, led by one Monaeses, the Parthian whom Antonius had trusted completely. When autumn came, Antonius had no choice but to retreat. Five hundred miles to Artaxata, dogged by Monaeses and the Parthian horde, who picked off the stragglers in thousands – mostly his auxiliary troops, who couldn't march at the rate of a Roman legion. But a Roman governor who employs auxiliary troops is honor-bound to protect them as if they were Roman, and Antonius deliberately abandoned them to save his legions. Perhaps I or Marcus Agrippa would have done the same in similar circumstances, but I doubt either of us would have lost a baggage train by letting it lag hundreds of miles behind the army.

'The retreat was accomplished and the army put into temporary camp in Carana at the end of November. Antonius then fled to a small Syrian port, Leuke Kome, leaving Publius Canidius to bring the troops, who were in desperate need of succor. Some perished on that last march in the aftermath of terrible cold; many had lost fingers and toes to frostbite. Of his hundred and forty-five thousand men, over a third died, the vast majority of them auxiliaries. Rome's honor was tainted, conscript fathers. I mention the loss of one particular man, a client-king appointed by Marcus

Antonius – Polemon of Pontus, who had greatly contributed to the victories of Publius Ventidius, and generously given forces to Antonius, including his own person. I add that I have, on Rome's behalf, decided that a little of Sextus Pompeius's hoard be spent on ransoming King Polemon, who does not deserve to die a Parthian captive. He will cost the Treasury a pittance – twenty talents.'

The weeping was audible now, many of the senators sitting with folds of toga pulled over their heads. A dark day for Rome.

'I said that Antonius's army was in desperate need of succor. But to whom did Antonius turn for succor? Where did he go for succor? Did he send to you, conscript fathers? Did he send to me? No, he did not! *He sent to Cleopatra of Egypt!* A foreigner, a woman who worships beast-gods, a non-Roman! Yes, he sent to her! And while he waited, did he inform the Senate and People of this disastrous campaign? No, he did not! He drank himself insensible for two solid months, only pausing dozens of times each day to rush outside his tent and ask, "Is she coming?" like a little boy crying for his mama. "I want my mama!" is what he really said, over and over again. "I want my mama, I want my mama!" Little boy Marcus Antonius, Triumvir of the East.

'And eventually she did come, conscript fathers of the Senate. The Queen of Beasts came bearing food, wine, physicians, healing herbs, bandages, exotic fruits: all the plenty of Egypt! And as the soldiers limped into Leuke Kome, she ministered to them. Not in Rome's name, but in *Egypt's* name! While Marcus Antonius, drunk, put his head in her lap and blubbered! Yes, blubbered!'

Poplicola leaped to his feet. 'That's not true!' he shouted. 'You lie, Octavianus!'

Again Octavian patiently waited for the hubbub to cease, a faint smile playing about his lips, sunlight on water. It was a beginning; yes, definitely it was a beginning. A few of the less wholeheartedly Antonian senators were angry enough to abandon him and his cause. All it had taken was the word 'blubbered'.

'Do you have a motion to move?' asked Quintus Laronius, one of Octavian's supporters.

'No, Laronius, I do not,' said Octavian strongly. 'I came to my divine father's Curia Hostilia today to tell a story, set the record straight. I have said many times before – and I repeat it now! – *I will not go to war against a fellow Roman*! For no reason, even this, will I so much as contemplate war against the Triumvir Marcus Antonius! Let him stew in his own juice! Let him continue to make mistake after mistake, until this House decides that, like Marcus

Lepidus, he should be removed from his magistracies and his provinces. I will not move that, conscript fathers, now or in the future.' He paused to look sorrowful. 'Unless, that is, Marcus Antonius rejects his citizenship and his homeland. Let us offer to Quirinus and Sol Indiges that Marcus Antonius never does that. There will be no debate today. This meeting is dismissed.'

He descended from the dais and walked down the black-and-white diamonds of the floor to the great bronze doors at the end, where his lictors and his Germans bunched around him. The doors had not been closed, a clever ploy, and, unsuspecting, the consuls had not insisted they were; the listeners outside, who also frequented the Forum Romanum, had heard it all. Within an hour, most of Rome would know that Marcus Antonius was no hero at all.

'I see a glimmer of hope,' he said to Livia Drusilla, Agrippa and Maecenas over dinner that afternoon.

'Hope?' his wife asked. 'Hope of what, Caesar?'

'Have you guessed?' he asked Maecenas.

'No, Caesar. Enlighten us, please.'

'Have you guessed, Agrippa?'

'Perhaps.'

'Yes, it would be you. You were with me at Philippi, heard much I've not voiced to anyone else.' Octavian fell silent.

'Please, Caesar!' Maecenas cried.

'It came to me suddenly, while I was speaking in the Senate. Extempore, given the subject matter. It's fun to tell stories, which should not be orated. Of course I've known Marcus Antonius all my life, and at one time I quite liked him, really. He was my antithesis – big, burly, friendly. The sort of fellow my health told me I couldn't be. But then, I suppose in pace with my divine father, I became disillusioned. Especially after Antonius massacred eight hundred citizens in the Forum Romanum and suborned my divine father's legions. Such heartbreaks! He couldn't be allowed to inherit. The worst of it was that he had absolutely no doubt that he would inherit, so I came as the rudest shock of his life. He set out to ruin me – but you know all this, so I'll skip to the present.'

He chose an olive carefully, popped it in his mouth, chewed and swallowed, while the others watched with bated breath.

'It was the bit where I likened Antonius to a little boy crying for his mother: "I want my mama!" And suddenly I saw a vision of the future, but dimly, as through a slice of amber. It all depends on two things. The first is Antonius's career of bad disappointments, from not inheriting to the Parthian expedition. He can't cope with disappointment, it shatters him. Destroys his ability to think clearly, exacerbates his temper, causes him to lean heavily upon his panders, and brings on a drinking binge.'

He sat up straight on his couch, held up one of his small, unlovely hands. 'The second is Queen Cleopatra of Egypt. It is upon her that everything turns, from his fate to my fate. If she comes to represent his mother to Antonius in literal fact, he will obey her every whim, dictate, request. That is his nature, perhaps because his real mother is such a . . . disappointment. Cleopatra is regnant, and born to it. Since the death of Divus Julius, she has been minus advice or assistance. And she has a small history with Antonius already – he dallied a winter in Alexandria, and she bore him a boy and a girl. Last winter she was with him in Antioch, and has borne him another boy. Under ordinary circumstances I would have simply listed her as one of Antonius's many royal conquests, but his behavior in Leuke Kome suggests that he sees her as someone he cannot do without – as his mama.'

'And what exactly is it that you see dimly, as through amber?' asked Livia Drusilla, eyes shining.

'A commitment. Of Antonius to Cleopatra. A non-Roman who will not be content with what relatively paltry gifts Antonius has bestowed upon her – Cyprus, Phoenicia, Philistia, Cilicia Tracheia and the balsam and bitumen concessions. He excluded Syrian Tyre and Sidon, and Seleuceia-in-Cilicia – the important entrepôts where the real money is. Though I will be going back to the Senate in about another month to complain of these bequests to the Queen of Beasts – don't you think that's a good name for her? From now on, I'm going to lump her name in with Antonius's constantly. Harping on her foreignness, her holding Divus Julius in thrall. Her high ambitions. Her designs on Rome through the person of her eldest son, whom she calls Caesar's son when the whole world knows the boy is base-born, the child of some Egyptian slave whom she used to slake her voracious sexual appetites. Ugh!'

'Jupiter, Caesar, that's genius!' cried Maecenas, rubbing his hands together gleefully. Then he frowned. 'But will it go far enough?' he asked. 'I can't see Antonius's abrogating his citizenship, nor even Cleopatra's encouraging him to. He's more useful to her as a Triumvir.'

'I can't answer that, Maecenas, the future is too clouded. However, he doesn't have to abrogate his citizenship formally. What we have to do is make it *seem* he has.' Octavian swung his legs off the back of his couch and waited until a clap produced a servant to tie on his shoes. 'I shall start my people talking,' he said, holding out his hand to Livia Drusilla. 'Come, my dear, let's look at the new fish.'

'Oh, Caesar, that one is pure gold!' she exclaimed, face awed. 'Not a flaw!'

'A female, and gravid.' He squeezed her fingers. 'What's her name? Any suggestions?'

'Cleopatra. And that huge fellow over there is Antonius.'

Along swam a much smaller carp, velvety black, with the lines of a shark. 'That's Caesarion,' Octavian said, pointing. 'See? He cruises below notice, still a child, but dangerous.'

'And that one,' said Livia Drusilla, indicating a pale gold fish, 'is Imperator Caesar Divi Filius. Most beautiful of all.'

EIGHTEEN

By May, the last of Antony's troops reached Leuke Kome and the tender ministrations of Cleopatra's hundreds of slave helpers; unaware of the political undercurrents surging below the surface of her presence alongside Antony, the soldiers were very grateful to her. Most of the frostbite victims were beyond saving, but a few still retained their blackened digits, and Egyptian medicine was better than Roman or Greek. As it was, some ten thousand of the legionaries would never pick up a sword again, or sustain a long march. To Antony's baffled surprise, his Athenian fleet came into Seleuceia Pieria early in that month to deliver forty-three thousand oaken chests (three ships had gone down in a gale off Cape Taenarum) containing Antony's share of Sextus Pompey's hoard. It was greeted with relief, for Cleopatra had brought no money with her, and swore she would not donate more funds to fruitless campaigns against the Parthians. Antony was able to give his maimed soldiers big pensions and load them aboard the galleys, returning to Athens and decommissioning; their seaworthy years were over. The windfall also enabled him to begin assembling a new army, liberally laced with the veterans of his first, bitterly disappointing endeavor.

'Why on earth did Octavianus do that?' Cleopatra asked.

'Do what, my love?'

'Send you your share of Sextus's treasure.'

'Because he's made a whole career out of shining goodness. It sits well with the Senate, and what does he need money for? He is Triumvir in Rome, he has the Treasury at his disposal.'

'It must be stuffed to the ceilings,' she said thoughtfully.

'So I gather from Octavianus's accompanying letter.'

'Which you haven't given me to read.'

'You're not entitled to read it.'

'I disagree. Who brought you aid in this benighted place? I did, not Octavianus! Give it to me, Antonius.'

'Say, please.'

'No, I will not! It is my *right* to read it! Hand it over.'

He poured a goblet of wine and drank deeply. 'You're getting too big for your shoes,' he said, burping. 'What do you want, a pair of military boots?'

'Perhaps,' she said, snapping her fingers. 'You're in my debt, Antonius, so hand it over.'

Scowling, he gave her the single sheet of Fannian paper, which she read, as Caesar had been able to do, at a glance. 'Pah!' she spat, screwing it up and throwing it into a corner of the tent. 'He's semi-literate at best!'

'Satisfied that there's nothing in it?'

'I never thought there was, but I am your equal in power, in rank, in wealth. Your full partner in our Eastern enterprise. I must be shown everything, just as I must be present at all your councils and meetings. Something Canidius understands, but not mere nothings like Titius and Ahenobarbus.'

'Titius I'll grant you, but Ahenobarbus? Far from a nothing. Come, Cleopatra, stop being so prickly! Show my colleagues that side of you that I alone seem to see – kind, loving, considerate.'

Her little foot, sheathed in a gilded sandal, tapped the earthen floor of the tent, and her face grew even grimmer. 'I am so tired of Leuke Kome, that's the trouble,' she said, biting her lip. 'Why can't we move to Antioch, where there is accommodation that doesn't creak and groan every time the wind blows?'

Antony blinked. 'No reason, really,' he said, sounding quite surprised. 'Let's move to Antioch. Canidius can carry on here, get the troops ready.' He sighed. 'It will be next year before I can lead them back to Phraaspa. That traitorous cur, Monaeses! I'll have his head, I swear it!'

'If you have his head, will you drink less?'

'Probably,' he said, and put the goblet down as if it held lava. 'Oh, don't you understand?' he cried, shuddering. 'I have lost my luck! If I ever had any luck. Yes, I did have luck – at Philippi. But only at Philippi, it seems to me now. Before and since – no luck at all. That's why I have to continue to fight the Parthians. Monaeses made off with my luck as well as my two Eagles. Four, if you include the two that Pacorus stole. I have to get them back, my luck and my Eagles.'

It goes around and around, she thought: always the same old conversation about lost luck and the triumph of Philippi. Drunkards do talk in circles, the same subject over and over, as if in it is some pearl of wisdom with the power to cure every misfortune or evil in the world. Two months of Leuke Kome, listening to Antonius go around and around, swallowing his own tail. Perhaps when we get to a new and different place, he will improve. Though he has no name for what ails him, I call it deep melancholy. His moods are flat, he sleeps far too long, as if he doesn't want to wake and set eyes on his life, even with me in it. Does he feel that he should have committed suicide, that night of threatened mutiny? Romans are strange, they have this honor thing that pushes them to fall on their swords. Life isn't priceless to them, it has a cut-off point involving *dignitas*, and they are not afraid of dying as most peoples are, including Egyptians. So I have to dig Antonius's melancholy out by the roots or it will strangle him. Give him back his *dignitas*. I need him, I need him! Whole and entire, the old Antonius. Capable of defeating Octavianus and putting my son on the throne of Rome, which has been vacant for five hundred years. Waiting for Caesarion. Oh, how I miss Caesarion! If we get as far as Antioch, I can work on getting Antonius to Alexandria. Once he's there, he will recover.

But Antioch held shocks, none of them pleasant. Antony found a pile of letters from Poplicola in Rome, each dated on its outside so he could read them in order.

The letters detailed Octavian's campaign against Sextus Pompey in graphic terms, though they made it clear that Poplicola's chief gripe was his exclusion from what he called a very smooth operation. Nor had Octavian hidden in the Italian equivalent of a marsh, even during heavy fighting after he finally landed at Tauromenium. The wheezes, he said cheerfully to anyone prone to listen, had quite gone since his marriage. Huh! thought Antony. Cold fish and cold fish swim well together.

The news of Lepidus's fate angered him; under the terms of their pact, he was entitled to vote on an issue like expelling Lepidus from all his public offices and provinces, but Octavian hadn't bothered to contact him, pleading as his excuse Antony's isolation in Media. Thirty legions! How had Lepidus managed to accumulate half that number in a backwater like Africa Province? And the Senate, including his, Antony's adherents, had voted to exile poor Lepidus from Rome herself! He pined in his villa at Circeii.

There was a letter from him too, full of excuses and self-pity. His wife, Brutus's sister Junia Minor (Junia Major was the wife of Servilius Vatia), had not always been faithful to him, and was making life hard now that she couldn't escape from him. Moan, moan, moan. Antony grew tired of Lepidus's woes, and tore his letter up half read. Perhaps Octavian had some right on his side; certainly the little worm had dealt smartly with Lepidus's troops. How well he did that sweet young lad act!

Octavian's version of the Lepidus incident was somewhat different, though he had things to say too about enlisting the enemy's legions in a Roman's own, as Lepidus had done with Sextus Pompey's.

'I thought it high time that the Senate and People of Rome saw clear as water that the days when enemy troops were treated leniently are over; leniency cannot help but rankle, especially when Rome's legionaries have to endure the presence alongside them of men they fought last *nundinum*. Knowing these detested men will be dowered with land when they retire, just as if they never took up swords against Rome. I have changed that. Sextus Pompeius's soldiers, sailors and oarsmen have been dealt with very harshly,' Octavian's letter said. 'It is not Roman custom to take prisoners, but neither is it Roman custom to free the conquered enemy as if they were Roman. Sextus Pompeius had few Romans in his legions or his crews. Those he did have were *hostis*. Under other conditions I might have sold them into slavery, but instead I chose to make an example of them.

'Sextus Pompeius himself escaped, together with Libo and two of my divine father's assassins, Decimus Turullius and Cassius Parmensis. They have fled eastward, thus becoming your problem, not mine. It is rumored they have sought asylum in Mitylene.'

Which was by no means all that Octavian had to say. He went on blandly, his words assured and strong; this was a new Octavian, victorious, dowered with superb luck and conscious of it. Not a letter Antony could spit at and tear up.

'You will have received your share of Sextus Pompeius's hoard together with my covering letter by now, and I take leave to tell you that this enormous sum of money, paid in coin of the Republic, cancels any obligation I have to send you twenty thousand soldiers. You are, of course, free to come to Italia to recruit them, but I have neither the time nor the inclination to do your dirty work for you. What I have done is choose two thousand of the very best men, all willing to serve with you in the East, and will ship them to Athens shortly. As I saw for myself that seventy of your war galleys were on their beams with rot and barnacles, I will donate you seventy newly built fives from my own fleets, as well as some excellent artillery and siege equipment to help replace what you lost in Media. No triumphs have been awarded for the campaign against Sextus Pompeius, who must be classified as Roman. I do, however, highly commend Marcus Agrippa, who proved as brilliant an admiral as he is a land general. Lucius Cornificius, junior consul this year, was brave and clever in command, as were Sabinus, Statilius Taurus and Messala Corvinus. Sicilia is at peace, charge of it given permanently to Marcus Agrippa, the only one gifted with an old style *latifundium* there. Taurus has gone to govern Africa Province; I sailed with him to Utica and supervised the start of his term, and can assure you that he will not exceed his mandate. In fact, nobody will exceed his mandate, from consuls through praetors to governors and junior magistrates. And I have given notice to Rome's legions that no more big bonuses will be paid to them. In future they fight for Rome, not any one man.'

And so on and so forth. Finishing the lengthy scroll, Antony tossed it to Cleopatra. 'Here, read this!' he snapped. 'The pup fancies himself a wolf, and leader of the pack at that.'

Done with it in a tenth the time it had taken Antony, she put it down with fingers that trembled slightly, and fixed her golden eyes on Antony's face. Not good, not good! While Antony failed in the East, Octavian had succeeded in the West. No half measures, either; a complete and stunning victory that had poured wealth into the Treasury, which meant that Octavian had the funds to equip and train fresh legions as he needed them, and maintain fleets too.

'He is patient' was her comment. 'Very patient. He waited six years to do it, but when he did, it was all-encompassing. I think this Marcus Agrippa must be an extraordinary man.'

'Octavianus is welded to him,' Antony growled.

'Rumor says they're lovers.'

'That wouldn't surprise me.' Antony shrugged, picked up the next letter, shorter by far. 'From Furnius, in Asia Province.'

No good news from Asia Province either. Furnius wrote that Sextus Pompey, Libo, Decimus Turullius and Cassius Parmensis had arrived in the port of Mitylene on the island of Lesbos at the end of last November, and had not been idle. Their stay there was not long; by January they were in Ephesus, and recruiting volunteers from among the veterans who, over the years, had taken up land in Asia Province. By March they had three full legions, and were ready to make a bid to conquer Anatolia. A frightened Amyntas, King of Galatia, had joined forces with Furnius and Marcus Titius. By the time Antony received this letter, Furnius fully expected that war would have broken out.

'You should have snuffed out Sextus Pompeius's light years ago,' said Cleopatra, opening an old wound.

'How could I, when he kept Octavianus busy and off my back?' Antony demanded, reaching for the wine flagon.

'*Don't!*' she said sharply. 'You haven't read Poplicola's latest letter yet. If you must drink, Antonius, do so after your business is finished.'

Childlike, he obeyed, which satisfied her that he needed her good opinion more than he needed the wine; she did not understand that Antony was not addicted to wine, that his drinking was a temporary thing. A thought popped into her mind: an amethyst! Amethysts had magical powers over wine, prevented dependence upon it. She would commission the royal jeweller in Alexandria to make him the most magnificent amethyst ring in the world. Once he wore it, he would overcome his need for wine.

Of course Poplicola had always known that Antony's campaign against the Parthians had failed; it was he who had spread the story far and wide throughout Rome that Antony had won a great victory, based on the theory that whoever got in first with one version of events would succeed. He had written earlier in jubilant mood to tell Antony that Rome and the Senate believed his version, and chuckled over the fact that none other than Octavian himself had voted Antony a thanksgiving for his 'victory'. The most recent of his letters was very different. The bulk of it was a verbatim report of Octavian's speech in the Senate describing Antony's campaign as an abysmal failure; the agents Octavian had sent to the East had found out every tiny detail.

By the time he had mumbled his way through the scroll, the tears were rolling down Antony's face; Cleopatra watched with sinking heart, snatched the scroll and read that biting, intensely political diatribe. Oh, how dared Octavian recount her own part in those events as malign! The Queen of Beasts! 'I want my mama!' Brilliant mud-slinging. How was she going to mend Antony now?

I curse you, Octavianus, I curse you! May Sobek and Tawaret suck you into their nostrils and drown you, chewed and trampled!

Then she saw her way, wondered that she hadn't thought of it before. Antony would have to be weaned away from Rome, made to see that his fate and his luck dwelled in Egypt, not in Rome. She would make a nest for him in Alexandria, so comfortable and flattering, so stuffed with diversions that he would never want to be anywhere else. He would have to marry her; what good fortune that a monogamous people like the Romans ignored foreign marriages as illegal! If, for the time being, Antony had to cleave to Octavia, that didn't matter. In reality his Egyptian union would count for far more among those to whom his private relationships held significance – his client-kings, his minor princes.

She sat with Antony's head in her lap and fixed her eyes on a bust of Caesar, the perfect partner taken from her. It was from Aphrodisias, whose sculptors and painters were unparalleled, and everything about it was right, from the shade of the pale gold hair to the piercing eyes, palest blue surrounded by inky dark rings. A wave of grief swept over her, was ruthlessly suppressed. Make do with what you have, Cleopatra, don't yearn for what might have been.

It will be war, it has to be war. The only question is, when? Octavianus lies through his teeth about no more civil wars – he will have to fight Antonius or lose what he has. But not yet, from that speech. He plans to train his legions to peak condition by subjugating the tribes of Illyricum, and he says up to three years of campaigns. That means we have three years to prepare, and then . . . we invade the West, we invade Italia. I will have to let Antonius finish with the Parthians inside his mind, in a way that will weld his legions without destroying them. For Antonius is not in Caesar's class as a general of troops. I must always have known that, but I believed that, with Caesar dead, no one alive could rival Antonius. But now that I know him better, I realize that the flaws he demonstrates as a man also affect his ability to general troops. Ventidius was his superior; so, I think, is Canidius. Let Canidius do the real work while Antonius, enjoying the reputation, dazzles the world with the illusory tricks of a magician.

First, the marriage. We do that as soon as I can send for Cha'em. Push Canidius off on the first stage of this silly campaign, see that Armenia is crushed and Media too intimidated to move. Keep Antonius out of the Kingdom of the Parthians proper. I will work to convince Antonius that, in conquering Armenia and Media Atropatene, he has conquered the Parthians. Befuddle him with wine, run things myself. Why shouldn't I be able to run a campaign as well as any Roman? Oh, Antonius, why couldn't you have been Caesar's equal? How easy it would have been!

One day, no more than ten years in the future, Caesarion must be King of Rome, for he who is King of Rome is king of the world. I will have him tear down the temples on the Capitol and build his palace there, with a golden hall in which he will sit in judgement. And Egypt's 'beast gods' will become Rome's gods. Jupiter Optimus Maximus will prostrate himself before Amun-Ra. I have done my duty to Egypt: three sons and one daughter. Nilus will continue to inundate. I will have the time to turn my attention to conquering Rome, and Antonius will be my partner in the enterprise.

Antony's tears had ceased; she lifted his head, smiled at him tenderly, and cleaned his face with a soft linen handkerchief.

'Better, my love?' she asked, kissing his brow.

'Better,' he said, humiliated.

'Have a glass of wine, it will do you good. You have things to do, an army to organize. Don't take any notice of Octavianus! What does he know about armies? A thousand talents to one mud brick, he'll fail in Illyricum.'

Antony gulped until the goblet was empty.

'Have some more,' crooned Cleopatra.

Late in June they married in the Egyptian rite; Antony was given the title of Pharaoh's Consort, which seemed to please him. Now that she had abandoned the idea of a sober Antony to share her throne, albeit as consort only, she relaxed a little, only then realizing how taxing it had been trying to keep Antony away from the wine since his return from Carana. A fruitless business.

She turned her attention to Canidius, having Antony summon him to a council comprised of the three of them, no one else. But she made sure Antony was sober; it was no part of her plans to expose the degree of his weakness to his commanders, though one day it was bound to happen. The only one who might have objected to such a small meeting, Ahenobarbus, had returned to Bithynia and was now embroiled in Furnius's war against Sextus Pompey, who had decided that Bithynia would suit him beautifully and plotted to kill the intractable Ahenobarbus before taking it over. A fate Ahenobarbus had no intention of letting happen.

Well schooled beforehand by Cleopatra, Antony began by outlining his plans for the coming campaign in a manner that didn't betray her careful coaching.

'I have twenty-five legions at my disposal,' he said to Publius Canidius in a voice that held no trace of slurring, 'but those in Syria are very under strength, as you know. Exactly how much under strength, Canidius?'

'If averaged out, only three thousand men. Five cohorts, though some are up at eight, and some down at two cohorts. I've called them legions, thirteen altogether.'

'Of which one, at Jerusalem, is at full strength. There are seven more in Macedonia, all full strength, two in Bithynia, also full strength, and three that belong to Sextus Pompeius, full strength.' Antony grinned, looked his old self. 'Kind of him to recruit on my behalf, isn't it? He'll be a dead man by the end of this year, which is why I lump his and Ahenobarbus's legions in my total. However, I think I must have thirty legions, not all of which will be full strength or experienced. What I propose to do is send the least numerous of the Syrian legions to Macedonia, and bring the Macedonian troops here for my campaign.'

Canidius looked dubious. 'I understand your reasons, Marcus Antonius, but I strongly advise you to leave one Macedonian legion where it is. Send for six, but don't send any of your Syrian men there. Wait until you've recruited five more legions, send them. I agree that inexperienced new soldiers will be all right in Macedonia – the Dardani and the Bessi haven't recovered from Pollio and Censorinus yet. You'll have your thirty legions.'

'Good!' said Antony, feeling his spirits soar higher than in months. 'I'll need ten thousand cavalry, Galatian and Thracian. I can't recruit horse from the Gauls anymore, Octavianus is in control and not inclined to cooperate. He denies me the four legions he owes me, the little turd!'

'How many legions will you take east?'

'Twenty-three, all full strength and experienced men. One hundred and thirty-eight thousand of them, including noncombatants. No auxiliaries this time, they're too big a nuisance. At least cavalry can keep up with the legions. And this time we march in square the whole way, with the baggage train in the middle. Where the ground is flat enough, *agmen quadratum*.'

'I agree, Antonius.'

'However, I think we have to do something this year, though I have to stay here until I see what happens to Sextus Pompeius. It will have to be you leading this year, Canidius. How many legions can you assemble to start out now?'

'Seven full strength if I merge cohorts.'

'Enough. It won't be a long campaign – whatever happens, do not get caught by winter unless you're in warm quarters. Amyntas can donate two thousand horsemen immediately – from his letter, they're almost here. I suspect had they not been, he would have kept them to deal with Sextus.'

'You're right, Sextus won't last,' Canidius said comfortably.

'Drive into Armenia proper from Carana. It's important that we teach Artavasdes of Armenia a little lesson this year. Then he'll be ripe for the plucking next year.'

'As you wish, Antonius.'

Cleopatra cleared her throat; the two men looked at her in surprise, having forgotten her presence. For Canidius's sake she tried to appear – well, if not humble, at least amenable, sensible. 'I suggest we start building fleets,' she said.

Astonished, Canidius couldn't conceal his reaction. 'What for?' he asked. 'We're not planning any marine expeditions.'

'Not now, I agree,' she said with composure, not allowing her displeasure to show. 'However, we may need them in the future. Ships take a long time to build, especially in the quantities we will need. Or perhaps it's best to say, might need.'

'Need for what?' Antony asked, as puzzled as Canidius.

'Publius Canidius has not read the transcript of Octavianus's speech to the Senate, so I acquit him of obstruction. But you have, Antonius, and I would have said that its message was clear – one day he will be sailing east to crush you.'

For a moment neither man said a word, Canidius conscious of a sinking in his belly. What was the woman up to?

'I have read the speech, Your Majesty,' he said. 'It was sent to me by Pollio, with whom I correspond whenever I can. But I can't see any threat to Marcus Antonius in it, beyond criticism that Octavianus is not qualified to level. In fact, he reiterates that he will not go to war against a fellow Roman, and I believe him.'

Her face had grown stony; when she spoke, her voice had ice in it. 'Allow me to say, Canidius, that I am far more politically skilled than you are. What Octavianus says is one thing. What he does is quite another. And I assure you that he intends to crush Marcus Antonius. Therefore we prepare, and we begin to prepare now – not next year, or the year after that. While you men go on your Parthian odyssey, I will do good work on the shores of Your Sea by commissioning the biggest warships possible.'

'Content yourself with fives . . . er, quinqueremes, madam!' Canidius said. 'Anything larger is too slow and clumsy.'

'Quinqueremes were what I had in mind,' she said haughtily.

Canidius sighed, slapped his hands on his thighs. 'Well, I daresay it can do no harm.'

'Who is going to pay for them?' Antony demanded suspiciously.

'I am, of course,' said Cleopatra. 'We must have at least five hundred war galleys, and at least that many troop transports.'

'*Troop transports?*' Canidius gasped. 'What for?'

'The name is self-explanatory, I would have thought.'

Mouth open to reply, Canidius shut it, nodded, and left.

'You confounded him,' said Antony.

'I am aware of that, though I fail to see why.'

'He doesn't know you, my dear,' Antony said, a little tiredly.

'Are you opposed?' she asked, teeth clenched.

The reddish eyes opened wide. 'I? *Edepol*, no! It's your money, Cleopatra. Spend it any way you want.'

'Have a drink!' she snapped, then, recovering her temper, gave him her most enchanting smile. 'In fact, for once I'll join you. My steward tells me that the vintage he bought from old Asander the wine merchant is particularly good. Did you know that Asander is a corruption of Alexander?'

'That's not a very clever effort at changing the subject, but I'll humor you.' He produced a grin. 'Though if you are going to bib, you'll have to bib on your own.'

'I beg your pardon?'

'My recovery is complete, I'm done with wine.'

Her mouth fell open. 'What?'

'You heard me. Cleopatra, I love you to distraction, but did you really think I haven't noticed your plan to keep me drunk?' He sighed, leaned forward earnestly. 'Though you think you know what my army went through in Media, you don't. Nor do you know what I went through. To know, you'd have to have been there, and you weren't. I, my army's commander, didn't keep them out of harm's way because I rushed into enemy lands like an enraged boar. I took credence in the whisperings of a Parthian agent, yet took no credence in the warnings of my legates. Julius Caesar was always at me for my rashness, and he was right. The failure of my Median campaign can be laid at no one's door save my own, and I know it. I am not a simpleton, or hopelessly dependent on wine. You just think I am! It was *necessary* for me to blot out my delinquency in Media by drinking myself into oblivion! That's the way I'm made! And now—well, it's passed. I say again, I love you more than life. I will never be able to stop

346

loving you. But you're not in love with me, for all your protestations, and your head is stuffed with schemes and machinations aimed at securing the gods know what for Caesarion. The entire East? The West as well? Is he to king it over Rome? You dream of it perpetually, don't you? Lumping your own ambitions on that poor boy's shoulders—'

'I do love you!' she cried, interrupting. 'Antonius, never think I don't! And Caesarion—Caesarion—' She floundered, too aghast at this Antony to summon up arguments.

He took her hands, chafed them. 'It's all right, Cleopatra. I understand,' he said gently, smiling. His eyes teared, his mouth quivered. 'And I, poor fool, will do whatever you want. That's the fate of any man in love with a masterful woman. Just grant me the right to do it lucidly.' The tears vanished, he laughed. 'Which is not to say that I won't take to the wine again! I can't help my tendency to hedonism, but I drink in binges. I can do without wine, which means that when I am most needed, I'll be there—for you, for Ahenobarbus or Poplicola—and for Octavia.'

She blinked, shook her head. 'You have surprised me,' she said. 'What else have you noticed?'

'That's my secret. I've commanded Plancus to govern Syria,' he said, going elsewhere. 'Sosius wants to return home. And Titius is taking my Syrian fleet to Miletus with a proconsular imperium. He's to deal with Sextus Pompeius.' He chuckled. 'See how right you always are, my love? I have need of fleets already!'

'What are Titius's orders?' she asked suspiciously.

'To bring Sextus to me here in Antioch.'

'For a ceremonious execution?'

'How you Eastern monarchs love an execution! It may be,' said Antony slyly, 'that since you're so set on building ships, I will have need of him as an admiral. They don't come any better.'

NINETEEN

'I have a commission for you, my dear,' said Octavian to his sister over dinner.

She paused with a tiny lamb cutlet in her hand, its thin but delectable crust of fat seeded with mustard and peppercorns. His remark interrupted her thoughts, which dwelled upon the change in Octavian's dinner menus since he had married Livia Drusilla. The daintiest, most delicious fare! Yet she had good reason to know that nothing was wasted, from the cook's exorbitant salary to the money spent on buying ingredients and viands; Livia Drusilla did the marketing herself, and drove a hard bargain. Nor did the cook come down with sick headaches or smuggle some of the goodies to his own kitchen favorites; Livia Drusilla watched him, hawklike.

'A commission, Caesar?' Octavia asked, carefully biting off more meat than fat; that way, the fat lasted.

'Yes. How would you like to take a trip to Athens to see your husband?'

Octavia's face lit up; she beamed. 'Oh, Caesar, yes, please!'

'I thought you wouldn't object.' He winked at Maecenas. 'I have an errand you can do better than anyone else.'

Her brow pleated. 'An errand? Is that a commission?'

'Sometimes,' Octavian said solemnly.

'What do I have to do?'

'Deliver Antonius two thousand picked troops – the finest of the finest – as well as seventy new warships, an outsized battering ram, three smaller rams, two hundred ballistas, two hundred large catapults, two hundred onagers, and two hundred scorpions.'

'Dear me! Am I to be the officer in command of all this . . . um . . . bounty?' she asked, eyes sparkling.

'I like nothing better than to see you look so happy, but no. Gaius Fonteius is anxious to rejoin Antonius, so he'll be officer in command,' Octavian said, crunching a stick of celery. 'You can carry a letter from me to him.'

'I'm sure he'll appreciate the gifts.'

'Not as much as he will appreciate a visit from you, *I'm* sure,' Octavian said, wagging a finger. His gaze traveled from Octavia to the couch Maecenas shared with Agrippa, dwelling upon Agrippa a little sorrowfully. It wasn't often that his schemes went awry, but this one certainly had, he thought. Where did I go wrong?

It had stemmed out of Agrippa's bachelor status, which Livia Drusilla had decided could not continue; if she deemed the expression in his eyes too fond when he looked at her, she kept that to herself, simply informing Octavian that it was high time Agrippa married. Unsuspecting, he turned her comment over in his mind and concluded she was, as usual, right. Now that he was loaded down with riches, land and property, no doting father could possibly judge Agrippa a fortune-hunter; he was, besides, very attractive in his person. It was a rare female from fifteen to fifty who did not become kittenish or flirtatious around Agrippa. While he, alas, never even noticed. No small talk, few social graces, that was Agrippa. Women swooned, he yawned – or, worse still, bolted from the room.

When Octavian taxed him with his bachelor status, he blinked and then looked uncomfortable.

'Are you hinting I should marry?' he asked.

'Actually, yes. You're the most important man in Rome after me, yet you live like one of those eastern hermits. A camp stretcher for a bed, more armor than togas, not even a female servant,' said Octavian. 'Whenever you itch—' he tittered, looked coy – 'you scratch with some country-bumpkin of a girl you can't possibly form a permanent union with. I'm not saying you ought to abandon the country-bumpkin girls, you understand, Agrippa. I'm merely saying that you ought to marry.'

'No one would have me,' he said bluntly.

'Ah, but there you're wrong! My dear Agrippa, you have looks, wealth and high status. You're a *consular*!'

'Yes, but I don't have the blood, Caesar, and I don't fancy any of those stuck-up girls named Claudia, Aemilia, Sempronia or Domitia. If they did say yes, it would only be for my friendship with you. The idea of a wife who looks down on me doesn't appeal.'

'Then look a little lower, but not much lower,' Octavian wheedled. 'I have the ideal wife for you.'

Agrippa looked suspicious. 'Is this Livia Drusilla at work?'

'No, word of honor, it isn't! This is all my own idea.'

'Then, who?'

Octavian took a deep breath. 'Atticus's daughter,' he said, looking triumphant. 'Perfect, Agrippa, truly! Not of senatorial rank, though I admit that's only because her *tata* prefers to make money by unsenatorial means. Connected by blood to the Caecilii Metelli, therefore highborn enough. And heiress to one of the biggest fortunes in Rome!'

'She's too young. Do you even know what she looks like?'

'She's seventeen, nearly eighteen, and yes, I have seen her. Handsome rather than pretty, a good figure, and extremely well educated, as you would expect of Atticus's daughter.'

'Is she a reader or a shopper?'

'A reader.'

The craggy face looked relieved. 'Well, that's one good thing. Is she dark, or fair?'

'Medium.'

'Oh.'

'Look, if I had a female relative old enough, you could have her with my blessing!' Octavian cried, hands flailing the air.

'Would you? Would you really, Caesar?'

'Yes, of course I would! But as I don't, will you or will you not take Caecilia Attica?'

'I'd never be game to ask.'

'I'll do the asking. Will you?'

'I don't seem to have much choice, so . . . yes, I will.'

And so it had been done, though Octavian hadn't realized just how reluctant the bridegroom was. Agrippa had been set in his ways at thirteen; at twenty-seven he was dipped in the concrete he so loved to experiment with. Unless in Octavian's company – and to some extent, Livia Drusilla's – he was dour, silent and eternally watchful. All had seemed well at the wedding, for the bride was, like all her friends, enamored of the magnificently glamorous and unattainable Marcus Vipsanius Agrippa.

A month into the marriage saw the tall, graceful lily (as Livia Drusilla had named her) wilted and browned. She poured her woes into Livia Drusilla's sympathetic ear, and Livia Drusilla in her turn poured them into Octavian's ear.

'It's a disaster!' she cried. 'Poor Attica thinks he doesn't care for her a scrap – he never *talks* to her! And his idea of making love is . . . is – I crave your pardon for being vulgar, my love! – resembles a stallion with a mare! He bites her on the neck and . . . and – well, I leave it to your imagination. Luckily,' she continued in tones of gloom, 'he doesn't avail himself of his conjugal pleasures very often.'

As this was a side of Agrippa he had never expected to know anything about, nor wanted to now, Octavian blushed and wished he was anywhere but sitting with his wife. That his own love-making talents left something to be desired he knew, but he also knew that Livia Drusilla's thrills came from power, and could rest comfortably. A pity that Attica was not so inclined – but then, she hadn't had six years of marriage to Claudius Nero to transform her girlish dreams into a woman's iron purpose.

'Then we will have to hope that Agrippa quickens her,' he said. 'A baby will give her someone else to interest her.'

'A baby is no substitute for a satisfactory husband,' said Livia Drusilla, extremely satisfied herself. She frowned. 'The trouble is that she has a confidant.'

'What do you mean? That Agrippa's marital affairs will become known far and wide?'

'If it were that simple, I wouldn't worry as much. No, her confidant is her old tutor, Atticus's freedman, Quintus Caecilius Epirota. According to her, the nicest man she knows.'

'Epirota? I know that name!' Octavian exclaimed. 'An eminent scholar. According to Maecenas, an authority on Virgilius.'

'Hmmm . . . I'm sure you're right, Caesar, but I don't think he'd offer her poetic consolation, somehow. Oh, she's virtuous! But for how long, if you take Agrippa off to Illyricum?'

'That is on the laps of the gods, my dear, and I for one have no intention of sticking my beak into Agrippa's marriage. We must hope that a baby comes along to keep her occupied.' He sighed. 'Perhaps a very young woman isn't right for Agrippa. Ought I to have suggested Scribonia?'

Be that as it may, by the time that Octavia came to dinner, together with Maecenas and his Terentia and Agrippa and his Attica, it was clear to most of Rome's upper class that Agrippa's marriage was not prospering. Looking at Agrippa's bleak expression, his oldest friend yearned to offer him words of comfort, but could not. At least, he reflected, Attica was pregnant. And he had had the necessary fortitude to drop a hint in Atticus's ear that his much-loved freedman Epirota ought to be kept far from his much-loved daughter. Women who read, he thought, are just as vulnerable as women who shop.

Octavia almost skipped home to the palace on the Carinae, she was so happy. To see Antonius at last! Two years had gone by since he left her on Corcyra; baby Antonia Minor, known as Tonilla, was walking and talking. A lovely little girl with her father's dark red hair and reddish eyes, but luckily neither his chin nor – thus far, at any rate – his nose. Oh, what a temper! Antonia was more her mother's child, whereas Tonilla was all her father's. Stop, Octavia, stop! Stop thinking of your children and think about your husband, whom you will be seeing soon. Such joy! Such pleasure! She went in search of her dresser, a very competent woman who much esteemed her position in the Antonian household, and was, besides, greatly attached to Octavia.

They were deep in a consultation about which dresses Octavia should take with her to Athens, and how many new dresses she ought to have made to delight her husband, when the steward came to tell her that Gaius Fonteius Capito had come to call.

She knew him, but not very well; he had been with them when she and Antony had last set sail, but seasickness had kept her in her cabin and her journey had been cut short at Corcyra. So she greeted the tall, handsome, impeccably garbed Fonteius with some reserve, not sure why he had come.

'Imperator Caesar says you are to take his gifts to Marcus Antonius in Athens and will sail with me,' he said, not attempting to sit down. 'I thought I should call to see if there is anything you specially need, either on the voyage or as cargo for Athens – a piece of furniture, or some non-perishable foods, perhaps?'

Her eyes, he thought, watching the expressions chase through them, are the most beautiful I have ever seen, though it isn't the unusual color that renders them so haunting; it's the sweetness in them, the all-embracing love. How can Antonius play her so false? Were she mine, I would cleave to her forever. Another contradiction: how can she be the full sister of Octavianus? And another: how can she manage to love Antonius *and* Octavianus?

'Thank you, Gaius Fonteius,' she was saying with a smile, 'I can think of nothing, really, except –' she looked fearful – 'the sea, and that is beyond anyone's ability to arrange.'

He laughed, took her hand and kissed it lightly. 'Lady, I will do my best! Father Neptune, Vulcan Earthshaker and the Lares

Permarini of voyages shall all have rich offerings that the seas be flat, the winds propitious, and our passage swift.'

Whereupon he departed, leaving Octavia to stare after him, conscious of a peculiar feeling of relief. What a nice man! With him in charge, things would go well, no matter how the sea behaved.

It behaved exactly as Fonteius had ordered when he made his offerings; even rounding Cape Taenarum was shorn of its dangers. But while Octavia thought that his concern for her welfare was just that, Fonteius knew how much of self was in his hopes; he wanted this lovely woman's company throughout the voyage, which meant no seasickness. He couldn't fault her, up to and including docking in the Piraeus. Pleasant, witty, easy to converse with, never prudish or what he called 'Roman matron' in her attitude – divine! No wonder Octavianus erected statues to her, no wonder ordinary people respected, honored and loved her! The two *nundinae* he had spent in Octavia's company from Tarentum to Athens would live in his memory for the rest of his life. Love? Was it love? Maybe, but he fancied it held none of the baser urges he associated with that word when it concerned the relationship between a man and a woman. Had she appeared in the middle of the night demanding the act of love, he would not have refused her, but she didn't appear; Octavia belonged to some higher plane, as much goddess as woman.

The worst was that he knew Antony wouldn't be in Athens to meet her, that he knew Antony was firmly in the clutches of Queen Cleopatra in Antioch. Octavia's brother knew it too.

'I have entrusted my sister to your care, Gaius Fonteius,' Octavian had said just before the cavalcade set off from Capua to Tarentum, 'because I think you more sincere than the rest of Antonius's creatures, and believe you a man of honor. Of course your main task is to escort these various military supplies to Antonius, but I require something more of you, if you're willing.'

It was a typically backhanded Octavian compliment – he was one of Antony's 'creatures' – but Fonteius took no offense, as he sensed this was simply an introduction to something else far more important that Octavian wished to say. And here it came:

'You are aware what Antonius is doing, with whom he is doing it, where he is doing it, and probably why he is doing it,' said Octavian in rhetorical vein. 'Unfortunately my sister has little idea what's going on in Antioch, and I haven't enlightened her because it's possible that Antonius is just . . . ah . . . filling in time by filling up Cleopatra. It's possible that he will return to my sister the

353

moment he knows she's in Athens. I doubt it, but must consider it. What I ask is that you remain in Athens in close touch with Octavia in case Antonius doesn't come. If he doesn't, Fonteius, poor Octavia will need a friend. News that Antonius's infidelity is serious will crush her. I trust you to be no more than a friend, but a caring one. My sister is part of Rome's luck, a figurative Vestal. If Antonius disappoints her, she must be returned home, yet not *hustled* home. Do you understand?'

'Completely, Caesar,' Fonteius said without hesitation. 'She can't be let leave Athens until all her hope is gone.'

Remembering that exchange, Fonteius felt his face twist; he knew the lady far better now than he had then, and found he cared desperately about her fate.

Well, this was Greece; his offerings should now be to Greek gods – Demeter the mother, Persephone the ravished daughter, Hermes the messenger, Poseidon of the deep and Hera the queen. Send Antonius to Athens, let him break his ties with Cleopatra! How could he prefer such a scrawny, ugly little woman to the beautiful Octavia? He couldn't, he just couldn't!

Octavia concealed her disappointment at the news that Antony was in Antioch, but learned enough of the awful campaign of Phraaspa to understand that he probably preferred to be with his troops at this moment. So she wrote to him immediately to tell him of her arrival in Athens, and of the bounty in her train, from soldiers to battering rams and artillery. The letter was replete with news of his children, her other nursery occupants, the family and events in Rome, and artlessly implied that, if he couldn't come to Athens, he would require her to travel on to Antioch.

Between the writing of it and Antony's reply, a matter of a full month, she had to suffer the renewal of friendships and acquaintances from her previous time in residence. Most of these were innocuous enough, but when the steward announced the arrival of Perdita to call on her, Octavia's heart sank. This elderly Roman matron was the wife of a merchant plutocrat, immensely rich and dangerously idle. Perdita was her nickname, one she flaunted with pride; it meant not so much that she herself was ruined, as that she contrived at the ruination of others. Perdita was a destroyer, a bringer of bad tidings.

'Oh, my poor, poor sweet dear!' she cried, swanning into the sitting room clad in gauzy wools of the newest color, a jarring magenta, her plethora of necklaces, bracelets, bangles and earrings clanking like prisoner's chains.

'Perdita. How nice to see you,' Octavia said mechanically, suffering the kisses on her cheeks, the squeezing of her hands.

'I think it's a disgrace, and I hope you tell him so when you see him!' Perdita cried, settling into a chair.

'What is a disgrace?' Octavia asked.

'Why, Antonius's shameless affair with Cleopatra!'

A smile curved Octavia's lips. 'Is it shameless?' she asked.

'My dear, he's *married* her!'

'Has he?'

'Indeed he has. They married in Antioch, the moment they arrived there from Leuke Kome.'

'How do you know?'

'Peregrinus has had letters from Gnaeus Cinna, Scaurus, Titius and Poplicola,' Perdita said: Peregrinus was her husband. 'It is quite true. She bore him another boy last year.'

Perdita stayed half an hour, stubbornly clinging to her chair despite her hostess's negligence in not offering her refreshments. During this time she poured out the entire story as she knew it, from Antony's months-long binge waiting for Cleopatra, to all the details of the marriage. Some of it Octavia already knew, though not the way Perdita painted events; she listened intently, her face giving nothing away, and rose as soon as she could to end the unpleasant interlude. No word of men's tendencies to take lovers when separated from their wives passed her lips, nor other remarks that would fuel Perdita's retelling of this morning's work. Of course the woman would lie, but those to whom she lied would find no confirmation of Perdita's version when they encountered Octavia. Who closed her sitting-room door to admission even by servants for a full hour after Perdita had clashed and clattered off into the Attic sun. Cleopatra, Queen of Egypt. Was this why her brother spoke of Cleopatra so scathingly, even over dinner? How much did others know, while she knew virtually nothing? Of the children her husband had sired on Cleopatra she was aware, including the boy born last year, but they hadn't chewed at her; she had simply assumed that the Queen of Egypt was a fertile woman who, like herself, did not take precautions against conceiving. Her own impressions had been of a woman who had loved Divus Julius passionately, wholeheartedly, and sought solace in his cousin to provide her with more offspring to safeguard her throne in the next generation. It had certainly never occurred to Octavia that Antony wouldn't philander; such was his nature, and how could he change that?

But Perdita spoke of an undying love! Oh, she oozed malice and spite, so why believe her? Yet the parasite had been inserted under Octavia's skin and was beginning to tunnel its way through her vitals toward her heart, her hopes, her dreams. She couldn't deny that her husband had called for aid from Cleopatra, nor that he was still in the arms of this fabulous monarch. But no, the moment he learned of her – Octavia's – presence in Athens, he would send Cleopatra back to Egypt and come to Athens. She was sure of it, positive of it!

Even so, during that hour alone she paced the room, struggled with the burrowing worm of Perdita's making, reasoned her way to sanity, called upon all her formidable resources of common sense. For it made no sense that Antony would have fallen in love with a woman whose chief claim to fame was her seduction of Divus Julius, an intellectual, an aesthete, a man of unusual and fastidious tastes. As much like Antony as chalk was like cheese. The usual metaphor, yet it didn't properly distinguish them. As much like Antony as a ruby was like a red glass bead? No, no, why was she wasting time on silly metaphors? The only thing Divus Julius and Antony had in common was Julian blood, and from what brother Caesar said, it was this alone that had spurred Cleopatra to seek out Antony. She had, brother Caesar revealed, once propositioned *him* because of his Julian blood; her children had to have Julian blood. To bed a ruling queen with the aim of providing her with children would have appealed enormously to Antony, and so Octavia had regarded the affair when first it came to her attention. But *love*? No, never! Impossible!

When Fonteius called on his usual quick daily visit, he found Octavia subtly blighted; there were shadows under those wonderful eyes, the smile had a tendency to slip, and her hands were aimless. He decided to be blunt.

'Who's been blabbing to you?' he demanded.

She shivered, looked rueful. 'Does it show?' she asked.

'Not to anyone save me. Your brother charged me with your welfare, and I have taken that charge to heart. Who?'

'Perdita.'

'Abominable woman! What did she tell you?'

'Nothing really that I didn't know, except for the marriage.'

'But it's not what she said, it's how she said it, yes?'

'Yes.'

He dared to take those purposeless hands, rub his thumbs over their backs in what might have been construed as comfort – or love. 'Octavia, listen to me!' he said very seriously. 'Don't think the worst, please. It's far too early and too ephemeral for you – or anyone! – to form conclusions. I'm a good friend of Antonius's, I *know* him. Perhaps not as well as you, his wife, but differently. It may well be that a marriage with Egypt was something he deemed necessary to his own rule as Triumvir of the East. It can't affect you – you're his legal wife. This invalid union is a symptom of his trials in the East, where nothing has gone as he imagined. It is, I think, a way of stemming the spate of his disappointments.' He released her hands before she could find their touch intimate. 'Do you understand?'

She looked better, more relaxed. 'Yes, Fonteius, I do. And I thank you from the bottom of my heart.'

'In future, you're not at home to Perdita. Oh, she'll come running the next time Peregrinus has a letter from one of his boon companions! But you won't see her. Promise?'

'I promise,' she said, smiling.

'Then I have good news. There's a performance of *Oedipus Rex* this afternoon. I'll give you a few moments to prink, then we're off to see how good the actors are. Rumor has it, they're terrific.'

A month after Octavia's letter went to Antioch, Antony's reply reached her.

What are you doing in Athens without the twenty thousand men I am owed by your brother? Here I am, preparing for an expedition back to Parthian Media, shockingly short of good Roman troops, and Octavianus has the presumption to send me two thousand only? It is too much, Octavia, far too much. Octavianus knows full well that I cannot return to Italia at the moment to recruit legionaries in person, and it was part of our agreement that he recruit me four legions. Legions I need badly.

Now, I receive a silly letter from you, burbling about this child and that child – do you think the nursery and its occupants concern me one scrap at such a time as this? What concerns me is Octavianus's broken agreement. Four legions, not four cohorts! The finest of the finest, indeed! And does your brother think I have need of a gigantic battering ram when I'm sitting not far from the cedars of the Libanus?

May a plague take him, and all associated with him!

She put the letter down, bathed in cold perspiration. No words of love, no terms of endearment, no reference to her arrival beyond a diatribe aimed at Caesar.

'He doesn't even tell me what he wants done with the men and supplies I've brought,' she said to Fonteius.

His face felt stiff, its skin prickling as if hit by a blast of sand in a dust storm. The big eyes fixed on him, so translucent that they were windows into her most private thoughts, filled with tears that began to course down her cheeks as if she didn't know they did. Fonteius reached into the sinus of his toga and pulled out his handkerchief, gave it to her.

'Cheer up, Octavia,' he said, voice hardly under control. 'I think two things, reading your letter. The first, that it reflects a side of Antonius that we both know – angry, impatient, thwarted. I can see and hear him rampaging up and down the room, coming out with a typical initial reaction to what he sees as Caesar's insult. You just happen to be the intermediary, the messenger he kills to vent his spleen. But the second is more serious. I think that Cleopatra sat listening, jotted down notes, and dictated this reply herself. Had Antonius replied, he would at least have indicated what he wants done with what is, after all, a donation of materials and engines of war, as well as soldiers, that he needs very badly. Whereas Cleopatra, a military tyro, wouldn't be bothered with a directive. *She* wrote it, not Antonius.'

An answer that made sense; Octavia mopped at her tears, blew her nose, gazed at Fonteius's wet handkerchief in dismay, and smiled. 'I have ruined it until it's laundered,' she said. 'I thank you, dear Fonteius. But what should I do?'

'Come to a performance of Aristophanes's *Clouds* with me, and then write to Antonius as if this letter was never sent. Ask him what he wants done with Caesar's gifts.'

'And ask when he intends to come to Athens? May I do that?'

'Definitely. He *must* come.'

Another month went by, of tragedies, comedies, lectures, excursions, any treat Fonteius could invent to help his poor darling pass the time, before Antony's reply arrived. Interesting, that not even Perdita could manage to make a scandal out of Fonteius's dancing attendance on Imperator Caesar's sister! Simply, no one would – or could – believe that Octavia was the stuff of unfaithful wives. Fonteius was her guardian; Caesar had made no secret of it, and ensured that his wishes were known even as far away as Athens.

By now everyone was talking about Antony's continuing passion for the woman Octavian had named the Queen of Beasts. Fonteius found himself caught in a cleft stick; half of him longed to come to Antony's defense, but the other half, by now deeply in love with Octavia, was concerned only with her wellbeing.

Antony's letter wasn't as great a shock as his first one.

Go back to Rome, Octavia! I have no business to take me to Athens in the foreseeable future, so it is pointless to wait there when you ought to be caring for your children in Rome. I say again, return to Rome!

As for the men and the supplies, ship them to Antioch immediately. Fonteius can come with them, or not, as he pleases. It seems from what I have heard that you need him more than I do.

I forbid you to come to Antioch yourself, is that clear? Go to Rome, not to Antioch.

Perhaps it was shock rendered her tearless; Octavia wasn't sure. The pain was terrible, but had a life of its own that was somehow not connected to her, Octavia, sister of Imperator Caesar and wife of Marcus Antonius. It ripped and tore, squeezed her dry, while all her mind could think of were his two little girls. They floated in an utterly dark place behind her eyes: Antonia, tall and sandy-fair; Mama Atia said she behaved like Divus Julius's Aunt Julia, who had been the wife of Gaius Marius. She was five now, going through a 'good' phase, though how she would eventually turn out was still a mystery. Whereas Tonilla the red of hair and eye was imperious, impatient, implacable, impassioned. Antonia hardly knew her *tata*, while Tonilla had never set eyes on him.

'You're just like your father!' Avia Atia would cry, tried beyond endurance by a tantrum or a torrent of feeling from Tonilla.

'You're just like your father,' Octavia would whisper very tenderly, loving the tiny volcano more because of it.

And now, she knew, it was all over. The day had come that once she had foreseen; for the rest of her life she would love him but have to exist without him. Whatever tied him to Egypt's Queen was very strong, perhaps unbreakable. And yet . . . and yet . . . somewhere in her depths Octavia knew that theirs wasn't a happy union, that Antony railed at it, half hated it. With me, she thought, he had peace and contentment. I soothed and calmed him. With Cleopatra, he has uncertainty and turmoil. She inflames him, goads him, torments him.

'That kind of marriage will madden him,' she said to Fonteius, showing him this letter too.

'Yes, it will,' Fonteius managed around the huge lump in his throat. 'Poor Antonius! Cleopatra will mold him to her liking.'

'What is her liking?' Octavia asked, looking hunted.

'I wish I knew, but I don't.'

'Why didn't he divorce me?'

Fonteius looked astonished, then chagrined. '*Edepol*! Why didn't it occur to me to wonder that? Yes, why didn't he divorce you? His letter almost demands that he should.'

'Come, Fonteius, think! You must know. Whatever it is has to be political.'

'This second letter hasn't come as a surprise, has it? You expected it to say what it does.'

'Yes, yes! But why no divorce?' she persisted.

'I think it means he hasn't quite burned his boats,' Fonteius said slowly. 'There's still a need in him to feel a Roman with a Roman wife. You're protection, Octavia. It may be too that in not divorcing you, he's making a bid for independence. The woman fixed her claws in him at a moment of deepest despair, when he would have turned for comfort to whomever was at hand – her.'

'She made sure of that.'

'Yes, obviously.'

'But why, Fonteius? What does she want of him?'

'Territory. Power. She's an Eastern monarch, granddaughter of Mithridates the Great. It's not the Ptolemy in her, they've been torpid and narrowly ambitious for generations, more concerned with filching the throne of Egypt off each other than in looking farther afield. Cleopatra is hungry for expansion – Mithridatic and Seleucid appetites.'

'How do you know so much about her?' Octavia asked curiously.

'I talked to people when I was in Alexandria and Antioch.'

'And what did you think of her when you met her?'

'Two things, more than any others. One, that she was utterly obsessed with her son by Divus Julius. The second, that she was a little like Thetis – able to change herself into whatever she felt necessary to achieve her ends.'

'Shark, cuttlefish – I forget the rest, only that Peleus hung on no matter what Thetis became.' She shivered. 'Indeed, poor Antonius! He's determined to hang onto her.'

360

He decided to change the subject, though he could think of nothing that would cheer her. 'And are you going home?' he asked.

'Oh, yes. I hate to impose, but could you find me a ship?'

'Better than that,' he said easily. 'Your brother charged me with your welfare, which means I'll be going with you.'

A relief, if not a joy; Fonteius watched her face relax a little, wishing with might and main that he, Gaius Fonteius Capito, could persuade her to love him. Quite a number of women had said they could love him, and two wives certainly had, but they were nothings. Long after he had ever expected to, he had found the woman of his heart, his dreams. But she loved another, and would go on doing so. Just as he would go on loving her.

'What a strange world we live in,' he said, and managed a wry laugh. 'Could you bear to see *The Trojan Women* this afternoon? I admit the subject is close to our present bone – women who have lost their men – but Euripedes is a true master, and the cast is splendid. Demetrius of Corinth is playing Hekabe, Doriscus is playing Andromache, and – they say he is amazing in the part – Aristogenes is Helen. Will you come?'

'Yes, please,' she said, smiling at him, even with her eyes. 'What are my woes, compared to theirs? At least I have my home, my children and my freedom. It will do me good to witness the plight of the Trojan women, especially as I've never seen the play. I've heard it tears at the heart, so I'll be able to weep for someone else's troubles.'

Octavian wept for his sister's troubles when she arrived in Rome a month later. It was September, and he was about to embark on his first campaign against the tribes of Illyricum. Dashing his tears away, he threw the two letters that Fonteius had given him on his desk and fought for composure. The battle won, he ground his teeth in anger, but not anger at Fonteius.

'Thank you for coming to see me before I could see Octavia,' he said to Fonteius, and held out his hand. 'You have acquitted yourself with honor and kindness to my sister, and I don't need her to tell me that. Is she . . . is she very depressed?'

'No, Caesar, that's not her way. Antonius's behavior has crushed her, but not defeated her.'

A verdict that Octavian agreed with, once he saw her.

'You must come and live here with me,' he said, his arm around her shoulders. 'Bring the children, of course. Livia

361

Drusilla is anxious that you have company, and the Carinae is too far away.'

'No, Caesar, that I cannot do,' Octavia said strongly. 'I am Antonius's wife, and will live in his house until he bids me go. Please don't nag or bully me about it! I won't change my mind.'

Sighing, he put her in a chair and drew another up close to hers, taking her hands. 'Octavia, he won't come home to you.'

'I know that, Little Gaius, but it makes no difference. I am still his wife, which means he expects me to care for his children and his house as a wife must when her husband is abroad.'

'What about money? He can't be providing for you.'

'I have my own money.'

That annoyed him, though his anger was reserved for Antony's emotional callousness. 'Your money is yours, Octavia! I'll have the Senate grant you sufficient from Antonius's stipend to care for his property here in Rome. His villas as well.'

'No, I beg you, don't do that! I'll keep a faithful account of what I spend, and he can pay me back when he comes home.'

'Octavia, he isn't coming home!'

'You can't say that for sure, Caesar. I don't claim to understand men's passions, but I do know Antonius. This Egyptian woman might be another Glaphyra – another Fulvia, even. He tires of women when they become importunate.'

'He has tired of you, my dear.'

'No, he hasn't,' she said valiantly. 'I am still his wife, he didn't divorce me.'

'That was to keep his tame senators and knights in his camp. No one can say he's permanently in the clutches of the Queen of Egypt when he hasn't divorced you, his true wife.'

'No one can say? Oh, come, Caesar! *You* can't say, is what you mean! I am not blind! You want Antonius to seem a traitor – for your own ends, not mine.'

'Believe that if you must, but it isn't true.'

'Here I stay' was all she said.

Octavian left her feeling neither surprise nor more than a minor irritation; he knew her as only a little brother could, following someone four years older as if tethered to a leash, privy to thoughts expressed aloud, girlish conversations with her friends, adolescent swoons and crushes. Antony had inspired those swoons long before she was old enough to love him as a woman did. When Marcellus applied to marry her, she had gone to her fate without a murmur of protest because she knew her duty and never dreamed of marriage

362

to Antony. He was so much in Fulvia's toils at the time that an eighteen-year-old as sensible as Octavia abandoned what hope she had ever cherished – probably none.

'She wouldn't move here?' asked Livia Drusilla when he returned.

'No.'

Livia Drusilla clicked her tongue. 'Tch! What a pity!'

He laughed, brushed his hand down her cheek affectionately. 'What nonsense! You're profoundly glad. A child lover you are not, wife, and you are well aware that those overindulged, under-disciplined children would swarm everywhere, did they live here, no matter how we tried to contain them.'

She giggled. 'Alas, too true! Though, Caesar, it isn't I who is out of the normal, it is Octavia. Children are greatly to be desired, and I would rejoice were I to fall pregnant. But Octavia makes a female cat look negligent. I'm surprised she consented to go to Athens without them.'

'She went without them because – keeping up the feline metaphor – she knows Antonius is a tomcat and feels the way you do about children. Poor Octavia!'

'Be sorry for her, Caesar, by all means, but don't lose sight of the fact that it's better her pain comes now than later.'

TWENTY

While Publius Canidius and his seven legions had penetrated Armenia and done good work, Antony had remained in Syria, ostensibly to oversee the war against Sextus Pompey in Asia Province and get a grand army together for his next campaign into Median Parthia. No more than an excuse; it had taken him that year to emerge, slowly and painfully, from the effects of his wine-induced furore. While Uncle Plancus governed Syria, Nephew Titius had deputed for Antony and taken an army to Ephesus to help Furnius, Ahenobarbus and Amyntas of Galatia subdue Sextus Pompey. It was Titius who cornered him in Phrygian Midaeum, and Titius who escorted him to the Asian coast at Miletus. There he was put to death at Titius's orders, an act Antony loudly deplored. He accused Uncle Plancus of putting Titius up to it, but Uncle Plancus stoutly insisted that the order, a secret one, had come from Antony, who should wear the blame. Not so! roared Antony.

Whose the blame was might never be known, but certainly Antony benefited from this short little war. He inherited the three good legions of bored veterans Sextus had recruited, and two splendid seafaring Romans in Decimus Turullius and Cassius Parmensis, the last of Divus Julius's assassins left alive. After they offered Antony their services and Antony accepted, Octavian wrote an almost hysterical letter to Antony.

'If nothing more was necessary to prove to me that you were a party to the plot to murder my divine father, Antonius, this is it,' said Octavian in his own small, meticulous hand. 'Of all the infamous, treacherous, disgusting acts of your hideous career, this is the worst. *Knowing* these two men are assassins, you have taken them into your service instead of publicly executing them. You do not deserve to hold a Roman magistracy, even of the lowliest kind.

You are not my colleague, you are my enemy, just as you are the enemy of all decent, honorable Roman men. You will pay for this, Antonius, so I swear by Divus Julius. You will pay.'

'Were you a party to the plot?' Cleopatra demanded.

Antony looked injured. 'No, of course I wasn't! Jupiter, it's ten years since Caesar was murdered, and ask me which I would prefer – two dead suspected assassins, or two live Roman admirals? There is no contest.'

'Yes, I see your logic. Still . . .'

'Still *what*?'

'I'm not sure I believe your denials about Caesar's murder.'

'Well, I don't happen to care whether you believe or you don't believe! Why don't you go home to Alexandria and rule in person for a change? Then I can deal with my war plans in peace.'

Cleopatra did as Antony suggested; within one *nundinum* the *Philopator* sailed for Alexandria with Pharaoh on board. Her willingness to leave him was evidence of her confidence that he had finally repaired the ravages that wine had wreaked upon his body and, more importantly, his mind. He really was extraordinary! Any other man of his age would have emerged showing physical scars of dissipation, but not Mark Antony. As fit as ever, certainly fit enough to conduct his ridiculous campaign. But this time he would not be marching for Phraaspa, of that she could be sure. Without the absent Canidius to back her up it had been hard going, but she had kept grinding away at Antony's ambitions over the months, shaping them into a different form. Of course she hadn't implied by word or look that he should turn his eyes westward to Rome; instead, she had harped upon the fact that Octavian was bound to come east now that he had conquered Sextus Pompey, whose execution had been her idea. A fat bribe to Lucius Munatius Plancus, another to his sister's boy, Titius, and the deed was done.

With Lepidus forced into retirement and Sextus Pompey gone for good, she had argued, there was no one to prevent Octavian's ruling the world except Mark Antony. It hadn't been difficult to convince Antony that Octavian *wanted* to rule the world, especially after she found an unexpected ally to reinforce her contentions. As if his nose had the ability to scent a vacant space around Antony, Quintus Dellius had appeared in Antioch to take the place that Gaius Fonteius had relinquished, full of mischief about Fonteius, who he swore was now Octavia's slave, a lovesick laughing stock. As Dellius utterly lacked Fonteius's integrity and suavity, he was no real substitute. However, he could be bought and, once a Roman noble had sold his services, he stayed bought. It was, apparently, a matter of honor, even were the honor tawdry. Cleopatra bought him.

She put Dellius to work in the slot Fonteius had vacated; once more he functioned as Antony's ambassador. The business of Ventidius and Samosata had faded from the forefront of Antony's mind, didn't seem such a crime anymore. Antony was, besides, missing Fonteius's manly company, so he seized upon Dellius as a substitute. Had Ahenobarbus been in Syria, things would have fallen out differently, but Ahenobarbus was busy in Bithynia. Nothing stood in Dellius's way. Or in Cleopatra's.

At the moment, Dellius was engaged in a task of Cleopatra's devising. Between the two of them, he and Cleopatra had experienced little trouble in convincing Antony that it was a task of great moment; he was to journey as Antony's ambassador to the court of Artavasdes of Media, and there propose an alliance between Rome and Media that ran counter to Parthian interests. Media proper, of which Phraaspa was the capital, belonged to the King of the Parthians; Artavasdes ruled Media Atropatene, smaller and less clement. Since all his borders save the one with Armenia were Parthian, Artavasdes was in conflict; self-preservation dictated that he should do nothing to offend the King of the Parthians, whereas ambition prompted him to cast hungry eyes on Media proper. When Antony's disastrous campaign had commenced, he and his Armenian namesake had been positive that no one could beat Rome, but by the time that Antony had set out from Artaxata on that terrible march, both Artavasdes thought differently.

In sending Dellius to Median Artavasdes, Cleopatra was trying to patch up an alliance that would keep this king quiet while his Armenian namesake was conquered for Rome. That it could be done was thanks to trouble at the court of ing Phraates, where princes of a minor Arsacid house were intriguing against him. No matter how many of your relatives you manage to kill, reflected Cleopatra, there are always some who lie so low you don't see them until it is too late.

Making Antony see that he didn't dare seize upon this Parthian turmoil by trying a second time to take Phraaspa was much harder, but she had eventually succeeded by dwelling constantly upon money. Those forty-four thousand talents that Octavian had sent him had been swallowed up by the cost of war – pay for the legions, arming the legions, buying the staples legionaries liked to eat from bread to pease porridge, horses, mules, tents – a thousand and one necessities. And somehow, whenever a general of any nationality equipped a new army, it was a seller's market; the general paid inflated prices for every commodity. As Cleopatra continued to refuse to pay for Parthian campaigns, and Antony had no more territory he could cede her in return for her gold, he was caught in her carefully laid trap.

'Content yourself with the complete conquest of all Armenia,' she said. 'If Dellius can draft a treaty with Median Artavasdes, your campaign will be a huge success, something you can trumpet to the Senate in tones that will make its rafters ring. You can't afford to lose another baggage train, nor the digits of your soldiers, which mean no marches into unknown country too far from Rome's own provinces to get help quickly. This campaign is simply to exercise your experienced men and toughen your recruits. You'll need them to face Octavianus, never forget that.'

He took it to heart, of that she had no doubt, therefore she could leave him to invade Armenia without needing to remain in Syria herself.

One other thing prompted her to go home: a letter from her Lord High Chamberlain, Apollodorus. Though it was not specific, it indicated that Caesarion was becoming troublesome.

Oh, Alexandria, Alexandria! How beautiful the city was after the filthy alleyways and slums of Antioch! Admittedly it held as many poor in slums as Antioch did – more, actually, as it was a bigger city – but every street was wide enough to let the air in, and the air was sweet, fresh, dry; neither too hot in summer nor too cold in winter. The slums were new, as well; Julius Caesar and his Macedonian enemies had virtually leveled the city fourteen years ago, obliging her to rebuild it. Caesar had wanted her to increase the number of public fountains and give the people free baths, but that she hadn't done – why should she? If she sailed into the Great Harbor, she came ashore inside the Royal Enclosure, and if she came in by road, she used Canopic Avenue. Neither route saw her needing to traverse the stews of Rhakotis: what her eyes didn't see, her heart didn't grieve about. Plague had reduced the population from three million to one million, but that had been six years ago; from somewhere a million people had appeared, most by the birth of babies, a smaller number by immigration. No native Egyptians could be found in Alexandria, but there were plenty of hybrids from interbreeding with poor Greeks; they formed a large servant class of free citizens who were not citizens, even after Caesar's urging her to bestow the Alexandrian citizenship on all its residents.

Apollodorus was waiting on the jetty in the Royal Harbor, but not, her eager eyes discovered, her eldest son. The light in them died, but she gave her hand to Apollodorus to kiss when he rose from his obeisance, and didn't object when he led her to one side, his face betraying his need to give her vital information right at this moment of her arrival.

'What is it, Apollodorus?'

'Caesarion,' he said.

'What has he done?'

'Nothing – as yet. It's what he plans to do.'

'Can't you and Sosigenes control him?'

'We try, Isis Reincarnated, but it becomes more and more difficult.' He cleared his throat and looked embarrassed. 'His balls have dropped, Majesty, and he regards himself as a man.'

She stopped in her tracks to turn wide gold eyes upon her most trusted servant. 'But . . . but he isn't yet thirteen!'

'Thirteen in three more months, Majesty, and growing like a weed. He is already four and a half cubits tall. His voice is breaking, his physique more a man's than a child's.'

'Ye gods, Apollodorus! No, don't tell me anymore, I beg you! Armed with this information, I think it's better that I form my own opinions.' She resumed walking. 'Where is he? Why didn't he meet me?'

'He's in the middle of drafting legislation he wanted to have finished before you arrived.'

'*Drafting legislation?*'

'Yes. He'll tell you all about it, Daughter of Ra, probably before you can so much as open your mouth to try to speak.'

Even forewarned, Cleopatra's first sight of her son took the breath from her body. In the year of her absence he had gone from child to youth, but without the awkwardness males usually suffered. His skin was clear and tanned, his thick mop of gold hair trimmed short rather than kept long as was the wont of adolescents, and, as Apollodorus had said, his body was a man's. *Already!* My son, my beautiful little boy, what happened to you? I have lost you forever, and my heart is broken. Even your eyes are changed – so stern and certain, so . . . inflexible.

All of which was as nothing compared to his likeness to his father. Here was Caesar the young man, Caesar as he must have been when he wore the *laena* and the *apex* of the Flamen Dialis, Rome's special priest of Jupiter Optimus Maximus. It had taken Sulla and his nineteenth birthday to free Caesar of that abominated priesthood, but here stood Caesar as he might have been did Gaius Marius not attempt to ban him from a military career. The long face, the bumpy nose, the sensuous mouth with the creases of humor in its corners – Caesarion, Caesarion, not yet! I am not ready.

He came across the wide expanse of floor between his desk and the spot where Cleopatra stood, transfixed, one hand holding a fat scroll, the other extended to her.

'Mama, how good to see you,' he said in a deep voice.

'I left a boy, I behold a man,' she managed.

He handed her the scroll. 'I've just completed it,' he said, 'but of course you must read it before I put it into force.'

The roll of paper felt heavy; she looked down at it, then at him. 'Don't I get a kiss?' she asked.

'If you want one.' He pecked her on the cheek, then, it seemed deciding this was not enough, he pecked her on the other cheek. 'There! Now read it, Mama, please!'

Time to assert her ascendancy. 'Later, Caesarion, when I have a moment. First, I'm going to see your brothers and sister. Then I intend to have dinner on dry land. And after that, a meeting with you, Apollodorus and Sosigenes, at which you may tell me all about whatever it is you've written in here.'

The old Caesarion would have argued; the new one didn't. He shrugged, took the scroll back. 'Actually that's good. I'll work on it a little more while you're otherwise engaged.'

'I hope you intend to be at dinner!'

'A meal I never eat – why put the cooks to the trouble of making a fancy meal I won't do justice to? I take fresh bread and oil, a salad, some fish or lamb, and eat while I work.'

'Even today, when I've just come home?'

The brilliant blue eyes twinkled; he grinned. 'I am to feel guilty, is that it? Very well, I'll come to dinner.' Off he went to sit behind his desk, the paper already unfurled, and bent his head to it the moment he groped for his chair and found it.

Her feet carried her to the nursery as if they belonged to a woman outside of herself, but here at least was sanity, normality. Iras and Charmian came running to hug her, kiss her, then stand off to watch their beloved mistress take in the sight of her three younger children. Ptolemy Alexander Helios and Cleopatra Selene

369

were putting a jigsaw puzzle together, a scene of flowers, grass and butterflies painted on thin wood that some master craftsman with a fret saw had cut into small, irregular pieces. The Sun twin was whanging away with a toy mallet at a piece that didn't fit, while his sister the Moon glared in outrage. Then she wrenched the mallet away from her brother and hit him on the head with it. Sun howled, Moon shrieked with joy; a moment later they were back working on the puzzle.

'The mallet head is made of cork,' whispered Iras.

How lovely they were! Five years old now, and so different in appearance that no one would have guessed that they were twins. The Sun was appropriately gold of hair and eye and skin, handsome in a more Eastern than Roman vein; it was easy to see that when he matured he would have a curved beak of a nose, high cheekbones. The Moon had dense, curly black hair, a delicate face and a pair of huge eyes the color of amber between long black lashes; it was easy to see that when she matured she would be very beautiful in no way save her own. Neither of them resembled Antony, or indeed their mother. The mingling of two disparate strains had produced children more physically attractive than either parent.

Little Ptolemy Philadelphus, on the other hand, was Mark Antony from head to feet: big, thickset, reddish hair and eyes, the nose that strove to meet the chin across a small, full mouth. He had been born in Roman October the year before last, which made him eighteen months old.

'He's a typical youngest child,' Charmian murmured. 'Makes no attempt to speak, though he walks like his daddy.'

'Typical?' Cleopatra asked, enveloping his wriggling body in a hug he clearly didn't appreciate.

'Youngests don't talk because their elders talk for them. He gabbles, they understand.'

'Oh.' She dropped Philadelphus in a hurry when he sank his milk teeth into her hand, stood flapping it in pain. 'He really is like his father, isn't he? Determined. Iras, have the court jeweller make him an amethyst bracelet. It guards against wine.'

'He'd tear it off, Majesty.'

'Then a close-fitting necklet, or a brooch – I don't care, as long as he wears an amethyst.'

'Does Antonius wear his?' Iras asked.

'He does now,' said Cleopatra grimly.

From the nursery she went to her bath, Charmian and Iras

accompanying her. In Rome, she knew, they told fabulous stories of her bath: that it was filled with ass's milk, that it was the size of a carp pond, that a miniature waterfall refreshed it, that its heat was tested by immersing a slave in it first. None of the tales that sprang out of her sojourn in Rome was true; the tub that Caesar found in Lentulus Crus's tent after Pharsalus was far more sumptuous. Cleopatra's was a rectangular tub of ordinary size, made of unpolished red granite. It was filled by slaves carrying amphorae of plain water, some hot, some cold; the recipe was standard, so the temperature scarcely varied.

'Does Caesarion mix with his little brothers and sister?' she asked as Charmian massaged her back, poured water over it.

'No, Majesty,' Charmian answered, sighing. 'He *likes* them, but they don't interest him.'

'Hardly surprising,' said Iras, preparing perfumed unguent. 'The age difference is too great for intimacy, and he was never treated as a child. That is the fate of Pharaoh.'

'True.'

An observation reinforced at dinner, which Caesarion attended in body but not in mind; that was elsewhere. If someone thrust food at him, he ate it; always the plainest of fare. Clearly the servants were educated in what to offer him. His intake of fish was consoling, and he did eat lamb, but poultry, young crocodile and other meats were ignored. Crisp bread, as snowy white as the bakers could make it, formed the largest part of his meal, dipped in olive oil or, at breakfast time, honey, he told his mother.

'My father ate plain,' he said in response to a chiding remark from Cleopatra aimed at persuading him to vary his diet more, 'and it didn't do him any harm, did it?'

'No, it didn't,' she admitted, giving up.

She held her councils in a room designed for them, having a big marble table that could seat her and Caesarion at its end, and take four men down either side; the far end was always vacant as an honorary place for Amun-Ra, who never managed to come. This day saw Apollodorus sitting opposite Sosigenes and Cha'em. Their queen took her seat, annoyed to find no Caesarion but, before she could say something scathing, in he strolled with both hands full of documents. A loud gasp went up; Caesarion went to the place of Amun-Ra and seated himself there.

'Take your designated chair, Caesarion,' Cleopatra said.

'This is my chair.'

'It belongs to Amun-Ra, and even Pharaoh is not Amun-Ra.'

'I have contracted an agreement with Amun-Ra that I represent him at all councils,' the lad said, unruffled. 'It is foolish to sit in a chair from which I cannot see the one face I need most to see, Pharaoh – yours.'

'We reign jointly, therefore we should sit together.'

'Were I your parrot, Pharaoh, we could. But now that I have become a man, I do not intend to be your parrot. When I think it necessary, I will disagree with you. I bow to your age and your experience, but you must bow to me as senior partner in our joint rule. I am male Pharaoh, it is my right to have the final word.'

A silence followed this level speech, during which Cha'em, Sosigenes and Apollodorus looked fixedly at the surface of the table and Cleopatra looked down its length at her rebel son. It was her own doing; she had elevated him to the throne, had him anointed and consecrated Pharaoh of Egypt and King of Alexandria. Now she didn't know what to do for the best, and doubted that she had sufficient influence with this stranger to reassert herself as the senior partner. Oh, pray this is not the beginning of a war between ruling Ptolemies! she thought. Pray this isn't going to be Ptolemy Pot Belly versus Cleopatra the Mother! But I see no corruption in him, no greed, no savagery. He's a Caesar, not a Ptolemy! Which means he will not subject himself to me, that he thinks himself wiser than me, for all my 'age and experience'. I must give way, I must give in.

'Your point is taken, Pharaoh,' she said without anger. 'I sit at this end, you at that end.' Unconsciously she rubbed her hand across the base of her neck, where, she had discovered in her bath, a swelling had arisen. 'Is there anything you wish to discuss about your conduct of State affairs while I was away?'

'No, all went smoothly. I dispensed justice without needing to consult previous cases, and none disputed my verdicts. The public purse of Egypt is properly accounted for, also the public purse of Alexandria. I have left it to the Recorder and the other magistrates of Alexandria to do all the necessary repairs to the city's buildings, and authorized repairs to various temples and precincts along the shores of Nilus as petitioned.' His face changed, became more animated. 'If you have no questions and have heard no complaints about my conduct, may I ask that you listen to my plans for the future of Egypt and Alexandria?'

'I have heard no complaints thus far,' Cleopatra said with caution. 'You may proceed, Ptolemy Caesar.'

He had put his bundles of scrolls on the table, and spoke now without consulting them. The room was dim because the day was drawing to a close, but wayward spears of light dancing with dust motes flickered in time to the swaying of palm fronds outside. One ray, steadier than the rest, illuminated the disc of Amun-Ra on the wall behind Caesarion's head; Cha'em took on his seer's look, said something in the back of his throat too strangled to understand, and put trembling hands on the table. Perhaps it was the fading light made his skin seem grey; Cleopatra didn't know, but did know that whatever vision had come to him would not be imparted to her. Which meant it had been malign.

'First, I shall deal with Alexandria,' said Caesarion briskly. 'There have to be changes – immediate changes. In future we will follow Roman practice by providing a free grain dole for the poor. Means-tested, of course. Further to grain, its price will not fluctuate to reflect its cost if bought from overseas when Nilus does not inundate. The additional expense will be absorbed by Alexandria's public purse. However, these laws apply only to the amount of grain a small family consumes during the course of one month – the *medimnus*. Any Alexandrian buying more than one *medimnus* a month will have to pay the going rate.'

He paused, chin up, eyes challenging, but no one spoke. He resumed. 'Those residents of Alexandria who are not at the moment entitled to the citizenship will be enfranchised. This applies to all free men, including freedmen. That way, there will be citizen rolls and the apparatus to issue grain chits, be they for free grain or that one subsidized monthly *medimnus*. All the city's magistracies from Interpreter down will be filled in the fairest way – by free election – and last for one year only. Any citizen, be he Macedonian, Greek, Jew, Metic or hybrid Egyptian, will be permitted to stand, and laws will be enacted to punish electoral bribery, as well as corruption while in office.'

Another pause, greeted by profound silence. Caesarion took that as a sign that opposition, when it came, would be implacable.

'Finally,' he announced, 'at every major intersection I will build a marble fountain. It will have several spouts for drawing water and a roomy pool for washing clothes. For washing persons, I will build public baths in each of the city's districts except Beta, where the Royal Enclosure already has adequate facilities.'

Time to switch from man to boy; eyes dancing, he looked at each set face around the table. 'There!' he cried, laughing now. 'Isn't all of that splendid?'

'Splendid indeed,' Cleopatra said, 'but manifestly impossible.'
'Why?'

'Because Alexandria cannot afford your program.'

'Since when did a democratic form of government cost more than a bunch of life-tenured Macedonians who are too busy feathering their own nests to spend the city's moneys where they should be spent? Why should public income support their plush existences? And since when should a youth be castrated in order to enter senior service with the King and Queen? Why can't women guard our virgin princesses? Eunuchs, in this day and age? It's abominable!'

'Unanswerable,' said Cha'em, mouth twitching at the look of horror on Apollodorus's face; he was a eunuch.

'And since when did universal suffrage cost more than select suffrage?' Caesarion demanded. 'Setting up an electoral apparatus will cost, yes. A free grain dole will cost. A subsidized grain ration will cost. Fountains and baths will cost. But if the nest-featherers are hauled down from their perches at the top of the roost and *every* citizen pays *all* his taxes instead of some people's taxes being winked at, I think the money can be found.'

'Oh, stop being a child, Caesarion!' Cleopatra said in weary tones. 'Just because you have a huge allowance to squander doesn't mean you understand high finance! Find money, piffle! You're a child, with a child's idea of how the world works.'

All the glee vanished; Caesarion's face took on a pinched, rigid hauteur. 'I am no child!' he said through his teeth, voice as cold as Rome in winter. 'Do you know how I spend my huge allowance, Pharaoh? I pay the wages of a dozen accountants and clerks! Nine months ago I commissioned them to investigate Alexandria's revenues and expenditures. Our Macedonian magistrates, from the Interpreter to their bureaucracy of nephews and cousins, are corrupt! *Rotten!*' One hand, a ruby ring flashing crimson fire, brushed the scrolls. 'It is all here, every last peculation, embezzlement, fraud, petty theft! Once the data were all in, I felt ashamed to call myself King of Alexandria!'

If silence could boom, this silence did. One part of Cleopatra exulted in her son's amazing precocity, but another part was so angry that her right palm itched to strike the little monster's face. How dared he! Yet how wonderful that he dared! And what could she answer? How was she going to get out of this with her dignity intact, her pride unhumbled?

Sosigenes postponed that evil moment. 'What I want to know

is, who gave you these ideas, Pharaoh? You certainly didn't get them from me, and I refuse to believe that they sprang fully armed from your own brow. So where did they come from?'

Even as he asked, Sosigenes was conscious of a twisting in his chest, a pang of pure sorrow for the lost boyhood of Caesarion. It has always been awesome to witness the evolution of this true prodigy, he thought, for, like his father, he is a true prodigy.

But it has meant no boyhood. As a tiny babe in arms he had talked in polished sentences; no one could fail to see what a mighty mind dwelled inside the infant Caesarion. Though his father had never once remarked on it, or indeed seemed to see it; perhaps the memories of his own early years closed his eyes. How had Julius Caesar been when he was twelve years old? How, for instance, had his mother treated him? Not the way Cleopatra treated Caesarion, Sosigenes decided in that minute slice of time waiting for Caesarion to answer. Cleopatra regarded her son as a god, so the depth of his intellect only served to increase her foolishness. Oh, if only Caesarion had been more—*ordinary*!

Well did Sosigenes remember persuading Cleopatra to let the five-year-old boy play with some of the children belonging to high-born Macedonians like the Recorder and the Accountant! Those boys had drawn back from Caesarion in fear, or punched and kicked him, or mocked him cruelly. All of which he had borne without complaint, as determined to conquer them as he was to conquer the woes of Alexandria today. But seeing their behavior, Cleopatra had banished all children, girls as well as boys, from contact with her son. In future, she had ordained, Caesarion must be content with his own company. Whereupon Sosigenes had produced a mongrel puppy. Horrified, Cleopatra would have had the creature drowned.

But Caesarion had walked in at that opportune moment, seen the dog, and become a little boy of seven. Face wreathed in smiles, his hands went out to hold the squirming scrap: thus had Fido entered Caesarion's life. Yet the boy knew Fido displeased his mother, and had been obliged to conceal the dog's importance to him from her. Again, that wasn't normal. Again, Caesarion was forced into adult behavior. A careworn old man lives within him, while the boy he has never been allowed to be withers save in secret moments spent far from his mother and the thrones he occupies as her equal. *Equal?* No, not that, never that! Caesarion is his mother's superior in every way, and that is a tragedy.

* * *

The lad's answer to the question came, and suddenly he was a little boy, face alight.

'Fido and I go ratting in the palace attics—terrific rats up there, Sosigenes! Some are nearly as big as Fido, I swear! They must like paper, because they've eaten through piles and piles of old records— some go back as far as the second Ptolemy! Anyway, a few months ago Fido found a box they hadn't managed to chew—malachite inlaid with lapis. Beautiful! When I opened it, I found it held all the documents my father wrote while he was in Egypt. Stuff for you, Mama! Advice, not love letters. Did you never read them?'

Face burning, Cleopatra remembered a donkey ride Caesar had made her take through the ruins of Alexandria, forcing her to see what had to be done, and in what order. Housing for the ordinary people first—only after that, temples and public buildings. Oh, and the seemingly endless lectures! How they had irritated her, when what she hungered for was love! Remorseless instructions as to what must be done, from citizenship for everyone to a free grain dole for the poor. She had ignored all of them save giving citizenship to the Jews and Metics for helping Caesar hold the Alexandrians at bay until his legions arrived. Meaning to get to all of them some-time. But her godhead had intervened, and his murder. After his death, she had deemed his reforms pointless. He had tried reforms in Rome, and they killed him for his hubris. So she had put his lists and orders and explanations—thousands upon thousands of words!—into that malachite box inlaid with lapis, and given it to a palace steward to store somewhere out of sight, out of mind.

What she hadn't counted on was a busy boy with a ratting dog. Oh, the damage his discovery had created! Caesarion was now infected with his father's disease; he wanted to change things so hallowed by the centuries that even those who would benefit didn't want change. Why hadn't she put those sheaves of paper in the fire? Then her son could have found nothing except rats.

'Yes, I read them,' she said.

'Then why didn't you act on them?'

'Because Alexandria has its own *mos maiorum*, Caesarion. Its own customs and traditions. The rulers of a place, be it a city or a nation, are not obligated to succor the poor, who are an affliction only starvation can cure. The Romans call their poor *proletarii*, meaning that they have absolutely nothing to give the State save children – not taxes, not prosperity. But the Romans also have a tradition of philanthropy, which is why they feed their poor at the State's expense. Alexandria has no such tradition, nor do other places.

And yes, I agree that our magistrates are corrupt, but the Macedonians are the original settlers, and feel entitled to the perquisites of office. Try to strip them of office, and you'll be torn to pieces in the agora – not by the Macedonians, but by the poor. The citizenship of Alexandria is precious, not to be given to the undeserving. As for elections – they are a farce.'

'I wish you could hear yourself. It's all hippo shit.'

'Don't be vulgar, *Pharaoh*.'

The expressions crossed his face like shivers over a horse's hide, childish at first – angry, frustrated, resisting – but slowly becoming adult – flintily determined, icily resolute. 'I will have my way,' he said. 'Later if not sooner, I will have my way. You can block me for a while because you can appeal to enough of Alexandria's citizens to block me. I am not a fool, Pharaoh, I do know the magnitude of the resistance there will be to my changes. But they *will* come! And when they do, they will not be confined to Alexandria. We are Pharaoh of a country a thousand miles long but only ten miles wide at most except for Ta-She, a country that has no free citizens at all. They belong to us, as does the land they till and the crops they harvest. As for money . . . ! We have so much we can never spend it, sitting beneath the ground outside Memphis. I will use it to improve the lot of Egypt's people.'

'They will not thank you,' she said, tight-lipped.

'Why should they? By rights it's their money, not ours.'

'We,' she said, biting off each word, 'are Nilus. We are son and daughter of Amun-Re, Isis and Horus reincarnated, Lords of the Two Ladies Upper and Lower Egypt, of the Sedge and Bee. Our purpose is to be fruitful, to bring prosperity to high and low alike. Pharaoh is God on earth, destined never to die. Your father had to die to assume his godhead, whereas you have been a god since your conception. You *must* believe!'

He gathered up his scrolls and rose to his feet. 'Thank you for listening to me, Pharaoh.'

'Give me your papers! I want to read them.'

That provoked a laugh. 'I think not,' he said, and left.

'Well, at least we know where we stand,' Cleopatra said to the others. 'On the edge of a precipice.'

'He will change as he matures,' Sosigenes comforted.

'Yes, he will,' said Apollodorus.

Cha'em said nothing.

'And do you agree, Cha'em?' she asked. 'Or did your vision tell you he won't change?'

'My vision made no sense,' Cha'em whispered. 'It was muddled, confused – truly, Pharaoh, it signified nothing.'

'I'm sure it did to you, but you won't tell me, will you?'

'I say again, there is nothing to tell.'

But he crept away showing his age and, as soon as he was far enough away not to be caught, he began to weep.

Cleopatra took supper in her rooms, but did not call for her two handmaidens; the day had been a long one that must have tired Charmian and Iras out. A junior girl – Macedonian, of course – waited on her while she picked without appetite at the food, then assisted her to shed her robes for sleep. Among those who were well off and owned many servants, it wasn't customary to wear clothes to bed. Those who did sleep clothed were either prudish, like the late Cicero's wife, Terentia, or those who didn't have sufficient servants to launder the sheets regularly. That she actually spent time thinking about this was Antony's fault; he despised women who wore a shift to bed, and had told her why, even who. Octavia, a modest rather than a prudish woman, was not averse to making love naked, he had said, but once the lovemaking was over, she donned a shift. Her excuse (for so it seemed to him) was that one of the children might need her urgently during the night, and she would not permit the servant who came to wake her to see her unclothed body. Though, according to Antony, her body was lovely.

That subject exhausted, Cleopatra's mind passed to the odder aspects of Antony's relationship with Octavia: anything, not to have to think about today!

He had refused to divorce Octavia, stubbornly dug his heels in when Cleopatra tried to persuade him that divorce was the best alternative. He was *her* husband now; the Roman marriage had no purpose. But it had emerged during the course of her exhortations that Antony was still fond of Octavia, and not merely because she was the mother of two of his Roman children. Both girls, therefore – to Cleopatra, at any rate – unimportant. Not to Antony, it seemed; he was already planning their marriages, though Antonia was about five at most, and Tonilla not yet two. Ahenobarbus's son, Lucius, was destined to wed Antonia, but Antony hadn't yet made up his mind about Tonilla's husband. As if any of that mattered! How could she prise him loose of his Roman connections? What use were they to Pharaoh's consort, Pharaoh's stepfather? What use was a Roman wife, even the sister of Octavian?

To Cleopatra, Antony's clinging to Octavia was a sign that he still hoped for an arrangement with Octavian that would permit each of them to have his share of empire. As if that boundary on the river Drina dividing West from East were a permanent fence, on either side of which dog Antony and dog Octavian could snarl and bare their teeth at each other without ever needing to fight. Oh, why couldn't Antony see that such an accommodation would never last? She knew it and Octavian knew it. Her agents in Rome were full of Octavian's ploys to discredit her in Roman and Italian eyes. He called her the Queen of Beasts, embroidered the tales of her bath, her private life, and alleged that she was corrupting Antony with drugs and wine. Turning him into her creature. Her agents reported that, thus far, Octavian's efforts to besmirch Antony fell on barren ground: no one really believed them – yet. His seven hundred senators remained faithful, their fondness for Antony fueled by their hatred for Octavian. A tiny crack had appeared in the solid wall of their devotion after the real story of the Parthian campaign became known, but only a handful of them had deserted him. Most had decided that the Eastern disaster was not Antony's fault; to admit that it was, was to admit Octavian was right – and that they could not do.

Antony . . . By now, starting his campaign against Artavasdes of Armenia, whom he must be allowed to conquer. But before he could contemplate marching against Artavasdes of Media Atropatene, Quintus Dellius *must* have succeeded in forging an alliance that no Roman general, including Antony, could possibly refuse. Though some aspects of the pact could not be written down, even imparted to Antony: they were between Egypt and Media, to the effect that, when Rome was conquered and absorbed into the new Egyptian empire, Median Artavasdes could strike at the King of the Parthians with all the might of forty or fifty Roman legions, and assume the throne he hungered for above all else. Cleopatra's price was peace, a peace that must last until Caesarion was grown enough to step into his father's boots.

There. The name had intruded at last, could not be avoided. If the events of this, her first day back in Alexandria, were taken as evidence of Caesarion's remarkable character, then he was going to grow into the same kind of military genius his father had been. His father's wishes drove him, and his father had been murdered three days before he was to set off for a five-year campaign against the Parthians. Caesarion would want to conquer east of the Euphrates and, once he had succeeded, he would rule from Oceanus

Atlanticus to the River of Ocean beyond India. A kingdom far bigger than Alexander the Great's at its peak. Nor would his army refuse to keep going east, nor would the structure of his satrapies be imperiled by rebellious marshals intent upon pulling his empire down, carving it up among themselves. For his marshals would be his brothers and his cousins from Antony's marriage to Fulvia. Welded into blood loyalty: united, not divided.

She saw none of this as impossible. All it required to bear fruit was iron determination on her part, and that she had. If her advisers were less hers, one of them at least might have asked her what would happen to this gauzy edifice of ambitions did her son turn out not to have his father's military genius? A question she would have brushed aside anyway. The boy was as precocious as his father, as gifted, as like him as the proverbial peas in a pod. He was a Julian, half of his blood Caesar's. And look at what Octavian, with far less Julian in him, had done at eighteen, nineteen, twenty. Assumed his inheritance, twice marched on Rome, forced the Senate to make him senior consul. A mere youth. But, beside Caesarion, Octavian paled into insignificance.

Only how was she to deflect Caesarion from a kind of idealism that she knew Caesar's pragmatism would have tempered? Caesar's plans for Alexandria and Egypt were experimental, things he felt he could enforce in Egypt through his domination of its ruler, Cleopatra. Thinking to point to the success of his programs in her kingdom when he tried the same reforms in Rome more seriously than time had permitted, he had not been able to find colleagues who believed in his ideas. Nor, she knew, would Caesarion. Therefore Caesarion had to be talked out of trying to implement his program.

She rose from her bed and went to the exquisite little room attached to her quarters wherein stood statues of Ptah, Horus, Isis, Osiris, Sekhmet, Hathor, Sobek, Anubis, Montu, Tawaret, Thoth, a dozen more. Some had the heads of beasts, that was true, but many did not. All of them were aspects of life along the river, not so different from Roman *numina* and elemental forces. More like them, in fact, than like Greek gods, who were humans on a giant scale. And hadn't the Romans needed to give some of their gods faces as the centuries wore on?

Sheathed in gold, the room was lined with these statues, painted in lifelike colors that glowed even in the weak lamp flames of night. In its center lay a rug from Persepolis; Cleopatra knelt on it, arms stretched in front of her.

'My father, Amun-Ra, my brothers and sisters in godhead, I humbly ask that you give your son and brother Ptolemy Caesar, who is Pharaoh, enlightenment. I humbly ask that you give me, his earthly mother, the ten years more that I need to bring him into the full glory that you intend. I offer you my life as security against his, and beseech your help in my difficult task.'

Her praying done, she continued to abase herself, and so fell asleep, only waking with the dawn and the coming of the disc of the sun. Cramped, bewildered, stiff.

On her way back to bed, hurrying before the servants came on duty, she passed her huge mirror of polished silver, and paused, startled, to stare at the woman reflected in it. As thin as ever, as small, as unlovely. Of body hair she had none: it was plucked with scrupulous care. She looked more child than woman, save for her face. Its shape had changed, lengthened, hardened, though it betrayed no lines or wrinkles. The face of a woman fully thirty-four, whose large golden-yellow eyes were shadowed with sadness. The light grew; she continued to stand looking at herself. No, not the body of a child! Three pregnancies, one with twins, had turned the skin of her belly to sloppy parchment: loose, crinkled, dully brown.

Why does Antonius love me? she asked her image, shocked. And why can't I love him?

Halfway through the morning she found Caesarion, resolved to have it out with him. As was his habit, he had gone down to the cove behind his palace to swim, and sat now on a rock looking like an ideal subject for Phidias or Praxiteles. All he wore was a loincloth, still wet enough to show his mother that he was indeed a man. The realization terrified her, but she was not one to give in to her feelings, and so sat on another rock where she could see his face. Caesar's face, more and more.

'I haven't come to scold, or nag, or criticize,' she said.

His brilliant smile showed regular white teeth. 'I didn't expect you had, Mama. What is it?'

'A petition, I think.'

'Then plead your case.'

'Give me time, Caesarion,' she said in her most honeyed voice. 'I need time, but I have less of it than you. You owe me time.'

'Time for what?' he asked warily.

'To prepare our people of Alexandria and Egypt for change.'

He frowned, displeased, but said nothing. She hurried on.

'I'm not going to tell you that you haven't lived long enough to have sufficient experience in dealing with people, be they subjects or colleagues – you would reject that. But you *must* take my age and experience into account as worth listening to! Truly, my son, people have to be educated to accept change. You can't issue pharaonic edicts that throw people into instant upheaval and expect no opposition. I admire the thoroughness of your investigations, and admit the truth of much you said. But what you and I know to be the truth isn't as obvious to others. Ordinary people, even Macedonian aristocrats, are set in their ways. They resist change the way a mule resists being led on a halter. A man or woman's world is circumscribed compared to our world – few of them travel, and those who do go no farther than the Delta, or Thebes for a holiday if they have the money. The Recorder has never been farther from Alexandria than Pelusium, so how do you think he sees the world? Does he care about Memphis, let alone Rome? And if that is true of him, how do you think lesser people will feel?'

His face grew mulish, but the eyes showed uncertainty. 'If the poor have free grain, Mama, I cannot think they'll revolt.'

'I agree, which is why I suggest you start with that. But not overnight, please! Spend the next year working out what your father would have called the logistics, put it down on paper, and bring it back to council then. Will you do that?'

Obviously the free grain dole was first on his list of priorities; she had guessed correctly. 'It won't take that long,' he said. 'Just a month or two.'

'Even the great Caesar's legislation took years to draft,' she countered. 'You can't cut corners, Caesarion. Deal with each change properly, meticulously, *perfectly*. Take Cousin Octavianus as your example – now there is a real perfectionist, and I am not too bigoted to admit it! You have so much time, my son. Do things gradually, please. Talk long before you act – people must be carefully prepared for change so that they don't feel it has been thrust upon them without warning. Please?'

His face had relaxed; now he smiled. 'All right, Mama, I take your point.'

'Your solemn word on it, Caesarion?'

'My solemn word.' He laughed, a clear, attractive sound. 'At least you didn't make me swear on the gods.'

'Do you believe in our gods enough to regard an oath taken in their name as sacred, binding unto death?'

'Oh, yes.'

'Well, I see you as a man of his word, a man who doesn't need to be bound by oaths.'

Off the rock, descending on her to hug her, kiss her. 'Oh, thank you, Mama, thank you! I will do as you say.'

And that, she thought, watching him leap from rock to rock as gracefully as a dancer, is exactly the way to handle him. Offer him a fraction of what he wants and convince him it is enough. For once I have acted wisely, seen my way unerringly.

A month later Cleopatra realized that she was constantly stroking her throat to check on that swelling. It didn't look or feel like a lump, but when Iras commented upon her new habit and inspected the swelling for herself, she insisted that her mistress consult a physician.

'*Not* a slimy Greek quack! Send for Hapd'efan'e,' Iras said. 'I mean it, Cleopatra! If you don't summon him, I will.'

The years had dealt kindly with Hapd'efan'e; he looked much as he had when he had followed Caesar around from Egypt to Asia Minor to Africa to Spain to Rome, keeping a stern eye on Caesar's 'epilepsy', which he had realized only happened if Caesar forgot to eat for long periods, something this captious and difficult patient was prone to do. After Caesar's death he returned to his homeland aboard Caesarion's ship, then, following a year as royal physician in Alexandria, he got permission to go back to the precinct of Ptah in Memphis. The order of physicians was under the patronage of Ptah's wife, Sekhmet; its members were shaven-headed, wore a white linen dress that commenced under the nipples and flared gently to a hem below the knee, and were required to be celibate. Travel had broadened him, both as man and doctor; he was now acknowledged as the finest diagnostician in Egypt.

First he examined Cleopatra carefully, feeling for a pulse, sniffing her breath, probing her bones, pulling down her lower eyelids, making her extend her hands to arm's length, observing her walk a straight line. Only then did he concentrate on the problem, feeling under her jaw and down the throat and neck.

'Yes, Pharaoh, it is a swelling, not a lump,' he said. 'The cause of the swelling is not encapsulated like a cyst – the edges simply fuse into unswollen tissue all around. I have seen its like among those who live in Egypt of the river, but rarely in Alexandria, the Delta and Pelusium. It is called a goitre.'

'Is it malignant?' she asked, dry-mouthed.

'No, Majesty. Which is not to say that it won't grow bigger. Most goitres get bigger, but very slowly, over years. Yours is new, so there is always a chance that its growth will be rapid. If so, then your eyes will start to pop out of their sockets like frog's eyes. No, no, do not panic! I doubt that this goitre is going to give you pop-eyes, but a physician who does not warn a patient of all eventualities is not a good practitioner of the medical arts. However, you are not quite symptom free, Majesty. You have the faintest hint of a vibrating tremor in the hands, and your heart is beating a little too fast. I want Iras to feel your pulse before you arise from your bed every morning –' he gave her and Charmian his sweetest smile – 'because Charmian is too dramatic. After a month, Iras will know how fast your heart beats, and be able to monitor it. The heart, you see, is tied inside your chest by vessels holding blood, which is why you can assess it by finding the wrist pulse. Did these vessels not exist, hearts would wander the way the Greeks think a womb does.'

'Is there a potion I can take? A god I can offer to?'

'No, Pharaoh.' He paused, coughed delicately. 'Your moods, Majesty. Are you more nervous than you used to be? More likely to be irritated by small things?'

'Yes, Hapd'efan'e, but only because my life has been very difficult these past two years.'

'Perhaps' was all he said, prostrating himself; he backed from the room on hands and knees.

'A relief to know it isn't a true malignancy,' Cleopatra said to Iras and Charmian.

'Yes indeed, but if it grows it will disfigure you,' said Iras.

'Bite your tongue!' Charmian cried, rounding on Iras fiercely.

'It wasn't said thoughtlessly, you silly spinster! Too busy worrying about losing your looks and all hopes of a husband to see that the Queen must be prepared before anything happens, that's you!'

Charmian stood gobbling, unable to get her retaliation out, while Cleopatra laughed, the first sound of genuine amusement she had uttered since she arrived home.

'Come, come!' she said when she was able. 'You're thirty-four, not fourteen – and you're *both* spinsters.' A frown replaced the smile. 'I have taken your youth and your chances of marriage from you, I am well aware of it. Whom do you meet except eunuchs and old men, serving me?'

Charmian forgot the insult, started to chuckle. 'I hear that Caesarion had words to say about eunuchs.'

'How do you know?'

'How couldn't we know, more like? Apollodorus is shattered.'

'Oh, that wretched boy!'

TWENTY-ONE

King Artavasdes of Armenia stood no chance of defeating the huge force Antony led against him, but he didn't give in tamely; which provided Antony with several decent battles to blood his inexperienced men and bring his experienced men to peak fitness. Now that he wasn't drinking any wine at all, his ability to general a battle returned, and with it, his confidence. Sober and in the pink of health, he admitted to himself that his proper course the year before last had been to remain in Carana with the remnants of his army, bring Cleopatra's aid to them there; instead, he had inflicted another five-hundred-mile march upon them before they had any succor at all. Still, what was done was done. No point in dwelling upon the past, the reinvigorated Antony told himself.

Titius was governing Asia Province in place of Furnius and Plancus remained in Syria, but Ahenobarbus had come on campaign, and Canidius was, as always, Antony's trusty right hand. Safely inside Artaxata, his army camped in comfort, his own mood sanguine, he began to plan his move against the other Artavasdes. There was time to invade and conquer before winter; Armenia had crumbled and its King was a prisoner by the beginning of Julius.

Then, before he could start his march into Media Atropatene, Quintus Dellius arrived in Artaxata accompanied by an enormous caravan that incorporated King Artavasdes of Media Atropatene himself, his harem, children, furniture, an impressive number of treasures including a hundred gigantic Median horses, and all of Antony's lost artillery and engines of war.

Very pleased with himself, the moment he set eyes on Antony, Dellius produced a draft of the treaty he had concluded with Median King Artavasdes.

Antony looked nonplussed, anger visibly rising. 'Who gave you the right to negotiate anything in my name?' he demanded.

The faunlike face creased into lines of surprise, the fawnish eyes widened in astonishment. 'Why, you did! Marcus Antonius, you must remember! You agreed with Queen Cleopatra that the best way to deal with Media Atropatene was to bring its Artavasdes on to Rome's side. You did, you did, I *swear* it!'

Something in his attitude convinced Antony, bewildered now. 'I don't remember issuing any such order,' he muttered.

'You were still sick,' Dellius said, wiping the sweat from his brow. 'That must be it, because you did order it done.'

'Yes, I was sick, I remember that. What happened in Media?'

'I persuaded King Artavasdes that his only course was to co-operate with Rome. His relations with the King of the Parthians have deteriorated since Monaeses went to Ecbatana and told Phraates that the Medians had made off with the entire contents of your baggage train – Monaeses had expected to share the plunder. To make matters worse, Phraates is threatened by rivals who happen to have Median blood on the distaff side. It wasn't difficult for Median Artavasdes to see that you would conquer Armenia unless he came to its rescue. Which he couldn't do, given the situation in his own lands. So I talked and talked until I made him see that his best alternative was to ally his kingdom with Rome.'

Antony's anger died; the memories were coming back. That was worrying – worse, frightening. How many other decisions, orders and momentous conversations didn't he remember?

'Give me the details, Dellius.'

'Artavasdes came himself to reinforce his sincerity, complete with his women and children. If you consent, he wishes to offer his four-year-old daughter, Iotape, as a bride for your Egyptian son, Ptolemy Alexander Helios. Five other children, including a son by his principal wife, will be handed over as hostages. There are many gifts, from Median horses to gold bullion and the precious stones of his kingdom – lapis lazuli, turquoise, jasper, carnelian and rock crystal. All your artillery is there, your engines and materials of war, even the eighty-foot battering ram.'

'So all I've lost are two legions and their Eagles.' Antony kept his tone neutral.

'No, their Eagles are with us. It appears Artavasdes didn't send them to Ecbatana immediately, and by the time that he would have, Monaeses had turned Phraates against him.'

Mood lightening, Antony chuckled. '*That* won't please dear Octavianus! He's made much of my four lost Eagles in Rome.'

A meeting with Median Artavasdes cheered Antony greatly. With little fuss and no rancor, the terms of the treaty as drafted by Dellius were redrafted, ratified and signed with the seals of Rome and Media Atropatene. This occurred after Antony had closely inspected the gifts contained in fifty wagons – gold, precious stones, chests of Parthian gold coins, several chests of exquisite jewellery. But perhaps no gift thrilled Antony as much as the hundred massive horses, tall enough and strong enough to sustain the weight of a cataphract. The artillery and materials of war were divided, half to go to Carana later with Canidius, the other half to go to Syria. Canidius was to winter in Artaxata with one-third of the army before taking up quarters in Carana.

Antony sat down to write to Cleopatra in Alexandria.

I miss you very much, my little wife, and can't wait to see you. First, however, I go to Rome to hold my triumph. Oh, the booty! As much as Pompeius Magnus had after he beat Mithridates. These Eastern kingdoms are awash in gold and jewels, even if they contain no statues worthy of Phidias or any other Greek. A six-cubit-high *solid gold* statue of Anaitis is bound for Rome and the temple of Jupiter Optimus Maximus, and it is but a small part of the Armenian plunder.

You will be pleased to know that Dellius concluded the treaty you wanted so badly – yes, Rome and Media Atropatene are now allies. Armenian Artavasdes is my prisoner and will walk in my triumph. It is a long time since a triumphing general has displayed a genuinely royal, reigning monarch of such high status. All Rome will marvel.

It is now but fifteen days until the Kalends of Sextilis, and I am shortly beginning my return to Rome. As soon as my triumph is over, I will sail for Alexandria, winter seas or not. There are many arrangements to be made, including a big garrison in Artaxata. There, I will leave Canidius and one-third of my troops. The other two-thirds I will march back to Syria and put into camp around Antioch and Damascus. The Nineteenth Legion will sail with me to Rome to represent my army at my triumph, its spears and standards wreathed in laurels. Yes, I was hailed Imperator on the field at Naxuana.

I am very well, except a little perturbed by some odd lapses of memory. Do you know, I didn't remember sending Dellius to see Median Artavasdes? I must rely upon you to confirm other things when they are drawn to my attention.

I send you a thousand thousand kisses, my Queen, and yearn to hold your tiny sparrow of a body in my arms. Are you well? Is Caesarion well? And our own children? Write to me at Antioch. There will be time because I am sending this by courier at the gallop. I love you.

Having formed a very affectionate alliance with an Armenian woman, Publius Canidius wasn't sorry to winter there. The lady was related in some vague way to the royal family, spoke fluent Greek, was extremely well read, and, though not in the first blush of youth, was beautiful. His Roman wife was not of exalted rank, could hardly read, and offered no real companionship. Clymene therefore seemed to Canidius a gift from the Armenian gods he had conquered, someone special just for him.

Antony and his two-thirds of the army marched via Carana for Syria; Ahenobarbus accompanied them as far as the Syrian Gates of the Amanus, then struck off overland for his province, Bithynia. Only Dellius, Cinna, Scaurus and a grandson of the slain Crassus continued in his train to Antioch.

There Antony found a letter from Cleopatra.

What do you mean, Antonius, triumph in Rome? Are you mad? Have you forgotten *everything*? Let me refresh your memory, then.

You vowed to me that you would return from your Armenian campaign to me in Alexandria, together with the spoils. You vowed to me that you would display your spoils in Alexandria. Nothing was said about a triumph in Rome, though I suppose I cannot very well stop your doing that if you must. But you vowed that Alexandria would come before Rome, and that your spoils would be donated to me as Queen and Pharaoh. What do you owe Rome and Octavianus, tell me that? He works against you incessantly, and as for me – I am the Queen of Beasts, the enemy of Rome. Every day he says it, every day the Roman people grow more angry. I have done nothing to them, but to hear Octavianus, you would think me Medea and Medusa combined. And now you are returning to Rome and Octavia, there to smarm us to your wife's brother and donate your hard-won spoils to a nation that will use them to tear me down?

I truly think you must be mad, Antonius, to condone the insults perpetually thrown my way by Octavianus and Rome, to want to ingratiate yourself with Egypt's foes by triumphing amid a brood of Roman snakes. Are you a man of no honor, to abandon me, your loyalest ally, friend – *and wife*! – in favor of people who sneer at you as well as at me, who deride you as my puppet, who believe that I have clothed you in women's garb and strut before you clad in men's armor? They say you are Achilles in the harem of King Lykomedes, face painted and skirts flowing. Do you really want to display yourself in front of people who say such things behind your back?

You vowed that you would come to Alexandria, and I hold you to that vow, husband. The citizens of Alexandria and the people of Egypt have seen Antonius, yes, but not as my consort. I deserted my kingdom to go to you in Syria, bringing with me a whole fleet of comforts for your *Roman* soldiers. May I remind you that *I* paid for that mission of mercy?

Oh, Antonius, do not let me down! Do not scorn me as you have scorned so many women. You said you loved me, then you married me. Am I, Pharaoh and Queen, to be discarded?

Hands shaking, Antony dropped the letter as if it were red-hot, unbearably painful. The cacophany of noises outside, Antioch going about its business, drifted through the open shutters of his study windows. Horrified, stunned, he stared at the brilliant rectangle of light that filled one such aperture, suddenly chilled to the bone despite the Syrian summer heat.

Did I vow? *Did I?* Why would she say I had, if I did not? Oh, what has happened to my memory? Has my mind turned to a cheese from the Alps, riddled with holes? It feels so clear, and of late I know it has been clear. I am my old self again. Yes, these two lapses I know of thus far happened in Lueke Kome and Antioch while I was recovering from the effects of the wine. It is to that period, and that period alone, that my omissions date. What did I do, what did I say? What else did I vow?

He got to his feet and began to pace, conscious of a sinking gut, a helplessness that he could lay at no one's door save his own. In the joyous flush of his newfound confidence, the disappearance of depression and anger, he had seen with perfect clarity where his choices lay, how to go about regaining his prestige in Rome. Egypt? Alexandria? What were they, except foreign places ruled by a foreign queen? Yes, he loved her, loved her enough to have married her, but he was neither Egyptian nor Alexandrian. He was a Roman. Every fiber of his being was Roman. And, he had thought in Artaxata, he could still patch up his differences with Octavian. Ahenobarbus and Canidius both believed it was possible; indeed, Ahenobarbus scoffed at Cleopatra's tales of Octavian's bruited scandalmongering. If such were true, Ahenobarbus had asked, why were seven hundred of the thousand senators of Rome still loyal to Antony? Why did the plutocrats and knight-businessmen cleave so strongly to Antony? Admittedly his dispositions in the East had been slow in coming, but they were in place now, and of enormous benefit to Roman commerce. Money would begin to flow into the Treasury as well; the tributes were finally going to be paid. Thus Ahenobarbus, with Canidius nodding agreement.

Now, in Antioch, he had neither man to reassure him; just Dellius and a group of more junior men, grandsons and great-nephews of famous men long dead. And could he rely on Dellius? Nothing came to mind to say the chastised Dellius could not be relied upon, but he was always ruled by self-interest, and not ethical or moral when he had been mortally offended, as in the affair of Ventidius and Samosata. If only Plancus were here! But he had gone off to Asia Province on a visit to Titius. There was no one to appeal to save Dellius. At least, thought Antony, Dellius is aware that I did have one memory lapse. He may recollect others.

'Did I vow to take the spoils of my campaign to Alexandria?' he asked Dellius a few moments later.

Since Dellius had also had a letter from Cleopatra, he knew exactly what to say. 'Yes, Marcus Antonius, you did,' he lied.

'Then for Jupiter's sake, Dellius, why didn't you mention it in Artaxata, or on the road south?'

Dellius coughed apologetically. 'Until we reached the Amanus, I was not in your company. Gnaeus Ahenobarbus dislikes me.'

'And after the Amanus?'

'I confess it slipped my mind.'

'You too, eh?'

'It happens to us all.'

'So I did make that vow?'

'Yes.'

'To which gods did I swear?'

'Tellus, Sol Indiges and Liber Pater.'

Antony groaned. 'But how would Cleopatra know them?'

'I have no idea, Antonius, except that she was Caesar's wife for several years, speaks Latin like a Roman, and lived in Rome. Certainly she had ample opportunity to know which Roman gods are the ones a Roman swears by.'

'Then I am bound. Terribly bound.'

'I fear so, yes.'

'How am I going to tell the others?'

'Don't,' said Dellius strongly. 'Put the Nineteenth into a good camp at Damascus – the weather's wonderful there – and tell your legates that you're off to Rome via Alexandria. You miss your wife, and want to show her the booty.'

'That's postponement as well as a lie.'

'Believe me, Marcus Antonius, it's the only way. Once you reach Alexandria, there are a dozen reasons why you might not be able to celebrate your triumph in Rome – illness, military crises.'

'*Why* did I vow it?' Antony cried, fists clenched.

'Because Cleopatra asked it of you, and you were in no fit state to deny her.' There! thought Dellius, I can at least pay you back that much, you Egyptian harpy.

Antony sighed, slapped his hands on his knees. 'Well, if I am to go to Alexandria, I had best leave before Plancus comes back. He'd question me more closely than juniors like Cinna and Scaurus.'

'Overland?'

'With all that plunder? I have no choice. The Jerusalem legion can meet me and act as my escort.' Antony grinned savagely. 'I can call on Herod and find out exactly what's going on.'

Ten miles a day in September, with no relief from the Syrian sun until the end of October, perhaps later still; the miles-long train of wagons lumbered south from Antioch and, at the River Eleutherus, passed into territory now owned by Cleopatra. It was an eight-hundred-mile journey that took two and a half months, Antony doggedly riding or walking at the train's pace, but not in complete idleness; he made excursions to see all the potentates, including the Alexandrian officials Cleopatra had put in charge of her territories. In that way he made it seem to those who followed his odyssey in some puzzlement that he was using this journey as an excuse to check up on southern Syria. The ethnarchs of Sidon and Tyre aired their grievances now that they were fully surrounded by Egyptian possessions; Cleopatra had put tollgates on all the roads leading from these two great emporiums and taxed any goods going out of them by land.

King Malchus of Nabataea came all the way to Accho Ptolemais to complain bitterly about Cleopatra's enforcement of the bitumen fisheries Antony had awarded her.

'I don't care if the woman is your wife, Marcus Antonius,' said a seething Malchus, 'she is despicable! Having discovered for herself that the overheads make bitumen only slightly profitable, she has had the temerity to sell me back my fisheries for the sum of two hundred talents a year! Which *Herod* is deputed to collect! Oh, not for himself – on her behalf. Wicked, wicked!'

'What do you expect me to do about it?' Antony asked, aware that he could do nothing and loathing the fact.

'You're her husband – and Rome's Triumvir! Command her to give me back my fisheries free and clear! They have belonged to Nabataea for time immemorial.'

'Sorry, I can't help you,' said Antony. 'Rome is no longer sovereign over your bitumen fisheries.'

The other half of this situation, Herod, was summoned to see him in Joppa. The same fate had befallen Herod; he could have his balsam gardens back – for two hundred talents a year – but only if he also collected two hundred talents a year from King Malchus.

'It's disgusting!' he cried to Antony. 'Disgusting! The woman ought to be flogged! You're her husband – flog her!'

'Were you her husband, Herod, she'd certainly be flogged,' Antony said, consumed with admiration for Cleopatra's cunning in keeping enmity between Herod and Malchus on the boil. 'Romans do not flog their wives, I'm afraid. Nor can you complain to me. I ceded the balsam gardens of Jericho to Queen Cleopatra, so it's her you have to apply to, not me.'

'Women!' was Herod's infuriated response to that.

'Which leads me to things other than balsam,' said Antony in the voice of a Roman governor, 'though they do concern women. I understand that you appointed a Zadokite named Ananeel as the High Priest of the Jews as soon as you took the throne. But your mother-in-law, Queen Alexandra, wanted the position for her son, Aristobulus, aged sixteen. Not so?'

'Yes!' Herod hissed, at his most malignant. 'And just who happens to be Alexandra's dearest friend? Why, Cleopatra! The pair of them conspired against me, knowing that I am too new to my throne to do what I would love to do – murder that interfering old sow,

Alexandra! Oh, she was very quick to suck up to Cleopatra! A guarantee of continued life! But I ask you, a sixteen-year-old high priest? Ludicrous! Besides, he's Hasmonaean, not Zadokite. It was Alexandra's first move in her crafty game to take my throne back for Aristobulus.' Herod stretched out his hands. 'I mean, Marcus Antonius, I've bent over backwards to conciliate my wife's relatives!'

'But you did bow to your mother-in-law's wishes, as I heard.'

'Yes, yes, last year I made Aristobulus the high priest! Not that it did him or his mother any good.' Herod assumed the mien of an unjustly condemned prisoner. 'Alexandra and Cleopatra hatched a plot to make it seem as if Aristobulus was in danger of his life – what rubbish! He was to flee Jerusalem and Judaea for refuge in Egypt. Then, after a short stay there, he was to return with an army and usurp my throne – the throne *you* gave me!'

'I have heard something of it,' said Antony carefully.

'Well, so far be it from the truth, that young Aristobulus happily accepted my invitation to go on a picnic.' Herod sighed, looked sorrowful. 'The whole family came along, including Alexandra, her daughter my wife, our four little sons, my own beloved mother – a merry group, I assure you. We chose a beautiful spot where the river widens into a big pool, very deep in places but not perilous unless a bather is too adventurous. Aristobulus was too adventurous – he went swimming without being able to swim.' The beefy shoulders rose and fell. 'Need I say more? He must have stumbled into a hole, because all of a sudden only his head was above water and he was screaming for help. Several of the guards swam to his rescue, but it was too late. He had drowned.'

Antony considered the story, knowing he would be interrogated when he reached Cleopatra. Of course he knew very well that Herod had contrived at the 'accidental' death, but there was absolutely no proof of it, thank all the gods. Women, indeed! This journey south was revealing more and more facets of Cleopatra, not as a person but as a monarch. Greedy for expansion, greedy for dominion, crafty in sowing enmity between her enemies, not above befriending a widowed queen whose husband and sons had warred against Rome. And how cleverly she had worked on him, Antony, to achieve her ends.

'I fail to see how an accidental drowning could be your doing, Herod, especially if, as you say, it occurred under the eyes of the lad's mother as well as the whole family.'

'Cleopatra wanted me tried and executed, didn't she?'

'She was displeased, that's true. As well that you and I . . . er . . .

missed each other in Laodiceia. Had we met then, I might have reacted differently. As it is, I've found no evidence to suggest that any of this was your doing, Herod. Furthermore, the position of high priest is in your gift. You may appoint whomsoever you want. But may I ask that you don't make it a lifetime job?'

'Splendid!' said Herod, beaming. 'In fact, I'll go even farther than that. I'll keep the sacred regalia in my possession, and *lend* them to the high priest whenever Mosaic law requires him to wear them. They are said to be magic, therefore I don't want him able to go among the people all dressed up to stir up trouble for me. I swear to you, Antonius, that I will *not* yield my throne! When you see Cleopatra, tell her that.'

'You may take it from me that Rome will not approve of any Hasmonaean resurgence in Judaea,' Antony said. 'The Hasmonaean royal house has spelled nothing but trouble, ask anyone from the late Aulus Gabinius on down.'

The wagon train continued on its way, especially wearying for Antony after Gaza fell behind; from this point the road branched inland across sere country that made watering many hundreds of oxen a hideous business. That it could not stick to the coast was because of the Nilus Delta, a hundred-and-fifty-mile-wide fan of unnegotiable swamps and waterways that no road traversed. The only way to reach Alexandria was to go south to Memphis at the Delta's apex, then turn north along the Canopic branch of Nilus.

At the end of November, the journey was finally over: Antony entered the world's biggest city through the Sun Gate at the eastern terminus of Canopic Avenue, where a horde of twittering officials took charge of the wagons and led them off to paddocks by Lake Mareotis. Antony himself rode into the Royal Enclosure. The Jerusalem legion had already begun its march back to Judaea; Antony had to trust that fear of Cleopatra would keep stickied fingers out of the treasures that every wagon contained.

She hadn't come to greet him at the Sun Gate, a fact that no doubt meant she was annoyed. The only person who had more agents than Octavian was Cleopatra, Antony reflected as he reached the main palace. Clearly she knew about everything he had done.

'Apollodorus, you nutless old darling,' he said as the lord high chamberlain appeared. 'Where is Her cranky Majesty?'

'In her sitting room, Marcus Antonius. How good to see you!'

Antony tossed his cloak on the floor with a grin and went to beard the lioness in her den.

'What do you mean by subjecting my satraps to quizzes and dictates about their conduct in territories that are no longer of any interest to Rome?' she demanded.

'What a welcome,' he said, flinging himself into a chair. 'I obey my orders – I uphold my vow – by bringing my booty to you in Alexandria, and all I get for my pains is a nasty question. I warn you, Cleopatra, that you can go too far. For eight hundred miles I've had to witness your machinations, your domination of peoples who are not Egyptian – you execute, you imprison, you put up tollgates to collect taxes to which you are not entitled, you set kings against each other, you sow discord. Isn't it time you remembered that you need me more than I need you?'

Her face froze, a flash of terror streaked through her eyes; for a long moment she said nothing while she battled to put some expression on her face that would conciliate him.

'I'm sober,' he said before she could find speech, 'and Marcus Antonius fit and well is not the cringing minion he becomes when the wine has conquered his ability to think. No wine has passed my lips since I last saw you. I have waged a successful war against a cunning foe. I have regained my confidence in myself. And I have found many reasons why, as Triumvir of the East and Rome's highest representative in the East, I must deplore Egypt's actions in the East. You have interfered in the activities of Roman possessions, of client-kings in Rome's service. Swaggering like a miniature Zeus, parading your might as if you had an army of a quarter of a million men and the genius of Gaius Julius Caesar at his peak.' He drew a breath, eyes gleaming red and angry. 'Whereas the truth is that, without me, you are nothing. You have no army. You are not a genius. In fact, I can see very little difference between you and Herod of Judaea. Both of you are feral, greedy and rat-cunning. But right at this moment, Cleopatra, I have more liking and respect for Herod than I do for you. At least Herod is an unashamed savage who wears no fancy disguises. While you trick yourself out as a seductress one day, as a goddess of succor the next day, as a tyrant, as a glutton, as a thief, and then – lo! – you revert to some softer guise. It stops here and it stops *now*, do you hear me?'

She had found the right expression: woe. Silent tears rolled down her face, her beautiful little hands wrenched at each other.

He laughed; it sounded genuine. 'Oh, really, Cleopatra! Can you do no better than tears? I've had four wives before you, so I'm no stranger to tears. A woman's most effective weapon, she's brought up to believe. Well, on Marcus Antonius they have no more power than water dripping on granite – any impression they make takes thousands of years, and that's more time than even goddesses on earth are given. I am serving you notice that you will return the balsam gardens to Herod free and clear, and the bitumen to Malchus, free and clear. You will shut up your tollgates outside Tyre and Sidon, and your administrators in the territories I *sold* you will cease enforcing Egyptian law. They have been told that they have no right to execute or imprison unless a Roman prefect adjudicates. Like all the other client-kings, you will pay Rome tribute, and you will confine your future activities to Egypt proper. Is that understood, madam?'

She had ceased weeping, was angry now. Yet she couldn't show that anger to this Mark Antony.

'What, trying to work out how you can persuade me to have a beaker of wine?' he mocked, feeling as if he could conquer the world now he had found the courage to stand up to Cleopatra. 'Persuade all you like, my dear. You won't succeed. Like the crew of Ulysses, my ears are stoppered up so I can't hear your siren song. Nor, if you fancy the role of Circe, will you turn me once again into a pig swilling in the liquid sty of your making.'

'I am glad to see you,' she whispered, rage evaporated. 'I love you, Antonius. I love you very much. And you're right, I have exceeded my mandate. It shall all be done as you wish, I solemnly vow it.'

'By Tellus, Sol Indiges and Liber Pater?'

'No, by Isis mourning for her dead Osiris.'

He held out his arms. 'Then come kiss me.'

She did rise to obey, but before she could reach Antony's chair, Caesarion erupted through the door.

'Marcus Antonius!' the lad cried, going to embrace him as he got up. 'Oh, Marcus Antonius, this is terrific! No one told me you'd come until I met Apollodorus in the hall.'

Antony held Caesarion off and stared, astonished. 'Jupiter, you could be Caesar!' he said, kissing both Caesarion's cheeks. 'You've turned into a man.'

'I'm glad *someone* can see that. My mother refuses to.'

'Well, mothers hate to see their sons grow up. You just have to forgive them, Caesarion. You're well, I can see that. Ruling more these days?'

'A little more, yes. I'm working on the logistics of a free grain dole for Alexandria's poor.'

'Excellent! Show me.'

And off they went together, almost of a height, Caesarion had grown in stature so much. He would never be a Hercules like Antony, but he was going to be taller, the deserted Cleopatra thought as they disappeared.

Her mind in turmoil, she went to gaze out of a window that faced the sea – Their Sea, and likely to remain Their Sea if her husband had anything to do with it. She had moved too quickly, she could see that now; but she had assumed that Antony would go back to the wine flagon. Instead, he showed no sign of lapsing. Had he not witnessed her actions in southern Syria, he might have been easier to cozen; rather, those actions had infuriated him, stimulated his man's desire to be the dominant half in a marriage. That slimy grub, Herod! What had he said to Antony to rouse him? And Malchus, and the twin cities of Phoenicia? The reports her agents had sent were not accurate, for none had mentioned Antony's commands about her own possessions, nor had any been privy to his talks with Malchus, Herod, Sidon or Tyre.

Oh, how right he was! Without him, she was nothing. No army, no genius as soldier or ruler. Now, more than ever in the past, she understood that her first – perhaps her only – task was to woo Antony away from his allegiance to Rome. All sprang from that.

I am not, she thought, beginning to pace, a monster in any of the guises he says I assume. I am a monarch whom destiny has put in a position of potential power at a moment in time when I can strike for complete autonomy, regain Egypt's lost territories, be a great figure on the world's stage. My ambitions are not even for myself! They are entirely for my son. Caesar's son. Heir to more than Caesar's name, immortalized already in his title, Ptolemy XV *Caesar*, Pharaoh and King. He must fulfill his promise, but it is too soon! For ten more years I must struggle to protect him and his destiny – I have no time to waste loving other people, people like Marcus Antonius. He senses it; these long months apart have struck off the shackles I forged to keep him chained to my side. What to do? What to do?

By the time that Antony rejoined her, jovial, loving, eager for bed, she had resolved on her course of action. Which was to talk Antony around, make him see that Octavian would never let him become undisputed First Man in Rome, therefore what use in continuing to cleave to Rome? She had to convince him – sober, possessed of his self-control – that the only way he could ever rule Rome alone was to go to war against Octavian the obstacle.

Her first step was to arrange for Antony to parade through Alexandria in as similar a way to a Roman triumph as she dared. That was easier because the only Roman of companion status he had brought with him was Quintus Dellius, under orders from her to deflect Antony's analytical powers away from the form of a Roman triumph. After all, he had no legions with him, not even a cohort of Roman troops. There would be no pageant floats, she decided, just huge flat-bedded wagons behind garlanded oxen that bore carefully designed scaffolds and frames on which to display this or that looted treasure. Nor would he ride in anything remotely resembling the antique four-wheeled chariot of a Roman triumphator; he would wear pharaonic armor and helmet and drive himself in a pharaonic two-wheeled chariot. Nor would there be a slave holding a laurel wreath over his head to whisper in his ear that he was but a mortal man. In fact, laurels had no place at all; she pleaded that Egypt had no true laurel trees. Her worst battle was to convince Antony that King Artavasdes of Armenia must be put in golden chains and led behind a donkey as a prisoner; in a Roman triumph the prisoners of high enough status to be part of the parade were decked out in all their royal finery and walked as if free men. Antony consented to the chains, thinking it removed any hint of a Roman triumph.

What he didn't count on was Quintus Dellius, whom Cleopatra had instructed to write a specific note to Poplicola in Rome.

What a scandal, Lucius! At last the Queen of Beasts has prevailed. Marcus Antonius has triumphed in Alexandria rather than in Rome. Oh, there were differences, but none to write home about. Instead, I am compelled to write home full of the similarities. Though he says the plunder is greater than Pompeius Magnus took from Mithridates, the truth is that, while it is indeed great, it is not *that* great. Even so, it belongs to Rome, not to Antonius. Who, at the end of his parade down Alexandria's wide streets to deafening cheers from thousands upon thousands of throats, entered the temple of Serapis and dedicated the spoils to – Serapis! Yes, they will remain in Alexandria, the property of its queen and boy king. By the way, Poplicola, Caesarion is the image of Caesar Divus Julius, so I hate to think what might happen to Octavianus were he ever to be seen in Italia, let alone Rome.

There were many evidences of the hand of the Queen of Beasts throughout. King Artavasdes of Armenia was led in chains, can you imagine it? Then, when the parade was ended, he was imprisoned rather than strangled. Not Roman custom at all. Antonius said not one word about the chains or the spared life. He is her dupe, Poplicola, her slave. All I can think is that she drugs him, that her priests concoct potions you and I, simple Romans, cannot even comprehend.

I leave it to you to decide how much of all this should be disseminated – Octavianus would make much of it, I fear to the point of declaring war on his fellow Triumvir.

There! thought Dellius, laying down his reed pen. That ought to prick Poplicola into tattling at least some of it – enough at any rate to filter as far as Octavianus. It gives him munitions, yet it exonerates Antonius. If war is what she wants, then war will eventually come. But it should be a war that, once Antonius wins it, will allow him to retain his Roman position and have no trouble in establishing sole rule. As for the Queen of Egypt, she will fade into obscurity. I know that Antonius is far from her slave; he still owns himself.

Dellius didn't have the intelligence to sniff out the most secret of Cleopatra's ambitions, nor to scent the depth of Octavian's subtlety. A paid servant of the Double Crown, he did as he was told without question.

Before he could find a messenger and a ship to send his short missive to Rome and Poplicola, he was writing a long postscript:

Oh, Poplicola, it goes from bad to worse! Utterly deluded, Antonius has just participated in a ceremony in the Alexandrian gymnasium, bigger since the city was rebuilt than the agora, and so the site of all public meetings. A huge podium was constructed inside the gymnasium, with five thrones upon its tiers. On top, one throne. Next step down, one throne. Step lower than that, three baby thrones. On the highest Caesarion sat, dressed in full pharaonic regalia. I have seen it often, but will briefly describe it for you: a red-and-white, two-part thing on the head, very big and heavy – the Double Crown, it is called. Pleated white linen dress, broad collar of gems and gold around the neck and shoulders, a wide, gem-studded gold belt, many bracelets, armlets, anklets, rings for fingers and toes. Hennaed palms, hennaed soles of the feet. Amazing. Female Pharaoh, Cleopatra, sat on the next step down. Same regalia, except that her dress was made of cloth of gold. On the step below her sat the three children she has borne Antonius. Ptolemy Alexander Helios was fitted out in the garb of a king of Parthia – tiara, rings of gold around the neck, frilly, jeweled blouse and skirt. His sister, Cleopatra Selene, was in something halfway between pharaonic and Greek; she sat in the middle. And on her other side sat a little boy not yet three, tricked out like a king of Macedonia – a wide-brimmed purple hat with the diadem tied around its crown, purple chlamys, purple tunic, purple boots.

The crowd was huge, overflowing the gymnasium, said to hold a hundred thousand – though, being familiar with the Circus Maximus, I doubt it. They had rigged up bleachers, but these were interrupted by athletic stuff. Cleopatra and her four children stood at the bottom of the dais at first, while none other than Marcus Antonius rode in on a magnificent Median horse, a dappled grey with black muzzle, mane and tail. Its tack was dyed *purple* leather, bossed and fringed in gold. He slid off the horse and walked to the dais. He was wearing a purple tunic and purple cloak, but at least his golden armor was Roman in style. I add that I, his legate, was seated close by, with a good view of proceedings. Antonius took Caesarion by the hand and led him up the steps of the dais to the top throne, and seated him. The crowd cheered loudly. Once the boy was in place, Antonius kissed him on both cheeks, then stood and roared out that by the authority of Rome, he proclaimed Caesarion King of Kings, ruler of the world. The crowd went wild. Then he took Cleopatra to her lower throne and seated her. She was proclaimed Queen of Kings, ruler of Egypt, Syria, the islands of the Aegean, Crete, Rhodes, all Cilicia and Cappadocia. Alexander Helios (his tiny fiancée was perched on the step alongside him) was proclaimed King of the East – everything east of the Euphrates, and everything south of Caucasus. Cleopatra Selene was proclaimed Queen of Cyrenaica and Cyprus, and little Ptolemy Philadelphus was proclaimed King of Macedonia, Greece, Thrace, and the lands around the Euxine Sea. Did I say Epirus? He got that too.

Throughout all this Antonius was as solemn as if he truly believed in what he was doing, though later he told me that he did it simply to shut down Cleopatra's nagging. The fact that as a goodly number of the lands mentioned belong to Rome, it boggled imagination to witness these five people pronounced sovereign over places they do not – and cannot – rule.

Oh, but the Alexandrians thought it was wonderful! I have rarely heard such cheers. After the crowning ceremony was over, the five monarchs climbed down from the dais and mounted a kind of wagon, just a flat-bed with five thrones atop it. I add that Egypt must be swimming in gold, because the ten thrones used were all of solid gold, studded with so many gems that they flashed and glittered more than a Roman whore in glass beads. This wagon, drawn by ten white Median horses – a load light enough that they didn't strangle – was paraded right down Royal Avenue, then right down Canopic Avenue, and ended its journey at the Serapeum, where the chief priest, a man named Cha'em, conducted some religious ritual. The people were feasted on ten thousand huge tables just groaning with food – something that had never been done before, I understand, and done at Antonius's request. It was an even wilder bun fight than a Roman public feast.

The two events – Antonius's 'triumph' and the donation of the world to Cleopatra and her children – have left me winded, Poplicola. I have nicknamed the latter the Donations. Poor Antonius! He's caught fast in that woman's toils, I swear it.

Again I leave it to you how much of this you disseminate, but of course Octavianus will have his own spies' reports, so I don't think you can conceal the matter for long. If you are aware what's afoot, you may have a fighting chance.

The letter went off to Rome; Dellius settled down in his delightful little palace inside the Royal Enclosure to spend the winter with Antony, his wife and family.

Antony and Caesarion were great friends, and elected to do everything together, be it crocodile- or hippo-hunting on Nilus, war exercises or chariot racing in the hippodrome, or swimming in the sea. Try though Cleopatra did, she couldn't trick Antony into guzzling wine; he refused to take so much as a sip of it, saying frankly that, once he tasted it, he would be lost. That he didn't trust her, was aware of her intentions, was manifest in the way he sniffed at the contents of his goblet to make sure it held water.

Caesarion noticed all of it, and grieved. Alone among them, he saw both sides. His mother, he knew, did everything to further not her own ends, but his, Caesarion's, while Antony, very much in love with her, strenuously resisted her attempts to turn him away from Rome. The trouble was, the youth reflected, that he wasn't sure he wanted what his mother wanted for him; he had no sense of destiny, for all that his father had, and his mother too. Thus far, his experience of his world told him that there was so much work to do in Alexandria and Egypt alone that he would never live to finish it, were he to live a hundred years. In a curious way he was more like Octavian than Caesar, for he yearned to have what he did perfect down to the finest detail, and shrank from the idea of taking additional burdens on his shoulders that would inevitably make it impossible for anything to be done properly. His mother didn't own this reluctance – how could she? Born and reared in a nest of vipers like Ptolemy Auletes, her idea of sovereignty was to leave the fiddling work of daily administration to others, and those others were as likely to be successful sycophants as truly talented.

He knew well what his mother's limitations were. He also knew why she was attempting to strip Antony of his Romanness, his independence and his judgement. Nothing else than world dominion would satisfy her, and she saw Rome as her enemy. Rightly so; a power as entrenched as Rome would not yield to her without war. Oh, if only he were older! Then he could face Cleopatra as her genuine equal, and inform her adamantly that what she wanted for him was not what he wanted. As it was, he had so far said nothing to her about his own sentiments, understanding that she would dismiss his opinions as those of a boy. But he wasn't a boy, he had never really been a boy! Owning his father's precocious intelligence and a kingly position from early childhood, he had lapped at knowledge like a starving dog at a pool of blood, not for any reason other than that he loved to learn. Every fact was taken in, stored for immediate recollection as needed, and, when sufficient knowledge on a subject had been assimilated, to analyze. But he was not enamored of power, and didn't know whether that was true of his father as well. Sometimes he suspected that it was; Caesar had risen to Olympian heights because not to rise would have seen him exiled and stripped of all mention in Rome's annals. Not a fate Caesar could tolerate. But he hadn't tried very hard to live, somehow Caesarion knew that. My *tata*, whom I remember as a toddling child so vividly that his face, his tall, strong body leap to the inside of my eyes this very moment. My *tata*, whom I miss desperately. Antonius is a marvelous man, but Caesar he is not. I need my *tata* here to advise me, and that cannot be.

Emboldened, he sought out Cleopatra and tried to tell her how he felt, but it fell out as he had expected. She laughed at him, pinched his cheek, kissed him lovingly, and told him to run away and do the things boys of his age should. Hurt, isolated, with no one he felt he could turn to, he moved farther from his mother mentally and began not to come to dinner. That he might have gone to Antony never occurred to him; he saw Antony as Cleopatra's quarry, didn't think that Antony's response would be any different from hers. The dinner omissions became more numerous in exact proportion to Cleopatra's increasingly remorseless browbeating of her husband, whom she treated, Caesarion thought, more like a son than a partner in her enterprises.

There were, however, enjoyable days, sometimes longer periods; in January the Queen took *Philopator* out of the shed and sailed down Nilus to the First Cataract, even though it was not the right season to inspect the Nilometer. For Caesarion, a wonderful trip. He had made the journey before, but when he was younger; now he was fully old enough to appreciate every nuance of the experience, from his own godhead to the simplicity of life along the mighty river. The facts were stored away; later, when he was Pharaoh in truth, he would give these people a better life. At his insistence they stopped in Coptus, and took the overland caravan route to Myos Hormus on the Sinus Arabicus; he had wanted to take the longer path to Berenice, far down the Sinus, but that Cleopatra refused to do. From Myos Hormus and Berenice the Egyptian fleets set out for India and Taprobane, here they returned bearing their cargoes of spices, peppercorns, ocean pearls, sapphires and rubies. Here too the Horn of Africa fleets were harbored; they carried ivory, cassia, myrrh and incense from the African coast around the Horn. Special fleets brought home gold and jewels sent overland to the Sinus from Aithiopai and Nubia; the country was too rugged and Nilus too convulsed by cataracts and rapids to use the river.

On their return journey, sailing now on the current, they paused at Memphis, entered the precinct of Ptah, and were shown the treasure tunnels that branched out a long way toward the pyramid fields. Neither Caesarion nor Antony had seen them, but Cha'em, their guide, was careful not to let Antony see where and how the entrance was accessed; he was led blindfold, and thought it a great joke until, his eyes freed, he beheld the wealth of Egypt. For Caesarion it was an even bigger shock; he hadn't begun to grasp how much there was, and spent the rest of the long journey marveling at his mother's parsimoniousness. She could afford to feed all of Alexandria to the point of gluttony, and yet she grumbled at his pathetic little free grain dole!

'I do not understand her,' he muttered to Antony as *Philopator* sailed into the Royal Harbor.

A remark that sent Antony into fits of laughter.

TWENTY-TWO

The conquest of Illyricum was to take three years, but the first of them, that same year Antony was supposed to have been senior consul, was the hardest, simply because it took a year to understand how to go about the business handily. As with any enterprise of Octavian's, it was meticulously planned insofar as any military venture could be. Governor of Italian Gaul for the duration of the Illyrian campaign, Gaius Antistius Vetus was to deal with the restless tribes living in the Vale of the Salassi on the northwestern frontier; though many hundreds of miles away from Illyricum, Octavian wanted no part of Italian Gaul at the mercy of barbarian tribes, and the Salassi were still a nuisance.

The actual Illyrian campaign was divided into three separate theaters: one on the sea, two on the land.

Back in favor, Menodorus was given command of the Adriatic fleets; his job was to scour the islands off Istria and Dalmatia and sweep the Liburnian pirates from the sea. Statilius Taurus was given command of the group of legates who drove east from Aquileia over the pass of Mount Ocra toward the town of Emona and, eventually, the headwaters of the Savus River. Here dwelled the Taurisci and their allies, who perpetually raided Aquileia and Tergeste. Agrippa was to strike southwest from Tergeste into the lands of the Delmatae and the town of Senia; from that point, Octavian would assume the command himself, turn east, cross the mountains and descend upon the Colapis River. Once on the river, he would march to Siscia, at the confluence of the Colapis and the Savus. This was the wildest, least-known country.

The propaganda commenced well in advance of the campaign, for Illyricum's subjugation was a part of Octavian's scheme to make it plain to the people of Italia and Rome that he, and he alone, cared about their safety as much as he cared about their welfare. Once Italian Gaul was freed from all outside threat, the entire alp-fringed Italian haunch would be as safe as the leg.

Leaving Maecenas to govern Rome under the indifferent eye of the consuls, Octavian sailed from Ancona to Tergeste, and thence rode overland to join Agrippa's legions as their nominal commander-in-chief. Illyricum came as a shock; used though he was to thick forests, these were, he sensed, more akin to the leafy wastelands of the German forests than anything Italia or other civilized places could produce. Wet, gloomy, dense beyond imagination, the gigantic trees stretched on forever, the rugged ground beneath their canopy so stripped of light that only ferns and fungi grew there. The people, Iapudes now, hunted deer, bear, wolf, aurochs and wildcat – some for food, some to safeguard their pathetic villages. Only in a few clearings did they break the soil to grow millet and spelt, the source of pallid bread. The women kept a few chickens, but the diet was monotonous and not particularly nourishing. Trade, which flowed through the sole emporium, Nauportus, consisted in bearskins, fur and gold panned from rivers like the Corcoras and the Colapis.

He found Agrippa at Avendo, which had surrendered at sight of the legions and so much formidable siege equipment.

Avendo was to be their last peaceful submission; as the legions began to cross the Capella Ranges, the forests proved to contain an undergrowth of shrubs and bushes too dense to penetrate without physically hacking a path.

'No wonder,' said Octavian to Agrippa, 'that countries much farther away from Italia than Illyricum have been pacified while Illyricum remains unconquered. I think even my divine father would have blanched at this terrible place.' He shuddered. 'We are also marching – if I may use that word ironically – at some risk of attack. The undergrowth makes it impossible to recognize the site of an ambush ahead of us.'

'True,' said Agrippa, waiting to see what Caesar suggested.

'Would it help if we sent some cohorts up on to the ridges on either side of our progress? They might have a chance of spotting raiders crossing a clearing.'

'Good tactics, Caesar,' Agrippa said, pleased.

Octavian grinned. 'Didn't think I had it in me, did you?'

'I never underestimate you, Caesar. Too full of surprises.'

The advance cohorts on the ridges foiled several ambushes; Terpo fell, Metulum lay ahead. This was the biggest settlement in the

406

area, with a well-fortified wooden stronghold atop a two-hundred-foot crag. Its gates were shut, its inhabitants defiant.

'Think you can take it?' Agrippa asked Octavian.

'I don't know, whereas I do know you can.'

'No, because I won't be here. Taurus is in a dilemma – is he to keep going east, or turn north toward Pannonia?'

'As Rome needs both east and north pacified, Agrippa, you'd better go and make up his mind for him. But I will miss you!'

Octavian surveyed Metulum carefully, and decided that his best line of attack was to build a mound from the valley floor all the way up to the log walls two hundred feet above. The legionaries dug away cheerfully, piled up the rock-larded earth to the specified height. But the Metulans, who had captured siege engines and apparatus from Aulus Gabinius years before, promptly used their excellent Roman spades and shovels to undermine the mound; riddled with tunnels, it fell apart. Octavian re-erected it, but not flat against Metulum's cliffs. Now it reared free, shored up on every side by stout planks. A second mound was raised alongside it. Able to turn their hands to anything, legionary artificers began constructing a wooden framework between the fortress cliffs and the two Roman mounds; when the scaffolding reached the height of the walls, it would carry two planked bridges from each mound to those walls. Each of the four gangways was wide enough to allow eight soldiers abreast, which would lend the assault great and immediate manpower.

Agrippa came back just in time to witness the attack upon Metulum's walls, and toured the siegeworks thoughtfully.

'Avaricum on a tiny scale, and flimsier by far,' he said.

Octavian looked devastated. 'I did it wrongly? It isn't what is needed? Oh, Marcus, let us not waste lives! If it isn't right, tear it down, please! You'll think of a better way.'

'No, no, it's fine,' Agrippa soothed. 'Avaricum was a city with *murus Gallicus* walls, and Caesar's log platform took a month to build, even for him. This will suffice for Metulum.'

For Octavian, much depended upon this Illyrian campaign, even above and beyond its political importance. Eight years had passed since Philippi, yet still people sneered that he was a coward, too afraid to face enemy troops. The asthma had finally disappeared, and he thought its recurrence unlikely in surroundings like these, wet and wooded. He believed that marriage to Livia Drusilla had cured him, for he remembered that his divine father's Egyptian physician, Hapd'efan'e, had said a happy domestic life was the best recipe for a cure.

Here in Illyricum he had to forge a new reputation – as a brave *soldier*. Not as a general, but as one who fought in the front lines with sword and shield, the same way his divine father had on many occasions. Somewhere he had to find an opportunity to be a front-line soldier, but so far he hadn't succeeded. The deed had to be spontaneous and dramatic, visible to those who fought around him – something truly remarkable, worthy of being recounted from legion to legion. Did that happen, he would be free of the canard of Philippi. Display battle scars for all to see.

His chance came when the attack on Metulum got under way at dawn on the day following Agrippa's return. Desperate to be rid of the Roman presence, the Metulans, undetected, had mined a way out of their citadel and emerged at the base of the scaffolding in the middle of the night. They sawed through the main support beams, but not completely; it was the weight of the legionaries, massing on the gangways, that caused the collapse.

Three of the four bridges broke and fell, soldiers plummeting to the valley floor in their dozens. By happy chance, Octavian was close to the remaining bridge. When his troops faltered and began to retreat, he seized a shield, drew his sword and ran to their front rank, halfway across.

'Come on, boys!' he shouted. 'Caesar's here, you can do it!'

The sight of him worked wonders; cheering, shrieking their war cry to Mars Invictus, the troops rallied and, with Octavian at their head, pounded along the gangway. They almost made it. Right under the wall the bridge gave way with a crackling roar; Octavian and the soldiers directly behind him fell into the valley.

I cannot die! a part of Octavian's mind kept repeating, but it was a cool mind still. As he tumbled off the structure he grabbed for the end of a shattered strut, held it for long enough to spot another below him, and so went down the two hundred feet in stages. His arm felt wrenched out of its socket, his hands and forearms were porcupined with splinters, and somewhere his right knee took a frightful blow, but when he wound up on the mossy ground buried under timber, he was still very much alive.

Frantic men tore the heap apart, screaming to their horrified companions that Caesar was injured but not dead. As they dragged him out, handling the right leg as gently as they could, Agrippa arrived, white-faced.

Octavian gazed up at the ring of faces around him, consumed with pain, determined not to be a sissy and show it.

'What's this?' he demanded. 'What are you doing here, Agrippa? Build more bridges and take this wretched little fortress!'

No stranger to Octavian's nightmares about cowardice, Agrippa grinned. 'Typical!' he roared in a stentorian voice. 'Caesar's badly wounded, but our orders are to take Metulum! Come on, boys, let's start again!'

The battle was over as far as Octavian was concerned; he was put on a stretcher and carried to the surgeon's tent to find it jammed with casualties, so many that they spilled out of it to lie everywhere around it. Some were appallingly still, others groaned, howled, cried out. When his stretcher-bearers would have pushed all the wounded aside to get Caesar immediate attention, Octavian stopped them.

'No!' he gasped. 'Put me down in turn! I will wait until the medics consider my wound the next to be treated.'

And from that they could not budge him.

Someone bound the knee tightly to staunch the bleeding, then he lay and took his turn, the soldiers trying to touch him for good luck, those with the strength crawling to take his hand.

Which didn't mean that when his turn came he was palmed off with an assistant surgeon. The chief surgeon, Publius Cornelius, attended to his knee in person, while an underling began to pluck the splinters from his hands and forearms.

When the packing bandage was removed, Cornelius grunted. 'A bad wound, Caesar,' he said, probing delicately. 'You've broken the kneecap, which has splintered in places and come through the skin. Luckily none of the main blood tubes has been torn, but there is a lot of slow bleeding. I'm going to have to pick out the fragments – a painful business.'

'Pick away, Cornelius,' Octavian said with a grin, aware that every other occupant of the huge tent was watching, listening. 'If I yell, sit on me.'

From where he got the fortitude to endure the next hour, he didn't know; as Cornelius worked on the knee he kept himself occupied in talking to the other wounded, joking with them, making nothing of his own plight. In fact, were it not for the agony, the entire experience was fascinating. How many commanders ever come into the surgeon's tent to see for themselves what war can do? he wondered. What I have seen today is yet one more reason why, when I am undisputed First Man in Rome, I will pile Pelion on top of Ossa to avoid war for the sake of war, war in order to secure a triumph after a governorship is over. My legions will garrison, not invade. They will only fight when there is no other alternative. These men are brave beyond imagining, and do not deserve to suffer needlessly. My plan to take Metulum was a poor one, I did not count upon the enemy's having sufficient intelligence to do what they did. And that makes me a fool. But a lucky fool. Because I have been badly wounded as a consequence of my bungle, the soldiers will not hold my bungle against me.

'You'll have to call it a day and return to Rome,' Agrippa said after Metulum capitulated.

The gangways had been rebuilt upon a stouter framework and guards posted to make sure no Metulan miners repeated their work; the very fact that Caesar had been severely wounded spurred the men to get inside Metulum. Which burned to the ground after some of its inhabitants panicked. No spoils, no captives to be sold into slavery.

'I fear you're right,' Octavian managed; the pain was worse than immediately after his injury. He plucked at his blankets, eyes sunk in their orbits. 'You'll have to carry on without me, Agrippa.' He laughed wryly. 'No impediment to success, I know! In fact, you'll do better.'

'Don't blame yourself, Caesar, please.' Agrippa frowned. 'Cornelius tells me that the knee looks inflamed, and asked me to persuade you to take some syrup of poppies to ease your pain.'

'When I am out of the district, perhaps, but until then I cannot. Syrup of poppies isn't available for a humble legionary, and some of them are in more agony than I am.' Octavian grimaced, shifted on his camp bed. 'If I am to scotch Philippi, I must keep up appearances.'

'As long as that means you survive, Caesar.'

'Oh, I will survive!'

It took five *nundinae* to transport a litter-bound Octavian to Tergeste, and another three to get him to Rome via Ancona. An infection set in that saw him traverse the Apennines in delirium, but the assistant surgeon who had traveled with him lanced the abscess that had formed, and by the time he was carried into his own house, he was feeling better.

Livia Drusilla covered him in tears and kisses, then told him that she would sleep elsewhere until he was fully out of danger.

'No,' he said strongly, 'no! All that has sustained me is the thought of lying next to you in our own bed.'

As delighted as she was worried, Livia Drusilla consented to share his bed provided that a curved cane roof was placed over the injured knee.

'Caecilius Antiphanes will know how to cure it,' she said.

'I shit on Caecilius Antiphanes!' Octavian growled, looking fierce. 'If I have learned nothing else on this campaign, my dear, I have learned that our army surgeons are infinitely more capable than every Greek physician in Rome. Publius Cornelius donated me the services of Gaius Licinius, and Gaius Licinius will continue to doctor me, is that clear?'

'Yes, Caesar.'

Whether because of Gaius Licinius's ministrations or because Octavian, at twenty-nine, was far healthier than he had been at twenty, once installed in his own bed with Livia Drusilla beside him, he mended rapidly. When first he ventured out and down to the Forum Romanum, he hobbled between two sticks, but two *nundinae* later he was getting along deedily on one stick, quickly discarded.

People cheered him; no one, even the staunchest of Antony's senators, spoke of Philippi again. The knee (a handy place to bear a nasty wound, he discovered) could be bared for inspection, tutted and exclaimed over now that bandages were unnecessary. Even the scars on his hands and forearms were impressive, as some of the splinters had been huge. His heroism was manifest.

Hard on the heels of his recovery came news that there had been trouble at Siscia, which Agrippa had reached and taken. He had left Fufius Geminus in command of a garrison, but the Iapudes attacked in force. Octavian and Agrippa set out to relieve it, only to find that Fufius Geminus had managed to contain the uprising without them.

Thus on New Year's Day the ceremonies could go ahead as planned; Octavian was to be senior consul, and Agrippa, though a consular, took on the duties of curule aedile.

In some ways this was to be the year of Agrippa's greatest glory, for he commenced a massive overhaul of Rome's water supply and sewerage. The Aqua Marcia's reconstruction was finished, and the Aqua Julia brought on line to augment water to the Quirinal and Viminal, until now largely reliant upon springs. Wonderful, yes, but insignificant compared to what Agrippa undertook in Rome's mighty sewers. Three underground streams had made this system of arched tunnels feasible; there were three outlets, one just below the Trigarium of the Tiber, at which point the river was clean and pure for swimming, one at the Port of Rome, and one, the most mammoth, where the Cloaca Maxima flowed out just to one side of the Wooden Bridge. Here the aperture (it had once been the outflow of the River Spinon) was big enough to permit entry into the Cloaca Maxima in a rowboat. All Rome marveled at the journeys Agrippa took in his rowboat, mapping the system, taking note of whereabouts the walls needed shoring up or repairing. There would be, promised Agrippa, no more backing up of the sewers when Father Tiber flooded. What was more, said that amazing man, he did not intend to relinquish supervision of sewers and water supply after he stepped down from office; as long as he lived, Marcus Agrippa would be hunched like a black dog outside the premises of the water companies and the drainage companies, which for far too long had tyrannized over Rome. Only Octavian managed to be half as popular among the people. Having cowed the water and sewerage companies, Agrippa then banished all magicians, prophets, soothsayers and medical quacks from Rome. He dusted off the sets of standard weights and measures and compelled all vendors of everything to abide by them, then went to work upon the building contractors. For a while he tried to keep the height of all insulae apartments to a hundred feet, but this, as he soon learned, was a task beyond even Marcus Agrippa. What he could do – and did – was to make sure that the adjutages leading off water pipes were of the proper size; no more lavish water for smart apartments on the Palatine and Carinae!

'What staggers me,' said Livia Drusilla to her husband, 'is how Agrippa manages all of this, yet can still campaign in Illyricum! Until this year, I had thought you were Rome's most indefatigable worker but, much and all as I love you, Caesar, I have to say that Agrippa does more.'

Octavian hugged her, kissed her brow. 'I take no offense, *meum mel*, because I know why that is. Did Agrippa only have a wife as dear as you at home, he wouldn't need to work so hard. As it is, he finds any excuse to avoid spending time with Attica.'

'You're right,' she said, looking sad. 'What can we do?'

'Nothing.'

'Divorce is the only answer.'

'He has to decide that for himself.'

Then Livia Drusilla's world was thrown upside down in a way neither she nor Octavian had expected. Tiberius Claudius Nero, a mere fifty years old, died so suddenly that it was left to his steward to discover the body, still hunched over his desk. The will, which Octavian opened, left everything he had to his elder son, Tiberius, but neglected to say what he wanted done with his boys. Young Tiberius was eight years old; his brother, Drusus, born after his mother married Octavian, was just turned five.

'I think, my dear, that we have to take them,' Octavian said to a shocked Livia Drusilla.

'Caesar, no!' she gasped. 'They have been reared to hate you! Nor do they like me, as far as I can gather – I never see them! Oh, no, please don't do this to me! Don't do it to yourself!'

Well, he had never had any illusions about Livia Drusilla; despite her protestations to the contrary, she was not maternal. Her children might not have existed, she thought of them so little, and when someone asked her how often she visited, she trotted out Nero's ban – she wasn't wanted. There were times when he wondered how hard she tried to fall pregnant by him, but her barren state wasn't a grief to him. And how lucky he was! The gods had given him Livia Drusilla's sons. If little Julia did not have sons, he would still have heirs to his name.

'It will be done,' he said in the voice that told his wife he would not budge. 'The poor boys have no one save – oh, I daresay cousins in a fairly remote degree. Neither the Claudii Nerones nor the Livii Drusi are lucky families. You are the mother of these children. People will expect us to take them.'

'I don't want this, Caesar.'

'I know. Nevertheless, it is already being done. I've sent for them and they should be here any moment. Burgundinus is preparing proper quarters for them – a sitting room, two sleeping cubicles, a schoolroom and a private garden. I believe the suite was young Hortensius's. Tomorrow I'll personally buy a pedagogue for them, while Burgundinus goes around to Nero's house to gather up their stuff. I'm sure there will be toys they'd hate to part with, as well as clothes and books. Though I will not take their present pedagogue, even if they are strongly attached to him. I mean to break them of their dislike for us, and that is better done under the aegis of strangers.'

'Why can't you put them with Scribonia and little Julia?'

'Because that is a house of women, a species they are not used to. Nero didn't have a woman in his house, even a laundress,' said Octavian. He went to kiss her, but she jerked her head away. 'Don't be silly, dear, please. Accept your fate as gracefully as Caesar's wife should.'

Her mind was racing to get ahead of his. How extraordinary, that he should set his heart on her sons! For he had, that was patent. So, loving him – and understanding that her future depended on him – she shrugged her shoulders, smiled and kissed him of her own volition.

'I suppose I needn't see a great deal of them,' she said.

'As much and as little as a good Roman mother ought. When I am out of Rome, I expect you to take my place with them.'

The boys arrived stiff and tearless, no red rims around their eyes to suggest that they had already wept themselves dry. Neither remembered his mother, neither had seen their stepfather, even in the Forum; Nero had kept them at home under strict supervision.

Tiberius was black of hair and eye, had an olive skin and quite regular features; he was tall for his age, but painfully thin. As if, thought Octavian, he didn't get enough exercise. Drusus was adorable; that he went straight to Octavian's heart lay in his likeness to his mother, though his eyes were bluer. A riot of black curls, a full mouth, high cheekbones. Like Tiberius, he was tall and thin – did Nero never let his children run around, get some muscle on their bones?

'I am sorry for your *tata*'s death,' Octavian said, unsmiling, striving to look sincere.

'I'm not,' said Tiberius.

'Nor am I,' said Drusus.

'Here is your mama, boys,' Octavian said, at a loss.

They bowed, eyes busy.

To Tiberius, this man and woman seemed friendly and relaxed, not at all what he had imagined after so many years of listening to his father talk about them with so much loathing. Had Nero been kind and approachable, his sentiments would have soaked into this older boy; instead, they had seemed unreal. Hurting from a savage beating, concealing both his tears and his sense of injustice, Tiberius would wish, wish, wish for liberation from his awful father, a man who drank too much wine and had forgotten he was ever a boy himself. Now liberation had come, though in the short hours since Nero's body had been discovered, Tiberius had expected to go from the frying pan into the fire. Instead, he found Octavian especially nice, perhaps because of his alien fairness, those enormous, tranquil grey eyes.

'You'll have your own rooms,' Octavian was saying, smiling now, 'and a terrific garden to play in. You must learn, of course,

414

but I want you to have plenty of time to run around. When you're older, I'll take you with me if I travel – it's important that you see the world. Will you like that?'

'Yes,' said Tiberius.

'Your face is creaky,' said Livia Drusilla, drawing him close. 'Does it ever smile, Tiberius?'

'No,' he said, finding her smell exquisite and her roundness hugely comforting. He pushed his head against her breasts and shut his eyes, the better to feel her, suck in that flowery scent.

Time for Drusus, who was gazing at Octavian as if at a bright gold statue. Squatting down to his level, Octavian stroked his cheek, sighed, winked away tears. 'Dear little Drusus,' he said, dropped to his knees and cuddled the child. 'Be happy with us!'

'It's my turn, Caesar,' Livia Drusilla said, but didn't let go of Tiberius. 'Come, Drusus, let me hold you.'

But Drusus clung to Octavian for comfort, refused to go.

Over dinner the astonished, vastly relieved new parents found out some of the reasons why the boys had survived Nero without becoming imbued with his hatred. The confidences were innocent, yet appalling; it had been a childhood of cold, impersonal, not always bearable inattention. Their pedagogue had been the least expensive one on Stichus's books, so neither boy could read or write very well. Though he had not beaten them, he was instructed to report their offenses to their father, who took great pleasure in wielding a switch. The drunker he was, the worse the beating. They had no toys at all, which made Octavian weep; he had been inundated with toys by his doting mama, had the best of everything in Philippus's house.

A cool and dispassionate man whom many called cold as ice, Octavian yet had a softer side that came to the fore whenever he was with children. Not a day went by when he was in Rome that he didn't snatch a few moments to see little Julia, an enchanting child now six years old. And while he hadn't yearned for sons – to do so would have been unRoman – he had yearned for the company of children – a characteristic he shared with his sister, whose nursery often saw Uncle Caesar, who was funny, jolly, full of ideas for new games. Now, watching his stepsons over dinner, he could tell himself again how lucky he was. Tiberius was clearly going to belong to Livia Drusilla, who seemed to have lost her dislike for her firstborn entirely. Ah, but dear little Drusus! We have one each, thought Octavian, so happy he felt as if he might burst.

Even the dinner itself was a wonder to the boys, who ate raven-ously, unconsciously revealing that Nero had rationed both the quality and the quantity of the food served to them. It was Livia Drusilla who cautioned against gorging, Octavian who urged them to try a little of this, a little of that. Luckily eyelids were drooping before the sweeties came in; Octavian carried Drusus and Burgundinus Tiberius to their sleeping cubicles, tucked them up warmly between down mattresses and down quilts; winter was still hanging on grimly.

'So how do you feel now, wife?' Octavian asked Livia Drusilla as they prepared to climb into their bed.

She squeezed his hand. 'Much better – oh, so much better! I am ashamed that I didn't try harder to visit them, but I never expected that Nero's hatred of us wouldn't impinge on his sons. How shab-bily he treated them! Caesar, they are *patrician*! He had every opportunity to turn them into our implacable enemies, and what did he do? Flogged them into hating him. Didn't care about their welfare – starved them, ignored them. I am very glad that he's dead and we can look after our boys properly.'

'Tomorrow I have to conduct his funeral.'

She put his hand on one breast. 'Oh, dear, I had forgotten! I suppose Tiberius and Drusus have to go?'

'I am afraid so, yes. I'll give the eulogy from the rostra.'

'I wonder, does Octavia have any black children's togas?'

Octavian chuckled. 'Bound to. I sent Burgundinus around to ask, at any rate. If she doesn't have a couple in storage, he'll buy them in the Porticus Margaritaria.'

Snuggling against him, she kissed his cheek. 'You must have Caesar's luck, Caesar! Who could ever have predicted that our boys would be ripe for our plucking? Today we've gained two important allies for your cause.'

The day after the funeral, Octavian took the boys to meet their cousins. Octavia, who had been at the funeral, was anxious to welcome them into the family fold.

Almost sixteen and on the verge of official manhood, Gaius Scribonius Curio was due to leave the nursery and become a *contu-bernalis*. A red-haired, freckled youth, he wanted to be Mark Antony's cadet, but Antony had refused him. So he was to go to Agrippa. The elder of Antony's two sons by Fulvia, Antyllus, was eleven, and already dying for a military career. The other son, Iullus, was eight. They were handsome boys, Antyllus with his father's reddish coloring, Iullus more like his dusky mother. Only in a household like Octavia's could they have been reared so successfully, for both boys were impetuous, adventurous and warlike. Octavia's gentle yet firm hand kept them, as she put it with a laugh, 'members of the *gens humana*.'

Her own daughter, Marcella, was thirteen, menstruating, and promising to be a great beauty. Dark like her father, she had her own nature, which was flirtatious, haughty and imperious. Marcellus was eleven, another darkly handsome child. He and Antyllus, his coeval, couldn't bear each other, and fought tooth and nail; nothing Octavia could do succeeded in making them like each other, so whenever Uncle Caesar was in town, he was called upon to administer whacks on the palm with a ruler. Privately Octavian considered Marcellus far the more likeable of the two, for he had a calm temperament and a better mind than Antyllus. Cellina, Octavia's younger girl by Marcellus Minor, was eight; she was golden-haired, blue-eyed and very pretty. A strong likeness existed between her and little Julia, who was a regular tenant of the nursery, as Octavia and Scribonia were good friends. Antonia, aged five, had sandy hair and greenish eyes – no beauty, alas, since she had Antony's nose and chin. Her nature was proud and aloof, and she considered her betrothal to Ahenobarbus's son, Lucius, beneath her. Surely, she was heard to complain often, there was someone better? The youngest child of all, Tonilla, had auburn hair and amber eyes, though luckily her features were Julian rather than Antonian. In character she was turning out to be resolute, intelligent and fierce.

Iullus and Cellina were much the same age as Tiberius; while Antonia and Drusus would shortly be six.

No matter what intrigues and squabbles occurred when this brood of children were not in Octavia's presence, they were well-mannered and cheerful. It soon became apparent that Drusus liked three-year-old Tonilla much better than he liked the whining Antonia; he proceeded to take her under his wing and enslave her. Things were more difficult for Tiberius, who turned out to be a shy child, unsure of himself and incapable of conversation. The kindest of the Marcelli, Cellina, befriended him immediately, seeming to sense his insecurities, while Iullus, discovering that Tiberius knew nothing of horse riding, dueling with a play-sword, or the history of Rome's wars, regarded him with visible contempt.

'Do you think you'll mind visiting Aunt Octavia?' Octavian asked as he led the boys home via the Forum Romanum, where he was greeted on all sides and stopped every few feet by someone anxious to obtain a favor or impart a morsel of political gossip. The boys were dazzled, not only by this first trip into the city, but also by Octavian's retinue: twelve lictors and a German guard. Despite the diatribes and maunderings against Octavian that their father had uttered over the years, it was clear in this one walk that Octavian – Caesar, they must learn to call him – was far more important than Nero.

Their pedagogue was a free man, a nephew of Burgundinus's named Gaius Julius Cimbricus. Like all the descendants of Divus Julius's beloved Burgundus, he was immensely tall and muscular, a fair, round-faced man with a snub nose and pale blue eyes. He was with them now, pointing out this and that, things he considered worthy of the boys' attention. There was much to like in him, and nothing to fear. Not only would he teach them in the schoolroom, he would also give them exercises to do in their garden, and, in time, instruct them in military exercises so that, when each boy turned twelve, he would be able to go to the Campus Martius for military exercises not quite unskilled.

'Do you think you'll enjoy visiting your Aunt Octavia?' asked Octavian a second time.

'Yes, Caesar,' Tiberius said.

'Oh, yes!' cried Drusus.

'And do you think you'll like Cimbricus?'

'Yes,' they chorused.

'Don't let your shyness overwhelm you, Tiberius. As soon as you grow used to your new life, it will fade.' Octavian gave his stepson a conspiratorial grin. 'Iullus is a bully, but once you get a bit of muscle on those long bones, you'll wallop him.'

A very comforting thought; Tiberius looked up at Octavian and essayed his first smile.

'As for you, young man,' Octavian said to Drusus, 'I don't see any sign of shyness. You were quite right to prefer Tonilla to Antonia, but I hope later on that you can find things in common with Marcellus, even though he's a bit older than you.'

Livia Drusilla greeted the boys with a kiss and sent them to the schoolroom with Cimbricus.

'Caesar, I've had a brilliant idea!' she cried as soon as they were alone.

'What?' he asked warily.

'A reward for Marcus Agrippa! Well, two rewards, actually.'

'Agrippa isn't in it for reward, dearest.'

'Yes, yes, I know that! Still, he ought to have rewards – they will keep him tied to you as the years go on.'

'He will never not be tied, because the feeling comes from who and what he is.'

'Yes, yes, *yes*! But wouldn't it be a great match for him if he married Marcella?'

'She's thirteen, Livia Drusilla.'

'Thirteen going on thirty, more like. In four more years she'll be seventeen – old enough for marriage. Fewer and fewer of the Famous Families adhere to the old custom of keeping girls at home until they're eighteen.'

'I'll certainly consider it.'

'Then there's Agrippa's daughter, Vipsania. I know that when old Atticus dies, his fortune will go to Attica, but I hear tell that if Attica should die, his will stipulates that everything must go to Agrippa,' Livia Drusilla said eagerly. 'That makes the child extremely eligible, and since Tiberius's inheritance is so paltry, I think he should marry Vipsania.'

'He's eight, and she's not yet three.'

'Oh, for pity's sake, Caesar, stop being so blockheaded! I am aware how old they are, but they'll be grown up enough to marry before you can say Alammelech!'

'Alammelech?' he asked, mouth twitching.

'It's a river in Philistia.'

'I know, but I didn't know that you knew.'

'Oh, go and jump in the Tiber!'

While his domestic existence was becoming more and more a joy to Octavian, his public and political doings were not bearing much fruit worth the picking. Monger rumors though they did, whisper calumnies against Mark Antony though they might, Octavian's agents failed to sway those seven hundred senators in their conviction that Antony was the man to follow. They genuinely believed that he would soon return to Rome; indeed, he had to, if only to celebrate a triumph for his victories in Armenia. His letters from Artaxata had boasted of huge plunder, from solid gold statues six cubits high to chests of Parthian gold coins and literally hundreds of talents of rock lapis lazuli and crystal. He was bringing the Nineteenth Legion with him, and had already demanded that Octavian find land for them to retire on.

If Antony's influence had extended no farther than the Senate, it might have been overcome, but the entire First and Second Classes, many thousands of men engaged in some kind of business or other, swore by Antony's brilliance, integrity, military genius. To make matters worse, tribute was coming into the Treasury at an ever-increasing rate, the *publicani* tax farmers and plutocrats of all description were buzzing around Asia Province and Bithynia like bees around flowers dripping nectar, and now it seemed there would be immense booty to add to the Treasury. The solid gold statue of Anaitis was to be Antony's gift to the temple of Jupiter Optimus Maximus, but most of the other works of art, as well as the jewellery, would be sold. The general, his legates and his legions would receive their legal shares, but the Treasury would get the rest. Though it was years since Antony had been in Rome for more than a few days – and the last visit of all had been five years ago – his popularity endured among the people who mattered. Did these people care about Illyricum? No, they didn't. It held no promise of commercial activities, and few who lived in Rome and had villas in Campania and Etruria cared a rush whether Aquileia was razed to the ground or Mediolanum flattened.

The only positive thing Octavian had managed to do was to make the name, Cleopatra, known to all Italia from highest to lowest. Of her, everyone believed the worst; the trouble was that they couldn't be brought to see that she controlled Antony. Had the enmity between Octavian and Antony not been so well known, Octavian might have established his point, but everyone who liked Antony simply dismissed Octavian's allegations as a part of that enmity.

Then Gaius Cornelius Gallus arrived in Rome. Good friend of Octavian's though he was, this impoverished poet with a warlike streak had begged Octavian's pardon and set out to serve as one of Antony's legates just in time to miss the retreat from Phraaspa. So he had idled in Syria while Antony drank, using his time to compose lyrical, beautiful odes in the style of Pindar, and writing occasionally to Octavian. Bemourning the fact that his purse was no heavier, he clung to Syria until Antony shook off the effects of the wine and marched for Armenia. His hatred of Cleopatra was hot and obdurate; no one rejoiced more than he did when she returned to Egypt and left Antony to do without her.

Thirty-four years old when he sought an interview with his erst-while friend, Octavian, Gallus was extremely handsome in a rather cruel way that was more an accident of physiognomy than a character trait. His love elegies, 'Amores', had already made him famous, and he was an intimate of Virgil's, with whom he had much in common racially; they were both Italian Gauls. He was not, therefore, a patrician Cornelius.

'I hope you can lend me some money, Caesar,' he said as he took the goblet of wine Octavian handed him. A rueful smile creased the corners of his splendid grey eyes. 'I'm not on the cadge, exactly,' he continued. 'It's just that I spent what I had on buying swift passage from Alexandria to Rome, knowing that winter would make news of what happened in Alexandria slow in reaching Rome.'

Octavian frowned. 'Alexandria? What were you doing there?'

'Trying to prise my entitled percentage of the Armenian spoils out of Antonius and that monstrous sow, Cleopatra.' He shrugged. 'I didn't succeed. Nor will anyone else.'

'The last I heard,' said Octavian, settling into his chair, 'Antonius was engaged in touring southern Syria – what, that is, he didn't sign over to Cleopatra.'

'A blind,' Gallus said, scowling. 'I'll bet no one in Rome knows yet that Antonius took every last sestertius of the Armenian spoils to Alexandria. Where he held a triumphal parade for the delectation of the citizens of Alexandria – and their queen, high on a golden dais at the junction of Royal and Canopic Avenues.' He drew a breath, drank deeply. 'After he triumphed, he dedicated everything to Serapis – his own share, his legates' shares, the legions' shares, and the Treasury's. Whereupon Cleopatra refused to pay any army shares, though Antonius managed to convince her that the troops *had* to be paid, and quickly. Men like me were so lowly that we weren't even invited to the public spectacles.'

'Ye gods!' Octavian said feebly, shocked to his marrow. 'He had the temerity to give away what isn't his to give away?'

'Oh, yes. Eventually I'm sure the entire army will be paid, but the Treasury won't be. I bore Alexandria after the triumph, but when Antonius held what Dellius calls the Donations, I felt such a hankering for Rome I had to come, still uncompensated.'

'Donations?'

'Oh, a wonderful ceremony in the new gymnasium! Acting on his authority as Rome's representative, Antonius publicly proclaimed Ptolemy Caesar the King of Kings and ruler of the world! Cleopatra was named Queen of Kings, and her three children by Antonius got most of Africa, the Parthian Kingdom, Anatolia, Thrace, Greece, Macedonia, and all the islands at the eastern end of Our Sea. Amazing, isn't it?'

Octavian sat with jaw dropped, eyes wide. 'Incredible!'

'Perhaps, but real for all that. It's fact, Caesar, *fact*!'

'Did Antonius offer his legates any explanation?'

'A curious one, yes. What Dellius knows is beyond me – he enjoys a special position. The rest of us – all junior legates – were told that he had vowed the spoils to Cleopatra, that his honor was involved.'

'And the honor of Rome?'

'Was nowhere to be found.'

During the course of the next hour, Octavian got the full tale out of Gallus, in the meticulous detail of one who saw his world as a poet does. The level of the wine flagon went down, but Octavian grudged neither that nor the hefty sum he would pay Gallus for getting this information to him ahead of everyone else in Rome. A fabulous trove! The winter this year had been early and very long; little wonder that so much time had elapsed. The triumph and the Donations had happened in December, and it was now April. However, Gallus warned, he had reason to believe that Dellius had written to Poplicola with all this news at least two months ago.

Finally, one last oddity was all that remained to be imparted. Octavian bent forward, elbows on his desk, chin propped on his hands. 'Ptolemy Caesar was proclaimed higher than his mother?'

'Caesarion, they call him. Yes, he was.'

'Why?'

'Oh, the woman dotes on him! Comparatively speaking, her sons by Antonius don't matter. Everything is for Caesarion.'

'Is he my divine father's son, Gallus?'

'Undoubtedly,' said Gallus firmly. 'The image of Divus Julius in every way. I'm not old enough to have known Divus Julius as a youthful man, but Caesarion looks as I imagine Divus Julius must have looked at the same age.'

'Which is?'

'Thirteen. He'll be fourteen in June.'

Octavian relaxed. 'Still a child, then.'

'Oh, no, anything but! He's well into puberty, Caesar – has a deep voice, the air of a grown man. I understand that his intellect is as profound as it is precocious. He and his mama have some spectacular differences of opinion, according to Dellius.'

'Ah!' Octavian rose to his feet and stretched out his arm to Gallus, shook Gallus's hand strongly and warmly. 'I cannot begin to tell you how grateful I am for your zeal, so I will let something more tangible speak for me. Go to Oppius's bank next *nundinum* and you will find a nice present. What's more, as I am now the custodian of my stepson's property, I can offer you Nero's house for the next ten years at a peppercorn rent.'

'And service in Illyricum?' asked the warrior poet eagerly.

'Definitely. Not much in the way of booty, but some very good fighting.'

The door shut behind a Gaius Cornelius Gallus floating several feet above the cobbles as he wended his way to Virgil's house, Octavian stood in the middle of his study floor, sorting out the mine of information into a sequence that enabled him to gauge it properly. That Antony could have done something as stupid as this flabbergasted him, would always remain the most mystifying aspect of the whole business. For he suspected that he would never know the why of it. *A vow*? That didn't make sense! As he had never believed his own propaganda, Octavian found himself almost uncertain what to do. *Almost*. Perhaps the harpy did drug Antony, though until this moment Octavian had been skeptical about potions able to overcome the most basic tenets of existence. And what was more basic to a Roman than Rome? Antony had dumped Rome's plunder in Cleopatra's lap without, it seemed, even considering whether or not she could be persuaded to pay his army the percentages due it from the spoils. Had he gone on his knees to beg before she consented at least to pay the common soldiers? Oh, Antonius, Antonius! How could you? What will my sister say? Such an insult!

However, there was one thing more important than all the rest lumped together: Ptolemy Caesar. Caesarion. Somehow Cleopatra made better sense knowing that she doted on this eldest son. A shock to learn for a fact that the boy was the image of his father, even to the early flowering, the intelligence. Fourteen in two months, only five years away from Caesarean audacity, Caesarean acumen. No one knew better than Octavian what Julian blood could do; he himself had struck out for power at eighteen, after all. *And succeeded!* This boy had so many advantages – used to wielding power already, strong-willed enough to clash with his mother, no doubt as fluent in Latin as she was, therefore capable of fooling Rome into thinking of him as genuinely Roman.

By the time Octavian opened his study door and went to find Livia Drusilla, his priorities were sorted out. Clever chicken, she went straight to the heart of the matter.

'Whatever you do, Caesar, you cannot let Italia or Rome set eyes on this boy!' she cried, hands clenched. 'He spells ruin.'

'I agree, but how do I prevent it?'

'Any way you can. First and foremost, by keeping Antonius in the East until your supremacy in Rome is paramount. For, if he comes, he'll bring Caesarion with him. It's his logical move. If the mother is so devoted to the boy, she won't object to being left in Egypt. It's her son who is King of Kings. Oh, all of the Antonian senators and knights will fall over backward when they see Divus Julius's blood son! The fact that he's a hybrid and not even a Roman citizen won't stop them: you know it and I know it. Therefore you *must* keep Antonius in the East at all costs!'

'Well, the Alexandrian triumph and the Donations are a starting point. It's my good luck that I have an unimpeachable witness in Cornelius Gallus.'

She looked anxious. 'But will he cleave to you? He deserted you for Antonius two years ago.'

'The result of ambition and penury. He's come back outraged, and I've paid him very well. He can caretake Nero's house, another perquisite. I think he knows where the best bread is.'

'You'll convene the Senate, of course?'

'Of course.'

'And have Maecenas and your agents tell the whole of Italia what Antonius has done?'

'That goes without saying. My gossip mill will grind Queen Cleopatra to dust.'

'What about the boy? Is there any way we can discredit him?'

'Oppius takes trips to Alexandria. That Cleopatra refuses to see him isn't nearly as well known. I'll have Oppius write a pamphlet about Caesarion, saying that he bears no likeness to my divine father.'

'And that he's actually the child of an Egyptian slave.'

He laughed. 'Perhaps I ought to have you write it.'

'I would, had I ever been to Alexandria.' She clasped her hands around Octavian's arm, shaking it. 'Oh, Caesar, we have never stood in greater danger!'

'Don't worry your beautiful head, dearest one. *I* am the son of Divus Julius! There will be no other.'

The news of the triumph and the Donations rocked Rome; few could believe it at first, but gradually others like Cornelius Gallus either returned in person or wrote letters long delayed by the wintry seas. Three hundred of Antony's senators left his ranks to sit as neutrals while the invective and accusations raged on the floor of the House. Knight-businessmen also deserted by the hundreds. But not enough. Never enough.

Had Octavian made Antony the butt of his campaign he might have won a bigger victory, but he was too shrewd. It was at Queen Cleopatra that he aimed his barbs, for he had seen his way clear; if war came, as seemed inevitable, it would not be war against Mark Antony. It would be war against a foreign foe – Egypt. Often he had longed for someone like Cleopatra to crush Antony, without its seeming that Antony was his true object. Now, in accepting Rome's spoils and forcing Antony to crown her and her children rulers of the world, Cleopatra stood forth as Rome's enemy.

'But it's not enough,' he said despondently to Agrippa.

'I think this is but the first trickle of pebbles in what will eventually be a landslide that brings the whole of the East down,' Agrippa comforted. 'Be patient, Caesar! You'll get there.'

Gnaeus Domitius Ahenobarbus and Gaius Sosius arrived in Rome in June. Both were to be consuls next year, which was something of a coup for Antony, whose adherents they were. Though everyone knew the elections were rigged, both men made a splash in their specially whitened togas as they walked around soliciting votes.

Ahenobarbus's first task was to read out a letter from Mark Antony to the Senate, which he did with the House doors wide open; it was vital that as many Forum frequenters as possible should hear what Antony had to say.

Considering its author, the letter was very long, which led Octavian (and others, some not always in sympathy with him) to think that its author had had help composing it. Naturally it had to be heard in full, which meant a lot of dozing. Since he had done his share of dozing in the past, Ahenobarbus was well aware of this tendency, and knew how to deal with it. He had read the letter many times himself, and marked the passages that must be heard by men wide awake. Therefore he droned when the contents were unimportant or (a great fault of this letter) tautologous, whereas each important part he announced with a bellow that made the House jerk and flutter, and continued to the end of that part shouting in a voice famous for its volume. Then he reverted to the drone and everybody could have another nice nap. Both the Antonians and the Octavians were so grateful for this technique that Ahenobarbus won a lot of friends.

Octavian sat on his ivory curule chair at the front of the curule magistrates' dais and tried very hard to keep awake, though when the entire House was dozing, he felt safe to doze too. The building was rather airless unless a high wind was blowing through the clerestory apertures high on its side walls, and no such wind blew today; it was early summer. However, staying awake was easier for him; he had a lot on his mind, and the background of soft snores was no impediment. To him, the beginning of the to-be-famous letter was the most interesting part.

'The East,' Antony (or Cleopatra?) said, 'is fundamentally alien to the Roman *mos maiorum*, therefore cannot be understood by Romans. Our civilization is the most advanced in the world; we freely elect the magistrates who govern us, and to ensure that no magistrate starts to think of himself as indispensable, his term in office is limited to one year. Only in times of great internal danger do we resort to longer, more dictatorial government, as at the moment, when we have three – I beg your pardon, conscript fathers, two – Triumvirs to oversee the activities of the consuls, praetors, aediles and quaestors, if not the tribunes of the plebs.

'We live by the rule of law, the process of which is formal and impartial—'

Sniggers broke out on every tier; Ahenobarbus waited until the noise abated, then resumed as if uninterrupted.

'. . . and enlightened in its penalties. We do not imprison for any crime. Minor offenses are dealt with by a fine; major ones, up to and including treason, by confiscation of property and exile to a specified distance from Rome.'

Ahenobarbus meticulously outlined the penal system, the kinds of citizens, the division of Roman government into executive and legislative arms, and the place of women in the Roman scheme of things.

'Conscript fathers, I have just detailed the *mos maiorum* and, in effect, the way a Roman sees the world.

'Picture then, if you can, a Roman governor with a proconsular imperium descending upon some Eastern province like Cilicia, Syria or Pontus. He assumes that his province thinks Roman, and when he dispenses justice or issues edicts, he thinks Roman.

'But,' roared Ahenobarbus, 'the East is *not* Roman! It does not think Roman! For instance, nowhere but in Rome are the poor fed at the State's expense. The poor are regarded as a nuisance, and let starve if they cannot afford to buy bread. Men and women are imprisoned in hideous dungeons, sometimes for offenses a Roman would consider worthy only of a trifling fine. Those in authority do as they please, for laws are scarce, and when present, often turn out to be differently applied, depending on the economic or social status of the accused—'

'It's the same in Rome!' Messala Corvinus yelled. 'Marcus Cacus of the Subura will pay a talent in fines for dressing as a woman and soliciting customers outside Venus Erucina's, while Lucius Cornelius Patricius gets off – in more ways than one!'

The House rocked with laughter; Ahenobarbus waited, unable to suppress his own amusement.

'Executions are common. Women have neither citizenship nor money. They cannot inherit, and what they earn has to be put in a man's name. They can be divorced, but not divorce. Official positions may be filled by election, but more commonly are filled by sortition, and, most commonly of all, by right of birth. Taxes are levied in an entirely different way from in Rome, each place having its own preferred system of taxation.'

Octavian's eyelids drooped; clearly Antony (or Cleopatra) was about to embark upon the minutiae. The amplitude of snores increased; Ahenobarbus began to drone.

'Rome cannot directly rule in the East!' Ahenobarbus roared. 'Rule must be through client-kings! Which is better, conscript fathers? A Roman governor enforcing Roman law on people who do not understand it, conducting wars that do not benefit the local people, and feathering his own nest – or a client-king who enforces laws his people understand, and who is not allowed to go to war at all? What Rome wants from the East is tribute, pure and simple. Time and time again it has been proved beyond a shadow of a doubt that the tribute flows better from a client-kingdom than from a Roman governor. Client-kings know how to squeeze their people, client-kings don't provoke rebellions.'

Back to the drone . . . Octavian yawned, eyes watering, and decided to do some mental gymnastics upon the subject of blackening Queen Cleopatra's reputation. He was absorbed in this when Ahenobarbus commenced to bellow again.

'To attempt to garrison the East with Roman troops is idiotic! They go native, conscript fathers! Look at what happened to the four legions of Gabiniani left to garrison Alexandria on behalf of its king, Ptolemy Auletes! When the late Marcus Calpurnius Bibulus recalled them to duty in Syria, they refused to obey. His two elder sons, protected only by lictors, insisted. With the result that the Gabiniani murdered them, the children of a senior Roman governor! Queen Cleopatra behaved in an exemplary way by executing the ringleaders and sending all four legions back to Syria—'

'Go on!' Maecenas interjected scornfully. 'Four legions have a total of two hundred and forty centurions. As Marcus Antonius has already pointed out, centurions are the legion's officers. Divus Julius, it is said, wept for the death of a centurion, but not for the death of a legate. And what did Cleopatra do? Why, the ten most incompetent heads rolled, but the other two hundred and thirty centurions were *never* sent back to Syria! She kept them in Egypt to stiffen her own army!'

'That is a lie!' Poplicola shouted. 'Take it back, you perfumed ponce!'

'Order,' said Octavian in a weary voice.

The House fell silent.

'Some places are Romanized or Hellenized enough to accept direct Roman rule, to be garrisoned by Roman troops. They are Macedonia, including Greece and coastal Thrace, Bithynia and Asia Province. Nowhere else. *Nowhere!* Cilicia never worked as a province, nor has Syria since Pompeius Magnus established it. But we haven't tried to incorporate places like Cappadocia and Galatia into provinces – nor should we! When Pontus was governed as a part of Bithynia, said government was a joke. How many times during his term did a governor of Bithynia ever get to Pontus? Once or twice, if at all!'

Here it comes, thought Octavian, straightening. We are about to hear Antonius's excuses for his actions.

'I make no apologies for my dispositions in the East,' said Ahenobarbus on Antony's behalf, 'because they are the right dispositions. I have given some of Rome's former direct possessions over to the rule of new client-kings, and strengthened the authority of client-kings who have always ruled. Before I lay down my present Triumvirate, I will complete my work by giving all of Anatolia save Asia Province and Bithynia to client-kings, and all of mainland Asia Minor as well. They will be governed by capable men of integrity and extreme loyalty to Rome, their suzerain.'

Ahenobarbus drew a long breath, then continued. 'Egypt,' he said, letting the word fall into a profound silence, 'is more an appanage of Rome than any other Eastern kingdom. By that I mean it is Rome's close cousin, too entwined with Rome's destiny to be of any danger. Egypt keeps no standing army, and has no ideas of conquest. The territories I have ceded to Egypt in Rome's name are better governed by Egypt, as all of them once belonged to Egypt for centuries. While King Ptolemy Caesar and Queen Cleopatra are busy establishing stable governments in these places, no tribute will be paid to Rome, but tribute *will* recommence at some date in the future.'

'What a comfort,' said Messala Corvinus.

Now the peroration, thought Octavian. It will be short, which is a mercy. Ahenobarbus reads well, but a letter can never replace a speech given in person. Especially by someone like Antonius, a very good orator.

'All Rome really wants from the East,' Ahenobarbus thundered, 'are trade and tribute! My dispositions will enhance both.'

He sat down to cheers and applause, though the three hundred who had deserted him after the Alexandrian triumph and Donations did not cheer or applaud. Antony had lost them for good with that last section of his letter, which all true Romans deemed evidence of Cleopatra's hold over him. It didn't take much imagination to deduce that what remained of Anatolia and mainland Asia Minor were to go to that wonderful appanage, that close cousin, Egypt.

Octavian rose, cuddling the folds of toga on his left shoulder with his left hand, moving until he found that ray of sunlight coming through a small hole in the roof. Once found, it lit up his hair brilliantly, and as it moved, he moved. What no one knew save Agrippa was that he had caused the hole to be made.

'What an astonishing document,' he said after the salutations were out of the way. 'Marcus Antonius, that fabulous authority on the East! A native of the place, one is tempted to say. In nature that might be so, since he is much addicted to lying on couches popping grapes into his mouth – liquid as well as solid – much addicted to scantily clad dancing girls, and much addicted to all things Egyptian. But then again, I may be wrong, for I am no kind of authority on the East. Um – let me see . . . How many years is it since Philippi, after which battle Antonius left for the East? Nine years, or thereabouts . . . Over the time since then, he has made three brief visits to Italia, two of them involving a trip to Rome. Only once did he remain in Rome for any length of time. That was five years ago, after Tarentum – you remember, conscript fathers, surely! Upon his return to the East after that, he dumped my sister, his wife, on Corcyra. She was heavily pregnant, but it was up to the good Gaius Fonteius to bring her home.

'Very well, nine years do indeed make Marcus Antonius an expert on the East, I have to admit that. For five years he has kept his Roman wife at home, while keeping his other wife, the Queen of Beasts, so close by his side that he cannot exist long without her there. She holds pride of place in Antonius's array of client-kings, for she at least has demonstrated her strength, her determination. Alas, I cannot say the same for the rest of his client-kings – a sorry lot. Amyntas the clerk, Tarcondimotus the brigand, Herod the savage, Antonius's son-in-law Pythodorus the slimy Greek, Cleon the brigand, Polemon the sycophant, Archelaus Sisenes, the son of his mistress – oh, I could go on and on!'

'Go off and off instead, Octavianus!' Poplicola yelled.

'*Caesar!* I am Caesar. Yes, a sorry lot. It is true that tribute is beginning to flow at last from Asia Province, Bithynia and Roman Syria, but where is the tribute from any of Antonius's sorry lot of client-kings? Especially that dazzling jewel, the Queen of Beasts? One presumes her money is better spent on buying potions to feed Antonius, for I cannot imagine that Antonius whole and intact would give away Rome's spoils as a gift to Egypt. Nor give away the entire world to the son of the Queen of Beasts and a pathetic slave.'

No one interjected; Octavian paused, positioned himself in the light properly, and waited patiently for a comment that did not come. On, then, to speak of the legions and offer his own solution to the problem of 'going native' – shuffle legions on garrison duty around from province to province.

'I do not intend to make your day a total ordeal, my fellow senators, so I will conclude by saying that if Marcus Antonius's legions – *his* legions! – have gone native, why does he expect me to find them retirement land in Italia? I would imagine that they would be happier if Antonius found them land in Syria. Or Egypt, where it seems he intends to settle himself permanently.'

For the first time since he had entered the House ten years ago, Octavian found himself heartily applauded; even some of Antony's four hundred clapped, while his own adherents and the three hundred neutrals gave him a standing ovation. And no one, not even Ahenobarbus, had dared to boo or hiss. He had cut too close to the bone for that.

He left the House on the arm of Gaius Fonteius, who had become suffect consul on the Kalends of May; his own consulship he had laid down on the second day of January, thus imitating Antony the year before. There would be more suffect consuls, but Fonteius was to continue in office until the end of the year, a signal honor. The consulship had turned into a triumviral gift.

As if he could read Octavian's mind, Fonteius sighed and said, 'It is a pity that each year has so many consuls these days. Can you see Cicero abdicating so that someone else got a turn?'

'Or Divus Julius, for that matter,' Octavian said with a grin. 'I do agree, despite my own abdication. But letting more men be consul removes the glare from a long-term triumvirate.'

'At least you cannot be accused of hungering for power.'

'While ever I am Triumvir, I have power.'

'What will you do when the Triumvirate expires?'

'Which it does at the end of this year. Why, I'll do something I don't think Antonius will do – I'll cease to use the title and put my curule chair on the front bench. My *auctoritas* and *dignitas* are so unassailable that I won't suffer for the lack of a title.' He cast Fonteius a shrewd glance. 'Where do you go from here?'

'Up onto the Carinae to visit Octavia,' Fonteius said easily.

'Then I'll go with you, if you don't object.'

'I'd be delighted, Caesar.'

Their progress through the Forum was hindered by Octavian's usual crowds, but when he gestured to the twenty-four lictors he and Fonteius had between them to plough on regardless, the German bodyguard closed ranks before and behind, and the walk proceeded at a brisk pace.

Passing the residence of the Rex Sacrorum on the Velia, Gaius Fonteius spoke again. 'Caesar, do you think Antonius will ever come back to Rome?'

'You think of Octavia,' said Octavian, well aware how Fonteius felt about her.

'Yes, I do, but more than her. Can't he see that he's losing ground more and more rapidly? I know senators who became physically ill when they learned of the Alexandrian triumph and the Donations.'

'He's not the old Antonius, that's all.'

'Do you honestly believe what you say about Cleopatra's hold over him?'

'I confess it started out as a political ploy, but it's almost as if the wish were father to the thought. His behavior is hard to credit under any other circumstances than Cleopatra's hold, yet for the life of me I can't find out why she has that hold. Above all things I am a pragmatist, so I tend to dismiss stratagems like drugs as impossible.' He smiled. 'However, I am not an authority on the East, so maybe such potions do exist.'

'It began on his last journey, if not before,' Fonteius said. 'He poured his heart out to me one stormy night on Corcyra – his loneliness, his disappointment, his conviction that he had lost his luck. Even then I think Cleopatra gnawed at him, but not in any dangerous way.' He snorted his contempt. 'A clever piece of work, the Queen of Egypt! I didn't like her. But then, she had no fondness for me either. Romans call her a harpy, but I think of her more as a siren – she has the most beautiful speaking voice. It charms the senses, it makes one believe everything she says.'

'Interesting,' said Octavian thoughtfully. 'Did you know that they have struck coins with their images on both sides?'

'*Together?*'

'Aye, together.'

'Then he is utterly lost.'

'So I think. But how do I convince those addle-pated senators of it? I need evidence, Fonteius, *evidence*!'

TWENTY-THREE

'"Your acts remain unratified,"' Cleopatra said, reading the letter from Ahenobarbus aloud. '"I began hammering at the House the moment I became senior consul, but Octavianus has a tame tribune of the plebs, Marcus Nonius Balbus of that obnoxious Picentine family, who keeps vetoing everything I try to do for you. Then when Sosius took the *fasces* from me on the Kalends of February, he moved a motion of censure against Octavianus, whom he accused of blocking your Eastern reforms. Three guesses what happened next: Nonius vetoed the motion."' She put the letter down, gold eyes fixed on Antony with that cold yet fierce flame that says the lioness is about to pounce. 'The only way you can regain your standing in Rome is to march against Octavianus.'

'If I do that, I'm the aggressor in a civil war. I'd be a traitor and declared *hostis*.'

'Rubbish! Sulla did it. So did Caesar. Both of them wound up ruling Rome. What's *hostis*, when it's boiled down? A decree of outlawry that has no teeth.'

'Sulla and Caesar ruled illegally, as dictators.'

'How one rules doesn't matter, Antonius!' she snapped.

'I abolished the dictatorship,' Antony said stubbornly.

'Then when you've defeated Octavianus, bring it back into law! Just as a temporary expedient, my dear,' she wheedled. 'Oh, surely you can see, Antonius, that if Octavianus isn't stopped, he'll move that your acts in the East be set aside – and no brave tribune of the plebs will veto *him*! After that, he can appoint his own clients to reign in all the kingdoms of the East.' She drew a breath, her eyes glowing. 'He will also move that Egypt be annexed as a province of Rome.'

'He wouldn't dare! Nor will I permit the setting aside of my arrangements,' Antony said between his teeth.

'You'd have to go to Rome personally to stiffen the Antonian backbones – they're rather sagging these days,' she said derisively, 'and to make that journey, you'd best have an army with you.'

'Octavianus will collapse. He can't keep on vetoing.'

There was just enough doubt in Antony's voice to tell Cleopatra she was starting to win the relentless argument. She had abandoned her plan to coax Antony into an outright invasion of Italy; he would listen to Octavian as the enemy, but never, it seemed, Rome. Alexandria and Egypt had burrowed into his heart, but alongside Rome rather than in place of Rome. Well, so be it. It didn't matter what the motive was, as long as Antony finally moved. If he didn't, she was indeed the nothing he had called her. Her agents in Rome reported that Octavian had settled all his veterans on good land in Italy and Italian Gaul, and that he enjoyed the approval of most Italians. But as yet he couldn't dominate the Senate beyond interposing a tribunician veto; between the four hundred loyal Antonians and the three hundred neutrals, Antony still had the edge on him. But was that edge enough?

'All right,' said Antony several days later, goaded beyond endurance, 'I'll move my armies and fleets closer to Italia. Ephesus.' He glanced at Cleopatra from under his brows. 'If, that is, I have the money. It's your war, Pharaoh, so you pay for it.'

'I'll happily pay. Provided I have the co-command. I want to attend every war council, I want to have my say, I want equal status with you. That means my opinions will count for more than any Roman opinion except yours.'

An intense weariness overwhelmed him; why did there always have to be conditions? Was he never to be free of Cleopatra the *dominatrix*? She could be so entrancing, so soft, such good company! But every time he thought that side of her had won, up reared her uglier head. She thirsted for power more than any man he had ever known, from Caesar to Cassius. And all for Caesar's son! Gifted beyond imagination, yet not, he sensed, after power. What would she do when Caesarion declined this Cleopatra-sculpted destiny? She knew nothing about the boy, nothing.

Nor did she know anything about Roman men, knowing only two Romans intimately. Neither Caesar nor Antonius was typical, as she would find out did she insist on having the co-command.

His sense of fair play said she ought to have the co-command, funding the enterprise, but none of his colleagues would accord her that privilege. His mouth opened with the intent of telling her what would inevitably happen, then closed with the words unuttered. Her face bore that flinty look that said she would hear no argument, a brewing storm roiled in her eyes. If he tried to tell her what experience would prove, they would have yet one more quarrel in too many. Was there a man ever born who could deal successfully with a masterful woman owning nigh unlimited power? Antony doubted it. Perhaps dead Caesar, but he had known her when she was very young, and had established an ascendancy over her that she didn't know how to destroy. Now, years later, she was set in stone. Far worse, she had seen him, Antony, at his nadir, sodden with wine to the point of coma, and had interpreted that episode as a demonstration of a core weakness. Yes, he could cow her by reminding her that she had no army or navy to achieve her ends, but the next day she would bounce back and start the nagging all over again.

I am caught, he thought, tangled in the web of her weaving, and there is no way to break free without abandoning my own bid for power. To some extent we want the same thing: the destruction of Octavianus. But she would go much farther, attempt to destroy Rome herself. That I will not let her do, yet right at this moment I cannot oppose her. I must bide my time, appear to give her everything she wants. Including the co-command.

'I agree,' he said, sounding decisive. Let everything be as Cleopatra wanted—for the time being. Experience would teach her that a command tent of Roman men would spurn her. Yet—could *he* spurn her? Living with her, sleeping in the same bed, could he spurn her? Time would show him that too.

He sat down to write to Ahenobarbus, using his now defunct title, Triumvir, and spelling out his demands from the Senate and People of Rome: complete authority in the East, which was to be absolutely divorced from senatorial supervision; the right to levy tribute as he saw fit; the appointment of client sovereigns; command of any legions Rome might send east of the Drina River; ratification of all his *actiones*; and one other ratification – the lands and titles he had granted to King Ptolemy XV Caesar, Queen Cleopatra, King Ptolemy Alexander Helios, Queen Cleopatra Selene and King Ptolemy Philadelphus.

'I have appointed King Ptolemy Caesar King of Kings and ruler of the world. No one can gainsay me. Furthermore, I would remind the Senate and People of Rome that King Ptolemy Caesar is the legitimate son of Divus Julius, and his heir at law. I want this formally acknowledged.'

Cleopatra was entranced; the ugly head vanished in a trice. 'Oh, my dearest Antonius, they'll shake in their shoes!'

'No, they'll shit themselves, my lovely lady. Now give me a thousand kisses.'

She gave them ardently, afire with her victory. Now things would happen! Antony was going to war; his letter to the Senate was an ultimatum.

Two documents sped to Rome: the letter, and the last will and testament of Marcus Antonius. Gaius Sosius lodged the will with the Vestal Virgins, custodian of all Roman citizen wills; a man's will was sacred, not to be opened until after his death, and the Vestals had kept a man's will since the time of the Kings. But when Ahenobarbus split the seal on Antony's letter and read it, he dropped the scroll as if it were red-hot. Some time passed before he could hand it voicelessly to Sosius.

'Ye gods!' Sosius whispered, dropping it in his turn. 'Is he mad? No Roman has the authority to do a half of this! Caesar's bastard, King of Rome? That's what he means, Gnaeus, that's what he means. And Cleopatra ruling in the bastard's name? Oh, he must be mad!'

'Either that, or permanently drugged.' Ahenobarbus looked decisive. 'I won't read this out, Gaius, I can't. I'm going to burn it and give a speech instead. Jupiter! What ammunition it would make for Octavianus! He'd swing the entire Senate onto his side without needing to lift a finger.'

'You don't suppose,' Sosius said hesitantly, 'that Antonius *designed* this to do just that? It's a declaration of war.'

'Rome doesn't need a civil war,' Ahenobarbus said wearily, 'though I suspect that Cleopatra would love one. Don't you see? Antonius didn't write this, Cleopatra did.'

Sosius sat and trembled. 'What do we do, Ahenobarbus?'

'As I said. We burn the letter, and I give the speech of my life to those pathetic dotards in the Senate. No one must ever know how complete Cleopatra's hold over Antonius is.'

'Defend Antonius to the hilt, yes. But how can we prise him loose of Cleopatra? He's too far away – oh, the wretched East! It's like chasing a rainbow. Two years ago it looked as if prosperity was returning – the tax farmers and businessmen were ecstatic. But in the last months I've noticed a change,' said Sosius.

'Antonius's client-kings are moving in, and moving Roman commerce out. And it's eighteen months since the Treasury had any Eastern tributes.'

'Cleopatra,' Ahenobarbus said grimly. 'It's Cleopatra. If we can't get Antonius away from the woman, we're lost.'

'So is he.'

By midsummer Antony had shifted his massive war machine from Carana and Syria to Ephesus. Cavalry, legions, siege equipment and baggage train made the slow plod across central Anatolia, finally coming along the winding turns of the River Maeander to Ephesus, where the camps spread around the beautiful little city farther than the sharpest eye could see. The boiling mass of men, animals and apparatus slowly settled to a simmer as local merchants and farmers did their best to make some kind of profit out of the disaster that army camps embodied. Fertile land that had grown wheat and grazed sheep was churned to unproductive mud or dust, depending on the weather, while Antony's junior legates, not a sensitive or sympathetic lot, made matters worse by refusing to discuss the state of affairs with any local person. Robbery and rape escalated dizzily; so did revenge murders, beatings and active and passive resistance to the invaders. Prices soared. Dysentery became pandemic. Some of the reasons why, in days now gone, a Roman governor had made big money out of threatening to billet his legions on a city unless the city paid him anything from a hundred to a thousand talents. The horrified city had scrambled to pay.

Antony and Cleopatra journeyed in *Philopator*, which anchored in Ephesus harbor to exclamations of wonder. There Antony left wife and ship to take another, smaller vessel to Athens; he had unfinished business there, he told Cleopatra, who discovered she couldn't restrain this sober Antony the way she had in Alexandria. Ephesus was firmly Roman territory, and she was not its ruler anymore than her ancestors had been, therefore it had no tradition of bowing down to Egypt. Whenever she left the governor's palace to inspect the city or one of the camps, men stared at her as if she gave deep offense. Nor could she punish them for their rudeness. Publius Canidius was an old friend, but the rest of the commanders and their legates who filled Ephesus to bursting point considered her a joke or an insult. No obeisances in Asia Province!

Her mood was an unhappy one, dating back to the day before *Philopator* sailed from Alexandria, when Caesarion had subjected her to a most unwelcome and unpleasant scene. He was being left behind to govern Egypt, a task he didn't want. Not because he hankered to go to war with his mother and stepfather – the reason for their absence was the core of the matter.

'Mama,' he said to Cleopatra, 'this is insanity! Don't you see that? You're challenging the might of *Rome*! I know Marcus Antonius is a great general and has a huge army, but even if all its resources are brought to bear, Rome can't be defeated. It took her a hundred and fifty years to crush Carthage, but Carthage *was* crushed—so badly it never rose again! Rome is patient, but it won't take her a hundred and fifty years to crush Egypt and Antonius's East. Please, I beg you, don't offer Caesar Octavianus the chance to come east! He'll regard Antonius's concentrating all his forces in Ephesus, so far from any troubled area, as a declaration of war. Please, please, Mama, I beg you, don't do this!'

'Nonsense, Caesarion,' she said comfortably as she moved from place to place supervising her packing. 'Antonius can't be beaten on land or on sea, I've made sure of that by providing a massive war chest. If we delay, Octavianus will only gather strength.'

He stood beside a very recent bust of himself that his mother had commissioned from Dorotheus of Aphrodisias, unconsciously twinning himself in his mother's eyes. Choerilus had painted the bust, got every nuance of skin and hair correct, and delineated the eyes brilliantly. The sculpture looked so alive it might open its lips and speak, but with the reality standing beside it so fired up and passionate, it faded into insignificance.

'Mama,' he persevered, 'Octavianus hasn't even begun to tap his resources. And, much though I love Marcus Antonius, he isn't the equal of Marcus Agrippa on land or on sea. Octavianus may occupy the command tent in name, but he'll leave the war-making to Agrippa. I warn you, Agrippa is the pivot of everything! He's formidable! Rome hasn't thrown up his equal since my father.'

'Oh, Caesarion, really! You worry so much that I don't take any notice of you anymore.' Cleopatra paused with one of Antony's favorite robes in her hands. 'Who is this Marcus Agrippa? A nothing, a nobody. Antonius's equal? Definitely not.'

'Then you at least stay here in Alexandria,' the lad pleaded.

She looked astonished. 'What are you thinking about? I'm paying for this campaign, which means I'm Antonius's partner in the enterprise. Do you think me a novice at waging war?'

'Yes, I do. Your only experience was when you sat on Mount Casius waiting for Achillas and his army. It was my father dragged you out of that mess, not your own nonexistent military ability.

If you accompany Marcus Antonius, his Roman colleagues will think he's under your control, and hate you. Romans are not used to foreigners in the command tent. I am not a fool, Mama. I know what they say in Rome about you and Antonius.'

She stiffened. 'And what do they say in Rome about us?'

'That you're a sorceress, that you've bewitched Antonius, that he's your plaything, your puppet. That it's you pushing him to clash with the Senate and People of Rome. That, if he was not your husband, none of what has happened would have happened,' Caesarion said valiantly. 'They call you the Queen of Beasts, and deem you the prime mover in this, not Antonius.'

'You go too far,' Cleopatra said, sounding dangerous.

'No, I don't go far enough if I haven't succeeded in talking you out of this! Especially out of personally participating. My dearest, loveliest mama, you act as if Rome were King Mithridates the Great. Rome is not – and never will be! – Eastern-minded. Rome is of the West. She seeks only to control the East for her own survival.'

She had watched him closely, eyes going back and forth as she tried to decide what was her best tack. Having arrived at it, she said, voice soothing, 'Caesarion, you're not yet fifteen. Yes, I admit you are a man. Still and all, a very young and inexperienced man. Rule Egypt wisely, and I'll give you additional powers when Antonius and I return wearing the laurels of victory.'

He ceased the struggle. Eyes full of tears, he stared at her, shook his head, and left the room.

'Silly boy,' she said fondly to Iras and Charmian.

'Beautiful boy,' from Charmian, sighing.

'Not a boy, and not silly,' from Iras, grimly. 'Haven't you realized, Cleopatra, that he's prophetic? You should take notice of what he says, not dismiss it.'

So she left on *Philopator* with Iras's words still ringing in her ears; it was those, rather than what Caesarion had actually said, that caused her unhappiness, a mood the attitude of Antony's colleagues in Ephesus only enhanced. But, autocrat that she was, all of it only served to make her haughtier, ruder, more overbearing.

Antony wasn't to blame for his ship's putting in to Samos; it developed a leak that couldn't wait for Athens to be attended to, and Samos was the closest island.

The League of Dionysiac Entertainers had made Samos its headquarters; while he waited, Antony thought he might as well see what was going on among the magicians, dancers, acrobats, freaks, musicians and others who lingered in their delightful cottages until some festival called them away. None at the moment, Callimachus the league president informed him, after showing him a wonderful trick that turned landbound beetles into twinkling butterflies.

'However, we've decided to put on a feast tonight in your honor. You will attend?'

Of course he would! Resisting the urge to drink wine was as nothing compared to his compulsion to seek merriment in the company of an assortment of entertainers. The only problem was, he soon learned, that sobriety severely curtailed his enjoyment; he took a cup of wine and proceeded to get drunk.

What happened during the days that followed this decision he didn't remember; it was true that wine affected his memory more and more as he grew older. Only his secretary, Lucilius, forced him back into the dismal world of sobriety – and that, by a single, simple sentence:

'The Queen is bound to find out.'

'Oh, Jupiter!' Antony groaned. '*Cacat!*'

The leak had been repaired *nundinae* ago, he discovered when Lucilius and his body servants half carried him aboard, shaking and stumbling. Had he really drunk that much? Or was it more quickly destructive? Under the hangover he was conscious of a new terror; that finally the years of dissipation were catching up with him. The days of lifting anvils were over. He had turned fifty-one, and his biceps when he flexed them felt a little soft, wouldn't pop up. Fifty-one! A venerable consular's age. And Octavian was a mere thirty, wouldn't be thirty-one until toward the end of September. Worse, all Octavian's best generals were young men, whereas his were like himself, becoming grizzled. Canidius was over sixty! Oh, where did the time go? He felt sick, had to rush to the rail and vomit.

His valet brought him water to drink, sponged his lips and chin. 'Are you coming down with something, *domine*?'

'Yes,' said Antony, shivering. 'Old age.'

But by the time his ship tied up in the Piraeus, Antony had regained a little of last year's physical wellbeing, even if his mood was unpleasant.

'Where is my wife, Octavia?' he demanded of his steward in the governor's palace.

The man looked blank – no, astonished. 'It is some years since the lady Octavia was in residence, Marcus Antonius.'

440

'What do you mean, some years? She's supposed to be here, along with twenty thousand soldiers from her brother!'

'I can only repeat, *domine*, that she isn't. Nor are there any soldiers billeted anywhere near Athens. If the lord Octavianus sent soldiers, they must have gone to Macedonia, or overland to Asia Province.'

Memory was coming back; yes, it was five years since Octavia had come with four cohorts of troops, not four legions. And he had commanded her to send the military gifts from Octavian to him in Antioch, and return home herself. *Five years*! Was it really so long? No, perhaps it was only four years ago. Or three? Oh, did it matter?

'I've been away from Rome too long,' he said to Lucilius as he settled behind his desk.

'The last time was Tarentum, six years ago,' said Lucilius from his own desk.

'Then it was four years ago that Octavia came to Athens.'

'Yes.'

'Take a letter, Lucilius . . . "To Octavia, from Marcus Antonius. I hereby divorce you. Remove yourself from my house in Rome and cease tenancy of any of my villas in Italia. I do not return your dowry and I decline to continue to support you or my Roman children. Accept this as binding and final."'

Keeping his eyes firmly on the sheet of paper, Lucilius wrote. Oh, dear lady! With this act, all hope of rescue for Antonius is lost . . . He lifted his head, got up, put the paper down in front of Antony. One of his superlative talents was handwriting so good it didn't need to be copied by a professional scribe.

Antony read it swiftly, then folded it. 'Wax, Lucilius.'

Red was the customary color for formal documents. Lucilius held the stick in the flame of a lamp so expertly that it wasn't discolored from the smoke, twisted it away the moment a blob the size of a denarius lay athwart the outer fold. Antony put his seal ring in it and pressed down hard. Hercules, surrounded by IMP· M· ANT· TRI·

'Get it on the next ship for Rome,' Antony said curtly, 'and find me a ship bound for Ephesus. My business in Athens is quite finished.' He smiled wryly. 'It never existed.'

There didn't seem to be an exact moment he could pinpoint as the actual burning of his Roman boats, Antony decided as he sailed from the Piraeus; just that it dated from his learning that he had

441

sworn to dedicate himself and his booty to Cleopatra and Alexandria. His love for Octavia and things Roman had not prospered, whereas his love for Cleopatra had become all-encompassing. Why that was he didn't really know, except that she lay at the core of his being, that he couldn't gainsay her even when her demands were preposterous. Some of it was due to his lapses of memory, yes, but they couldn't be blamed for it either. Maybe the great Queen had moved herself holus-bolus into his heart because she at least could find merit in him; she at least thought him powerful and worth cultivating. Rome belonged to Octavian, so why not let Rome go entirely? That was what it boiled down to, when all was said and done. If he wanted to be the First Man in Rome, he would have to conquer Octavian on a battlefield. And Cleopatra saw that clearly, always had. His dangerous binge on Samos and its awful aftermath of illness, fresh lapses of memory, had taught him that his best years were past, even though he knew it was no more than a binge. Irresistible, when his real reason for sailing from Ephesus to Athens had been to escape his love, his bane, his vows to Cleopatra.

So, he had thought, arriving in Athens more or less healed, why not burn his Roman boats? Everyone from Cleopatra to Octavian wanted it, expected it, would have nothing less from him. Now he must get back to Ephesus before Cleopatra created fresh problems.

But before he could reach Ephesus the presence of Cleopatra was having repercussions. First Saturninus and Arruntius departed for Rome, declaring that they would rather serve a man they hated than any kind of foreigner; at least Octavian was a *Roman*! Then Atratinus followed, together with a group of junior legates who were infuriated by the way Cleopatra toured their camps finding fault, even had scathing words to say about sloppy gear or major centurions who didn't snap to attention when she addressed them.

When Atratinus reached Rome, Ahenobarbus and Sosius listened to his complaints with dismay.

Things were not good in Rome either. The Treasury was almost empty, thanks to the cost of finding good land for so many thousands of veterans. The multimillions of sesterces that Sextus Pompeius's vaults had yielded were spent, incredible as that seemed. Land came expensive, and very few legionaries agreed to retire in foreign locations like the Spains, the Gauls and Africa. They too were Roman, welded to Italian soil. Yes, the retirees were content – but at huge cost to the nation.

However, there could be no denying that Octavian was slowly gaining the ascendancy in the Senate and among the plutocrats and knight-businessmen; opportunities in Antony's East were dwindling, and those men and firms that had been prospering two years ago were now disintegrating. Polemon, Archelaus Sisenes, Amyntas and the smaller Antonian-appointed dynasts had grown confident enough to legislate to make it impossible for Roman commerce to flourish. Egged on, as everybody knew, by Cleopatra, the spider at the centre of the web.

'What are we going to do?' Sosius asked Ahenobarbus after the angry Atratinus had gone.

'I've been thinking about that ever since Antonius's letter, Gaius, and I believe there's only one thing left to do.'

'Well, go on!' Sosius cried eagerly.

'We have to reinforce the Romanness of Antonius's rule in the East, that's the first prong of this two-tined fork,' Ahebobarbus said. 'The second is to make Octavianus look illegal.'

'*Illegal*? How on earth can you do that?'

'By removing the government from Rome to Ephesus. You and I are the consuls of the year. Most of the praetors are also Antonian. I doubt we'll prise any tribunes of the plebs off their bench, but if half the Senate goes with us, we'll be an undisputed government-in-exile. Yes, Sosius, we leave Rome for Ephesus! Thus making Ephesus the centre of government, and infusing Antonius's circle with, say, five hundred trusty Romans. More than enough to force Cleopatra to return to Egypt, where she belongs.'

'That was what Pompeius Magnus did after Caesar – oops, Divus Julius! – crossed the Rubicon into Italia proper. He took the consuls, the praetors and four hundred senators to Greece.' Sosius frowned. 'But in those days the Senate was smaller, nor did it contain so many *novi homines*. Today's Senate is a thousand strong, and two-thirds New Men. Most of them Octavianus's men. If we are to look like a government-in-exile, we'll have to persuade at least five hundred senators to go with us, and I don't think we will.'

'Nor do I, actually. I'm aiming for the four hundred do-or-die Antonians. Not a majority, but impressive enough to convince most people that Octavianus is operating illegally if he tries to form a government to replace us,' said Ahenobarbus, looking smug.

'Once you do that, Gnaeus, you're starting a civil war.'

'I know. But civil war is inevitable anyway. Why else has Antonius moved his entire army and navy to Ephesus? Do you think Octavianus hasn't interpreted the move correctly? I loathe the man, but I'm well aware of his brilliance. A warped counterpart of Caesar's mind lives inside Octavianus's head.'

'How do you know it's in the head?'

'What?' Ahenobarbus asked blankly.

'The mind.'

Ahenobarbus waved his hands around, exasperated. 'Sosius, we're not discussing the location of the *animus*! We're discussing how best we can help Antonius out of his Egyptian mire and back inside Rome!'

'Yes, yes, of course. Pardon me. We'd best act in a hurry, then. If we don't, Octavianus will prevent our leaving Italia.'

But Octavianus didn't. His agents reported the sudden convulsion of activity by certain senators – bank withdrawals, the salting away of assets to prevent their being garnished, packing up of houses, wives, children, pedagogues, tutors, nurserymaids, valets, maids, hairdressers, cosmeticians, cooks, seamstresses, skivvies, and body-guards. But he made no move of any kind, didn't even mention it in the House or on the rostra of the Forum Romanum. He had gone out of Rome early in spring, but he was back, alert as a bird dog, yet absolutely inactive.

So Ahenobarbus, Sosius, ten praetors and three hundred members of the Senate hastened down the Via Appia to Tarentum on horseback or in gigs, leaving their dependents to travel in litters together with hundreds of ox-drawn wagons of servants, furni-ture, fabrics, fans, follies and foodstuffs. Everything eventually sailed from Tarentum, Tarentum being the nearer port for voyages heading for Athens around Cape Taenarum or for Patrae on the Gulf of Corinth.

Only three hundred senators! Ahenobarbus was disappointed that he couldn't persuade a quarter of the loyal Antonians, let alone any of the neutrals, but the tally was respectable enough, he was sure, to make it impossible for Octavian to form a working government without huge ructions. A judgement largely made out of his own exclusivity; Ahenobarbus was a Palatine man with a Palatine man's elitist view of Rome.

Antony was delighted to see them, and promptly set up an anti-Senate in Ephesus city hall. Indignant merchants of wealth who had only a *socius* standing were evicted from their mansions; luckily Ephesus was a big emporium and provided Antony with enough residences to accommodate this huge influx of important men and their families. The local plutocrats relocated in Smyrna, Miletus

444

and Priene, which led to the disappearance of commercial shipping from the harbor; another blessing: more war galleys could anchor there. What would happen to the city when the Roman assemblage departed didn't worry Antony or his confrères: a pity; Ephesus was to take years to regain its prosperity.

Cleopatra wasn't at all pleased at the advent of Ahenobarbus and the government-in-exile, who adamantly refused to permit her to attend the anti-Senate.

Which led her to snarl an imprudent statement to Ahenobarbus. 'You'll be sorry for this when I sit in judgement on the Capitol!'

'You'll not judge me, madam!' he snarled back. 'If you sit in judgement on the Capitol, I'll be dead – and all good Romans with me! I warn you, Cleopatra, that you'd better put such ideas out of your head, because it will never happen!'

'Don't you dare address me by my given name!' she said in freezing tones. 'You address me as "Your Majesty" – and bow!'

'In a pig's eye I do, *Cleopatra*!'

She went straight to Antony, who had returned from Athens in a dull, lacklustre mood that she deduced was the result of his binge on Samos; Lucilius had reported.

'I want to attend the Senate, and I want that oaf Ahenobarbus disciplined!' she cried, standing with fists clenched by her sides and her mouth a thin red strip.

'My dear, you can't possibly attend the Senate – it's sacred to Quirinus, the god of Roman men. Nor am I in any position to . . . er . . . discipline men as august as Gnaeus Domitius Ahenobarbus. Rome isn't ruled by a king, it's a democracy. Ahenobarbus is my equal, as are all Roman men, no matter how poor or undistinguished. In the eyes of the law, Roman men are level. *Primus inter pares*, Cleopatra – all I can be is first among my equals.'

'Then that must change.'

'That can't change. Ever. Did you really tell him that you would sit in judgement on the Capitol?' Antony asked, frowning.

'Yes. Once you've beaten Octavianus and Rome is ours, I will sit there as Caesarion's deputy until he's old enough.'

'Even Caesarion won't be able to do that. He's not a Roman, that's one reason. And the other is that no living man or woman inhabits the Capitol. It's sacred to our Roman gods.'

She stamped her foot. 'Oh, I don't understand you! One moment you appoint my son King of Kings, the next you have speech with a few Romans and you're all Roman again! Make up your mind! Am I to continue to finance my son's bid for the world, or am I going to pack up and go back to Alexandria? You're a fool, Antonius! A big, bumbling, indecisive idiot!'

In answer, Antony turned his shoulder; time would prove to her that, when he defeated Octavian, Rome would go on as Rome always had – a republic owning no king. In the meantime, she was footing the bill, whole and entire. That didn't make her the owner of a Roman army, but it did make her the owner of this campaign. Oh, he could compel her to return to Egypt. That was what every angry legate instructed him to do, more and more of them with each passing day. But if he sent her home, she would take her war chest with her, all twenty thousand gold talents of it. Some, like Atratinus, had told him openly that he should simply kill the sow, confiscate her war chest, and annex Egypt into the Empire. Knowing himself unable to do any of that, he bore Cleopatra's diatribes in silence and reminded his legates who was paying. But some, like Atratinus, had ended in preferring Octavian's rule to Cleopatra's.

'How can I send her home?' he asked Canidius, one of her two Roman supporters.

'You can't, Antonius, I know that.'

'Then why do so many others demand that I do it?'

'Because they're not used to foreigners or women in command, and they've failed to get it through their thick heads that she who pays the musicians calls the tune.'

'Will they ever get it through their thick heads?'

Canidius laughed at the genuinely funny question. 'No, they won't. An affirmative would mean sophistication, Hellenistic attitudes – all the qualities they don't possess.'

Cleopatra's other supporter was Lucius Munatius Plancus, whom she had bought with a lavish bribe. This investment also gained her Marcus Titius, his nephew, though Titius, more openly feral than Plancus, found it difficult to hide his dislike and contempt for his uncle's new employer. What Cleopatra didn't understand about Plancus was his unerring ability to choose the winning side in any clash between potential Roman First Men. Like the present Lucius Marcius Philippus's grandfather, he was a born tergiversator, saw no disgrace in changing sides whenever instinct prompted it.

And, as he said to Titius at the end of a month in Ephesus, 'I am beginning to see that Antonius remains hamstrung when it comes to dealing with That Woman. I think it's nonsense that she drugs him, or even charms him the way a Marsian does a snake. No, it's his deficiencies that bind him to her – he's a henpecked husband, and we all know plenty of them. He'd rather kidnap Cerberus from the doors of Hades than stand up to her, be it over a trifle or a huge ultimatum. While I fancied myself in love with Fulvia, I had a taste of it – she could bluff, bully or bludgeon me into doing *anything*, and, like Cleopatra, she tried to occupy the command tent. Well, her only reward was to be divorced from Antonius for her temerity, but Cleopatra? She's his mama, his lover, his best friend *and* his co-commander.'

'Maybe that's the core of it,' said Titius thoughtfully. 'All Rome has known Antonius for twenty years as a pure force of nature. He got it up ten times a night every night, he left a trail of broken hearts, bastards and cuckolded husbands in his wake, he knocked heads together as if they were melons, he drove chariots drawn by lions – he's a legend rapidly on his way to becoming a myth. He made a difference in the Senate, he served valorously at Pharsalus and won Philippi brilliantly. He's adulated! And now all of us who love him are discovering that our idol has feet of clay – Cleopatra dominates him utterly. A crushing blow.'

'The inescapable power of Nemesis . . . He's paying for a legendary life. Well, Titius, we watch and wait. I still have friends in Rome, they'll keep me informed as to how Octavianus deals with this coming crisis. The moment the scales tip in favor of Octavianus, we decamp.'

'Perhaps we should decamp now.'

'No, I think not,' said Plancus.

Much of Cleopatra's perceived arrogance and rudeness stemmed from an insecurity both new and alarming; the culture she came from and the circumstances of her life to date had never imbued her with any consciousness that a woman, especially a queen, was inferior to a man. It never occurred to her that, entering the world of Roman men, neither her status nor her untold wealth could make them see her as their equal. Her basic mistake was to assume that it was her foreignness that provoked their antipathy; that it was her sex was so incredible she never considered it. Thus, when she aped the behavior of her Roman enemies inside Antony's circle, she aped to make herself seem more Roman, less foreign. Wearing a plumed helmet, a cuirass over a shirt of chain mail and a short sword on a jeweled baldric, she marched around military head-quarters cursing as foully as any legate, under the impression that, when they cast her looks of loathing, they did so because she hadn't succeeded in being Roman enough. When she toured the camps before Antony returned from Athens, clad in her armor and mouthing her oaths, the legionaries laughed at her openly, the centurions tried to stifle their guffaws, the military tribunes looked her up and down as if she were a freak, the junior legates spat insults at her and proceeded to ignore her. On one occasion she demanded of the legion commander that he flog his *primipilus* centurion for insubordination; the man flatly refused, unintimidated.

'Run away and play with dolls, not toy soldiers!' he snapped.

He had given her the answer, but she didn't see it. Not her foreignness: the fact that feminine lips spewed obscenities and a feminine body wore military gear. Women didn't interfere with the doings of men, not in person and right under men's noses.

When Antony did return from Athens she demanded retribution, but he declined to act, preferring to tell her to stay away from the camps if she didn't want to look a fool; it never occurred to him that she did not understand the cause of Roman eminity. If she didn't quite obey him, she made sure that in future the only camps she visited belonged to Antony's non-Roman allies. Ah, they knew how to treat her! Polemon's son Lycomedes (Polemon himself had gone back to Pontus to guard the far East against the Medes and Parthians), Amyntas of Galatia, Archelaus Sisenes of Cappadocia, Deiotarus Philadelphus of Paphlagonia and the rest of the client-kings who had come to Ephesus fawned upon her.

She had noticed that Herod of Judaea hadn't appeared, nor sent an army; once her complaints about her treatment had been summarily dismissed upon Antony's return, she drew his attention to Herod's absence, which perturbed him sufficiently to write the King of the Jews a letter. Herod's answer was swift and full of flowery, obsequious phrases that, stripped bare and summed up, said matters in Jerusalem prevented his presence as much as they did the sending of an army. Open rebellion was a whisker away so, a thousand pardons, but . . . True enough, though not the real reason for Herod's delinquency. Herod's instinct for survival was as exquisitely tuned as Plancus's, and it was telling Herod that Antony might not win this war. To hedge his bets, he had sent a nice letter to Octavian in Rome, together with a gift for the temple of Jupiter Optimus Maximus – an ivory sphinx carved by Phidias himself. It had once belonged to Gaius Verres, who had looted it from his province of Sicily, and had been given as a fee to Hortensius for defending Verres (unsuccessfully) on many charges of extortion. From Hortensius it went to one of the Perquitieni for a thousand talents; bankrupted, that Perquitienus sold it for a hundred talents to a Phoenician merchant, whose widow, an artistic ignoramus, sold it to Herod for ten talents. Its real worth, Herod estimated, was anywhere between four and six thousand talents, and he had heard that Antony was showering artworks on Cleopatra. Queen Alexandra knew he had it, and if she tattled to Cleopatra, it would not long remain his. Hating his Egyptian neighbor with all his being, he decided the best place for it was Rome – in a public place of great sanctity. To get it from Jupiter Best and Greatest, Cleopatra would indeed have to sit in judgement upon the Capitol. It represented an investment for the future of his kingdom and himself. If Antony won . . . oh, perish the thought, tied as he was to Cleopatra! Not knowing that he echoed the sentiments of Atratinus, Herod decided that Antony's only way out of his present predicament was to kill Cleopatra and annex Egypt into the Empire.

As the army and the fleets commenced to move from Ephesus to Greece at the end of summer, Antony hit upon the best present of all to give Cleopatra, to take her mind off the constant feuding and fighting in the command tent: he sent to Pergamum and ordered that the two hundred thousand scrolls in its library be packed up and sent to Alexandria.

'A little recompense for Caesar's burning your books,' he said. 'Many of them are duplicates, but there are some volumes unique to Pergamum.'

'Silly!' she said fondly, ruffling his hair. 'It was a book warehouse on the waterfront that burned, not Alexandria's library. That's in the museum.'

'Then I'll give them back to Pergamum.'

She sat up straight. 'Indeed you will not! If they remain in Pergamum, some Roman governor will confiscate them for Rome.'

TWENTY-FOUR

'I've heard a peculiar rumor,' said Maecenas to Octavian when Octavian returned to Rome in April.

Knowing that Ahenobarbus and Sosius were ardently Antonian and also determined to stay in office for the entire year, Octavian had felt it prudent to leave Rome just after the New Year and stay away until he saw whether the doughty couple could swing the Senate around. They hadn't thus far succeeded, and Octavian's exquisitely sensitive instincts said they wouldn't now. Rome was safe for him, would continue to be safe for him.

'Rumor?' he asked.

'That Ahenobarbus and Sosius have been rendered impotent by their master in Alexandria. Antonius ordered Ahenobarbus to read out a treasonous letter to the Senate, but he didn't dare.'

'Do you have the letter?'

'No. Ahenobarbus burned it and gave a speech instead. Then, when Sosius held the *fasces* in February, he spoke. Limp oratory.'

'*Limp?* the adjective I heard was "fiery"!'

'It couldn't achieve its objective, to turn the Senate around. There were icicles on the Curia Hostilia eaves, yet Sosius sweated. In fact, both our consuls are as restive and restless as stabled mules smelling smoke.'

'Restive *and* restless?'

'Yes. Keeping up the muley metaphor, try to lead them, and they balk. Restive. But they can't stay still. Restless. I've put our consuls' behavior down to yet another rumor – that they intend to flee into exile, taking the Senate with them.'

'Leaving me to govern Rome and Italia without legal authority, a repetition of Pompeius Magnus's conduct after Divus Julius crossed the Rubicon. Not very original.' Octavian shrugged. 'Well, this time it won't work. I'll have a quorum in the Senate, and be able to appoint suffect consuls. How many senators do you think our pretty pair will cozen into going with them?'

'Not above three hundred, though most of the praetors will go – it's an Antonian year for government.'

'So, I'll still have a hundred die-hard Antonians in Rome to stick daggers in my back.'

'They would all have gone, and a lot of the neutrals with them, save for Cleopatra. It's that lady you have to thank for your being able to make a quorum. While she lingers in Antonius's vicinity like a bad smell, Caesar, you'll always have die-hard Antonians hovering around your back with daggers drawn, because they won't hover around Cleopatra.'

'And is it true that Antonius is moving his legions and fleets to Ephesus?'

'Oh, yes. Cleopatra insists. She's with him.'

'Which means she's opened her money bags at last. How happy Antonius must be!' The long-lashed lids fell over Octavian's eyes. 'But how foolish! Can he really be contemplating civil war, or is this a ploy to push me into moving my legions east of the Drina?'

'I honestly don't think it much matters what Antonius thinks. It's Cleopatra set on war.'

'She's a foreigner. If I could wipe Antonius off this slate, it would be a foreign war against a foreigner bent on invading Italia and sacking Rome. Especially if Antonius's forces move from Ephesus west to Greece or Macedonia.'

'A foreign war is far preferable. However, it's a Roman army moving to Ephesus, and a Roman army possibly going on to Greece. Cleopatra has no troops of her own, just fleets, and those not in the majority. Sixty enormous fives and sixty mixed threes and twos out of five hundred war vessels.'

'I need whatever that letter from Antonius contained, Maecenas! Bother Ahenobarbus! Why did he have to be consul this year? He's intelligent. A stupid man would have read the letter out despite its treasonous content.'

'Sosius isn't stupid either, Caesar.'

'Then they're best separated from Rome and Italia. They can do us less harm in Ephesus.'

'You mean you'll not oppose their leaving the country?'

'Definitely. While ever they're here, they'll make my life harder. Only where am I going to find the money to fight a war? And who will condone another civil one?'

'No one,' said Maecenas.

'Exactly. Everyone will see it as a struggle for supremacy between two Romans, whereas we know it's a struggle against the Queen of Beasts. But we can't *prove* that! Whatever we say about Antonius comes out sounding like an excuse to wage civil war. My reputation is in question! I've been quoted too many times as saying that I would never go to war against Antonius. Now I look like a hypocrite.'

Agrippa spoke; until now he had sat and listened. 'I know a civil war won't be condoned, Caesar, and I feel for you. But I hope you realize that you'll have to start preparing for one now. At the rate things in the East are going, it will come on next year. That means you can't demobilize the Illyrian legions. You will also have to gather fleets.'

'But how do I pay the legions? And how do I build extra war galleys? I've spent the entire contents of the Treasury most of it settling on a hundred thousand veterans on good land!' Octavian cried.

'Borrow from the plutocrats. Their tongues are hanging out at the prospect,' said Agrippa.

'And plunge Rome back into staggering debt? Nearly half of what I put in the Treasury went to pay exorbitant interest to those selfsame plutocrats. No, I won't give the knights that much power over the State ever again.'

'Then tax,' said Maecenas.

'I daren't! Not, at least, what I'd have to tax.'

'Have you worked the amount out already?' Maecenas asked.

'Of course I have. One of Antonius's most telling slurs against me is that I'm more an accountant than a general. To keep thirty legions under the Eagles and provide a total of four hundred ships, I'd have to tax every Roman citizen from highest to lowest one-quarter of his annual income,' Octavian said.

Agrippa gaped. 'Twenty-five per cent?'

'That's what a quarter is.'

'There'd be blood on the streets,' said Maecenas.

'Tax the women too,' Agrippa said. 'Attica has an income of two hundred talents a year. Once his cancer carries Atticus off – that can't be too far away – she'll go up to five hundred talents. And I'm his major heir, so his money is safely for you.'

'Oh, come, Agrippa! Don't you remember what the women did when the Triumvirs tried to tax them eleven years ago? Hortensia is still very much alive, she'd lead another revolt. And do you fancy giving women the vote? Because we'd have to.'

'I don't see what difference there is between being ruled by Cleopatra and by Rome's own women,' Agrippa said. 'You're right, Caesar. It will have to be men only.'

Now owning an impressive majority in the House, Octavian had Lucius Cornelius Cinna and a cousin of Messala Corvinus's, Marcus Valerius Messala, appointed the new consuls. Rather than appoint new praetors, he closed the courts. By no means all of the remaining seven hundred senators were his creatures, but Octavian behaved as if they were, announcing that he himself would be senior consul next year, with Messala Corvinus as his junior. If war was to come on next year, Octavian needed all the authority he could muster.

'Democracy is a hollow word as long as Cleopatra and her minion Marcus Antonius threaten Rome, I am aware of that,' Octavian said to the House, 'but I pledge you my oath, conscript fathers, that as soon as this threat from the East evaporates, I will return proper government to the Senate and People of Rome. For Rome herself comes first, far ahead of mere men, no matter what their names or political viewpoints. I govern at the moment because someone has to! Though my Triumvirate has lapsed, it is some years since the Senate and People have had experience in government, whereas I have never been out of it these eleven years.'

He drew a breath, surveyed the tiers to either side of the curule dais, upon which he had replaced his ivory chair. 'What I wish to emphasize this morning is that I do not blame Marcus Antonius for the present situation. I blame Cleopatra – her, and her alone! It is she who marches steadily westward, not Antonius, who is her puppet, her marionette. The jig he dances is Egyptian! What have I or Rome done to deserve the threat of an army, a navy? Rome and I have acquitted ourselves of our duty without ever once menacing Antonius in the East! So why does he menace the West? The answer is, he doesn't! Cleopatra does!'

And so on, and so forth. Octavian said nothing new, and in saying nothing new, failed to carry a hundred of the neutrals as well as the hundred Antonians left. Nor, when he announced that he would impose a twenty-five per cent tax upon the incomes of all Roman men, could he carry the House. It erupted into fury, spilled into the streets and gratified the knight-businessmen by personally leading the bloody riots that ensued. Having no choice, Octavian went on to proscribe the three hundred and four members of Antony's anti-Senate in Ephesus. That gave him sufficient funds from the auction and sale of their Italian property to pay the Illyrian legions.

A much richer man after Atticus cut his terminal illness short by falling on the sword he had never used in life, Agrippa insisted on commissioning two hundred ships.

'But not clumsy big fives,' he said to Octavian. 'I'm going to use Liburnians, none but Liburnians. They're small, maneuverable, swift and cheap. Naulochus showed how good they are.'

A small man, Octavian wasn't quite convinced by this argument. 'Doesn't size matter in any way?' he asked.

'No,' said Agrippa flatly.

Midsummer saw a slight reversal of the eastward traffic in senators when some returned to Rome full of tales of That Woman and her pernicious influence over Antony; they did Octavian's cause more good than all his own oratory could. However, none of these refugees could offer ironbound proof that the coming war was Cleopatra's idea. All of them had to admit, when pressed, that Antony still occupied the command tent ahead of the Queen. It really did seem as if it were Antony intent upon civil war.

Then came the sensational news that Antony had divorced his Roman wife. Octavia sent immediately for her brother.

'He has divorced me,' she said, handing Octavian the curt note. 'I am to quit his house and take the children with me.'

Her eyes were tearless, but they held the stricken expression of a dying animal; Octavian's hand went out to her.

'Oh, my dear!'

'I had two years, the happiest of my life. My only trouble now is that I don't have enough money to settle the family somewhere else, unless I jam us into Marcellus's house.'

'You'll come to my house,' he said instantly. 'It's vast enough to provide a whole wing for you and the children. Besides, it will please Tiberius and Drusus to have their playmates living under the same roof, with a more motherly person than Livia Drusilla to supervise all our children. I think I'll take Julia from Scribonia and install her too.'

'Oh! Ah . . . um . . . if I'm to have Julia as well as Tiberius and Drusus, I'll need another pair of motherly hands – Scribonia's.'

Octavian looked wary. 'I doubt Livia Drusilla would approve.'

Privately Octavia thought Livia Drusilla would approve of any measure that meant she wouldn't be bothered by a tribe of young children. 'Ask her, Caesar, please!'

Livia Drusilla saw Octavia's point at once. 'An excellent idea!' she said, smiling the sphinx's smile. 'Octavia can't take the burden alone, but it's no use looking at me. I fear mine is not a maternal nature.' She looked delicately deferring. 'Ah . . . unless, that is, you don't wish to set eyes on Scribonia?'

'I?' He looked astonished. '*Edepol*, what does she matter to me? After Clodia, I quite liked her. Then she turned shrewish, I don't know why. Age, probably. But I see her every time I visit Julia, and we get along together splendidly these days.'

Livia Drusilla giggled. 'The *domus Livia Drusilla* seems like to be a harem! How wonderfully Eastern. Cleopatra would approve.'

Pouncing on her, he bit her neck playfully, then forgot all about Scribonia, Octavia, children and harems.

The fly in the ointment came from a different source: Gaius Scribonius Curio, aged eighteen, announced that he wouldn't be moving house; he was going east to join Mark Antony.

'Oh, Curio, must you?' Octavia asked, dismayed. 'It will grieve Uncle Caesar dreadfully.'

'Caesar's no uncle of mine!' the youth said scornfully. 'I belong in Antonius's camp.'

'If you go, how can I persuade Antyllus not to go?'

'Easily. He's not yet a man.'

'But that's easier said than done,' she said to Gaius Fonteius, who had volunteered to help her move house.

'When does Antyllus turn sixteen?'

'Not forever. He was born the year Divus Julius died.'

'Then he's barely thirteen.'

'Yes. But oh, so wild and impulsive! He'll run away.'

'At thirteen, he'll be caught. For young Curio, it's a very different matter. He's of age and master of his own fortune.'

'How can I tell Caesar?'

'You won't have to. I will,' said Fonteius, who would have done anything to spare his Octavia pain.

Her divorce made her eligible – theoretically – but Fonteius was too wise to speak of his own love. As long as he said nothing, his place in her life was secure; the moment he voiced what he felt, she would send him away. Better then to wait for time to cure her malady. If even time had that power. He didn't know.

The defection of Saturninus, Arruntius and Atratinus, among others, did not make huge inroads into Antony's band of followers, but when Plancus and Titius deserted, they left a noticeable gap.

'It's Pompeius Magnus's war camp all over again,' said Plancus to Octavian once he reached Rome. 'I wasn't with Magnus, but they say everyone had a different opinion, and Magnus couldn't control them. So that by the time Pharsalus happened, he was powerless to enforce the Fabian tactics he favored. Labienus generaled, and lost. No one could beat Divus Julius, though Labienus thought he could. Oh, the quarrels and squabbles! As nothing compared to the goings-on in Antonius's war camp, believe me, Caesar. That Woman insists on having her say, airs her opinions as if they had more weight than Antonius's, and thinks nothing of deriding him in front of his legates, his senators – even his centurions. He takes it all! Fawns on her, runs after her – she lies on his couch in the *locus consularis*, if you please! How Ahenobarbus hates her! They scrap like a pair of wildcats, spitting, snarling – yet Antonius won't put her in her place. One day at dinner she got a cramp in her foot, and would you believe that Antonius fell on his knees before her to rub the foot better? You could have heard a moth land on a down pillow, the dining room was so silent and still. Then he resumed his place as if nothing had happened! I think that episode was what made Titius and I decide the time had come to depart.'

'I hear all kinds of weird rumors in Rome, Plancus, so many that I don't know what to believe,' Octavian said, wondering what Plancus's price was going to be.

'Believe the worst of them and you won't go far wrong.'

'Then how can I convince these donkeys here in Rome that it's Cleopatra's war, not Antonius's?'

'You mean they still think Antonius commands?'

'Yes. They simply can't stomach the idea that a foreigner is capable of dominating the great Marcus Antonius.'

'Nor could I, until I saw it for myself.' Plancus tittered. 'Perhaps you ought to arrange for tours to Samos – that's where they are at the moment, en route to Athens – for the unbelievers. Once seen, never forgotten.'

'Levity, Plancus, does not become you.'

'Seriously, then, Caesar. I could *perhaps* offer you better ammunition, but there is a price.'

Dear, unapologetic Plancus! Straight out with it, no dancing around. 'Name your price.'

'A suffect consulship next year for my nevvy, Titius.'

'He's none too popular in Rome since he executed Sextus.'

'He did the deed, yes, but the order came from Antonius.'

'I can certainly procure him the job, but I can't protect him from his detractors.'

'He can afford bodyguards. Is it a done deal, then?'

'Yes. Now what can you offer me in return?'

'When Antonius was in Antioch, still in the last stages of his recovery from wine, he made his will. Whether it remains his last, I don't know, but Titius and I witnessed it. I believe he took it off to Alexandria with him when he went – Sosius carried it to Rome, at any rate.'

Octavian frowned. 'What has Antonius's will to do with it?'

'Everything,' said Plancus simply.

'Not an adequate answer. Expatiate.'

'He was in a good mood when we witnessed it, and passed a few remarks that made both Titius and me think it was a highly suspect document. Treasonous, in fact, if a document not seen until after its author's death can be held treasonous. Antonius clearly didn't think posthumous treason exists, hence his unguarded comments.'

'Be more specific, Plancus, please!'

'I can't. Antonius was too obscure. But Titius and I think it would profit you to take a look at Antonius's will.'

'How can I do that? A man's will is sacrosanct.'

'That's your problem, Caesar.'

'Can't you tell me anything about its contents? Exactly what remarks did he make?'

Already standing, Plancus twitched folds of toga into place, apparently absorbed. 'We really ought to design a garment more suitable for sitting in than the toga . . . How he loved Alexandria and That Woman . . . Yes, togas are a nuisance . . . How her son ought to have his rights . . . Oh, bother! There's a mark on it!' And out he sailed, still primping.

Not so treasonous, then. Except that Plancus had genuinely seemed to think Antony's will would help him. Since any suffect consulship for Titius was many months into the future, Plancus would surely have known that, if he dangled a false bait under Octavian's nose, Titius would never sit on the curule dais. But how to gain access to Antony's will? *How?*

'I remember that Divus Julius told me the Vestals held over two million wills – upstairs, downstairs, in part of the basement,' he said to Livia Drusilla, the only one to whom he could confide such incendiary news. 'They have a system. Wills from provinces and foreign countries in one area, Italian wills in another, and Roman wills somewhere else. But Divus Julius didn't elaborate on the system, and at the time I wasn't to know how important the subject would become, so I didn't push him to elaborate. Stupid, stupid!' He thumped a fist on his knee.

'Don't worry, Caesar, you'll attain your ends.' Livia Drusilla's large, striped navy-blue eyes turned contemplative; she sat thinking, then chuckled. 'You might begin by doing something nice for Octavia,' she said then, 'and, since I am a notoriously jealous wife, you will have to do it for me too.'

'You, jealous of Octavia?' he asked, amazed.

'But people outside our intimate circle of friends aren't to know how matters stand between Octavia and me, are they? All Rome is indignant over the divorce – silly man! He ought never to have evicted her and the children, it damages him more than all your canards about Cleopatra's influence over him.' The beautiful face took on a soft, dreamy expression. 'It would be splendid if your agents could tell the people of Rome and Italia how much you love your sister and your wife, with what tender consideration you regard them. I am sure that if you were to let Lepidus take up residence in the Domus Publica, Lepidus would be so grateful that he would propose a tiny honor for Octavia and me as a thank-you.'

He was staring at her with that dazzled air she could provoke when the subtlety of her mind outstripped his. 'I wish I knew where you're going, my dearest one, but I don't.'

'Think of the hundreds of statues of Octavia you've erected throughout Rome and Italia, and the statues of me that have joined them. Wouldn't it be wonderful if a line could be added to their inscriptions? Some stunning new honor?'

'I'm still in the dark.'

'Persuade Lepidus Pontifex Maximus to award Octavia and me the status of Vestal Virgins in perpetuity.'

'But you're not Vestals! Or virgins, for that matter!'

'Honorary, Caesar, *honorary*! Announce it with fanfares of trumpets in the marketplaces from Mediolanum and Aquileia to Rhegium and Tarentum! Your sister and your wife are exemplary beyond description, so much so that their marital chastity and conduct put them in the same league as the Vestals.'

'Go on!' he said eagerly.

'Our Vestal Virgin status will permit us to come and go in the Vestal side of the Domus Publica at – pardon my pun – will. There's no need to involve Octavia if I have that privilege too, because I can find out for you exactly where Antonius's will is stored. Appuleia won't suspect my motives – why should she? Her mother is your half-sister, she dines with us regularly, she likes me very much. I can't steal the will for you, but if I find out where it is, you can lay your hands on it quickly.'

His hug left her crushed and breathless, but she didn't mind being crushed and breathless. Nothing pleased Livia Drusilla more than being able to suggest a course of action that Caesar had not thought of for himself.

'Livia Drusilla, you're brilliant!' he cried, releasing her.

'I know,' she said, giving him a little push. 'Now start the business, my love! It's going to take a few *nundinae*, and we can't afford to wait too long.'

The heartache of losing his triumviral status wasn't nearly as painful to Lepidus as his exile from the city of Rome, so when he had a visit from Octavian and heard what he had to do in order to move back into the Domus Publica, he agreed without hesitation to elevate Octavia and Livia Drusilla to Vestal Virgin rank. This was not a hollow honor. It endowed both women with sacrosanctity and inviolability; they could walk anywhere without threat, as no man, be he the lowest and most predatory, would dare to touch a Vestal Virgin. If he did, he was doomed for all eternity – he would be *sacer* – unholy, stripped of his citizenship, flogged and beheaded, and all his property down to the meanest pottery beaker would be confiscated. His wife and children would starve.

All Rome and Italia rejoiced; if their approval was more on Octavia's behalf than on Livia Drusilla's, the latter lady did not care a rush. Instead, she invited herself to dinner in the Vestals' dining room to meet her fellow priestesses.

Appuleia the Chief Vestal was a cousin of Octavian's, and knew Livia Drusilla well, starting with the time when, young and pregnant, she had been sheltered in the Atrium Vestae before her marriage to Octavian.

'An omen,' Appuleia said to her as the seven settled to eat on chairs around a table. 'I was so worried, I can confess that now. Oh, the relief when your stay didn't have any religious consequences! It was an omen of this, I'm sure.'

Not a clever woman, Appuleia, yet the terrific reverence in which she was held had molded her into much of what was expected from a Chief Vestal. She was clad in pure white, a long-sleeved dress overlaid with a tunic slit up each side, the *bulla* medal on a chain around her neck, her hair hidden by a crown of seven rolled coils of wool atop each other, and the whole rounded off by a veil so fine it floated. She ruled her little flock with a rod of iron, mindful of the fact that Vestal chastity was Rome's luck. From time to time a man (like Publius Clodius) had impugned some Vestal's chastity and brought her to trial, but that wasn't going to occur under the reign of Appuleia!

All the Vestals were seated around the table, liberally loaded with tasty food and a flagon of sparkling white wine from Alba Fucentia. The two underage Vestals drank water from the well of Juturna, whereas the other three, clad like Appuleia, were at liberty to partake of the wine. Livia Drusilla, the seventh, had not presumed to clothe herself as a Vestal, though she did wear white.

'My husband has spoken a little of your testamentary industry,' Livia Drusilla said when the children had gone, 'but only in a vague way. Might it be possible for me to tour sometime?'

Appuleia's face lit up. 'Of course! Any time.'

'Ah . . . now?'

'If you wish, certainly.'

So Livia Drusilla undertook the tour Divus Julius had made when he assumed the title of Pontifex Maximus, was shown the many racks of vellum upon which the details of a will were entered, led upstairs to see the staggering number of pigeonholes, downstairs to the basement, and through the storage facilities on the ground floor. It was fascinating, especially to a woman like this one, so meticulous and organized herself.

'Do you have a special area for senators?' she asked after much marveling as she walked around.

'Oh, yes. They're here, on this floor.'

'And if they've been consuls, do you distinguish them from mere senators?'

'Of course.'

Livia Drusilla managed to look both coy and conspiratorial. 'I wouldn't dream of asking you to show me my husband's will,' she said, 'but I would dearly love to see one of equal status. Where, for instance, is the will of Marcus Antonius?'

'Oh, he's in a special place,' Appuleia answered at once, no suspicion crossing her mind. 'Consul and Triumvir, but not really a part of Rome. He's here, all by himself.'

She took Livia Drusilla over to a rack of pigeonholes beyond the screen which fenced off the lodgement office from strictly Vestal territory, and without hesitation withdrew a hefty scroll from a shelf it alone occupied. 'There you are,' she said, handing Livia Drusilla the document.

Octavian's wife balanced it experimentally, turned it over to look at the red seal: Hercules, IMP· M· ANT· TRI· Yes, this was Antony's will. She gave it back immediately, laughing.

'He must have many bequests,' she said.

'All the great ones do. The shortest one of all was Divus Julius's – such sagacity, such crispness!'

'Do you get to read them, then?'

Appuleia looked horrified. 'No, no! Naturally we see a will after its author is dead, when his or her executor comes to take it. The executor must open it in our presence because we have to put V.V. at the end of each clause. That way, it cannot be added to after it leaves us.'

'Brilliant!' said Livia Drusilla. She pecked Appuleia on the cheek and squeezed her hand. 'I must go, but one last, most important question – is any will ever opened before its author dies, my dear?'

Another look of horror. 'No, never! That would be to break our vows, and that we'd never do.'

Back to the *domus Livia Drusilla*, where Livia Drusilla found her husband in his study. One glance at her face, and he sent his scribes and clerks out.

'Well?' he asked.

'I held Antonius's will in my hand,' she said, 'and I can tell you exactly where it's stored.'

'So we're that much ahead. Do you think Appuleia would let me open it?'

'Not even if you convicted her of unchastity and buried her in an underground chamber with a jug of water and a loaf of bread. I'm afraid you'll have to wrest it from her – and the others.'

'*Cacat!*'

'I suggest that you take your Germans to the Atrium Vestae in the middle of the night, Caesar, and cordon off the whole area outside its lodgement doors. It will have to be soon, because I was told that Lepidus will be taking up residence in the Pontifex Maximus's side of the Domus Publica very shortly. There's bound to be a racket, and you don't want Lepidus rushing over from his side to see what's amiss. Tomorrow night, no later.'

* * *

461

Octavian had to do a lot of pounding on the doors before a frightened face opened one a crack and peered around it – the housekeeper. Two Germans thrust the woman away and ushered their master in amid a blaze of torches as other Germans followed him.

'Good!' Octavian said to Arminius. 'With any luck, I'll get it before the Vestals appear. They'll have to dress.'

He almost made it.

'What do you think you're doing?' Appuleia demanded from the door that led back into the Vestals' private apartments.

Antony's will in his hand, Octavian propped. 'I'm confiscating a treasonous document,' he said loftily.

'Treasonous, my foot!' the Chief Vestal snapped, striding to impede his exit. 'Give that back, Caesar Octavianus!'

For answer, he passed it over his head to Arminius, so tall that, when he held it high, Appuleia couldn't reach it.

'You are *sacer*!' she gasped as three more Vestals entered.

'Nonsense! I'm a consular doing my duty.'

Appuleia produced a chilling scream. 'Help, help, help!'

'Shut her up, Cornel,' Octavian said to another German.

When the three other Vestals commenced screaming, they too were held and silenced by Germans.

Octavian gazed at the four in that flickering glare of light, his eyes as coldly luminous as a black leopard's. 'I am removing this will from your custody,' he said, 'and there's nothing you can do to prevent me. For your own safety, I suggest that you say no word of what's happened here to anybody. If you do, I cannot answer for my Germans, who have no reverence for Vestals, and love to deflower virgins of any sort. *Tacete*, ladies. I mean it.'

And he was gone, leaving Rome's luck weeping and wailing.

He convened the Senate on the first permissible day, looking smugly triumphant. Lucius Gellius Poplicola, who had elected to remain in Rome to be a nuisance to Octavian, felt the hairs on his arms and neck rise as a frisson of icy fear streaked down his spine. What was the little worm up to now? And why did Plancus and Titius seem bursting with glee?

'For two years I have spoken to the members of this House about Marcus Antonius and his dependence upon the Queen of Beasts,' Octavian began, standing in front of his curule chair with a fat scroll in his right hand. 'Nothing I have said has been able to convince many of you here today that I have spoken the truth. "Give us proof!" you yammer, over and over again. Very well, I have proof!' He held up the scroll. 'I have in my hand the last will and testament of Marcus Antonius, and it contains all the proof even the most ardent of Antonius's followers can demand.'

'Last will and testament?' Poplicola asked, bolt upright.

'Yes, last will and testament.'

'A man's will is sacrosanct, Octavianus! No one can broach it while its author lives!'

'Unless it contains treasonous statements.'

'Even should it! Is a man to be deemed a traitor for what he says after his death?'

'Oh, yes, Lucius Gellius. Definitely.'

'This is illegal! I refuse to let you proceed!'

'How can you stop me? If you continue to interject, I'll have my lictors throw you out. Now sit down and listen!'

Poplicola looked around to see every face alight with curiosity, and acknowledged himself beaten. For the moment. Let the young monster do his worst, then . . . He sat, scowling.

Octavian unrolled the will, but didn't read from it; he had no need to, for he knew it off by heart.

'I have heard some of you call Marcus Antonius the most Roman of all Romans. Dedicated to the advancement of Rome, brave, bold, eminently capable of extending Roman rule to blanket the entire East. Which is why he asked for – and received! – the East as his purlieu after Philippi. That was just ten years ago. During those ten years, Rome has hardly seen him, so thoroughly and zealously has he pursued his command. Or so those of you like Lucius Gellius Poplicola would have it. But while he may have gone east with the best of intentions, his frame of mind didn't last. Why? What happened? I can sum up the answer in one word: Cleopatra. Cleopatra, the Queen of Beasts. A mighty sorceress, steeped in occult worship and the arts of love and poison. Do you not remember King Mithridates the Great, who poisoned himself with a hundred potions every day, and took a hundred antidotes? When he tried to kill himself with poison, it wouldn't work. One of his bodyguards had to run him through with a sword. I would also remind you that King Mithridates was the grandfather of Cleopatra. The blood in her veins is naturally inimical to Rome.

'They met first in Tarsus, where she cast her spell – but not effectively enough. Though she bore him twins, Antonius stayed free of her until the winter of the year that saw him apportion out Rome's client-kingdoms in Antioch. He joined her in revelry, but when spring came he couldn't leave her – she wouldn't let him. Instead, she became a camp follower quite as tawdry as any other eastern harlot! Yes, she went with him as he and his gigantic army marched for the uppper Euphrates. Strutting in ludicrous parody of some august commander-in-chief! Then Antonius came to his senses and ordered her to return home. *Brave* Antonius. Momentarily, cowed, she went. Oh, why couldn't our brave Antonius continue to stand up to her?' Octavian shrugged. 'A question for which I have no answer.'

Poplicola had subsided into a slump, his arms folded across his chest; Plancus on the front benches and Titius on the middle tier couldn't stop wriggling in anticipation, Octavian noted. He resumed declaiming to a silent House.

'There is no need to dwell upon the disastrous campaign he waged against Parthian Media, for it is the period after his awful retreat that should interest us more than the loss of one-third of a Roman army. Antonius did what Antonius does best – swilled wine until it broke his mind. Demented and helpless, he appealed for succor to . . . Cleopatra. Not to Rome, but Cleopatra. Who came to Leuke Kome bearing gifts beyond imagination – money, food, arms, medicines, servants in thousands and physicians in scores. From Leuke Kome the pair moved to Antioch, where Antonius finally got around to making a will. One copy was lodged here in Rome, the other in Alexandria, where Antonius wound up last winter. But by then he was utterly under Cleopatra's sway, drugged and dominated. He didn't need to drink wine anymore, he had better things to swallow, from Cleopatra's potions to her blandishments. With the result that, in spring of this year coming to an end, he moved his entire army and navy to . . . Ephesus. Ephesus! A thousand miles west of where it is really needed – on a line from Armenia Parva to southern Syria, there to guard against Parthian incursions. Why then did he move his army and navy to Ephesus? And why then has he since moved both to Greece? Is Rome a threat to him? Or Italia? Have any armies and navies west of the Drina River made warlike gestures in his direction? No, they have not! And you do not need to take my word for that – it is manifest to the least among you!'

His eyes swept the back tiers, where the *pedarii* sat under a ban of silence. Then, slowly and carefully, he descended from the curule dais and took up a place in the middle of the floor.

'I do not believe for one moment that Marcus Antonius has committed these acts of aggression against his homeland voluntarily.

No Roman would, save those who were outlawed unjustly and sought to return – Gaius Marius, Lucius Cornelius Sulla, Divus Julius. But has Marcus Antonius been declared *hostis*? No, he has not! To this very day, his status remains what it has always been – a Roman of Rome, the last of many generations of Antonii who have served their country. Not always wisely, but always with patriotic zeal.

'So what has happened to Marcus Antonius?' Octavian asked in ringing tones, though this was one speech that didn't need to rouse the senators from a gentle doze. They were wide awake, listening avidly. 'Again, the answer lies in one word – Cleopatra. He is her plaything, her puppet – yes, all of you could chant the list along with me, I know that! But most of you have never believed me, I know that too. Today I am able to offer you proof that what I say is actually a diminished version of Antonius's perfidies, done at Cleopatra's dictate. A foreigner, a woman, a worshipper of beasts! And a mighty sorceress, capable of bewitching one of the strongest, most Roman Romans.

'You know that the woman, the foreigner, has an eldest son whose paternity she attributes to Divus Julius. A youth now aged fifteen, who sits beside her on the Egyptian throne as Ptolemy XV *Caesar*, if you please! To a Roman, he is a bastard and not a Roman citizen. For those of you who believe he is the son of Divus Julius, I can offer proof that he is not – that he is the son of a slave Cleopatra took for her amusement. She is of an amorous disposition, has many lovers, and always has had many lovers. Whom she uses first as sexual partners, then as victims of her poisons – yes, she experiments on them until they die! As died the slave who fathered her eldest son.

'How is this relevant, you ask? Because she inveigled poor Antonius into declaring this bastard boy King of Kings, and now she goes to war against Rome to seat him on the Capitol! There are men sitting here, conscript fathers, who can attest on oath that her favorite threat is that they will suffer when she takes her throne on the Capitol and passes judgement in her son's name! Yes, she expects to use Antonius's army to conquer Rome and turn it into Ptolemy XV Caesar's kingdom!'

He cleared his throat. 'But is Rome to continue to be the world's greatest city, the centre of law, justice, commerce and society? No, Rome is not! The capital of the world is to be removed to Alexandria! Rome is to be let dwindle into nothing.'

The scroll flapped open, dangled from Octavian's hand held high all the way to the black-and-white tiles of the floor. A few of the senators jumped at the noise, so sudden was it, but Octavian ignored them, sweeping on.

'The proof lies in this document, Antonius's last will and testament! It leaves everything he has, including his Roman and Italian property, investments and money, to Queen Cleopatra. Whom he swears he loves, loves, loves, *loves*! His one and only wife, the centre of his being. He attests that Ptolemy XV Caesar is the *legitimate* son of Divus Julius, and heir to everything Divus Julius left to me, his Roman son! He insists that his famed Donations be honored, which makes Ptolemy XV Caesar the King of Rome! Rome, who has no king!'

The murmurs were beginning; the will was open, it could be examined by anyone who wanted to verify what Octavian was saying.

'What, conscript fathers, are you outraged? So you should be! But these are not the worst things that Antonius's will have to say! That is contained in the burial clause, which instructs that, no matter where his death might occur, his body is to be given over to the Egyptian embalmers who travel with him everywhere, and be embalmed according to the Egyptian technique. Then he instructs that he be entombed *in his beloved Alexandria*! Alongside his beloved wife, Cleopatra!'

Tumult ensued as senators leaped from their stools, their ivory chairs, shaking their fists and howling.

Poplicola waited until they quietened. 'I don't believe one word of it!' he shouted. 'The will is a forgery! How else could you have laid your hands on it, Octavianus?'

'I wrested it from the Vestal Virgins, who defended it well,' Octavian said calmly. He tossed it to Poplicola, who scooped it up and tried to re-roll it. 'Don't bother with the beginning or the middle, Lucius Gellius. Go to the end. Examine the seal.'

Hands shaking, Poplicola looked at the seal, intact because Octavian had carefully cut around it, then went to the clause dealing with treatment and disposition of Antony's body. Gulping, shuddering, he flung the screed away, clattering. 'I must go to him and try to make him see sense,' he said, rising clumsily to unsteady feet. Then, weeping openly, he turned to the tiers and held out his trembling hands. 'Who will come with me?'

Not many. Those who left with Poplicola were hissed and reviled; the House was convinced at last that Marcus Antonius was no longer a Roman, that he was bewitched, under Cleopatra's spell – and preparing to march on his homeland for her sake.

* * *

'Oh, what a triumph!' Octavian said to Livia Drusilla when he returned home, riding on the shoulders of Agrippa and Cornelius Gallus, who made a well-matched pair of ponies. But at his door he dismissed them, together with Maecenas and Statilius Taurus, asking them to dinner on the morrow. Something as juicy as this victory must first be shared with his wife, whose devious scheme had made his task so much easier. For he knew that Appuleia and her companions could not have been forced into showing him whereabouts the will was stored, and he wouldn't have dared ransack the place. He had had to know exactly where the will was.

'Caesar, I never doubted the outcome,' she said, snuggling against him. 'You will always control Rome.'

He grunted, hunched his shoulders unhappily. 'That's still debatable, *meum mel*. The news of Antonius's treachery will make it easier to collect my taxes, but they'll remain unpopular until I can convince the whole country that the alternative is to be reduced to an Egyptian possession under Egyptian law. That the free grain dole will go, the circuses will go, commercial activity will go, Roman autonomy will go for every class of citizen. They haven't understood that yet, and I fear I won't be able to explain it to them before the Egyptian axe falls, wielded by Antonius's capable hands. They *must* be made to see that this is not a civil war! It's a foreign war in Roman guise.'

'Have your agents repeat it *ad nauseam*, Caesar. Hold up Antonius's conduct to them in the simplest terms – people need simplicity if they are to understand,' Livia Drusilla said. 'But it is more than that, isn't it?'

'Oh, yes. I am not a triumvir anymore, and if the early days of the war should go against me, some aspiring wolf on the front benches will spill me – Livia Drusilla, my hold on power is so tenuous! What if Pollio should come out of retirement with Publius Ventidius at his shoulder?'

'Caesar, Caesar, don't be so glum! You have to demonstrate publicly that this war is a foreign one. Is there no way?'

'One, though it isn't enough,' he said. 'When the Republic was very young, the Fetiales were sent to the foreign aggressor to negotiate a settlement. Their chief was the *pater patratus*, who had with him the *verbenarius*. This man carried herbs and soil gathered on the Capitol; the herbs and soil gave the Fetiales a magical protection. But then that became too awkward, and a big ceremony was conducted at the temple of Bellona instead. I mean to revive the ceremony and have as many people as possible witness it. A start, yet by no means a finish.'

'How do you know all that?' she asked curiously.

'Divus Julius told me. He was a great authority on our ancient religious rites. There were a group of them interested in the subject – Divus Julius, Cicero, Nigidius Figulus and Appius Claudius Pulcher, I think. Divus Julius said to me, laughing, that he had always itched to perform the ceremony, but never had the time.'

'Then you must do it for him, Caesar.'

'I shall.'

'Good! What else?' she asked.

'I can't think of anything else except widely disseminated propaganda. And that won't make my own position less precarious.'

Her eyes widened, stared for a long moment into space, then she drew a breath. 'Caesar, I'm the granddaughter of Marcus Livius Drusus, the tribune of the plebs who almost averted the Italian War by legislating the Roman citizenship for all Italians. Only his murder prevented him from doing it. I remember being shown the knife – a wicked little thing used to cut leather. Drusus took days to die, screaming in agony.'

Arrested, he watched her face intently, not sure whereabouts she was going, but feeling in the pit of his stomach that what she was saying would be of enormous importance. Sometimes his Livia Drusilla had the second sight – or if it wasn't quite that, it was frightening, otherworldly. 'Go on,' he prompted.

'Drusus's murder wouldn't have been necessary had he not done something extraordinary, something that raised his status so high only murder could tear him down. He secretly exacted a sacred oath of personal allegiance from all the Italian non-citizens. Had his legislation been passed, he would have had the whole of Italia in his clientele, and been so powerful that he could have ruled as a dictator in perpetuity had he been so inclined. Whether he was, will never be known.' She sucked in her cheeks and looked fey. 'I wonder – would it be possible for you to ask the people of Rome and Italia to swear an oath of personal allegiance to you?'

He had frozen; now he began to tremble. Sweat broke out on his brow, washed into his eyes and stung like the bite of an acid. 'Livia Drusilla! What made you think of that?'

'Being his granddaughter, I suppose, even if my father was Drusus's adopted son. It's always been one of the family stories, you see. Drusus was the bravest of the brave.'

'Pollio – Sallustius – someone is bound to have preserved the form of the oath in a history of those times.'

She smiled. 'There's no need to give the game away to the likes of them. I can recite the oath off by heart.'

'Don't! Not yet! Write it down for me, then help me amend it to suit my own needs, which aren't Drusus's. I'll arrange for the Fetial ceremony as soon as I can, and start the agents talking. I'll hammer away at the Queen of Beasts, have Maecenas dream up fabulous vices for her to practice, compile a list of lovers and hideous crimes. When she walks in my triumphal parade, no one must pity her. She's such a wispy little thing that some who see her might be tempted to pity her unless she's known to be a fusion of harpy, Fury, siren and gorgon – a veritable monster. I'll sit Antonius backward on an ass, and put cuckold's horns on his head. Deny him the chance to look noble – or Roman.'

'You're drifting from the subject,' she said gently.

'Oh! Yes, I am. I'm to be senior consul in the New Year, so toward the end of December I'll put posters up in every city, town and village from the alps to the instep, the toe and the heel. It will announce the oath, and humbly beg that any who wish to take it, take it. No coercion, no rewards. It must be pristine, a transparently voluntary thing. If people want to be free of the threat of Cleopatra, then they must swear to stand by me until I've done the job to my satisfaction. And if enough people swear, no one will dare to spill me, strip me of my imperium. If men like Pollio decline to take it, I will exact no punishment, either at the time or in the future.'

'You must always be above exacting retribution, Caesar.'

'I am aware of that.' He laughed. 'Just after Philippi, I thought deeply upon men like Sulla and my divine father, tried to see where they had gone wrong. And I realized that they loved to live splashily, extravagantly, as well as rule the Senate and the Assemblies with a rod of iron. Whereas I decided to be a quiet, unostentatious man, and rule Rome like a dear, kind old daddy.'

Bellona was Rome's original god of war, and went back to times when Roman gods were pure forces having neither faces nor sex. Her other name was Nerio, an even more mysterious entity entwined with Mars, the later war god. When Appius Claudius the Blind inaugurated the temple to get Bellona on side during the Etruscan and Samnite wars, he put a statue of her in the building; both were handsome and well kept-up, painted in vivid colors regularly revitalized. As war was not something that could be discussed within the *pomerium* of the city, Bellona's precinct was on the Campus Martius outside the sacred boundary, and it was spacious. Like all Roman temples, it was elevated on a high podium. To get inside involved climbing twenty steps in two flights of ten; upon the wide sweep of the platform between the two flights stood, exactly in the middle, a square column of red marble four feet high. At the bottom of the steps was a full *iugerum* of flagging, its margins marked with phallic plinths upon which stood the statues of great Roman generals: Fabius Maximus Cunctator, Appius Claudius Caecus, Scipio Africanus, Aemilius Paullus, Scipio Aemilianus, Gaius Marius, Caesar Divus Julius and many others, each so beautifully painted that it looked alive.

When the College of Fetiales, twenty strong, assembled on Bellona's steps, they performed to a packed audience of senators, knights, men of the Third, Fourth and Fifth Classes, and some Head Count paupers. Though the Senate had to be accommodated in whole, Maecenas had carefully chosen the rest near enough to witness events so as to spread them right across the social strata. That way, men of the Subura and Esquiline were represented as generously as men of the Palatine and Carinae.

All the other priestly colleges attended, plus every lictor on duty in Rome, so it was a colorful spectacle of togas striped in red and purple, round capes and ivory *apex* helmets, pontifices and augurs with togas pulled up to veil their heads.

The Fetiales wore dull red togas over naked torsos, as was the custom in the beginning, their heads bare too. The *verbenarius* held herbs and soil gathered from the Capitol, standing closest to the *pater patratus*, whose role was confined to the very end of the ritual. Most of the lengthy proceedings were declaimed in a language so old that no one understood it anymore, and by a Fetial who had perfected the gibberish; no one wanted to make a mistake, as even the slightest error meant the whole business had to be started all over again. The sacrificial victim was a small boar which a fourth Fetial killed with a flint knife older than Egypt.

Finally the *pater patratus* strode into the temple and emerged toting a leaf-shaped spear whose shaft was black with age. He walked down the upper flight of ten steps and stood in front of the little column, spear lifted to throw, its silver head glinting in the chilly, brilliant sun.

'Rome, thou art threatened!' he cried in Latin. 'Here before me is Enemy Territory, guarded by Rome's generals! I declare that the name of Enemy Territory is Egypt! With the casting of this spear, we, the Senate and People of Rome, embark upon a holy war against Egypt in the persons of Egypt's King and Queen!'

The spear left his hand, flew over the top of the column and landed in the *iugerum* of open space called Enemy Territory. A single flag had been dislodged, and the *pater patratus* was a superb warrior; the spear stuck, quivering, with its head buried in the soil beneath the lifted flag. A huge cheer arose as people tossed tiny woollen dolls at the spear.

Standing off to one side with the rest of the College of Pontifices, Octavian gazed on all this and was content. Ancient, impressive, absolutely a part of the *mos maiorum*. Rome was now officially at war, but not against a Roman. The enemy was the Queen of Beasts and Ptolemy XV Caesar, rulers of Egypt. Yes, yes! How lucky that he had managed to make Agrippa the *pater patratus*, and didn't Maecenas make a good – if flabby – *verbenarius*?

He walked home surrounded by hundreds of clients, thoroughly enjoying himself for a change. Even the plutocrats – why were the richest always the most reluctant to pay tax? – seemed to be in charity with him today, though that couldn't last beyond the first tax payment. He had completed his arrangements for the payments of tax using the citizen rolls, which detailed a man's income and were upgraded every five years. By rights the censors did this, but censors had been thin on the ground for some decades. The Triumvir in the West for the last decade, Octavian had taken over censorial duties and made sure every citizen income was current. To collect his new tax was a complicated business that meant big premises – the Porticus Minucia on the Campus Martius.

He intended to make the first payment day something of a festival. There could be no rejoicing, but there ought to be a patriotic atmosphere. The colonnades and grounds of the Porticus Minucia were decked with scarlet SPQR flags, posters of a female figure, bare-breasted, with a jackal's head and clawlike hands twisting SPQR into a mangled mess; another showed a cretinously ugly youth wearing the Double Crown, and said, below, THIS IS THE SON OF DIVUS JULIUS? IT CANNOT BE!

As soon as the sun was well above the Esquiline, a procession appeared, led by Octavian in the full glory of his priestly toga, his head crowned by laurels, the sign of a triumphator. Behind him came Agrippa, also crowned, toting the curlicued staff of an augur and wearing his red and purple particolored toga. Then came Maecenas, Statilius Taurus, Cornelius Gallus, Messala Corvinus,

Calvisius Sabinus, Domitius Calvinus, the bankers Balbi and Oppius, and a host of Octavian's loyalest adherents. However, that was insufficient for Octavian, who had inserted three women between himself and Agrippa; Livia Drusilla and Octavia wore the robes of a Vestal Virgin, which rather put Scribonia, the third, in the shade. Octavian made a great show of paying over two hundred talents as his twenty-five per cent, though no bags of coins were tendered. Just a scrap of paper, a draft on his bankers.

Livia Drusilla stepped forward to the table. 'I am a Roman citizen!' she cried loudly. 'As a woman, I do not pay taxes, but I wish to pay this tax, for it is needed to stop Cleopatra of Egypt turning our beloved Rome into a desert, denuded of people and of money! I give this cause two hundred talents!'

Octavia gave the same speech and the same amount of money, though Scribonia could give only fifty talents. No matter; by now the rapidly gathering crowd was cheering so loudly that it quite drowned out Agrippa, paying eight hundred talents.

A good day's work.

But not as finicking and patient as the work Octavian and his wife put into drafting the Oath of Allegiance.

'Ohhh!' sighed Octavian, looking at the original oath sworn to Marcus Livius Drusus sixty years ago. 'If only I dared make people swear to be my clients, as Drusus did!'

'The Italians had no patrons at that time, Caesar, because they weren't Roman citizens. Today, everyone has a patron.'

'I know, I know! How many gods should we use?'

'More than Sol Indiges, Tellus and Liber Pater. Drusus used more, though I wonder at his using Mars, since – at the time, at any rate – there was no element of war.'

'Oh, I think he knew it would come to war,' Octavian said, pen poised. 'The Lares and Penates, do you think?'

'Yes. And Divus Julius, Caesar. He reinforces your status.'

The oath was pinned up all over Italia, from the alps to the instep, the toe and the heel, on New Year's Day; in Rome it graced the Forum wall of the rostra, the urban praetor's tribunal, all the crossroads that had a shrine to the Lares, and every marketplace – meat, fish, fruit, vegetables, oil, grain, pepper and spices, and the spaces inside the major gates from Capena to Quirinalis.

'I swear by Jupiter Optimus Maximus, by Sol Indiges, by Tellus, by Liber Pater, by Vesta of the hearth, by the Lares and Penates, by Mars, by Bellona and Nerio, by Divus Julius, by the gods and heroes who founded and assisted the people of Rome and Italia in their struggles, that I will hold as my friends and foes those whom Imperator Gaius Julius Caesar Divi Filius holds as his friends and foes. I swear that I will work for the benefit of Imperator Gaius Julius Caesar Divi Filius in his conduct of the war against Queen Cleopatra and King Ptolemy of Egypt, and work for the benefit of all others who take this oath, even at the cost of my life, my children, my parents and my property. If through the work of Imperator Gaius Julius Caesar Divi Filius the nation of Egypt is defeated, I swear that I will bind myself to him, not as his client but as his friend. This oath I take upon myself to pass on to as many others as I can. I swear faithfully in the knowledge that my faith will bring its just rewards. And if I am forsworn, may my life, my children, my parents and my property be taken from me. So be it. So do I swear.'

Publication of the oath caused a sensation, for Octavian had not announced it in advance; it simply appeared. By it stood an agent of Maecenas's or Octavian's, primed to answer questions and hear it sworn. A scribe sat nearby to take down the names of those who took it. By now the news of Mark Antony's involuntary treachery had spread everywhere; the people knew that he was not to blame, and knew too that Egypt pursued the war. Antony was Cleopatra's catspaw, her instrument of destruction kept caged and drugged to serve her both sexually and in the field. The canards about her multiplied until she was seen as an inhuman monster who even used her bastard son Ptolemy 'Caesar' as her sexual object. The Egyptian rulers practiced incest as a matter of course, and what could possibly be less Roman? If Mark Antony condoned it, he was no Roman anymore.

The oath resembled a wavelet far out to sea; a few took it at once and, having taken it, persuaded others to do so, until it became a tidal wave of swearing. Octavian's legions all took it, as did the crews and oarsmen of his ships. And finally, knowing that not to swear was fast becoming evidence of treason, the whole Senate took it. Except for Pollio, who refused. True to his word, Octavian exacted no retribution. Objection to the tax ceased; all that people wanted now was the defeat of Cleopatra and Ptolemy, understanding that their defeat meant the tax would end.

Agrippa, Statilius Taurus, Messala Corvinus and the rest of the generals and admirals were sent to their commands, while in Rome Octavian too prepared to leave.

'Maecenas, you will govern Rome and Italia in my name,' he said, not realizing that he had grown and changed over the past few months. He had turned thirty-one the previous September, and his face was set now; it looked strong yet tranquil, still quite beautiful in a masculine mold.

'The Senate will never permit it,' Maecenas said.

Octavian grinned. 'The Senate won't be present to object, my dear Maecenas. I'm taking it with me on campaign.'

'Ye gods!' said Maecenas feebly. 'Seven hundred senators is a recipe for madness.'

'Not at all. I'll have work for every one of them, and while they're under my supervision, they can't sit in Rome brewing vats of mischief.'

'You're right.'

'I'm always right.'

PART V

War

32–30 B.C.

MARCUS VIPSANIUS AGRIPPA

TWENTY-FIVE

Cleopatra labored under terrible handicaps, handicaps that only increased when she and Mark Antony left Ephesus bound for Athens. At root of her worry was a conviction that Antony wasn't telling her all his thoughts or plans; whenever she fantasized about delivering her judgements from the Capitol in Rome, a tinge of amusement crept into his eyes that knowledge of him told her was evidence of disbelief. Yes, he had concluded that Octavian had to be stopped, and that war was the only way left to stop him, but about his plans for Rome she couldn't be so sure. And though he always sided with her in those command tent disputes, he did so as if they didn't really matter—that to humor her was more important than keeping his legates happy. He had also developed considerable agility at sidestepping her accusations of disloyalty when she did voice her suspicions. Ageing he might be, subject to lapses of memory he was, but did he truly believe in his heart of hearts that Caesarion would be King of Rome? She wasn't sure.

Only nineteen of Antony's thirty Roman legions sailed for western Greece, the other eleven assigned to garrison Syria and Macedonia. However, Antony's land forces were augmented by forty thousand foot and horse donated by client-kings, most of whom had come in person to Ephesus—there learning that they were not to accompany Antony and Cleopatra to Athens. Instead, they were to make their own way to the designated theater of war in western Greece. Which didn't sit well with any of them.

It was Mark Antony himself who had separated his progress from that of his client-kings, fearing that, were they to witness Cleopatra's autocracy in the command tent, they would make matters worse for him by siding with her against his Roman generals. Only he knew how desperate his plight was, for only he knew the full extent of his Egyptian wife's determination to have her say. And it was all so silly! What Cleopatra wanted and what his Roman generals wanted was usually much the same thing; the trouble was that neither she nor they would admit it.

Gaius Julius Caesar would have pinpointed Antony's weaknesses as a commander, whereas only Canidius had that kind of perception, and Canidius, low-born, was largely ignored. Simply, Antony could general a battle, but not a campaign. His cheerful trust that things would go well betrayed him when it came to the logistics and problems of supply, perpetually neglected. Besides, Antony was too concerned with keeping Cleopatra happy to think of equipment and supplies; he devoted his energies to dancing attendance on her. To his staff it looked like weakness, but Antony's real weakness was his inability to kill her and confiscate her war chest. Both his love for her and his sense of fair play negated that.

So she, not understanding, gloried in her ascendancy over Antony, deliberately provoking his marshals by demanding this or that from him as proof of his devotion to her. Without seeing that her conduct was making Antony's task much harder—and making her own presence more abominable with every passing day.

In Samos he had a brainwave and insisted on remaining there to revel; his legates went on to Athens and he had Cleopatra to himself. If she deemed him drunk, so much the better; most of the wine in his goblet was emptied surreptitiously into his solid gold chamber pot, a gift from her. Her own, she pointed out gleefully, had an eagle and the letters SPQR on its bottom so that she could piss and shit on Rome. That earned her a tirade and a broken chamber pot, but not before it traveled to Italia as a canard Octavian exploited to the limit.

One more handicap lay in her growing conviction that Antony was not a military genius after all, though she failed to see that her own conduct made it impossible for Antony to enter on this war with his old zest, his rightful position of authority. He had his way in the end, yes, but the constant brawling sapped his spirits.

'Go home,' he said to her wearily over and over again. 'Go home and leave this war to me.'

But how could she do that when she saw through him? Were she to leave for Egypt, Antony would reach an accommodation with Octavian, and all her plans would fail.

In Athens he refused to travel farther west, dreading the day when Cleopatra rejoined his army. Canidius was an excellent second-in-command, he could manage things in western Greece.

His own main duty, Antony thought, was to protect his legates from the Queen. An activity so demanding that he neglected his correspondence with Canidius, not as difficult as it would have been for a man less addicted to pleasure than Antony. On the subject of supplies he ignored every letter.

The news of Octavian's seizing and reading of his will took Antony's breath away.

'I, *treasonous?*' he asked Cleopatra incredulously. 'Since when do a man's posthumous dispositions brand him a traitor? Oh, *cacat*, this is more than enough! I have been stripped of my legal triumvirate and all my imperium! How dare the Senate side with that disgusting little *irrumator*? He's the one who committed sacrilege! No one can open the will of a man still living, but he did! And they have forgiven him!'

'You'll have your revenge when we conquer,' Cleopatra soothed.

Then came publication of Octavian's Oath of Allegiance. Pollio sent a copy of it to Athens, together with a letter that told of his own refusal to take the oath.

'Antonius, he is so crafty!' the letter said. 'No reprisals have been visited upon those who refuse to swear—he intends future generations to be impressed by his *clementia*, shades of his divine father! He even sent notices to the magistrates of Bononia and Mutina—your cities, stuffed with your clients!—saying that no one was to be compelled to swear. I gather that the oath is to be extended to Octavianus's provinces, which are not so lucky. Every provincial is to swear whether he wants to or not—no choice like Bononia, Mutina, and me.

'I can tell you, Antonius, that people are swearing in huge numbers, absolutely voluntarily. The men of Bononia and Mutina are swearing mightily—and not because they felt themselves intimidated. Because they are so fed up with the uncertainties of the last few years that they would swear on a clown's *centunculus* if they thought that might bring stability. Octavianus has divorced you from the coming war—you are merely the drugged, drunken dupe of the Queen of Beasts. What fascinates me most is that Octavianus hasn't stopped at citing Egypt's queen. He names King Ptolemy XV Caesar alongside her as equal aggressor.'

Cleopatra's face was ashen when she put Pollio's missive down with shaking fingers. 'Antonius, how can Octavianus do that to Caesar's *son*? His blood son, his true heir—and a mere child!'

'Surely you can see that for yourself,' Ahenobarbus said; he and the other seniors in command had come to Athens as fast as they could, for the same news had reached them. 'Caesarion turned sixteen last June – he's a man now. He's also co-ruler of Egypt.'

'But he's *Caesar's* son! His *only* son!'

'And the living image of his father,' said Ahenobarbus flatly. 'Octavianus knows full well that if Rome and Italia set eyes on the lad, he'll be overwhelmed with followers. The Senate will scramble to make him a Roman citizen and strip Octavianus of his so-called daddy's wealth – *and* all his clients, which is far more important.' Ahenobarbus glared. 'You would have done better, Cleopatra, to have stayed in Egypt and sent Caesarion on this campaign. There would have been less rancor in the councils.'

She shrank, in no condition to contend with Ahenobarbus. 'No, if what you say is true, I was right to keep Caesarion in Egypt. I must conquer for him, and only then display him.'

'You're a fool, woman! As long as Caesarion remains at the arse-end of Our Sea, he's invisible. Octavianus can issue leaflets describing him as totally unlike Caesar, and get no arguments. And if Octavianus should get as far as Egypt, your son by Caesar will die unseen.'

'Octavianus will never reach Egypt!' she cried.

'Of course he won't,' said Canidius, stepping in. 'We'll beat him now in western Greece. I have it on good authority that Octavianus has settled on sixteen full-strength legions and seventeen thousand German and Gallic horse. They represent his only land forces. His navy consists of two hundred big fives that did well at Naulochus, plus two hundred miserable little Liburnians. We outnumber him in all aspects.'

'Well said, Canidius. We cannot possibly lose.' Then she shivered. 'Some issues can only be settled by a war, but the outcome is always uncertain, isn't it? Look at Caesar. He was always outnumbered. They say this Agrippa is almost as good.'

Immediately after Pollio's letter they moved to Patrae, on the mouth of the Gulf of Corinth in western Greece; by now the entire army and navy had arrived, sailing around the westernmost peninsula of the Peloponnese, into the Adriatic.

Though several hundred galleys were left to garrison Methone, Corcyra and other strategic islands, the main fleet numbered some four hundred and eighty of the most massive quinqueremes ever built. These leviathans had eight men to an oar in three banks, were completely decked, and had ramming beaks of solid bronze

480

surrounded by oak beams; their hulls were reinforced with belts of squared timber, plated and belted with iron to serve as buffers should they be rammed. They were two hundred feet long and fifty feet wide in the beam, stood ten feet above the water amidships and twenty-five feet above it at stern and prow. Each had a crew of a hundred and fifty men excluding marines, and bristled with tall towers carrying artillery pieces. All this rendered them impregnable, an asset in defense; but they crept along at the pace of a snail, no asset in attack. Antony's flagship, the *Antonia*, was even bigger. Sixty of Cleopatra's ships were of this size and design, but the second sixty were roomy triremes with four men to an oar in three banks, and could move at a fast clip, especially when under sail as well as oar power. Her flagship, the *Caesarion*, though daintily daubed and gilded, was swift and designed more for flight than fight.

When everything was in train, Antony sat back complacently, finding nothing wrong in issuing orders so broad that much of the detail was left up to the ability of individual legates, some good, some mediocre, and some hopeless.

He had put himself on a line running between the island of Corcyra and Methone, a Peloponnesian port just to the north of Cape Acritas. Bogud of Mauretania, a refugee from his brother, was given command of Methone, while the other big naval base, on the island of Leucas, was given to Gaius Sosius. Even Cyrenaica in Africa had been garrisoned. Lucius Pinarius Scarpus, a great-nephew of Divus Julius's, held it with a fleet and four legions. This was necessary to safeguard grain and food shipments from Egypt. Huge caches of foodstuffs were put on Samos, at Ephesus and at many ports on the eastern coast of Greece.

Antony had decided to ignore western Macedonia and northern Epirus: to try to hold them would stretch his front and thin out the density of his troops and ships, therefore let Octavian have them and the Via Egnatia, the great eastern road. Dread of a too-long, too-thin front obsessed him so much that he even vacated Corcyra. His main base was the Bay of Ambracia; this vast, rambling, almost landlocked body of water had a mouth into the Adriatic less than one mile wide. The southern promontory at the mouth was called Cape Actium, and here Antony put his command camp, his legions and auxiliaries fanned around it for many miles of swampy, unhealthy, mosquito-ridden ground. Though it hadn't been in camp very long, the land army was approaching dire straits. Pneumonia and the ague were pandemic, even the hardiest men had bad colds, and food was beginning to run short.

His supply chain had not been well organized, and anything that Cleopatra suggested to rectify its deficiencies was either ignored or deliberately sabotaged. Not that either she or Antony spared supply much thought, sure that their policy of keeping the food-stuffs on the eastern side of the landmass was good strategy; Octavian would have to round the Peloponnese to get at the caches. But what they failed to take into account was the high, rugged, rather impassable range of mountains that ran like a fat spine down from Macedonia to the Gulf of Corinth and separated eastern Greece from the west. The roads were mere tracks, where they existed at all.

Alone among the legates, Publius Canidius saw the imperative necessity of bringing most of these food and grain caches around the Peloponnese by ship, but Antony, in a stubborn mood, took many days to approve the order, which then had to make the voyage east before it could be executed. And that took time.

Time, it turned out, that Antony and Cleopatra didn't have. It was so well known that late winter and early spring saw the advantages lie with those on the east side of the Adriatic that no one in Antony's command tent believed Octavian and his forces would – or could – cross the Adriatic until summer. But this year all the watery gods from Father Neptune to the Lares Permarini were on Octavian's side. Very brisk westerlies blew, as unusual as they were unseasonal. They meant a following wind and a following sea for Octavian, but a head wind and a head sea for Antony, who was powerless to prevent Octavian's sailing – or landing wherever he pleased.

While the troop transports poured across the Adriatic from Brundisium, Marcus Agrippa detached half his four hundred galleys and struck at Antony's base of Methone. He was completely victorious, especially because, having killed Bogud, destroyed half his ships and pressed the other half into his own service, Agrippa went on to do the same thing to Sosius at Leucas. Sosius himself escaped, a very small joy. For Antony and Cleopatra were now completely cut off from any grain and foodstuffs coming by sea, no matter where their point of origin. Suddenly the only way to feed the land and sea forces was overland, but Antony was adamant that his Roman soldiers were not going to be made beasts of burden – or even lead beasts of burden! Let Cleopatra's indolent Egyptians do something for a change! Let them organize the overland trek!

Every donkey and mule in the east of the country was commandeered and loaded to maximum tolerance. But Egyptian overseers,
it turned out, had scant respect for animals, neglected to water
them, and indifferently watched them die as the cavalcades came
over the mountains of Dolopia. So Greek men by the thousands
were forced at swordpoint to shoulder bags and jars of supplies
and walk the eighty hideous miles between the end of the Gulf of
Malis and the Bay of Ambracia. Among these wretched porters was
a Greek named Plutarch, who survived his ordeal and entertained
his grandchildren ever after with lurid tales of dragging wheat over
eighty awful miles.

By the end of April, Agrippa controlled the Adriatic, and all Octavian's
troops had been safely landed around Epirote Toryne, in the lee of
Corcyra. After deciding to make Corcyra his main naval base,
Octavian pressed on south with his land forces in an attempt to
surprise Antony at Actium.

Until this moment, all Antony's wrong decisions had stemmed
out of the adverse effect Cleopatra had on his legates. But now he
committed a cardinal mistake: he penned up every ship he had
within the Bay of Ambracia, a total of four hundred and forty
vessels even after his losses at Agrippa's hands. Given the size and
slowness of his ships, it was impossible except under the most ideal
conditions to get the bottled-up fleets out of the bay through a
gullet less than a mile wide. And while Antony and Cleopatra sat
impotent, the rest of their bases fell to Agrippa: Patrae, the entire
Gulf of Corinth, and the western Peloponnese.

Octavian's effort to move fast enough to surprise Antony's land
army failed; it was wet, the ground was boggy, and his men were
sickening with colds. Acting on reports from his scouts, Antony
and the assassin Decimus Turullius set out with several legions and
Galatian cavalry and defeated the leading legions; Octavian was
compelled to halt.

Desperately needing a victory, Antony made sure his soldiers
hailed him Imperator on the field (for the fourth time in his career)
and grossly inflated his success. Between illness and increasingly
poor rations, morale in his camps was extremely low. His command
chain was severely disaffected, for which he had Cleopatra to thank.
She made no attempt to keep in the background, toured the area
regularly to carp and criticize, and comported herself with icy
hauteur. According to her lights, she did nothing wrong; though
her association with Romans now dated back a full sixteen years,

she still hadn't managed to grasp the concept of egalitarianism, which incorporated no automatic reverence for any man or woman, even one born to wear the ribbon of the diadem. Blaming her for the mess they were in, ordinary legionaries jeered, booed and hissed at her, yammered like a thousand little dogs. Nor could she command that they be punished. Their centurions and legates simply ignored her.

Octavian finally camped on good dry ground near the north headland of the bay, connecting his vast compound to a supply base on the Adriatic shore by 'long walls' fortifications. An impasse ensued, with Agrippa blockading the bay from the sea and Octavian depriving Antony of the chance to relocate where his own ground was less swampy. Hunger reared its ugly head higher, and desperation followed it.

On a day when the westerlies blew less constantly, Antony sent out a part of his fleet under the command of Tarcondimotus. Agrippa came bustling to meet it with his trusty Liburnians and trounced it. Tarcondimotus himself was killed; only a sudden change in wind direction from east to west enabled most of the Antonian fleet to struggle back inside its prison.

Agrippa was puzzled by the fact that the sally had been led by a client-king and that no vessel held any Roman troops, but interpreted the move as doubt in Antony's mind that he could win.

In actual fact it stemmed out of dissent in the councils that a despondent Mark Antony still held regularly. Antony and the Romans wanted a land battle, but Cleopatra and the client-kings wanted a sea battle. Both factions could see that they were trapped in a no-win situation, and both factions were beginning to see that they had to abandon the invasion of Italia in favor of returning to Egypt to regroup and think out a better strategy. If they were to do this, however, they had first to defeat Octavian badly enough to enable a mass retreat.

Sufficient food kept trickling in over the mountains to keep starvation at bay, but short rations had to be enforced. In this respect Cleopatra suffered a defeat that was rapidly alienating the non-Roman contingents, fully seventy thousand strong. Antony was furtively feeding bigger portions to his sixty-five thousand Roman soldiers – but not furtively enough. The secret leaked to the client-kings, who objected strenuously and loathed him for it. And deemed Cleopatra weak, since she was unable to persuade or hector Antony into ceasing this unfair practice.

Ague and enteric fever ran through the camps as summer came

in. No one, Roman or non-Roman, had the forethought – or the enthusiasm – to drill the land forces or exercise the sea forces. Almost a hundred and forty thousand Antonian men sat around, idle, hungry, ill and discontented. Waiting for someone at the top to think of a way out. They didn't even clamor for a battle, a sure sign that they had given up.

Then Antony thought of a way out. Rousing himself from gloom, he summoned his staff and explained.

'We're quite lucky here, we're close to the river Acheron,' he said, pointing to a map. 'And here is Octavianus – not nearly as lucky. He has to bring fresh water from the river Oropus, a long way from his camps. It's ducted through halves of hollowed tree trunks, which he's replacing with terra-cotta pipes that Agrippa brings from Italia. But at this moment, his water situation is precarious. So we're going to cut off his supply and oblige him to withdraw from his present position to one nearer the Oropus. Unfortunately the distance we have to travel to achieve surprise negates a full-scale infantry attack, at least in the beginning.'

He continued, using his right index finger to illustrate the relevant areas, and he sounded very confident; the mood in the command tent lightened, especially when Cleopatra kept silent.

'Therefore, Deiotarus Philadelphus, you'll take your cavalry and the Thracian cavalry – Rhoemetalces will be second-in-command – and spearhead the action. I know you'll have a very long detour around the east of the bay, but Octavianus won't be watching anything happening there, it's too distant. Marcus Lurius will take ten of the Roman legions and follow as hard on your heels as he can. In the meantime I'll take rafts of infantry across the bay and set them up in a camp just under Octavianus's walls. He won't be particularly dismayed and, when I offer battle, he'll ignore me. He's too firmly entrenched to be alarmed. When your infantry, Lurius, meet Deiotarus Philadelphus's cavalry, you'll rip miles of Octavianus's ducting out and then plunder his northern food caches. Once he hears what's happening, he'll pull out to relocate along the Oropus. And while he's in the middle of that – and while Agrippa is helping him – we'll evacuate for Egypt.'

Excitement spread; it was an excellent maneuver, with a very good chance of succeeding. But disaffection had grown amain since news that the Roman troops were being better fed; a Thracian commander deserted, went to Octavian, and gave the scheme away in great detail. Octavian was able to intercept the cavalry with some of his own Germans. There was no battle. Deiotarus Philadelphus and Rhoemetalces went over to Octavian on the spot, and then, combined with the Germans, went to crush the approaching foot soldiers, who turned and fled in the direction of Actium.

When he heard of the disaster, Antony marshaled the last of his horse, the contingent from Galatia under Amyntas, and set out in person to turn his legions around. But when Amyntas met up with his colleagues and the Germans, he deserted, offering himself and his two thousand horse troopers to Octavian.

Thwarted and despairing, Antony took his legions back to Actium, convinced that no land engagement could be won in this awful place.

'I don't know how to break free!' he wept to Cleopatra, head in her lap, hopes as black and shriveled as a mummy. 'The gods have deserted me, so has my luck! If the winds had blown as they always do, Octavian would never have been able to cross the Adriatic! But they blew to favor him, and undid all my plans! Cleopatra, Cleopatra, what am I to do? It's all over!'

'Hush, hush,' she crooned, stroking the stiff, curly hair, and noticing for the first time that it was greying. Frosted almost overnight!

She too had acknowledged that same impotence, a terrible dread that her own gods as well as Rome's had taken Octavian's side in this. Why else had he been able to cross the Adriatic out of season? And why else had he been gifted with a commander as great as Agrippa? But, most urgent question of all, why hadn't she abandoned Marcus Antonius to his inevitable fate, fled home to Egypt? *Loyalty?* No, surely not! What did she owe Antony, after all? He was her dupe, her tool, her weapon! She had always known that! So why now was she cleaving to him? He didn't have the skill or the stomach for this quest, he never had. Simply, loving her, he had tried to be what she needed. It's Rome, she thought, stroking, stroking. Not even a monarch as great and powerful as Cleopatra of Egypt can dig the Roman out of a Roman. I almost succeeded. But only almost. I couldn't do it to Caesar, and I can't do it to Antonius. So why am I here? Why, over these last *nundinae*, have I found myself growing softer with him, stopped flogging him?

Then it dawned upon her with the terror of some sudden natural catastrophe—an avalanche, a wall of water, an earthquake: *I love him!* Cradling him protectively, she kissed his face, his hands, his wrists, and, stupefied, recognized the identity of this new emotion that had crept upon her so stealthily, invaded her, conquered her. *I love him, I love him!* Oh, poor Marcus Antonius, finally you have your revenge! I love you as much as you love me—utterly, boundlessly. My walled-up heart has convulsed, cracked, gaped open to admit Marcus Antonius, the wedge that did it his own love for me. He has offered me his Roman spirit, gone out into a night so dense and black that he sees nothing beyond me. And I, in taking his sacrifice, have come to love him. Whatever the future holds, it is the same future for both of us. I cannot desert him.

'Oh, Antonius, I love you!' she cried, embracing him.

As summer wore on, legates deserted Antony in dozens, senators in hundreds flocked to join Octavian. It was as easy as rowing across the bay, for Antony refused to stop them. Their pleas for asylum always revolved around That Woman, the cause of ruin. Though a spy reported a curious thing to Cleopatra: Rhoemetalces of Thrace grew particularly caustic in his criticisms of Antony until Octavian rounded on him, furious.

'*Quin taces*!' he snapped. 'Just because I like treason does not mean I must like traitors.'

For Antony, the worst blow came late in Julius; making no secret of his loathing for Cleopatra – hoarsely declaiming it, in fact – Ahenobarbus quit.

'Not even for you, Antonius, can I stand another day of That Woman. You're aware that I'm ill, but you probably don't know that I'm dying. And I want to die in a properly Roman environment, free from the slightest whiff of That Woman. Oh, what a fool you are, Marcus! Without her, you would have won. With her, you don't have a chance.'

Weeping, Antony watched the rowboat carry Gnaeus Domitius Ahenobarbus across the bay, then sent all Ahenobarbus's possessions after him. Cleopatra's strenuous objections fell on deaf ears.

The day after Ahenobarbus left, Quintus Dellius followed him, together with the last of the senators.

The day after that, Octavian sent Antony a graceful letter. 'Your most devoted friend, Gnaeus Domitius Ahenobarbus, died peacefully last night. I want you to know that I had welcomed him and treated him with great consideration. As I understand it, his son, Lucius, is betrothed to your older daughter by my sister Octavia. The betrothal will be honored, I gave Ahenobarbus my word. It will be interesting to watch the offspring of a couple linking the blood of Divus Julius, Marcus Antonius and the Ahenobarbi, don't you agree? A metaphorical tug-of-war, given that the Ahenobarbi have always opposed the Julii.'

'I miss him, I miss him!' Antony said, uncontrolled tears rolling down his face.

'He was my obdurate enemy,' Cleopatra said, tight-lipped.

On the Ides of Sextilis Cleopatra summoned a council of war. So few of us, so few! she thought as she tenderly inserted Mark Antony into his ivory curule chair.

'I have a plan,' she announced to Canidius, Poplicola, Sosius and Marcus Lurius, the only senior legates left. 'However, it may be that someone else also has a plan. If so, I would like to hear it before I speak.' Her tone was humble, she sounded sincere.

'I have a plan,' Canidius said, very grateful for this unexpected opportunity to air it without needing to call a council himself. It was months since he had been able to place any confidence in Antony, who had turned into a remnant of what he used to be. *Her* fault, no one else's. And to think that once he had championed her! Well, no more of that.

'Speak, Publius Canidius,' she said.

Canidius too was looking old, despite his trim body and love of physical work. However, he hadn't lost any of his frankness. 'The first thing we have to do is abandon the fleet,' he said, 'and by that I don't mean we save as many as the flagships. *All* the ships, including Queen Cleopatra's, must be abandoned.'

Stiffening, Cleopatra opened her mouth, then shut it. Let Canidius finish outlining his ridiculous plan, then strike.

'We withdraw the land army by forced marches into Macedonian Thrace, where we'll have room to maneuver, room to give battle on ground of our choosing. We'll be in a perfect position to gather additional troops from Asia Minor, Anatolia and even Dacia. We can utilize the seven Macedonian legions, at present around Thessalonica – good men, Antonius, as you know. I suggest the area behind Amphipolis, where the air is clean and dry. This year has been wet enough to ensure no dust storms, as happened when we fought Philippi. The harvest will be in by the time we get there, and it's going to be a plentiful one. The move will give our sick soldiers time to regain strength, and morale will soar by the very fact that we're leaving this terrible place. Into the bargain, I doubt Octavianus and Agrippa can march at Caesar's speed – Octavianus, I've heard, is running out of money. He might even decide against fighting a campaign so far from Italia with the winter coming on and uncertain supply lines. We'll be marching overland, whereas he'll have to get his fleets from the Adriatic to the upper Aegean.

We're not going to need fleets, but with us blocking the Via Egnatia, he'll have to rely on ships for supply.'

Canidius stopped, but when Cleopatra would have spoken, he held up his hand so commandingly that she didn't. The others were hanging on his every word, the fools!

'Your Majesty,' Canidius went on, addressing her now, 'you know I have been your strongest supporter. But not anymore. Time has proved that a campaign is no place for a woman, most especially when that woman occupies the command tent. Your presence has sown dissent, anger, opposition. Through your presence, we have lost valuable men and even more valuable time. Your presence has sapped the Roman troops of their vitality, their will to win. Your presence has created so many problems that, even were you a Julius Caesar – which you are definitely not – your presence is a frightful burden to Antonius and his generals. Therefore I say adamantly that you must return to Egypt at once.'

'I will do no such thing!' Cleopatra cried, jumping to her feet. 'How dare you, Canidius! It's my money has kept this war going, and my money means *me*! I will not go home until this war is won!'

'You miss my point, Your Majesty. Which is that we cannot win this war while ever you are here. You are a woman trying to fill a man's military boots, and you haven't succeeded. You and your antics have cost us dearly, and it's high time you realized that. If we are to win, you must go home immediately!'

'I will not!' she said through her teeth. 'What's more, how can you even suggest that we abandon the fleets? They've cost ten times what the land army has, and you want to hand them over to Octavianus and Agrippa? That's tantamount to handing them the whole world!'

'I didn't say they'd be handed over to the enemy, Majesty. What I implied – but will now say outright – is that we burn them.'

'*Burn them?*' She gasped, hands going to her throat and that growing lump. '*Burn them?* All those trees, all that work, all that money, going up in smoke? Never! No, and no, and no! We have over four hundred quinqueremes in fighting condition, and many more transports than that! We have no cavalry left, you idiot! That means the land army is in no position to fight – it's utterly crippled! If anything is to be abandoned, let it be the infantry!'

'Land battles are decided by infantry, not cavalry,' said Canidius, not about to give in to this crazy woman and her passion for getting her money's worth. 'We burn the fleets, and we march for Amphipolis.'

Antony sat silent while the verbal battle raged, Cleopatra fighting alone against Canidius backed by Poplicola, Sosius and Lurius. What they said seemed to hum, float, wax and wane, strike colors off the walls that bled into each other. Unreal, thought Antony.

'I will not go home! You will not burn my fleets!' she was screaming, flecks of foam at the corners of her mouth.

'Go home, you woman! We must burn the fleets!' the men were shouting, fists clenched, some brandished at her.

Finally Antony bestirred himself; one hand came down on the table, sent it vibrating. 'Shut your mouths, all of you! Shut up and sit down!'

They sat, all of them trembling with rage and frustration.

'We will not burn the fleets,' Antony said in a tired voice. 'The Queen is right, they must be saved. If we burn all our ships, nothing will stand between Octavianus and the eastern end of Our Sea. Egypt will fall, because Octavianus will simply bypass us at Amphipolis. He'll sail straight for Egypt, and Egypt will fall because we won't be able to get there first if we have to march overland. Think of the distance! A thousand miles to the Hellespont, another thousand miles through Anatolia, and a third thousand to Alexandria. Maybe Caesar could have covered them in three or four months, but his troops would have died for him, whereas ours would grow tired of forced marches in a month, and desert.'

His argument was unassailable; Canidius, Poplicola, Sosius and Lurius subsided, while Cleopatra sat with eyes downcast and no expression of triumph. At last she understood that it was her sex these fools couldn't bear, that it was neither her foreignness nor her money. All their hatred was for a *woman*. Romans didn't like women, which was why they left them at home even if they were doing nothing more important than staying in a country villa! Finally she had the answer to the puzzle.

'I didn't know it was my sex,' she said to Antony after his four generals had departed, muttering darkly, but convinced he was right. 'How could I have been so blind?'

'Oh, because your own life has never lifted that veil.'

A silence fell, but not an uncomfortable one. Cleopatra sensed a change in Antony, as if the bitterness and protracted length of the argument between her and his four remaining friends had penetrated his detachment, pushed some energy back into him.

'I don't think that I want to share *my* plan with Canidius and the others anymore,' she said, 'but I would like to air it with you. Will you listen?'

'Gladly, my love. Gladly.'

'We can't win here, I know that,' she said, but briskly, as if it didn't concern her. 'I also understand that the land army is useless. Your own Roman troops are as loyal as ever, and there have been no desertions among them. So, if possible, they should be saved. What I want to do is break out of Ambracia and make a run for Egypt. And there's only one way to do that. Our fleets must offer battle. A battle you must lead in person aboard the *Antonia*. I'll leave it to you and your friends to work out the details because I have no skill in naval matters. What I want to do is load as many of your Roman troops as will fit in my transports, while you load others aboard your fleetest galleys. Don't bother with the quinqueremes, they're so slow they'll be caught.'

He was listening alertly, eyes fixed on her face. 'Go on.'

'This is our secret, Marcus my love. You can't speak of it even to Canidius, whom you will keep on land to command whatever infantry are left. Put Poplicola, Sosius and Lurius in command of your fleets: that will keep them busy. As long as they know you're there in person, they won't smell a dead rat. I'll be aboard *Caesarion*, just far enough behind the lines to see where a gap opens. And the moment that gap opens, we're running for Egypt with your troops. You'll have to keep a pinnace near the *Antonia* – when you see me sailing, you'll follow. You'll catch up with me quickly, and come aboard *Caesarion*.'

'I'll look like a deserter,' Antony said, frowning.

'Not once it's known that you acted to save your legions.'

'My dear love, I can improve on your plan. I have a fleet and four good legions in Cyrenaica with Pinarius Scarpus. Give me one ship and I'll sail for Paraetonium to collect Pinarius and my men. We'll meet again in Alexandria.'

'Paraetonium? That's in Libya, not Cyrenaica.'

'Which is why I'm sending a ship to Cyrenaica this moment. I'll order Pinarius to march for Paraetonium at once.'

'Given that we can't save all eleven of your legions here, we can do with four more,' she said with satisfaction. 'So be it, Marcus. I'll have that ship on *Caesarion*'s beam, waiting. But, before you board, you must farewell me on *Caesarion*, please.'

'That's no hardship,' he said with a laugh, and kissed her.

The secret leaked, as was inevitable when on the Kalends of September the legions were loaded, packed like sardines, aboard Cleopatra's transports and any others deemed capable of sailing swiftly. Other evidence of something more than a sea battle had occurred before this: all but the massive fives had their sails stowed, and huge amounts of water and food. Canidius, Poplicola, Sosius, Lurius and the rest of the legates assumed that, hard on the heels of the engagement, they were making a bid to get to Egypt. This was reinforced when every unseaworthy or unnecessary vessel was beached and burned far enough away from Ambracia's mouth to dissipate the smoke before Octavian could see it. What no one suspected was that the engagement too was smoke, that it would not be fought to a conclusion. Proud Romans that they were, Poplicola, Sosius and Lurius could not have borne a plan that meant no all-out fight. Canidius, who did see through the smoke, said nothing to his colleagues, but simply concentrated on getting what troops could not be fitted aboard the transports on the march before Octavian woke up to what was going on.

TWENTY-SIX

At the end of the Adriatic summer, the wind was more predictable than at any other season: it blew from the west in the morning, and about midday veered northwest, picking up in strength the more to the north it turned.

Octavian and Agrippa had not missed the signs of an impending battle, though no spy had reported to them about the sails, water and food aboard every transport that Antony and Cleopatra possessed; had they known those things, they might have planned countermoves for flight. As it was, they just assumed the enemy was tired of sitting still and had resolved to gamble all on defeating Agrippa at sea.

'Antonius's strategy is simple,' Agrippa said to Octavian in their command tent. 'He has to turn my line of ships at its northern-most end and drive it southward – that is, away from your land camp and my own base on the Bay of Comarus. His land army will invade your camp and my naval base with a good chance of winning. My strategy is equally simple. I have to prevent his turning my line downwind. Whoever wins the race to do the turning will also win the battle.'

'Then the wind favors you slightly more than it does him,' Octavian said, on tiptoe from excitement.

'Yes. What also favors me is size, Caesar. Those monstrous fives of Antonius's are too slow. He's Antaeus the giant, we're Hercules the comparative midget,' Agrippa said with a grin, 'and what he seems to have forgotten is that Hercules lifted Antaeus free of his mother, the earth. Well, there's no earth for Antaeus to draw strength from in a battle fought on water.'

'Find me a flotilla to command at the south end of your line,' Octavian said. 'I refuse to sit this battle out on dry land, and have everyone call me craven. But if I'm far enough away from the main thrust, I can't interfere with your tactics even by the most innocent mistake. How many of our legionaries do you plan to use, Agrippa? Given that, if Antonius wins, he'll invade our camp and port?'

'Thirty-five thousand. Every ship will have the *harpax* for hauling those elephants in from a distance, and as many *corvus* gangplanks as possible. We have the advantage in that our troops have been trained as marines – Antonius never bothered to do that. But, Caesar, there's no use sitting at the south end of our line. Better to be aboard my own Liburnian as my second-in-command. I trust you not to countermand my orders.'

'Why, thank you for the compliment! When will it happen?'

'Tomorrow, by all the signs. We'll be ready.'

On the second day of September, Mark Antony came out of the Bay of Ambracia in six squadrons, leading the northernmost one himself. His right, which was his north, comprised three of the six squadrons, each numbering fifty-five massive fives; Poplicola was his second-in-command. Agrippa lay on his oars farther from the shore than Antony had expected, which meant he had to row for longer than he wanted. By mid-morning he achieved the distance and lay on his oars, resting the oarsmen. Only at midday, when the wind began to veer to the north, could the battle begin.

Cleopatra and her transports took advantage of the longer distance, moving into the mouth as though keeping herself in reserve, and trusting to Agrippa's unexpected distance from the shore to conceal the troop-carrying nature of her ships.

The wind began to change; both sides put their backs to the oars and rowed desperately for the north, the galleys at the north end of both sides strung out in a line that saw longer intervals between Antony's fives than between Agrippa's Liburnians.

The race was a tie. Neither side managed to turn the other downwind. Instead, the two end squadrons became locked in combat. The *Antonia* and Agrippa's flagship, the *Divus Julius*, were the first to engage, and within moments six nippy little Liburnians had grappled the *Antonia* and were hauling it in. When he had the time to look, Antony discovered that ten of his galleys were also in trouble, grappled by Liburnians. Some were on fire; scant matter that they couldn't be rammed and sunk, when fire would do it. Soldiers from his six limpetlike

Liburnians began pouring on to *Antonia*'s deck; Antony decided to abandon ship. He could see that Cleopatra and her transports had broken out of the bay and were heading south under sail, helped by the brisk nor'westerly. A leap into the pinnace and he too was away, dodging between the Liburnians in a craft famous for its speed.

No one aboard the *Divus Julius* took any notice of the pinnace, half a mile away by the time that the *Antonia* surrendered. Lucius Gellius Poplicola and the other two squadrons of Antony's right promptly surrendered without engaging, while Marcus Lurius, in command of Antony's centre, turned his ships around and rowed back into the bay. At the south end of his line and commanded by Gaius Sosius, Antony's left followed Lurius's example.

It was a debacle, a laughing stock of a battle. Of the more than seven hundred ships on the sea, less than twenty had clashed.

So incredible was it, in fact, that Agrippa and Octavian were convinced this oddest of all outcomes was a trick, that on the morrow some other tactic would be employed. Thus all that night Agrippa's fleet lay on its oars out to sea, losing any chance they might have had to catch Cleopatra and forty thousand Roman troops.

When the next day produced no clever stratagem, Agrippa rowed home to Comarus and he and Octavian went to see their captives.

From Poplicola they learned the shocking truth: that Antony had deserted his command to follow the fleeing Cleopatra.

'It's all That Woman's fault!' Poplicola shrilled. 'Antonius never meant to fight! As soon as the *Antonia* was finished, he got over its side into a pinnace and hared off to catch Cleopatra.'

'Impossible!' Octavian exclaimed.

'I tell you, I saw it myself! And when I did, I thought, why should I imperil my soldiers and crews? Surrender suddenly seemed more honorable. I hope you take due note of my good sense.'

'I'll put it on your memorial,' Octavian said genially, and to his German, 'I want him executed immediately. See to it.'

Only Sosius was spared this fate; Arruntius interceded for him, and Octavian listened.

As it turned out, Canidius had tried to persuade the land army to attack Octavian's camp, but no one save he wanted a fight. Nor would the troops strike camp and march for the East. Canidius himself vanished while the legion representatives negotiated a peace with Octavian, who sent the foreign levies home and found land in Greece and Macedonia for the Romans.

'For I'll not have a one of you polluting Italia with your stories,' Octavian told the legion representatives. 'Clemency's my policy, but you'll never go home. Be like your master Antonius, and learn to love the East.'

Gaius Sosius was made to swear the Oath of Allegiance, and warned that he was never to contradict whatever Octavian's 'official' version of Actium turned out to be. 'I have spared you on one condition – silence all the way to the pyre. And remember that I can light it at any time.'

'I need a walk,' Octavian said to Agrippa two *nundinae* after Actium, 'and I want company, so don't make excuses. Cleaning up is properly in train, you're not needed.'

'You come before anyone and anything, Caesar. Where do you want to walk?'

'Anywhere but here. Faugh! The stink of shit, piss and so many men is unbearable. I could bear it better if there were a bit of blood, but there isn't. The bloodless battle of Actium!'

'Then let's ride first, up into the north until we're far enough away from Ambracia to *breathe*.'

'An excellent idea!'

They rode for two hours, which carried them farther than the dimple of the Bay of Comarus; when the forest closed in, Agrippa stopped by a brook sparkling in the dappled sunlight. It tumbled over its rocky bottom in breaks of foam, the mossy ground around it giving off a sweetly earthy smell.

'Here,' Agrippa said.

'We can't walk here.'

'I know, but there are two lovely rocks over there. We can sit on them facing each other, and talk. Talk, not walk. Isn't that what you really want to do?'

'Brave Agrippa!' Octavian laughed, sat down. 'You're right, as always. Here is peace, solitude, reflection. The only source of turbulence is the stream, and it's a melody.'

'I brought a skin of watered wine, that Falernian you like.'

'Trusty Agrippa!' Octavian drank, then passed the skin to his friend. 'Perfect!'

'Cough it up, Caesar.'

'At least these days that carries no implication of asthma.' He sighed, stretched out his legs. 'The bloodless battle of Actium – ten

496

enemy ships engaged out of four hundred, and only two of them fired until they sank. Perhaps a hundred dead, if that many. And for this I've taxed the people of Rome and Italia twenty-five per cent, the second year's contribution even now being collected? I will be cursed, perhaps even torn in pieces when all I can show for their money is a battle that was no battle. I can't even produce Marcus Antonius or Cleopatra! They stole a march on me, sailed away. And, like a fool, I believed better of Antonius, lingered to defeat him instead of flying in pursuit.'

'Come, Caesar, that's all done with. I know you, which means I know you'll manage to turn Actium into a triumph.'

'I've been racking my mind for days, and I want to try out my ideas on you because you'll answer me truthfully.' He picked up a series of pebbles and began to lay them out on his rock. 'I can see no alternative other than to deliberately inflate Actium into something that Homer would yearn to hymn. The two fleets came together like titans, clashed all down the line from north to south – that's why Poplicola, Lurius and the rest perished. Only Sosius survived. Let Arruntius think his pleas spared Sosius – now you know better. Antonius fought heroically aboard *Antonia* and was winning his part of the engagement when, out of the corner of his eye, he noticed Cleopatra treacherously leaving both the battle – and him. So much drug was still in his body that he suddenly panicked, commandeered a pinnace and set off after her like a lovesick dog a bitch. Many of his admirals saw him go after Cleopatra, crying out to her –' Octavian raised his voice to a falsetto – '"Cleopatra, don't leave me! I beg you, don't leave me!" Dead men were floating everywhere, the sea was red with blood, spars and shrouds tangled on the water, but the pinnace that held Marcus Antonius forged onward to Cleopatra. After that, Antonius's admirals lost heart. And you, Agrippa, superlative in combat, crushed your adversaries.'

'It works so far,' said Agrippa, taking another swig from the wineskin. 'What happens next?'

'Antonius reaches Cleopatra's ship and climbs on board. Pray pardon the switch to the present tense – it always helps me when I'm embroidering something whose truth will never be known,' said the master of embroidery. 'But suddenly he comes to his senses, sees in his mind's eye the disaster he left so cravenly –≠I'll teach that *irrumator* Antonius to accuse me of cowardice at Philippi! Now it's his turn . . . He sees the disaster he left so cravenly. He howls in anguish, pulls his *paludamentum* over his head, and sits on the deck for three days without moving. Cleopatra feeds him antidotes, pleading with him to go to her cabin, but he won't move, too devastated at his heedless treachery. *Thousands* of men dead, and he responsible!'

'It sounds like one of those trashy epic poems that young girls buy,' said Agrippa.

'Yes, it does, doesn't it? But would you care to bet that all of Rome and Italia won't buy this one?'

'I'm not so silly. They'd buy it even on expensive paper. Once Maecenas adds some flowery phrases it will be faultless.'

'Certainly it ought to lighten the resentment against me for going to war. People like value for their money.'

'A touchy subject, Caesar. How on earth are you going to pay your debts? Now that Cleopatra's defeated, you have no excuse for continuing to levy your tax. Yet, while she's alive, you'll have no peace. She'll be arming to have another try, whether Antonius is with her or not. It's Divus Julius's alleged son she wants to rule the world, not Antonius. So . . . money?'

'Proximately, I'm going to squeeze Antonius's client-kings until they go Tyrian purple and their eyes bug out. Ultimately, I'll invade Egypt.'

Agrippa glanced at the sun between the trees and rose to his feet. 'Time to ride back, Caesar. We don't want to be caught out here in the dark. According to Atticus – and he should know – the woods are full of bears and wolves.'

Some three hundred of Antony's warships were undamaged, though all the troop transports had gone with Cleopatra. At first Octavian thought to burn all of them; he had fallen in love with the deadly little Liburnian, and become convinced that all future naval warfare would be Liburnian. Massive quinqueremes were obsolescent. Then he decided to retain sixty of Antony's leviathans as a deterrent against piracy, growing at the western end of Our Sea. He sent them to Forum Julii, Caesar's seaport colony of veterans on the coast where the Gallic Province met Liguria. The rest were beached and burned inside Ambracia, yielding such a vast number of ramming beaks that many of them had to be burned too. The most imposing were saved to adorn a column in front of the Temple of Divus Julius in the Forum Romanum, while others were sent throughout Italia to remind the taxpayers that the threat had been very real.

Agrippa was to return to Italia and commence placating the

veterans, who of late years always became truculent after service had involved a big victory. The Senate was sent home too, and went thankfully; it had not been a comfortable sojourn overseas, even for those who had populated Antony's anti-Senate. Clemency was the order of the day; once Antony's admirals were executed, the inarguable ruler of Rome announced that only three men still at large would face decapitation: Canidius, Decimus Turullius and Cassius Parmensis, the latter two because they were the last of Divus Julius's assassins left alive.

Octavian himself planned to march his legions overland for Egypt, calling in on the client-kings as he progressed. But it was not to be. Frantic word came from Rome that Lepidus's son Marcus was plotting to usurp him. Having started his legions east under the command of Statilius Taurus, Octavian himself braved the winter gales of the Adriatic and returned to Italia. The crossing was the worst since that memorable one just after Divus Julius had been murdered, but now that the asthma had ceased to plague him, Octavian survived it reasonably well.

From Brundisium he traveled up the Via Appia for Rome at the gallop in a four-mule gig, swerving onto the Via Latina at Teanum Sidicinum to avoid the ague-riddled Pomptine Marshes. He was there within a *nundinum*, only to find it had been a wasted trip. Gaius Maecenas had dealt with the insurrection even before Agrippa had arrived. Marcus Lepidus and his wife, Servilia Vatia, suicided.

'How odd,' Octavian said to Maecenas and Agrippa. 'Servilia Vatia was once betrothed to me.'

True to form, the veterans were restless and talking revolt. Octavian dealt with them by walking fearlessly through the vast camps around Capua wearing a toga and a laurel wreath upon his head. Smiling and waving, loudly proclaiming their valor and loyalty to anyone in hearing distance, he sought out the right men and sat down to some hard bargaining. Because a legion's representatives were always the least satisfactory troops, as lazy as greedy, he talked money and land.

'In another seven or eight years, land won't be a part of a veteran's retirement package,' he said, 'so be grateful that all of you here today will get good land. I am establishing a military *aerarium*, a treasury separate and distinct from the one under Saturn's Temple in Rome. The State will put money into it and that money will be invested at ten per cent. The soldiers will also contribute. At this moment my actuaries are working out how much money it will need to contain in order to keep solvent even as it pays out pensions. They will be generous pensions, accompanied by a lump sum determined by a man's service record.'

'Waffle for the future!' said Tornatius, the chief of the group, with studied rudeness. 'We're here for land and big cash bonuses – *now*, Caesar.'

'I know you are,' Octavian said cordially, 'but I'm not in a position to oblige you until I get to Egypt and defeat the Queen of Beasts. That's where the plunder is that can give you what you ask.' He lifted one hand. 'No, Tornatius, no! There's no point in arguing and even less point in aggressive behavior. At the moment Rome and I don't have a sestertius to give you. While you remain in camp you will be fed and made comfortable, but should any of you go on a rampage, you'll be treated as traitors. *Wait!* Be patient! Your rewards will come, but not yet.'

'It's not good enough,' said Tornatius.

'It has to be good enough. I've issued edicts to every town and city in Campania that, if any soldiers try to sack and pillage them, every measure of reprisal is condoned by the Senate and People of Rome. They will not suffer rebellious soldiers, Tornatius, and I doubt you have sufficient influence with all my legionaries to mount a full-scale uprising.'

'You're bluffing,' Tornatius muttered.

'No, I am not. I'm in the process of issuing edicts to every camp around Capua even as we speak. They will inform the men of my predicament and ask them to be patient. On the whole, most men are reasonable. They will see my point.'

Tornatius and his colleagues subsided, and remained quiet after they realized that the bulk of the soldiers were prepared to wait the two years Octavian asked for.

'Did you take their names?' he asked Agrippa.

'Of course, Caesar. They'll quietly disappear.'

'I had hoped you'd be able to stay home,' Livia Drusilla said to her husband.

'No, dearest one, that was never a possibility. I cannot let Cleopatra start arming. Even now that the Senate is back, I'm safe against insurrection. Once the Capuan troops realize that their representatives somehow never return to the ranks, they'll behave. And with Agrippa in Capua regularly, no ambitious senator will be able to raise an army.'

'People are getting used to having you at the head of Rome,' she said, smiling. 'I even hear some of them say that you're good luck, that you've managed against all the odds to keep them safe – against Sextus Pompeius, and now Cleopatra. Antonius is hardly mentioned.'

'I have no idea where he is, because he isn't in Alexandria with That Woman.'

A mystery that was solved not many days later when a letter came from Gaius Cornelius Gallus in Cyrenaica.

'The moment I arrived in Cyrene, Pinarius surrendered his fleet and four legions to me,' Gallus wrote. 'He had received orders from Antonius to march east across Libya to Paraetonium, but it seems he didn't fancy emulating Cato Uticensis by trudging hundreds of miles along a desert coast. So he stayed put. When he showed me his orders from Antonius, I could see why he didn't march. Antonius wants a land battle, he's not finished yet. I have sent for transports, Caesar, and once they arrive I'll load the legions aboard for a voyage to Alexandria, escorted by Pinarius's fleet. Though not before the spring, and not before I get word from you when to start. Oh, I forgot to tell you that Antonius himself intended to meet Pinarius and his forces in Paraetonium.'

'Typical poet,' said Agrippa, grunting. 'No logic.'

'How is Attica?' Octavian asked, changing the subject.

'Very poorly, has been ever since her *tata* fell on his sword. Funny, that. She behaves more like his widow than his daughter. Won't eat, drinks far too much, neglects little Vipsania as if she didn't like the child. I'm having her watched because I don't want her slashing her wrists in the bath. Her money will come to me. I tried to persuade her to leave it to Vipsania – you'd have no trouble procuring an exemption from the *lex Voconia de mulierum hereditatibus* – but she refused. However, if anything does happen to her, I'll dower Vipsania with her fortune.'

So it was that Octavia inherited yet another child: Attica took poison and died in agony three days after Agrippa talked of her to Octavian, leaving his sister to take Vipsania in. A man of his word, Agrippa transferred Attica's funds to the child, which made her an extremely eligible marital prize.

Octavian had discovered a love of children in himself that, while it couldn't rival Octavia's, was strong and protective. When Antyllus tried to run away and was brought back, he wasn't punished. And whenever Octavian was home to dinner, the entire nursery partici- pated in the meal. Since Vipsania's addition made twelve of them,

Octavia hadn't exaggerated when she had told her brother that she needed a second pair of motherly hands.

For Livia Drusilla, it was time to plan which child would marry which; she cornered Octavian and forced him to listen.

'Of course Antyllus and Iullus will have to find brides elsewhere,' she said, that competent, positive look on her face that told Octavian he wasn't supposed to argue. 'Tiberius can marry Vipsania. Her fortune is immense, and he likes her.'

'And Drusus?' he asked.

'Tonilla. They like each other too.' She cleared her throat and looked stern. 'Marcellus should marry Julia.'

He frowned. 'They're first cousins, Livia Drusilla. Divus Julius didn't approve of first cousins marrying.'

'Your daughter, Caesar, is an uncrowned queen. No matter who her husband is, if he isn't to be a part of the family, he will be a threat to you. He who marries Caesar's daughter is your heir.'

'You're right, as always.' He sighed. 'Very well, let it be Marcellus and Julia.'

'Antonia is taken care of – Lucius Ahenobarbus. Not the match I would have chosen, but she was in her father's hand when the betrothal contract was drawn up, and you've promised to honor it.'

'And Atia's daughter, Marcia?' He still hated thinking about her and his mother's treachery.

'I leave that to you.'

'Then she'll marry a nobody, preferably a provincial. Maybe even a mere *socius*. After all, Antonius married a daughter to a *socius*, Pythodorus of Tralles. Which leaves Marcella.'

'I thought of Agrippa for her.'

'*Agrippa?* He's almost old enough to be her father!'

'I know that, silly! But she's in love with him, haven't you noticed? Moons and sighs and spends all day looking at the bust of him she bought in the market.'

'It won't last. Agrippa's not right for a young girl.'

'*Gerrae!* She's dark, Attica was mousy; she's cuddly, Attica was angular; she's gorgeous, Attica was . . . er, undistinguished. And it will elevate him to the ranks of Rome's First Family, where he belongs. How else is he to get there?'

He knew when he was beaten. 'Very well, my dear. Marcella shall marry Agrippa. But *not* until she's eighteen, which will give her another year to fall out of love with him. If she should, Livia

502

Drusilla, the marriage will not take place, so we won't mention it for the time being. Is that understood?'

'Perfectly,' she purred.

Short of money but trusting to get some from the client-kings, Octavian sailed to Ephesus, reaching it in May at the same time as his legions and cavalry arrived.

All the client-kings were there, including Herod, oozing charm and virtue.

'I knew you'd win, Caesar, which is why I resisted all Marcus Antonius's blandishments and bullying,' he said, fatter and more toadlike than ever.

Octavian eyed him with amusement. 'Oh, no one can deny that you're a sharp fellow,' he said. 'I suppose you want rewards?'

'Of course, but none that won't benefit Rome.'

'Name them.'

'The balsam gardens of Jericho, the bitumen fisheries of the Palus Asphaltites, Galilaea, Idumaea, both sides of the Jordanus, and the coast of Your Sea from the River Eleutherus to Gaza.'

'In other words, all of Coele Syria.'

'Yes. But your tribute will be paid the day it's due, and my sons and grandsons will be sent to Rome to be educated as Romans. No client-king is loyaler than I, Caesar.'

'Or shrewder. All right, Herod, I agree to your terms.'

Archelaus Sisenes, whose contributions to Antony failed by and large to materialize, was allowed to keep Cappadocia, and was given Cilicia Tracheia, a part of Cleopatra's grant. Amyntas of Galatia kept Galatia, but Paphlagonia was incorporated into the Roman province of Bithynia, while Pisidia and Lycaonia went to Asia Province. Polemon of Pontus, who had succeeded in safeguarding the Eastern borders against the Medes and Parthians, was also let keep his kingdom, expanded to include Armenia Parva.

None of the rest fared nearly as well, and some lost their heads. Syria was to be a province of Rome all the way to the new borders of Judaea, but the cities of Tyre and Sidon were freed of direct supervision in return for tribute. Malchus of Nabataea lost the bitumen, but nothing else; in return for what Octavian saw as leniency, Malchus was to watch the Egyptian fleets in the Sinus Arabicus and deal with any unusual activity there.

Cyprus was attached to Syria, Cyrenaica to Greece, Macedonia and Crete. Cleopatra's territory had shrunk to Egypt proper.

And in June, Octavian and Statilius Taurus loaded the army aboard transports, their destination Pelusium, the entrance to Egypt. Auster, the south wind, was late in coming, so sailing was feasible. Cornelius Gallus was to approach Alexandria from Cyrenaica. All was in train for the final defeat of Cleopatra, Queen of Beasts.

TWENTY-SEVEN

Antony and Cleopatra ended in sailing together to Paraetonium. He had not yet left the *Caesarion* when Cassius Parmensis boarded it to tell them that the densely packed soldiers were drinking the water much faster than the *praefectus fabrum* had estimated. Therefore the whole fleet would have to put in at Paraetonium to top up the barrels.

Antony's mood was better than Cleopatra had expected. There were no signs of that grey melancholy he had fallen into during those last months at Actium, nor did he have defeat on his mind.

'You just wait, my love,' he said to her jovially as the fleet prepared to sail from Paraetonium, its water barrels topped up and the soldiers' bellies full of bread, something unavailable at sea. 'You just wait. Pinarius can't be far away. The moment he arrives, Lucius Cinna and I will be following you to Alexandria. By sea. Pinarius has enough transports to hold his twenty-four thousand men, and a good fleet to augment the Alexandrian one.' A hard kiss on her mouth, and he was gone, sentenced to kick his heels in Paraetonium until Pinarius hoved in view.

Only two hundred miles to Alexandria and Caesarion – how much Cleopatra had missed them! All was not yet lost, she told herself; we can still win this war. In hindsight she could see that Antony was no admiral, but on land she believed he had a fighting chance. They would march to Pelusium and defeat Octavian there, on Egypt's frontier. Between the Roman soldiers and her Egyptian army they would marshal a hundred thousand men, more than enough to crush Octavian, who didn't know the lie of the land. It should be possible to split his force in two and beat each half in a separate engagement . . .

Only how to suppress indignation among the Alexandrians? Though they had been more tractable of recent years, she knew their volatility of old, and feared an uprising if their Queen were to slink into harbor a beaten woman, accompanied not by her Egyptian fleets, but by a refugee Roman army. So before the city appeared she summoned her captains and Antony's legates and gave succinct instructions, pinning her hopes on the fact that news of Actium would not yet have reached the Alexandrians.

Garlanded and decorated, the transports entered the Great Harbor amid the sound of victory paeans, ostensible conquerors returning home. However, Cleopatra took no chances. The fleet was anchored in the roads and its occupants kept aboard until a camp could be made near the hippodrome; she herself sailed *Caesarion* all around the harbor foreshores, standing high in the prow, her cloth-of-gold dress vying to outdo the glittering splendor of her jewels. Cheers erupted as the Alexandrians rushed to see her; limp with relief, she knew she had fooled them.

When she drew into the Royal Harbor, she could see Caesarion and Apollodorus standing on the jetty, waiting.

Oh, he had *grown*! Taller than his father now, broad in the shoulders, slender but well-muscled. His thick hair hadn't darkened, though his face, long and high in the cheekbones, had lost all trace of its boyish contours. He was Gaius Julius Caesar to the life! Love poured out of her in a spate akin to downright worship; her knees trembled until her legs wouldn't hold her up without support, her eyes were blinded by sudden tears. Charmian on one side and Iras on the other, she managed to walk the gangway and into his arms.

'Oh, Caesarion, Caesarion!' she said between sobs. 'My son, it is beyond joy to see you!'

'You lost,' he said.

Her breath caught. 'How do you know?'

'It's written all over you, Mama. If you won, why has none of your fleet come with you and why are these transports crewed by Roman troops? Most of all, where is Marcus Antonius?'

'I left him and Lucius Cinna in Paraetonium,' she said, taking his arm and compelling him to walk alongside her. 'He's waiting for Pinarius to get there from Cyrenaica with his fleet and four more legions. Canidius was left at Ambracia – the rest deserted.'

He said nothing in reply, simply walked with her into the big palace, then transferred her to Charmian and Iras. 'Bathe and rest, Mama. We'll meet for a late dinner.'

Bathe she did, but quickly. There could be no rest, though a late dinner was very welcome because it gave her time to do what had to be done. Only Apollodorus and her palace eunuchs were let into the secret, which had to be kept at all costs from Caesarion; he would never approve. The Interpreter, the Recorder, the Night Commander, the Accountant, the Judge and every nepotistic appointee in their departments were rounded up and executed. Gang leaders vanished from the stews of Rhakotis, demagogues from the agora. She had her story prepared for the questions Caesarion was bound to ask when he noticed that all the bureaucrats were new men. The old ones, she would explain, had been seized by a fit of patriotism and gone off to serve with the Egyptian army. Oh, he wouldn't believe her for a moment, but, lacking the ruthlessness to imagine her chosen path, he would assume that they had fled to avoid Roman occupation.

The late dinner was sumptuous; the cooks were as elated as the rest of Alexandria. If, when most of it was returned uneaten to the kitchens, they wondered, no one enlightened them.

Her murders done, Cleopatra felt better and looked composed. She told the story of Ephesus, Athens and Actium without any attempt to excuse her own folly. Apollodorus, Cha'em and Sosigenes listened too, more moved than Caesarion, whose face remained impassive. He has aged ten years hearing this terrible news, thought Sosigenes, yet he apportions no blame.

'Antonius's Roman friends and legates wouldn't defer to me,' she said, 'and though they harped on my sex, I thought it was my foreignness at the root of their animosity. But I was wrong! It was my sex. They wouldn't be ordered around by a woman, no matter how exalted her station. So they never stopped badgering Antonius to send me back to Egypt. Not understanding why, I refused to go.'

'Well, it's all in the past and can't matter now,' Caesarion said with a sigh. 'What do you plan to do next?'

'What would you do?' she asked, suddenly curious.

'Send Sosigenes as ambassador to Octavianus and try to make peace. Offer him as much gold as he wants to leave us be in our little corner of Their Sea. Give him hostages as a guarantee and permit the Romans to send inspectors regularly to make sure we're not secretly arming.'

'Octavianus won't leave us be, take my solemn word for that.'

'What does Antonius think?'

'Regroup and fight on.'

'Mama, that's pointless!' the young man cried. 'Antonius is past his prime and I don't have the experience to lead in his stead. If what you say about being a woman is true, then these Roman troops here in Alexandria will never follow you. Sosigenes must lead a delegation to Rome, or wherever Octavianus is, and try to negotiate a peace. The sooner the better.'

'Let's wait until Antonius returns from Paraetonium,' she pleaded, her hand on Caesarion's arm. 'Then we can decide.'

Shaking his head, Caesarion got up. 'It must be now, Mama.' She said no.

Her son's attitude had spoken volumes, opened her senses and mind to what she should have seen before she left for Ephesus. Every ounce of her energy and mental resources had gone into her plans for his future, that brilliant, triumphant, glorious future as King of Kings, ruler of the world. Now for the first time she heard what he had been trying to tell her for two years. Hers, the hunger for that glowing future, putting herself in his shoes in the mistaken belief that *no one* could resist its lure, least of all a youth with godly descent, a royal background, the mind of a genius. His military exercises had proven him no coward, so it wasn't fear for his skin that deterred him. What Caesarion lacked was ambition. And, lacking it, he would never be King of Kings in anything but name; he wasn't driven. Egypt and Alexandria were enough, he wanted no more.

Oh, Caesarion, Caesarion! How could you do this to me? How can you turn your back on power? Where did the combination of my blood and Caesar's blood go wrong? Two of the most driven people ever to walk this globe have produced a brave but gentle, strong but unambitious child. It has all been for nothing, and I haven't even the consolation of thinking I can replace my first-born with Alexander Helios or Ptolemy Philadelphus, devoid not of ambition but of sufficient intelligence. Mediocre. It is Caesarion who makes Nilus rise into the Cubits of Plenty year after year, it is Caesarion who is Horus and Osiris. And he doesn't want his destiny. He who is not mediocre yearns for mediocrity. What an irony. Oh, what a tragedy!

'When I used to say that he was a child one couldn't spoil, I didn't understand what that meant,' she said to Cha'em after that silent dinner was over and Apollodorus and Sosigenes, pale-faced, had vanished.

'But now you understand,' the old man said, voice tender.

'Yes. Caesarion wants for nothing because he wants nothing. Had Amun-Ra put him into the body of an Egyptian hybrid and set him to baking bread or sweeping the streets, he would have accepted his lot with grace and gratitude, happy to be earning enough to eat, rent a tiny house in Rhakotis, marry and have children. If some perceptive baker or street superviser saw his merits and raised him up a little, he would have been ecstatic not for his own sake, but for his children's sake.'

'You have seen the truth.'

'But what of you, Cha'em? Did you see Caesarion's character and nature that time when you went the color of ashes and refused to explain your vision to me?'

'Something like that, Daughter of Ra. Something like that.'

Antony returned to Alexandria a month later, just before the Alexandrians learned about the defeat at Actium. No one demonstrated in the streets, no one formed a mob to move on the Royal Enclosure. They wept and wailed, nothing more, though some had lost sons, nephews, cousins who had manned the Egyptian fleets. Cleopatra issued an edict explaining that few of these men were lost for good; if Octavianus wanted to sell them into slavery, she would buy them, or, if Octavianus released them, she would bring them home as soon as possible.

During the month she waited for Antony, she fretted about him as never before; love had invaded her heart, and that meant fear, doubt, perpetual worry. Was he well? How was his mood? What was happening in Paraetonium?

All of that she had to find out from Lucius Cinna. Antony refused to go near the palaces; he clambered over the side of his ship into shallow water and waded ashore at a tiny beach adjacent to the Royal Harbor. He had spoken to no one since they sailed from Paraetonium, Cinna said.

'Truly, lady, I've never seen him like this, so depressed.'

'What happened?'

'We had word that Pinarius had surrendered to Cornelius Gallus in Cyrenaica. A terrible blow for Antonius, but worse followed. Gallus is sailing for Alexandria with his own four legions and the four that belonged to Pinarius. He has plenty of transports and two fleets, his own and Pinarius's. So there are eight legions and two fleets bearing down on Alexandria from the west. Antonius wanted to stay in Paraetonium and engage Gallus there, but . . . well, you can see for yourself why he couldn't, Your Majesty.'

'Not enough time to fetch the troops from Alexandria. So he has convinced himself he should have kept his legions in Paraetonium. But to have made that decision, Cinna, he would have had to be a seer!'

'We have all tried, lady, but he won't listen.'

'I must go to him. Please see Apollodorus and tell him to find you accommodation.' Cleopatra patted Cinna on the arm and started to walk to the cove where she could see the hunched figure of Mark Antony sitting with his arms around his knees and his chin on his hands. Desolate. Alone.

Every omen is against us, she thought, her cloak flapping around her wildly. The day was cloudy and the wind much colder than an ordinary Alexandrian winter breeze. This was a gale that chilled to the bone. White foam ruptured the grey waters of the Great Harbor, the clouds streamed low and dense from north to south; Alexandria was going to get rain.

He stank of sweat, but not, thank all the gods, of wine. His beard had grown into the spiky stage and his hair stood up in a stiff umbel, uncut; no Roman wore a beard or long hair save after a death or some other huge calamity. Mark Antony was mourning.

She squatted down beside him, shivering. 'Antonius? Look at me, Antonius! *Look at me!*'

In answer he pulled his *paludamentum* over his head and tugged it down to hide his face.

'Antonius, my love, speak to me!'

But he would not, nor unveil his face.

At the end of what must have been more than an hour, it began to rain, a hard and steady downpour that soaked them. Then he spoke—but only, she felt, to get rid of her.

'See that little promontory over there beyond the Akro?'

'Yes, my love, of course I do. Soter Point.'

'Build me a one-roomed house on it, a room just big enough for me. No servants. I want no congress with men or women, including you.'

'Think you to emulate Timon of Athens?' she asked, horrified.

'Aye. The new Marcus Antonius is both misanthrope and misogynist, just like Timon of Athens. My one-roomed house will be my Timonium, and no one is to come near it. Do you hear me? No one! Not you, not Caesarion, not my children.'

'You'll be dead of a chill before it's finished,' she said, glad of the rain; it disguised her tears.

'All the more reason to hurry, then. Now go away, Cleopatra! Just go away and leave me alone!'

'Let me send you food and drink, please!'

'Don't. I want nothing.'

Caesarion was waiting, so anxious for a report that he would not leave her room; she had to change out of her wet clothing behind a screen, talking to him as Charmian and Iras rubbed her icy body with rough linen towels to warm it.

'Tell me, Mama!' came his voice, over and over. The sound of his feet pacing. 'What is the truth? Tell me, tell me!'

'That he has turned into Timon of Athens,' she said through the screen for the tenth time. 'I am to build him a one-roomed house on the end of Soter Point – he intends to call it his Timonium.' She came out from behind the screen. 'And no, he doesn't want to see you or me, he doesn't want food or wine, he won't even condone the presence of a servant.' She was weeping again. 'Oh, Caesarion, what am I to do? His soldiers know he's back, but what will they think when he doesn't visit them? Won't lead them?'

He dried her eyes, put a comforting arm about her. 'Hush, Mama, hush! There's no point in crying. Was it this bad while you were away? I know he was suicidal after the retreat from Phraaspa, and I know he tried to drown himself in wine. But you haven't told me what he was like while there was such turmoil in his command tent. Just what his friends and legates were like, which isn't the same thing. Tell me about you and Antonius. As honestly as you can. I'm not a boy anymore in *any* way.'

Jerked out of her grief, she stared at him in astonishment. 'Caesarion! You mean there have been women?'

He laughed. 'Would you rather there had been men?'

'Men were good enough for Alexander the Great, but in that respect Romans are very strange. Your father would be glad if your lovers were women, certainly.'

'Then he has nothing to complain of. Here, sit down.' He put her into a chair and sat cross-legged at her feet. 'Tell me.'

'He stuck to me through thick and thin, my son. No loyaler husband has ever lived than he. Oh, how they browbeat him! Day after day, on and on and on. Send me home to Egypt, they wouldn't have a woman in the command tent, I was a foreigner – a thousand thousand reasons why I should not have been there with him. And I was stupid, Caesarion. Very stupid. I resisted, I refused to go home. And I browbeat him too. They would *not* be dominated by a woman! But Antonius championed me, he never once gave in. And at the end, when even Canidius turned against me, he still refused to send me away.'

'Was his refusal from loyalty – or love?'

'Both, I think.' Her hands went out, clasped his feverishly. 'But that was not the worst of it for him, Caesarion. I . . . I . . . I didn't love him, and he knew it. It was his greatest sorrow. I treated him like dirt! Ordered him around, humiliated him in front of legates who didn't know him well and, being Romans, looked at him in contempt because he let me order him around – I, a *woman*! I made him kneel at my feet in front of them, I snapped my fingers to summon him, I snatched him out of conferences to take me on picnics. No wonder they hated me! But he never did.'

'When did you realize that you loved him, Mama?'

'At Actium, in the midst of mass desertions among the client-kings and his legates, and after several minor defeats on land. The scales fell from my eyes, I can describe it no other way. I looked down at his head, and saw that he had gone grey almost overnight. Suddenly I was suffering for him and with him, as if he were I. And . . . the scales fell. In a moment, a breath. Yes, I realize now that my feelings had actually changed more slowly, but at the time it came like a thunderclap. Then things happened so quickly that I never did have sufficient time to show him the depth of my love.' She emitted a small, sad sound. 'Now perhaps I never will have the time.'

Caesarion pulled her out of the chair and clasped her between his knees, rubbing her back as if she were a child. 'He'll come around, Mama. This will pass, you'll have a chance to show him.'

'How did you become so wise, my son?'

'Wise? *I?* No, not wise. Just able to see. There are no scales over my eyes, there never were. Now go to bed, Mama, my dearest, sweetest Mama. I'll build him his one-roomed house in a single day.'

Caesarion was as good as his promise; Mark Antony's little 'Timonium' was erected in a single day. A man whose face Antony didn't know shouted to him, keeping his distance, that food and drink would be placed outside his door, then went away.

Hunger and thirst would come, of course, little though he felt the pangs of either when he pushed the door open and stood surveying this prison cell. For so it was. Not until he had faced his mental torments could he venture out, and when he entered, Antony had no idea how long this odyssey of the mind would take.

He could see as if illuminated by a brilliant light what was wrong, yet every step of it had to be detailed in . . .

Poor, silly Cleopatra! Grasping at him as if at a savior, when every member of his world must surely have been able to see that Marcus Antonius could save no one. If he couldn't save himself, what chance did he have of saving others?

Caesar—the true Caesar, not that posturing boy in Rome—had always known, of course. Why else had he passed over the one everybody assumed would be his heir? It all began there, with that rejection. His response had been predictable: he would go east to fight the Parthians, do what Caesar hadn't lived to do. Earn immortality as Caesar's equal.

But then the plan had foundered, mired in his own deficiencies. Somehow there had always seemed to be enough time for revels, so he had reveled. But there wasn't time. Not with Octavian doing so well in Italia, against all odds. Octavian, always Octavian! Gazing around the unrendered walls of his Timonium, Antony saw at last why his plans had foundered. He should have ignored Octavian, continued with the Parthian campaign instead of persecuting Caesar's heir. Oh, the wasted years! *Wasted!* Intrigues aimed at securing Octavian's downfall, season upon season frittered away encouraging Sextus Pompey in his futile designs. He need not have remained in Greece to secure it; if Octavian were to win against Sextus Pompey, his own presence could not prevent that. Nor had it, in the end. Octavian had outmaneuvered him, won in spite of him. While the years went on and the Parthians grew stronger.

Mistakes, one after the other! Dellius had led him astray, Monaeses had led him astray. And Cleopatra. Yes, Cleopatra . . .

Why had he gone to Athens instead of staying in Syria that spring when the Parthians had invaded? Fearing Octavian more than he feared the true, the natural enemy. Imperiling his own standing in Rome, commencing the erosion of his power base and his spirit. And now, eleven years after Philippi, he had nothing left save shame.

How could he look Canidius in the face? Caesarion? His Roman friends still living? So many dead, thanks to him! Ahenobarbus, Poplicola, Lurius . . . Men like Pollio and Ventidius driven into retirement as a result of his mistakes . . . How could he look a man of Pollio's stature in the face ever again?

And at that conclusion he remained for a long time, pacing up and down the packed-earth floor, remembering to eat and drink only when he reeled in exhaustion, or paused to wonder what clawed beast chewed in his belly. The shame, the shame! He, so admired and loved, had let all of them down, flogging himself on to conspire at the demise of Octavian when such was neither his duty nor his best course. The shame, the shame!

Only when that unusually cold winter was finally blowing itself out did he reach a calm placid enough to think of Cleopatra.

Yet what was there to think about? Poor, foolish Cleopatra! Strutting around the command tent aping the conduct of hoary Roman marshals in the field, deeming herself their equal in military prowess just because she was footing the bill.

And all of it for Caesarion, King of Kings. Caesar in a new guise, blood of her blood. Yet how could he, Antony, oppose her, when all he wanted to do was please her? Why else had he embarked on this insane venture to conquer Rome, than love of Cleopatra? In his mind she had replaced that Parthian campaign after his retreat from Phraaspa.

She was wrong, I was right. Crush the Parthians first, then move on Rome. That was our best alternative, but she could never see it. Oh, I love her! How mistaken we can be, when we put our objectives to the test! I gave in to her when I should not have. I let her queen it over my friends and colleagues when I should have confiscated her war chest and sent her packing to Alexandria. But I never had the strength, and that too is a shame, a humiliation. She has used me because I let her use me. Poor, silly Cleopatra! But how much the poorer and sillier does that make Marcus Antonius?

When March came in and the Alexandrian weather returned to halcyon, Antony opened the door of his Timonium.

Clean-shaven, his hair trimmed short – oh, it was so grey! – he appeared unannounced in the palace, roaring for Cleopatra.

'Antonius, Antonius!' she cried, covering his face with kisses. 'Oh, now I can live again!'

'I'm starved for you,' he whispered in her ear, then set her gently to one side to embrace an overjoyed Caesarion. 'I won't say what everyone must tell you, boy, but you make me feel young again, my arse smarting from the toe of Caesar's boot. Now I'm grizzled and you're grown up.'

'Not grown enough to serve as a senior legate – but then, nor are Curio and Antyllus. They're both here in Alexandria, waiting for you to come out of your Timonian shell.'

'Curio's son? My own eldest? *Edepol*, they're men too!'

Caesarion beamed. 'We'll all meet for a splendid dinner tomorrow, not before. You and Mama need time together first.'

After the most wonderful hours of love she had ever known, Cleopatra lay along the sleeping Antony's side, a stick insect trying to envelop a tree trunk, she thought wryly. Afire with love for him, she poured it out in words, then held nothing of herself back, drowned instead in fabulous sensations she had last felt when Caesar held her. But that was a traitorous thought, so she put it away and struggled to give Antony acts of love that would make him see how much she loved him.

He had told her all that he was prepared to, anxious mostly to assure her that he hadn't binged, that his body was fit and his mind clear.

'I was waiting for the sky to fall in,' he ended, 'alone, passive, utterly broken. And then at dawn this morning I awoke healed. I don't know why, or how. I just woke up thinking that, though we can't win this war now, Cleopatra, we can give Octavianus a run for his money. You tell me that my legions here are still for me, and your own army is in camp on the Pelusiac arm of Nilus. So when Octavianus comes, we'll be waiting.'

The perfection of the mood between them didn't last very long; the outside world impinged and destroyed it.

Worst was the news that Canidius brought not far into March. He had traveled alone and overland from Epirus to the Hellespont, crossed into Bithynia, rode the length of Cappadocia and passed through the Amanus without being recognized. Even the last leg through Syria and Judaea had been uneventful. He too had aged – white of hair, blue eyes faded – but his loyalty to Antony hadn't faltered, and he had come to terms with the presence of Cleopatra.

'Actium has been blown up into the most colossal sea battle ever fought,' he told a dinner table that held young Curio and Antyllus as well as Caesarion. 'Many, many thousands of your Roman troops died, Antonius – did you know that? So many that a mere handful survived to be taken prisoner. You yourself, however, fought on even after the *Antonia* went up in flames. Then you saw the Queen deserting you for Egypt, leaped into a pinnace and pursued her frantically, abandoning your men. You forced your way through hundreds of dying Roman soldiers, ignoring their pleas to stay, intent only on catching up to Cleopatra. When you did and she hauled you aboard her ship, you howled like an impaled dog, sat down on the deck, covered your head, and refused to move for three days. The Queen confiscated your sword and dagger, you were so out of your mind with guilt at deserting your men. Of course Rome and Italia are now absolutely convinced that you're at best a slave to Cleopatra. Your most faithful adherents have abandoned you. Pollio, even, though he won't fight against you.'

'Is Octavianus in Rome?' Caesarion asked, breaking the appalled silence.

'He was, but briefly. He's setting out with more legions and fleets to join those he has waiting in Ephesus. I heard that he will have thirty legions, though no more cavalry than the seventeen thousand he has always had. It seems he's to sail from Ephesus to Antioch, maybe even to Pelusium. The Etesian Winds won't be blowing, but Auster has been very late of recent years.'

'When do you think he'll arrive?' Antony asked, voice calm, demeanor unruffled.

'In Egypt, perhaps June. Word has it that he won't cross the Nilus Delta by sea. He intends to march from Pelusium to Memphis overland, and approach Alexandria from the south.'

'Memphis? That's peculiar,' said Caesarion.

Canidius shrugged. 'All I can think, Caesarion, is that he wants Alexandria completely isolated, unable to draw upon any reinforcements. It's sound strategy, if cautious.'

'It seems wrong to me,' Caesarion maintained. 'Is Agrippa the author of this strategy?'

'I don't think Agrippa is present. Statilius Taurus is to be Octavianus's second-in-command, and Cornelius Gallus will advance from Cyrenaica.'

'A pincer movement,' said Curio, airing his knowledge.

Antony and Canidius concealed their smiles, Caesarion looked exasperated. Really! A pincer movement! How perceptive of Curio.

Now that Antony had regained his senses, a huge weight was lifted from Cleopatra's shoulders, but she couldn't summon up her old reserves of spirit and energy. The lump in her throat was still growing a little, her feet and lower legs kept puffing up, she was short of breath and had an occasional attack of confusion. All of which Hapd'efan'e blamed on the goitre, without knowing how to treat it. The best he could do was order her to lie on a bed or a couch with her feet elevated whenever the oedema occurred, usually after she sat for too long at her desk.

Her vengefulness and arrogance had made intractable enemies out of the two men on her Syrian border, Herod and Malchus, and Cornelius Gallus had blocked Egypt's west. Therefore she had to look farther afield for allies. An embassage set out for the King of the Parthians, bearing many gifts and a promise of assistance when the Parthians next invaded Syria. But what could she do for Median Artavasdes? He was steadily growing in power as he inched into Parthian Media by exploiting the feuds in the Parthian court. Armenian Artavasdes, who had been brought to Alexandria to walk in Antony's triumphal parade, was still held captive. Cleopatra executed him and sent his head to Media, with ambassadors under instructions to assure the King that his little daughter, Iotape, would remain betrothed to Alexander Helios, and that Egypt relied on Media to keep the Romans at bay along the Armenian borders; to help defray the costs of this policy, she sent gold.

As time drew on and reports came in that Octavian was still coming, Cleopatra was spurred to invent wilder and wilder schemes. In April she portaged a small fleet of speedy warships across the sands from Pelusium to Heroönopolis at the head of the Sinus Arabicus. What consumed her most now was Caesarion's safety, and she could see no possibility of that unless she sent him to the Malabar coast of India, or to the big pear-shaped island below it, Taprobane. Whatever happened, Caesarion must be sent somewhere to finish his growing; only as a fully mature man could he come back to conquer Octavian. But no sooner was the fleet anchored in Heroönopolis than Malchus of Nabataea descended and burned every galley to the water line. Undeterred, she portaged another fleet to the Sinus Arabicus, but sent the ships to Berenice, far out of reach of Malchus. With them went fifty of her most trusted servants, under orders to wait in Berenice until Pharaoh Caesar arrived. Then they were to sail for India.

Since it was impossible to revive the Society of Inimitable Livers, Cleopatra hit upon the idea of founding the Society of Companions in Death. The object was much the same: to revel, drink, eat—but also to forget for a few hours at a time the fate that was rapidly descending. Though Companions in Death, reflecting its name, was never the riotous, feckless succession of celebrations that Inimitable Livers had been. Hollow, forced, frenetic.

Antony was sober despite his intake of wine, moderate at most, for he preferred to spend his days with his legions, training them to peak performance. Caesarion, Curio and Antyllus were always with him when he was in military mode, though not so keen to be Companions in Death. At their age, they refused to believe that death was possible; anybody else could die, they could not.

At the beginning of May came news from Syria that devastated Antony. On his way to Athens he had found a hundred genuine Roman gladiators stranded on Samos, and hired them to fight in the victory games he intended to celebrate after he defeated Octavian. He paid them and gave them the use of two ships, but Actium ruined his plans. On hearing of Antony's defeat, the gladiators resolved to go to Egypt and fight for him there, soldiers of the sawdust no longer, but *real* soldiers. They got as far as Antioch, where Titus Didius, Octavian's new governor, detained them. Then Messala Corvinus arrived with the first of Octavian's legions, and ordered them crucified. A cruel and lingering death reserved for slaves and pirates, no others. It was Corvinus's way of saying that any gladiators who fought for Mark Antony were slaves, not free men.

For some reason beyond Cleopatra's ability to plumb, this sad little story affected Antony as neither Actium nor Paraetonium had seemed to. He wept inconsolably for several days, and when at last the paroxysm of grief was over, he seemed to have lost his interest, energy, spirit. A depression descended, but masked under a huge enthusiasm for the Society of Companions in Death, whose revels he now entered into feverishly, drinking himself senseless. The legions were neglected, the Egyptian army forgotten, and when Caesarion constantly reminded him that he had to buckle down and keep both armies on their toes, Antony ignored him.

At precisely this moment, the priests and nomarchs of Nilus from Elephantine to Memphis – a thousand miles – came to Pharaoh Cleopatra and offered to fight to the death of every last Egyptian. Let all of Nilotic Egypt rise up in Pharaoh's defence! they cried, on their knees with faces pressed to the golden floor of her audience chamber.

Adamant, unbendable, she kept refusing until they went home in despair, convinced that Roman rule would be the end of Egypt. But they didn't go before they had seen her tears. No! she wept, she would not let Egypt become a bloodbath for the sake of two Pharaohs who had hardly any Egyptian blood in their veins.

'A senseless sacrifice I cannot accept,' she said, weeping.

'Mama, you had no right to refuse their offer without me,'

Caesarion said when he found out. 'My answer would have been the same, but in not requiring my presence you stripped me of my entitlements. Why do you think your behavior spares me pain? It doesn't. How can I rule with my proper godhead if you persist in shielding me? My shoulders are broader than yours.'

In between trying to jolly Antony out of his gloom and keeping an eye on the three young men, Caesarion, Curio and Antyllus, Cleopatra was very busy completing her tomb, which she had started when she ascended the throne at seventeen, as was custom and tradition. It was inside the Sema, a large compound within the Royal Enclosure where all the Ptolemies were buried, and where Alexander the Great lay encased in a transparent crystal sarcophagus. One of her two brother-husbands was there (she had murdered him to elevate Caesarion to the throne); the other, drowned, was under the waters of Pelusiac Nilus. Each Ptolemy had his own tomb, as did the various Berenices, Arsinoës and Cleopatras who had reigned. None was a gigantic edifice, though pharaonic in form: an innermost chamber for the sarcophagus, canopic jars and guardian statues, plus three little outer chambers filled with food, drink, furniture and an exquisite reed boat for sailing the River of Night.

Since Cleopatra's tomb was to hold Antony as well, it was twice the size of the others. Her own side was finished; it was Antony's side that the craftsmen labored over frantically. Made of sombre red Nubian granite, it was polished like a mirror and rectangular in shape, its outside walls unadorned save for her and Antony's cartouches. Two massive bronze doors worked with sacred symbols closed both its sets of chambers, opening into an anteroom that led through two doors into the sides. A speaking tube penetrated the five-foot-thick masonry adjacent to the left leaf of the outer doors.

Until she and Antony lay fully embalmed within it, an aperture would remain high on the door wall, reached by scaffolding made from bamboo; a winch and a long, roomy basket enabled persons and items to be conveyed in and out of the interior. The embalmment process took ninety days, so it would be fully three months between death and the sealing up of the opening high on the door wall; embalmer priests would shuttle to and fro with their instruments and natron, the sour, acrid salts they obtained from Lake Tritonis on the margin of the Roman African province. Even that was ready, the priests housed in a special building together with their gear.

Antony's inner chamber was connected to hers through a door, and both were beautiful: emblazoned with murals, gold, gems; every solace that Pharaoh and her consort might wish for in the Realm of the Dead. Books for them to read, scenes of their lives to smile at, every last Egyptian god, a wonderful mural of Nilus. The food, furniture, drink and boat were already installed; it would not be long now, Cleopatra knew.

In the rooms reserved for Antony stood his desk and his ivory curule chair, his best suits of armor, an array of togas and tunics, citruswood tables on pedestals of ivory inlaid with gold. His miniature temples, which held the wax images of all his ancestors who had reached the office of praetor were there, and a bust of himself on a hermed pillar that he particularly liked; the Greek sculptor had sheathed his head in the jaws of a lion skin, its paws knotted over the top of his chest and two red eyes glaring above his skull. The only things missing from his section were a workmanlike suit of armor and one purple-bordered toga, all he would need now before the end.

Of course Caesarion knew what she was doing, fully realized that it meant she thought she and Antony would soon be dead, but he said nothing, nor tried to dissuade her. Only the most foolish pharaoh would not take death into account; it didn't mean that his mother and stepfather were contemplating suicide, only that they would be ready to step into the Realm of the Dead properly accoutred and equipped, whether their deaths came as the result of Octavian's invasion, or didn't occur for another forty years. His own tomb was abuilding, as was fit and proper; his mother had put it next to Alexander the Great, but he had relocated it in a small, unobtrusive corner.

One part of him was thrilled at the prospect of battle, but another fretted and chewed over the fate of his people if they were to be left without Pharaoh. Old enough to remember the famine and pestilence of those years between his father's death and the birth of the twins, he had an enormous sense of responsibility, and knew that he must live no matter what happened to his mother and her consort. He was sure that he would be permitted to live if he went about the negotiations skillfully, and was prepared to give Octavian whatever amount of treasure he demanded. Living Pharaoh was more important by far to Egypt than tunnels choked with mere stuff. His ideas and opinions about Octavian were private, never transmitted to Cleopatra, who would not agree with them nor think well of him for them. For he understood Octavian's dilemma, and could not blame him for his actions. Oh, Mama, Mama! So much hubris, so much ambition! Because she had dared the might of Rome, Rome was coming. A new era was about to begin for Egypt, an era that he had to control. Nothing in Octavian's conduct said he was a tyrant; he was, Caesarion divined, a man with a mission, to secure Rome from her enemies and provide her people with safety and prosperity. With those goals in mind, he would do whatever he must, but no more. A reasonable man, a man who could be talked to and made see the good sense of a stable Egypt under a stable ruler who would never be a danger. Egypt, Friend and Ally of the Roman People, Rome's most loyal client-kingdom.

Caesarion turned seventeen on the twenty-third day of June. Cleopatra wanted to give him a big party, but he refused to hear of it.

'Just something small, Mama. The family, Apollodorus, Cha'em, Sosigenes,' he said firmly. 'No Companions in Death, please! Try to talk Antonius out of that.'

Not as difficult a task as she had expected; Mark Antony was wearing out, running down.

'If that's the kind of celebration the boy wants, he shall have it.' The red-brown eyes produced a rare twinkle. 'Truth to tell, my dearest wife, I'm more Death than Companion these days.' He sighed. 'It won't be long now that Octavianus has reached Pelusium. Another month, perhaps a little more.'

'My army wouldn't stand,' she said through her teeth.

'Oh, come, Cleopatra, why should it? Landless peasants, a few grizzled, knotted old Roman centurions who date back to Aulus Gabinius – I wouldn't ask them to give up their lives anymore than Octavianus wishes that. No indeed, I'm glad they didn't fight.' He looked wry. 'And gladder still that Octavianus simply sent them home. He's acting more like a tourist than a conqueror.'

'What's to stop him?' she asked bitterly.

'Nothing, and that's an irrefutable fact. I think we should send an ambassador to him immediately and ask for terms.'

Even a day earlier she would have flown at him, but that was yesterday. One look at her son's birthday face had told her that Caesarion didn't want the soil of his country soaked in the blood of his subjects; he would consent to a last-ditch stand by the Roman legions in camp at the hippodrome, but only because those troops hungered for a battle. They had been denied it at Actium, so they wanted it here. Victory or defeat didn't matter, just the chance to fight.

Yes, what it boiled down to was what Caesarion wanted, and that was peace at any price. So be it. Peace at any price.

'Who will Octavianus see?' she asked.

'I thought, Antyllus,' Antony said.

'*Antyllus*? He's a child!'

'Exactly. What's more, Octavianus knows him well. I can't think of a better ambassador.'

'No, nor can I,' she said, after thinking it over. 'However, it means you'll have to write a letter. Antyllus isn't bright enough to negotiate.'

'I know. And yes, I'll write the letter.' He stretched his legs, ran a hand through his hair, whiter now than grey. 'Oh, my dearest girl, I'm so tired! I just want it to be over.'

This lump in her throat was on the inside; she swallowed. 'And I, my love, my life. I am so sorry for the torment I inflicted on you, but I didn't understand – no, no, I must stop trying to make excuses! I must take the blame squarely, without flinching, without excuses. If I had stayed in Egypt, things might have gone very differently.' She pressed her forehead against his, too close to see his eyes. 'I didn't love you enough, so now I suffer – oh, terribly! I love you, Marcus Antonius. I love you more than life, I won't live if you don't. All I want is to wander the Realm of the Dead with you forever. We will be together in death as we never have in life, because there is peace, contentment, a most wonderful ease.' She lifted her head. 'You do believe that?'

'I do.' His little white teeth flashed. 'That's why it's better to be an Egyptian than a Roman. Romans don't believe in a life after death, which is why they don't fear death. It's just an eternal sleep, that's how Caesar looked at it. And Cato, and Pompeius Magnus, and the rest. Well, while they sleep, I'll be walking the Realm of the Dead with you. Forever.'

Octavianus,

I am sure you don't want more Roman deaths, and from the way you treated my wife's army, you don't want enemy deaths either.

I suppose by the time my eldest son reaches you, you will be in Memphis. He bears this letter because I know it will arrive on your desk rather than some legate's. The boy is eager to do me this service, and I am happy to let him.

Octavianus, let us not continue this farce. I admit freely that I was the aggressor in our war, if war it can be called.

Marcus Antonius has not shone too brightly, so much is sure, and now he wishes an end.

If you permit Queen Cleopatra to rule her kingdom as Pharaoh and Queen, I will undertake to fall on my sword. A good end to a pathetic struggle. Send your answer back with my boy. I will wait three *nundinae* for it. If by then I have received no answer, I will know you refuse me.

The three *nundinae* passed, but no word came from Octavian. What worried Antony was that Antyllus didn't return, but he decided that Octavian would detain the boy until his victory was complete, then – what did one do with the sons of the proscribed? Banishment was the usual practice, but Antyllus had lived with Octavia for years. Her brother wouldn't banish one of her brood. Nor deny him an income big enough to live as an Antonian must.

'Did you really think Octavianus would accept whatever terms you laid out in your letter?' Cleopatra asked. She hadn't seen it, nor had she demanded to see it; the new Cleopatra understood that men's business belonged to men.

'I suppose not,' said Antony, shrugging. 'I wish Antyllus would contact me.'

How to tell him the boy is dead? she asked herself. Octavian couldn't make terms, he needed the Treasure of the Ptolemies. Did he know where to find it? No, of course not. Which wouldn't deter him from digging more holes in the sands of Egypt than there were stars in the sky. And Antyllus? A nuisance, alive. Sixteen-year-old lads moved like quicksilver and had a certain guile; Octavian wouldn't run the risk of keeping him alive to escape and report the enemy dispositions to his father. Yes, Antyllus was dead. Did it matter whether she broached the subject to his father or held her counsel? No, it did not. Therefore why drop another burden of grief on his shoulders, so bowed over, so . . . *frail*? Not an adjective she had ever thought to apply to Mark Antony.

Instead she broached the subject of a different young man – Caesarion. 'Antonius, we have perhaps three *nundinae* left before Octavianus reaches Alexandria. At some point close to the city I presume you'll fight a battle, is that right?'

He shrugged. 'The soldiers want it, so yes.'

'Caesarion can't be let fight.'

'In case he dies?'

'Yes. I can see no possibility that Octavianus will allow me to rule Egypt, but nor will he let Caesarion rule. I have to get Caesarion

523

away to India or Taprobane before Octavianus starts to hunt him down. I have fifty good men and a small, swift fleet at Berenice. Cha'em gave my servants sufficient gold to permit Caesarion a good life at the end of his voyage. When he's a fully grown man, he can come back.'

He studied her intently, a frown bringing his brows together. Caesarion, always Caesarion! Still, she was right. If he stayed, Octavian would hunt him down and kill him. Had to. No rival as like Caesar as this Egyptian son could be let live.

'What do you want of me?' he asked.

'Your support when I tell him. He won't want to go.'

'He won't, but he must. Yes, I'll support you.'

Both of them were astonished when Caesarion agreed at once.

'I see your point, Mama, Antonius,' he said, blue eyes wide. 'One of us must live, yet none of us will be let live. If I skulk in India for ten years, Octavianus will have let Egypt go on its way. As a province, not a client-kingdom. But if the people of Nilus know that Pharaoh is alive, they'll welcome me when I return.' The eyes filled with tears; his face twisted. 'Oh, Mama, Mama, not to see you ever again! I must, yet I can't. You will walk in Octavianus's triumphal parade and then die at the hands of the strangler. I must, yet I can't!'

'You can, Caesarion,' said Antony strongly, clasping him by the forearm. 'I don't doubt your love for your mother, but nor do I doubt your love for your people. Go to India and stay there until the time's right to come back. Please!'

'Oh, I'll go. It's the sensible thing to do.' He gave each of them Caesar's smile, and walked out.

'I can hardly believe it,' said Cleopatra, stroking her lump. 'He did say he'll go, didn't he?'

'Yes, he did.'

'It must be tomorrow.'

Tomorrow it was; robed like a banker or a bureaucrat of the middle order, Caesarion set off with the appropriate two servants, all three mounted on good camels.

Cleopatra stood on the Royal Enclosure battlements watching while ever she could see her son on the Memphis road, waving a red scarf, smiling brilliantly. Pleading a headache, Antony remained in the palace.

There Canidius found him, pausing in the doorway to take in the sight of Marcus Antonius stretched full length on a couch, an arm across his eyes. 'Antonius?'

Antony swung his legs to the floor and sat up, blinking.

'Are you unwell?' Canidius asked.

'A headache, but not from wine. My life burdens me.'

'Octavianus won't cooperate.'

'Well, we've known that since the Queen sent him her sceptre and diadem to Pelusium. I wish the town had been as sluggish as the army! A lot of good Egyptians died – how did they ever think to resist a Roman siege?'

'He couldn't afford a siege, Antonius, which is why he stormed the place.' Canidius peered at Antony, puzzled. 'Don't you remember? You are unwell!'

'Yes, yes, I remember!' Antony laughed, a grating sound. 'I have too much on my mind, that's all. He's in Memphis, isn't he?'

'He was in Memphis. Now? Coming up the Canopic Nilus.'

'What has my son to say about him?'

'Your son?'

'Antyllus!'

'Antonius, we haven't heard from Antyllus in a month.'

'We haven't? How odd! Octavianus must have detained him.'

'Yes, I daresay that's what happened,' Canidius said gently.

'Octavianus sent a servant with letters, didn't he?'

'Yes,' said Cleopatra from the doorway. She walked in and sat opposite Antony, her eyes signalling Canidius frantically.

'What was the fellow's name?'

'Thyrsus, dear.'

'Refresh my memory, Cleopatra,' Antony said, obviously very confused. 'What was in the letters Octavianus sent you?'

Canidius had slumped into a chair, staring amazed.

'The public one ordered me to disarm and surrender; the one for my eyes only said that Octavianus will work out a solution satisfactory to all parties,' Cleopatra said levelly.

'Oh, yes! Yes, of course that was it . . . Ah – didn't I have to do something for you? Something about the commander of the garrison at Pelusium?'

'He sent his family to Alexandria for safekeeping and I had them arrested. Why should *his* family avoid the suffering visited on Pelusium? But then Caesarion –' she stopped, wrung her hands – 'said I was too angry to dispense justice, and handed them to you.'

'Oh! Oh. And did I dispense justice to the family?'

'You freed them. That was no justice.'

Canidius listened to the exchange, feeling as if he had been hit by a poleaxe. All this was over, in the past! Ye gods, Antony was . . . was half-demented! His memory had gone. And how was he, Canidius, going to discuss war plans with a forgetful old man? Broken! Shattered into a thousand pieces. Unfit for command.

'What did you want, Canidius?' Antony was asking.

'Octavianus is nearly here, Antonius, and I have seven legions at the hippodrome raring for a fight. Are we to fight?'

Up leaped Antony, transformed in a moment from forgetful old man to general of troops: eager, alert, interested. 'Yes! Yes, of course we fight,' he said, and commenced to roar. 'Maps! I need maps! Where are Cinna, Turullius, Cassius?'

'Waiting, Antonius. Dying to fight.'

Cleopatra saw the visitor out.

'How long has this been going on?' Canidius asked.

'Since he returned from Phraaspa, what – four years ago?'

'Jupiter! Why didn't I see it?'

'Because it happens in spasms, and usually when his guard is down, or he has a headache. Caesarion left today, so it's a bad day. But don't worry, Canidius. He's already snapping out of it, and by tomorrow he'll be everything he was at Philippi.'

Cleopatra didn't speak lightly. Antony pounced as Octavian's advance guard of cavalry arrived in the suburb of Canopus, where the hippodrome was located. This was the old Antony, full of dash and fire, incapable of putting a foot – or a man – wrong. The cavalry routed, Antony's seven legions charged into battle singing their war paeans to Hercules Invictus, patron god of the Antonii as well as of war.

He returned to Alexandria at dusk, still in his armor, to be greeted by an ecstatic Cleopatra.

'Oh, Antonius, Antonius, nothing is too good for you!' she cried, covering his face with kisses. 'Caesarion! How I wish Caesarion could see you now!'

She still hadn't learned, poor lady. When Canidius, Cinna, Decimus Turullius and the others arrived in much the same sweaty, bloody condition as Antony, she ran from one to another, smiling so widely that Cinna for one found the performance revolting.

'It wasn't a major engagement,' Antony tried to tell her when she spun past him on one of her gyrations. 'Save your joy for the big battle that's still to come.'

But no, no, she wouldn't listen. The whole city was rejoicing as at a major engagement, and Cleopatra was utterly absorbed in planning a victory feast for the morrow in the Gymnasium – the army would be there, she would decorate the bravest soldiers, the legates must be ensconced in a golden pavilion on sumptuously fat cushions, the centurions in something only slightly less plush . . .

'They're both mad,' said Cinna to Canidius. 'Mad!'

He tried to restrain her, but Antony the man, the beloved, had vanished before her conviction that, in winning this minor battle, the war was won and over, that her kingdom was safe, that Octavian was no threat anymore. Professional soldiers all, the legates watched an impotent Antony succumb to Cleopatra's crazy joy and spend what was left of his energy in convincing her that seven legions would never fit inside the Gymnasium.

The feast was held with only the men to be decorated there from the ranks, though all four-hundred-plus centurions came, the military tribunes, the junior legates, and all of Alexandria that could squeeze in. There were also prisoners to accommodate, men Cleopatra insisted be put in chains and stood in a place from which the Alexandrians could jeer and throw rotten vegetables. If nothing else could have turned the legions away from her, that did. Un-Roman, barbaric. An insult to men as Roman as any.

Nor would she listen to advice about the decorations she insisted that she must bestow; instead of the plain oak-leaf crown for valor, the man who had saved the lives of his fellows and held the ground on which it happened until the conflict was over found himself presented with a golden helmet and cuirass by a slightly pop-eyed, plain little woman who *kissed* him!

'Where's me oak leaves? Gimme me oak leaves!' the soldier demanded, hugely offended.

'*Oak leaves?*' Her laugh tinkled. 'Oh, my dear boy, a silly crown of oak leaves instead of a golden helmet? Be sensible!'

He dropped the golden gear on the edge of the crowd and went immediately to Octavian's army, so angry that he knew he would kill her did he stay. Antonius's wasn't a Roman army: it was a combination of dancing girls and eunuchs.

'Cleopatra, Cleopatra, when will you learn?' Antony demanded in real pain that night after the ridiculous affair was finished and the Alexandrians had gone home, sated.

'What do you mean?'

'You shamed me in front of my men!'

'*Shamed you?*' She drew herself up and prepared for her own battle. 'What do you mean, shamed you?'

'It's not your place to conduct a military celebration, nor to tamper with Rome's *mos maiorum* and give a soldier gold instead of oak leaves. Nor clap Roman soldiers in manacles. Do you know what those prisoners said when I invited them to join my legions? They said they'd prefer to die. Die!'

'Oh, well, if that's how they feel, I'll oblige them!'

'You'll do nothing of the kind. For the last time, madam, keep your nose out of men's affairs!' Antony roared, trembling. 'You've turned me into a ponce, a . . . a *saltatrix tonsa* trolling for custom outside Venus Erucina's!'

Her rage died in the time it took lightning to strike; jaw dropped, eyes drowning, she stared at him in genuine dismay. 'I . . . I thought you'd want it,' she whispered. 'I thought it would enhance your standing if your ranker soldiers, your centurions and tribunes saw how great the rewards were going to be once our war is won. And haven't we won it? Surely it was a victory?'

'Yes, but a little victory, not a big one. And for Jupiter's sake, woman, save your golden helmets and cuirasses for Egyptian soldiers! Roman ones would rather have a grass crown.'

And so they parted, each to weep, but for very different reasons.

On the morrow they kissed and made up; this was no time to remain at odds with each other.

'If I swear on my father Amun-Ra that I won't interfere in whatever military things you do, Marcus, will you consent to fight that major battle?' she asked, hollow-eyed from lack of sleep.

From somewhere he conjured up a smile, pulled her close and inhaled the exquisite fragrance of her skin, that light, flowery fragrance she distilled from Jericho balsam. 'Yes, my love, I'm going to fight my last battle.'

She stiffened, drew back to look at him. '*Last* battle?'

'Yes, *last* battle. Tomorrow, at dawn.' He drew a breath, looked stern. 'I won't be coming back, Cleopatra. No matter what happens, I won't be coming back. We may win, but it's only one battle. Octavianus has won the war. I intend to die on the field with as much valor as I can. That way, the Roman element is gone and you can treat with Octavianus without needing to consider me. I'm his embarrassment, not you – you're a foreign enemy with whom he can deal plainly, as a Roman does. He may require you to walk in his triumphal parade, but he'll not execute you or your children by me. I doubt he'll let you rule Egypt, which means that after his triumph is over he'll put you and the children to live in an Italian fortress town like Norba or Praeneste. Very comfortably. And there you can wait for Caesarion to return.'

Her face had drained of color, concentrated now in those huge gold eyes. 'Antonius, no!' she whispered.

'Antonius, yes. It's what I want, Cleopatra. You can ask for my body and he'll give it to you. He's not a vengeful man – what he does is expedient, rational, carefully thought-out. Don't deny me the chance of a good death, my love, please!'

The tears felt hot, burning her cheeks as they ran down to the corners of her mouth. 'I won't deny you your good death, my most beloved. One last night in your living arms, I ask for that and nothing more.'

He kissed her once and left for the Hippodrome, there to make his battle dispositions.

Aimless, killed inside, she walked through the palace to the door that led across palmy gardens to the Sema, Charmian and Iras in her wake as always. They hadn't asked any questions; there was no need after seeing Pharaoh's face. Antony was going to die in the battle, Caesarion was gone to India, and Pharaoh was rapidly approaching that dim horizon that separated living Nilus from the Realm of the Dead.

At her tomb she commanded the attention of those who still worked on Antony's side, issuing orders to have everything ready for his body at dusk tomorrow. That done, she stood in the little anteroom just inside the great bronze doors and stared at them, then turned to look at the outermost of her own chambers, where a beautiful bed had been situated, and a bath, a corner for her private bodily functions, a table and two chairs, a desk stacked with finest papyrus paper, reed pens and cakes of ink, a chair. Everything Pharaoh would require in the afterlife. But, she thought, it was also properly appointed for Pharaoh in this life.

That preyed on her, her caged impotence between Antony's death and Octavian's decision about her and her children. She had to hide! Hide until she found out what Octavian's decision was. If he found her where she could be captured, she would be incarcerated and her children probably murdered immediately. Antony kept insisting that Octavian was a merciful man, but to Cleopatra he was Basiliskos, the lethal reptile. Certainly he wanted her alive for his triumphal parade: ergo, a dead Queen of Beasts was the last kind he wanted. But if she took her own life now, her children would undoubtedly suffer. No, she could not take her own life until she had made her children safe. For one thing, Caesarion would not yet have reached harbor on the Sinus Arabicus; it would be *nundinae* before he sailed away. As for Antony's children – she was their mother, caught by the intangible bond that fused a woman and her children together forever.

The idea had come when her eyes chanced upon the bed. Why not hide inside her tomb? Admittedly it could still be entered through the aperture, but before Octavian could order men to enter, she would be screaming down the speaking tube that if any minions tried to enter that way, they would find her dead of poison. The last type of death Octavian could condone in her; all his many enemies would be clamoring that he had poisoned her. Somehow she had to stay alive and a free agent with choices for long enough to get his oath that her children would live and prosper independently of Rome. In the event that the Master of Rome refused to agree, she would poison herself so publicly and so shockingly that the odium of the deed would destroy his political image ever after.

'I shall stay here,' she said to Charmian and Iras. 'Put a dagger on that table, another dagger near the speaking tube, and go to Hapd'efan'e immediately. Tell him I want a phial of pure *aconitas*. Octavianus will never lay hands on a living Cleopatra.'

An order that Charmian and Iras mistook, thinking that their mistress meant to die – oh, the agony of it! – almost at once. So a shocked Apollodorus mistook Cleopatra's intentions in turn when the two weeping women entered the palace. 'Where is the Queen?'

'In her tomb,' sobbed Iras, hurrying off to find Hapd'efan'e.

'She's going to die before Octavianus reaches Alexandria!' Charmian managed through spasms of tears.

'But – Antonius!' Apollodorus said, devastated.

'Antonius intends to die in tomorrow's battle.'

'Will the Daughter of Ra be dead by then?'

'I don't know! Perhaps, probably – I don't know!' Charmian hurried off to find fresh food for her mistress in the tomb.

Within an hour, everyone in the palace knew that Pharaoh was about to die; her appearance in the dining room astonished Cha'em, Apollodorus and Sosigenes.

'Majesty, we have heard,' said Sosigenes.

'I don't intend to die today,' said Cleopatra, amused.

'Please, Majesty, think again!' Cha'em beseeched.

'What, no visions about my death, son of Ptah? Rest easy! Death is nothing to fear. No one knows that better than you.'

'And the lord Antonius? Will you tell him?'

'No, I will not, gentlemen. He's still a Roman, he won't understand. I want our last night together to be perfect.'

*   *   *

In the middle of that last night Antony and Cleopatra spent in each other's arms, serene, awash with love, senses unbearably heightened, the gods quit Alexandria. They heralded their going with a faint shudder, a sigh, an immense groan that dwindled away like dying thunder in the far distance.

'Serapis and the Alexandrian gods are like us, my dearest Antonius,' she whispered against his throat.

'It's just a tremor,' he said indistinctly, half asleep.

'No, the gods refuse to stay in a Roman Alexandria.'

After that he slept, but Cleopatra couldn't. The room was faintly lit with lamps so that she could lift herself on one elbow to gaze down at him, drink in the sight of his beloved face, the almost silvery curls a wonderful contrast against his ruddy skin, the planes of his bones sharpened because he had lost weight. Oh, Antonius, what I have done to you, and none of it good, or kind, or understanding! Tonight has been so peaceful that I am wrapped in your forgiveness – you never did hold my conduct against me. I used to wonder why that was, but now I realize that your love for me was great enough to forgive anything, everything. All I can do in return is make the eternity of death something beyond all human sensation, a golden idyll in the realm of Amun-Ra.

But then she must have dozed, because he was rising, a dim black outline against the pallid pearl of dawn. She watched his manservant help him into his armor: the padded scarlet tunic over the scarlet loincloth, the scarlet leather underdress, the plain contoured steel of the cuirass, skirt and sleeves of red leather straps, the shortish boots laced tightly, their tongues tooled with steel lions folded down over the criss-crossed laces. Giving her a wide grin, he tucked his steel helmet under his arm and flung the scarlet *paludamentum* back to fall free of his shoulders.

'Come, wife,' he said. 'Wave me goodbye.'

She tucked her finest handkerchief, sprinkled with her own perfume, into the armhole of his cuirass and walked with him out into the clear, cool air, alive with birdsong.

Canidius, Cinna, Decimus Turullius and Cassius Parmensis were waiting; Antony stepped upon a stool to reach saddle height, kicked his dappled grey Public Horse in the ribs, and galloped off for the five-mile ride to the hippodrome. It was the last day of Julius.

As soon as he had disappeared from sight, she moved into her tomb, Charmian and Iras with her. The three of them working in unison, they lowered the bars over the inside of the double doors until only Antony's famous eighty-foot ram could have burst them.

Of fresh food there was plenty, Cleopatra discovered, as well as baskets of figs, olives, dates and small bread rolls baked to a special formula that kept them at much the same consistency for many days. Not that she expected to be inside for many days.

The worst was going to be tonight, when Antony's body was returned to her; he would go straight to his own sarcophagus room, there to submit voicelessly to the horrific talents of the embalming priests. But first she would have to look on his dead face – O Amun-Ra and all your gods, let it look peaceful, in no pain! Let his life have ceased quickly!

'I am glad,' said Charmian, shivering, 'that the aperture lets in plenty of air. Oh, it's so gloomy!'

'Light more lamps, silly,' was the practical Iras's answer.

Antony and his generals rode in the direction of Canopus, smiling with satisfaction at the prospect of battle. The area had been populated for many years, traditionally by wealthy foreign merchants, though their houses were not interspersed between tombs, like the houses to the west of the city, where the necropolis was. Here were gardens, plantations, stone mansions with pools and fountains, groves of black oak and palms. Beyond the hippodrome, spanning the low dunes near the sea – less desirable for a rich man's house – lay the Roman camp, two miles on each ramrod-straight side, entrenched, ditched, walled.

Good! thought Antony as they neared, seeing that the soldiers were already outside and in formation. Between their front ranks and Octavian's front ranks lay half a mile of space. Eagles flashed, cohort flags fluttered in many colors, the scarlet *vexillum proponere* stood hard by Octavian's Public Horse as he sat, surrounded by his marshals, waiting. Oh, I love this moment! Antony's mind went on as he threaded his way among his troops, cavalry making their usual fuss and clatter on the flanks. I love the eerie feel of the air, the faces of my men, the potential of so much power.

Then, in a tiny moment, it was over. His own *vexillarius*, encrusted flag aloft, dipped it and walked toward Octavian's army. Every *aquilifer* with his Eagle did the same, every *vexillarius* of every cohort, while his soldiers, crying quarter, followed, swords reversed, white kerchiefs tied around their *pila*.

How long Antony sat his jigging, prancing horse he didn't know, but when his mind cleared enough to look sideways at his marshals, they had gone. Vanished, whereabouts he had no idea. With the stiff, jerky gestures of a marionette, he turned the grey's head and galloped for Alexandria, the tears coursing down his face and flying away like raindrops in a gale.

'Cleopatra, Cleopatra!' he shouted the moment he entered the palace, his helmet clanging and bouncing down a flight of stairs when he dropped it. 'Cleopatra!'

Apollodorus came, then Sosigenes, and finally Cha'em. But Cleopatra did not.

'Where is she? Where's my wife?' he demanded.

'What happened?' Apollodorus asked, shrinking.

'My army deserted, which no doubt means my fleet has too,' he said curtly. 'Where is the Queen?'

'In her tomb,' said Apollodorus. There! It was spoken.

His face went grey, he staggered. 'Dead?'

'Yes. She didn't seem to think she'd see you alive again.'

'Nor would she, had my army fought.' He shrugged, untied the strings of his *paludamentum*, which fell to the floor in a puddle of bright red. 'Well, it makes no difference.' He undid the straps of his cuirass; another clang as it hit the marble. The sword came out of its scabbard, a nobleman's sword with an ivory eagle handle. 'Help me get the leather off,' he commanded Apollodorus. 'Come on, man, I'll not ask you to push the sword in! Just get me down to my tunic.'

But it was Cha'em who stepped forward, took off the leather underdress and its *pteryges* straps.

The three old men stood watching transfixed as Antony put the tip of his *gladius* against his midriff, the fingers of his left hand groping to find the bottom of his ribcage. Satisfied, he clasped the ivory eagle in both hands, drew in an audible gulp of air, and pushed with all his might. Only then did the three old men move, flying to help him as he subsided to the floor, gasping, blinking, frowning not in pain but in anger.

'*Cacat!*' he said, lips drawn back to show his teeth. 'I missed the heart. Should have been there . . .'

'What can we do?' Sosigenes asked, weeping.

'Stop blubbering, for one thing. The sword's in my liver or lights, I'm going to take some time dying.' He groaned. '*Cacat*, it hurts! Serves me right . . . The Queen – take me to her.'

'Stay here until you die, Marcus Antonius,' Cha'em pleaded.

'No, I want to die looking at her. Take me to her.'

Two embalmer priests went up in the basket first, their apparatus around them, then stood on the shelf of the aperture while two more embalmer priests got Antony into the basket, its base stuffed with white blankets. Priests on the ground outside winched the basket up; at the aperture they pulled it across on a set of rails until they could lower it into the tomb, where the first two embalmer priests steadied it down.

Cleopatra was waiting, expecting to see a lifeless Antony beautifully arranged in a death that bore no visible stigmata.

'Cleopatra!' he gasped. 'They said you were dead!'

'My love, my love! You're still alive!'

'Isn't that a joke?' he asked, trying to chuckle through a coughing gurgle. '*Cacat!* There's blood in my chest.'

'Put him on my bed,' she said to the priests, and hovered, a nuisance, until he was placed to her liking. The scarlet padded tunic didn't betray the blood as the white blankets on which he lay did, but she had seen plenty of blood in her thirty-nine years and was not horrified at it. Until, priest-physicians that they were, they peeled off the tunic intending to bind the wound more tightly, stop the hemorrhage. When she saw that magnificent body rent by a wide, thin tear below the ribs, Cleopatra had to clench her teeth to prevent the cry of protest, the first stab of grief. He was going to die – well, she had expected that. But not the reality. The pain in his eyes, the spasm of agony that suddenly bent him like a bow as the priests fought to bind him. His hand crushed her fingers, ground the bones together, but she knew that touching her gave him strength, so she suffered it.

Once he was made as comfortable as he could be, she drew up a chair to the side of the bed and sat there talking to him in a soft, crooning voice, and his eyes, bright with pleasure, never left her face. Moment after moment, hour after hour, helping him to cross the River, as he put it, still at the core of him a Roman.

'Will we really walk together in the Realm of the Dead?'

'Very soon now, my love.'

'How will I find you?'

'I will find you. Just sit somewhere beautiful and wait.'

'A nicer fate than eternal sleep.'

'Oh, yes. We will be together.'

'Caesar's a god too. Will I have to share you?'

'No, Caesar belongs to the Roman gods. He won't be there.'

It was a long time before he summoned up the courage to tell her what had happened at the hippodrome.

'My troops deserted, Cleopatra. To the last man.'

'So there was no battle.'

'No. I fell on my sword.'

'A better alternative than Octavianus.'

'So I thought. Oh, but it's wearying! Slow, too slow.'

'It will be over soon, my dearest love. Did I tell you that I love you? Did I tell you how very much I love you?'

'Yes, and at long last I believe you.'

The transition from life to death when it came was so subtle that she didn't realize it had happened until, chancing to look closely at his eyes, she found the pupils huge and covered with a thin patina of gold. Whatever was Marcus Antonius had left; she held a husk in her arms, the part of him he had abandoned.

A scream ripped the air: her scream. She howled like an animal, tore out her hair in handfuls, ripped at her bodice until her breasts were bare and gouged them with her nails, howling and wailing, beating at herself, demented.

When it seemed to Charmian and Iras that she would do herself a serious damage, they summoned the embalmer priests and forced syrup of poppies down Cleopatra's throat. Only after she fell into a drugged stupor could the priests remove the body of Mark Antony to his sarcophagus room, there to commence the embalming.

Darkness had fallen; it had taken Antony eleven hours to die, but at the end he was the old Antony, the great Antony. In death he found himself at last.

TWENTY-EIGHT

Caesarion continued down the Memphis road tranquilly, though his two servants, both elderly Macedonian men, urged him to ride for Schedia and there take ferry for Leontopolis on the Pelusiac Nile. That would avoid all risk of encountering Octavian's army, they said; it was also a shorter way to Nilus.

'What rubbish, Praxis!' the young man laughed. 'The shortest way to Nilus is the Memphis road.'

'Only when it does not contain a Roman army, Son of Ra.'

'And don't call me that! I'm Parmenedes of Alexandria, a junior banker going to inspect the royal bank accounts at Coptus.'

A pity that Mama had insisted he take two watchdogs, Caesarion thought, though they couldn't make any difference in the end. He knew exactly where he was going and what he was going to do. *Not* leave Mama in the lurch, first and foremost – what kind of son would consent to do that? Once they had been tied together by a cord that had poured her blood into him as he lay enveloped in the soft warm fluid she had made for him. And, even after the cord was cut, an invisible one capable of stretching over the whole world still bound them. Of course she was thinking of him when she sent him off to a part of the globe so alien he would comprehend neither the customs nor the language. But he was thinking of her when he set off with the full intention of going somewhere else to do something very different.

At the fork where the Schedia road took most of the traffic he said a cheerful farewell to the several other travelers nearby, flicked his camel with a switch, and galloped off down the Memphis road. 'Brrrr! Brrrr!' he urged the beast, legs hooked firmly around the front of the saddle to prevent falling; the gait was unusual, both legs on one side driving forward together, which meant a rocking progress akin to a ship in a beam-on swell.

'We must catch him,' said Praxis, sighing.

'Brrrr! Brrrr!' and off the two men went in pursuit of the rapidly disappearing Caesarion.

Not very many miles farther on, and just as his watchdogs were closing the gap between them, Caesarion saw Octavian's army. He curbed in the camel and reduced its pace to an amble, then moved off the road itself. No one took any notice of him; both troops and officers were engrossed in their marching songs, for they knew the thousand-mile march was almost over and a good camp awaited them – proper legionary food, Alexandrian girls to give themselves willingly or unwillingly, no doubt lots of little gold votive objects no one high up would miss.

> One-two, one-two,
> Antonius we've done for you!
> Three-four, three-four,
> We're a-knocking on your door!
> Five-six, five-six,
> Antonius counts for nix!
> Seven-eight, seven-eight,
> Antonius, meet your fate!
> Nine-ten, nine-ten,
> We've been there and back again!
> Caesar, Caesar!
> Men or women, a cock-teaser!
> Alexandria!
> Alexandria!
> Al-ex-an-dria!

Fascinated, Caesarion noted how the soldiers varied the rhythm of their words to keep up that inflexible left-right, left-right march, and then, as he moved slowly down the line, realized that each cohort had its own song, and that some soldier with a good voice and a keen mind made up new words to sing between the choruses. He had seen Antony's army, both here in Egypt and in Antioch, but his troops had never sung marching songs. Probably because they weren't on the march, he thought. It stirred him, even when the words were not very complimentary to his mother, who seemed to be the favorite subject. Witch, bitch, sow, cow, Queen of Beasts, whore of priests.

Ah! There was the general's scarlet *vexillum proponere*, its shaft held in a deep tube by a man who wore a lion skin; when the general pitched his tent, it would fly outside. Octavianus, at last! Like the rest of his legates, he was on foot, and clad rather drably in a leather underdress of plain brown. The golden hair gave him away even if the scarlet banner had not. So – *small*! Not above five and a half feet, thought Caesarion, amazed. Slender, well tanned, beautiful in the face yet not effeminate, his little and ugly hands moving in time to the (polite) song ahead.

'Caesar Octavianus!' he called, pulling off his hood. 'Caesar Octavianus, I come to treat!'

Octavian stopped dead, which ground the half of his army behind him to a halt, while those in front continued until a junior legate mounted on a horse went forward.

For a wild, spinning moment, Octavian genuinely thought that he beheld Divus Julius as Divus Julius must look were he endowed with Greek materialization. Then his dazed eyes took in the fawn wool of the disguise, the youth of Divus Julius's features, and understood that this was Caesarion. Cleopatra's son by his divine father. Ptolemy XV Caesar of Egypt.

Two older men on camels were bearing down; suddenly Octavian turned to Statilius Taurus.

'Capture them – and put up the boy's hood, Taurus! *Now!*'

While the army dropped its burdens from backs and shoulders long used to the weight, and parties went off to nearby Lake Mareotis to fetch water, Octavian's command tent was hastily erected. There could be no getting out of including his marshals in the coming interview, at least at its start; Messala Corvinus and Statilius Taurus had both glimpsed the bared golden head, the manifestation of Divus Julius's . . . ghost?

'Take the two others away and kill them immediately,' he said to Taurus, 'then come back to me. Let no one speak to them before they die, so stay to see the deed done, is that clear?'

Three men traveled with Octavian of choice rather than for any military prowess, of which they had none. One was a nobleman, the other two his own freedmen. Gaius Proculeius was the half-brother of Maecenas's brother-in-law, Varro Murena, a man famous for his erudition and pleasant nature. Gaius Julius Thyrsus and Gaius Julius Epaphroditus had been Octavian's slaves, and served him so well that upon their manumission he had taken them not only into his service but his confidence. For such a one as Octavian, the unalleviated company of military men like his senior legates for months on end would have driven him mad. Hence Proculeius, Thyrsus and Epaphroditus. As all Octavian's marshals from Sabinus through Calvinus to Corvinus understood that their master was an eccentric, no one found it offensive or off-putting to discover that Octavian on campaign was prone to dine by himself: that is, with Proculeius, Thyrsus and Epaphroditus.

The shock Octavian had suffered took a little time to wear off, for many reasons: first and foremost that he had located the Treasure of the Ptolemies by following his divine father's outline of its whereabouts to the letter. An exercise he undertook with his two freedmen; no noble Roman was ever going to see what lay in hundreds of little rooms to each side of that warren of tunnels that started in the precinct of Ptah, reached by pressing a certain cartouche and descending into lightless bowels. After wandering for several hours like a slave admitted to the Elysian Fields, he had assembled his 'mules' – Egyptian men blindfolded until well inside the tunnels, then set to removing what Octavian felt he was going to need to put Rome back on her feet: gold in the main, with some blocks of lapis lazuli, rock crystal and alabaster to give to sculptors to fashion wonderful works of art that would adorn Rome's temples and public places. Back in the sunlight, his own cohort of troops killed the Egyptians and took charge of the wagon train already on its way to Pelusium and the voyage home. The soldiers might guess at the contents of the crates by their sheer weight, but none would open one, for each was sealed with the sphinx.

The load that had lifted from Octavian's mind at sight of more wealth than he had dreamed existed left him exhilarated, so free and carefree that his legates couldn't work out what it was about Memphis had changed him so. He sang, he whistled, he almost skipped with joy as the army started up the road to the lair of the Queen of Beasts, Alexandria. Of course in time it would dawn upon them what must have happened in Memphis, but by then they – and all that gold – would be back in Rome, all opportunities lost to pop a little something into the sinuses of their togas.

So when Caesarion hailed him not thirty-five miles from the hippodrome and the outskirts of Alexandria, he hadn't yet worked out all his strategies. The gold was on its way to Rome, yes, but what was he going to do with Egypt and its royal family? With Mark Antony? What would best safeguard the Treasure of the Ptolemies? How many knew how to access it? Whom had Cleopatra told about it among her would-be allies, from the King of the

Parthians to Artavasdes of Armenia? Oh, curse the boy for this unexpected and unannounced appearance! In full sight of his army!

When Statilius Taurus returned, Octavian nodded curtly.

'Bring him in, Titus. Yourself.'

Caesarion entered with his head still covered, but quickly shed the robe to stand revealed in a plain leather riding tunic. So tall! Taller even than Divus Julius had been. Octavian's marshals sucked in a collective breath, staggered.

'What are you doing here, King Ptolemy?' Octavian asked from the ivory curule chair in which he had seated himself. There would be no handshakes, no cordial welcomes. No hypocrisy.

'I have come to treat.'

'Did your mother send you?'

The young man actually laughed, revealing yet another layer of his likeness to Divus Julius. 'No, of course not! She thinks I'm well on my way to Berenice, where I am to sail for India.'

'You would have done better to obey her.'

'No. I cannot leave her – would not leave her to face you all alone.'

'She has Marcus Antonius.'

'If I read him aright, he will be dead.'

Octavian stretched, yawned until his eyes watered. 'Very well, King Ptolemy, I will treat with you. But not with so many ears listening. Gentlemen legates, you are dismissed. Remember the oath you swore to my person. I want no whisper of this going one man farther, nor are you to discuss today among yourselves. Is that understood?'

Statilius Taurus nodded; he and the other legates left.

'Sit down, Caesarion.'

Proculeius, Thyrsus and Epaphroditus ranged themselves along the tent wall out of eyeshot of both participants in this drama, hardly breathing from their terror.

Caesarion sat, his blue-green eyes the only part of him that did not belong to Divus Julius.

'What do you think you can accomplish that Cleopatra cannot?'

'A tranquil atmosphere, to begin with. You do not hate me – how can you, when we have never met? I want to bring about a peace of benefit to you as well as to Egypt.'

'Outline your proposals.'

'That my mother retire to private life in Memphis or Thebes. That her children by Marcus Antonius go with her. That I rule in Alexandria as king and in Egypt as pharaoh. In the clientele of

Gaius Julius Caesar Divi Filius, as his loyalest, most faithful client-king. I will give you all the gold you ask for, as well as wheat to feed Italia's multitudes.'

'Why should you rule more wisely than your mother did?'

'Because I am Gaius Julius Caesar's blood son. I've already started to rectify the mistakes that many generations of the House of Ptolemy have made – I've instituted a free grain dole for the poor, I've extended the citizenship of Alexandria to all its residents, and I'm in the process of establishing democratic elections.'

'Hmmm. Very Caesarean, Caesarion.'

'I found his papers, you see – the ones detailing his plans for Alexandria and Egypt to bring them out of a stagnation that has lasted in Egypt proper for millennia. I saw that his ideas were right, that we wallowed in an unpitying sink of privileges for the upper classes.'

'Oh, you do sound like him!'

'Thank you.'

'We share a divine father, that's true,' Octavian said, 'but you look far more like him.'

'So my mother has always said. Antonius too.'

'Hasn't it occurred to you what that means, Caesarion?'

The young man looked blank. 'No. What could it mean, apart from its reality?'

'*Its reality.* In a nutshell, that's the problem.'

'Problem?'

'Yes.' Octavian sighed, steepled his crooked fingers. 'If it were not for the accident of your appearance, King Ptolemy, I might well have agreed to treat with you. As it is, I have no choice. I must put you to death.'

Caesarion gasped, started to rise, subsided. 'You mean I will walk with my mother in your triumphal parade and then go to the strangler? But why? What makes my death necessary? For that matter, what makes my mother's death necessary?'

'You mistake me, son of Caesar. You'll never walk in my triumphal parade. In fact, I wouldn't let you within a thousand miles of Rome. Has no one ever enlightened you?'

'About what?' Caesarion demanded, looking exasperated. 'Stop playing with me, Caesar Octavianus!'

'Your likeness to Divus Julius presents a threat to me.'

'I, a threat because of a *likeness*? That's insane!'

'Anything but insane. Listen to me, and I will enlighten you – how odd, that your mother never did! Perhaps she thought that if you knew, you would supplant her on the Capitol immediately. No, sit and listen! I speak frankly of Cleopatra not to goad you, but because she has been my unrelenting enemy. My dear boy, I have had to fight tooth and nail, with might and main, to establish my ascendancy in Rome. *For fourteen years!* I started when I was eighteen, adopted as my divine father's Roman son. I took up my inheritance and hewed to it, though many men have opposed me, including Marcus Antonius. I am now thirty-two, and – once you are dead – safe at last. I had no youth like yours. I was sickly and weak. Men mocked my courage. I strove to look like Divus Julius – practiced his smile, wore high boots to seem taller, copied his speech and his style of rhetoric. Until finally, as the earthly image of Divus Julius faded in men's memories, they thought he must have looked like me. Are you beginning to understand, Caesarion?'

'No. I suffer for your tribulations, cousin, but I fail to see what my appearance has to do with anything.'

'Appearance is the fulcrum upon which my career has turned. You're not a Roman and you haven't been brought up a Roman. You are a foreigner.' Octavian leaned forward, his eyes blazing. 'Let me tell you why the Romans, a pragmatic and sensible people, deified Gaius Julius Caesar. A most un-Roman thing to do. They *loved* him! It has been said of many generals that their soldiers would die for them, but only of Gaius Julius Caesar that all the people of Rome and Italia would have died for him. When he walked the Forum Romanum, the alleyways and stews of Rome or some other Italian city, he treated the people he encountered as his equals – he joked with them, he listened to their small tales of woe, he tried to help. Born and brought up in the slums of the Subura, he moved among the Head Count as one of them – he spoke their argot, he slept with their women, he kissed their smelly babies and wept when their plights moved him, as often happened. And when those conceited, unmitigated snobs and money-lovers murdered him, the people of Rome and Italia couldn't bear to lose him. *They* made him a god, not the Senate! In fact, the Senate – led by Marcus Antonius! – tried every way it knew to crush Caesar-worship. Without success. His clients were legion, and I inherited them together with his wealth.'

He got up, came around his desk to stand in front of the troubled-looking youth, stared down at him.

'Let the people of Rome and Italia set eyes on you, Ptolemy Caesar, and they will forget everything else. They will take you to their hearts and bosoms in a frenzy of joy—and I? I will be forgotten overnight. The work of fourteen years will be forgotten. The sycophantic Senate will suck up to you, make you a Roman citizen and probably gift you with the consulship the next day. You will rule not only Egypt and the East, but Rome, undoubtedly in any form you choose, from *dictator perpetuus* to *rex*. Divus Julius himself began to soften up our *mos maiorum*, then we three Triumvirs softened it up even more, and now that I have ejected Antonius from all hope of rivalry, I am the undisputed master of Rome. Provided, that is, that neither Rome nor Italia sets eyes on you. I fully intend to rule Rome and her possessions as an autocrat, young Ptolemy Caesar. For Rome at last is in just the right condition to embrace autocratic rule. Did the people see you in Rome, they would accept you. But you would rule as your mama has trained you – as a king, sitting on the Capitol dispensing justice, Minos at the gates of Hades. You see nothing wrong in that, for all your liberal programs of reform in Alexandria and Egypt. Whereas my rule will be invisible. I will wear no diadem or tiara to proclaim my status, nor will I allow my dear wife to queen it. We will continue to inhabit our present house and let Rome think she governs democratically. That is why you must die. To keep Rome Roman.'

The emotions had chased across Caesarion's face one after another – amazement, grief, thoughtfulness, anger, sadness, comprehension. But neither confusion nor puzzlement.

'I see,' he said slowly. 'I do see, and cannot blame you.'

'Well, you're the divine Caesar's actual son, and from all I've been told, you've inherited his intellectual brilliance. I'm sorry I will never see whether you've also inherited his military genius, but I have some very good marshals and fear not the King of the Parthians, whom I intend to conciliate, not attack. One of the cornerstones of my rule will be peace. War is inherently the most wasteful of human activities, from lives to money, and I will not permit the Roman legions to dictate the shape of Rome or who rules her.'

He was talking now, Caesarion sensed, in order to postpone the execution of an execution.

Oh, Mama! Why didn't you confide in me? Didn't you know what Caesar's truly Roman son has just told me? Antonius surely must have, but Antonius was your puppet. Not because you drugged him, or he was sometimes the worse for wine, but because he loved you. You should have told me. But then again, you may not have seen it, and Antonius may have been too busy proving himself worthy of your love to deem my predicament important . . .

Caesarion closed his eyes, disciplined himself to *think*, to bend that formidable intellect upon his plight. Was there even the remotest chance of escape? Feeling his belly empty of hope, he sighed. No, there was no chance of escape. The most he could do was make it difficult for Octavian to kill him, rush out of the tent crying that he was Caesar's son—no wonder Taurus had stared at him! But was that what his father would want from his non-Roman son? Or would Caesar require an ultimate sacrifice from him? He knew the answer, and sighed again. Octavianus was Caesar's true son by Caesar's own will and dictate; no mention of his other son in Egypt. And when all was done, what Caesar had prized above everything else in his life was *dignitas*. *Dignitas!* That most Roman of all qualities, a man's personal share of achievements, deeds, strength. Even in his last moments Caesar had preserved his *dignitas* intact; instead of continuing to fight, he had used the tiny fraction of time he had left to draw one fold of toga over his face, and another down past his knees. So that Brutus, Cassius and the rest wouldn't witness the expression on his dying face, or catch a glimpse of his genitalia.

Yes, thought Caesarion, I too will preserve my *dignitas!* I will die owning myself, my face and genitals covered. I will be worthy of my father.

'When will I die?' he asked, voice calm.

'Now, inside this tent. I have to do the job myself, as I trust no one else to do it. If my lack of expertise makes your death more painful, I am sorry for it.'

'My father said, "Let it be sudden." As long as you bear that in mind, Caesar Octavianus, I'll be content.'

'I cannot decapitate you.' Octavian was very pale, nostrils flaring as he struggled to discipline his mouth. He produced a twisted smile. 'I have not that kind of muscular strength, or so much steel. Nor do I wish to see your face. Thyrsus, hand me that cloth and that cord.'

'How, then?' Caesarion asked, on his feet.

'A sword up under your ribs into your heart. Don't try to run, it can't alter your fate.'

'I can see that. More public, but much messier. However, I will run unless you agree to my conditions.'

'Name them.'

'That you be kind to my mother.'

'I will be kind.'

'And my little brothers, my sister?'

'Not a hair of their heads will be harmed.'

'Have I your oath?'

'You have.'

'Then I am ready.'

Octavian draped the cloth over Caesarion's head and tied the cord around his neck to keep the makeshift hood in place. Thyrsus handed him a sword; Octavian tested the blade and found it sharp as a razor. Then he looked at the earthen floor of the tent and frowned, nodded to the sheet-white Epaphroditus.

'Give me a hand, Ditus.'

Octavian took Caesarion's arm. 'Move with us,' he said, and looked at the white cloth. 'How brave you are! Your breathing is shallow and steady.'

A voice issued from under the hood that might have been Mark Antony's. 'Stop chattering and get on with it, Octavianus!'

Four paces away was a bright red Persian rug; Epaphroditus and Octavian moved Caesarion to stand on it, and there could be no more delays. Get on with it, Octavianus, get on with it! He positioned the sword and drove it under and up in one swift stroke with more strength than he had known he possessed; Caesarion gave a sigh and crumpled at the knees, Octavian following him down, his hands still around the ivory eagle because he couldn't let go.

'Is he dead?' he asked, head twisted to look up. 'No, no! Don't uncover his face, whatever you do!'

'The artery in his neck doesn't beat, Caesar,' said Thyrsus.

'Then I did it well. Roll him up in the carpet.'

'Let go the sword, Caesar.'

A shock went through him; his fingers relaxed, he let go of the eagle at last. 'Help me up.'

Thyrsus had rolled the body inside the rug, but it was so long that the feet protruded. Big feet, like Caesar's.

Octavian collapsed into the nearest chair and sat with his head between his knees, gasping. 'Oh, I didn't want to do that!'

'It had to be done,' said Proculeius. 'What now?'

'Send for six noncombatants with shovels. They can dig his grave right here.'

'Inside the tent?' Thyrsus asked, looking sick.

'Why not? Get a move on, Ditus! I don't want to have to spend the night here, and I can't issue orders until the boy is safely buried. Has he a ring?'

Thyrsus scrabbled inside the rug, emerged with it.

Taking it in one hand – good, good, he wasn't trembling – Octavian stared at it. What the Egyptians called the Uraeus was carved on it, a rearing hooded cobra. The stone was an emerald, and around the edge it said something in hieroglyphs. A bird, an eye drooping a tear, some wavy lines, another bird. Good, it would do. If he had to show it as proof of Caesarion's fate, it would do. He slipped it into his purse.

An hour later the legions and cavalry were marching again, though not far up the Alexandria road; Octavian had decided to camp for a few days and lull Cleopatra into believing that her son had escaped, was on his way to India. Behind them, where the tent had stood for such a brief time, was an area of smooth, carefully tamped soil; under it, a full six cubits down, lay the body of Ptolemy XV Caesar, Pharaoh of Egypt and King of Alexandria, wrapped in a carpet soaked with his blood.

What goes around comes around, thought Octavian that night in the same tent on different ground. That Woman has a legend already, and a part of it is that she was smuggled in to see Caesar wrapped in a carpet. According to Caesar, it was a cheap rush mat, but the historians are turning it into a very fine rug. Now it's all finished, with her hopes and dreams back inside a carpet. And I can relax at last. My greatest threat has gone forever. He died well, though, I have to give him that.

After the debacle on the last day of Julius, when Antony's army surrendered, Octavian decided not to enter Alexandria like a conqueror, at the head of his miles of legions, his enormous mass of cavalry. No, he would enter Cleopatra's city quietly, unobtrusively. Just himself, Proculeius, Thyrsus and Epaphroditus – with his German bodyguard, of course. No point in risking an assassin's dagger for the sake of anonymity.

He left his senior legates at the hippodrome trying to take a census of Antony's troops and make some sort of order out of a considerable chaos. However, he noted, the people of Alexandria were making no attempt to flee. That meant they were reconciled to the presence of Rome and would be there to listen to his band of heralds when they announced the fate of Egypt. He had heard from Cornelius Gallus, not many miles away to the west, and sent him instructions that his fleets were to bypass Alexandria's two harbors to anchor in the roads off the hippodrome.

'How beautiful!' said Epaphroditus as the four approached the Sun Gate shortly after dawn on the Kalends, the first day of Sextilis.

And indeed it was, for the Sun Gate at this eastern end of Canopic Avenue was built of two massive pylons joined by a lintel, very square and Egyptian to any who had seen Memphis. But the colors dazzled in the golden light of the rising sun, the plain white of the stone gilded at this moment every morning.

Publius Canidius was waiting in the middle of the extremely wide street just inside the gate, mounted on a bay horse. Octavian rode alongside him and stopped.

'Do you plan another escape, Canidius?'

'No, Caesar, I've done with running. I'm turning myself over to you with just one request. That you honor my courage by making mine a quick death. I could have fallen on my sword, after all.'

The cool grey eyes rested on Antony's marshal reflectively. 'Decapitation, but no flogging. Will that do?'

'Yes. Will I remain a citizen of Rome?'

'No, I am afraid not. There are still some senators to cow.'

'So be it.' Canidius kicked his horse in the ribs and moved to ride on. 'I'll turn myself over to Taurus.'

'Wait!' Octavian cried sharply. 'Marcus Antonius – where is he?'

'Dead.'

The grief washed over Octavian more strongly and suddenly than he had expected; he sat on his striking little creamy Public Horse and wept bitterly while the Germans gazed around Canopic Avenue in wonder and his three boon companions wished they were somewhere else.

'We were cousins, and it need not have come to this.' Octavian mopped at his eyes with Proculeius's handkerchief. 'Oh, Marcus Antonius, you poor dupe!'

The ornate wall of the Royal Enclosure cordoned Canopic Avenue off from the jumble of palaces and buildings within it; near its end where it fused into the craggy flank of the Akro, a theater that had once been a fortress, stood the Royal Enclosure gates. Nobody manned them; they gaped open to admit all.

'We really need a guide to this labyrinth,' Octavian said, halting inside to gaze at the splendor everywhere.

As if he could express a wish for anything and have it come

true, an elderly man emerged from between two small marble palaces in the Greek Doric style, walked toward them holding a long golden staff in his left hand. A very tall and handsome man, he was dressed in a pleated linen robe dyed purple, belted at the waist by a wide gold affair studded with gems; it matched the collar around his neck, the bracelets on each bare, sinewy forearm. His head was uncovered save by long grey ringlets held in place by a broad band of gold-worked purple tapestry.

'Time to dismount,' said Octavian, sliding to the ground, which was paved with polished fawn marble. 'Arminius, guard the gates. If I need you, I'll send Thyrsus. Don't believe anyone else.'

'Caesar Octavianus,' said the newcomer, bowing deeply.

'Just Caesar will do. Only my enemies add the Octavianus. You are?'

'Apollodorus, Lord High Chamberlain to the Queen.'

'Oh, good. Take me to her.'

'I fear that isn't possible, *domine*.'

'Why? Has she fled?' he asked, clenching his fists. 'Oh, plague take the woman! I want the business over!'

'No, *domine*, she is here, but in her tomb.'

'Dead? Dead? She can't be dead, I don't want her dead!'

'No, *domine*. She is in her tomb, but alive.'

'Take me there.'

Apollodorus turned and headed into the bewildering maze of buildings, Octavian and his friends following. After a short walk they encountered another of those high walls smothered in vivid two-dimensional pictures and the curious writing Memphis had told Octavian was hieroglyphic in nature. Each sticklike symbol was a word but, to his eyes, it was unintelligible.

'We are about to enter the Sema,' said Apollodorus, pausing. 'Here the members of the House of Ptolemy are buried, together with Alexander the Great. The Queen's tomb is against the sea wall, here.' He pointed to a blockish, red stone structure.

Octavian eyed the huge bronze doors, then the scaffolding and winch mechanism, the basket. 'Well, at least it won't be hard to get her out,' he said. 'Proculeius, Thyrsus, go in through the opening at the top of that scaffolding.'

'If you do that, *domine*, she will hear your coming and die before your men can reach her,' Apollodorus said.

'*Cacat*! I need to speak to her, and I want her alive!'

'There is a tube – here, beside the doors. Blow down it, and it will alert Her Majesty that someone on the outside has things to say.'

Octavian blew.

Back came a voice, astonishingly distinct, though reedy. 'Yes?' it asked.

'I am Caesar, and I wish to have speech with you. Open the doors and come out.'

'No, no!' came two screeched words. 'I will not speak to Octavianus! To anyone but Octavianus! I will not come out, and if you try to enter, I will kill myself!'

Octavian gestured to Apollodorus, who looked exhausted. 'Tell Her nuisance Majesty that Gaius Proculeius is here with me, and ask her if she'll speak to him.'

'Proculeius?' came the thin clear voice. 'Yes, I'll speak to Proculeius. Antonius told me on his deathbed that I could trust Proculeius, but no one else. Let him talk.'

'She won't know one voice from another down that thing,' Octavian whispered to Proculeius.

But apparently she could tell the difference between voices, for when Octavian, having let her have speech with Proculeius, tried to take over the bizarre conversation, she recognized him and would not communicate. Nor would she talk to Thyrsus or Epaphroditus.

'Oh, I don't believe this!' Octavian cried. He rounded on Apollodorus. 'Bring wine, water, food, chairs and a table. If I have to coax Her nuisance Majesty out of this fortress, then at least let us be comfortable.'

But for poor Proculeius comfort wasn't possible; the tube was too high up on the wall for him to sit in a chair, though some hours into the business Apollodorus appeared with a tall stool that Octavian suspected he had had made for the purpose, hence the delay. Proculeius's orders were to assure Cleopatra that she was safe, that Octavian had no intention of killing her, and that her children were safe. It was the children who gnawed at her, not only their safety but their fate. Until Octavian agreed to let one of them rule in Alexandria and another in Thebes, she would not come out. Proculeius argued, entreated, coaxed, beseeched, reasoned, argued over again, fawned, badgered, all to no effect.

'Why this farce?' Thyrsus asked Octavian as darkness fell and palace servants came with torches to light the area. 'She must know you can't promise her what she asks! And why won't she speak directly to you? She knows you're here!'

'Because she's afraid that if she speaks directly to me, no one else will hear what we say. This is her way of putting her words on some kind of permanent record – she knows Proculeius is a scholar, a writer of events.'

'Surely we can enter from above during the darkness?'

'No, she's not tired enough yet. I want her so worn down and weary that her guard drops. Only then can we enter.'

'At the moment, Caesar, your main trouble is me,' Proculeius said. 'I'm flagging dreadfully, my mind is reeling. I am ready to do anything for you, but my body is giving up.'

At which moment Gaius Cornelius Gallus arrived, his handsome face fresh, his grey eyes alert. Octavian had an idea.

'Ask Her nuisance Majesty if she'll talk to a different but equally prestigious writer,' he said. 'Tell her you're sick, or that I've called you away – something, anything!'

'Yes, I'll talk to Gallus,' said the voice, not as strong now that twelve hours had elapsed.

The discussion went on until the sun came up and continued into the morning: twenty-four hours. Luckily the little precinct in front of the doors was well shaded from the summer sun.

Her voice had grown very weak; she sounded now as if she hadn't much more energy to command, but with Octavia for a sister, Octavian knew how hard a woman would fight for her children.

Finally, well after noon, he nodded. 'Proculeius, take over again. That will wake her up, focus her attention on the tube. Gallus, take my two freedmen and enter the tomb through the aperture. I want it done with absolute stealth – no jingling pulleys, no creaks, no stage whispers. If she succeeds in killing herself, you're nose-deep in the shit with my hand on your heads.'

Cornelius Gallus was a catlike man, very silent and supple; when all three men stood on the aperture wall he elected to shinny down a rope on his own. In the waning torchlight he saw Cleopatra and her two companions clustered around the speaking tube, the Queen gesturing passionately as she talked, all her attention focused on Proculeius. One servant woman held her right side in the armpit to prop her up, the other her left side. Gallus moved like lightning. Even so, she gave a great cry and lunged for the dagger on a table next to her; he wrenched it from her and held her easily, despite the two exhausted maids, tearing and beating at him. Then Thyrsus and Epaphroditus joined him and the three women were restrained.

A thirty-eight-year-old man in the pink of health, Gallus left the women to the care of the freedmen and tilted the two mighty bronze bars up and away from the doors, then opened them. Light streamed in; he blinked, dazzled.

By the time the women were brought outside, literally held up, Octavian himself had disappeared. It was no part of his plans to confront the Queen of Beasts yet, or for many days to come.

Gallus carried the Queen in his arms to her private rooms, the two freedmen carrying Charmian and Iras. The *homo novus* senior legate had found himself shocked at Cleopatra's appearance once the light of day fell on her: robes stiff and crusted with blood, breasts bared and covered with deep lacerations, hair a tangled mess between patches of oozing scalp.

'Has she a physician?' he asked Apollodorus, hovering.

'Yes, *domine*.'

'Then send for him at once. Caesar wants your Queen whole and healthy, Chamberlain.'

'Are we to be allowed to minister to her?'

'What did Caesar say?'

'I did not presume to ask.'

'Thyrsus, go and find out,' Gallus ordered.

The answer came at once: Queen Cleopatra was not to be let leave her private quarters, but anyone she needed could go to her there, and anything she asked for was to be supplied.

Cleopatra lay, golden eyes huge and hollowed, on a couch, no regal figure now.

Gallus went over to her. 'Cleopatra, can you hear me?'

'Yes,' she croaked.

'Give her wine, someone!' he snapped, and waited until she had swallowed some. 'Cleopatra, I have a message for you from Caesar. You are free to move about your apartments, eat whatever you like, have knives on hand for paring fruit or meat, see whomever you wish. But if you take your life, your children will be put to death immediately. Is that clear? Do you understand?'

'Yes, I understand. Tell Caesar that I won't attempt to harm myself. I must live for my children.' She lifted herself on an elbow as a shaven-headed Egyptian priest entered, followed by two acolytes. 'May I see my children?'

'No, that isn't possible.'

She flopped back, covered her eyes with a graceful hand. 'But they are still alive?'

'You have my word on that, and Proculeius's.'

'If women want to rule as sovereigns,' said Octavian to his four companions over a late dinner, 'they should never marry and produce offspring. It is a very rare female indeed who can overcome mother

551

love. Even Cleopatra, who must have murdered hundreds of people – including a sister and a brother – can be controlled by a simple threat to her children. A king of kings is capable of murdering his children, but not the Queen of Kings.'

'What's your purpose, Caesar? Why not let her put paid to her existence?' Gallus asked, part of his mind composing an ode. 'Unless it's all to have her walk in your triumph?'

'The last captive I want in my triumph is Cleopatra! Can't you see our sentimental grannies and mamas all along the route of the parade beholding this poor, scrawny, pathetic little woman? Her, a threat to Rome? Her, a witch, a seductress, a whore? My dear Gallus, they'd weep for her, not hate her. Buckets of tears, rivers of tears, oceans of tears. No, she dies here in Alexandria.'

'Then why not now?' Proculeius asked.

'Because first, Gaius, I have to break her. She has to be subject to a new form of war – the war of nerves. I must play on her sensibilities, harrow her with worry for her children, keep her on a knife blade.'

'I still don't understand,' said Proculeius, brow knitted.

'It's all to do with the manner of her death. However she accomplishes it, it must be seen by the entire world as her own choice, and not a murder done at my instigation. I must emerge from this pristine, the noble Roman who treated her well, gave her all kinds of latitude once she was back in her palace, never once threatened her with death. If she takes poison, I will be blamed. If she stabs herself, I will be blamed. If she hangs herself, I will be blamed. Her death must be so Egyptian that no one suspects my hand in it.'

'You haven't seen her,' said Gallus, reaching for a squab crusted with strange, tasty spices.

'No, nor do I intend to. Yet. First, I must break her.'

'I like this country,' Gallus said, tongue titillated by the perverse mixture of flavors in the squab's crunchy skin.

'That's excellent news, Gallus, because I'm leaving you here to govern it in my name.'

'Caesar! Can you do that?' the gratified poet asked. 'Won't it be a province at the command of the Senate and People?'

'No, that cannot be allowed to happen. I want no peculating proconsul or propraetor sent here with the Senate's blessing,' Octavian said, chewing what he thought was the Egyptian equivalent of celery. 'Egypt will belong to me personally, just as Agrippa virtually owns Sicilia nowadays. A trifling reward for my victory over the East.'

'Will the Senate oblige you?'

'It had better.'

The four men were gazing at him, it seemed in a new light; this was not the man who had struggled futilely against Sextus Pompey for years, nor gambled all on his homeland's willingness to take an oath to serve him. This was Caesar Divi Filius, sure to be a god one day, and undeniable master of the world. Hard, cool, detached, far-sighted, not in love with power for power's sake, Rome's indefatigable champion.

'So what do we do for the present?' Epaphroditus asked.

'You take up station in the big corridor outside the Queen's apartments, and keep a register of all who enter to see her. No one is to bring her children. Let her stew for a few *nundinae*.'

'Shouldn't you be leaving for Rome in a hurry?' Gallus asked, anxious to be left to his own devices in this wonderful land.

'I don't move until I have achieved my purpose.' Octavian rose. 'It's still light outside. I want to see the tomb.'

'Very nice,' Proculeius commented as they passed through the chambers that led to Cleopatra's sarcophagus room, 'but there are more valuable things in the palace. Do you think she did that deliberately, so that we'd let her keep her trappings for the afterlife they believe in?'

'Probably.' Octavian surveyed the sarcophagus room and the sarcophagus itself, a single piece of alabaster with a likeness of the Queen on its upper half, painted exquisitely.

A noisome smell issued from a door at the back of the room; Octavian passed into Antony's sarcophagus room and stopped dead, eyes dilated on horror. Something resembling Antony lay on a long table, its body buried in natron salts, the face still visible because, had they known it, Antony's brain had to be removed in small gobbets through his nostrils and the cranial cavity filled with myrrh, cassia and crumbled sticks of incense.

Octavian gagged; the embalmer priests looked up briefly, then returned to their work. 'Antonius, mummified!' he said. 'No Roman death, but the one he wanted. I believe it takes three months to finish the job. Only then will they remove the natron and wrap him in bandages.'

'Will Cleopatra want the same?'

'Oh, yes.'

'And will you let this disgusting process continue?'

'Why not?' Octavian asked indifferently, turning to leave.

'So that's why the aperture in the wall. To let the embalmers come and go. Once it's finished – for both of them – they'll bar the doors and wall up the opening,' said Gallus, leading the way.

'Yes. I want both of them reduced to this. That way, they belong to old Egypt and will not become *lemures* to haunt Rome.'

As the days dragged on and Cleopatra refused to cooperate, Cornelius Gallus had an inspiration about why Octavian would not see the Queen: he was afraid of her. His relentless propaganda campaign against the Queen of Beasts had conquered even him; if he came face to face with her, he wasn't sure the power of her sorcery wouldn't overcome him.

At one stage she began to starve herself, but Octavian put a stop to that by threatening to kill her children. The same old ploy, but it always worked. Cleopatra began to eat again. The war of nerves and will went on between them remorselessly, neither participant showing any sign of giving in.

However, Octavian's intransigence worked more powerfully on Cleopatra than she knew; had she only been able to step back far enough from her predicament, she would have seen that Octavian didn't dare kill her children, all very much under age. Perhaps it was her conviction that Caesarion had succeeded in escaping that blinded her; but, whatever the reason, she continued to be convinced that her children stood in peril.

Then, as Sextilis wore down toward its end and September loomed with the threat of equinoctial gales, Octavian sought out Cleopatra in her quarters.

She was lying listlessly on a couch, the scratches, bruises and other relics of her grief at Antony's death healed. When he entered she opened her eyes, stared, turned her head away.

'Go,' Octavian said curtly to Charmian and Iras.

'Yes, go,' said Cleopatra.

He drew up a chair beside the couch and sat, his eyes busy; several busts of Divus Julius dotted the room, and one splendid bust of Caesarion, a likeness taken not long before he died, for it was more man than youth.

'Like Caesar, isn't he?' she asked, following his gaze.

'Yes, very.'

'Better to keep him in this part of the world, safely away from Rome,' she said, voice at its most melodious. 'His father always intended that his destiny be in Egypt – it was I who took it upon myself to expand his horizons, not knowing that he had no wish for empire. He'll never be a danger to you, Octavianus – he is happy to rule Egypt as your client-king. The best way you can safeguard your own interests in Egypt is to put him on both thrones and ban all Romans from entering the country. He will see to it that you have whatever you want – gold, grain, tribute, paper, linen.' She sighed and stretched a little, conscious of her pain. 'No one in Rome need even know that Caesarion exists.'

His eyes turned from the bust to her face.

Oh, I had forgotten how beautiful his eyes! she thought – as much silver as grey, so filled with light, and rimmed with such thick, long, crystal lashes. Why then do they never give away his thoughts? Anymore than his face does. A lovely face, reminiscent of Caesar's, but not angular, the shape of the bones beneath more secretive. And, unlike Caesar, he is going to keep that mop of golden hair.

'Caesarion is dead.' He repeated it: 'Caesarion is dead.'

She didn't answer. Her eyes went to his and locked there, still as a stagnant pond and gone a greenish brown; the color emptied out of her face from hairline to neckline in a flash, leaving the beautiful skin grey-white.

'He came to see me while I was marching up the Alexandria road from Memphis; he was mounted on a camel, with two elderly companions. Head full of ideas that he could persuade me to spare you and the dual kingdom. So young! So deluded about the honorableness of men! So sure he could convince me. He told me that you'd sent him away, that he was supposed to sail from Berenice to India. And as I had already located the Treasure of the Ptolemies – yes, lady, Caesar betrayed you and told me how to find it before he died – I didn't need to torture its whereabouts out of him. Not that he would have told me, no matter how extreme the torture. A very brave young man, I had no trouble seeing that. However, he could not be permitted to live. One Caesar at a time is enough, and I am that Caesar. I killed him myself and buried him alongside the Memphis road in an unmarked grave.' He twisted the knife. 'His body was wrapped in a carpet.' Then he fumbled in the purse at his belt and handed her something. 'His ring.'

'You murdered Caesar's *son*?'

'With regret, but yes. He was my cousin, I have blood guilt. But I am prepared to live with the nightmares.'

Her body writhed, shuddered. 'Is it enjoyment in witnessing my pain makes you say these things to me? Or is it policy?'

'Policy, of course. In the flesh you're a damnable nuisance to me, Queen of Beasts. You'd be dead, except that I cannot be seen to have had anything to do with your death – very difficult!'

'You don't want me for your triumph?'

'*Edepol*, no! If you looked like an Amazon I'd happily make you walk in it, but not looking like an abused, half-starved kitten.'

'What about the other young men? Antyllus? Curio?'

'Put to death, along with Canidius, Cassius Parmensis and Decimus Turullius. I spared Cinna – he's a nothing.'

The tears were rolling down her face. 'And what of Antonius's children?' she whispered.

'They're well. Unharmed. Missing their mother, their father, their big brother. I have told them you're all dead – let them do their crying now, while seemly.' His gaze moved to a statue of Caesar Divus Julius in the guise of an Egyptian pharaoh – very peculiar. 'I am not enjoying this, you know. It gives me no joy to cause you so much suffering. But I am doing it nonetheless. *I* am Caesar's heir! And I intend to rule the world of Our Sea from end to end and side to side. Not as a king or even as a dictator, but as a simple senator endowed with all the powers of the tribunes of the plebs. *So right!* It will take a Roman to rule the world as it should be ruled. Someone who enjoys not the power, but the *job*.'

'Power is a ruler's prerogative,' she said, not comprehending.

'Nonsense! Power is like money – a tool. You're fools, you oriental autocrats. None of you loves the job, the work.'

'You're taking Egypt.'

'Naturally. Not as a province, swarming with Romans. I need to monitor the Treasure of the Ptolemies properly. In time the people of Egypt – in Alexandria, the Delta and along Nilus – will come to think of me as they think of you. And I'll administer Egypt better than you. You frittered this beautiful land of plenty away on war and personal ambition, you spent money on ships and soldiers in the mistaken belief that numbers always win. What wins is work. Plus, Divus Julius would say, organization.'

'How smug you Romans are! You'll kill my children?'

'Not at all! Instead, I'm going to make Romans out of them. When I sail for Rome they'll come with me. My sister Octavia will rear them. The loveliest and sweetest of women! I never could forgive that clod Antonius for hurting her.'

'Go away,' she said, turning her back on him.

He was preparing to leave when she spoke again.

'Tell me, Octavianus, would it be possible to send to the country for some fruit?'

'Not if you doctor it with poison,' he said sharply. 'I will have every piece of it sampled by your own maids, right at the spot I indicate with my finger. The slightest suggestion that you died of poison, and I'll be blamed. And don't get any grandiose ideas! If you try to make it look as if I murdered you, I'll strangle all three of your remaining children. I mean it! If I'm to be blamed for your death, what matters it if I murder your children?' He thought of something else, and said, 'They're not even very nice children.'

'No poison,' she said. 'I have lit upon the one way to die which will absolve you of all blame. It will be clear to the world that I chose the way myself, of my own volition. I will die as Pharaoh of Egypt, fitting and proper.'

'Then you may send for your fruit.'

'One more thing.'

'Yes?'

'I will eat this special fruit in my tomb. You may inspect the manner of my death after it is done. But I insist that you let the embalmer priests finish their work on Antonius and me. Then have the tomb sealed. If you yourself are not in Egypt, it must be done by your deputy.'

'As you wish.'

The bust of Caesarion filled her eyes; no more tears, the time for them was over. My beautiful, beautiful boy! How much you were your father's son, yet how little. You duped me so cleverly that I had no suspicion of your intentions. Trust *Octavianus*? But you were too naive to see the threat you were to him, too little a Roman. And now you lie in an unmarked grave, no tomb around you, no boat to sail the River of Night, no food or drink, no comfortable bed. Though I think I can forgive Octavianus everything except the carpet. His snide little poke. What he doesn't know is that his vengeance gave you a sarcophagus of a kind, enough to hold your Ka for a while.

'Send for Cha'em,' she said when Iras and Charmian came in.

He had always had the ageless look of a priest of Ptah, this chief of the order exiled from his precinct to serve Pharaoh, but these days he wore something of the air of a mummy.

'I don't need to tell you that Caesarion is dead.'

'No, Daughter of Ra. The day you queried me I saw that he would live only until his eighteenth year.'

'They wrapped him up and buried him alongside the Memphis road where there should be some signs that the army paused. Of course now you will be returning to Ptah's precinct, shepherding your carts and barrows and laden donkeys. Find him, Cha'em, and hide him inside the mummy of a bull. They won't detain you long if they detain you at all. Take him to Memphis for a secret entombment. We will beat Octavianus yet. When I am in the Realm of the Dead, I must see my son in all his glory.'

'It shall be done,' said Cha'em.

Charmian and Iras were weeping. Cleopatra let them have their cry, then waved them to silence. 'Be quiet! The time draws near, I need certain things done. Have Apollodorus send for a basket of the sacred figs. *Complete*. Do you understand?'

'Yes, Majesty,' Iras whispered.

'What clothes will you wear?' Charmian asked.

'The Double Crown. My best collar, girdle and bracelets. The pleated white dress with the beaded coat I wore for Caesar years ago. No shoes. Henna my hands and feet. Give all of it to the priests against the day when they put me in my sarcophagus. My beloved Antonius's dress armor they have already, the set he wore when he crowned my children.'

'The children?' Iras asked, reminded. 'What of them?'

'Going to Rome to live with Octavia. I don't envy her.'

Charmian smiled through her tears. 'Not when it comes to Philadelphus! I wonder if he's kicked Octavianus's shins?'

'Probably.'

'Oh, madam!' Charmian cried, at a loss. 'It was never meant to end like this!'

'Nor would it, had I not encountered Octavianus. The blood of Gaius Julius Caesar is very strong. Now leave me.'

One is supposed, thought Cleopatra, wandering the room yet keeping her gaze on the bust of Caesarion, to think of one's whole life at this moment, but I do not want to. I can only think of Caesarion, his fluffy gold head against my breast as he took in my milk with big, long gulps. Caesarion, playing with his wooden Trojan horse – he knew the name of every one of the fifty dolls in its belly. Caesarion, determined to have his entitlements as Pharaoh. Caesarion, lifting up his arms to his father. Caesarion, laughing with Antonius. Always and forever, Caesarion.

Oh, but I am glad it's over! I cannot bear to walk this vale of tears a moment longer. The mistakes, the griefs, the shocks, the struggles. Widowhood. And for what? A son I didn't understand, two men I didn't understand. Yes, life is a vale of tears. I am so very grateful for the chance to leave it on my own terms.

The basket of figs came with a note from Cha'em that said everything had been done as she commanded, that Horus would greet her when she came, that Ptah himself had furnished the instrument.

She bathed scrupulously, shrugged on a plain dress, walked with Charmian and Iras to her tomb. Birds sang in a new dawn, the scented breeze of Alexandria blew gently.

A kiss for Iras, a kiss for Charmian; Cleopatra shed her robe and stood naked.

When she lifted the lid on the basket of figs they stirred as the immense king cobra cruised the confines of his prison. There! Now! Cleopatra took his body in both her hands just below his flaring hood as he surged, rearing out of the basket, and offered him her breasts. He struck with an audible thud, a blow so powerful that she staggered, dropped him. He writhed away immediately to hide in a dark corner; eventually he found his way out through a conduit.

Charmian and Iras sat with her while she died, not a long process, but an agonizing one. Rigors, convulsions, a restless coma. Her dying done, the two women set about their own.

From the shadows the embalmer priests came forward to take Pharaoh's body and stretch it upon a bared table. The knife with which they made the incision in her flank was obsidian; through the rent they removed liver, stomach, lungs and intestines. Each was washed, rolled and stuffed with crushed herbs and spices save for frankincense, forbidden, then placed in a canopic jar amid natron and resin. The brain would come later, after the Roman conqueror paid his visit.

By the time he came in with Proculeius and Cornelius Gallus, she was covered in mounds of natron save for her chest and head; they knew the Romans wanted to see how she had died.

'Ye gods, look at the size of the fang punctures!' Octavian said, pointing to them. Then, to the chief embalmer: 'Where did you put her heart? I should like to see her heart.'

'The heart is not removed, Great One, nor the kidneys,' said the man, bowing low.

'She doesn't even look human.'

Octavian was clearly unaffected, but Proculeius went pale, excused himself, and left.

'Things shrink when the life goes out of them,' said Gallus. 'I know she was a tiny woman, but now she's like a child.'

'Barbaric!' Octavian walked out.

He was vastly relieved, and delighted at her solution to their dilemma: a snake! Perfect! Proculeius and Gallus had seen the fang marks, would publicly attest to the manner of Cleopatra's death. What a monster the thing must be! he thought. I wish I had seen it, preferably with a sword in my hand.

Late that night, a little tipsy – it had been a harrowing month – Octavian stood back to let his valet pull the covers down so he could climb into bed. There, coiled in the middle of it, was seven feet of cobra as thick as a man's arm. Octavian screamed.

PART VI

Metamorphosis

29–27 B.C.

CAESAR AUGUSTUS
AETATIS XXXVI

TWENTY-NINE

When Cleopatra's three living children embarked for Rome in the care of the freedman Gaius Julius Admetus, they sailed alone; like Divus Julius when he had left Egypt, Octavian decided he may as well tidy up Syrian Asia and Anatolia before returning to Rome. A stipulated amount of the gold he had sent to the Treasury was to be sold to buy silver for minting into denarii and sesterces: neither too much nor too little. The last thing Octavian wanted was inflation after so many years of depression.

A wearisome business, my sweetest girl, yet I feel you will approve of my logic; yours is its only rival. Store your desires in a place you will not forget, have them ready for me when I come home. Not for many months, alas. If I settle the East properly, I need not return there for years.

It is hard to credit that the Queen of Beasts is dead and in her tomb, there to be reduced to an effigy made out of what looks like Pergamum parchment glued together. Similar to the puppets that people so love when the traveling shows come to town. I saw some mummies in Memphis, all bandaged up. The priests weren't happy when I commanded them to unwrap the things, but obeyed because they were not of the highest class of dead. Just a wealthy merchant, his wife and their cat. I can't decide whether it is the muscle that wastes away, or the fat that melts away. One or the other does, leaving the face fallen in, as happened to Atticus. One does see that it is the relic of a human being, and can make assumptions about character, beauty, et cetera. I am bringing some of these mummies to Rome and will display them on a float in my triumphal parade, together with a few priests so that the people can see every stage of the gruesome process. The Queen of Beasts is welcome to this fate, but the thought of Antonius chews at me. Undoubtedly it is a mummified Marcus Antonius who has stimulated such fascination among those of us who were in Egypt. Proculeius tells me that Herodotus described the business in his treatise but, as he wrote in Greek, I never read him myself.

I have left Cornelius Gallus to administer Egypt as *praefectus*. He's very pleased, so much so that the poet has vanished, temporarily at least. All he can talk about are the expeditions he wants to make – south into Nubia and beyond that to Meroë – west into the eternal desert. He is also convinced that Africa is a mighty island, and intends to sail right around it in Egyptian ships that are built to go to India. I don't mind these giddy essays into exploration, as they will keep him busy. Far rather them, than learn he has spent his time sniffing around Memphis in search of buried treasure. The affairs of the country have been well taken care of by a team of officials I personally chose.

This comes to you with Cleopatra's young children, a ghastly trio of miniature Antonii with a dash of Ptolemy. They need heavy discipline that Octavia won't be prepared to administer, but I'm not worried. A few months of living with Iullus, Marcellus and Tiberius will tame them. After that, we shall see. I hope to marry Selene to a client-king when she's grown, whereas the boys present a more difficult problem. I want all memory of their origins erased, so you are to tell Octavia that Alexander Helios will henceforth be known as Gaius Antonius, and Ptolemy Philadelphus as Lucius Antonius. What I hope is that the boys are on the dull side. As I am not confiscating Antonius's properties in Italia, Iullus, Gaius and Lucius will have a decent income. Luckily so much was cashed in or sold that they will never be hugely rich and therefore a danger to me.

Only three of Antonius's marshals were executed. The rest are nothings, grandsons of famous men long dead. I pardoned them on condition that they swore the oath to me in a slightly modified form. Which is not to say that their names won't go down on my secret list. An agent will be assigned to watch each of them, certainly. I am Caesar, but no Caesar.

As to your request to have some of Cleopatra's clothing and jewellery, my dearest Livia Drusilla, all of it will come to Rome, but to be displayed in my triumph. Once that is over, you and Octavia may choose some items that I will buy for you, thus ensuring that the Treasury is not cheated. There will be no more sticky fingers.

Keep well. I will write again from Syria.

From Antioch, Octavian went to Damascus, and from there sent his ambassador to King Phraates in Seleuceia-on-Tigris. The man, a pretender to the Parthian throne named Arsaces, was loath to put his head back inside the lion's jaws, but Octavian was adamant. As Syria held Roman legions from one end to the other, Octavian was sure the King of the Parthians would do nothing foolish, including harming the Roman conqueror's ambassador.

So as winter began at the end of that year when Cleopatra's dreams had died, Octavian met with a dozen Parthian noblemen in Damascus and hammered out a new treaty: everything east of the Euphrates River to be in the domain of the Parthian Empire, and everything west of the Euphrates to be in the domain of the Roman Empire. Armed troops would never cross that mighty body of milky blue water.

'We had heard that you were wise, Caesar,' said the chief Parthian ambassador, 'and our new pact confirms it.'

They were strolling the fragrant gardens for which Damascus was famous, an incongruous couple: Octavian in a purple-bordered toga; Taxiles in a frilly skirt and blouse, a series of gold rings around his neck, and a little round brimless hat encrusted with ocean pearls upon his corkscrewed black locks.

'Wisdom is mostly common sense,' said Octavian, smiling. 'I have had a career so checkered that it would have foundered dozens of times were it not for two things – my common sense and my luck.'

'So young!' Taxiles marveled. 'Your youth fascinates my King more than anything else about you.'

'Thirty-three last September,' said Octavian rather smugly.

'You will be at the head of Rome for decades to come.'

'Definitely. I hope I can say the same for Phraates?'

'Just between you and me, Caesar, no. The court has been in turmoil since Pacorus invaded Syria. I predict that there will be many kings of Parthia before your reign ends.'

'Will they adhere to this treaty?'

'Yes, categorically. It frees them to deal with pretenders.'

* * *

Armenia had fallen away since the war of Actium took place; Octavian started the exhausting journey up the Euphrates to Artaxata, fifteen legions following him on what seemed to some of the soldiers to be a march they were doomed to repeat forever. But this was to be the last time.

'I have handed responsibility for Armenia to the King of the Parthians,' Octavian said to Artavasdes of Media, 'on condition that he stays on his side of the Euphrates. Your part of the world is shadowy because it lies north of the Euphrates headwaters, but my treaty fixes the boundary hereabouts as a line between Colchis on the Euxine Sea and Lake Matiane. Which gives Rome Carana and the lands around Mount Ararat. I am returning your daughter Iotape to you, King of the Medes, for she should marry a son of the King of the Parthians. Your duty is to keep the peace in Armenia and Media.'

'And all done,' said Octavian to Proculeius, 'without loss of life or limb.'

'You need not have gone to Armenia in person, Caesar.'

'True, but I wanted to see the lie of the land for myself. In years to come when I am sitting in Rome, I may need to have first-hand knowledge of every Eastern land. Otherwise some new military man hungry for fame might hoodwink me.'

'No one will ever do that, Caesar. What will you do with all the client-kings who sided with Cleopatra?'

'Not demand money from them, for sure. If Antonius hadn't tried to tax these people money they just do not have, things might have turned out very differently. Antonius's dispositions themselves are excellent, and I can see no merit in overturning them simply to assert my own might.'

'Caesar's a puzzle,' said Statilius Taurus later to Proculeius.

'How so, Titus?'

'He doesn't behave like a conqueror.'

'I don't believe he thinks of himself as a conqueror. He's simply fitting together the pieces of a world he can hand to the Senate and People of Rome as finished, complete in every way.'

'Huh!' Taurus grunted. 'Senate and People of Rome, my arse! He has no intention of letting go the reins. No, what puzzles me, old chap, is how he intends to rule, as rule he must.'

He was holding his fifth consulship when he pitched camp on the Campus Martius accompanied by his two favorite legions, the

Twentieth and the Twenty-Fifth. Here he was obliged to stay until he had celebrated his triumphs – three all told: for the conquest of Illyricum, for victory at Actium and for the war in Egypt.

Though none of the three could hope to rival some of the triumphs of the past, each of them far outstripped any predecessors when it came to propaganda. His pageant Antonys were shambling oafs of elderly gladiators, his Cleopatras gigantic German women who controlled their Antonys with dog collars, leashes and lashes.

'Wonderful, Caesar!' said Livia Drusilla after the triumph for Egypt was over and her husband came home from the lavish feast in Jupiter Optimus Maximus.

'Yes, I thought so,' he said complacently.

'Of course some of us remembered Cleopatra from her days in Rome, and were amazed at how much she'd grown.'

'Yes, she sucked Antonius's strength and elephanted.'

'What an interesting verb!'

Then came the work, which was what Octavian loved the most. He had departed from Egypt the owner of seventy legions, an astronomical total that only gold from the Treasure of the Ptolemies enabled him to retire comfortably. After careful consideration he had decided that in future Rome needed no more than twenty-six legions; none of them was to be stationed in Italia or Italian Gaul, which meant that no ambitious senator of a mind to supplant him would have troops conveniently close by. And at last these twenty-six legions were to constitute a standing army that would serve under the Eagles for sixteen years and under the flags for a further four years. Each of the forty-four legions he discharged was disbanded and scattered from one end of Our Sea to the other, on land confiscated from towns that had backed Antony. These veterans would never live in Italia.

Rome herself began the transformations that Octavian had vowed: from brick to marble. Every temple was repainted in its proper colors, the squares and gardens were beautified, and the plunder from the East was dispersed to adorn temples, forums, circuses, marketplaces. Wondrous statues and paintings, fabulous Egyptian furniture. A million scrolls were to be put in a public library.

Naturally the Senate voted Octavian all kinds of honors; he accepted very few, and disliked it when the House persisted in calling him '*dux*' – leader. Secret hankerings he had, but they were not of a blatant nature; the last thing he wanted was to look a naked despot. So he lived as befitted a senator of his rank, but never flamboyantly. He knew he couldn't continue to rule without the connivance of the Senate, yet he knew just as certainly that somehow he had to draw that body's teeth without seeming to have grown any himself. It was a help to control the *fiscus* and the army, two powers he had no intention of laying down, but they did not endow him with a shred of personal inviolability. For that, he needed the powers of a tribune of the plebs – not for a year or a decade, but for life. To that end he had to work, gradually accruing them until finally he had the greatest one of all – the power of the veto. He, the least musical of all men, had to sing the Senate a siren song so seductive they would lie on their oars forever.

When Marcella turned eighteen she married Marcus Agrippa, consul for the second time; she hadn't fallen out of love with her dour, uncommunicative hero, and entered the union convinced that she would captivate him.

Octavia's nursery never seemed to diminish in size, despite the departure of Marcella and Marcellus, her two oldest. She had Iullus, Tiberius and Marcia, all aged fourteen; Cellina, Selene, Selene's twin the newly named Gaius Antonius, and Drusus, all twelve; Antonia and Julia, eleven; Tonilla, nine; the newly named Lucius Antonius, seven; and Vipsania, aged six. Twelve children altogether.

'I am sorry to see Marcellus go,' Octavia said to Gaius Fonteius, 'but he has his own house and should take up residence in it. He is to be a *contubernalis* on Agrippa's staff next year.'

'What about Vipsania now that Agrippa's married?'

'She's to stay with me – a wise decision, I think. Marcella won't want a reminder of her last few years in the nursery, and Vipsania would be that. Besides, Tiberius would mope.'

'How are Cleopatra's children surviving?' Fonteius asked.

'Much better!'

'So Gaius and Lucius Antonius, so called, finally grew tired of being drubbed by Tiberius, Iullus and Drusus?'

'Once I steeled myself to turn a blind eye, yes. That was good advice, Fonteius, little though I liked it at the time. Now all I have to do is persuade Gaius Antonius not to overeat – oh, he is a glutton!'

'So was his father in many ways.' Fonteius leaned his back against a column in the new, exquisite gardens that Livia Drusilla had created around old Hortensius's carp ponds, and crossed his arms rather defensively. Now that Mark Antony was dead and the tomb in Alexandria sealed forever, he had resolved to try his luck with Octavia, who had had many years to mourn her last husband. At forty, her childbearing days were probably finished, and the nursery would receive no further additions. Unless they were grandchildren. Why not try? She and he had been such good friends that he had grown past thinking she would turn away from him for the sake of Antony's memory.

Such a handsome man! she was thinking as she watched him, her sensitive nature divining that he had something on his mind.

'Octavia . . .' he said, then stopped.

'Yes?' she prompted, curious. 'Do tell me!'

'You must know how much I love you. Would you marry me?'

The shock dilated her pupils, tensed her body. She sighed, shook her head. 'I thank you for the offer, Gaius Fonteius, and most of all for the love. But I cannot.'

'You don't love me?'

'Yes, I do. It's crept up on me year by year, and you've been so very patient. But I cannot marry you, or anyone else.'

'Imperator Caesar,' he said, mouth tight.

'Yes, Imperator Caesar. He has held me up to all the world as the epitome of wifely devotion, of motherly care. And well do I remember how he reacted when our mother fell from grace! Were I to marry again, Rome would be disappointed in me.'

'Then can we be lovers?'

She thought about that, her generous mouth curved in a smile. 'I shall ask him, Gaius, but his answer will be no.'

'Ask him, nonetheless!' He went to sit on the edge of a pond, his fine eyes filled with light, mouth smiling at her. 'I will have an answer, Octavia, even if it is no. Ask him – *now*!'

Her brother was working at his desk—when was he not? He looked up, brows raised.

'May I see you in private, Caesar?'

'Of course.' A wave sent the clerks scurrying out. 'Well?'

'I have received a proposal of marriage.'

That provoked a frown of displeasure. 'From whom?'

'Gaius Fonteius.'

'Ah!' He steepled his fingers. 'A good man, one of my most trusted adherents. Would you want to marry him?'

'Yes, but only with your consent, brother.'

'I cannot consent.'

'*Why?*'

'Oh, come, Octavia, you know why! It isn't that marriage to you puts him too high, it's that it puts you too low.'

Her shoulders slumped; she sat in a chair and hung her head. 'Yes, I realize that. But it is very hard, Little Gaius.'

The childhood name brought tears to his eyes; he winked them away. 'How, hard?' he asked.

'I would so much like to be married. I have given you many years of my life, Caesar, without complaint or expectation of reward. I've let you elevate me to a status that makes me equal to the Vestals. But I am not yet decrepit, and I feel that I do deserve some reward.' She lifted her head. 'I am not you, Caesar. I do not wish to be higher than everyone else. I want to feel a man's arms around me again. I want to be desired and needed in a more personal way than by children.'

'It's not possible,' he said through his teeth.

'What if we became lovers, then? Very quietly and secretly, with the utmost discretion. Give me that at least!'

'I would like to, Octavia, but we live in a transparent pool. Servants gossip, my agents gossip. It can't be done.'

'Yes, it can! The gossip about us goes on incessantly – your mistresses, my lovers – Rome buzzes! Do you think that Rome doesn't already deem Fonteius my lover, when we spend so much time together? What would change, except that a fiction would become a fact? It's old and hoary, Caesar, hardly worth one tattling tongue.'

He had listened inscrutably, eyelids down; now they lifted and he smiled Little Gaius's sweetest smile. 'All right, take Fonteius as your lover. But no others, and never publicly by look or gesture or word. I do not *like* the prospect, but you don't have a promiscuous bone in your body.' He slapped his hands on his knees. 'I'll enlist Livia Drusilla. Her aid will be invaluable.'

Octavia shrank. 'Caesar, no! She wouldn't approve!'

'Actually, she would. Livia Drusilla never forgets that there is *one* mother in our family.'

The last part of that year was fraught with crises neither Octavian nor Agrippa had foreseen. As always, a Famous Family lay at the root of them, this time the Licinii Crassi. It was a clan as old as the Republic, and its present leading member made a bid for power so clever that he couldn't see how it could fail. But that upstart, that imposter Octavian dealt with him brilliantly – constitutionally, and through the Senate Marcus Licinius Crassus had assumed would support him. It did not.

Crassus's sister, Licinia, was the wife of Cornelius Gallus, thus linking Cornelius Gallus to events. While governor of Egypt he had accomplished great things as an explorer; his success went to his head so hugely that he inscribed his exploits on the pyramids, the temples of Isis and Hathor, and various monuments in Alexandria. He had also erected gigantic effigies of himself everywhere, an action forbidden to all Romans, whose statues were never to exceed the size of a man. Even Octavian was careful to observe this; that his friend and adherent Gallus had not came as a shock. Summoned to Rome to answer for his hubris, Cornelius Gallus and his wife committed suicide halfway through trial for treason before the Senate.

Never one to ignore such lessons, Octavian sent none but very ordinary men of low birth to govern Egypt from that moment on, and ensured that ex-consuls governing provinces were sent to regions devoid of large armies. Ex-praetors inherited the armies; since they wanted to be consuls, they were more likely to behave themselves. Triumphs would become the entitlement of Octavian's own family, none other.

'Crafty,' said Maecenas. 'Your senatorial sheep went along like lambs – baa, baa, baa.'

'The new Rome cannot be let raise ambitious men in ways that display their colors to the knights, let alone the common people. Let them win military laurels by all means, but in the service of the Senate and People of Rome, not to enhance their own families,' Octavian said. 'I have worked out how to castrate the nobility, old or new makes no difference. They may live as fat as they like, but never attain public fame. I'll allow them guts, but never glory.'

'You need another name besides Caesar,' Maecenas said, eyes fixed on a beautiful bust of Divus Julius looted from Cleopatra's palace. 'It hasn't escaped me that you don't care for dux or princeps. Imperator is better let die, and Divi Filius isn't necessary anymore. But what name?'

'Romulus!' Octavian cried eagerly. 'Caesar Romulus!'

'Impossible!' Maecenas squawked.

'I *like* Romulus!'

'You may like it all you wish, Caesar, but it is the name of the founder of Rome – and Rome's first king.'

'I want to be called Caesar Romulus!'

A stand from which Octavian refused to be budged, no matter how hard Maecenas and Livia Drusilla argued. Finally they went to Marcus Agrippa, in Rome these days because he was consul of the old year and to be consul again in the new year.

'Marcus, convince him that he can't be Romulus!'

'I'll try,' said Agrippa, 'but I make no promises.'

'I don't know what all the fuss is about,' Octavian said sulkily when approached. 'I need a name befitting my status, and I can't think of one that does the job half as well as Romulus.'

'Would you change your mind if someone found a better name?'

'Yes, of course I would! I'm not blind to the kingly implications of Romulus!'

'Find him a better name,' said Agrippa to Maecenas.

It was Virgil the poet who thought of it.

'How about,' Maecenas asked delicately, 'Augustus?'

Octavian blinked. '*Augustus?*'

'Yes, Augustus. It means the highest of the high, the most glorious of the glorious, the greatest of the greatest. And it's never been used as a cognomen by anyone – anyone at all.'

'Augustus.' Octavian rolled it on his tongue, savoring it. 'Augustus . . . Yes, I like it. Very well, let it be Augustus.'

On the thirteenth day of January, when Octavian was thirty-five years old and consul for the seventh time, he convened the Senate. 'It is time that I laid down all my powers,' he told it. 'The dangers are over. Marcus Antonius, poor dupe, has been dead two and a half years, and with him the Queen of Beasts, who vilely corrupted him. The little panics and passing terrors of the time since have also died, mere nothings compared to the might and glory of Rome. I have been Rome's faithful guardian, her indefatigable champion. So now, on this day, conscript fathers, I give you notice that I am relinquishing all my provinces – the grain islands, the Spains, the Gauls, Macedonia and Greece, Asia Province, Africa, Cyrenaica, Bithynia and Syria. I hand them to the Senate and People of Rome. All I wish to keep is my *dignitas*, which entails my status as a consular, as your princeps senatus, and my personal rank as an honorary tribune of the plebs.'

The House flew into a spontaneous uproar. 'No, no!' drummed in Octavian's ears from everywhere, a staccato booming.

'No, great Caesar, no!' came Plancus's voice, the loudest. 'Keep your trusty hands on Rome, we beg you!'

'Aye, aye, aye!' from all sides.

The farce went on for some hours, a shrinking Octavian trying to protest that he wasn't needed anymore, and the House insisting that he was. Finally Plancus, stout turncoat, adjourned the matter unresolved until the House met again in three days.

On the sixteenth day of January, the House, in the person of Lucius Munatius Plancus, addressed its brightest luminary.

'Caesar, your hand will always be needed,' said Plancus, at his most mellifluous. 'Therefore we beg that you retain your *imperium maius* over all Rome's provinces, and that you continue as her senior consul for the forseeable future. Your scrupulous attention to the welfare of the Republic has not escaped us, and we rejoice that under your care the Republic has been infused with new vigor, rejuvenated for all time.'

He went on for another hour, eventually coming to an end in a thunderous voice that echoed around the chamber. 'As a special mark of this body's thanks, we wish to give you the name of Caesar Augustus, and recommend a law that no other man is ever to use it! Caesar Augustus, highest of the high, bravest of the brave! Caesar Augustus, the greatest man in the history of the Roman Republic!'

'I accept.' What else was there to say?

'Caesar Augustus!' Agrippa roared, and embraced him. First among his adherents, first among his friends.

Augustus walked out of Divus Julius's Curia Hostilia in the midst of a host of senators, but arm in arm with Agrippa. In the foyer he hugged his wife and sister, then strode to the edge of the steps and lifted both hands to the cheering crowd.

There has already been a Romulus, he thought. I am Augustus, and unique.

FINIS

GLOSSARY

aedes
The house of a god not sanctified by the rite of augury during its consecration. Vesta, a god of women, had an *aedes*, not a temple. It was round and situated in the Forum Romanum.

aerarium
A repository for public moneys.

ether
That part of the upper atmosphere permeated by godly forces, or the air immediately surrounding a god. It also meant the blue sky of daylight.

agora
An open space inside a Greek city used for public gatherings. It was usually surrounded by colonnades.

Anatolia
Roughly, modern Asian Turkey.

animus
Quoting the Oxford Latin Dictionary: "The mind as opposed to the body, the mind or soul as constituting with the body the whole person." To a Roman, it did not mean an immortal soul; it was simply the animating force that endowed awareness.

Apollonia
The southern terminus of the Via Egnatia on the Adriatic coast of Macedonia. It lay near the mouth of the modern Vijosë River in Albania. The northern terminus was Dyrrachium.

Apulia, Apulian
That part of southeastern Italia wherein the Apennines flatten and the boot's "spur" is located. An Apulian was considered an uneducated, brainless bumpkin.

Armenia Parva
Little Armenia. It lay west of Armenia proper, around the head-waters and upper courses of the Euphrates River, and was high, extremely mountainous and inhospitable.

Arretium
Modern Arezzo, on the Arno River.

575

augur
A member of the College of Augurs, fifteen men at this time. His duties concerned divination rather than prognostication, and he was elected for life by his fellow augurs. He inspected the stipulated object or signs to ascertain whether or not a projected undertaking had the approval of the gods, be it a meeting, a proposed new law, or any other public business. A protocol governing interpretation existed, so an augur "went by the book" rather than claimed to have psychic powers. He wore the red-and-purple-striped toga, and carried a staff, the *lituus*, topped by a curlicue.

aurochs
Bos primigenia, the wild ox of Europe, extinct for a millennium. It was black in color, stood six feet at the shoulder, and was equipped with a formidable pair of forward-curving horns.

auxiliaries
Troops serving in a Roman army without owning the Roman citizenship. They were usually mounted, but could be foot soldiers.

ballista
At this time, a piece of artillery designed to hurl boulders or stones. The missile was placed in a spoon-shaped arm that was put under extreme tension by a tightly wound rope spring; when the spring was released, the arm shot into the air and came to rest against a thick pad, propelling the missile a long distance. It was accurate when expertly fired by trained artillerymen.

basilica
A large building devoted to public activities such as courts of law. It was lit by clerestory windows high up on its sides.

beak
In Latin, *rostrum*. Of oak or bronze, the beak projected forward of a ship's bow just below the waterline, and was used to hole or damage an enemy vessel by a procedure called "ramming."

Belgae
The fearsome confraternity of tribes inhabiting the northwestern region of Long-haired Gaul, adjacent to the Rhine. They were of mixed Germano-Gallic blood; among many tribes were the Nervii, who fought on foot, and the Treveri, who were mounted.

boni
Literally, the plural of "good", but used of the men who formed the ultra-conservative rump of the Senate – "the good men."

Bononia
A town on the Via Aemilia in Italian Gaul. Modern Bologna.

Burdigala
A Gallic city at the apex of the mouth of the Garumna (Garonne) River in Aquitania. Now called Bordeaux.

cacat!
Shit!

caligae
Legionary footwear, open to the air but more supportive than a sandal, as they were laced tightly around the ankles. The very thick leather sole was studded with metal hobnails, thus raising the marching foot too high off the ground to pick up painful gravel. The shoe's open nature kept the foot healthy. In icy or snowy weather, the legionary wore thick socks, rabbit skins or similar inside it.

Campania
The fabulously rich and fertile volcanic basin that lay between the mountains of Samnium and the Tuscan Sea, and extended from Tarracina in the north to a point just south of the Bay of Naples. Strong Greek and Samnite elements in its population made it a grudging subject of Rome's, always prone to insurrection.

capite censi
See entry on Head Count.

Capua
The largest inland city of Campania. It had a long history of broken pledges to Rome, but by the time of this book, it had become the centre of a huge martial industry catering for the needs of the army camps and gladiator schools scattered around it.

Carrhae
Modern Harran in the extreme south of Turkey on its Syrian border. It was the site of a terrible Roman defeat, when the Parthians cut the seven legions of Marcus Licinius Crassus to pieces.

catapult
At this time, a piece of artillery that shot wooden bolts or sharpened logs. The principle was the same as that of the crossbow. Small catapults were known as scorpions.

censor
The most senior of all Roman magistracies, though not the most powerful, as it did not have imperium (q.v.). A censor had to have been consul first, and only famous consulars stood for the censorship. Two censors were elected for a period of five years, the *lustrum*. They inspected the citizen rolls, decided a man's economic status, regulated membership in the Senate, and held a full census of all Romans worldwide. Usually they

could not get on together, and were prone to resign long before their *lustrum* was ended.

centunculus
A gaudy patchwork coat of many colors worn by a clown.

centurion
A regular professional officer in a Roman legion. He enjoyed his status without social denigration. Promotion was up from the ranks. Centurion seniority was graduated in a manner so tortuous that no modern scholar has succeeded in working out how many grades there were, or how they progressed. The ordinary centurion was in command of a century (80 soldiers and 20 noncombatant citizens). The *pilus prior* commanded a cohort; the *primipilus* a legion.

chlamys
The cloaklike outer garment worn by Greek men.

Classes
There were five Classes, numbered from First to Fifth. Membership was economic, and decided by the censors.

client, clientele
A man of free or freed status (he did not have to be a Roman citizen) who pledged himself to a man he called his patron was a client in the patron's clientele. The client undertook in the most solemn and binding way to obey the wishes and serve the interests of his patron in return for various favors (usually gifts of money, or jobs, or legal assistance). Whole towns could be in one man's clientele, like Bononia and Mutina, in the clientele of Antony.

client-king
A king who pledged his nation to Rome – or to a Roman.

cohort
The tactical unit of the legion, comprising 6 centuries of troops. In normal circumstances, there were 10 cohorts to the legion.

comitium, comitia
A gathering of men politically empowered to vote. A *comitium* might be legislative, and pass laws or plebiscites; judiciary, and hear trials; or religious, and endow a magistrate with his imperium, elect the Pontifex Maximus, approve adoptions, and various other situations.

confarreatio
The oldest and strictest of the three forms of Roman marriage. It was unpopular, for two reasons: the first, that it gave a woman absolutely no freedom or independence; and the second, that it virtually negated the possibility of divorce.

conscript fathers
By this time, a courtesy title for senators. It originated under the Kings of Rome, who called their councilmen "fathers." Later, when they were adlected by the censors, they were considered as conscripted. Thus, "conscript fathers."

consul
The most senior of regular Roman magistrates holding imperium (q.v.). Modern scholars refer to holding the consulship, as the term "consulate" is a diplomatic one. Two consuls were elected, and served for one year; the man with more votes was senior to his colleague. They entered office on January 1st, with the senior holding the *fasces* (q.v.) for January, then alternating month by month with his junior. A consul's imperium overruled other magistrates, except in earlier days by the dictator, and at this time, by those holding *imperium maius* (q.v.).

consular
A man who had been consul.

contubernalis
A noble youth serving his obligatory year of military service as a cadet on the general's staff. It was a step toward a political career rather than a military one.

Corcyra Island
Modern Corfu or Kerkyra, off the Adriatic coast of Greece.

Cornelia the Mother of the Gracchi
Few Republican women earned fame, but Cornelia was worshipped as an unofficial goddess. She was the daughter of Scipio Africanus and Aemilia Paulla, and married Tiberius Sempronius Gracchus. By him she had twelve children, of whom only three survived. The two males were the famous Brothers Gracchi, one murdered, the other forced to commit suicide. Her granddaughter married a Fulvius, and produced Fulvia, wife to Clodius, then Curio, and finally Mark Antony. Throughout her very long life Cornelia was never heard to complain, despite her plethora of tragedies. It was this exemplary fortitude that earned her goddess status, as she was seen as all that a Roman woman should be, yet rarely was.

cunnus, cunni
A choice Latin obscenity: cunt.

curator annonae
The magistrate in charge of the grain supply.

curule chair
Curule magistrates sat on a chair carved out of ivory, the curule chair. When extended, its legs formed a broad X. It had no back but low arms,

and could be folded up. Only consuls and prectors definitely used it, though there is debate about curule aediles.

denarius, denarii
The most commonly used Roman coin, made of silver, and about the size of a dime. There were 4 sesterces to the denarius; 6,250 denarii made up one talent.

diadem
The Hellenistic symbol of sovereignty. It was a white ribbon about an inch wide, worn around the head and tied on the occiput. Its two ends were fringed, and strayed down upon the shoulders.

Dionysus or Dionysos
A Greek deity, originally of Thracian origin, and having bloodily orgiastic rites. By this time, a much milder god who was patron of wine and revelry.

domine, domina
Latin for my lord, my lady.

domus
A man's urban dwelling if a house rather than an apartment; it also meant a man's home or household whole and entire.

Druidism
The major Celtic religion, mystical and animist. It was frowned on by Romans, who deplored its bizarre qualities; in particular, human sacrifice as a part of augury.

duumvir
One of two magistrates in charge of a Roman town or *municipium*.

Eagle
When Gaius Marius enlisted paupers in his army, he gave each of his legions a silver eagle carried aloft by an *aquilifer*, and introduced worship of the Eagle to give these propertyless troops something tangible to fight for. The ploy worked brilliantly.

Ecastor!
The socially acceptable epithet used by women: akin to "Darn!"

Ecbatana
Modern Hamadan, in Iran.

Edepol!
The socially acceptable epithet used by men: akin to "Damn!"

Elysian Fields
Romans had no real belief in the intact survival of an individual after death, though they did believe in an underworld populated by shades, characterless and mindless effigies of the dead. The Elysian Fields contained the most virtuous shades, who could enjoy a brief return to life after they drank human blood.

Epirus
On the west coast of Greece – more or less modern Albania.

Euxine Sea
The modern Black Sea.

Fabian tactics
Named after Fabius Maximus Cunctator, who dogged Hannibal's army through peninsular Italy for seventeen years without ever offering outright battle. It still means avoiding battle.

Fannian paper
A Roman businessman named Fannius invented a cheap way to turn poor-grade papyrus paper into something akin to the most expensive kinds. He made a huge fortune.

fasces
A cylindrical bundle of red-dyed birch rods tightly bound together in a criss-cross pattern by red leather thongs. Carried by a man called a lictor, it indicated a magistrate's degree of imperium (q.v.) – six for a praetor, twelve for a consul. Within Rome, the *fasces* contained only the rods, indicating the magistrate's power to chastise, but outside the city it also held a single-bladed axe to indicate that the magistrate had the power to decapitate. Mussolini revived the term for his party, hence the modern "Fascist."

fasti
A list of days, as in the Roman calendar, or a list of consuls.

feliciter
"Good luck!" or "Much happiness!"

fiscus
A purse of money or a moneybag: it referred to State moneys.

"five"
Slang for the quinquereme (q.v.).

flamen
A Roman priest having a specific job. There were three major flaminates: Dialis (Jupiter), Martialis (Mars), and Quirinalis (Quirinus). The *flamen*

was shackled with taboos, particularly the *flamen Dialis*, who was forbidden to see death, touch iron, have knots or buckles on his person, and many more. The *flamen* wore a circular poncholike cape, the *laena*, and the *apex*, which was a close-fitting ivory helmet surmounted by a spike bearing an impaled disc of wool.

forum
The Roman public meeting place, also applied to major markets – fish, meat, fruit and vegetables, etc.

freedman
A manumitted slave. He was obliged to wear a conical skullcap, the "cap of liberty." If his former master was a Roman, then he was automatically in his master's clientele, and had little right to exercise his franchise. However, he could make money, and so rise high in the Classes.

Gades
Modern Cadiz, in Spain.

Galatia
In the third century B.C., an enclave of Gauls settled in the rich grassy regions of Anatolia between the Sangarius and Halys Rivers. Its ancient capital, Ancyra, is now Ankara.

garum
A highly esteemed flavoring obtained from fish; as far as we know, it stank a treat. The best *garum* was from Spain.

Gaul, Gauls
Any region inhabited by Celtic peoples was a Gaul. Romans did not call these people Celts: they were Gauls.

gens humana
The human family.

Gerrae!
Utter rubbish, nonsense.

gig
A Roman conveyance with two wheels. It was drawn by mules, in any number from one to four.

gorgon
A mythical monster, female in sex. She had hair of living snakes, and a glance that turned men to stone. There were three gorgons, the most famous one Medusa.

Halys River
The modern Kizil Irmak River of central Turkey.

harpy
A mythical monster, female in sex. She had the body of a bird of prey and the head of a woman.

Head Count
The *capite censi*. Those Romans too impoverished to belong to the Fifth Class. When holding a census, the censors simply counted their heads. They could vote, and could wear the toga.

Hellespont
The straits between Europe and Asia, flowing from the Sea of Marmara to the Aegaean Sea.

herm
A pedestal adorned with male genitalia. In Christian times hermed pedestals were defaced, portrayal of the genitals being considered obscene.

hostis
An enemy of the Roman State. If declared *hostis*, a citizen was stripped of his property and citizenship, possibly also his life.

Ides
One of the three enumerated days in a Roman month. It fell on the 13th of January, February, April, June, Sextilis (August), September, November and December. In March, May, Julius and October, it fell on the 15th.

Ilium
The Roman name for Troy.

Illyricum
The upper, eastern coast of the Adriatic Sea, and extending well inland. Istria, Liburnia and Dalmatia were a part of it.

imperator
Properly, the commanding general of a Roman army. By this time, it had come to mean only those commanders hailed "imperator" on the battlefield. It entitled a man to celebrate a triumph (q.v.).

imperium
The degree of authority vested in a curule magistrate. If he went on to hold a promagistracy, it was extended, though not necessarily to the same degree. The number of lictors preceding a man denoted his imperium – 6 for a praetor, 12 for a consul.

imperium maius
Unlimited imperium, so high that its holder was superior to all save a dictator, whether in Rome or in a province. Until this time it was relatively rare, but during the last decades of the Republic, the Senate awarded it to quite a number of men.

inepte
A fool, idiot, someone mentally dull.

insula
It meant an island, but also a tall apartment building, which was always surrounded by alleyways.

irrumator
A mortal insult! The man performing fellatio on another man, thus on his knees before him.

Italia
The leg and foot of the Italian boot. It terminated at the rivers Arnus and Rubicon.

Italian Gaul
The haunch of the Italian leg: everything between the Alps and the two rivers of the Italian boundary. Watered by the Padus (Po) River, it was extremely rich and fertile. However, its bounty could not be exported to Italia proper because of the Apennine mountain chain on land, and perverse winds on the sea.

iugerum, iugera
The Roman unit of land acreage. One *iugerum* was equal to 0.623 of an acre, or 0.252 of a hectare.

Julius
The old Roman month of Quinctilis became Julius after Julius Caesar was assassinated.

Kalends
One of the three enumerated days of the Roman month. It was the first day.

knights
The Ordo Equester, or equestrian order. When Rome was very young, some men formed the cavalry, and because horses were expensive, the State bought their mounts. However, by the time of this book, a knight was merely a prominent businessman, a member of the First Class. Thus it was a social and economic distinction.

Lares and Penates
The Roman household gods or gods of the field – of granaries and storage cupboards, all things that enabled a family to live safely and comfortably.

Lares Permarini
The Lares who presided over Romans voyaging on the sea.

laserpicium
A substance obtained from a north African shrub called silphium. It was used to relieve indigestion after over-indulgence, and was extremely expensive.

latifundium, latifundia
A large tract of land, usually public, leased for grazing rather than growing. *Latifundia* were the chief reason why Italia was not able to feed itself wheat, as they deprived the small farmer of his land. They reduced employment and encouraged urban drift.

lectus medius
Roman dining couches were arranged facing each other in a U that might contain as few as three or as many as fifteen. The host's couch, the *lectus medius*, formed the bottom of the U.

legate
Deputy generals or commanders in a Roman army, as used herein.

legion
The smallest unit in a Roman army capable of fighting a war on its own: that is, it was complete within itself in terms of manpower, equipment and function. A full-strength legion contained 4,800 soldiers divided into 10 cohorts of 6 centuries; it also held 1,200 noncombatant Roman citizen servants and 60 centurions, plus artificers and artillerymen. It had 600 mules as pack animals, and 60 ox-drawn wagons for bulk supplies.

lemur, lemures
Shades. Creatures from the underworld.

lex, leges
A law, laws. The name of the man promulgating the law was usually attached to it, as lex Annia, lex Voconia, etc. Feminine gender.

lex Voconia de mulierum hereditatibus
Passed in 169 B.C., it severely limited a woman's right to inherit a large fortune. However, the Senate could override it by decree.

Liburnian
So called because the pirates of Liburnia used it. Its exact dimensions are hard to surmise, but as Agrippa used Liburnians in sea battles, it must have been about the size of a trireme, or "three". Which meant it was decked and able to carry marines in goodly number. Certainly it was swift and easy to manoeuvre.

Liguria
The mountainous maritime region between Italian Gaul and the Gallic Province. A poor area, it was famous for its greasy wool, tamped into felt and waterproof ponchos.

locus consularis
The right-hand end position on the host's couch, the most important.

Long-haired Gaul
So called because its inhabitants wore their hair very long, a mark of barbarity. It was, roughly, most of modern France and Belgium excluding the Rhone Valley and the Mediterranean coast. Its people were tribal, divided into Celtae and Belgae.

Macedonia
It bordered the eastern Adriatic below Illyricum, went east across the mountains of Candavia, and ended at the Strymon River. In ancient times it was much larger than it is today. Its main artery was the Via Egnatia (q.v.).

maiestas
"Little" treason. "Big" treason, *perduellio*, had fallen into disuse by the time of this book. A man convicted *maiestate* could hope to keep his life, perhaps also his citizenship, but never his money, property, or right to live in Rome.

maniple
In earlier times, the tactical unit of the legion. It comprised two centuries of troops. Gaius Marius made the cohort supreme, and the maniple became a mere parade ground unit.

Massilia
Modern Marseilles.

Mauretania
Modern Morocco.

medicus
A pun on "medius" (middle) and "medicus" (doctor) that called the middle finger, used for rectal examination, the "medicus".

mentula
A choice Latin obscenity: prick.

mentulam caco
A particularly obscene phrase: "I shit on your prick!"

meretrix
A harlot.

meum mel
A Latin endearment: "my honey."

modius, modii
The customary Roman measure of grain. It weighed 13 pounds, and was sufficient to make one large loaf a day for six days. The free grain dole gave a recipient five *modii* a month. The Greek measure, a *medimnus*, consisted of five *modii*.

mos maiorum
Almost indefinable for us. It was the established order of things: the way things had always been, and always would be. It represented an unwritten constitution of sorts.

municipium
A district that did not have full autonomy in Roman eyes.

Mutina
A town on the Via Aemilia in Italian Gaul. Modern Modena. It lay in the clientele of Mark Antony.

Narbo
Modern Narbonne, in France.

nefas
Unholy, sacrilegious.

nemes
An Egyptian headdress made of cloth bound across the forehead, joined at the nape of the neck, and flaring out on either side behind the ears.

Nones
One of the three enumerated days in a Roman month. If the Ides fell on the 13th, it fell on the 5th; if the Ides were on the 15th, it fell on the 7th.

numen, numina, **numinous**
Truly Roman gods were faceless, sexless, and best described as forces rather than entities. They governed everything from the opening and

closing of a door to rain and wind, to war and public prosperity. They had no mythology. The pathways of these forces were a push-pull relationship between the universe of men and that of the gods, hence the Roman habit of making contracts with their gods.

nundinum, nundinae
There were eight days in a Roman week, every eighth day being a market day called the *nundinus*. A calendar was affixed to the rostra in the Forum Romanum.

oppidum
A Gallic fortress, considered by Romans to be hideously ugly.

Our Sea
In Latin, *Mare Nostrum*. The Mediterranean, whole and entire.

Padus River
The Po River of northern Italy.

Palus Asphaltites
The Dead Sea, so called because it produced lumps of bitumen that could be "fished" from its waters – a valuable commodity.

Paraetonium
Thought to be modern Mersa Matruh, in western Egypt.

Parthians
Parthia itself was a land to the east of the Caspian Sea, so to the Romans the enemy was "the Parthians" rather than the country. The Kingdom of the Parthians was enormous, stretching from the Indus River to the Euphrates River. Much of it was inhospitable.

Patrae
Modern Patras, on the Gulf of Corinth in Greece.

phalerae
Round, chased, ornamented silver or gold discs about 3 or 4 inches in diameter. They were decorations for military valor, mounted in three rows of three upon a fancy harness, and worn over the mail shirt or cuirass.

Pharsalus
In Grecian Thessaly. Here Caesar defeated Pompey the Great.

Phraaspa
Somewhere around modern Zanjan, in Iran.

Picenum
The calf muscle of the Italian leg. It was famous for producing disruptive political figures; the people were looked down on by Romans as Gauls. A sore point with the Picentine Pompey the Great.

pilum, pila
The legionary's spear. It had a small, pyramidal, barbed head and an iron shaft for half its length; this was fastened to a wooden shaft by a weak pin that severed connection when it lodged in an enemy, thus preventing his throwing it back. Gaius Marius invented it.

pinnace
An open boat rowed by about eight men. Very swift.

plebeian, Plebs
The huge majority of Roman citizens were plebeian; patricians were thin on the ground by the time of this book.

plethron
The Greek measure of land acreage.

pomerium
The sacred boundary of the city of Rome, marked by stones called *cippi*, and different from the Servian Walls; the Aventine Mount and the Capitol lay outside it. Religiously, Rome herself existed only within the *pomerium*; all outside it was Roman territory.

pontifex, pontifices
The Roman priest, inducted into the College of Pontifices. The head of the College was the Pontifex Maximus, who shared the State-owned Domus Publica with the Vestal Virgins. A priest wore the red-and-purple-striped toga, also called "particolored".

praefectus fabrum
The individual, usually a civilian, who purchased the items to equip Roman legions, from tent pegs to mules to mail shirts, food and clothing. He tended to be a banker by profession.

praetor
The second highest Roman magistrate owning imperium. His duties concerned the law courts and litigation. He served for one year.

pro-
Proconsul, propraetor, proquaestor, promagistrate. This was a man who had passed out of office, but retained imperium. If a proconsul or propraetor, he probably governed a province.

proletarii
The poor, who had nothing to give Rome except children. After Gaius Marius, not quite true; a *proletarius* could be a soldier.

pronuba
The bride's chief attendant at her wedding.

proscription
The act of stripping a man of his property, probably also his citizenship, and perhaps his life. Usually he was on the losing side in a civil war. A list of the proscribed was posted on the rostra in the Forum Romanum.

province
A region belonging to Rome and directly governed by Rome.

Public Horse
The horse bought by the State in earlier times; though Romans no longer fielded their own cavalry, the Famous Families all prized possession of a Public Horse.

publicani
A business company licensed by the Treasury to "farm" the taxes and tributes of a province – that is, to collect them on behalf of the Treasury. As *publicani* always collected more money than the Treasury stipulated, tax-farming was highly profitable.

quaestor
The most junior magistrate, owning no imperium. The office let him enter the Senate. He looked after the State's moneys, be they a governor's or an institution's or the Treasury's.

quinquereme
A very popular war galley coming to be deemed too slow and clumsy, though it had the advantages of massive weight and ability to carry artillery as well as marines. Apparently the "five" had either five men on one oar, or five men spread over the three oars of one bank. The top bank was always located in an outrigger or platform jutting over the water: the middle bank's oars poked through ports well up the ship's beams; and the bottom bank's oars protruded through a leather valve very close to the water-line. The ship was always decked, and accommodated about 120 marines. It had about 270 oarsmen, who were professionals; the galley-slave was a Christian idea. There were 30 sailors to work the rigging, as the five carried a huge sail.

quin taces
Shut up! in the singular.

Rex Sacrorum
During the time of the Kings of Rome, he was the high priest. As he also happened to be the King, the new Republic decided to reduce his importance by inventing the Pontifex Maximus, who outranked him.

Rhegium
Modern Reggio, at the tip of the Italian boot's toe.

Rhenus River
The Rhine.

Rhodanus River
The Rhône, in France.

rostra
A raised dais in the forum, used for oratory and conducting big meetings. It was named for the ship's beaks that decorated a column adjacent to it.

Rubicon River
The eastern boundary of Italia proper. Modern authorities differ on the identity of this river, as extensive drainage schemes were carried on around Ravenna in later times.

saltatrix tonsa
Literally, a barbered dancing-girl. In fact, a man who dressed as a woman and sold his sexual favors in a public place. There was a law, the *lex Scantinia*, that made it a capital offense.

satrapy
Territory belonging to a suzerain or over-ruler, but administered as a distinct entity on the suzerain's behalf. The man designated to rule a satrapy was a **satrap**.

Senate
The upper house, so to speak. At this time it held a thousand men, who were either admitted through election as quaestors, or adlected by the censors, or by the Triumvirs. The Senate could not pass a law, only decree that a law should be passed; the power to legislate belonged to the Assemblies, now virtually defunct. The Triumvirs legislated with mere lip-service to the Assemblies.

senatus consultum
A decree issued by the Senate.

Serapis
A peculiarly hybrid god invented for the citizens of Alexandria by its first Ptolemy and the then high priest of Ptah, one Manetho. The aim was to

weld Greek and Egyptian religious ideas together so that Alexandria could have a local god of suitably Greek nature. His precinct lay in Rhakotis, the worst section of the city, a hint that Serapis was a god for the lower classes.

sestertius, sesterces
This minute silver coin was the official unit of Roman bookkeeping. Four of them made one denarius. 25,000 made one talent.

sinus
Geographically, a gulf. A sinus was also that part of a toga sitting in loose folds on a man's right hip; he used it as a pocket for his handkerchief and documents. However, his money purse was always firmly attached to a belt around his tunic.

siren
Mythical women of great allure who lived on dangerous reefs and rocks. They bewitched sailors with the beauty of their songs, thus causing them to run their ships aground.

Skenite Arabs
A tribe of Arabs who inhabited the area east of the Euphrates in the vicinity of Zeugma and Nicephorium. They were a nomadic desert people who found little to admire in the Romans.

socius
A free man who was a native of a Roman province without owning the Roman citizenship.

Sol Indiges, Tellus and Liber Pater
This trio of numinous Roman gods governed the swearing of oaths. If they were invoked, even the most cynical of Romans adhered to his oath, no matter what the cost.

sortition
Choosing the holders of public positions by casting lots.

sow
A unit of smelted metal. Iron, copper, tin, silver and gold were all kept as sows, perhaps a talent in weight.

Subura
A declivity between the Viminal and Esquiline Mounts of Rome. It was a famous stew having the poorest inhabitants, but Suetonius says that Julius Caesar lived there as a child.

suffect consul
A consul who was appointed by the Senate rather than elected; it had been a last resort upon the death of an incumbent or other severe circumstances,

but under the Triumvirs suffect consulships became a way of rewarding loyalty.

sui iuris
In control of one's own affairs and fate. Used of women who kept control of their own money and property.

tace
The singular of "Shut up!"

tacete
Shut up! in the plural.

talent
Traditionally, the weight a man could carry upon his own back. About 56 pounds (25 kilograms).

Taprobane
The island of Sri Lanka (Ceylon).

tata
Latin for "daddy."

Thrace
The long stretch of country between the Strymon River and the area around the Hellespont and the Thracian Bosporus. It thrust far inland, and was, apart from the people of its Mediterranean coast, populated by barbarians.

transport
A ship designed to carry troops. If empty, it was rowed by a crew; if occupied by legionaries, these hapless men had to row. Since legionaries had a horror of the sea, their generals felt that rowing gave them something to do.

tribune of the plebs
A magistrate who, though elected, did not represent the whole Roman People – just the Plebs. This meant that tribunes of the plebs did not operate under the auspices, and could hold no kind of imperium. However, they were inviolate and sacrosanct in the carrying out of their duties, and they had one tremendous political weapon: the veto, which they could exercise against a law, an undertaking, or a magistrate. They had been famous for legislating, but by this time little did they pass into law.

triumph
A Roman general whose troops hailed him as imperator on the field of battle was entitled to apply to the Senate for a triumph, not easily gainsaid. Upon his return to Rome he featured as the star of a huge

parade that displayed his deeds and booty for the crowd. Some triumphs were spectacular, others run-of-the-mill.

Tyrian purple
The most expensive and desired of all purple dyes. It was made from a little tube inside the shellfish *murex* by the city of Tyre, in Syria. The color was almost black, but shot with subtle flashes of a deep purple-red.

verpa
A Latin obscenity referring to the penis and its foreskin.

via
A main road, as the Via Latina, Via Valeria, Sacra Via.

via Egnatia
The great eastern road that ran from two branches at Dyrrachium and Apollonia on the Adriatic coast and shortly thereafter merged to continue for almost a thousand miles across Macedonia and the coast of Thrace to Byzantium in a northerly direction and the Hellespont in its southern branch. It was built about 146 B.C. by the Romans, to facilitate movement of troops.

vicus
A city street or less important road than a via. A city street on an incline was called a **clivus**.

villa
A man's country estate, incorporating a vast residence. The old Getty Museum in Malibu, California, was a brilliant reconstruction of Caesar's father-in-law Lucius Piso's villa at Herculaneium, and was a true wonder of the world. I deplore its closure, as no villa exists anywhere in Europe that is not in ruins. Our times are the poorer for its lack.